THE EDGE
&
COMEBACK

Dick Francis has written forty-one international bestsellers and is widely acclaimed as one of the world's finest thriller writers. His awards include the Crime Writers' Association's Cartier Diamond Dagger for his outstanding contribution to the crime genre, and an honorary Doctorate of Humane Letters from Tufts University of Boston. In 1996 Dick Francis was made a Mystery Writers of America Grand Master for a lifetime's achievement and in 2000 he received a CBE in the Queen's Birthday Honours list.

Dick Francis

THE EDGE
&
COMEBACK

PAN BOOKS

The Edge first published 1988 by Michael Joseph Ltd
Comeback first published 1991 by Michael Joseph Ltd

This omnibus edition published 2002 by Pan Books
an imprint of Pan Macmillan Ltd
Pan Macmillan, 20 New Wharf Road, London N1 9RR
Basingstoke and Oxford
Associated companies throughout the world
www.panmacmillan.com

ISBN 0 330 41509 3

The author is grateful to the estate of Dylan Thomas and the publishers
J.M. Dent & Sons for permission to quote lines from 'Do Not Go Gentle
Into That Good Night' From *The Poems*.

A CIP catalogue record for this book is available from
the British Library.

Printed and bound in Great Britain by
Mackays of Chatham plc, Chatham, Kent

THE EDGE

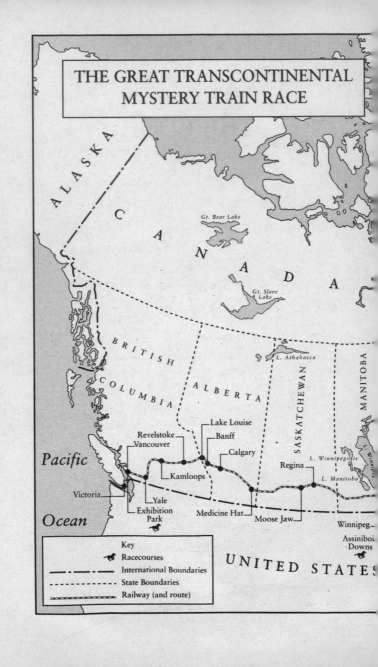

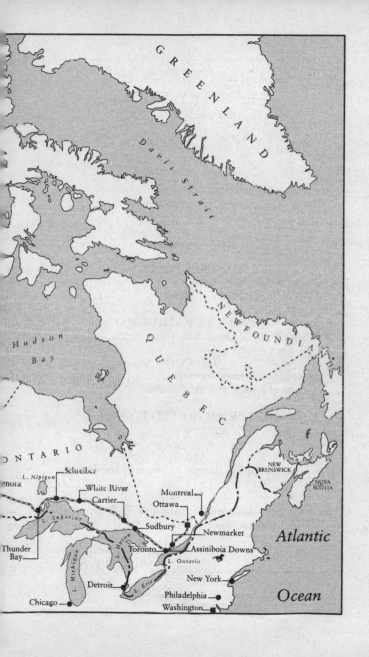

The villains in this story are imaginary.
The good guys may recognize their own virtues!

Many thanks to

SHANNON WRAY
formerly of Penguin Books, Canada, who started the
train rolling

SHEILA BOWSLAUGH
and Sam Blyth of Blyth & Co, travel entrepreneurs

BILL COO
Manager of Travel Communications, VIA Rail,
and the staff of Union Station, Toronto

HOWARD SHRIER and TED BISAILLION
actor/writers

and
Col. Charles (Bud) Baker, Chairman of the Ontario
Jockey Club,

Krystina Schmidt, caterer; American Railtours Inc.,
operators of private rail cars,

and John Jennings, who travelled the trains with horses.

CHAPTER ONE

I was following Derry Welfram at a prudent fifty paces when he stumbled, fell face down on the wet tarmac and lay still. I stopped, watching, as nearer hands stretched to help him up, and saw the doubt, the apprehension, the shock flower in the opening mouths of the faces around him. The word that formed in consequence in my own brain was violent, of four letters and unexpressed.

Derry Welfram lay face down, unmoving, while the fourteen runners for the three-thirty race at York stalked closely past him, the damp jockeys looking down and back with muted curiosity, minds on the business ahead, bodies shivering in the cold near-drizzle of early October. The man was drunk. One could read their minds. Mid-afternoon falling-down drunks were hardly unknown on racecourses. It was a miserable, uncomfortable afternoon. Good luck to him, the drunk.

I retreated a few unobtrusive steps and went on watching. Some of the group who had been nearest to Welfram when he fell were edging away, looking at the departing horses, wanting to leave, to see the race. A few shuffled from foot to foot, caught between a wish to desert and shame at doing so, and one, more civic-minded, scuttled off for help.

I drifted over to the open door of the paddock bar, from where several customers looked out on the scene. Inside, the place was full of dryish people watching life on closed-circuit television, life at second hand.

One of the group in the doorway said to me, 'What's the matter with him?'

'I've no idea.' I shrugged. 'Drunk, I dare say.'

I stood there quietly, part of the scenery, not pushing through into the bar but standing just outside the door under the eaves of the overhanging roof, trying not to let the occasional drips from above fall down my neck.

The civic-minded man came back at a run, followed by a heavy man in a St John's Ambulance uniform. People had by now half-turned Welfram and loosened his tie, but seemed to step back gladly at the approach of officialdom. The St John's man rolled Welfram fully on to his back and spoke decisively into a walkie-talkie. Then he bent Welfram's head backwards and tried mouth-to-mouth resuscitation.

I couldn't think of any circumstance which would have persuaded me to put my mouth on Welfram's. Perhaps it was easier between absolute strangers. Not even to save his life, I thought, though I'd have preferred him alive.

Another man arrived in a hurry, a thin raincoated

2

man I knew by sight to be the racecourse doctor. He tapped the ambulance man on the shoulder, telling him to discontinue, and himself laid first his fingers against Welfram's neck, then his stethoscope against the chest inside the opened shirt. After a long listening pause, perhaps as much as half a minute, he straightened and spoke to the ambulance man, meanwhile stuffing the stethoscope into his raincoat pocket. Then he departed, again in a hurry, because the race was about to begin and the racecourse doctor, during each running, had to be out on the course to succour the jockeys.

The ambulance man held a further conversation with his walkie-talkie but tried no more to blow air into unresponsive lungs, and presently some colleagues of his arrived with a stretcher and covering blanket, and loaded up and carried away, decently hidden, the silver hair, the bulging navy-blue suit and the stilled heart of a heartless man.

The group that had stood near him broke up with relief, two or three of them heading straight for the bar.

The man who had earlier asked me, asked the new-comers the same question. 'What's the matter with him?'

'He's dead,' one of them said briefly and unneces-sarily. 'God, I need a drink.' He pushed his way into the bar, with the doorway spectators, me among them, following him inside to listen. 'He just fell down and died.' He shook his head, 'Strewth, it makes you think.'

He tried to catch the barman's eye. 'You could hear his breath rattling... then it just stopped... he was dead before the St John's man got there... Barman, a double gin... make it a treble...'

'Was there any blood?' I asked.

'Blood?' He half looked in my direction. ''Course not. You don't get blood with heart attacks... Barman, a gin and tonic... not much tonic... get a shunt on, will you?'

'Who was he?' someone said.

'Search me. Just some poor mug.'

On the television the race began, and everyone, including myself, swivelled round to watch, though I couldn't have said afterwards what had won. With Derry Welfram dead my immediate job was going to be much more difficult, if not temporarily impossible. The three-thirty in those terms was irrelevant.

I left the bar in the general break-up after the race and wandered about inconclusively for a bit, looking for other things that were not as they should be and, as on many days, not seeing any. I particularly looked for anyone who might be looking for Derry Welfram, hanging around for that purpose outside the ambulance-room door, but no one arrived to enquire. An announcement came over the loudspeakers presently asking for anyone who had accompanied a Mr D. Welfram to the races to report to the clerk of the course's office, so I hung about outside there for a while also, but no one accepted the invitation.

Welfram the corpse left the racecourse in an ambulance en route to the morgue and after a while I drove away from York in my unremarkable Audi, and punctually at five o'clock telephoned on my car phone to John Millington, my immediate boss, as required.

'What do you mean, he's dead?' he demanded. 'He can't be.'

'His heart stopped,' I said.

'Did someone kill him?'

Neither of us would have been surprised if someone had, but I said, 'No, there wasn't any sign of it. I'd been following him for ages. I didn't see anyone bump into him, or anything like that. And there was apparently no blood. Nothing suspicious. He just died.'

'Shit.' His angry tone made it sound as if it were probably my fault. John Millington, retired policeman (Chief Inspector), currently Deputy Head of the Jockey Club Security Service, had never seemed to come to terms with my covert and indeterminate appointment to his department, even though in the three years I'd been working for him we'd seen a good few villains run off the racecourse.

'The boy's a blasted amateur,' he'd protested when I was presented to him as a fact, not a suggestion. 'The whole thing's ridiculous.'

He no longer said it was ridiculous but we had never become close friends.

'Did anyone make waves? Come asking for him?' he demanded.

'No, no one.'

'Are you sure?' He cast doubt as always on my ability.

'Yes, positive.' I told him of my vigils outside the various doors.

'Who did he meet, then? Before he snuffed it?'

'I don't think he met anybody, unless it was very early in the day, before I spotted him. He wasn't searching for anyone, anyway. He made a couple of bets on the Tote, drank a couple of beers, looked at the horses and watched the races. He wasn't busy today.'

Millington let loose the four-letter word I'd stifled. 'And we're back where we started,' he said furiously.

'Mm,' I agreed.

'Call me Monday morning,' Millington said, and I said, 'Right,' and put the phone down. Tonight was Saturday. Sunday was my regular day off, and Monday too, except in times of trouble. I could see my Monday vanishing fast.

Millington, in common with the whole Security Service and the Stewards of the Jockey Club, was still smarting from the collapse in court of their one great chance of seeing behind bars arguably the worst operator still lurking in the undergrowth of racing. Julius Apollo Filmer had been accused of conspiring to murder a stable lad who had been unwise enough to say loudly and drunkenly in a Newmarket pub that he knew things about Mr effing-blinding Filmer that would get the said arsehole chucked out of racing quicker than Shergar won the Derby.

The pathetic stable lad turned up in a ditch two days later with his neck broken, and the police (Millington assisting) put together a watertight-looking conspiracy case, establishing Julius Filmer as paymaster and planner of the crime. Then, on the day of his trial, odd things happened to the four prosecution witnesses. One had a nervous breakdown and was admitted in hysteria to a mental hospital, one disappeared altogether and was later seen in Spain, and two became mysteriously unclear about facts that had been razor-sharp in their memories earlier. The defence brought to the witness box a nice young man who swore on oath that Mr Filmer had been nowhere near the Newmarket hotel where the conspiracy was alleged to have been hatched but had instead been discussing business with him all night in a motel (bill produced) three hundred miles away. The jury was not allowed to know that the beautifully-mannered, well-dressed, blow-dried, quietly spoken youth was already serving time for confidence tricks and had arrived at court in a Black Maria.

Almost everyone else in the court – lawyers, police, the judge himself – knew that the nice young man had been out on bail on the night in question, and that even though the actual murderer was still unknown, Filmer had beyond doubt arranged the stable lad's killing.

Julius Apollo Filmer smirked with satisfaction at the

'Not Guilty' verdict and clasped his lawyer in a bear-hug. Justice had been mocked. The stable lad's parents wept bitter tears over his grave and the Jockey Club ground its collective teeth. Millington swore to get Filmer somehow, anyhow, in the future, and had made it into a personal vendetta, the pursuit of this one villain filling his mind to the exclusion of nearly everything else.

He had spent a great deal of time in the Newmarket pubs going over the ground the regular police had already covered, trying to find out exactly what Paul Shacklebury, the dead stable lad, had known to the detriment of Filmer. No one knew – or no one was saying. And who could blame anyone for not risking a quick trip to the ditch.

Millington had had more luck with the hysterical witness, now back home but still suffering fits of the shivers. She, the witness, was a chambermaid in the hotel where Filmer had plotted. She had heard, and had originally been prepared to swear she had heard Filmer say to an unidentified man, 'If he's dead, he's worth five grand to you and five to the hatchet, so go and fix it.'

She had been hanging fresh towels in the bathroom when the two men came in from the corridor, talking. Filmer had been abrupt with her and bundled her out and she hadn't looked at the other man. She remembered the words clearly but hadn't of course seen their significance until later. It was because of the word 'hatchet' that she remembered particularly.

A month after the trial Millington got from her a half-admission that she'd been threatened not to give evidence. Who had threatened her? A man she didn't know. But she would deny it. She would deny every-thing, she would have another collapse. The man had threatened to harm her sixteen-year-old daughter. Harm . . . he'd spelled out all the dreadful programme lying ahead.

Millington, who could lay on the syrup if it pleased him, had persuaded her with many a honeyed promise (that he wouldn't necessarily keep) to come for several days to the races, and there, from the safety of various strategically placed security offices, he'd invited her to look out of the window. She would be in shadow, seated, comfortable, invisible, and he would point out a few people to her. She was nervous and came in a wig and dark glasses. Millington got her to remove the glasses. She sat in an upright armchair and twisted her head to look over her shoulder at me, where I stood quietly behind her.

'Never mind about him,' Millington said. 'He's part of the scenery.'

All the world went past those windows on racing afternoons, which was why, of course, the windows were where they were. Over three long sessions during a single week on three different racecourses Millington pointed out to her almost every known associate and friend of Filmer's, but she shook her head to them all. At the fourth attempt, the following week, Filmer himself strolled past, and I thought we'd have a repeat of the hysterics: but though our chambermaid wobbled and wept and begged for repeated assurances he would never know she had seen him, she stayed at her post. And she astonished us, shortly after, by pointing towards a group of passing people we'd never before linked with Filmer.

'That's him,' she said, gasping. 'Oh my God . . . that's him . . . I'd know him anywhere.'

'Which one?' Millington said urgently.

'In the navy . . . with the grey sort of hair. Oh my God . . . don't let him know . . .' Her voice rose with panic.

I could hear the beginnings of Millington's reassurances as I fairly sprinted out of the office and through to the open air, slowing there at once to the much slower speed of the crowd making its way from paddock to stands for the next race. The navy suit with the silvery hair above it was in no hurry, going along with the press. I followed him discreetly for the rest of the afternoon, and only once did he touch base with Filmer, and then as if accidentally, as between strangers.

The exchange looked as if navy-suit asked Filmer the time. Filmer looked at his watch and spoke. Navy-suit nodded and walked on. Navy-suit was Filmer's man, all right, but was never to be seen to be that in public: just like me and Millington.

I followed navy-suit from the racecourse in the going-home traffic and telephoned from my car to Mill ington.

'He's driving a Jaguar,' I said, 'licence number A 576 FDD. He spoke to Filmer. He's our man.'

'Right.'

'How's the lady?' I asked.

'Who? Oh, her. I had to send Harrison all the way back to Newmarket with her. She was half off her rocker again. Have you still got our man in sight?'

'Yep.'

'I'll get back to you.'

Harrison was one of Millington's regular troops, an ex-policeman, heavy, avuncular, near to pensioned retirement. I'd never spoken to him, but I knew him well by sight, as I knew all the others. It had taken me quite a while to get used to belonging to a body of men who didn't know I was there; rather as if I were a ghost.

I was never noticeable. I was twenty-nine, six foot tall, brown-haired, brown-eyed, twelve stone in weight with, as they say, no distinguishing features. I was always part of the moving race crowd, looking at my racecard, wandering about, looking at horses, watching races, having a bet or two. It was easy because there were always a great many other people around doing exactly the same thing. I was a grazing sheep in a flock. I changed my clothes and general appearance from day to day and never made acquaintances, and it was lonely quite often, but also fascinating.

I knew by sight all the jockeys and trainers and very many owners, because all one needed for that was eyes and racecards, but also I knew a lot of their histories from long memory, as I'd spent much of my childhood and teens on racecourses, towed along by the elderly race-mad aunt who had brought me up. Through her knowledge and via her witty tongue I had become a veritable walking data bank; and then, at eighteen, after her death, I'd gone world-wandering for seven years. When I returned, I no longer looked like the unmatured youth I'd been, and the eyes of the people who had known me vaguely as a child slid over me without recognition.

I returned to England finally because at twenty-five I'd come into inheritances from both my aunt and my father, and my trustees were wanting instructions. I had been in touch with them from time to time, and they had despatched funds to far-flung outposts fairly often, but when I walked into the hushed book-lined law office of the senior partner of Cornborough, Cross and George, old Clement Cornborough greeted me with a frown and stayed sitting down behind his desk.

'You're not . . . er . . . ?' he said, looking over my shoulder for the one he'd expected.

'Well . . . yes, I am. Tor Kelsey.'

'Good Lord.' He stood up slowly, leaning forward to extend a hand. 'But you've changed. You . . . er . . .'

'Taller, heavier and older,' I said, nodding. Also sun-tanned, at that moment, from a spell in Mexico.

'I'd ... er ... pencilled in lunch,' he said doubtfully.

'That would be fine,' I said.

He took me to a similarly hushed restaurant full of other solicitors who nodded to him austerely. Over roast beef he told me that I would never have to work for a living (which I knew) and in the same breath asked what I was going to do with my life, a question I couldn't answer. I'd spent seven years learning how to live, which was different, but I'd had no formal training in anything. I felt claustrophobic in offices and I was not academic. I understood machines and was quick with my hands. I had no overpowering ambitions. I wasn't the entrepreneur my father had been, but nor would I squander the fortune he had left me.

'What have you been doing?' old Cornborough said, making conversation valiantly. 'You've been to some interesting places, haven't you?'

Travellers' tales were pretty boring, I thought. It was always better to live it. 'I mostly worked with horses,' I said politely. 'Australia, South America, United States, anywhere. Racehorses, polo ponies, a good deal in rodeos. Once in a circus.'

'Good heavens.'

'It's not easy now, though, and getting harder, to work one's passage. Too many countries won't allow it. And I won't go back to it. I've done enough. Grown out of it.'

13

'So what next?'

'Don't know.' I shrugged. 'Look around. I'm not getting in touch with my mother's people, so don't tell them I'm here.'

'If you say so.'

My mother had come from an impoverished hunting family who were scandalized when at twenty she married a sixty-five-year-old giant of a Yorkshireman with an empire in second-hand car auctions and no relatives in *Burke's Peerage*. They'd said it was because he showered her with horses, but it always sounded to me as if she'd been truly attracted. He at any rate was besotted with her, as his sister, my aunt, had often told me, and he'd seen no point in living after she was killed in a hunting accident, when I was two. He'd lasted three years and died of cancer, and because my mother's family hadn't wanted me, my aunt Viv Kelsey had taken me over and made my young life a delight.

To Aunt Viv, unmarried, I was the longed-for child she'd had no chance of bearing. She must have been sixty when she took me, though I never thought of her as old. She was always young inside; and I missed her dreadfully when she died.

Millington's voice said, 'The car you are following . . . are you still following it?'

'Still in sight.'

'It's registered to a Derry Welfram. Ever heard of him?'

'No.'

14

Millington still had connections in the police force and seemed to get useful computerized information effortlessly.

'His address is down as Parkway Mansions, Maida Vale, London,' he said. 'If you lose him, try there.'

'Right.'

Derry Welfram obligingly drove straight to Parkway Mansions and others of Millington's minions later made a positive identification. Millington tried a photograph of him on each of the witnesses with the unreliable memories and, as he described to me afterwards, 'They both shit themselves with fear and stuttered they'd never seen the man, never, never.' But they'd been so effectively frightened, both of them, that Millington could get nothing out of them at all.

Millington told me to follow Derry Welfram if I saw him again at the races, to see who else he talked to, which I'd been doing for about a month on the day the navy-suit fell on its buttons. Welfram had talked intensely to about ten people by then and proved he was comprehensively a bearer of bad news, leaving behind him a trail of shocked, shivering, hollow-eyed stares at unwelcome realities. And because I had an ingenious camera built into binoculars (and another that looked like a cigarette lighter) we had recognizable portraits of most of Welfram's shattered contacts, though so far identifications for less than half. Millington's men were working on it.

Millington had come to the conclusion that Welfram

was a frightener hired to shake out bad debts: a rent-a-thug in general, not solely Filmer's man. I had seen him speak to Filmer only once since the first occasion, which didn't mean he hadn't done so more often. There were usually race meetings at three or more different courses in England each day, and it was a toss-up, sometimes, to guess where either of the quarries would go. Filmer, moreover, went racing less often than Welfram, two or three times a week at most. Filmer had shares in a great many horses and usually went where they ran; and I checked their destinations every morning in the racing press.

The problem with Filmer was not what he did, but catching him doing it. At first sight, second sight, third sight he did nothing wrong. He bought racehorses, put them in training, went to watch them run, enjoyed all the pleasures of an owner. It was only gradually, over the ten years since Filmer had appeared on the scene, that there had been eyebrows raised, frowns of disbelief, mouths pursed in puzzlement.

Filmer bought horses occasionally at auction through an agent or a trainer but chiefly acquired them by deals struck in private, a perfectly proper procedure. Any owner was always at liberty to sell his horses to anyone else. The surprising thing about some of Filmer's acquisitions was that no one would have expected the former owner to sell the horse at all.

I had been briefed about him by Millington during my first few weeks in the Service, but then only as someone to be generally aware of, not as a number one priority.

'He leans on people,' Millington said. 'We're sure of it, but we don't know how. He's much too fly to do anything where we can see him. Don't think you'll catch him handing out bunches of money for information, nothing crude like that. Look for people who're nervous when he's near, right?'

'Right.'

I had spotted a few of those. Both of the trainers who trained his horses treated him with caution, and most of the jockeys who rode them shook his hand with their fingertips. The Press, who knew they wouldn't answer questions, hardly bothered to ask them. A deferential decorative girlfriend jumped when he said jump, and the male companion frequently in attendance fairly scuttled. Yet there was nothing visibly boorish about his general manner at the races. He smiled at appropriate moments, nodded congratulations to other owners in the winners' enclosures and patted his horses when they pleased him.

He was in person forty-eight, heavy, about five foot ten in height. Millington said the weight was mostly muscle, as Filmer spent time three days a week raising a sweat in a gym. Above the muscle there was a well-shaped head, large flat ears and thick black hair flecked with grey. I hadn't been near enough to see the colour of his eyes, but Millington had them down as greenish brown.

Rather to Millington's annoyance I refused to follow Filmer about much. For one thing, in the end he would have been certain to have spotted me, and for another it wasn't necessary. Filmer was a creature of habit, moving from car to lunch to bookmaker to grandstand to paddock at foreseeable intervals. At each track he had a favourite place to watch the races from, a favourite vantage point overlooking the parade ring and a favourite bar where he drank lager mostly and plied the girlfriend with vodka. He rented a private box at two racecourses and was on the waiting list at several more, where his aim seemed to be seclusion rather than the lavish entertainment of friends.

He had been born on the Isle of Man, that tax-haven rock out of sight of England in the stormy Irish Sea, and had been brought up in a community stuffed with millionaires fleeing the fleecing taxes of the mainland. His father had been a wily fixer admired for fleecing the fled. Young Julius Apollo Filmer (his real name) had learned well and outstripped his father in rich pickings until he'd left home for wider shores; and that was the point, Millington said gloomily, at which they had lost him. Filmer had turned up on racecourses sixteen or so years later giving his occupation as 'company director' and maintaining a total silence about his source of considerable income.

During the run-up to the conspiracy trial, the police had done their best to unravel his background further, but Julius Apollo knew a thing or two about offshore companies and had stayed comfortably ravelled. He still officially lived on the Isle of Man, though he was never there for long. During the flat season he mostly divided his time between hotels in Newmarket and Paris, and in the winter he dropped entirely out of sight, as far as the Security Service was concerned. Steeplechasing, the winter sport, never drew him.

During my first summer with the Service he had bought, to everyone's surprise, one of the most promising two-year-olds in the country. Surprise, because the former owner, Ezra Gideon, was one of the natural aristocrats of racing, a much respected elderly and extremely wealthy man who lived for his horses and delighted in their successes. No one had been able to persuade him to say why he had parted with the best of his crop or for what price: he bore its subsequent high-flying autumn, its brilliant three-year-old season and its eventual multi-million-pound syndication for stud with an unvaryingly stony expression.

After Filmer's acquittal, Ezra Gideon had again sold him a two-year-old of great promise. The Jockey Club mandarins begged Gideon practically on their knees to tell them why. He said merely that it was a private arrangement: and since then he had not been seen on a racecourse.

On the day Derry Welfram died I drove homewards to London wondering yet again, as so many people had wondered so often, just what leverage Filmer had used on Gideon. Blackmailers had gone largely out of business since adultery and homosexuality had been blown wide open, and one couldn't see old-fashioned upright Ezra Gideon as one of the newly fashionable brands of transgressor, an insider-trader or an abuser of children. Yet without some overwhelming reason he would never have sold Filmer two such horses, denying himself what he most enjoyed in life.

Poor old man, I thought. Derry Welfram or someone like that had got to him, as to the witnesses, as to Paul Shacklebury dead in his ditch. Poor old man, too afraid of the consequences to let anyone help.

Before I reached home the telephone again purred in my car and I picked up the receiver to hear Millington's voice.

'The boss wants to see you,' he said. 'This evening at eight, usual place. Any problem?'

'No,' I said. 'I'll be there. Do you know... er... why?'

'I should think,' Millington said, 'because Ezra Gideon has shot himself.'

CHAPTER TWO

The boss, Brigadier Valentine Catto, Director of Security to the Jockey Club, was short, spare, and a commanding officer from his polished toecaps to the thinning blond hair on his crown. He had all the organizational skills needed to rise high in the army, and he was intelligent and unhurried and listened attentively to what he was told.

I met him first on a day when old Clement Cornborough asked me again to lunch to discuss in detail, as he said, the winding up of the trust he'd administered on my behalf for twenty years. A small celebration, he said. At his club.

His club turned out to be the Hobbs Sandwich Club, near the Oval cricket ground, a Victorian mini-mansion with a darkly opulent bar and club rooms, their oak-panelled walls decorated with endless pictures of gentlemen in small cricket caps, large white flannels and (quite often) side-whiskers.

The Hobbs Sandwich, he said, leading the way through stained-glass panelled doors, was named for two great Surrey cricketers from between the wars, Sir Jack Hobbs, one of the few cricketers ever knighted, and Andrew Sandham, who had scored one hundred and seven centuries in first-class cricket. Long before I was born, he said.

I hadn't played cricket since distant days at school, nor liked it particularly even then: Clement Cornborough proved to be a lifelong fanatic.

He introduced me in the bar to an equal fanatic, his friend Val Catto, who then joined us for lunch. Not a word about my trust was spoken. The two of them talked cricket solidly for fifteen minutes and then the friend Catto began asking questions about my life. It dawned on me uneasily after a while that I was being interviewed, though I didn't know for what; and I learned afterwards that in conversation one day during the tea interval of a cricket match Catto had lamented to Cornborough that what he really needed was someone who knew the racing scene intimately, but whom the racing scene didn't know in return. An eyes-and-ears man. A silent, unknown investigator. A fly on racing's wall that no one would notice. Such a person, they had sighed together, was unlikely to be found. And that when a few weeks later I walked into Cornborough's office (or at least by the time I left it) the lawyer had suffered a brainwave which he passed on to his friend Val.

The Hobbs Sandwich lunch (of anything but sandwiches) had lasted through a good chunk of the afternoon, and by the end of it I had a job. I hadn't taken a lot of persuading, as it seemed interesting to me from the start. A month's trial on both sides, Brigadier Catto said, and mentioned a salary that had Cornborough smiling broadly.

'What's so funny?' the Brigadier asked. 'That's normal. We pay most of our men that at the start.'

'I forgot to mention it. Tor here is ... um ...' He paused, perhaps wondering whether finishing the sentence came under the heading of breaking a client's right to confidentiality, because after a short while he went on, 'He'd better tell you himself.'

'I accept the salary,' I said.

'What have you not told me?' Catto asked, suddenly very much the boss, his eyes not exactly suspicious but unsmiling: and I saw that I was not binding myself to some slightly eccentric friendly cricket nut, but to the purposeful, powerful man who had commanded a brigade and was currently keeping horse racing honest. I was not going to be playing a game, he was meaning, and if I thought so we would go no further.

I said wryly, 'I have a private income after tax of about twenty times the salary you're offering, but I'll take your money all the same, sir, and I'll work for it.'

He listened to the underlying declaration of commitment and good faith, and after a long pause he smiled briefly and nodded.

'Very well,' he said. 'When can you start?'

I had started the next day at Epsom races, relearning

the characters, reawakening sleeping memories, hearing
Aunt Viv's bright voice in my ear about as clearly as if
she were alive. 'There's Paddy Fredericks. Did I tell
you he used to be married to Betsy who's now Mrs
Glovebinder? Brad Glovebinder used to have horses
with Paddy Fredericks but when he pinched Betsy, he
took his horses away too . . . no justice in the world.
Hello Paddy, how are things? This is my nephew
Torquil, as I expect you remember, you've met him
often enough. Well done with your winner, Paddy . . .'
and Paddy had taken us off for a drink, buying me a
Coke.

I came face to face unexpectedly with the trainer
Paddy Fredericks that first day at Epsom and he hadn't
known me. There hadn't been a pause or a flicker. Aunt
Viv had been dead nearly eight years and I had changed
too much; and I had been reassured from that early
moment that my weird new non-identity was going to
work.

On the grounds that racing villains made it their
business to know the Security Service comprehensively
by sight, Brigadier Catto said that if ever he wanted to
speak to me himself, it would never be on a racecourse
but always in the bar of the Hobbs Sandwich, and so
it had been for the past three years. He and Clement
Cornborough had sponsored me for full membership
of the club and encouraged me to go there occasionally
on other days on my own, and although I'd thought
the Brigadier's passion for secrecy a shade obsessive I

had fallen in with his wishes and come to enjoy it, even if I'd learned a lot more about cricket than I really wanted to.

On the night of Derry Welfram's death, I walked into the bar at ten to eight and ordered a glass of Burgundy and a couple of beef sandwiches which came promptly because of the post-cricket-season absence of a hundred devotees discussing leg-breaks and insider politics at the tops of their voices. There were still a good number of customers, but from late September to the middle of April one could talk all night without laryngitis the next day, and when the Brigadier arrived he greeted me audibly and cheerfully as a fellow member well met and began telling me his assessment of the Test team just assembled for the winter tour abroad.

'They've disregarded Withers,' he complained. 'How are they ever going to get Balping out if they leave our best in-swinger biting his knuckles at home?'

I hadn't the faintest idea, and he knew it. With a gleam of a smile he bought himself a double Scotch drowned in a large glass of water, and led the way to one of the small tables round the edge of the room, still chatting on about the whys and wherefores of the selected team.

'Now,' he said without change of speed or volume, 'Welfram's dead, Shacklebury's dead, Gideon's dead, and the problem is what do we do next?'

The question. I knew, had to be rhetorical. He never

25

called me to the Hobbs Sandwich to ask my advice but always to direct me towards some new course of action, though he would listen and change his requirements if I put forward any huge objections, which I didn't often. He waited for a while, though, as if for an answer, and took a slow contemplative mouthful of weak whisky.

'Did Mr Gideon leave any notes?' I asked eventually.

'Not as far as we know. Nothing as helpful as telling us why he sold his horses to Filmer, if that's what you mean. Not unless a letter comes in the post next week, which I very much doubt.'

Gideon had been frightened beyond death, I thought. The threat must have been to the living: an ongoing perpetual threat.

'Mr Gideon has daughters,' I said.

The Brigadier nodded. 'Three. And five grandchildren. His wife died years ago, I suppose you know. Am I reading you aright?'

'That the daughters and grandchildren were hostages? Yes. Do you think they could know it?'

'Positive they don't,' the Brigadier said. 'I talked with his eldest daughter today. Nice, sensible woman, about fifty. Gideon shot himself yesterday evening, around five they think, but no one found him for hours as he did it out in the woods. I went down to the house today. His daughter, Sarah, said he's been ultra-depressed lately, going deeper and deeper, but she didn't know what had caused it. He wouldn't discuss

26

it. Sarah was in tears, of course, and also of course feeling guilty because she didn't prevent it; but she couldn't have prevented it, it's almost impossible to stop a determined suicide, you can't force people to go on living. Short of imprisonment, of course. Anyway, if she was any sort of a hostage, she didn't know it. It wasn't that sort of guilt.'

I offered him one of my so far uneaten sandwiches. He took one absent-mindedly and began to chew, and I ate one myself. The problem of what to do about Filmer lay in morose wrinkles across his brow and I'd heard he considered the collapse of the conspiracy trial a personal failure.

'I went to see Ezra Gideon myself after you and John Millington flushed out Welfram,' he said. 'I showed Ezra your photograph of Welfram. I thought he would faint, he went so white, but he still wouldn't speak. And now, God damn it, in one day we've lost both contacts. We don't know who Filmer will get to next, or if he's already active again, and we'll have the devil's own job spotting another frightener.'

'He won't have found one himself yet, I shouldn't think,' I said. 'Certainly not one as effective. They aren't that common, are they?'

'The police say they're getting younger.'

He looked unusually discouraged for someone whose success rate in all other fields was impressive. The lost battle rankled: the victories had been shrugged off. I drank some wine and waited for the commanding officer to emerge from the worried man, waited for him to unfold the plan of campaign.

He surprised me, however, by saying, 'I didn't think you'd stick this job this long.'

'Why not?'

'You know damn well why not. You're not dim. Clement told me the pile your father left you simply multiplied itself for twenty years, growing like a mushroom. And still does. Like a whole field of mushrooms. Why aren't you out there picking them?'

I sat back in my chair wondering what to say. I knew very well why I didn't pick them, but I wasn't sure it would sound sensible.

'Go on,' he said. 'I need to know.'

I glanced at his intent eyes and sensed his concentration, and realized suddenly that he might mean in some obscure way to base the future plan on my answer.

'It isn't so easy,' I said slowly, 'and don't laugh, it really isn't so easy to be able to afford anything you want. Short of the Crown Jewels and trifles like that. Well . . . I don't find it easy. I'm like a child loose in a sweetshop. I could eat and eat . . . and make myself sick . . . and greedy . . . and a jellyfish. So I keep my hands off the sweets and occupy my time following crooks. Is that any sort of answer?'

He grunted non-committally. 'How strong is the temptation?'

'On freezing cold days in sleet and wind at, say,

28

Doncaster races, very strong indeed. At Ascot in the sunshine I don't feel it.'

'Be serious,' he said. 'Put it another way. How strong is your commitment to the Security Service?'

'They're really two different things,' I said. 'I don't pick too many mushrooms because I want to retain order . . . to keep my feet well planted. Mushrooms can be hallucinogenic, after all. I work for you, for the Service, rather than in banking or farming and so on, because I like it and I'm not all that bad at what I do, really, and it's useful, and I'm not terribly good at twiddling my thumbs. I don't know that I'd die for you. Is that what you want?'

His lips twitched. He said, 'Fair enough. How do you feel about danger nowadays? I know you did risky enough things on your travels.'

After a brief pause, I said, 'What sort of danger?'

'Physical, I suppose.' He rubbed a thumb and forefinger down his nose and looked at me with steady eyes. 'Perhaps.'

'What do you want me to do?'

We had come to the point of the meeting, but he backed away from it still.

I knew in a way that it was because of what he'd called the mushrooms that he'd grown into the way of speaking to me as he did, proposing but seldom giving straight orders. He would have been more forthright if I'd been a junior army officer in uniform. Millington, who didn't know about the mushrooms, could uninhibitedly boss me around like a sergeant-major, and did so pretty sharply under pressure.

Millington mostly called me Kelsey and only occasionally, on good days, Tor. ('Tor? What sort of name is that?' he'd demanded at the beginning. 'Short for Torquil,' I said. '*Torquil?* Huh. I don't blame you.') He always referred to himself as Millington ('Millington here,' when he telephoned) and that was how I thought of him: he had never asked me to call him John. I supposed that a man who had served in a strongly hierarchical organization for a long time found surnames natural.

The Brigadier's attention still seemed to be focused on the glass he was slowly revolving in his hands, but finally he put it down precisely in the centre of a beer mat as if coming to a precise conclusion in his thoughts.

'I had a telephone call yesterday from my counterpart in the Canadian Jockey Club.' He paused again. 'Have you ever been to Canada?'

'Yes,' I said. 'Once, for a while, for maybe three months, mostly in the west. Calgary . . . Vancouver . . . I went up by boat from there to Alaska.'

'Did you go to the races in Canada?'

'Yes, a few times, but it must be about six years ago . . . and I don't know anyone—' I stopped, puzzled, not knowing what kind of response he wanted.

'Do you know about this train?' he said. 'The Transcontinental Mystery Race Train? Ever heard of it?'

'Um,' I said, reflecting. 'I read something about it the

other day. A lot of top Canadian owners are going on a jolly with their horses, stopping to race at tracks along the way. Is that the one you mean?'

'It is indeed. But the owners aren't all Canadian. Some of them are American, some are Australian and some are British. One of the British passengers is Julius Filmer.'

'Oh,' I said.

'Yes, oh. The Canadian Jockey Club has given its blessing to the whole affair because it's attracting worldwide publicity and they are hoping for bumper attendances, hoping to give all Canadian racing an extra boost. Yesterday, my counterpart, Bill Baudelaire, told me he'd been talking with the company who are arranging everything – they've had regular liaison meetings, it seems – and he found there was a late addition to the passenger list, Julius Filmer. Bill Baudelaire of course knows all about the conspiracy fiasco. He wanted to know if there wasn't some way we could keep the undesirable Mr Filmer off that prestigious train. Couldn't we possibly declare him *persona non grata* on all racetracks, including and especially Canadian. I told him if we'd had any grounds to warn Filmer off we'd have done it already, but the man was acquitted. We can't be seen to disgrace him when he's been declared not guilty, we'd be in all sorts of trouble. We can't warn him off for buying two horses from Gideon. These days, we can't just warn him off because we want to, he can only be warned off for transgressing against the rules of racing.'

All the frustrated fury of the Jockey Club vibrated in his voice. He wasn't a man to take impotence lightly.

'Bill Baudelaire knows all that, of course,' he went on. 'He said if we couldn't get Filmer off the train, would we please get one of our grandees *on*. Although the whole thing is sold out, he twisted the arms of the promoters to say they would let him have one extra ticket, and he wanted one of our stewards, or one of the Jockey Club department heads, or me myself, to go along conspicuously, so that Filmer would know he was being closely watched and would refrain from any sins he had in mind.'

'Are you going?' I asked, fascinated.

'No, I'm not. You are.'

'Um . . .' I said a shade breathlessly, 'I hardly fit the bill.'

'I told Bill Baudelaire,' the Brigadier said succinctly, 'that I would send him a passenger Filmer *didn't* know. One of my men. Then if Filmer does try anything, and after all it's a big if, we might have a real chance of finding out how and what, and catching him at it.'

My God, I thought. So simple, put like that. So absolutely impossible of performance.

I swallowed. 'What did Mr Baudelaire say?'

'I talked him into agreeing. He's expecting you.'

I blinked.

'Well,' the Brigadier said, 'not you by name.

Someone. Someone fairly young, I said, but experienced. Someone who wouldn't seem out of place ...' his teeth gleamed briefly ' ... on the millionaires' express.'

'But—' I said, and stopped dead, my mind full of urgent reservations and doubts that I was good enough for a job like that. Yet on the other hand, what a lark.

'Will you go?' he asked.

'Yes,' I said.

He smiled. 'I hoped you might.'

Brigadier Catto, who lived ninety miles from London in Newmarket, was staying overnight, as he often did, in a comfortable bedroom upstairs in the club. I left him in the bar after a while and drove the last half-mile home to where I lived in a quiet residential street in Kennington.

I had looked in that district for somewhere to put down a few roots on the grounds that I wouldn't be bothered to use the club much if I lived on the other side of London. Kennington, south of the Thames, rubbing shoulders with the grittiness of Lambeth and Brixton, was not where the racing crowd panted to be seen, and in fact I'd never spotted anyone locally that I knew by sight on the racecourse.

I'd come across an advertisement: 'House share available, for single presentable yuppy. Two rooms, bath, share kit, mortgage and upkeep. Call evenings', and although I'd been thinking in terms of a flat on my own, house sharing had suddenly seemed attractive, especially after the loneliness of work. I'd presented myself by appointment, been inspected by the four others in residence, and let in on trial, and it had all worked very well.

The four others were currently two sisters working in publishing (whose father had originally bought the house and set up the running-mortgage scheme), one junior barrister who tended to stutter, and an actor with a supporting role in a television series. The house rules were simple: pay on the dot, show good manners at all times, don't pry into the others' business, and don't let overnight girl/boy friends clog up any of the three bathrooms for hours in the morning.

There was a fair amount of laughter and camaraderie, but we tended to share coffee, beer, wine and saucepans more than confidences. I told them I was a dedicatedracegoerandnooneaskedwhetherIwonorlost.

The actor, Robbie, on the top floor, had been of enormous use to me, though I doubted he really knew it. He'd invited me up for a beer early one evening a few days after I went to live there, and I'd found him sitting before a brightly lit theatrical dressing table creating, as he said, a new make-up for a part he'd accepted in a play. I'd been startled to see how a different way of brushing his hair, how a large false moustache and heavier eyebrows had changed him.

'Tools of the trade,' he said, gesturing to the grease-paints and false hair lying in neat rows and boxes before him. 'Instant stubble, Fauntleroy curls – what would you like?'

'Curls,' I said slowly.

'Sit down, then,' he said cheerfully, getting up to give me his place, and he brought out a butane hair curler and wound my almost straight hair on to it bit by bit there and then, and within minutes I looked like a brown poodle, tousled, unbrushed, totally different.

'How's that?' he said, bending to look with me into the looking-glass.

'Amazing.' And easy, I thought. I could do it in the car, any time.

'It suits you,' Robbie said. He knelt down beside me, put his arm round my shoulders, gave me a little squeeze and smiled with unmistakable invitation into my eyes.

'No,' I said matter-of-factly. 'I like girls.'

He wasn't offended. 'Haven't you ever tried the other?'

'It's just not me, dear,' I said, 'as one might say.'

He laughed and took his arm away. 'Never mind, then. No harm in trying.'

We drank the beer and he showed me how to shape and stick on a bold macho moustache, holding out a pair of thick-framed glasses for good measure. I regarded the stranger looking back at me from the glass and said I'd never realized how easy it was to mislead.

'Sure thing. All it takes is a bit of nerve.'

And he was right about that. I bought a butane hair curler for myself, but I took it with me for a week in the car before I screwed myself up to stop in a lay-by on the way to Newbury races and actually use it. In the three years since then, I'd done it dozens of times without a thought, brushing and damping out the effects on the way home.

Sundays I usually spent lazily in my two big bright rooms on the first floor (the barrister directly above, the sisters below) sleeping, reading, pottering about. For about a year some time earlier I'd spent my Sundays with the daughter of one of the Hobbs Sandwich members, but it had been a mutual passing pleasure rather than a grand passion for both of us, and in the end she'd drifted away and married someone else. I supposed I too would marry one day: knew I would like to: felt there was no hurry this side of thirty.

On the Sunday morning after meeting the Brigadier in the club I began to think about what I should pack for Canada. He'd told me to be what I spent so much time not being, a rich young loafer with nothing to do but enjoy myself. 'All you need to do is talk about horses to the other passengers and keep your eyes open.'

'Yes,' I said.

'Look the part.'

'Yes, right.'

'I've caught sight of you sometimes at the races, you

know, looking like a stockbroker one day and a hillbilly the next. Millington says he often can't see you, even though he knows you're there.'

'I've got better with practice, I suppose, but I never really do much. Change my hair, change my clothes, slouch a bit.'

'It works,' he said. 'Be what Filmer would expect.'

It wasn't so much what Filmer would expect, I thought, looking at the row of widely assorted jackets in my wardrobe, but what I could sustain over the ten days the party was due to take before it broke up.

Curls, for instance, were out, as they disappeared in rain. Stuck-on moustaches were out in case they came off. Spectacles were out, as one could forget to put them on. I would have to look basically as nature had ordained and be as nondescript and unnoticeable as possible.

I sorted out the most expensive and least worn of my clothes, and decided I'd better buy new shirts, new shoes and a cashmere sweater before I went.

I telephoned Millington on Monday morning as instructed and found him in his usual state of disgruntlement. He had heard about the train. He was not in favour of my going on it. The Security Service (meaning the Brigadier) should have sent a properly trained operative, an ex-policeman preferably. Like himself, for instance. Someone who knew the techniques of investigation and could be trusted not to destroy vital evidence through ignorance and clumsiness. I listened without interruption for so long that, in the end, he said sharply, 'Are you still there?'

'Yes,' I said.

'I want to see you, preferably later this morning. I'll have your air ticket. I suppose you do have an up-to-date passport?'

We agreed to meet, as often before, in a reasonably good small snack bar next to Victoria Station, convenient for both Millington who lived a couple of miles south-west across Battersea Bridge, and for me a few stops down the line to the south.

I arrived ten minutes before the appointed time and found Millington already sitting at a table with a mug of brown liquid and several sausage rolls in progress. I took a tray, slid it along the rails in front of the glass-fronted serving display and picked a slice of cheesecake from behind one of the small hinged doors. I actually approved of the glass-door arrangement: it meant that with luck one's cheesecake wouldn't have been sneezed on by the general public, but only by a cook or two and the snack bar staff.

Millington eyed my partially hygienic wedge and said he preferred the lemon meringue pie himself.

'I like that too,' I said equably.

Millington was a big beer-and-any-kind-of-pie man who must have given up thankfully on weight control when he left the police. He looked as if he now weighed

about seventeen stone, and while not gross was definitely a solid mass, but with an agility also that he put
to good use in his job. Many petty racecourse crooks
had made the mistake of believing Millington couldn't
snake after them like an eel through the crowds, only
to feel the hand of retribution falling weightily on their
collar. I'd seen Millington catch a dipping pickpocket
on the wing: an impressive sight.

The large convenience-food snack bar, bright and
clean, was always infernally noisy, pop music thumping
away to the accompaniment of chairs scraping the floor
and the clatter of meals at a gallop. The clientele were
mostly travellers, coming or going on trains lacking
buffet cars, starving or prudent; travellers checking
their watches, gulping too-hot coffee, uninterested in
others, leaving in a hurry. No one ever gave Millington
and me a second glance, and no one could ever have
overheard what we said.

We never met there when there was racing at places
like Plumpton, Brighton, Lingfield and Folkestone: on
those days the whole racing circus could wash through
Victoria Station. We never met, either, anywhere near
the Security Service head office in the Jockey Club, in
Portman Square. It was odd, I sometimes thought, that
I'd never once been through my employer's door.

Millington said, 'I don't approve of you travelling
with Filmer.'

'So I gathered,' I said. 'You said so earlier.'

'The man's a murderer.'

He wasn't concerned for my safety, of course, but thought me unequal to the contest.

'He may not actually murder anyone on the train,' I said flippantly.

'It's no joke,' he said severely. 'And after this he'll know you, and you'll be no use to us on the racecourse, as far as he's concerned.'

'There are about fifty people going on the trip, the Brigadier said. I won't push myself into Filmer's notice. He quite likely won't remember me afterwards.'

'You'll be too close to him,' Millington said obstinately.

'Well,' I said thoughtfully, 'it's the only chance we've ever had so far to get really close to him at all. Even if he's only going along for a harmless holiday, we'll know a good deal more about him this way.'

'I don't like wasting you,' Millington said, shaking his head.

I looked at him in real surprise. 'That's a change,' I said.

'I didn't want you working for us, to begin with,' he said, shrugging. 'Didn't see what good you could do, thought it was stupid. Now you're my eyes. The eyes in the back of my head that the villains have been complaining about ever since you started. I've got the sense to know it. And if you must know, I don't want to lose you. I told the Brigadier we were wasting our trump card, sending you on that train. He said we might be playing it, and if we could get rid of Filmer, it was worth it.'

I looked at Millington's worried face. I said slowly, 'Do you, and does the Brigadier, know something about Filmer's travel plans that you've not told me?'

'When he said that,' Millington said, looking down at his sausage rolls, 'I asked him that same question. He didn't answer. I don't know of anything myself. I'd tell you, if I did.'

Perhaps he would, I thought. Perhaps he wouldn't.

The next day, Tuesday, I drove north to Nottingham for a normal day's hard work hanging around doing nothing much at the races.

I'd bought the new clothes and a new suitcase and had more or less packed ready for my departure the next morning, and the old long-distance wanderlust that had in the past kept me travelling for seven years had woken from its recent slumber and given me a sharp nudge in the ribs. Millington shouldn't fear losing me to Filmer, I thought, so much as to the old seductive tug of moving on, moving on . . . seeing what lay round the next corner

I could do it now, I supposed, in five-star fashion, not backpacking; in limousines, not on buses; eating haute cuisine, not hot dogs; staying in Palm Beach, not dusty backwoods. Probably I'd enjoy the lushness for a while, maybe even for a long while, but in the end, to stay real, I'd have to get myself out of the sweet-shop and do some sort of work, and not put it off and off until I no longer had a taste for plain bread.

I was wearing, perhaps as a salute to plain bread, a well-worn leather jacket and a flat cloth cap, the bin-oculars-camera slung round my neck, a racecard clutched in my hand. I stood around vaguely outside the weighing room, watching who came and who went, who talked to whom, who looked worried, who happy, who malicious.

A young apprentice with an ascendant reputation came out of the weighing room in street clothes, not riding gear, and stood looking around as if searching for someone. His eyes stopped moving and focused, and I looked to see what had caught his attention. He was looking at the Jockey Club's paid steward, who was acting at the meeting as the human shape of authority. The steward was standing in social conversation with a pair of people who had a horse running that day, and after a few minutes he raised his hat to the lady and walked out towards the parade ring.

The apprentice calmly watched his departing back, then made another sweep of the people around. Seeing nothing to worry about he set off towards the stand the jockeys watched the races from and joined a youngish man with whom he walked briefly, talking. They parted near the stands, and I, following, transferred my attention from the apprentice and followed the other man instead; he went straight into the bookmakers' enclosure in front of the stands, and along the rows of bookmakers to the domain of Collie Goodboy who was shouting his offered odds from the height of a small platform the size of a beer crate.

The apprentice's contact didn't place a bet. He picked up a ledger and began to record the bets of others. He spoke to Collie Goodboy (Les Morris to his parents) who presently wiped off the offered odds from his board, and chalked up new ones. The new odds were generous. Collie Goodboy was rewarded by a rush of eager punters keen to accept the invitation. Collie Goodboy methodically took their money.

With a sigh I turned away and wandered off up to the stands to watch the next race, scanning the crowds as usual, watching the world revolve. I ended up standing not far from the rails dividing the bookmakers' section of the stands (called the Tattersalls enclosure) from the club, the more expensive end. I often did that, as from there one could see the people in both enclosures easily. One could see also who came to the dividing rails to put bets on with the row of bookmakers doing business in that privileged position. The 'rails' bookmakers were the princes of their trade; genial, obliging, fair, flint-hearted, brilliant mathematicians.

I watched as always to see who was betting with whom, and when I came to the bookmaker nearest to the stands, nearest to me, I saw that the present customer was Filmer.

I was watching him bet, thinking of the rail journey ahead, when he tilted his head back and looked straight up into my eyes.

CHAPTER THREE

I looked away instantly but smoothly, and presently glanced back.

Filmer was still talking to the bookmaker. I edged upwards through the crowd behind me until I was about five steps higher and surrounded by other racegoers.

Filmer didn't look back to where I'd been standing. He didn't search up or down or sideways to see where I had gone.

My thumping heart quietened down a bit. The meeting of eyes had been accidental: had to have been. Dreadfully unwelcome, all the same, particularly at this point.

I hadn't expected him to have been at Nottingham, and hadn't looked for him. Two of his horses were certainly down to run, but Filmer himself almost never went to the Midland courses of Nottingham, Leicester or Wolverhampton. He had definite preferences in racecourses, as in so much else: always a creature of habit.

I made no attempt to shadow him closely, as it wasn't

necessary: before the following race he would be down in the parade ring to watch his horse walk round and I could catch him up there. I watched him conclude his bet and walk away to climb the stands for the race about to start, and as far as I could see he was alone, which also was unusual, as either the girlfriend or the male companion was normally in obsequious attendance.

The race began and I watched it with interest. The chatty apprentice wasn't riding in it himself, but the stable that employed him had a runner. The runner started third favourite and finished third last. I switched my gaze to Collie Goodboy, and found him smiling. A common, sad, fraudulent sequence that did racing no good.

Filmer stepped down from the stands and headed in the direction of the saddling boxes, to supervise, as he always did, the final preparation for his horse's race. I drifted along in his wake to make sure, but that was indeed where he went. From there to the parade ring, from there to place a bet with the same bookmaker as before, from there to the stands to watch his horse race. From there to the unsaddling enclosure allotted to the horse that finished second.

Filmer took his defeat graciously, making a point as always of congratulating the winning owner, in this case a large middle-aged lady who looked flushed and flattered.

Filmer left the unsaddling enclosure with a smirk of

self-satisfaction and was immediately confronted by a young man who tried to thrust a briefcase into his hand.

Julius Apollo's face turned from smug to fury quicker than Shergar won the Derby, as Paul Shackle-bury would have said. Filmer wouldn't take the case and he practically spat at the offerer, his black head going forward like a striking cobra. The young man with the briefcase retreated ultra-nervously and in panic ran away, and Filmer, regaining control of himself, began looking around in the general direction of stewards and pressmen to see if any of them had noticed. He visibly sighed with relief that none of them showed any sign of it – and he hadn't looked my way at all.

I followed the demoralized young man, who still held on to the briefcase. He made straight for the men's cloakroom, stayed there for a fair time and came out looking pale. Filmer's effect on people's guts, I reflected, would put any laxative to shame.

The shaken youth with the briefcase then made his nervous way to a rendezvous with a thin, older man who was waiting just outside the exit gate, biting his nails. When the thin man saw the briefcase still in the nervous youth's possession he looked almost as furious as Filmer had done, and a strong argument developed in which one could read the dressing-down in the vigorous chopping gestures, even if one couldn't hear the words.

Thin man poked nervous man several times sharply

DICK FRANCIS

in the chest. Nervous man's shoulders drooped. Thin
man turned away and walked off deep into the car
park.

Nervous man brought the briefcase with him back
through the gate and into the nearest bar, and I had to
hang around for a long time in the small crowd there
before anything else happened. The scattered clientele
was watching the television: nervous man shuffled from
foot to foot and sweated, and kept a sharp lookout at
the people passing by outside in the open air. Then,
some time after Filmer's second runner had tried and
(according to the closed-circuit commentary) lost,
Filmer himself came past, tearing up betting tickets and
not looking pleased.

Nervous man shot out from his waiting position just
inside the door of the sheltering bar and offered the
briefcase again, and this time Filmer took it, but in
fierce irritation and with another sharp set of glances
around him. He saw nothing to disturb him. He was
leaving after the fifth of the six races and all forms of
authority were still engaged to his rear. He gripped the
case's handle and strode purposefully out on his way
to his car.

Nervous man shuffled a bit on the spot a bit more
and then followed Filmer through the exit gate and
into the car park. I tagged along again and saw both
of them still making for their transport, though in different directions. I followed nervous man, not Filmer,
and saw him get into the front passenger seat of a car

already occupied by thin man, who still looked cross. They didn't set off immediately and I had time to walk at a steady pace past the rear of their car on the way to my own which was parked strategically, as ever, near the gate to the road, for making quick following getaways. I memorized their number plate in case I later lost them; and out on the road, comfortably falling into place behind them, I telephoned Millington.

I told him about the briefcase and read him the number plate still ahead in my sight.

'The car's going north, though,' I said. 'How far do you want me to go?'

'What time's your flight tomorrow?'

'Noon, from Heathrow. But I have to go home first to pick up my gear and passport.'

He thought for a few moments. 'You'd better decide for yourself. If he gets on the motorway to Scotland . . . well, don't go.'

'All right.'

'Very interesting,' Millington said, 'that he didn't want to be seen in public accepting that briefcase.'

'Very.'

'Anything special about it?'

'As far as I could see,' I said, 'it was black, polished, possibly crocodile, with gold clasps.'

'Well, well,' Millington said vaguely. 'I'll get back to you with that car number.'

The thin man's car aimed unerringly for the motorway in the direction of Scotland. I decided to keep on going at least until Millington called back, which he did with impressive speed, telling me that my quarry was registered to I. J. Horfitz, resident of Doncaster, address supplied.

'All right,' I said, 'I'll go to Doncaster.' An hour and a bit ahead, I thought, with plenty of time to return.

'Does that name Horfitz ring any bells with you?' Millington asked.

'None at all,' I said positively. 'And by the way, you know that promising young apprentice of Pete Shaw's? All that talent? The silly young fool passed some verbal info to a new character on the racecourse who turned out to be writing the book for Collie Goodboy. Collie Goodboy thought it good news.'

'What was it, do you know?'

'Pete Shaw had a runner in the second race, third favourite, finished nearly last. The apprentice knew the score, though he wasn't riding it.'

'Huh,' Millington said. 'I'll put the fear of God into the lot of them, Pete Shaw, the owner, the jockey, the apprentice and Collie Goodboy. Stir them up and warn them. I suppose,' he said as an afterthought, 'you didn't get any photos? We haven't any actual proof?'

'Not really. I took one shot of the apprentice talking to Collie's man, but they had their backs to me. One of Collie's man with Collie. One of Collie's board with the generous odds.'

'Better than nothing,' he said judiciously. 'It'll give them all an unholy fright. The innocent ones will be livid and sack the guilty, like they usually do. Clean their own house. Save us a job. And we'll keep a permanent eye on that stupid apprentice. Ring me when you get to Doncaster.'

'OK. And I took some more photos. One of the nervous young man with the briefcase, one of him with the thin man . . . er . . . I. J. Horfitz possibly, I suppose, and one of Filmer with the briefcase, though I'm not sure if that one will be very clear, I had almost no time and I was quite far away, and I was using the cigarette lighter-camera, it's less conspicuous.'

'All right. We need that film before you go. Um . . . er . . . you'd better give me a ring when you're on the way back, and I'll have thought of somewhere we can meet tonight. Right?'

'Yes,' I said. 'Right.'

'This Horfitz person, what did he look like?'

'Thin, elderly, wore a dark overcoat and a black trilby, and glasses. Looked ready for a funeral, not the races.'

Millington grunted in what seemed to me to be recognition.

'Do you know him?' I asked.

'He was before your time. But yes, I know him. Ivor Horfitz. It must be him. We got him warned off for life five years ago.'

'What for?'

'It's a long story. I'll tell you later. And I don't think after all you need to spend all that time going to Doncaster. We can always find him, if we want to. Turn round at the next exit and come back to London, and I'll meet you in that pub at Victoria. Not the snack bar; the pub.'

'Yes, right. See you in about . . . um . . . two and a half hours, with luck.'

Two and a half hours later, beer-and-pork-pie time in a dark far corner in a noisy bar, Millington's preferred sort of habitat.

I gave him the exposed but undeveloped film, which he put in his pocket saying, 'Eyes in the back of my head,' with conspicuous satisfaction.

'Who is Horfitz?' I said, quenching the long drive's thirst in a half-pint of draught. 'Did you know he knew Filmer?'

'No,' he said, answering the second question first. 'And Filmer wouldn't want to be seen with him, nor to be seen in any sort of contact.'

'What you're saying,' I said slowly, 'is that the messenger, the nervous young man, is also known by sight to the stewards . . . to you yourself probably . . . because if he were an unidentifiable stranger, why should Filmer react so violently to being seen with him; to being seen accepting something from him?'

Millington gave me a sideways look. 'You've learned a thing or two, haven't you, since you started?' He patted the pocket containing the film. 'This will tell us if we know him. What did he look like?'

'Fairly plump, fairly gormless. Sweaty. Unhappy. A worm between two hawks.'

Millington shook his head. 'Might be anyone,' he said.

'What did Horfitz do?' I asked.

Millington bit into pork pie and took his time, speaking eventually round escaping crumbs of pastry.

'He owned a small stableful of horses in Newmarket and employed his own trainer for them, who naturally did what he was told. Very successful little stable in a quiet way. Amazing results, but there you are, some owners are always lucky. Then the trainer got cold feet because he thought we were on to him, which we actually weren't, we'd never reckoned him for a villain. Anyway, he blew the whistle on the operation, saying the strain was getting too much for him. He said all the horses in the yard were as good as interchangeable. They ran in whatever races he and Horfitz thought they could win. Three-year-olds in two-year-old races, past winners in maidens-at-starting, any old thing. Horfitz bought and sold horses continually so the yard never looked the same from week to week, and the stable lads came and went like yo-yos, like they do pretty much anyway. They employed all sorts of different jockeys. No one cottoned on. Horfitz had some nice long-priced winners but no bookmakers hollered foul. It was a small unfashionable stable, see? Never in the newspapers. Because they didn't run in big races, just small ones at tracks the press don't go to, but you can win as much by betting on those as on any others. It was all pretty low-key, but we found out that Horfitz had made literally hundreds of thousands, not just by betting but by selling his winners. Only he always sold the real horses which fitted the names on the racecard, not the horses that had actually run. He kept those and ran them again, and sold the horses in whose names they'd run, and so on and so on. Audacious little fiddle, the whole thing.'

'Yes,' I agreed, and felt a certain amount of awe at the energy and organization put into the enterprise.

'So when the trainer ratted we set a few traps with his help and caught Horfitz with his pants down, so to speak. He got warned off for life and swore to kill his trainer, which he hasn't done so far. The trainer was warned off for three years with a severe caution, but he got his licence back two years ago. Part of the bargain. So he's in business again in a small way but we keep his runners under a microscope, checking their passports every time they run. We're a lot hotter at checking passports randomly all over the place now, as of course you know.'

I nodded.

Then Millington's jaw literally dropped. I looked at the classic sign of astonishment and said, 'What's the matter?'

'Gawd,' he said. 'What a turn-up. Can you believe it? Paul Shacklebury, that murdered stable lad, he was working for Horfitz's old trainer.'

I left Millington frowning with concentration over a replenished pint while he tried to work out the significance of Horfitz's old trainer employing a lad who was murdered for knowing too much about Filmer. What had Paul Shacklebury known, Millington demanded rhetorically for the hundredth time. And, more to the minute, what was in the briefcase, and why was Horfitz giving it to Filmer?

'Work on the sweating messenger,' I suggested, getting up to go. 'He might crack open like the trainer. You never know.'

'Maybe we will,' Millington said. 'And Tor . . . look out for yourself on the train.'

He could be quite human sometimes, I thought.

I flew to Ottawa the next day and gave in to temptation at Heathrow to the extent of changing my ticket from knees-against-chest economy to full-stretch-out first class. I also asked the Ottawa taxi driver who took me into the city from the airport to find me a decent hotel; he cast a rapid eye over my clothes and the new suitcase and said the Four Seasons should suit.

It suited. They gave me a small pleasant suite and I telephoned straight away to the number I'd been given for Bill Baudelaire. He answered himself at the first ring, rather to my surprise, and said yes, he'd had a telex to confirm I was on my way. He had a bass voice with a lot of timbre even over the wires and was softly Canadian in accent.

He asked where I would be in an hour and said he

55

would come around then to brief me on the matter in hand, and I gathered from his circumspect sentences that he wasn't alone and didn't want to be understood. Just like home, I thought comfortably, and unpacked a few things, and showered off the journey and awaited events.

Outside, the deepening orange of the autumn sunshine was turning the green copper roofs of the turreted stone government buildings to a transient shimmering gold, and I reflected, watching from the windows, that I'd much liked this graceful city when I'd been here before. I was filled with a serene sense of peace and contentment, which I remembered a few times in the days lying ahead.

Bill Baudelaire came when the sky had grown dark and I'd switched on the lights, and he looked round the suite with quizzical eyebrows.

'I'm glad to see old Val has staked you to rooms befitting a rich young owner.'

I smiled and didn't enlighten him. He'd shaken my hand when I opened the door to him and looked me quickly, piercingly up and down in the way of those used to assessing strangers instantly and with no inhibitions about letting them know it.

I saw a man of plain looks but positive charm, a solid man much younger than the Brigadier, maybe forty, with reddish hair, pale blue eyes and pale skin pitted by the scars of old acne. Once seen, I thought, difficult to forget.

He was wearing a dark grey business suit with a cream shirt and a red tie out of step with his hair, and I wondered if he were colour-blind or simply liked the effect.

He walked straight across the sitting room, sat in the armchair nearest to the telephone and picked up the receiver.

'Room service?' he said. 'Please send up as soon as possible a bottle of vodka and . . . er . . .' He raised his eyebrows in my direction, in invitation.

'Wine,' I said. 'Red. Bordeaux preferably.'

Bill Baudelaire repeated my request with a ceiling price and disconnected.

'You can put the drinks on your expense sheet and I'll initial it,' he said. 'You do have an expense sheet, I suppose?'

'I do in England.'

'Then start one here, of course. How are you paying the hotel bills?'

'By credit card. My own.'

'Is that usual? Never mind. You give all the bills to me when you've paid them, along with your expense sheet, and Val and I will deal with it.'

'Thank you,' I said. Val would have a fit, I thought, but then on second thoughts, no he probably wouldn't. He would pay me the agreed budget; fair was fair.

'Sit down,' Bill Baudelaire said, and I sat opposite him in another armchair, crossing one knee over the other. The room seemed hot to me with the central heating, and I wasn't wearing a jacket. He considered me for a while, his brow furrowing with seeming uncertainty.

'How old are you?' he said abruptly.

'Twenty-nine.'

'Val said you were experienced.' It wasn't exactly a question, nor a matter of disbelief.

'I've worked for him for three years.'

'He said you would look this part . . . and you do.' He sounded more puzzled than pleased, though. 'You seem so polished . . . I suppose it's not what I expected.'

I said, 'If you saw me in the cheaper sections of a racecourse, you would think I'd been born there, too.'

His face lightened into a smile. 'Right, then. I'll accept that. Well, I've brought you a whole lot of papers.' He glanced at the large envelope that he had put on the table beside the telephone. 'Details about the train and about some of the people who'll be on it, and details about the horses and the arrangements for those. This has all been an enormous undertaking. Everyone has worked very hard on it. It's essential that it retains a good, substantial, untarnished image from start to finish. We're hoping for increased worldwide awareness of Canadian racing. Although we do of course hit world headlines with the Queen's Plate in June or July, we want to draw more international horses here. We want to put our programmes more on the map. Canada's a great country. We want to maximize our impact on the international racing circuit.'

'Yes,' I said, 'I do understand.' I hesitated. 'Do you have a public relations firm working on it?'

'What? Why do you ask? Yes, we do, as a matter of fact. What difference does it make?'

'None, really. Will they have a representative on the train?'

'To minimize negative incidents? No, not unless . . .' he stopped and listened to what he'd said. 'I'm using their jargon, damn it. I'll watch that. So easy to repeat what they say.'

A knock on the door announced the drinks in the charge of an ultra-polite slow-moving waiter who knew where to find ice and mixers in the room's own refrigerator. The waiter took his deliberate time over uncorking the wine, and Bill Baudelaire, stifling impatience, said we would do the pouring ourselves. When the tortoise waiter had gone he gestured to me to help myself, and on his own account fixed a lengthy splash of vodka over a tumblerful of cubes.

He had suggested to the Brigadier that I should meet him first here in Ottawa, as he had business in that city which couldn't be postponed. It would also, they both thought, be more securely private, as everyone going on the train in the normal way would be collecting in Toronto.

'You and I,' Bill Baudelaire said over his vodka, 'will fly to Toronto tomorrow evening on separate planes, after you've spent the day absorbing all the material I've brought you and asking any questions that arise. I

59

propose to drop by your sitting room here again at two o'clock for a final briefing.'

'Will I be able to get in touch with you fairly easily after tomorrow?' I asked. 'I'd like to be able to.'

'Yes, indeed. I'm not going on the train myself, as of course you know, but I'll be at Winnipeg for the races there, and at Vancouver. And at Toronto, of course. I've outlined everything. You'll find it in the package. We can't really discuss anything properly until you've read it.'

'All right.'

'There's one unwelcome piece of news, however, that isn't in there because I heard it too late to include. It seems Julius Filmer had bought a share in one of the horses travelling on the train. The partnership was registered today and I was told just now by telephone. The Ontario Racing Commission is deeply concerned, but we can't do anything about it. No regulations have been broken. They won't let people who've been convicted of felonies such as arson, fraud or illegal gambling own horses, but Filmer hasn't been convicted of anything.'

'Which horse?' I said.

'Which horse? Laurentide Ice. Quite useful. You can read about it in there.' He nodded to the package. 'The problem is that we made a rule that only owners could go along to the horse car to see the horses. We couldn't have everyone tramping about there, both for security reasons and for preventing the animals being upset. We thought the only comfort left to us about Filmer's being on the train was that he wouldn't have access to the horse car, and now he will.'

'Awkward.'

'Infuriating.' He refilled his glass, with the suppressed violence of his frustration. 'Why for God's sake couldn't that goddam crook have kept his snotty nose out? He's trouble. We all know it. He's planning something. He'll ruin the whole thing. He practically said as much.' He looked me over and shook his head. 'No offence to you, but how are you going to stop him?'

'It depends what needs to be stopped.'

His face lightened suddenly to a smile as before. 'Yes, all right, we'll wait and see. Val said you don't miss things. Let's hope he's right.'

He went away after a while and with a great deal of interest I opened the package and found it absolutely fascinating from start to finish.

'The Great Transcontinental Mystery Race Train', as emblazoned in red on the gold cover of the glossy prospectus, had indeed entailed an enormous amount of organization. Briefly, the enterprise offered to the racehorse owners of the world a chance to race a horse in Toronto, to go by train to Winnipeg, and race a horse there, to stop for two nights at a hotel high in the Rockies, and to continue by train to Vancouver, where they might again race a horse. There was accommodation for eleven horses on the train, and for forty-eight human VIP passengers.

At Toronto, Winnipeg and Vancouver there would be overnight stays in top-class hotels. Transport from train to hotels to races and back to the train was also included as required. The entire trip would last from lunch at Toronto races on the Saturday, to the end of the special race day at Vancouver ten days later.

On the train there would be special sleeping cars, a special dining car, two private chefs and a load of good wine. People who owned their own private rail cars could, as in the past, apply for them to be joined to the train.

Every possible extra luxury would be available if requested in advance, and in addition, for entertainment along the way, an intriguing mystery would be enacted on board and at the stopovers, which passengers would be invited to solve.

I winced a shade at that last piece of information: keeping eyes on Filmer would be hard enough anyhow without all sorts of imaginary mayhem going on around him. He himself was mystery enough.

Special races, I read, had been introduced into the regular programmes at Woodbine racecourse, Toronto, at Assiniboia Downs, Winnipeg, and at Exhibition Park, Vancouver. The races had been framed to be ultra-attractive to the paying public, with magnificent prize money to please the owners. The owners of the horses and indeed all the train passengers would be given VIP treatment at all the racecourses, including lunch with the presidents.

It wasn't to be expected that owners would want to run the horses on the train three times in so short a span.

Any owner was free to run a horse just once. Any owner (or any other passenger on the train) was free to bring any other of his horses to Toronto, Winnipeg or Vancouver by road or by air to run in the special races. The trip was to be a light-hearted junket for the visitors, a celebration of racing in Canada.

In smaller print after all that trumpeting came the information that accommodation was available also for one groom for each horse. If owners wanted space for extra attendants, would they please specify early. Grooms and other attendants would have their own dining and sleeping cars and their own separate entertainments.

Stabling had been reserved at Toronto, Winnipeg and Vancouver for the horses going by train, and they would be able to exercise normally at all three places. In addition, during the passengers' visit to the mountains, the horses would be stabled and exercised in Calgary. The good care of the horses was of prime importance, and a veterinarian would be at once helicoptered to the train if his services should become necessary between scheduled stops.

Next in the package was a pencilled note from Bill Baudelaire:

All eleven horse places were sold out within two weeks of the first major announcement.

All forty-eight VIP passenger places were sold within a month.
There are dozens of entries for the special races.
This is going to be a success!

After that came a list of the eleven horses, with past form, followed by a list of their owners, with nationalities. Three owners from England (including Filmer), one from Australia, three from the United States and five from Canada (including Filmer's partner).

The owners, with husbands, wives, families and friends, had taken up twenty-seven of the forty-eight passenger places. Four of the remaining twenty-one places had also been taken by well-known Canadian owners (identified by a star against their names), and Bill Baudelaire, in a note pencilled at the bottom of this passenger list had put, 'Splendid response from our appeal to our owners to support the project!'

There were no trainers mentioned on the passenger list, and in fact I later learned that the trainers were making their own way by air as usual to Winnipeg and Vancouver, presumably because the train trip was too time-consuming and expensive.

Next in the package came a bunch of handouts from the three racecourses, from the Canadian railway company and from the four hotels, all shiny pamphlets extolling their individual excellences. Finally, a fat brochure with good colour plates put together by the travel organizers in charge of getting the show on the railroad, a job which seemed well within their powers since they apparently also arranged safaris to outer deserts, treks to the Poles and tours to anywhere anyone cared to go.

They also staged mysteries as entertainment; evenings, weekends, moving or stationary. They were experts from much practice.

For the Great Transcontinental Mystery Race Train, they said, they had arranged something extra special. 'A mystery that will grab you by the throat. A stunning experience. All around you the story will unfold. Clues will appear. BE ON YOUR GUARD.'

Oh great, I thought wryly. But they hadn't finished. There was a parting shot.

'BEWARE! MANY PEOPLE ARE NOT WHAT THEY SEEM.'

CHAPTER FOUR

'How can they stage a play on a train?' I asked Bill Baudelaire the next day. 'I wouldn't have thought it would work.'

'Mysteries are very popular in Canada. Very fashionable,' he said, 'and they don't exactly stage a play. Some of the passengers will be actors and they will make the story evolve. I went to a dinner party . . . a mystery dinner party . . . not long ago and some of the guests were actors, and before we knew where we were, we were all caught up in a string of events, just as if it were real. Quite amazing. I went because my wife wanted to. I didn't think I would enjoy it in the least, but I did.'

'Some of the passengers . . .' I repeated slowly. 'Do you know which ones?'

'No, I don't,' he said, more cheerfully than I liked. 'That's part of the fun for everyone, trying to spot the actors.'

I liked it less and less.

'And of course the actors may be hiding among the other lot of passengers until their turn to appear comes.'

'What other lot of passengers?' I said blankly.

'The racegoers.' He looked at my face. 'Doesn't it say anything about them in the package?'

'No, it doesn't.'

'Ah.' He reflected briefly. 'Well, in order to make the trip economically viable, the rail company said we should add our own party to the regular train which sets off every day from Toronto to Vancouver, which is called the Canadian. We didn't want to do that because it would have meant we couldn't stop the train for two nights in Winnipeg and again for the mountains, and although the carriages could be unhitched and left in a siding, we'd be faced with security problems. But our own special train was proving extremely, almost impossibly, expensive. So we advertised a separate excursion . . . a racegoing trip . . . and now we have our own train. But it has been expanded, with three or four more sleeping cars, another dining car, and a dayniter or two according to how many tickets they sell in the end. We had an enormous response from people who didn't want to pay what the owners are paying but would like to go to the races across Canada on vacation. They are buying their tickets for the train at the normal fare and making their own arrangements at the stops . . . and we call these passengers the racegoers, for convenience.'

I sighed. I supposed it made sense. 'What's a day-niter?' I said.

'A car with reclining seats, not bedrooms.'

'And how many people altogether will be travelling?'

'Difficult to say. Start with forty-eight owners . . . we call them owners to distinguish them from the racegoers . . . and the grooms. Then the actors and the people from the travel company. Then the train crew and stewards, waiters, chefs and so on. With all the racegoers . . . well, perhaps about two hundred people altogether. We won't know until we start. Probably not then, unless we actually count.'

I could get lost among two hundred more easily than among forty-eight, I thought. Perhaps it might not be too bad. Yet the owners would be looking for actors . . . for people who weren't what they seemed.

'You asked about contact,' Bill Baudelaire said.

'Yes.'

'I've discussed it with some of our Jockey Club, and we think you'll simply have to telephone us from the stops.'

I said with some alarm, 'How many of your Jockey Club know I'm going on the train?'

He looked surprised. 'I suppose everyone in the executive office knows we'll have a man in place. They don't know exactly who. Not by name. Not yet. Not until I'd met you and approved. They don't and won't know what you look like.'

'Would you please not tell them my name,' I said.

He was half bewildered, half affronted. 'But our Jockey Club are sensible men. Discreet.'

'Information leaks,' I said.

He looked at me broodingly, vodka and ice cubes tinkling in a fresh glass. 'Are you serious?' he said.

'Yes, indeed.'

His brow wrinkled. 'I'm afraid I may have mentioned your name to one or two. But I will impress on them not to repeat it.'

It was too late, I supposed, for much else. Perhaps I was getting too obsessed with secrecy. Still . . .

'I'd rather not telephone direct to the Jockey Club,' I said. 'Couldn't I leave messages where only you will get them? Like your own home?'

His face melted into an almost boyish grin. 'I have three teenage daughters and a busy wife. The receiver is almost never in the cradle.' He thought briefly, then wrote a number on a sheet of a small notepad and gave it to me.

'Use this one,' he said. 'It's my mother's number. She's always there. She's not well and spends a good deal of time in bed. But her brains are intact. She's quick-witted. And because she's ill, if she calls me at the office she gets put straight through to me or else she gets told where to find me. If you give her a message, it will reach me personally with minimum delay. Will that do?'

'Yes, fine,' I said, and kept my doubts hidden. Carrier pigeons, I thought, might be better.

'Anything else?' he asked.

'Yes . . . do you think you could ask Laurentide Ice's owner why he sold a half-share to Filmer?'

'It's a she. I'll enquire.' He seemed to have hesitations in his mind but he didn't explain them. 'Is that all?' he said.

'My ticket?'

'Oh yes. The travel company, Merry & Co, they'll have it. They're still sorting out who's to sleep where, since we've added you in. We'll have to tell *them* your name, of course, but all we've said so far is that we absolutely have to have another ticket and even if it looked impossible it would have to be done. They'll bring your ticket to Union Station in Toronto on Sunday morning and you can pick it up there. All the owners are picking theirs up then.'

'All right.'

He stood up to go. 'Well . . . bon voyage,' he said, and after a short pause added, 'Perhaps he won't try anything.'

'Hope not.'

He nodded, shook my hand, finished the last of his vodka at a gulp and left me alone with my thoughts.

The first of those was that if I were going across a whole continent by train I might as well start out as I meant to go on. If there was a train from Ottawa to Toronto I would take it instead of flying.

There was indeed a train, the hotel confirmed.

Leaving at five-fifty, arriving four hours later. Dinner on board.

Ottawa had shovelled its centre-of-town railway station under a rug, so to speak, as if railways should be kept out of sight like the lower orders, and built a great new station several miles away from anywhere useful. The station itself, however, proved a delight, a vast airy tent of glass set among trees with the sun flooding in with afternoon light and throwing angular shadows on the shiny black floor.

People waiting for the train had put their luggage down in a line and gone to sit on the seats along the glass walls, and thinking it a most civilized arrangement I put my suitcase at the rear of the queue and found myself a seat also. Filmer or not, I thought, I was definitely enjoying myself.

Dinner on the train was arranged as in aeroplanes with several stewards in shirtsleeves and deep-yellow waistcoats rolling first a drinks trolley, then a food trolley down the centre aisle, serving to right and left as they went. I watched them idly for quite a long time, and when they'd gone past me I couldn't remember their faces. I drank French wine as the daylight faded across the flying landscape and ate a better-than-many-airlines dinner after dark, and thought about chameleons; and at Toronto I took a cab and booked into another in the chain of the Four Seasons Hotels, as I had told Bill Baudelaire I would.

In the morning, a few hundred thoughts later, I fol-

71

lowed the hotel porter's directions and walked to the offices of the travel organizers, Merry & Co, as given in their brochure.

The street-level entrance was unimposing, the building deceptively small, but inside there seemed to be acres of space all brightly lit, with pale carpeting, blond woods and an air of absolute calm. There were some green plants, a sofa or two and a great many desks behind which quiet unhurried conversations seemed to be going on at a dozen telephones. All the telephonists faced the centre of the huge room, looking out and not at the walls.

I walked to one desk whose occupant wasn't actually speaking on the wire, a purposeful-looking man with a beard who was cleaning his nails.

'Help you?' he asked economically.

I said I was looking for the person organizing the race train.

'Oh yes. Over there. Third desk along.'

I thanked him. The third desk along over there was unoccupied.

'She'll be back in a minute,' comforted the second desk along. 'Sit down if you like.'

There were chairs, presumably for clients, on the near side of the desks. Comfortable chairs, clients for the pampering of, I thought vaguely, sitting in one.

The empty desk had a piece of engraved plastic on it announcing its absent owner's name: Nell. A quiet voice behind me said, 'Can I help you?' and I stood up politely and said, 'Yes, please.'

She had fair hair, grey eyes, a sort of clean look with a dust of freckles, but she was not as young, I thought, as her immediate impression, which was about eighteen.

'I came about the train,' I said.

'Yes. Could you possibly compress it into five minutes? There's such a lot still to arrange.' She walked round to the back of her desk and sat, looking down at an array of list upon list.

'My name is Tor Kelsey,' I began.

Her head lifted fast. 'Really? The Jockey Club told us your name this morning. Well, we've put you in because Bill Baudelaire said he'd cancel the whole production if we didn't.' The unemphatic grey eyes assessed me, not exactly showing that she didn't think the person she saw to be worth the fuss, but pretty near. 'It's the dining car that's the trouble,' she said. 'There are only forty-eight places. We have to have everyone seated at the same time because the mystery is acted before and after meals, and two or three of those places are taken by actors. Or are supposed to be, only now there isn't room for them either, as my boss sold too many tickets to late applicants, and you are actually number forty-nine.' She stopped briefly. 'I suppose that's our worry, not yours. We've given you a roomette for sleeping, and Bill Baudelaire says anything you ask for will we please let you have. We said what would you ask for and he didn't know. Maddeningly unhelpful. Do you yourself know what you want?'

'I'd like to know who the actors are, and the story they're going to enact.'

'No, we can't do that. It'll spoil it for you. We never tell the passengers anything.'

'Did Bill Baudelaire tell you,' I asked, 'why he so particularly wanted me on the train?'

'Not really.' She frowned slightly. 'I didn't give it much thought, I've so much else to see to. He simply insisted we take you, and since the Jockey Club are our clients, we do what the client asks.'

'Are you going on the train?' I asked.

'Yes, I am. There has to be someone from the company to sort out the crises.'

'And how good are you at secrets?'

'I keep half a dozen before breakfast every day.'

Her telephone rang quietly and she answered it in a quiet voice, adding her murmur to the hum of other murmurs all round the room. I realized that the quiet was a deliberate policy, as otherwise they would all have been shouting at the tops of their lungs and not hearing a word their callers said.

'Yes,' she was saying. 'Out at Mimico before ten. Four dozen, yes. Load them into the special dining car. Right. Good.' She put the phone down and without pause said to me, 'What secret do you want kept?'

'That I'm employed by the Jockey Club ... to deal with crises.'

74

'Oh.' It was a long sound of understanding. 'All right, it's a secret.' She reflected briefly. 'The actors are holding a run-through right now, not far away. I've got to see them sometime today, so it may as well be at once. What do you want me to tell them?'

'I'd like you to say that your company are putting me on the train as a trouble-spotter, because a whole train of racing people is a volatile mass looking for an excuse to explode. Say it's a form of insurance.'

'Which it is,' she said.

'Well, yes. And I also want to solve your problem of the forty-ninth seat. I want to go on the train as a waiter.'

She didn't blink but nodded. 'Yes, OK. Good idea. Quite often we put one of the actors in as a waiter, but not actually on this trip, luckily. The rail company are very helpful when we ask. I'll fix it. Come on, then, there's such a lot still to do.'

She moved quickly without seeming to, and presently we were skimming round corners in her small blue car, pulling up with a jerk outside the garage of a large house.

The rehearsal, if you could call it that, was actually going on in the garage itself, which had no car but a large trestle table, a lot of folding chairs, a portable gas heater and about ten men and women standing in groups.

Nell introduced me without mentioning my name. 'We're taking him on the train as company eyes and ears. Anything you think might turn into trouble, tell him or me. He's going as a service attendant, which will mean he can move everywhere through the train without questions. OK? Don't tell the paying passengers he's one of us.'

They shook their heads. Keeping the true facts from the passengers was their daily occupation.

'OK,' Nell said to me. 'I'll leave you here. Phone me later.' She put a large envelope she was carrying on to the table, waved to the actors and vanished, and one of them, a man of about my own age with a mophead of tight, light brown curls came forward, shook my hand and said, 'She's the best in the business. My name's David Flynn, by the way, but call me Zak. That's my name in the mystery. From now on, we call each other by the mystery names, so as not to make mistakes in front of the passengers. You'd better have an acting name, too. How about . . . um . . . Tommy?'

'It's all right by me.'

'Right, everybody, this is Tommy, a waiter.'

They nodded, smiling, and I was introduced to them one by one by the names they would use on the train.

'Mavis and Walter Bricknell, racehorse owners.' They were middle-aged, dressed like the others in jeans and casual sweaters. 'They're married in real life too.'

David/Zak went briskly along the row, an enormously positive person, wasting no time. 'Ricky . . . a groom in the mystery, though he'll be travelling with the racegoers, not the grooms. His part in the mystery finishes at Winnipeg, and he'll be getting off there. This is Raoul, racehorse trainer for the Bricknells, their guest on the train. Ben, he's an old groom who has ridden a few races.' Ben grinned from a small, deeply-lined face, looking the part. 'This is Giles: don't be taken in by his good looks, he's our murderer. This is Angelica, who you won't see much of as she's the first victim. And Pierre, he's a compulsive gambler in love with the Bricknells' daughter, Donna, and this is Donna. And last, this is James Winterbourne, he's a big noise in the Ontario Jockey Club.'

I don't think I jumped. The big name in the Ontario Jockey Club wore a three-day beard and a red trilby hat, which he lifted to me ceremoniously. 'Alas,' he said, 'I'm not travelling. My part ends with giving the train an official blessing. Too bad.'

David/Zak said to me, 'We're walking through the first scene now. Everyone knows what to do. This is Union Station. This is the gathering point for the passengers. They're all here. Right, guys, off we go.'

Mavis and Walter said, 'We're chatting to other passengers about the trip.'

Pierre and Donna said, 'We're having a quiet row.'

Giles said, 'I'm being nice to the passengers.'

Angelica: 'I am looking for someone called Steve. I ask the passengers if they've seen him. He is supposed to be travelling, but he hasn't turned up.'

Raoul said, 'I put my two cents' worth into Pierre and Donna's quarrel as I want to break them up so

I can marry her myself. For her father's money, of course.'

Pierre said, 'Which I furiously point out.'

Donna: 'Which I don't like, and am near to tears.'

Ben: 'I ask Raoul for a handout, which I don't get. I tell a lot of people he's stingy, after I worked for him all those years. The passengers are to find me a nuisance. I tell them I'm travelling on the racegoers' part of the train.'

James Winterbourne said, 'I ask for attention and tell everybody that we have horses, grooms, racegoers and all your owners and friends on the train. I hope everyone will have a great time on this historic re-enactment, etc., etc., for the glory of Canadian racing.'

Ricky said, 'I arrive. One of the station staff – who will be Jimmy (not here now) in staff uniform – tries to stop me, but I run in among the passengers, bleeding all over the place, shouting that some thugs tried to hijack one of the horses off the train, but I shouted and the maintenance men in the loading yard chased them away. I think the owners should know.'

Zak said, 'Jimmy runs off to fetch me and I stride in and tell everyone not to be worried, all the horses are safe and on the train, but to make sure things are all right in future I will go on the train myself. I am the top security agent for the railway.' He looked round the company. 'All right so far? Then James Winterbourne calms everyone down and tells them to board the train at Gate 6, Track 7. I'll check that that's still right, on Sunday morning, but that's what we've been told so far.'

The Bricknells said, 'We ask you which horse they were trying to hijack, but you don't know. We try to find Ricky, to ask him. He's not our groom, but we are always anxious sort of people.'

'Right,' Zak said. 'So we are all on board. It'll take a good half-hour. Ricky gets bandaged by Nell in plain view, beside the train. The train leaves at twelve. Then everyone gathers shortly afterwards in the dining room for champagne. We do scene two next, just before lunch.'

They 'walked through' scene two, which was shorter and chiefly established Zak as being in charge, and had Ricky coming to say that he didn't know which of the horses the horse-nappers had been making for . . . they had come into the horse car wearing masks, brandishing clubs. . . . Ricky had been alone out there in the loading yard as all the other grooms had gone back to the station's coffee shop.

The Bricknells were a twitter. Angelica was distraught that Steve hadn't turned up. Who cared about a horse, where was Steve?

Who was Steve? Zak asked. Angelica said he was her business manager. What business? Zak asked. None of yours, Angelica tartly said.

'Right,' Zak said, 'about now it has dawned on the thickest passenger that this is all fiction. They'll be smiling. So lunch is next. Everyone gets the afternoon to relax. Our next scene is during drinks before dinner. That's the one we rehearsed before Nell came. Right. We may have to change things a bit as we go along, so we'll do the rest of the final walk-throughs in one of the bedrooms, a day at a time.'

The others thought this reasonable and began to put on their coats.

'Don't you have a script?' I asked Zak.

'No formal words to learn, if that's what you mean. No. We all know what we've got to establish in each scene, and we improvise. When we plan a mystery, the actors get a brief outline of what's going to happen and basically what sort of people they are, then they invent their own imaginary life stories, so that if any passenger asks questions in conversations, they have the answers ready. I'd advise you to do it, too. Invent a background, a childhood . . . as near as possible to the real thing is always easiest.'

'Thanks for the tip,' I said. 'Will you let me know your plans each day, and also tell me instantly if anything odd happens you don't expect? Even small things, really.'

'Yes, sure. Ask Nell, too. She knows the story. And there are some actors who weren't here today because they don't get activated until later on the trip. They're on the passenger list. Nell will point them out.'

He stifled a yawn and looked suddenly very tired, a complete contrast to two minutes earlier, and I suspected he was one of those people who could turn cnergy on and off like a tap. One of Aunt Viv's best friends had been an elderly actor who could walk down to the theatre like a tired old pensioner and go out on the stage and make the audience's hair stand on end with his power.

David Flynn, offering me a lift if I needed one, was beginning to move with a sort of lassitude that one would never have seen in Zak. He picked up Nell's large envelope, opened it and distributed its contents to the others: luggage labels saying 'Merry & Co', and photocopied sheets of 'Information and Advice to Passengers'.

Scene dressing, I supposed. I asked him if he would be going anywhere near the Merry & Co office and he said he would detour that way and was as good as his word.

'Do you do this all the time?' I asked on the way.

'Act, do you mean? Or mysteries?'

'Either.'

'Anything I'm offered,' he said frankly. 'Plays. Commercials. Bit parts in series. But I do mostly mysteries now that they're so popular, and nearly all for Merry & Co. I write the stories to suit the occasion. I was engaged for a doctors' convention last week, so we did a medical crime. Just now it's racing. Next month I've got to think up something for a fishing club weekend train trip to Halifax. It keeps me employed. It pays the bills. It's quite good fun. It's not Stratford-upon-Avon.'

'What about the other actors?' I asked. 'The ones in the garage.'

'Much the same. It's work. They like the train trips, even if it does mean shouting all the scenes against the wheel noise when we're going along, because the dining cars are so long. Not by any means the right shape for a stage. We don't always use the same actors, it depends on the characters, but they're all friendly, we never take anyone who can't get along. It's essential to be tolerant and generous, to make our sort of improvisation work.'

'I'd no idea mysteries were such an industry.'

He gave a small sideways smile. 'They have a lot in England too, these days.'

'Um . . .' I said, as he braked to a halt outside the Merry & Co offices. 'How English do I sound to you?'

'Very. An educated Englishman in an expensive suit.'

'Well, the original plan was for me to go on the train as a wealthy owner. What would you think of my accent if I were dressed as a waiter in a deep-yellow waistcoat?'

'Harvest gold, that's what they call that colour,' he said thoughtfully. 'I wouldn't notice your accent so much, perhaps. There are thousands of English immigrants in this country, after all. You'll get by all right, I should think.'

I thanked him for the lift and got out of the car. He yawned and turned that into a laugh, but I reckoned the tiredness was real. 'See you Sunday, Tommy,' he said, and I dryly said, 'Sure thing, Zak.' He drove away with a smile and I went into the Merry & Co office where the earlier calm had broken up into loud frenetic activity on several telephones.

'How *could* twenty-five of our bikers all burst their tyres at once?'

'They won't reach Nuits-St Georges tonight.'

'Any suggestions for alternative hotels?'

'Where do we *find* fifty new tyres, assorted, in France? They've cut them to ribbons, they say.'

'It was sabotage. It has to be.'

'They rode over a cattle grid which had spikes.'

Nell was sitting at her desk talking on her telephone, one hand pressed to her free ear to block out the clamour.

'Why didn't the fools pick up their bikes and walk across?'

'Nobody told them. It was a new grid. Where *is* Nuits-St Georges? Can't we get a bus to go and pick up the bikes? What bus company do we use in that part of France?'

'Why isn't our French office dealing with all this?'

I sat on Nell's client chair and waited. The hubbub subsided: the crisis was sorted. Somewhere in Burgundy, the bikers would be transported to their dinners on sturdier wheels, and new tyres would be found in the morning.

Nell put her receiver down.

'You arrange cycling tours?' I said.

'Sure. And trips up Everest. Not me personally, I do mysteries. Do you need something?'

'Instructions.'

'Oh, yes. I talked to VIA. No problems.'

VIA Rail, I had discovered, was the company that operated Canada's passenger trains, which didn't mean that it owned the rails or the stations. Nothing was simple on the railways.

'VIA,' Nell said, 'are expecting you to turn up at Union Station tomorrow morning at ten to get fitted for a uniform. Here's who you ask for.' She passed me a slip of paper. 'They've got hand-picked service people going on this trip, and they'll show you what to do when you meet them at the station on Sunday morning. You'll board the train with them.'

'What time?' I asked.

'The train comes into the station soon after eleven. The chefs and crew board soon after. Passengers board at eleven-thirty, after the reception in the station itself. The train leaves at twelve. That's thirty-five minutes earlier than the regular daily train, the Canadian, which will be on our heels as far as Winnipeg.'

'And the horses will have boarded, I gather, out in a loading area.'

'Yes, at Mimico, about six miles away. That's where they do maintenance and cleaning and put the trains together. Everything will be loaded there. Food, wine, flowers, everything for the owners.'

'And the grooms?'

'No, not them. They're being shipped back to the station by bus after they've settled the horses in. And you might like to know we've another addition to the train, a cousin of our boss, name of Leslie Brown, who's going as horsemaster, to oversee the horses and the grooms and keep everything up that end in good order.'

'Which end?'

'Behind the engine. Apparently horses travel better there. No swaying.'

While she was talking, she was sorting postcards into piles: postcards with names and numbers on.

'Do you have a plan of the train?' I asked.

She glanced up briefly and didn't exactly say I was a thundering nuisance, but looked as if she thought it. Still, she shuffled through a pile of papers, pulled out a single sheet and pushed it across the desk towards me.

'This is what we've asked for, and what they say we'll get, but the people at Mimico sometimes change things,' she said.

I picked up the paper and found it was written in a column.

Engine
Generator/boiler
Baggage car
Horse car
Grooms/sleeping

	Grooms/dining/dome	
(Racegoers)		Sleeping
	"	Sleeping
	"	Sleeping
	"	Dayniter
	"	Dining
(Owners)	Sleeping (Green)	26
"	Sleeping (Manor)	24
"	Sleeping (Mount)	16
"	Special dining	
"	Dome car (Park)	8
"	Private car	4
		78 if full

(Owners includes actors, Company
and VIA executives, chefs and service
crew, most in Green.)

'Do you have a plan of who sleeps where?' I asked.

For answer she shuffled through the same pile as before and gave me two sheets stapled together. I looked first, as one does, for my own name; and found it.

She had given me a room – a roomette – that was right next door to Filmer.

CHAPTER FIVE

I walked back to the hotel and at two o'clock local time telephoned to England, reckoning that seven o'clock Friday evening was perhaps a good time to catch Brigadier Catto relaxing in his Newmarket house after a busy week in London. I was lucky to catch him, he said, and he had news for me.

'Remember Horfitz's messenger who gave the briefcase to Filmer at Nottingham?' he asked.

'I sure do.'

'John Millington has identified him from your photographs. He is Ivor Horfitz's son, Jason. He's not bright, so they say. Not up to much more than running errands. Delivering briefcases would be just about his mark.'

'And he got that wrong, too, according to his father.'

'Well, there you are. It doesn't get us anywhere much, but that's who he is. John Millington has issued photos to all the ring inspectors, so that if they see him they'll report it. If Horfitz plans on using his son as an on-course errand boy regularly, we'll make sure he knows we're watching.'

'He'd do better to find someone else.'

'A nasty thought.' He paused briefly. 'How are you doing, your end?'

'I haven't seen Filmer yet. He's staying tomorrow night at a hotel with most of the owners' group, according to the travel company's lists. Presumably he'll be at the official lunch with the Ontario Jockey Club at Woodbine tomorrow. I'll go to the races, but probably not to the lunch. I'll see what he's doing, as best I can.' I told him about Bill Baudelaire's mother, and said, 'After we've started off on the train, if you want to get hold of me direct, leave a message with her, and I'll telephone back to you or John Millington as soon as I'm able.'

'It's a bit hit or miss,' he grumbled, repeating the number after I'd dictated it.

'She's an invalid,' I added, and laughed to myself at his reaction.

When he'd stopped spluttering, he said, 'Tor, this is impossible.'

'Well, I don't know. It's an open line of communication, after all. Better to have one than not. And Bill Baudelaire suggested it himself. He must know she's capable.'

'All right then. Better than nothing.' He didn't sound too sure, though, and who could blame him. Brigade commanders weren't accustomed to bedridden grandmothers manning field telephones. 'I'll be here at home on Sunday,' he said. 'Get through to me, will you, for last-minute gen both ways, before you board?'

'Yes, certainly.'

'You sound altogether,' he said with a touch of disapproval, 'suspiciously happy.'

'Oh! Well . . . this train looks like being good fun.'

'That's not what you're there for.'

'I'll do my best not to enjoy it.'

'Insubordination will get you a firing squad,' he said firmly, and put down his receiver forthwith.

I put my own receiver down more slowly and the bell rang again immediately.

'This is Bill Baudelaire,' my caller said in his deep-down voice. 'So you arrived in Toronto all right?'

'Yes, thank you.'

'I've got the information you asked for about Laurentide Ice. About why his owner sold a half-share.'

'Oh, good.'

'I don't know that it is, very. In fact, not good at all. Apparently Filmer was over here in Canada at the end of last week enquiring of several owners who had horses booked on the train if they would sell. One of them mentioned it to me this morning and now I've talked to the others. He offered a fair price for a half-share, they all say. Or a third-share. Any toehold, it seems. I would say he methodically worked down the list until he came to Daffodil Quentin.'

'Who?'

'The owner of Laurentide Ice.'

'Why is it bad news?' I asked, taking the question from the disillusionment in his voice.

'You'll meet her. You'll see,' he said cryptically.

'Can't you tell me?'

He sighed audibly. 'Her husband, Hal Quentin, was a good friend of Canadian racing, but he died this time last year and left his string of horses to his wife. Three of them so far have died in accidents since then, with Mrs Quentin collecting the insurance.'

'Three!' I said. 'In a year?'

'Exactly. They've all been investigated but they all seem genuine. Mrs Quentin says it's a dreadful coincidence and she is most upset.'

'She would be,' I said drily.

'Anyway, that is who has sold a half-share to Julius Filmer. What a pair! I phoned just now and asked her about the sale. She said it suited her to sell, and there was no reason not to. She says she is going to have a ball on the train.' He sounded most gloomy, himself.

'Look on the bright side,' I said. 'If she's sold a half-share she can't be planning to push Laurentide Ice off the train at high speed for the insurance.'

'That's a scurrilous statement.' He was not shocked, however. 'Will you be at Woodbine tomorrow?'

'Yes, but not at the lunch.'

'All right. If we bump into each other, of course it will be as strangers.'

'Of course,' I agreed; and we said goodbyes and disconnected.

Daffodil Quentin, I reflected, settling the receiver in its cradle, had at least not been intimidated into selling. No one on the business end of Filmer's threats could be looking forward to having a ball in his company. It did appear that in order to get himself on to the train as an owner, he had been prepared to spend actual money. He had been prepared to fly to Canada to effect the sale, and do the return to England to collect the briefcase from Horfitz at Nottingham on Tuesday, and to fly back to Canada, presumably, in time for tomorrow's races.

I wondered where he was at that moment. I wondered what he was thinking, hatching, setting in motion. It was comforting to think that he didn't know I existed.

I spent the rest of the afternoon doing some shopping and walking and taxi-riding around, getting reacquainted with one of the most visually entertaining cities in the world. I'd found it architecturally exciting six years earlier, and it seemed to me now not less but more so, with glimpses of its slender tallest-in-the-world free-standing tower with the onion bulge near its top appearing tantalizingly between angular highrises covered with black glass and gold. And they had built a whole new complex, Harbourfront, since I'd been there before, a new face turned to Lake Ontario and the world.

At six, having left my purchases at the hotel, I went back to Merry & Co's warm pale office and found many of the gang still working. Nell, at her desk, naturally on the telephone, pointed mutely to her client chair, and I sat there and waited.

Some of the murmurers were putting on coats, yawning, switching off computers, taking cans of cold drinks out of the large refrigerator and opening them with the carbonation hissing. Someone put out a light or two. The green plants looked exhausted. Friday night; all commercial passion spent. Thank God for Fridays.

'I have to come in here tomorrow,' Nell said with resignation, catching my thought. 'And why I ever said I'd have dinner with you tonight I cannot imagine.'

'You promised.'

'I must have been mad.'

I'd asked her after she'd shown me the train's sleeping arrangements (which perhaps had been my subconscious making jumps unbeknown to me), and she'd said, 'Yes, all right, I have to eat,' and that had seemed a firm enough commitment.

'Are you ready?' I asked.

'No, there are two more people I positively must talk to. Can you ... er ... wait?'

'I'm quite good at it,' I said equably.

A few more lights went out. Some of those remaining shone on Nell's fair hair, made shadows of her eyes and put hollows in her cheeks. I wondered about her, as one does. An attractive stranger; an unread book; a beginning, perhaps. But there had been other beginnings, in other cities, and I'd long outgrown the need to hurry. I might never yet have come to the conventional ending, but the present was greatly OK, and as for the future . . . we could see.

I listened without concentration to her talking to someone called Lorrimore. 'Yes, Mr Lorrimore, your flowers and your bar bottles will already be on the train when it comes into the station. . . . And the fruit, yes, that too. . . . The passengers are gathering at ten-thirty for the reception at the station. . . . Yes, we board at eleven-thirty and leave at twelve. . . . We're looking forward to meeting you too . . . goodbye, Mr Lorrimore.' She glanced over at me as she began to dial her next number, and said, 'The Lorrimores have the private car, the last car on the train. Hello, is that Vancouver racecourse . . .?'

I listened to her discussing entry arrangements for the owners. 'Yes, we're issuing them all with the special club passes . . . and yes, the other passengers from the train will be paying for themselves individually, but we're offering them group transport. . . .' She put down the receiver eventually and sighed. 'We've been asked to fix moderate-price hotels and bus transport for so many of the racegoers that it's like duplicating the whole tour. Could you wait for just one more call . . . or two?'

We left the darkened office almost an hour later and

93

even then she was still checking things off in her mind and muttering vaguely about not forgetting scissors and clips to go with the bandages for Ricky. We walked not very far to a restaurant called the Fluted Point People that she'd been to before and whose menu I had prospected earlier. Not very large, it had tables crammed into every cranny, each dimly lit by a candle lantern.

'Who are the Fluted Point People,' I asked, 'in general?'

'Heaven knows,' Nell said.

The waiter, who must have been asked a thousand times, said the fluted point people had lived on this land ten thousand years ago. Let's not worry about them, he said.

Nell laughed and I thought of ten thousand years and wondered who would be living on this land ten thousand years ahead. Fluted points, it transpired, described the stone tools in use over most of the continent: would our descendants call us the knife and fork people?

'I don't honestly care,' Nell said, to those questions. 'I'm hungry right now in Toronto today.'

We did something about that in the shape of devilled smoked salmon followed by roast quail. 'I hope this is all on your expense account,' she said without anxiety as I ordered some wine, and I said, 'Yes, of course,' untruthfully and thought there was no point in having money if one didn't enjoy it. 'Hamburgers tomorrow,' I said, 'to make up for it.'

Nell nodded as if that were a normal bargain she well understood and said with a galvanic jump that she had forgotten to order a special limousine to drive the Lorrimores around at Winnipeg.

'Do it tomorrow,' I said. 'They won't run away.'

She looked at me with a worried frown of indecision, and then round the comfortable little candlelit restaurant, and then at the shining glass and silver on the table and then back to me, and the frown dissolved into a smile of self-amusement.

'All right. Tomorrow. The Lorrimores may be the icing on this cake but they've meant a lot of extra work.'

'Who are the Lorrimores?' I asked.

She looked at me blankly and answered obliquely, 'Where do you live?'

'Ah,' I said. 'If I lived here, I would know the Lorrimores?'

'You certainly wouldn't ask who they are.'

'I live in London,' I said. 'So please tell me.'

She was wearing, as so many women in business tended to, a navy suit and white blouse of such stark simplicity as to raise questions about the warmth of the soul. Women who dressed more softly, I thought inconsequentially, must feel more secure in themselves, perhaps.

'The Lorrimores,' Nell said, showing no insecurity, 'are one of the very richest families of Toronto. Of Ontario. Of Canada, in fact. They are the society magazines' staple diet. They are into banking and good works. They own mansions, endow art museums, open charity balls and entertain heads of state. There are quite a few of them, brothers, sisters and so on, and I'm told that in certain circles, if Mercer Lorrimore accepts an invitation and comes to your house, you are made for life.' She paused, smiling. 'Also he owns great racehorses, is naturally a pillar of the Ontario Jockey Club and has this private railcar which used to be borrowed regularly by campaigning politicians.' She paused again for breath. 'That's who's honouring our train – Mercer Lorrimore, the big chief of the whole clan, also Bambi, his wife, and their son Sheridan and their daughter Xanthe. What have I left out?'

I laughed. 'Do you curtsy?'

'Pretty nearly. Well, to be honest, Mercer Lorrimore sounds quite nice on the telephone but I haven't met him yet or any of the others. And he phones me himself. No secretaries.'

'So,' I said, 'if Mercer Lorrimore is on the train, it will be even more in the news from coast to coast?'

She nodded. 'He's going For the Benefit of Canadian Racing in capital letters on the Jockey Club's PR hand-out.'

'And is he eating in the dining car?' I asked.

'Don't!' She rolled her eyes in mock horror. 'He is supposed to be. They all are. But we don't know if they'll retreat into privacy. If they stay in their own car, there might just be enough room for everyone else to sit down. It's a shambles in the making though, and it was made by my boss selling extra tickets himself when he knew we were full.' She shook her head over it, but with definite indulgence. The boss, it appeared, ranked high in her liking.

'Who did he sell them to?' I asked.

'Just people. Two friends of his. And a Mr Filmer, who offered to pay double when he found there was no room. No one turns down an extra profit of that sort.' She broke open a roll with the energy of frustration. 'If only there was more room in the dining car, we could have sold at least six more tickets.'

'David ... er ... Zak was saying the forty-eight-seater was already stretching the actors' vocal cords to the limit against the noise of the wheels on the rails.'

'It's always a problem.' She considered me over the candle flame. 'Are you married?' she said.

'No. Are you?'

'Actually, no.' Her voice was faintly defensive, but her mouth was smiling. 'I invested in a relationship which didn't work out.'

'And which was some time ago?'

'Long enough for me to be over it.'

The exchange cleared the ground, I thought, and maybe set the rules. She wasn't looking for another relationship that was going nowhere. But dalliance? Have to see ...

'What are you thinking?' she asked.

'About life in general.'

She gave me a dry look of disbelief but changed the subject back to the almost as compelling matter of trains, and after a while I asked her the question I'd had vaguely in mind all day.

'Besides the special passes for the races, and so on,' I said, 'is there anything else an owner of a horse is entitled to? An owner, that is to say, of one of the horses travelling on the train?'

She was puzzled. 'How do you mean?'

'Are they entitled to any privileges that the other people in the special dining car don't have?'

'I don't think so.' Her brow wrinkled briefly. 'Only that they can visit the horse car, if that's what you mean.'

'Yes, I know about that. So there's nothing else?'

'Well, the racecourse at Winnipeg is planning a group photograph of owners only, and there's television coverage of that.' She pondered. 'They're each getting a commemorative plaque from the Jockey Club when we get back on the train at Banff after the days in the mountains.' She paused again. 'And if a horse that's actually on the train wins one of the special races, the owner gets free life membership of the clubs at all three racecourses.'

The last was a sizeable carrot to a Canadian, perhaps, but not enough on its own, surely, to attract Filmer. I sighed briefly. Another good idea down the drain. So I was left with the two basic questions: why was Filmer on the train, and why had he worked so hard to be an owner? And the answers were still I don't know and I don't know. Highly helpful.

We drank coffee, dawdling, easy together, and she said she had wanted to be a writer and had found a job with a publisher ('which real writers never do, I found out') but was very much happier with Merry & Co, arranging mysteries.

She said, 'My parents always told me practically from birth that I'd be a writer, that it ran in the family, and I grew up expecting it, but they were wrong, though I tried for a long time, and then I was also living with this man who sort of bullied me to write. But, you know, it was such a *relief* the day I said to myself, some time after we'd parted and I'd dried my eyes, that I was not really a writer and never would be and I'd much rather do something else. And suddenly I was liberated and happier than I could remember. It seems so stupid, looking back, that it took me so long to know myself. I was in a way brainwashed into writing, and I thought I wanted it myself, but I wasn't good enough when it came to the point, and it was such hard work, and I was depressed so much of the time.' She half laughed. 'You must think I'm crazy.'

'Of course not. What did you write?'

'I was writing for a women's weekly magazine for a while, going to interview people and writing up their lives, and making up lives altogether sometimes if I couldn't find anyone interesting or lurid enough that week. Don't let's talk about it. It was awful.'

'I'm glad you escaped.'

'Yes, so am I,' she said with feeling. 'I look different, I feel different, and I'm much healthier. I was always getting colds and flu and feeling ill, and now I don't.' Her eyes sparkled in the light, proving her right. 'And you,' she said, 'you're the same. Light-hearted. It shows all over you.'

'Does it, indeed?'

'Am I right?'

'On the button, I suppose.'

And we were lucky, I thought soberly, paying the bill. Light-heartedness was a treasure in a world too full of sorrows, a treasure little regarded and widely forfeited to aggression, greed and horrendous tribal rituals. I wondered if the Fluted Point People had been light-hearted ten thousand years ago. But probably not.

Nell and I walked back to where she had parked her car near the office: she lived twenty minutes' drive away, she said, in a very small apartment by the lake.

To say good night we kissed cheeks and she thanked me for the evening, saying cheerfully that she would see me on Sunday if she didn't sink without trace under all the things she still had to do on the next day, Saturday. I watched her tail lights recede until she turned a corner, then I walked back to the hotel, slept an untroubled night, and presented myself next morning at ten sharp in the Public Affairs office, at Union Station.

The Public Affairs officer, a formidably efficient lady, had gathered from Nell that I was one of the actors, as they had helped with actors before, and I didn't change that understanding. She wheeled me back into the cavernous Great Hall of the station (which she briskly said was 250 feet long, 84 feet wide and had a tiled arched ceiling 88 feet above the floor) and led me through a heavy door into an undecorated downstairs duplication of the grandeur upstairs, a seemingly endless basic domain where the food and laundry and odd jobs of the trains got seen to. There was a mini power station also, and painting and carpentering going on all over the place.

'This way,' she said, clattering ahead on snapping heels. 'Here is the uniform centre. They'll see to you.' She pushed open a door to let me through, said briefly, 'Here's the actor,' to the staff inside, and with a nod abandoned me to fate.

The staff inside were good-natured and equally efficient. One was working a sewing machine, another a computer, and a third asked me what collar size I took.

There were shelves all round the room bearing hundreds of folded shirts of fine light grey and white vertical stripes, with striped collars, long striped sleeves and buttoned cuffs. 'The cuffs must remain buttoned at all times unless you are washing dishes.'

Catch me, I thought mildly, washing dishes.

There were two racks of the harvest gold waistcoats on hangers. 'All the buttons must be fastened at all times.'

There were row on row of mid-grey trousers and mid-grey jackets tidily hung, and boxes galore of grey, yellow and maroon striped ties.

My helper was careful that everything he gave me should fit perfectly. 'VIA Rail staff at all times are well turned out and spotlessly clean. We give everyone tips on how to care for the clothes.'

He gave me a grey jacket, two pairs of grey trousers, five shirts, two waistcoats (which he called vests), two ties and a grey raincoat to go over all, and as he passed each garment as suitable he called out the size to the man with the computer. 'We know the sizes of every VIA employee right across Canada.'

I looked at myself in the glass in my shirtsleeves and yellow waistcoat, and the waiter Tommy looked back. I smiled at my reflection. Tommy looked altogether too pleased with himself, I thought.

'Comfortable?' my helper asked.

'Very.'

'Don't vary the uniform at all,' he said. 'Any variation would mark you out straight away as an actor.'

'Thank you.'

'This uniform,' he said, 'trousers, shirt, tie and vest, is worn by all male service attendants and assistant service attendants when on duty. That's to say, the sleeping-car attendants and the dining-car staff, except that sometimes they wear aprons in the dining car.'

'Thank you,' I said again.

'The chief service attendant, who is in charge of the

dining car, wears a grey suit, not a vest or an apron. That's how you'll know him.'

'Right.'

He smiled. 'They'll teach you what to do. Now, we'll lend you a locker for these clothes until Sunday morning. Collect the clothes and put them on in the changing room here before boarding, and take your own clothes with you on to the train. When you've finished with the VIA uniform, please see that we get it back.'

'Right,' I said again.

When I'd put my own clothes on once more, he took me along a few passages into a room with ultra-narrow lockers into which Tommy's clothes barely slotted. He locked the metal door, gave me the key, showed me the way back into the Great Hall and smiled briefly.

'Good luck,' he said. 'Don't spill anything.'

'Thank you,' I said, 'very much.'

I went back to the hotel and had them arrange a car with a driver to take me to Woodbine, wait through the afternoon and bring me back. No trouble at all, they said, so as it was a nice bright autumn day with no forecast of rain I curled my hair and put on some sunglasses and a Scandinavian patterned sweater to merge into the crowd at the races.

It actually isn't easy to remember a stranger's face after a fleeting meeting unless one has a special reason for doing so, or unless there is something wholly distinctive about it, and I was reasonably certain no one going on the train would know me again even if I inadvertently stood next to them on the stands. I had spectacular proof of this, in fact, almost as soon as I'd paid my way into the paddock, because Bill Baudelaire was standing nearby, watching the throng coming in, and his eyes paused on me for a brief second and slid away. With his carroty hair and the acne scars, I thought, *he* would have trouble getting lost in a crowd.

I walked over to him and said, 'Could you tell me the time sir, please?'

He glanced at his watch but hardly at me and said, 'One twenty-five,' in his gravelly voice, and looked over my shoulder towards the gate.

'Thank you,' I said. 'I'm Tor Kelsey.'

His gaze sharpened abruptly on my face and he almost laughed.

'When Val told me about this I scarcely believed him.'

'Is Filmer here?' I asked.

'Yes. He arrived for the lunch.'

'OK,' I said. 'Thanks again.' I nodded and walked on past him and bought a racecard, and when in a moment or two I looked back, he had gone.

The racecourse was packed with people and there were banners everywhere announcing that this was the opening event of The Great Transcontinental Mystery Race Train's journey. Race Train Day, they economically said. There was a splendid colour photograph of a train crossing a prairie on the racecard's cover. There were stalls selling red and white Race Train T-shirts, with a horse face to face with a locomotive across the chest. There were Race Train flags and scarves and baseball caps; and a scatter of young ladies with Support Canadian Racing sashes across their bosoms were handing out information leaflets. The PR firm, I thought with amusement, were leaving no one in any doubt.

I didn't see Filmer until just before the Race Train's special race, which had been named without subtlety The Jockey Club Race Train Stakes at Woodbine. I'd spent some of the afternoon reading the information in the racecard about the owners and their horses and had seen that whereas all the owners were on the train's passenger list, none of the horses were. We would be taking fresh animals to Winnipeg and Vancouver.

Filmer wasn't on the racecard as an owner, but Mrs Daffodil Quentin was, and when she came down to see the saddling of her runner, Filmer was with her, assiduous and smiling.

Daffodil Quentin had a big puffball hair arrangement of blonde curls above a middle-aged face with intense shiny red lipstick. She wore a black dress with a striped chinchilla coat over it: too much fur, I briefly thought, for the warmth of the afternoon sun.

There was hardly time to identify all the other owners as the pre-race formalities were over much more quickly than in England, but I did particularly look for and sort out Mercer Lorrimore.

Mercer Lorrimore, darling of the glossy mags, was running two horses in the race, giving it his loyal support. He was a man of average height, average build, average weight, and was distinguishable chiefly because of his well-cut, well-brushed full head of white hair. His expression looked reasonable and pleasant, and he was being nice to his trainer.

Beside him was a thin well-groomed woman whom I supposed to be his wife, Bambi: and in attendance were a supercilious-looking young man and a sulking teenage girl. Son and daughter, Sheridan and Xanthe, no doubt.

The jockeys were thrown up like rainbow thistle-down on to the tiny saddles and let their skinny bodies move to the fluid rhythm of the walking thoroughbreds. Out on the track with the horses' gait breaking into a trot or canter they would be more comfortable standing up in the stirrups to let the bumpier rhythms flow beneath them, but on the way out from the parade ring they swayed languorously like a camel train. I loved to watch them: never grew tired of it. I loved the big beautiful animals with their tiny brains and their over-whelming instincts and I'd always, all over the world, felt at home tending them, riding them and watching them wake up and perform.

The Lorrimore colours were truly Canadian, bright red and white like the maple leaf flag. Daffodil Quentin's colours weren't daffodil yellow but pale blue and dark green, a lot more subdued than the lady.

She and Filmer and all the other owners disappeared upstairs behind glass to watch the race, and I went down towards the track to wait and watch from near where the lucky owner would come down to greet his winner.

There were fourteen runners for the mile-and-a-half race and I knew nothing about the form of any of them except for the information on the racecard. In England I knew the current scene like a magnified city map, knew the thoroughfares, the back alleys, the small turnings. Knew who people knew, who they would turn to and turn away from, who they lusted after. In Canada, I was without radar and felt blind.

The Race Train Stakes at Woodbine, turning out to be hot enough in the homestretch to delight the Ontario Jockey Club's heart, was greeted with roars and screams of encouragement from the stands. Lorrimore's scarlet-and-white favourite was beaten in the last stride by a streak in pale blue and dark green and a good many of the cheers turned to groans.

Daffodil Quentin came down and passed close by me in clouds of chinchilla, excitement and a musky scent. She preened coquettishly, receiving compliments and the trophy, and Filmer, ever at her side, gallantly kissed her hand.

A let-off murderer, I thought, kissing an unproven

insurance swindler. How very nice. Television cameras whirred and flash photographers outdid the sun.

I caught sight of Bill Baudelaire scowling, and I knew what John Millington would have said.

It was enough to make you sick.

CHAPTER SIX

On Saturday evening and early Sunday morning I packed two bags, the new suitcase from England and a softer holdall bought in Toronto.

Into the first I put the rich young owner's suit, cashmere pullover and showy shirts and into the second the new younger-looking clothes for off-duty Tommy, jeans, sweatshirts, woolly hat and trainers. I packed the Scandinavian jersey I'd worn at Woodbine into the suitcase just in case it jogged anyone's memory, and got dressed in dark trousers, open-necked shirt and a short zipped navy jacket with lighter blue bands round waist and wrists.

The rich young owner's expensive brown shoes went away. Tommy, following instructions from the uniform department, had shiny new black ones, with black socks.

Into Tommy's holdall went the binoculars-camera and the hair curler (one never knew), and I had the cigarette lighter-camera as always in my pocket. Tommy also had the rich young owner's razor and toothbrush, along with his underclothes, pyjamas and stock of fresh films. The suitcase, which held my passport, had a Merry & Co label on it addressed to the Vancouver Four Seasons Hotel; the holdall had no identification at all.

With everything ready, I telephoned Brigadier Catto in England and told him about Daffodil Quentin and the touching little scene in the winners' circle.

'Damn!' he said. 'Why does that sort of thing always happen? Absolutely the wrong person winning.'

'The general public didn't seem to mind. The horse was third favourite, quite well backed. Daffodil Quentin seems to be acceptable to the other owners, who of course probably don't know about her three dead horses. They're bound to take to Filmer too, you know how civilized he can seem, and I don't suppose news of the trial got much attention here since it collapsed almost before it began. Anyway, Filmer and Daffodil left the races together in what looked like her own car, with a chauffeur.'

'Pity you couldn't follow them.'

'Well, I did actually, in a hired car. They went to the hotel, where Filmer and the other owners from the train are staying, and they went into the bar for a drink. After that, Daffodil left in her Rolls and Filmer went upstairs. Nothing of note. He looked relaxed.'

The Brigadier said, 'You're sure they didn't spot you at the hotel?'

'Quite sure. The entrance hall of the hotel was as

big as a railway station itself. There were dozens of people sitting around waiting for other people. It was easy.'

It had even been easy following them from the racecourse, as when I went out to where my driver had parked his car I had a clear view from a distance of Daffodil at the exit gate being spooned into a royal blue Rolls-Royce by Filmer and her chauffeur. My driver, with raised eyebrows but without spoken question, agreed to keep the Rolls in sight for as long as possible, which he did without trouble all the way back to the city. At the hotel I paid him in cash with a bonus and sent him on his way, and was in time to see Filmer's back view receding into a dark-looking bar as I walked into the big central hall lobby.

It had been an exercise without much in the way of results, but then many of my days were like that, and it was only by knowing the normal that the abnormal, when it happened, could be spotted.

'Would you mind telling me,' I said diffidently to the Brigadier, 'whether Filmer has made a positive threat to disrupt this train?'

There was a silence, then, 'Why do you ask?'

'Something Bill Baudelaire said.'

After a pause he answered, 'Filmer was seething with anger. He said the world's racing authorities could persecute him all they liked but he would find a spanner to throw in their works, and they'd regret it.'

111

'When did he say that?' I asked. 'And why . . . and who to?'

'Well . . . er . . .' He hesitated and sighed. 'Things go wrong, you know. After the acquittal, the Disciplinary Committee of the Jockey Club called Filmer to Portman Square to warn him as to his future behaviour, and Filmer said they couldn't touch him, and was generally unbearably arrogant. As a result, one of the committee lost his temper and told Filmer he was the scum of the earth and no one in racing would sleep well until he was warned off, which was the number one priority of the world's racing authorities.'

'That's a bit of an exaggeration,' I commented, sighing in my turn. 'I suppose you were there?'

'Yes. You could have cut the fury on both sides with a knife. Very vicious, all of it.'

'So,' I said regretfully, 'Filmer might indeed see the train as a target.'

'He might.'

The trouble and expense he had gone to to get himself on board looked increasingly ominous, I thought.

'There's one other thing you might care to know,' the Brigadier said. 'John saw Ivor Horfitz's son Jason hanging around outside the weighing-room at Newmarket yesterday and had a word with him.'

When Millington had a word with people they could take days to recover. In his own way, he could be as frightening as Derry Welfram or Filmer himself.

'What happened?' I asked.

'John spoke to him about the inadvisability of running errands on racecourses for his warned-off father, and said that if Jason had any information, he should pass it on to him, John Millington. And apparently Jason Horfitz then said he wouldn't be passing on the information he had to anybody else as he didn't want to end up in a ditch.'

'*What?*' I said.

'John Millington pounced on that but he couldn't get another word out of the wretched Jason. He turned to jelly and literally ran away, John says.'

'Does Jason really know,' I said slowly, 'what Paul Shacklebury knew? Did he *tell* Paul Shacklebury whatever it was he knew? Or was it just a figure of speech?'

'God knows. John's working on it.'

'Did he ask Jason what was in the briefcase?'

'Yes, he did, but Jason either didn't know or was too frightened to speak. John says he was terrified that we even knew about the briefcase. He couldn't believe we knew.'

'I wonder if he'll tell his father.'

'Not if he has any sense.'

He hadn't any sense, I thought, but he did have fear, which was almost as good a life preserver.

'If I hear anything more,' the Brigadier said, 'I'll leave a message with ...' his voice still disapproved ' ... with Mrs Baudelaire senior. Apart from that ... good luck.'

I thanked him and hung up, and with considerable contentment took my two bags in a taxi to Union Station.

The train crew were already collecting in the locker room when I made my way there and introduced myself as Tommy, the actor.

They smiled and were generous. They always enjoyed the mysteries, they said, and had worked with an actor among them before. It would all go well, I would see.

The head waiter, head steward, chief service attendant, whatever one called him, was a neat small Frenchman named Emil. Late thirties, perhaps, I thought, with dark bright eyes.

'Do you speak French?' he asked first, shaking my hand. 'All VIA employees have to be able to speak French. It is a rule.'

'I do a bit,' I said.

'That is good. The last actor, he couldn't. This time the chef is from Montreal, and in the kitchen we may speak French.'

I nodded and didn't tell him that, apart from my school days, my working French had been learned in stables, not kitchens, and was likely to be rusty in any case. But I'd half-learned several languages on my travels, and somehow they each floated familiarly back at the first step on to the matching soil. Everything in bilingual Canada was written in both English and French and I realized that since my arrival I'd been reading the French quite easily.

'Have you ever worked in a restaurant?' Emil asked.

'No, I haven't.'

He shrugged good-humouredly. 'I will show you how to set the places, and to begin with, this morning, perhaps you will serve only water. When you pour anything, when the train is moving, you pour in small amounts at a time, and you keep the cup or glass close to you. Do you understand? It is always necessary to control, to use small movements.'

'I understand,' I said, and indeed I did.

He put a copy of the timetable into my hands and said, 'You will need to know where we stop. The passengers always ask.'

'OK. Thanks.'

He nodded with good humour.

I changed into Tommy's uniform and met some others of the crew: Oliver, who was a waiter in the special dining car, like myself, and several of the sleeping-car attendants, one to each car the whole length of the train. There was a smiling Chinese gentleman who cooked in the small forward dining car where the grooms, among others, would be eating, and an unsmiling Canadian who would be cooking in the main central dining car for the bulk of the racegoers and the crew themselves. The French chef from Montreal was not there, I soon discovered, because he was a she, and could only be found in the women's changing room.

Everyone put on the whole uniform including the grey raincoat on top, and I put on my raincoat also; I packed Tommy's spare garments and my own clothes into the holdall, and was ready.

Nell had said she would meet me this Sunday morning in the coffee shop in the Great Hall, and had told me that the crews often went there to wait for train time. Accordingly, accompanied by Emil and a few of the others, I carried my bags to the coffee shop where everyone immediately ordered huge carrot cakes, the speciality of the house, as if they were in fear of famine.

Nell wasn't there, but Zak and some of the other actors were, sitting four to a table, drinking pale-looking orange juice and not eating carrot cake because of the calories.

Zak said Nell was along with the passengers in the reception area, and that he wanted to go and see how things were shaping.

'She said something about you checking a suitcase through to Vancouver in the baggage car,' he added, standing up.

'Yes, this one.'

'Right. She said to tell you to bring it along to where the passengers are. I'll show you.'

I nodded, told Emil I'd be back, and followed Zak down the Great Hall and round a corner or two and came to a buzzing gathering of people in an area like an airport departure lounge.

An enormous banner across a latticed screen left no one in any doubt. Stretching for a good twelve feet it read in red on white THE GREAT TRANSCONTINENTAL MYSTERY RACE TRAIN, and in blue letters a good deal smaller underneath, THE ONTARIO JOCKEY CLUB, MERRY & CO AND VIA RAIL PRESENT A CELEBRATION OF CANADIAN RACING.

The forty or so passengers already gathered in happy anticipation wore name badges and carnations and held glasses of orange juice convivially.

'There was supposed to be champagne in the orange juice,' Zak said drily. 'There isn't. Something to do with the Sunday drink law.' He searched the throng with his eyes from where we stood a good twenty paces away out in the station. 'There's Ben doing his stuff, see? Asking Raoul to lend him money.'

I could indeed see. It looked incredibly real. People standing around them were looking shocked and embarrassed.

Zak was nodding his mop of curls beside me and had begun snapping his fingers rather fast. I could sense the energy starting to flow in him now that this fiction was coming alive, and I could see that he had used make-up on himself; not greasepaint or anything heavy, more a matter of darkening and thickening his eyebrows and darkening his mouth, emphasizing rather than disguising. An actor in the wings, I thought, gathering up his power.

I spotted Mavis and Walter Bricknell being fussy and anxious as intended, and saw and heard Angelica asking if anyone had seen Steve.

'Who's Steve?' I asked Zak. 'I forget.'

'Her lover. He misses the train.'

Pierre and Donna began to have their row which made a different bunch of passengers uncomfortable. Zak laughed. 'Good,' he said, 'that's great.'

Giles-the-murderer, who had been in the coffee shop, strolled along into the mêlée and started being frightfully nice to old ladies. Zak snapped his fingers even faster and started humming.

The crowd parted and shifted a little and through the gap I saw Julius Apollo Filmer, another murderer, being frightfully nice to a not-so-old lady, Daffodil Quentin.

I took a deep breath, almost of awe, almost on a tremble. Now that it was really beginning, now that I was going to be near him, I felt as strung up and as energized as Zak, and no doubt suffered the same compelling anxiety that things shouldn't go wrong.

Daffodil was playfully patting Filmer's hand.

Yuk, I thought.

Ben the actor appeared beside them and started his piece, and I saw Filmer turn a bland face towards him and watched his mouth shape the unmistakable words, 'Go away.'

Ben backed off. Very wise, I thought. The crowd

came together again and hid Filmer and his flower and I felt the tension in my muscles subside, and realized I hadn't known I had tensed them. Have to watch that, I thought.

The Lorrimores had arrived, each wearing yesterday's expression: pleasant, aloof, supercilious, sulky. Mercer was entering into the spirit of things, Bambi also but more coolly. Sheridan looked as if he thought he was slumming. The young daughter, Xanthe, could have been quite pretty if she'd smiled.

James Winterbourne, actor, had discarded his red felt trilby and had shaved off the stubble and was drifting around being welcoming in his role as a member of the Jockey Club. And the real Jockey Club was there, I saw, in the person of Bill Baudelaire, who was known to one or two of the owners with whom he was chatting. I wondered how much he would fret if he didn't see me among the passengers, and I hoped not much.

Nell emerged from the noise of the crowd and came across towards us, a clipboard clasped to her chest, her eyes shining. She wore another severe suit, grey this time over a white blouse, but perhaps in honour of the occasion had added a long twisted rope of coral, pearls and crystal.

'It's all happening,' she said. 'I can hardly believe it, after all these months. I won't kiss you both, I'm not supposed to know you yet, but consider yourselves kissed. It's all going very well. Pierre and Donna are having a humdinger of a row. How does she manage to cry whenever she wants to? Is that the suitcase for Vancouver? Put it over there with those others which are being checked right through. Mercer Lorrimore is sweet, I'm so relieved. We haven't had any disasters yet, but there must be one on the way. I'm as high as a kite and there's no champagne in the orange juice.'

She stopped for breath and a laugh and I said, 'Nell, if Bill Baudelaire asks you if I'm here, just say yes, don't say where.'

She was puzzled but too short of time to argue. 'Well . . . OK.'

'Thanks.'

She nodded and turned to go and take care of the passengers, and the James Winterbourne character came out to meet her and also to talk to Zak.

'It's too much,' he complained, 'the real goddam Chairman of the Ontario Jockey Club has turned up to do the "bon voyage" bit himself. I'm out of a job.'

'We did ask him first,' Nell said. 'We suggested it right at the beginning, before it all grew so big. He's obviously decided he should be here after all.'

'Yes, but . . . what about my fee?'

'You'll get it,' Zak said resignedly. 'Just go back and jolly things along and tell everyone what a great trip they're going to have.'

'I've been doing that,' he grumbled, but returned obediently to his task.

'As a matter of fact,' Nell said, her brow wrinkling, 'I suppose I did get a message days ago to say the

Chairman was coming, but I didn't know it meant him. I didn't know who it meant. It was a message left for me while I was out. "The Colonel is coming." I didn't know any colonels. Is the Chairman a colonel?'

'Yes,' I said.

'Oh well, no harm done. I'd better go and see if he needs anything.' She hurried off, unperturbed.

Zak sighed. 'I could have saved myself that fee.'

'How do you mean?'

'Oh, Merry & Co pay me a lump sum to stage the mystery. I engage the actors and pay them, and whatever is left at the end is mine. Not much, sometimes.'

Voices were suddenly raised over in the crowd and people began scattering to the edges of the area, clearing the centre and falling silent. Zak and I instinctively went nearer, he in front, I in his shadow.

On the floor, sprawling, lay the actor Raoul, with Donna and Pierre bending down to help him up. Raoul dabbed at his nose with the back of his hand, and everyone could see the resulting scarlet streak.

Mavis Bricknell began saying loudly and indignantly, 'He hit him. He hit him. That young man hit our trainer in the face. He had no right to knock him down.'

She was pointing at Sheridan Lorrimore, who had turned his back on the scene.

I glanced at Zak for enlightenment.

'That,' he said blankly, 'wasn't in the script.'

*

Nell smoothed it over.

Sheridan Lorrimore could be heard saying furiously and fortissimo to his father, 'How the hell could I know they were acting? The fellow was being a bore. I just bopped him one. He deserved it. The girl was crying. And he was crowding me, pushing against me. I didn't like it.'

His father murmured something.

'Apologize?' Sheridan said in a high voice. 'Apol – oh, all right. I apologize. Will that do?'

Mercer drew him away to a corner, and slowly, haltingly, the general good humour resurfaced. Ironic compliments were paid to Pierre, Donna and Raoul for the potency and effect of their acting and Raoul played for sympathy and looked nobly forgiving, holding a handkerchief to his nose and peering at it for blood, of which there seemed to be not much.

Zak cursed and said that Pierre had in fact been going to knock Raoul to the ground at a slightly later time, and now that would have to be changed. I left him to his problems because it was coming up to the time when Emil had said the crew should board the train, and I was due back in the coffee shop.

The carrot cakes had been reduced to crumbs and the coffee cups were empty. The bussed consignment of grooms had arrived and were sitting in a group wearing Race Train T-shirts above their jeans. Emil looked at his watch and another crew member arrived and said the computer in the crew's room downstairs was showing that the special train had just pulled into the station, Gate 6, Track 7, as expected.

'*Bon*,' Emil said, smiling. 'Then, Tommy, your duties begin.'

Everyone picked up their travelling bags and in a straggle more than a group walked back towards the passengers' assembly area. As we approached we could hear the real Chairman of the Ontario Jockey Club welcoming everyone to the adventure and we could see Zak and the other actors waiting for him to finish so that they could get on with the mystery.

Jimmy the actor was dressed in a maroon VIA Rail station uniform, Zak was intent, and Ricky, due on in gory glory at any moment, was checking in a small handmirror that 'blood' was cascading satisfactorily from a gash on his head.

Zak flashed a glance at the crew, saw me and gave me a thumbs-up sign. The Chairman wound up to applause. Zak tapped Ricky, who had put the mirror in his pocket, and Ricky went into the 'I've been attacked' routine most convincingly.

Emil, the crew and I wasted no time watching. We went on past and came to Gate 6, which was basically a staircase leading to ground level, where the rails were. Even though it was high morning, the light was dim and artificial outside as acres of arched roof far above kept out the Canadian weather.

The great train was standing there, faintly hissing, silver, immensely heavy, stretching away in both directions for as far as one could see in the gloom. In the Merry & Co office, I'd learned that each carriage (built of strong unpainted corrugated aluminium with the corrugations lying horizontally) was eighty-five feet long; and there were fifteen carriages in all, counting the horses, the baggage and the Lorrimores. With the engines as well, this train covered more than a quarter of a mile standing still.

Two furlongs, I thought frivolously, to put it suitably. Three times round the train more than equalled the Derby.

There was another long banner, duplication of the one in the station, fastened to the side of the train, telling all the passengers what they were going on, if they were still in any doubt. The crew divided to right and left according to where their jobs were and, following Emil, I found myself climbing up not into the dining car but into one of the sleeping cars.

Emil briefly consulted a notebook, stowed his travel bag on a rack in a small bedroom and directed me to put my bag in the one next door. He said I should remove my raincoat and my jacket and hang them on the hangers provided. That done, he closed both doors and we descended again to the ground.

'It's easier to walk along outside while we are in the station,' he explained. He was ever precise. We walked along beside the wheels until the end of the train was in sight and finally walked past the dining car and at the end of it swung upwards through its rear door into the scene of operations.

The special dining car lived up to its name with a blue and red carpet, big blue padded leather chairs, polished wood gleaming in the lights and glass panels engraved with birds. There were windows all down both sides with blue patterned curtains at intervals and green plants lodged above, behind pelmets. Ten feet wide, the car was long enough to accommodate six oblong tables down each side of a wide aisle with four chairs at each: forty-eight seats, as promised. All quiet, all empty. All waiting.

'Come,' Emil said, leading the way forward through the splendour, 'I show you the kitchen.'

The long, silvery, all-metal kitchen was already occupied by two figures dressed in white trousers and jackets topped by high white paper hats: the diminutive lady chef from Montreal and a tall willowy young man who introduced himself as Angus, the special chef employed by the outside firm of top-class caterers who were providing for this journey the sort of food not usually served on trains.

It seemed to my amused eyes that the two chefs were in chilly unfriendliness, marking out their territories, each, in the normal course of events, being accustomed to being the boss.

Emil, who must have picked up the same signals, spoke with a true leader's decisiveness. 'In this kitchen this week,' he said to me, 'Angus is to command.

Simone will assist.' Angus looked relieved, Simone resentful. 'This is because,' Emil said, as if it clinched matters, which it did, 'Angus and his company have designed *le menu* and provided the food.'

The matter, everyone could see, was closed. Emil explained to me that on this trip the linen, cutlery and glasses had been provided by the caterers, and without more ado he showed me first, where to find everything and second, how to set a table.

He watched me do the second table in imitation of his manner. 'You learn fast,' he said approvingly. 'If you practise, they will not tell you are not a waiter.'

I practised on about half of the remaining tables while the two other dining-room stewards, the real regular service attendants, Oliver and Cathy, set the rest. They put things right with a smile when I got them wrong, and I fell into their ways and rhythm of working as well as I could. Emil surveyed the finished dining room with a critical eye and said that after a week I would probably be able to fold a napkin tidily. They all smiled: it seemed that my napkins were already OK, and I felt quite ridiculously pleased, and also reassured.

Outside the windows, the red hat of a porter trundling luggage went by, with, in its wake, the Lorrimores.

'They're boarding,' Emil said. 'When the train departs, our passengers will all come here for the champagne.' He bustled about with champagne flutes and ice and showed me how to fold a napkin round the neck of a bottle and how to pour without drips. He seemed to have forgotten about only letting me loose on water.

There were voices outside as the train came alive. I put my head out of the rear door of the dining car and, looking forward, saw all the passengers climbing upwards into the sleeping cars, with porters following after with their bags. Several people were embarking also into the car behind the dining car, into the car which comprised three bedrooms, a bar, a large lounge area and an upstairs glass-domed observation deck, the whole lot known, I'd discovered, as the dome car.

Forward by the gate through which the passengers were crowding, Nell was doing her stuff with bandages on the convincing bloodiness of Ricky. The little scene concluded, she walked aft, looking inward through the windows, searching for someone, who in fact turned out to be me.

'I wanted to tell you,' she said, 'the Conductor – he's like the captain of a ship – knows that you're our security guard, sort of, and he's agreed to help you with anything you want, and to let you go everywhere in the train without question, including the engines, as long as the two engineers – they're the train-drivers – permit it, which he says they will once he's talked to them. Say you are Tommy, when you see him.'

I gazed at her with admiration. 'You're marvellous,' I said.

'Yes, aren't I?' She smiled. 'Bill Baudelaire did ask about you. I said you were here and you'd boarded early. He seemed satisfied. Now I've got to sort out all the people who persist in putting themselves into the wrong bedrooms . . .' She had gone before she'd finished the sentence, climbing into the sleeping car forward of the kitchen and vanishing from view.

Filmer's bedroom was in that car.

It had been easy to get myself moved away from sleeping next door to him: it had happened naturally with my demotion to crew. However much I might want to keep tabs on him, bumping into him several times a day in the corridor hardly seemed the best route to anonymity.

People started coming into the dining room and sitting at the tables regardless of the fact that we were still in the station.

'Where do we sit?' a pleasant-faced woman asked Emil, and he said, 'Anywhere, madam.' The man with her demanded a double Scotch on the rocks and Emil told him that alcohol was available only after departure. Emil was courteous and helpful. I listened, and I learned.

Mercer Lorrimore came through into the dining car followed by his wife, who looked displeased.

'Where do we sit?' Lorrimore said to me, and I answered, 'Anywhere, sir,' in best Emil fashion, which drew a fast appreciative grin from Emil himself.

Mercer and Bambi chose a centrally located table and were soon joined by their less-than-happy offspring, Sheridan audibly saying, 'I don't see why we have to sit in here when we have our own private car.'

Both mother and daughter looked as if they agreed with him but Mercer, smiling round clenched molars, said with surprising bitterness, 'You will do what I ask or accept the consequences.' And Sheridan looked furious but also afraid.

They had spoken as if I weren't there, which in a way I wasn't, as other passengers were moving round me, all asking the same questions. 'Anywhere, madam. Anywhere, sir,' I said, and 'I'm afraid we can't serve alcohol before departure.'

Departure came from one instant to the next, without any whistles blowing, horns sounding or general ballyhoo. One moment we were stationary, the next sliding forward smoothly, the transition from rest to motion of a quarter of a mile of metal achieved as if on silk.

We emerged from the shadow of the station into the bright light of noon, and Daffodil Quentin under her sunburst of curls made an entrance from the dome car end, looking about her as if accustomed to people leaping up to help.

'Where do we sit?' she asked, not quite looking at me, and I said, 'Anywhere, madam. Wherever you like.'

She found two seats free not far from the Lorrimores and, putting herself on one chair and her handbag on the other, said with *bonhomie* to the elderly couple already occupying the table, 'I'm Daffodil Quentin.

Isn't this fun?' They agreed with her warmly. They knew who she was: she was yesterday's winner. They started talking with animation, like almost everyone else in the car. There was no cool period here of waiting for the ice to break. Any ice left after the previous day's racing had been broken conclusively in the scenes out in the station, and the party had already gelled and was in full swing.

Emil beckoned me towards the kitchen end, and I went up there into the small lobby with a serving counter, a space that made a needed gap between the hot glittering galley and the actual dining area. The lobby led on the left to the kitchen and on the right to the corridor to the rest of the train, along which desultory passengers were appearing, swaying gently now to the movement of gathering speed.

Behind the counter, Emil was opening bottles of Pol Roger. Oliver and Cathy were still taking glasses from a cardboard container and arranging them on small trays.

'Would you mind polishing some of these smeary glasses?' Emil said to me, pointing at a trayful. 'It would be of great help.'

'Just tell me,' I said.

'Polish them,' he said.

'That's better.'

They all laughed. I picked up a cloth and began polishing the tall flutes, and Filmer emerged from the corridor and crossed into the dining room without glancing our way.

I watched him walk towards Daffodil, who was waving to him vigorously, and take the place saved by her handbag. He had his back to me, for which I was grateful. Prepared for the closeness of him, I was still unprepared, still missing a breath. It wouldn't do, I thought. It was time for a bit of bottle, not for knocking knees.

Every seat in the dining car filled up and still people were coming. Nell, arriving, took it in her stride. 'Bound to happen. All the actors are here. Give everyone champagne.' She went on down the car, clipboard hugged to her chest, answering questions, nodding and smiling, keeping the class in order.

Emil gave me a tray of glasses. 'Put four on each table. Oliver will follow you to fill them. Start at the far end and work back.'

'OK.'

Carrying a tray of glasses would have been easier if the floor had been stable but I made it to the far end with only a lurch or two and delivered the goods as required. Three or four people without seats were standing at the far dome car end, including the actress Angelica. I offered them all glasses as well, and Angelica took one and went on bellyaching to all around her about how Steve had let her down and she should never have trusted the louse, and it was a tribute to her acting that there was a distinct drawing aside of skirts in the pursed mouths of those around her who were fed up with hearing about it.

Oliver, on my heels, was delivering them solace in Pol Roger's golden bubbles.

I came with acute awareness to the table where Filmer was sitting with Daffodil and, careful not to look directly at either of them, put my last four glasses in a row on the tablecloth.

At once Filmer said, 'Where have I seen you before?'

CHAPTER SEVEN

About fifty conclusions dashed through my head, all of them disastrous. I had been so sure he wouldn't know me. Stupid, arrogant mistake.

'I expect it was when we were over in Europe and went to the Derby Eve dinner in London,' the elderly woman said. 'We sat at the head table . . . We were guests of dear Ezra Gideon, poor man.'

I moved away, sending wordless prayers of thankfulness to anyone out there listening. Filmer hadn't even glanced at me, still less had known me. His head, when I'd finally looked at him, was turned away from me towards his companions, as was Daffodil's also.

Filmer's own thoughts must anyway have been thrown in a tangle. He was himself directly responsible for Gideon's suicide, and now he found himself sitting with Gideon's friends. Whether or not he felt an ounce of embarrassment (probably not), it had to be enough to make him unaware of waiters.

I fetched more glasses and dealt some of them to the Lorrimores who were an oasis of silence in the chattering mob and paid me absolutely no attention: and from then on I felt I had indeed chosen the right role and could sustain it indefinitely.

When everyone was served, Zak the investigator appeared like a gale-force wind and moved the mystery along through Scene Two, disclosing the details of the attempted kidnap of one of the horses and leaving a tantalizing question mark in the shape of *which one*? To the amusement of the audience, he quizzed several of the real passenger owners: 'Which is your horse, sir? Did you say Upper Gumtree?' He consulted a list. 'Ah yes. You must be Harvey Unwin from Australia? Do you have any reason to believe that your horse might be the target of international intrigue?'

It was skilfully and entertainingly acted. Mercer Lorrimore in his turn and with a smile said his horse was called Voting Right, and no, he'd had no advance notice of any attack. Bambi smiled thinly, and Sheridan said in a loud voice that he thought the whole thing was stupid; everyone knew there hadn't been any goddam kidnap attempt and why didn't Zak stop messing around and piss off.

Into a gasping horrified silence while Mercer struggled for words, Zak smiled brilliantly and said, 'Is it indigestion? We'll get you some tablets,' and he patted Sheridan compassionately on the shoulder.

It brought the house, or rather the train, down. People laughed and applauded and Sheridan looked truly murderous.

'Now, Sparrowgrass,' Zak said, consulting his list and very smoothly carrying on, 'who owns Sparrowgrass?'

The elderly gentleman sitting with Filmer said, 'I do. My wife and I.'

'So you are Mr and Mrs Young? Any relation to Brigham? No? Never mind. Isn't it true that someone tried to burn down the barn your Sparrowgrass was stabled in a month ago? Could the two attacks be linked, would you say?'

The Youngs looked astounded. 'How ever did you know that?'

'We have our sources,' Zak said loftily, and told me afterwards his source was the *Daily Racing Form*, busily read recently for background help with his story. It impressed the passengers most satisfactorily.

'I'm sure no one's trying to kidnap my horse,' Young said, but with a note of doubt in his voice that was a triumph for Zak.

'Let's hope not,' he said. 'And finally, who owns Calculator?'

The actors Walter and Mavis Bricknell put up their hands in agitation. 'We do. What's wrong with him? We must go at once to make sure. The whole thing's most upsetting. Have you proper guards now looking after the horses?'

'Calm down, sir, calm down, madam,' Zak said as to children. 'Merry & Co have a special horsemaster looking after them. They will all be safe from now on.'

He concluded the scene by saying that we would

soon be stopping at Newmarket, but that British owners shouldn't get off the train as they would find no races there. (Laughter.) Lunch was now on its way, he added, and he hoped everyone would return for drinks at five-thirty when there would be Interesting Developments as per their printed programmes. The passengers clapped very loudly, to encourage him. Zak waved, retreated and set off down the corridor, flat-footed almost at once after his bounce in the dining car, and already with drooping shoulders consulting his notebook about what he needed to do next. How often, I wondered, had he had to deal with the likes of Sheridan? From his demeanour, often enough.

Emil told me to collect the champagne glasses, pour the water and put a pot of breadsticks on each table. He himself was opening wine. Oliver and Cathy began bringing plates of smoked salmon and bowls of vichyssoise soup on trays from the kitchen and offering a choice.

The seating problem more or less sorted itself out. Mavis and Walter, pretending 'their horse's welfare meant more to them than eating', set off up the train to eat in the racegoers' dining car, and so did Angelica, 'too upset to sit down'. A few others like Raoul, Pierre and Donna, left discreetly, until Nell, counting heads, could match all paying passengers with a place. Giles-the-murderer, I was interested to see, was still in the dining room, still being overpoweringly nice: it was apparently essential to the drama that he should be liked.

We stopped at Newmarket briefly. No British owners got off. (A pity.) The soup gave place to a fricassee of chicken with lemon and parsley.

I was promoted from Aquarius to Ganymede, forsaking water for wine. Emil quite rightly didn't trust me to clear dirty plates, which involved fancy juggling with knives and forks. I was allowed with the others to change ashtrays, to deliver maple hazelnut praline mousse and to take tea and coffee to the cups, already laid. Filmer ignored my presence throughout and I was extremely careful not to draw his attention by spilling things.

By the end I had a great admiration for Emil, Oliver and Cathy, who had neatly served and cleared three full courses with the floor swaying beneath their feet and who normally would have taken my few jobs also in their stride.

When nearly all the passengers (including Filmer) had left, heading for their own rooms or the observation car, we cleared the tables, spread fresh cloths and began thinking of food for ourselves. At least, I did. The others made for the kitchen with me following, but once there Oliver took off his waistcoat, donned an apron and long yellow gloves, and began washing dishes. A deep endless sinkful of three courses for forty-eight people.

I watched him in horror. 'Do you always do this?' I asked.

'Who else?'

Cathy took a cloth to do some drying.

'No machines?' I protested.

'We're the machines,' she said.

Catch me, I thought ruefully, washing dishes. I picked up one of the cloths and helped her.

'You don't have to,' she said. 'But thanks.'

Angus the chef was cleaning up his realm at the far end of the long hot kitchen and Simone was unpacking fat beef sandwiches which we all ate standing up while working. There was an odd sort of camaraderie about it all, as if we were the front-line troops in battle. They were entitled to eat after the last sitting in the central dining car, Emil said, rinsing glasses, but usually they went only for dinner, if then; I could see why, as after the sandwiches on that first day we ate the all-too-few left-over portions of the Lucullan lunch we had served. 'There's never anything thrown away,' Cathy said, 'when we do trips like this.'

The dishes finally finished and stowed in their racks, it appeared that we were free for a blessed couple of hours: reassembly on the dot of five-thirty.

I don't know what the others did but I made straight towards the front of the packed train, threading an unsteady way through seemingly endless sleeping cars (passing my own berth), through the still busy central dining car, the full and raucous open-seat dayniter, three more sleeping cars, the crowded dome car (dining room, kitchen, lounge, observation deck), another sleeping car, and finally reaching the horses. In all, a little less than a quarter of a mile's walk, though it felt like a marathon.

I was stopped at the horse-car entrance by a locked door and, in response to my repeated knocking, by a determined female who told me I wasn't welcome.

'You can't come in,' she said bluntly, physically barring my way. 'The train crew aren't allowed in here.'

'I'm working for Merry & Co,' I said.

She looked me up and down. 'You're an attendant,' she said flatly. 'You're not coming in.'

She was quivering with authority, the resolute governess guarding the pass. Maybe forty, I judged, with regular features, no make-up and a slim wiry figure in shirt, sweater and jeans. I knew an immovable object when I saw it, and I retreated through the first sleeping car, where grooms in T-shirts lolled in open day compartments (shut off by heavy felt curtains for sleeping), on my way to consult with the Chinese chef in the forward dome car's kitchen.

'The Conductor?' he said in answer to my question. 'He is here.' He pointed along the corridor towards the dining section. 'You're lucky.'

The Conductor, in his grey suit with gold bars of long service on his left sleeve, was sitting at the first table past the kitchen, finishing his lunch. There were other diners at other tables, but he was alone, using his lunch break to fill in papers laid out on the cloth. I slid into one of the seats opposite him and he raised his eyes enquiringly.

'I'm from Merry & Co,' I said. 'I believe you know about me.'

'Tommy?' he said, after thought.

'Yes.'

He put a hand across the table, which I shook.

'George Burley,' he said. 'Call me George.'

He was middle-aged, bulky, close cropped as to hair and moustache and with, I discovered, a nice line in irony.

I explained about the impasse at the door of the horse car.

His eyes twinkled, 'You've met the dragon-lady, eh? Ms Leslie Brown. They sent her to keep the grooms in order. Now she tries to rule the train, eh?'

He had the widespread Canadian habit of turning the most ordinary statement into a question. It's a nice day, eh?

'I hope,' I said politely, 'that your authority outranks hers.'

'You bet your life,' he said. 'Let me finish these papers and my lunch and we'll go along there, eh?'

I sat for a while watching the scenery slide by, wild uninhabited stretches of green and autumn-blazing trees, grey rocks and blue lakes punctuated by tiny hamlets and lonely houses, all vivid in the afternoon sunshine, a panoramic impression of the vastness of Canada and the smallness of her population.

'Right,' George said, shuffling his papers together. 'I'll just finish my coffee, eh?'

'Is there,' I asked, 'a telephone on the train?'

He chuckled. 'You bet your life. But it's a radio phone, eh? It only works near cities where they have receiver/ transmitters. At small stations, we have to get off and use the regular phones on the ground, like the passengers do at longer stops.'

'But can anyone use the train telephone?' I asked.

He nodded. 'It's a payphone by credit card, eh? Much more expensive. Most people stretch their legs and go into the stations. It's in my office.' He antici-pated my question. 'My office is in the first sleeping car aft of the central dining car.'

'My roomette is there,' I said, working it out.

'There you are, then. Look for my name on the door.'

He finished his coffee, slid his papers into a folder and took me forward again to the horse car. The dragon answered belligerently to his knock and stared at me disapprovingly.

'He is Tommy,' George said. 'He is a security guard for Merry & Co, eh? He has the run of the *whole* train under my authority.'

She bowed in her turn to an irresistible force and let us in with raised eyebrows and an air of power suspended, not abdicated. She produced a clipboard with a sheet of ruled paper attached. 'Sign here,' she said. 'Everyone who comes in here has to sign. Put the date and time.'

I signed 'Tommy Titmouse' in a scrawl and put the time. Filmer, I was interested to see, had been to see his horse before departure.

We walked forward into the horse car with George pointing things out.

'There are eleven stalls, see? In the old days they carried twenty-four horses in a car, but there was no centre aisle, eh? No passage for anyone between stops. They don't carry horses by train much now. This car was built in 1958, eh? One of the last, one of the best.'

There was a single stall lengthwise against the wall on each side of the entrance door, then a space, then two more box-stalls, one on each side, then a space where big sliding doors gave access to the outer world for loading and unloading. Next came a wider central space with a single box on one side only. Then two more boxes and another space for loading, then two more boxes and a space, and finally another box on each side of the far forward door. Eleven boxes, as promised, with a central aisle.

The boxes were made of heavy green-painted panels of metal slotted and bolted together, dismantleable. In the wide centre space, where one box alone stood along one wall, there was a comfortable chair for the redoubtable Ms Brown, along with a table, equipment lockers, a refrigerator and a heavy plastic water tank with a tap low down for the filling of buckets. George opened the top lid of the tank and showed me a small plank floating on the surface.

'It stops the water sloshing about so much, eh?'

Eh indeed, I thought.

There were dozens of bales of hay everywhere possible, and a filled hay-net swinging gently above each horse's head. A couple of grooms sat around on bales while their charges nibbled their plain fare and thought mysterious equine thoughts.

Each box had the name of its occupant thoughtfully provided on a typewritten card slotted into a holder on the door. I peered at a few of them, identifying Filmer and Daffodil's Laurentide Ice as a light grey colt with brittle-looking bones, the Lorrimores' Voting Right as an unremarkable bay, and the Youngs' Sparrowgrass as a bright chestnut with a white star and sock.

'Come on,' George said. 'Meet the engineers, eh?' He wasn't a horse man, himself.

'Yes. Thank you.'

He opened the forward door of the horse van with a key, and with a key also let us through into the baggage car.

'The doors are kept locked, eh?'

I nodded. We swayed down the long baggage car, which was half empty of freight and very noisy, and George, having told me to remove and lay aside my waistcoat in case I got oil on it, unlocked the door at the far end. If I'd thought it noisy where we were, where we went made talking impossible.

George beckoned and I followed through a door into the heat of the rear section of the engines, the section containing among other things the boiler which provided steam to heat the whole train. George pointed wordlessly to an immense tank of water and with amusement showed me the system for telling the quantity of the contents. At intervals up the huge cylinder there were normal taps, the sort found over sinks. George pointed to the figures beside each, which were in hundreds of gallons, and made tap-turning motions with his hands. One turned on the taps, I understood with incredulity, to discover the level of the contents. Supremely logical, I supposed, if one had never heard of gauges.

We went on forward into a narrow passage beside yards of hot hammering engine of more than head height, throbbingly painful to the senses, and then passed over a coupling into another engine, even longer, even noisier, even hotter, the very stuff of hell. At the forward end of that we came to a glass-panelled door, which needed no key, and suddenly we were in the comparative quietness of the drivers' cab, right at the front of the train.

There was fresh cool air there, as the right-hand window, next to the bank of controls in front of the engineer's seat, was wide open. When I commented on it, George said that that window was open always except in blizzards, eh?

Through the wide forward unopening windows there was a riveting view of the rails stretching ahead, signals shining green in the distance, trees flashing back at a useful seventy miles an hour. I'd never been in the cab of a moving train before, and I felt I could have stayed there all day.

At the controls sat a youngish man in no sort of uniform, and beside him sat an older man in cleanish overalls with grease on his fingers.

George made introductions. 'Robert', that was the younger, and 'Mike', the elder. They nodded and shook hands when George explained my position. 'Give him help, if he asks for it.'

They said they would. George patted Robert on the shoulder and pointed out to me a small white flag blowing stiffly outside to the right of the front windows.

'That flag shows this is a special train. Not in the timetable. It's so all railwaymen along the way don't think the Canadian is running thirty minutes early.'

They all thought it a great joke. Trains never ran early the world over. Late was routine.

Still chuckling, George led the way back through the glass door into the inferno. We inched again past the thundering monster and its second string to the rear, and emerged at last into the clattering reverberating peace of the baggage car where I was reunited with my waistcoat. My suitcase, I was interested to see, stood in a quiet row of others, accessible enough if I wanted it.

George locked the baggage car door behind us and we stood again in the quiet horse car which looked homely and friendly with the horses' heads poking forward over the doors. It was interesting, I thought, that as far as they were able in their maybe four-foot-wide stalls, most of them were standing diagonally across the space, the better to deal with the motion; and they all looked alert and interested, sure signs of contentment.

I rubbed the noses of one or two under the frowning suspicious gaze of Ms Brown who was not pleased to be told that she should let me in whenever I asked, eh?

George chuckled his way out of the horse car and we meandered back down the train together, George stopping to check for news with each sleeping-car attendant and to solve any problems. There was a sing-song in progress in the dome car and the racegoers in the dayniter had formed about four separate card schools with cash passing briskly.

The overworked and gloomy chef in the main dining car had not lost his temper altogether and only a few passengers had grumbled that the roomettes were too cramped; the most usual disgruntlement, George said.

No one was ill, no one was drunk, no one was fighting. Things, George said eventually, were going so smoothly that one should expect disaster any time now, eh?

We came at last to his office which was basically a roomette like my own: that is to say, it was a seven-by-four-foot space on one side of a central corridor, containing a washbasin, a folding table and two seats, one of which concealed what the timetable coyly called 'facilities'. One could either leave the sliding door open and see the world go by down the corridor, or close oneself into a private cocoon; and at night, one's bed descended from the ceiling and on to the seat of the facilities which effectively put them out of use.

George invited me in and left the door open.

'This train,' he said, settling himself into the armchair and indicating the facilities for me, 'is a triumph of diplomacy, eh?'

He had a permanent smile in his eyes, I thought, much as if he found the whole of life a joke. I learned later that he thought stupidity the norm for human behaviour, and that no one was as stupid as passengers, politicians, pressmen and the people who employed him.

'Why,' I asked, 'is it a triumph?'

'Common sense has broken out.'

I waited. He beamed and in a while went on, 'Except for the engineers, the same crew will stay with the train to Vancouver!'

I didn't to his eyes appear sufficiently impressed.

'It's unheard of, eh?' he said. 'The unions won't allow it.'

'Oh.'

'Also the horse car belongs to Canadian Pacific.'

I looked even blanker.

He chuckled. 'The Canadian Pacific and VIA Rail, who work so closely together, get along like sandpaper, good at friction. Canadian Pacific trains are freight trains, eh?, and VIA trains carry passengers, and never the two shall mix. This train is a mix. A miracle, eh?'

'Absolutely,' I said encouragingly.

He looked at me with twinkling pity for my lack of understanding of the really serious things in life.

I asked if his telephone would work at the next big stop which came under the heading of serious to me.

'Sudbury?' he said. 'Certainly. But we will be there for an hour. It's much cheaper from the station. A fraction of the price.'

'But more private here.'

He nodded philosophically. 'Come here as soon as we slow down coming to Sudbury, eh? I'll leave you here. I have to be busy in the station.'

I thanked him for everything and left the orbit of his beaming smile knowing that I was included in the universality of stupid behaviour. I could see a lot more of George, I thought, before I tired of him.

My own door, I found, was only two doors along from his, on the right-hand side of the train when facing forward. I went past without stopping, noting that there were six roomettes altogether at the forward end of the car: three each side. Then the corridor bent to the side to accommodate four enclosed double bedrooms and bent back again through the centre of open seating with sleeping curtains, called sections. The six sections of that car were allocated to twelve assorted actors and crew, most of them at that point reading, talking or fast asleep.

'How's it going?' Zak said, yawning.

'All quiet on the western front.'

'Pass, friend.'

I smiled and went on down the train, getting the feel of it now, understanding the way it was put together, beginning to wonder about things like electricity, water supply and sewage. A small modern city on the move, I thought, with all the necessary infrastructure.

All the doors were closed in the owners' sleeping cars (there were almost no open sections in those), the inhabitants there having the habit of privacy. The rooms could have been empty, it was impossible to tell, and in fact when I came to the special dining car I found a good number of the passengers sitting at the unlaid tables, just chatting. I went on through into the dome car where there were three more bedrooms before one came to the bar, which was furnished with tables, seating and barman. A few people sat there also, talking, and some again were sitting around in the long lower lounge to the rear.

From there a short staircase went up to the

observation lounge, and I went up there briefly. The many seats there were almost full, the passengers enjoying their uninterrupted view of a million brilliant trees under blue skies and baking in the hot sunshine streaming through the glass roof.

Mr Young was up there, asleep. Julius Apollo wasn't, nor anywhere else in public view.

I hadn't seen Nell at all either. I didn't know where she'd put herself finally on her often-revised allocation of sleeping space, but wherever she was, it was behind a closed door.

To the rear of the dome car there was only the Lorrimores' private car, which I could hardly enter, so I retraced my steps, intending to retreat to my own roomette and watch the scenery do its stuff.

In the dining car I was stopped by Xanthe Lorrimore who was sitting alone at a table looking morose.

'Bring me some Coke,' she said.

'Yes, certainly,' I said, and went to fetch some from the cold locker in the kitchen, thanking my stars that I'd happened to see where the soft-drink cans were kept. I put the can and a glass on one of the small trays (Emil's voice in my ear saying, 'Never ever carry the object. Carry the tray.') and returned to Xanthe.

'I'm afraid this is on a cash bar basis,' I said, putting the glass on the table and preparing to open the can.

'What does that mean?'

'Things from the bar are extra. Not included in the fare.'

'How ridiculous. And I haven't any money.'

'You could pay later, I'm sure.'

'I think it's stupid.'

I opened the can and poured the Coke, and Mrs Young, who happened to be sitting alone at the next table, turned round and said to Xanthe sweetly that she, Mrs Young, would pay for the Coke, and wouldn't Xanthe come and join her?

Xanthe's first instinct was clearly to refuse but, sulky or not, she was also lonely, and there was an undemanding grandmotherliness about Mrs Young that promised an uncritical listening ear. Xanthe moved herself and her Coke and unburdened herself of her immediate thought.

'That brother of mine,' she said, 'is an asshole.'

'Perhaps he has his problems,' Mrs Young said equably, digging around in her capacious and disorganized handbag for some money.

'If he was anyone else's kid, he'd be in jail.'

The words came out as if propelled irresistibly from a well of compressed emotion. Even Xanthe herself looked shocked at what she'd let out, and feebly tried to weaken the impact. 'I didn't mean literally, of course,' she said. But she had.

Mrs Young, who had paused in her search, finally found her purse and gave me a dollar.

'If there's any change, keep it,' she said.

'Thank you, madam.'

I had no choice but to leave and I made for the

151

kitchen carrying the dollar on the tray like a trophy anchored by a thumb. From there I looked back to see Xanthe begin to talk to Mrs Young, at first slowly, with brakes on, and then faster and faster, until all the unhappiness was pouring out like a flood. I could see Xanthe's face and the back of Mrs Young's head. Xanthe, it seemed to me, was perhaps sixteen, but probably younger: certainly not older. She still had the facial contours of childhood, with a round chin and big-pupilled eyes: also chestnut hair in abundance and a growing figure hidden within a bulky white top with a pink glittering pop-slogan on the front, the badge of youth.

They were still talking when I continued on my way back to my roomette where I sat in comfortable privacy for a while reading the timetable and also reflecting that although I still had no answers to the old questions, I now had a whole crop of new ones, the most urgent being whether or not Filmer had already known the Youngs were friends of Ezra Gideon. Whether the Youngs were, in fact, a target of some kind. Yet Filmer hadn't chosen to sit at their table; it had been the random fortuitous decision of Daffodil. Perhaps if it hadn't happened so handily by chance, he would have engineered a meeting. Or was the fact of their friendship with Gideon just an unwelcome coincidence, as I had at first supposed? Time, perhaps, would tell.

Time told me more immediately that it was five-thirty, the hour of return to the dining room, and I returned to find every single seat already taken, the passengers having learned fast. Latecomers stood in the entrances, looking forlorn.

Filmer, I saw at once, was placed opposite Mercer Lorrimore. Daffodil, beside him, was opposite Bambi who was being coolly gracious.

Xanthe was still sitting across from Mrs Young, now rejoined by her husband. Sheridan, as far as I could see, was absent. Giles-the-murderer was present, sitting with the Youngs and Xanthe, being nice.

Emil, Oliver, Cathy and I went round the tables pouring wine, tea or coffee into glasses or cups on small trays with small movements, and when that was done Zak bounded into the midst of things, vibrating with fresh energy, to get on with the mystery.

I didn't listen in detail to it all, but it revolved round Pierre and Donna, and Raoul the racehorse trainer who wanted to marry her money. Zak had got round the pre-empted Pierre hitting-Raoul-to-the-ground routine by having Donna slap Raoul's face instead, which she did with a gusto that brought gasps from the audience. Donna was clearly established as the wittering Bricknells' besotted daughter, with Raoul obviously Mavis's favourite, and Pierre despised as a no-good compulsive gambler. Mother and daughter went into a sharp slanging match, with Walter fussing and trying to stop them. Mavis, in the end, started crying.

I looked at the passengers' faces. Even though they knew this lot were all actors, they were transfixed. Soap

153

opera had come to life within touching distance. Racing people, I'd always thought, were among the most cynical in the world, yet here some of the most experienced of them were moved and involved despite themselves.

Zak, keeping up the tension, said that at the last of our brief stops at minor stations he had been handed a telex about Angelica's missing friend Steve. Was Angelica present? Everyone looked around, and no, she wasn't. Never mind, Zak said, would someone please tell her that she must telephone Steve from Sudbury, as he had serious news for her.

A lot of people nodded. It was amazing.

Dressed in silk and ablaze with jewellery, apparently to prove that Donna's inheritance was no myth, Mavis Bricknell stumbled off towards the toilet room at the dome car's entrance saying she must repair the ravages to her face, and presently she came back, screaming loudly.

Angelica, it appeared, was lying on the lavatory floor, extremely dead. Zak naturally bustled to investigate, followed by a sizeable section of the audience. Some of them soon came back smiling weakly and looking unsettled.

'She can't really be dead,' someone said solemnly. 'But she certainly looks it.'

There was a lot of 'blood' all over the small compartment, it appeared, with Angelica's battered head in shadow beyond the essential facility. Angelica's eyes

154

were just visible staring at the wall, unblinking. 'How can she do that?' several said.

Zak came back, looked around him, and beckoned to me.

'Stand in front of that door, will you, and don't let anyone go in?'

I nodded and went through the crowd towards the dome car. Zak himself was calling everyone back into the dining room, saying they should all stay together until we reached Sudbury, which would be soon. I could hear Nell's voice announcing calmly that everyone had time for another drink. There would be an hour's stop in Sudbury for everyone to stretch their legs if they wanted to, and dinner would be served as soon as the train started again.

I went across the clattering, windy linkage space between the dining and dome cars and stood outside the toilet room. I wasn't actually pleased with Zak as I didn't want to risk being identified as an actor, but that, I supposed, would be a great deal better than the truth.

It was boring in the passage but also, it proved, necessary, as one or two passengers came back for a look at the corpse. They were good-humoured enough when turned away. Meanwhile the corpse, who must have had to blink in the end, could be heard flushing water within.

When we began to slow down I knocked on the door. 'Message from Zak,' I said.

The door opened a fraction. Angelica's greasepaint make-up was a pale bluish grey, her hair a mass of tomato ketchup.

'Lock the door,' I said. 'Zak will be along. When you hear his voice outside, unlock it.'

'Right,' she said, sounding cheerfully alive. 'Have a nice trip.'

CHAPTER EIGHT

Angelica left the train on a stretcher in the dusk under bright station lights, her tomato head half covered by a blanket, and one lifeless hand, with red fingernails and sparkling rings, artistically drooping out of concealment on the side where the train's passengers were able to look on with fascination.

I watched the scene through the window of George Burley's office while I talked to Bill Baudelaire's mother on the telephone.

The conversation had been a surprise from the beginning, when a light young female voice had answered my call.

'Could I speak to Mrs Baudelaire, please?' I said.

'Speaking.'

'I mean . . . Mrs Baudelaire senior.'

'Any Mrs Baudelaire who is senior to me is in her grave,' she announced. 'Who are you?'

'Tor Kelsey.'

'Oh yes,' she replied instantly. 'The invisible man.'

I half laughed.

'How do you do it?' she asked. 'I'm dying to know.'

'Seriously?'

'Of course, seriously.'

'Well . . . say if someone serves you fairly often in a shop, you recognize them when you're in the shop, but if you meet them somewhere quite different, like at the races, you can't remember who they are.'

'Quite right. It's happened to me often.'

'To be easily recognized,' I said, 'you have to be in your usual environment. So the trick about invisibility is not to have a usual environment.'

There was a pause, then she said, 'Thank you. It must be lonely.'

I couldn't think of an answer to that, but was astounded by her perception.

'The interesting thing is,' I said, 'that it's quite different for the people who work in the shop. When they get to know their customers, they recognize them easily anywhere in the world. So the racing people I know, I recognize everywhere. They don't know that I exist . . . and that's invisibility.'

'You are,' she said, 'an extraordinary young man.'

She stumped me again.

'But Bill knew you existed,' she said, 'and he told me he didn't recognize you face to face.'

'He was looking for the environment he knew . . . straight hair, no sunglasses, a good grey suit, collar and tie.'

'Yes,' she said. 'If I meet you, will I know you?'

'I'll tell you.'

'Pact.'

This, I thought with relief and enjoyment, was some carrier pigeon.

'Would you give Bill some messages?' I asked.

'Fire away. I'll write them down.'

'The train reaches Winnipeg tomorrow evening at about seven-thirty, and everyone disembarks to go to hotels. Please would you tell Bill I will not be staying at the same hotel as the owners, and that I will again not be going to the President's lunch, but that I will be at the races, even if he doesn't see me.'

I paused. She repeated what I'd said.

'Great,' I said. 'And would you ask him some questions?'

'Fire away.'

'Ask him for general information on a Mr and Mrs Young who own a horse called Sparrowgrass.'

'It's on the train,' she said.

'Yes, that's right.' I was surprised, but she said Bill had given her a list to be a help with messages.

'Ask him,' I said, 'if Sheridan Lorrimore has ever been in any trouble that he knows of, apart from assaulting an actor at Toronto, that should have resulted in Sheridan going to jail.'

'Gracious me. The Lorrimores don't go to jail.'

'So I gathered,' I said dryly, 'and would you also ask which horses are running at Winnipeg and which at Vancouver, and which in Bill's opinion is the really best horse on the train, not necessarily on form, and which has the best chance of winning either race.'

'I don't need to ask Bill the first question, I can answer that for you right away, it's on this list. Nearly all the eleven horses, nine to be exact, are running at Vancouver. Only Upper Gumtree and Flokati run at Winnipeg. As for the second, in my own opinion neither Upper Gumtree nor Flokati will win at Winnipeg because Mercer Lorrimore is shipping his great horse Premiere by horse-van.'

'Um . . .' I said. 'You follow racing quite a bit?'

'My dear young man, didn't Bill tell you? His father and I owned and ran the *Ontario Raceworld* magazine for years before we sold it to a conglomerate.'

'I see,' I said faintly.

'And as for the Vancouver race,' she went on blithely, 'Laurentide Ice might as well melt right now, but Sparrowgrass and Voting Right are both in with a good chance. Sparrowgrass will probably start favourite as his form is consistently good, but as you ask, very likely the best horse, the one with most potential for the future, is Mercer Lorrimore's Voting Right, and I would give that one the edge.'

'Mrs Baudelaire,' I said, 'you are a gem.'

'Beyond the price of rubies,' she agreed. 'Anything else?'

'Nothing, except . . . I hope you are well.'

'No, not very. You're kind to ask. Goodbye, young man. I'm always here.'

She put the receiver down quickly as if to stop me from asking anything else about her illness, and it reminded me sharply of my Aunt Viv, bright, spirited and horse-mad to the end.

I went back to the dining car to find Oliver and Cathy laying the tables for dinner, and I helped them automatically, although they said I needn't. The job done, we repaired to the kitchen door to see literally what was cooking and to take the printed menus from Angus to put on the tables.

Blinis with caviare, we read, followed by rack of lamb or cold poached salmon, then chocolate mousse with cream.

'There won't be any over,' Cathy sighed, and she was right as far as the blinis went, though we all ate lamb in the end.

With ovens and gas burners roaring away, it was wiltingly hot even at the dining-room end of the kitchen. Down where the chef worked, a temperature gauge on the wall stood at 102° Fahrenheit, but tall willowy Angus, whose high hat nearly brushed the ceiling, looked cool and unperturbed.

'Don't you have air-conditioning?' I asked.

Angus said, 'In summer, I dare say. October is however officially winter, even though it's been warm this year. The air-conditioning needs freon gas, which has all leaked away, and it won't be topped up again until spring. So Simone tells me.'

Simone, a good foot shorter and with sweat trickling down her temples, mutely nodded.

The passengers came straggling back shedding overcoats and saying it was cold outside, and again the dining car filled up. The Lorrimores this time were all sitting together. The Youngs were with the Unwins from Australia and Filmer and Daffodil shared a table with a pair Nell later identified to me as the American owners of the horse called Flokati.

Filmer, extremely smooth in a dark suit and grey tie, solicitously removed Daffodil's chinchillas and hung them over the back of her chair. She shimmered in a figure-hugging black dress, diamonds sparkling whenever she moved, easily outstripping the rest of the company (even Mavis Bricknell) in conspicuous expenditure.

The train made its smooth inconspicuous departure and I did my stuff with water and breadsticks.

Bambi Lorrimore put her hand arrestingly on my arm as I passed. She was wearing a mink jacket and struggling to get out of it.

'Take this back into our private car, will you?' she said. 'It's too hot in here. Put it in the saloon, not the bedroom.'

'Certainly, madam,' I agreed, helping her with alacrity. 'I'd be glad to.'

Mercer produced a key and gave it to me, explaining that I would come to a locked door.

'Lock it again when you come back.'

'Yes, sir.'

He nodded and, carrying the coat away over my arm, I went back through the dome car and with a great deal of interest into the private quarters of the Lorrimores.

There were lights on everywhere. I came first to a small unoccupied sleeping space, then a galley, cold and lifeless. Provision for private food and private crew, but no food, no crew. Beyond that was the locked door, and beyond that a small handsome dining room to seat eight. Through there, down a corridor, there were three bedrooms, two with the doors open. I took a quick peek inside: bed, drawers, small bathroom with shower. One was clearly Xanthe's, the other by inference Sheridan's. I didn't go into the parents' room but went on beyond it to find myself in the rear part of the carriage, at the very end of the train.

It was a comfortable drawing room with a television set and abundant upholstered armchairs in pastel blues and greens. I went over to the rear door and looked out, seeing a little open boarding platform with a polished brass-topped balustrade and, beyond, the Canadian Pacific's single pair of rails streaming away into darkness. The railroad across Canada, I'd learned, was single track for most of the way. Only in towns and at a few other places could trains going in opposite directions pass.

I put the mink coat on a chair and retraced my journey, locking the door again and eventually returning the key to Mercer who nodded without speech and put it in his pocket.

Emil was pouring wine. The passengers were scoffing the blinis. I eased into the general picture again and became as unidentifiable as possible. Few people, I discovered, looked directly at a waiter's eyes, even when they were talking to him.

About an hour after we'd left Sudbury we stopped briefly for under five minutes at a place called Cartier and then went on again. The passengers, replete with the lamb and chocolate mousse, lingered over coffee, and began to drift away to the dome car's bar lounge. Xanthe Lorrimore got up from the table after a while and went that way, and presently came back screaming.

This time, the real thing. She came stumbling back into the dining car followed by a commotion of people yelling behind her.

She reached her parents who were bewildered as well as worried.

'I was nearly killed,' she said frantically. 'I nearly stepped off into space. I mean, I was *nearly killed*.'

'Darling,' Mercer said calmingly, 'what has exactly happened?'

'You don't understand.' She was screaming, trembling, hysterical. 'I nearly stepped into space because our private car *isn't there.*'

It brought both of the Lorrimores to their feet in an incredulous rush, but they had only to look at the faces crowding behind her to know it was true.

'And they say, all those people say...' she was gasping, half unable to get the words out, terribly frightened, '... they say the other train, the regular Canadian, is only half an hour behind us, and will smash into ... will smash into ... don't you *see*?'

The Lorrimores, followed by everyone still in the dining room, went dashing off into the dome car, but Emil and I looked at each other, and I said, 'How do we warn that train?'

'Tell the Conductor. He has a radio.'

'I'll go,' I said. 'I know where his office is. I'll find him.'

'Hurry then.'

'Yes.'

I hurried. Ran. Reached George's office.

No one there.

I went on, running where I could, and found him walking back towards me through the dayniter. He instantly took in that I brought bad news and steered me at once into the noisy outside coupling space between the dayniter and the central dining car.

'What is it?' he shouted.

'The Lorrimores' private car is unhitched ... it's

somewhere back on the track, and the Canadian is coming.'

He moved faster than I would have thought anyone could on a train and was already talking into a radio headset when I reached his office.

'The private car was there at Cartier,' he said. 'I was off the train there and saw it. Are you sure it's not in sight?' He listened. 'Right, then radio to the Canadian and warn the Conductor he'll not be leaving Cartier, eh? I'll get this train stopped and we'll go back for the lost car. See what's what. You'd better inform Toronto and Montreal. They won't think this is very funny on a Sunday evening, eh?' He chuckled and looked at me assessingly as I stood in his doorway. 'I'll leave someone here manning the radio,' he continued. 'Tell him when you've got the Canadian understanding the situation, eh?'

He nodded at the reply he heard, took off the headset and gave it to me.

'You are talking to the despatcher in Schreiber,' he said, ' – that's ahead of us, this side of Thunder Bay – and he can radio straight to the Canadian following us. You can hear the despatcher without doing anything. To transmit, press the button.' He pointed, and was gone.

I put on the headset and sat in his chair and presently into my ears a disembodied voice said, 'Are you there?'

I pressed the button. 'Yes.'

'Tell George I got the Canadian and it will stop in

Cartier. There's a CP freight train due behind it but I got Sudbury in time and it isn't leaving there. No one is happy. Tell George to pick up that car and get the hell out.'

I pressed the button. 'Right,' I said.

'Who are you?' asked the voice.

'One of the attendants.'

He said, 'Huh,' and was quiet.

The Great Transcontinental Mystery Race Train began to slow down and soon came to a smooth stop. Almost in the same instant, George was back in his doorway.

'Tell the despatcher we've stopped and are going back,' he said, when I'd relayed the messages. 'We're eleven point two miles out of Cartier, between Benny and Stralak, which means in an uninhabited wilderness. You stay here, eh?' And he was gone again, this time towards the excitement in the tail.

I gave his message to the despatcher and added, 'We're reversing now, going slowly.'

'Let me know when you find the car.'

'Yes.'

It was pitch dark through the windows; no light in the wilderness. I heard afterwards from a lot of excited chattering in the dining room that George had stood alone outside the rear door of the dome car on the brink of space, directing a bright hand-held torch beam down the track. Heard that he had a walkie-talkie radio on which he could give the engineer instructions to slow down further, and to stop.

He found the Lorrimores' car about a mile and a half out of Cartier. The whole train stopped while he jumped down from the dome car and went to look at the laggard. There was a long pause from my point of view, while the lights began flickering in the office and the train exceedingly slowly reversed, before stopping again and going into a sudden jerk. Then we started forward slowly, and then faster, and the lights stopped flickering, and soon after that George appeared in his office looking grim, all chuckles extinguished.

'What's the matter?' I said.

'*Nothing*,' he said violently, 'that's what's the matter.' He stretched out a hand for the headset which I gave him.

He spoke into it. 'This is George. We picked up the Lorrimores' car at one point three miles west of Cartier. There was no failure in the linkage.' He listened. 'That's what I said. Who the hell do they have working in Cartier, eh? Someone uncoupled that car at Cartier and rigged some way of pulling it out of the station into the darkness before releasing it. The brakes weren't on. You tell Cartier to send someone right away down the track looking for a rope or some such, eh? The steam heat pipe wasn't broken, it had been unlocked. That's what I said. The valve was closed. It was no goddam accident, no goddam mechanical failure, someone deliberately unhitched that car. If the Lorrimore girl hadn't found out, the Canadian would have crashed into it. No, maybe not at high speed, but at twenty-five, thirty miles an hour the Canadian can do a lot of damage. Would have made matchsticks of the private car. Might have killed the Canadian engineers, or even derailed the train. You tell them to start looking, eh?'

He took off the headset and stared at me with rage.

'Would you,' he said, 'know how to uncouple one car from another?'

'No, of course not.'

'It takes a railwayman.' He glared. 'A railwayman! It's like a mechanic letting someone drive off in a car with loose wheel nuts. It's criminal, eh?'

'Yes.'

'A hundred years ago,' he said furiously, 'they designed a system to prevent cars that had broken loose from running backwards and crashing into things. The brakes go on automatically in a runaway.' He glared. 'That system had been bypassed. The Lorrimores' brakes weren't on. That car was deliberately released on level ground, eh? I don't understand it. What was the point?'

'Maybe someone doesn't like the Lorrimores,' I suggested.

'We'll find the bastard,' he said, not listening. 'There can't be many in Cartier who know trains.'

'Do you get much sabotage?' I asked.

'Not like this. Not often. Once or twice in the past.

169

But it's mostly vandals. A kid or two throwing rocks off a bridge. Some stealing, eh?'

He was affronted, I saw, by the treachery of one of his own kind. He took it personally. He was in a way ashamed, as one is if one's countrymen behave badly abroad.

I asked him about his communication system with the engineer. Why had he gone up the train himself to get it stopped if he had a walkie-talkie?

'It crackles if we're going at any speed. It's better to talk face to face.'

A light flashed on the ship-to-shore radio and he replaced his headset.

'George here,' he said, and listened. He looked at his watch and frowned. 'Yes. Right. Understood.' He took off the headset, shaking his head. 'They're not going to go along the track looking for a rope until both the Canadian and the freight train have been through. If our saboteur's got an ounce of sense, by that time there won't be anything incriminating to find.'

'Probably not already,' I said. 'It's getting on for an hour since we left Cartier.'

'Yeah,' he said. His good humour was trickling back despite his anger, the gleam of irony again in his eye. 'Better than that fellow's fake mystery, eh?'

'Yes . . .' I said, thinking. 'Is the steam pipe the only thing connecting one car to the next? Except the links, of course.'

'That's right.'

170

'What about electricity . . . and water?'

He shook his head. 'Each car makes its own electricity. Self-contained. They have generators under the floors . . . like dynamos on bicycles . . . that make electricity from the wheels going round. The problem is that when we're going slowly, the lights flicker. Then there are batteries for when we're stopped, but they'd only last for forty five minutes, eh?, if we weren't plugged into the ground supply at a station. After that we're down to emergency lighting, just the aisle lights and not much else for about four hours, then we're in the dark.'

'And water?' I asked.

'It's in the roof.'

'Really?' I said, surprised.

He patiently explained. 'At city stations, we have water hydrants every eighty-five feet, the length of the cars. One to each car. Also the main electricity, same thing, eh? Anyway, the water goes up under pressure into the tanks in the roof and feeds down again to the washrooms by gravity.'

Fascinating, I thought. And it had made unhitching the Lorrimores' car a comparatively quick and easy job.

'The new cars,' George said, 'will be heated by electricity, not steam, so we'll be doing away with the steam pipe, eh? And they'll have tanks for the sewage, which now drops straight down on to the tracks, of course.'

'Canada's railways,' I said politely, 'will be the envy of the world.'

He chuckled. 'The trains between Montreal and Toronto are late three-quarters of the time and the new engines break down regularly. The old rolling stock, like this train, is great.'

He picked up the headset again. I raised a hand in farewell and went back to the dining room where the real mystery had easily usurped Zak's, though some were sure it was part of the plot.

Xanthe had cheered up remarkably through being the centre of sympathetic attention, and Filmer was telling Mercer Lorrimore he should sue the railway company for millions of dollars for negligence. The near-disaster had galvanized the general consciousness to a higher adrenalin level, probably because Xanthe had not, in fact, been carried off like Angelica.

Nell was sitting at a table with a fortyish couple who she later told me owned one of the horses in the box-car, a dark bay called Redi-Hot. The man beckoned to me as I stood around vaguely, and asked me to fetch cognac for him, vodka with ice for his wife and . . . what for Nell?

'Just Coke, please,' she said.

I went to the kitchen where I knew the Coke was, but made frantic question mark signals to Nell about the rest. Emil, the chefs, Oliver and Cathy had finished cleaning up and had all gone off duty. I had no alcohol-divining rod to bend a twig in the direction of brandy or Smirnoff.

Nell said something to the owners and came to join me, stifling laughter.

'Yes, very funny,' I said, 'but what the hell do I do?'

'Take one of the small trays and get the drinks from the bar. I'll explain they have to pay for them.'

'I haven't seen you for five minutes alone today,' I complained.

'You're downstairs, I'm up.'

'I could easily hate you.'

'But do you?'

'Not yet,' I said.

'If you're a good little waiter, I'll leave you a tip.'

She went back to her place with a complacent bounce to her step, and with a curse, but not meaning it, I took the Coke and a glass to her table and went on into the dome car for the rest. After I'd returned and delivered the order someone else asked for the same service, which I willingly performed again, and yet again.

On each trip I overheard snatches of the bar-room conversations and could hear the louder buzz of continuing upheaval along in the lounge, and I thought that after I'd satisfied everyone in the dining room I might drift along to the far end with my disarming little tray.

The only person not wholly in sympathy with this plan was the bartender who complained that I was supposed to be off duty and that the passengers should come to the bar to buy the drinks themselves; I was siphoning off his tips. I saw the justice of that and offered to split fifty-fifty. He knew very well that, without my running to and fro, the passengers mostly wouldn't be bothered to move to drink, so he accepted fast, no doubt considering me a mug as well as an actor.

Sheridan Lorrimore, who was sitting at a table apart from his parents, demanded I bring him a double Scotch at once. He had a carrying voice, and his sister from two tables away turned round in disapproval.

'No, no, you're not supposed to,' she said.

'Mind your own business.' He turned his head slightly towards me and spoke in the direction of my tie. 'Double Scotch, at the double.'

'Don't get it,' Xanthe said.

I stood irresolute.

Sheridan stood up, his ready anger rising. He put out a hand and pushed my shoulder fiercely.

'Go on,' he said. 'Damn well do as I say. Go and get my drink.'

He pushed again quite hard and as I turned away I heard him snigger and say, 'You have to kick 'em, you know.'

I went into the dome car and stood behind the bar with the bartender, and felt furious with Sheridan, not for his outrageous behaviour but because he was getting me noticed. Filmer had been sitting with his back to me, it was true, but near enough to overhear.

Mercer Lorrimore appeared tentatively in the bar doorway and came in when he saw me.

'I apologize for my son,' he said wearily, and I had a convincing impression that he'd apologized countless times before. He pulled out his wallet, removed a twenty-dollar note from it and offered me the money.

'Please don't,' I said. 'There's no need.'

'Yes, yes. Take it.'

I saw he would feel better if I did, as if paying money would somehow excuse the act. I thought he should stop trying to buy pardons for his son and pay for mental treatment instead. But then, perhaps he had. There was more wrong with Sheridan than ill temper, and it had been obvious to his father for a long time.

I didn't approve of what he was doing, but if I refused his money I would be more and more visible, so I took it, and when he had gone off in relief back towards the dining car I gave it to the barman.

'What was that all about?' he asked curiously, pocketing the note without hesitation. When I explained, he said, 'You should have kept the money. You should have charged him triple.'

'He would have felt three times as virtuous,' I said, and the barman looked at me blankly.

I didn't go back to the dining car but forward into the lounge, where again the sight of my yellow waistcoat stirred a few thirsts, which I did my best to accommodate. The barman was by now mellow and helpful and said we were rapidly running out of the ice that had come aboard in bags in Sudbury.

Up in the dome, the uncoupling of the private car had given way to speculation about whether the northern lights would oblige: the weather was right, apparently. I took a few drinks up there (including some for Zak and Donna, which amused them), and on my way down the stairs saw the backs of Mercer and Bambi, Filmer and Daffodil, as they walked through the lounge towards the door to the private car. Mercer stood aside to let Bambi lead the other two through the short noisy joining section, and then, before going himself, he looked back, saw me and beckoned.

'Bring a bowl of ice, will you?' he said when I reached him. 'To the saloon.'

'Yes, sir,' I said.

He nodded and departed, and I relayed the request to the barman who shook his head and said he was down to six cubes. I knew there were other bags of cubes in the kitchen refrigerator, so, feeling that I had been walking the train for a lifetime, I went along through the dining room to fetch some.

There weren't many people still in there, though Xanthe was still being comforted and listened to by Mrs Young. Nell sat opposite Sheridan Lorrimore who seemed to be telling her that he had wrapped his Lamborghini round a tree recently and had ordered a new one.

'Tree?' Nell said, smiling.

He looked at her uncomprehendingly. Sheridan wasn't a great one for jokes. I fetched a bag of ice and a bowl from the kitchen, swayed back to the bar and in due course took the bowl of ice (on a tray) to the saloon.

The four of them were sitting in armchairs, Bambi talking to Daffodil, Mercer to Filmer.

Mercer said to me, 'You'll find glasses and cognac in the cupboard in the dining room. And Benedictine. Bring them along here, will you?'

'Yes, sir.'

Filmer paid me no attention. In the neat dining room, the cupboards had glass fronts with pale green curtains inside them. In one I found the bottles and glasses as described, and took them aft.

Filmer was saying, 'Will Voting Right go on to the Breeders' Cup if he wins at Winnipeg?'

'He's not running at Winnipeg,' Mercer said. 'He runs at Vancouver.'

'Yes, I meant Vancouver.'

Daffodil with enthusiasm was telling a cool Bambi that she should try some face cream or other that helped with wrinkles.

'Just leave everything,' Mercer said to me. 'We'll pour.'

'Yes, sir,' I said, and retreated as he began the ultimate heresy of sloshing Rémy Martin's finest on to rocks.

Mercer would know me everywhere on the train, I thought, but none of the other three would. I hadn't met Filmer's eyes all day; had been careful not to; and it seemed to me that his attention had been exclusively focused upon what he had now achieved, a visiting-terms acquaintanceship with Mercer Lorrimore.

There was now loud music in the lounge, with two couples trying to dance and falling over with giggles from the perpetual motion of the dance floor. Up in the dome, the aurora borealis was doing its flickering fiery best on the horizon, and in the bar there was a group playing poker in serious silent concentration. Playing for thousands, the barman said.

Between the bar and the dining room there were three bedrooms, and in one of those, with the door open, was a sleeping-car attendant, dressed exactly like myself.

'Hello,' he said, as I paused in the doorway. 'Come to help?'

'Sure,' I said. 'What do I do?'

'You're the actor, aren't you?' he asked.

'It's hush-hush.'

He nodded. 'I won't say a word.'

He was of about my own age, perhaps a bit older, pleasant-looking and cheerful. He showed me how to fold up the ingenious mechanism of the daytime arm-chairs and slide them under a bed which pulled out from the wall. A top bunk was then pulled down from the ceiling, complete with ladder. He straightened the bedclothes and laid a wrapped chocolate truffle on each pillow, a goodnight blessing.

'Neat,' I said.

He had only one more room to do, he said, and he should have finished long before this but he'd been badly delayed in the car on the other side of the dining car, which he had in his care also.

I nodded – and several thoughts arrived simultaneously in a rush on my mental doorstep. They were that Filmer's bedroom was in that car. Filmer was at that moment with the Lorrimores. The only locks on the bedroom doors were inside, in the form of bolts to ensure privacy. There was no way of preventing anyone from walking in if a room were empty.

I went along to the sleeping car on the far side of the kitchen and opened the door of the abode of Julius Apollo.

CHAPTER NINE

By virtue of having paid double and possibly treble, Filmer had a double bedroom all to himself. Only the lower bunk had been prepared for the night: the upper was still in the ceiling.

For all that he could be expected to stay in the Lorrimores' car for at least fifteen more minutes I felt decidedly jittery, and I left the door open so that if he did come back unexpectedly I could say I was merely checking that everything was in order. My uniform had multiple advantages.

The bedrooms were small, as one would expect, though in the daytime, with the beds folded away, there was comfortable space. There was a washbasin in full view, with the rest of the plumbing in a discreet little closet. For hanging clothes there was a slot behind the bedheads about eight inches wide, enough in Filmer's case for two suits. Another two jackets hung on hangers on pegs on the wall.

I searched quickly through all the pockets, but they were mostly empty. There was only, in one inner pocket, a receipt for a watch repair which I replaced where I found it.

There were no drawers: more or less everything else had to be in his suitcase which stood against the wall. With an eye on the corridor outside, I tried one of the latches and wasn't surprised to find it locked.

That left only a tiny cupboard above the hanging space, in which Julius Apollo had stored a black leather toilet bag and his brushes.

On the floor below his suits, pushed to the back of the hanging space, I found his briefcase.

I put my head out of the door which was directly beside the hanging space, and looked up and down the corridor.

No one in sight.

I went down on hands and knees, half in and half out of the doorway, with an excuse ready of looking for a coin I'd dropped. I put a hand into the hanging space and drew the briefcase to the front; and it was of black crocodile skin with gold clasps, as I'd seen at Nottingham races.

The fact of its presence was all I was going to learn, however, as it had revolving combination locks which were easy enough to undo, but only if one had two hours to spend on each lock, which I hadn't. Whether or not the briefcase still contained whatever Horfitz had given Filmer at Nottingham was anyone's guess, and dearly though I would have liked to look at the contents, I didn't want to risk any more at that point.

I pushed the black case deep into the hanging space again, stood up outside the door, closed it and went back to the scenes of jollity to the rear.

It was, by this time, nearly midnight. The Youngs were standing up in the dining room, ready to go to bed. Xanthe, however, alarmed by the departure of her new-found friend, was practically clinging to Mrs Young and with an echo of the earlier hysteria was saying that she couldn't possibly sleep in the private car, she would have nightmares, she would be too scared to stay, she was sure whoever had uncoupled the car before would do it again in the middle of the night, and they would all be killed when the Canadian crashed into them, because the Canadian was still there behind us, wasn't it, wasn't it?

Yes, it was.

Mrs Young did her best to soothe her, but it was impossible not to respect her fears. She had undoubtedly nearly been killed. Mrs Young told her that the madman who had mischievously unhitched the car was hours behind us in Cartier, but Xanthe was beyond reassurance.

Mrs Young appealed to Nell, asking if there was anywhere else that Xanthe could sleep, and Nell, consulting the ever-present clipboard, shook her head doubtfully.

'There's an upper berth in a section,' she said slowly, 'but it only has a curtain, and no facilities except at the end of the car, and it's hardly what Xanthe's used to.'

'I don't care,' Xanthe said passionately. 'I'll sleep on the floor or on the seats in the lounge, or *anywhere*. I'll sleep in that upper berth ... please let me.'

'I don't see why not, then,' Nell said. 'What about night things?'

'I'm not going into our car to fetch them. I'm *not*.'

'All right,' Nell said. 'I'll go and ask your mother.'

Mrs Young stayed with Xanthe, who was again faintly trembling, until at length Nell returned with both a small grip and Bambi.

Bambi tried to get her daughter to change her mind, but predictably without success. I thought it unlikely that Xanthe would ever sleep in that car again, so strong was her present reaction. She, Bambi, Nell and the Youngs made their way past me without looking at me and continued on along the corridor beside the kitchen, going to inspect the revised quarters which I knew were in the sleeping car forward of Filmer's.

After a while Bambi and Nell returned alone, and Bambi with an unexcited word of gratitude to Nell walked a few paces forward and stopped beside her son, who had done nothing to comfort or help his sister and was now sitting alone.

'Come along, Sheridan,' she said, her tone without peremptoriness but also without affection. 'Your father asks you to come.'

Sheridan gave her a look of hatred which seemed not in the least to bother her. She stood patiently waiting until, with exceedingly bad grace, he got to his feet and followed her homewards.

Bambi, it seemed to me, had taught herself not to care for Sheridan so as not to be hurt by him. She too, like Mercer, must have suffered for years from his boorish behaviour in public, and she had distanced herself from it. She didn't try to buy the toleration of the victims of his rudeness, as Mercer did: she ignored the rudeness instead.

I wondered which had come first, the chill and disenchantment of her worldly sophistication, or the lack of warmth in her son: and perhaps there was ice in both of them, and the one had reinforced the other. Bambi, I thought, was a highly inappropriate name for her; she was no innocent wide-eyed smooth-skinned fawn but an experienced, aloof, good-looking woman in the skin of minks.

Nell, watching them go, sighed and said, 'She didn't kiss Xanthe goodnight, you know, or give her even a hug to comfort her. Nothing. And Mercer's so nice.'

'Forget them.'

'Yes. . . . You do realize the press will be down on this train like a pack of hunting lions at the next stop?'

'Lionesses,' I said.

'What?'

'It's the females who hunt in a pack. One male sits by, watching, and takes the lion's share of the kill.'

'I don't want to know that.'

'Our next stop,' I said, 'will be fifteen minutes at

184

White River in the middle of the night. After the delay, we'll aim to arrive at four-oh-five, depart four-twenty.'

'And after that?'

'Except for a three-minute pause in a back-of-beyond, we stop at Thunder Bay for twenty-five minutes at ten-fifty tomorrow morning.'

'Do you know the whole timetable by heart?'

'Emil told me to learn it. He was right when he said the question I would have to answer most was "When do we reach so and so?" . . . and if I were a regular waiter he said I would know the answers, even though we're thirty-five minutes earlier everywhere than the regular Canadian.'

'Emil is cute,' she said.

I looked at her in surprise. I wouldn't have thought of Emil as cute. Small, neat, bright and generous, yes. 'Cute?' I asked.

'I would hope,' she said, 'that you don't think so.'

'No.'

'Good.' She was relieved, I saw.

'Weren't you sure?' I asked curiously. 'Am I so . . . ambivalent?'

'Well . . .' There was a touch of embarrassment. 'I didn't mean to get into this sort of conversation, really I didn't. But if you want to know, there's something about you that's secret . . . ultra private . . . as if you didn't want to be known too well. So I just wondered. I'm sorry . . .'

'I shall shower you with ravening kisses.'

She laughed. 'Not your style.'

'Wait and see.' And two people didn't, I thought, drift into talking like that after knowing each other for such a short while unless there was immediate trust and liking.

We were standing in the tiny lobby between the kitchen and the dining room, and she still had the clipboard clasped to her chest. She would have to put it down, I thought fleetingly, before any serious ravening could take place.

'You always have jokes in your eyes,' she said. 'And you never tell them.'

'I was thinking about how you use your clipboard as chain-mail.'

Her own eyes widened. 'A lousy man in the magazine office squeezed my breast ... Why am I telling you? It was years ago. Why should I care? Anyway, where else would you carry a clipboard?'

She put it down, all the same, on the counter, but we didn't talk much longer as the revellers from the rear began coming through to go to the bedrooms. I retreated into the kitchen and I could hear people asking Nell what time they could have breakfast.

'Between seven and nine-thirty,' she said. 'Sleep well, everybody.' She put her head into the kitchen. 'Same to you, sleep well. I'm off to bed.'

'Goodnight,' I said, smiling.

'Aren't you going?'

'Yes, in a while.'

'When everything's . . . safe?'

'You might say so.'

'What exactly does the Jockey Club expect you to *do*?'

'See trouble before it comes.'

'But that's practically impossible.'

'Mm,' I said. 'I didn't foresee anyone uncoupling the Lorrimores.'

'You'll be fired for that,' she said drily, 'so if you sleep, sleep well.'

'Tor would kiss you,' I said. 'Tommy can't.'

'I'll count it done.'

She went away blithely, the clipboard again in place: a habit, I supposed, as much as a defence.

I walked back to the bar and wasted time with the barman. The intent poker school looked set for an all-night session, the dancing was still causing laughter in the lounge and the northern lights were entrancing the devotees in the dome. The barman yawned and said he'd be closing the bar soon. Alcohol stopped at midnight.

I heard Daffodil's voice before I saw her, so that when Filmer came past the door of the bar I was bending down with my head below the counter as if to be tidying things there. I had the impression they did no more than glance in as they passed, as Filmer was saying ' . . . when we get to Winnipeg.' 'You mean Vancouver,' Daffodil said. 'Yes, Vancouver.' 'You always get them mixed . . .' Her voice, which had been raised, as his had been, so as to be heard while one of them walked ahead of the other, died away as they passed down the corridor, presumably en route to bed.

Giving them time to say goodnight, as Daffodil's room was one of the three just past the bar, I slowly followed. They were nowhere in sight as I went through to the dining car, and Filmer seemed to have gone straight to his room, as there was a thread of light shining along the bottom of his door; but Daffodil, I discovered, had after all not. Instead of being cosily tucked up in her bunk near the bar, she surprisingly came walking towards me from the sleeping car forward of Filmer's, her diamonds lighting small bright fires with every step.

I stood back to let her pass, but she shimmered to a stop before me and said, 'Do you know where Miss Lorrimore is sleeping?'

'In the car you've just come from, madam,' I answered helpfully.

'Yes, but where? I told her parents that I would make sure she was all right.'

'The sleeping-car attendant will know,' I said. 'If you would like to follow me?'

She nodded assent and as I turned to lead the way I thought that at close quarters she was probably younger than I'd assumed, or else that she was older but immature: an odd impression, fleeting and gone.

The middle-aged sleeping-car attendant was dozing but dressed. He obligingly showed Daffodil the upper berth where Xanthe was sleeping, but the thick felt curtains were closely fastened, and when Daffodil called the girl's name quietly, there was no response. The slightly fatherly attendant said he was sure she was safely asleep, as he'd seen her returning from the washroom at the end of the car and climbing up to her bunk.

'I guess that will do,' Daffodil said, shrugging off someone else's problem. 'Goodnight, then, and thank you for your help.'

We watched her sway away holding on to the rails, her high curls shining, her figure neat, her intense musky scent lingering like a memory in the air after she herself had gone. The sleeping-car attendant sighed deeply at so much opulent femininity and philosophically returned to his roomette, and I went on up the train into the next car, where my own bed lay.

George Burley's door, two along from mine, was wide open, and I found he was in residence, dressed but asleep, quietly snoring in his armchair. He jerked awake as if with a sixth sense as I paused in his doorway and said, 'What's wrong, eh?'

'Nothing that I know of,' I said.

'Oh, it's you.'

'I'm sorry I woke you.'

'I wasn't asleep ... well, napping, then. I'm used to that. I've been on the railways all my life, eh?'

'A love affair?' I said.

'You can bet your life.' He rubbed his eyes, yawning.

'In the old days there were many big railway families. Father to son . . . cousins, uncles . . . it got handed down. My father, my grandfather, they were railwaymen. But my sons, eh? They're behind desks in big cities tapping at computers.' He chuckled. 'They run the railways too now from behind desks, eh? They sit in Montreal making decisions and they've never heard a train's call at night across the prairie. They've missed all that. These days the top brass fly everywhere, eh?' His eyes twinkled. Anyone who wasn't a wheels-on railwayman was demonstrably stupid. 'I'll tell you,' he said, 'I hope to die on the railways.'

'Not too soon, though.'

'Not before White River, at any rate.'

I said goodnight and went to my own room where I found the sleeping-car attendant had duly lowered my bed and laid a chocolate truffle on the pillow.

I ate the chocolate. Very good.

I took off the yellow waistcoat with its white lining and hung it on a hanger, and I took off my shoes, but rather like George I still felt myself to be on duty, so I switched off the light and lay on top of the bedclothes watching the black Canadian land slide by, while the free northern show went on above for hours in the sky. There seemed to be wide horizontal bands of light which slowly changed in intensity, with brighter spots growing and fading in places mysteriously against the deeps of eternity. It was peaceful more than frenetic, a mirage of slow dawns and sunsets going back to the

Fluted Point people: humbling. In the context of ten thousand years, I thought, what did Filmer and his sins matter? Yet all we had was here and now, and here and now ... always through time ... was where the struggle towards goodness had to be fought. Towards virtue, morality, uprightness, order: call it what one liked. A long, ever-recurring battle.

In the here and now we stopped without incident at White River. I saw George outside under the station lights and watched him set off towards the rear of the train. Apparently the Lorrimores were still safely with us as he came back presently without haste or alarm, and after a while the train made its usual unobtrusive departure westwards.

I slept for a couple of hours and was awakened while it was still dark by a gentle rapping on my door: it proved to be Emil, fully dressed and apologetic.

'I didn't know if I should wake you. If you are serious about this, it is time to set the tables for breakfast.'

'I'm serious,' I said.

He smiled with seeming satisfaction. 'It is much easier with four of us.'

I said I would come at once and made it, washed, shaved and tidy, in roughly ten minutes. Oliver and Cathy were already there, wide awake. The kitchen was filled with glorious smells of baking and Angus, with languid largesse, said he wouldn't notice if we ate a slice or two of his raisin bread, or of his apple and walnut. Simone said dourly that we were not to eat the croissants as there wouldn't be enough. It was all rather like school.

We set the plates, put fresh water and carnations in bud vases, one flower to each table, and folded pink napkins with precision. By seven-fifteen, the first break-fasters were addressing themselves to eggs Benedict and I was pouring tea and coffee as to the service born.

At seven-thirty, in struggling daylight, we stopped briefly in a place identified in suitably small letters on the small station as Schreiber.

It was from here, I reflected, looking through the windows at a small scattered town, that the despatcher had spoken to George and me the previous evening: and while I watched, George appeared outside and was met by a man who came from the station. They conferred for a while, then George returned to the train, and the train went quietly on its way.

A spectacular way: all through breakfast, the track ran along the north shore of Lake Superior, so close that at times the train seemed to be overhanging the water. The passengers oohed and aahed, the Unwins (Upper Gumtree) sitting with the owners of Flokati, the Redi-Hots with a couple talking incessantly of the prowess of their horse, Wordmaster, also on the train.

Filmer came alone to sit at an untenanted table, ordering eggs and coffee from Oliver without looking at him. Presently the Youngs appeared and with smiling acquaintanceship joined Filmer. I wondered if he thought immediately of Ezra Gideon, the Youngs' dear friend, but his face showed nothing but politeness.

Xanthe ambled in in a tousled yawning state and yesterday's clothes and flopped into the empty chair beside Filmer. Interestingly he made no attempt to save the seat for Daffodil, but seemed to echo Mrs Young's enquiries about how Xanthe had slept.

Like a log, it appeared, although she seemed to regret not reporting constant nightmares. Mr Young looked bored, as if he had tired of the subject a long time ago, but his wife retained her sweet comforting expression without any visible effort.

I waited with hovering impatience for Nell to arrive, which she did at length in a straight black skirt (worse and worse) with a prim coffee blouse and unobtrusive gold earrings. She had drawn her fair hair high into an elaborate plait down the back of her head and fastened it at the bottom with a wide tortoiseshell clasp: it looked distinguished and competent, but nowhere near cuddly.

People I hadn't yet identified beckoned her eagerly to join them, which she did with the ravishing smile she had loosed once or twice in my direction. She told Cathy she would pass on the eggs but would like croissants and coffee, and presently I was bringing them to her as she sat with eyes demurely downwards, studiously ignoring my existence. I set butter, jam and breads before her. I poured into her cup. She told her table companions it was nice having hand-picked attendants all the way to Vancouver.

I knew it was a game but I could cheerfully have strangled her. I didn't want them noticing me even a little. I went away and looked back, and met her eyes, which were laughing. It was the sort of look between us which would have started alert interest in me if I'd spotted it between others, and I thought I was near to losing my grip on what I was supposed to be doing, and that I'd better be more careful. I hadn't needed to serve her: I'd taken the tray from Cathy. Temptation will be your downfall, Tor, I thought.

Except for Xanthe, Mercer was the only Lorrimore to surface for breakfast, and he came not to eat but to ask Emil to send trays through to his own private dining room. Emil himself and Oliver delivered the necessary, although Emil on his return said he hoped this wasn't going to happen at lunch and dinner also, because it took too much time. Room service was strictly not available, yet one didn't disoblige the Lorrimores if one could help it.

Daffodil arrived after everyone else with each bright curl in place and pleasantly sat across the aisle from the Filmer/Young table, asking for news of Xanthe's night. The only people not bothering to ask, it seemed, were the near-victim's own family. Xanthe chattered and could be heard telling Daffodil she felt snug and safe behind her curtain. The next time I went slowly past their table, refill coffee pot at the ready, the conversation was back to the journey, with Xanthe this time saying she basically thought horse racing boring and she wouldn't have come on this trip if her father hadn't made her.

'How did he make you?' Filmer said interestedly.

'Oh!' She sounded suddenly flustered and evaded an answer. 'He made Sheridan come, too.'

'But why, if you both didn't want to?' That was Daffodil's voice, behind my back.

'He likes us where he can see us, he says.' There was a note of grudge and bitterness but also, it seemed to me, a realistic acknowledgement that father knew best: and judging from Sheridan's behaviour to date, under his father's long-suffering eye was certainly the son's safest place.

The conversation faded into the distance and I paused to refill the Unwins' cups, where the talk was about Upper Gumtree having the edge over Mercer's Premiere that was coming to Winnipeg by road.

George Burley presently came into the dining car and spoke for a while to Nell, who subsequently went from table to table, clipboard in place, repeating what he'd said.

'We're stopping at Thunder Bay for longer than scheduled, as there'll be an investigation there about the Lorrimores' car being uncoupled. We'll be there about an hour and a half, as we're not going on until after the regular Canadian has gone through. The Canadian will be ahead of us then all the way to Winnipeg.'

'What about lunch?' Mr Young asked. Mr Young, though thinnish, had a habit of eating half his wife's food as well as his own.

'We'll leave Thunder Bay at about a quarter to one,' Nell said, 'so we'll have lunch soon after. And a more leisurely dinner before we get to Winnipeg, instead of having to crowd it in early. It will all fit in quite well.' She was smiling, reassuring, keeping the party from unravelling. 'You'll be glad to stretch your legs for a bit longer in Thunder Bay, and some of you might visit your horses.'

The owner of Redi-Hot, who seemed to spend most of his time reading a guide book, told Mr and Mrs Wordmaster, who looked suitably impressed, that Thunder Bay, one of Canada's largest ports, was at the far west end of the St Lawrence–Great Lakes Seaway and should really be called what the locals called it, The Lakehead. Grain from the prairies was shipped from there to throughout the world, he said.

'Fancy that,' said Mrs Wordmaster, who was English.

I retreated from this scintillating conversation and helped Oliver and Cathy clear up in the kitchen, and shortly before eleven we slid to a halt in the port that was halfway across Canada on some rails parallel with but a little removed from the station buildings.

Immediately a waiting double posse of determined-looking men advanced from the station across two intervening tracks, one lot sprouting press cameras, the other notebooks. George stepped down from the train to meet the notebook people, and the others fanned out and began clicking. One of the notebook crowd climbed aboard and came into the dining car, inviting anyone who had seen anyone or anything suspicious the previous evening to please unbutton, but of course no one had, or no one was saying, because otherwise the whole train would have known about it by now.

The investigator said he would try his luck with the scenery-watchers in the dome car, with apparently the same result, and from there he presumably went in to see the Lorrimores, who apart from Xanthe were still in seclusion. He then reappeared in the dining car with an interested crowd of people following him and asked to speak to Xanthe, who up until then had kept palely quiet.

He identified her easily because everyone looked her way. Filmer was still beside her: the passengers tended all the time to linger at the tables, talking, after the meals had been cleared, rather than return to the solitude of their bedrooms. Nearly everyone, I would have guessed, had been either in the dining room or the dome car all morning.

Mrs Young squeezed Xanthe's hand encouragingly from across the table while the half-child half-young-woman shivered her way through the dangerous memory.

'No,' she said, with everyone quiet and attentively

listening, 'no one suggested I went to our car . . . I just wanted to go to the bathroom. And I could . . . I . . . could have been killed.'

'Yes . . .' The investigator, middle-aged and sharp-eyed, was sympathetic but calming, speaking in a distinct voice that carried easily through the dining car, now that we weren't moving. 'Was there anyone in the dome car lounge when you went through?'

'Lots of people.' Xanthe's voice was much quieter than his.

'Did you know them?'

'No. I mean, they were on this trip. Everyone there was.' She was beginning to speak more loudly, so that all could hear.

A few heads nodded.

'No one you now know was a stranger?'

'No.'

Mrs Young, intelligent besides comforting, asked, 'Do you mean it's possible to uncouple a car while you're actually on the train? You don't have to be on the ground to do it?'

The investigator gave her his attention and everyone leaned forward slightly to hear the answer.

'It's possible. It can be done also while the train is moving, which is why we want to know if there was anyone in the dome car who was unknown to you all. Unknown to any of you, I should say.'

There was a long, respectful, understanding silence.

Nell said, 'I suppose I know most of our passengers by sight by now. I identified them all at Toronto station when I was allocating their sleeping quarters. I didn't see anyone yesterday evening who puzzled me.'

'You don't think,' Mrs Young said, putting her finger unerringly on the implication, 'that the car was unhitched by *someone in our party*?'

'We're investigating all possibilities,' the investigator said without pompousness. He looked around at the ranks of worried faces and his slightly severe expression softened. 'The private car was deliberately uncoupled,' he said, 'but we're of the preliminary opinion that it was an act of mischief committed by someone in Cartier, the last place you stopped before Miss Lorrimore found the car was missing. But we do have to ask if the saboteur could have been on the train, just in case any of you noticed anything wrong.'

A man at the back of the crowd said, 'I was sitting in the dome car lounge when Xanthe came through, and I can tell you that no one had come the other way. I mean, we all knew that only the Lorrimores' car was behind the dome car. If anyone except the Lorrimores had gone that way and come back again . . . well . . . we would have noticed.'

Another nodding of heads. People noticed everything to do with the Lorrimores.

I was watching the scene from the kitchen end of the dining car, standing just behind Emil, Cathy and

199

Oliver. I could see Xanthe's troubled face clearly, and also Filmer's beside her. He seemed to me to be showing diminishing interest in the enquiry, turning his tidily brushed head away to look out of the window instead. There was no tension in him: when he was tense there was a rigidity in his neck muscles, a rigidity I'd watched from the depths of the crowd during the brief day of his trial and seen a few times since, as at Nottingham. When Filmer felt tense, it showed.

Even as I watched him, his neck went rigid.

I looked out of a window to see what he was looking at, but there seemed to be nothing of great note, only the racegoing passengers streaming off their forward carriages en route to write postcards home from the station.

Filmer looked back towards Xanthe and the investigator and made a small gesture of impatience, and it seemed to trigger a response from the investigator because he said that if anyone remembered any helpful detail, however small, would they please tell him or one of his colleagues, but meanwhile everyone was free to go.

There was a communal sigh as the real-life investigation broke up. Zak, I thought, would be finding the competition too stiff, the fiction an anti-climax after the fact. He hadn't appeared for this scene: none of the actors had.

Most of the passengers went off to don coats against what appeared to be a cold wind outside, but Filmer climbed down from the door of the dome-car end of the dining car without more protection than his carefully casual shirt and aristocratic tweed jacket. He paused irresolutely, not scrunching, as the others were beginning to, across the two sets of rails between our train and the station but meandering at an angle forward in the direction of the engine.

Inside, I followed him, easily keeping pace with his slow step. I thought at first that he was merely taking an open-air path to his own bedroom, but he went straight past the open door at the end of his sleeping car, and straight on past the next car also. Going to see his horse, no doubt. I went on following: it had become a habit.

At the end of the third car, just past George Burley's office, he stopped, because someone was coming out from the station to meet him: a gaunt man in a padded short coat with a fur collar, with grey hair blowing in disarray in the wind.

They met between George's window and the open door at the end of the car and although at first they looked moderately at peace with each other, the encounter deteriorated rapidly.

I risked them seeing me so as to try to hear, but in fact by the time I could hear them they were shouting, which meant I could listen through the doorway without seeing them or being seen.

Filmer was yelling furiously, 'I said before Vancouver!'

The gaunt man with a snarl in his Canadian voice said, 'You said before Winnipeg, and I've done it and I want my money.'

'Coo-ee,' trilled Daffodil, teetering towards them in chinchillas and high-heeled boots. 'Are we going to see Laurentide Ice?'

CHAPTER TEN

Blast her, I thought intensely. Triple bloody shit, and several other words to that effect.

I watched through George's window as Filmer made great efforts to go towards her with a smile, drawing attention away from the gaunt-faced man, who returned to the station.

Before Winnipeg, before Vancouver. Julius Apollo had mixed them up yet again. 'You said before Winnipeg, and I've done it and I want my money.' Heavy words, full of threat.

What before Winnipeg? What had he done?

What indeed.

It couldn't have been the Lorrimores' car, I thought. Filmer had shown no interest and no tension; had been obviously uninvolved. But then he would have been calm, I supposed, if he hadn't been expecting anything to happen except before Vancouver. He hadn't been expecting the Lorrimores' car to be uncoupled before either city, of that I was certain. He had instead been cultivating his acquaintanceship with Mercer, a game plan that would have come to an abrupt end if the Lorrimores had deserted the trip, which they would have done at once if the Canadian had ploughed into their home-from-home.

If not the Lorrimores' car, what else had happened? What had happened before Winnipeg that Filmer had intended to happen before Vancouver? In what way had the gaunt man already earned his money?

Anyone's guess, I thought.

He could have robbed someone, bribed a stable lad, nobbled a horse . . .

Nobbled a horse that was going to run at Winnipeg, instead of one running at Vancouver?

From the fury in their voices, the mistake had been devastating.

Only Flokati and Upper Gumtree were due to run at Winnipeg . . . Laurentide Ice was running at Vancouver against Voting Right and Sparrowgrass. . . . Could Filmer have been so stupid as to get the horses' names wrong in addition to the cities? No, he couldn't.

Impasse. Yet . . . gaunt-face had done *something*.

Sighing, I watched the Youngs walk past the window en route, I supposed, to the horse car. Soon after, the Unwins followed. I would have liked to have checked at once on the state of the horses, but I supposed if there were something wrong with any of them I would hear soon enough.

I wished I'd been able to take a photograph of gaunt-face, but I'd been more keen to listen.

If he'd done something to or around the horses, I thought, then he had to have travelled with us on the train. He hadn't just met us in Thunder Bay. If he'd been on the train and had walked with the other race-goers towards the station, Filmer could have seen him through the window ... and just the sight of him had caused the tensing of the neck muscles ... and if Filmer hadn't yet paid him for whatever ... then he would come back to the train ...

I left George's office and went two doors along to my roomette to dig my telescopic-lens binoculars-camera out of Tommy's holdall, and I sat and waited by the window for gaunt-face's return.

What happened instead was that after a while Filmer and Daffodil appeared in my view, making a diagonal course towards the station buildings, and pretty soon afterwards, accompanied by a lot of bell-ringing and warning hooters, a huge bright yellow diesel engine came grinding and groaning past my window followed by long corrugated silver coaches as the whole of the regular Canadian rolled up the track next to the race train and stopped precisely alongside.

Instead of a nice clear photographic view of the station, I now faced the black uninformative window of someone else's roomette.

Frustration and damnation, I thought. I tucked the binoculars into the holdall again and without any sensible plans wandered back towards the dining car. If I went on like this, I would fulfil the gloomiest fears of Bill Baudelaire, the Brigadier and, above all, John Millington. 'I *told* you we should have sent an ex-policeman . . .' I could hear his voice in my ear.

. It occurred to me, when I reached Julius Apollo's door, that the Canadian would be standing where it was for the whole of the twenty-five minutes of its daily scheduled stop. For twenty-five minutes . . . say twenty-two by now . . . Filmer would stay over in the station. He would not walk round either end of the lengthy Canadian to return to his room.

Would he?

No, he would not. Why should he? He had only just gone over there. I had twenty minutes to see what I could do about his combination locks.

If I'd paused for more thought I perhaps wouldn't have had the nerve, but I simply opened his door, checked up and down the corridor for observers (none) and went inside, shutting myself in.

The black briefcase was still on the floor at the back of the hanging space, under the suits. I pulled it out, sat on one of the armchairs, and with a feeling of unreality started on the right-hand lock. If anyone should come in, I thought confusedly . . . if the sleeping-car attendant for instance came in . . . whatever excuse could I possibly find?

None at all.

The right-hand combination wheels were set at one-three-seven. I methodically went on from there,

one-three-eight, one-three-nine, one-four-zero, trying
the latch after each number change.

My heart hammered and I felt breathless. I was used
to long-distance safety in my work, and in the past to
many physical dangers, but never to this sort of risk.

One-four-one, one-four-two, one-four-three.... I
tried the latch over and over and looked at my watch.
Only two minutes had gone. It felt like a lifetime.
One-four-four, one-four-five.... There were a thousand possible combinations ... one-four-six, one-four-
seven ... in twenty minutes I could perhaps try a
hundred and fifty numbers.... I had done this process
before, once, but not under pressure, when Aunt Viv
had set a combination on a new suitcase and then
forgotten it ... one-four-eight, one-four-nine ... my
face sweating, my fingers slipping on the tiny wheels
from haste ... one-five-zero, one-five-one ...

With a snap the latch flew open.

It was incredible. I could hardly believe it. I had
barely started. All I needed now was double the luck.

The left-hand combination numbers stood at seven-
three-eight. I tried the latch. Nothing.

With just a hope that both locks opened to the
same sesame, I turned the wheels to one-five-one and
tried it. Nothing. Not so easy. I tried reversing it to
five-one-five. Nothing. I tried comparable numbers,
one-two-one, two-one-two, one-three-one, three-one-
three, one-four-one, four-one-four ... six ... seven ...
eight ... nine ... three zeros.

Zilch.

My nerve deserted me. I rolled the left-hand wheels back to seven-three-eight and with the latch closed again set the right-hand lock to one-three-seven. I polished the latches a bit with my shirtsleeve, then I put the briefcase back exactly as I'd found it and took my leaf-trembling self along to the dining car, already regretting, before I got there, that I hadn't stayed until the Canadian left, knowing that I'd wasted some of the best and perhaps the only chance I would get of seeing what Filmer had brought with him on the train.

Perhaps if I'd tried one-one-five, or five-five-one . . . or five-one-one, or five-five-five . . .

Nell was sitting alone at a table in the dining car working on her interminable lists (those usually clipped to the clipboard) and I sat down opposite her feeling ashamed of myself.

She glanced up. 'Hello,' she said.

'Hi.'

She considered me. 'You look hot. Been running?'

I'd been indulging in good heart exercise while sitting still. I didn't think I would confess.

'Sort of,' I said. 'How's things?'

She glanced sideways with disgust at the Canadian.

'I was just about to go over to the station when *that* arrived.'

That, as if taking the hint, began quietly to roll, and within twenty seconds, we again had a clear view of the station. Most of the train's passengers, including

Filmer and Daffodil, immediately started across the tracks to reboard. Among them, aiming for the race-goers' carriages, was gaunt-face.

God in heaven, I thought. I forgot about him. I forgot about photographing him. My wits were scattered.

'What's the matter?' Nell said, watching my face.

'I've earned a D minus. A double D minus.'

'You probably expect too much of yourself,' she said dispassionately. 'No one's perfect.'

'There are degrees of imperfection.'

'How big is the catastrophe?'

I thought it over more coolly. Gaunt-face was on the train, and I might have another opportunity. I could undo one of the latches of Filmer's briefcase and, given time, I might do the other. Correction: given nerve, I might do the other.

'OK,' I said, 'let's say C minus, could do better. Still not good.' Millington would have done better.

Zak and Emil arrived together at that point, Emil ready to set the tables for lunch, Zak in theatrical exasperation demanding to know if the actors were to put on the next scene before the meal as originally planned, and if not, when?

Nell looked at her watch and briefly thought. 'Couldn't you postpone it until cocktail time this evening?'

'We're supposed to do the following scene then,' he objected.

'Well . . . couldn't you run them both together?'

He rather grumpily agreed and went away saying they would have to rehearse. Nell smiled sweetly at his departing back and asked if I'd ever noticed how *important* everything was to actors? Everything except the real world, of course.

'Pussycat,' I said.

'But I have such tiny, indulgent claws.'

Oliver and Cathy arrived and with Emil began spreading tablecloths and setting places. I got to my feet and helped them, and Nell with teasing amusement watched me fold pink napkins into water lilies and said, 'Well, well, hidden depths,' and I answered, 'You should see my dishwashing,' which were the sort of infantile surface remarks of something we both guessed might suddenly become serious. The surface meanwhile was safe and shimmering and funny, and would stay that way until we were ready for change.

As usual, the passengers came early into the dining car, and I faded into the scenery in my uniform and avoided Nell's eyes.

The passengers hadn't over-enjoyed their sojourn in the station, it appeared, as they had been fallen upon by the flock of pressmen who had taken Xanthe back again to the brink of hysteria, and had asked Mercer whether it wasn't unwise to flaunt the privilege of wealth in his private car, and hadn't he invited trouble by adding it to the train? Indignation on his behalf was thick in the air. Everyone knew he was public-spiritedly on the trip For the Sake of Canadian Racing.

The Lorrimores, all four of them, arrived together to murmurs of sympathy, but the two young ones split off immediately from their parents and from each other, all of them gravitating to their various havens: the parents went to join Filmer and Daffodil of their own free will, Xanthe made a straight piteous line to Mrs Young, and Sheridan grabbed hold of Nell, who was by this time standing, saying that he needed her to sit with him, she was the only decent human being on the whole damn train.

Nell, unsure of the worth of his compliment, nevertheless sat down opposite him, even if temporarily. Keeping Sheridan on a straight or even a wavy line definitely came into the category of crisis control.

Sheridan had the looks which went with Julius's name, Apollo: he was tall, handsome, nearly blond, a child of the sun. The ice, the arrogance, the lack of common sense and of control, these were the darkside tragedy. A mini psychopath, I thought, and maybe not so mini, at that, if Xanthe thought he should be in jail.

The Australian Unwins, sitting with the rival owners of Flokati, were concerned about a lifelessness they had detected in Upper Gumtree due to the fact that on the train their horse had been fed a restricted diet of compressed food nuts and high-grade hay and the Flokati people were cheerfully saying that on so long a stretch without exercise, good hay was best. Hay was calming. 'We don't want them climbing the walls,' Mr Flokati said. Upper Gumtree had looked asleep, Mrs Unwin remarked with disapproval. The Flokati people beamed wide, trying to look sympathetic. If Upper Gumtree proved listless, so much the better for Flokati's chances.

It seemed that all of the owners had taken the opportunity of visiting the horses while the train was standing still, and listen though I might I could hear no one else reporting trouble.

Upper Gumtree, it seemed to me, might revive spectacularly on the morrow, given oats, fresh air and exercise. His race was still more than forty-eight hours away. If gaunt-face had in fact given Upper Gumtree something tranquillizing, the effects would wear off long before then.

On reflection, I thought it less and less probable that he had done any such thing: he would have to have bypassed the dragon-lady, Leslie Brown, for a start. Yet presumably at times she left her post . . . to eat and sleep.

'I said,' Daffodil said to me distinctly, 'would you bring me a clean knife? I've dropped mine on the floor.'

'Certainly, madam,' I said, coming back abruptly to the matter in hand and, realizing with a shock that she had already asked me once, I fetched her a knife fast. She merely nodded, her attention again on Filmer, and he, I was mightily relieved to see, had taken no notice of the small matter. But how could I, I thought ruefully, how could I have possibly stopped concentrating when I was so close to him? Only one day ago the proximity had had my pulse racing.

The train had made its imperceptible departure and was rolling along again past the uninhabited infinity of rocks and lakes and conifers that seemed to march on to the end of the world. We finished serving lunch and coffee and cleared up, and as soon as I decently could I left the kitchen and set off forward up the train.

George, whom I looked for first, was in his office eating a fat ragged beef sandwich and drinking diet Coke.

'How did it go,' I asked, 'in Thunder Bay?'

He scowled, but half-heartedly. 'They found out nothing I hadn't told them. There was nothing to see. They're thinking now that whoever uncoupled the private car was on it when the train left Cartier.'

'On the private car?' I said in surprise.

'That's right. The steam tube could have been disconnected in the station, eh? Then the train leaves Cartier with the saboteur in the Lorrimores' car. Then less than a mile out of Cartier, eh?, our saboteur pulls up the rod that undoes the coupling. Then the private car rolls to a stop, and he gets off and walks back to Cartier.'

'But why should anyone do that?'

'Grow up, sonny. There are people in this world who cause trouble because it makes them feel important. They're ineffective, eh?, in their lives. So they burn things . . . and smash things . . . paint slogans on walls . . . leave their mark on something, eh? And wreck trains. Put slabs of concrete on the rails. I've seen it done. Power over others, that's what it's about. A grudge against the Lorrimores, most like. Power over them, over their possessions. That's what those investigators think.'

'Hm,' I said. 'If that's the case, the saboteur wouldn't have walked back to Cartier but up to some vantage point from where he could watch the smash.'

George looked startled. 'Well . . . I suppose he might.'

'Arsonists often help to put out the fires they've started.'

'You mean he would have waited around . . . to help with the wreck? Even to help with casualties?'

'Sure,' I said. 'Pure, heady power, to know you'd caused such a scene.'

'I didn't see anyone around,' he said thoughtfully, 'when we went back to the car. I shone the lamp . . . there wasn't anyone moving, eh?, or anything like that.'

'So, what are the investigators going to do?' I asked.

His eyes crinkled and the familiar chuckle escaped. 'Write long reports, eh? Tell us never to take private cars. Blame me for not preventing it, I dare say.'

He didn't seem worried at the idea. His shoulders and his mind were broad.

I left him with appreciation and went forward into the central dining car where all the actors were sitting in front of coffee cups and poring over typed sheets of stage directions, muttering under their breaths and sometimes exclaiming aloud.

Zak raised his eyes vaguely in my direction but it would have been tactless to disrupt the thoughts behind them, so I pressed on forward, traversing the dayniter and the sleeping cars and arriving at the forward dome car. There were a lot of people about everywhere, but no one looked my way twice.

I knocked eventually on the door of the horse-car and, after inspection and formalities that would have done an Iron Curtain country proud, was admitted again by Ms Brown to the holy of holies.

Rescrawling 'Tommy Titmouse' on her list I was interested to see how long it had grown, and I noticed that even Mercer hadn't been let in without signing. I asked the dragon-lady if anyone had come in who wasn't an owner or a groom, and she bridled like a thin turkey and told me that she had conscientiously checked every visitor against her list of bona fide owners, and only they had been admitted.

'But you wouldn't know them all by sight,' I said.

'What do you mean?' she demanded.

'Supposing for instance someone came and said they were Mr Unwin, you would check that his name was on the list and let him in?'

'Yes, of course.'

'And suppose he wasn't Mr Unwin, although he said he was?'

'You're just being difficult,' she said crossly. 'I cannot refuse entry to the owners. They were given the right to visit, but they don't have to produce passports. Nor do their wives or husbands.'

I looked down her visitors' list. Filmer appeared on it twice, Daffodil once. Filmer's signature was large and flamboyant, demanding attention. No one had written Filmer in any other way: it seemed that gaunt-face hadn't gained entry by giving Filmer's name, at least. It didn't mean he hadn't given someone else's.

I gave Leslie Brown her list back and wandered around under her eagle eye looking at the horses. They swayed peacefully to the motion, standing diagonally across the stalls, watching me incuriously, seemingly content. I couldn't perceive that Upper Gumtree looked any more sleepy than any of the others: his eyes were as bright, and he pricked his ears when I came near him.

All of the grooms, except one who was asleep on some hay bales, had chosen not to sit in the car with their charges, and I imagined it was because of Leslie Brown's daunting presence: racing lads on the whole felt a companionable devotion to their horses, and I would have expected more of them to be sitting on the hay bales during the day.

'What happens at night on the train?' I asked Leslie Brown. 'Who guards the horses then?'

'I do,' she said tartly. 'They've given me a roomette or some such, but I take this thing seriously. I slept in here last night, and will do so again after Winnipeg, and after Lake Louise. I don't see why you're so worried about anyone slipping past me.' She frowned at me, not liking my suspicions. 'When I go to the bathroom, I leave one groom in here and lock the horses' car door behind me. I'm never away more than a few minutes. I insist on one of the grooms being in here at all times. I am very well aware of the need for security, and I assure you that the horses are well guarded.'

I regarded her thin obstinate face and knew she believed to her determined soul in what she said.

'As for the barns at Winnipeg and the stabling at Calgary,' she added righteously, 'they are someone else's responsibility. I can't answer for what happens to the horses there.' She was implying, plain enough, that no one else could be trusted to be as thorough as herself.

'Do you ever have any fun, Ms Brown?' I asked.

'What do you mean?' she said, raising surprised eyebrows. 'All this is fun.' She waved a hand in general round the horse car. 'I'm having the time of my life.' And she wasn't being ironic: she truly meant it.

'Well,' I said a little feebly, 'then that's fine.'

She gave two sharp little nods, as if that finished the matter, which no doubt it did, except that I still looked for gaps in her defences. I wandered one more time round the whole place, seeing the sunlight slant in through the barred unopenable windows (which would keep people out as well as horses in), smelling the sweet hay and the faint musty odour of the horses themselves, feeling the swirls of fresh air coming from the rows of small ventilators along the roof, hearing the creaking and rushing noises in the car's fabric and the grind of the electricity-generating wheels under the floor.

In that long, warm, friendly space there were animals worth at present a total of many millions of Canadian dollars: worth more if any of them won at Winnipeg or Vancouver. I stood for a long while looking at Voting Right. If Bill Baudelaire's mother knew her onions, in this undistinguished-looking bay lay the dormant seed of greatness.

Maybe she was right. Vancouver would tell.

I turned away, cast a last assessing glance at Laurentide Ice, who looked coolly back, thanked the enthusiastic dragon for her co-operation (prim acknowledgement) and began a slow walk back through the train, looking for gaunt-face.

I didn't see him. He could have been behind any of the closed doors. He wasn't in the forward dome car, upstairs or down, nor in the open dayniter. I sought out and consulted separately with three of the sleeping-car attendants in the racegoers' sleeping cars who frowned in turn and said that first, the sort of jacket I was describing was worn by thousands, and second, everyone tended to look gaunt outside in the cold air. All the same, I said, if they came across anyone fitting that description in their care, please would they tell George Burley his name and room number.

Sure, they each said, but wasn't this an odd thing for an actor to be asking? Zak, I improvised instantly at the first enquiry, had thought the gaunt man had an interesting face and he wanted to ask if he could use him in a scene. Ah, yes, that made sense. If they found him, they would tell George.

When I got back to George, I told him what I'd asked. He wrinkled his brow. 'I saw a man like that at Thunder Bay,' he said. 'But I probably saw several men like that in all this trainload. What do you want him for?'

I explained that I'd told the sleeping-car attendants that Zak wanted to use him in a scene.

'But you?' George said. 'What do you want him for yourself?'

I looked at him and he looked back. I was wondering how far I should trust him and had an uncomfortable impression that he knew what I was thinking.

'Well,' I said finally, 'he was talking to someone I'm interested in.'

I got a long bright beam from the shiny eyes.

'Interested in . . . in the line of duty?'

'Yes.'

He didn't ask who it was and I didn't tell him. I asked him instead if he himself had talked to any of the owners' party.

'Of course I have,' he said. 'I always greet passengers

eh?, when they board. I tell them I'm the Conductor, tell them where my office is, tell them if they've any problems to bring them to me.'

'And do they? Have they?'

He chuckled. 'Most of the complaints go to your Miss Richmond, and she brings them to me.'

'Miss Richmond . . .' I repeated.

'She's your boss, isn't she? Tall pretty girl with her hair in a plait today, eh?'

'Nell,' I said.

'That's right. Isn't she your boss?'

'Colleague.'

'Right, then. The sort of problems the owners' party have had on this trip so far are a tap that won't stop dripping, a blind that won't stay down in one of the bedrooms, eh?, and a lady who thought one of her suitcases had been stolen, only it turned up in someone else's room.' He beamed. 'Most of the owners have been along to see the horses. When they see me, they stop to talk.'

'What do they say?' I asked. 'What sort of things?'

'Only what you'd expect. The weather, the journey, the scenery. They ask what time we get to Sudbury, eh? Or Thunder Bay, or Winnipeg, or whatever.'

'Has anyone asked anything that was different, or surprised you?'

'Nothing surprises me, sonny.' He glowed with irony and bonhomie. 'What would you expect them to ask?'

I shrugged in frustration. 'What happened before Thunder Bay that shouldn't have?'

'The Lorrimores' car, eh?'

'Apart from that.'

'You think something happened?'

'Something happened, and I don't know what, and it's what I'm here to prevent.'

He thought about it, then said, 'When it turns up, you'll know, eh?'

'Maybe.'

'Like if someone put something in the food, eh?, sooner or later everyone will be ill.'

'George!' I was dumbstruck.

He chuckled. 'We had a waiter once years ago who did that. He had a grudge against the world. He put handfuls of ground-up laxative pills into the chocolate topping over ice cream and watched the passengers eat it, and they all had diarrhoea. Dreadful stomach pains. One woman had to go to hospital. She'd had two helpings. What a to-do, eh?'

'You've frightened me stiff,' I said frankly. 'Where do they keep the fodder for the horses?'

He stared, his perpetual smile fading.

'Is that what you're afraid of? Something happening to the horses?'

'It's a possibility.'

'All the fodder is in the horse car,' he said, 'except for some extra sacks of those cubes most of the horses are having, which are in the baggage car. Some of the horses have their own special food brought along with them, sent by their trainers. One of the grooms had a whole set of separate bags labelled "Sunday evening", "Monday morning" and so on. He was showing them to me.'

'Which horse was that for?'

'Um . . . the one that belongs to that Mrs Daffodil Quentin, I think. The groom said one of her horses died of colic or some such recently, from eating the wrong things, and the trainer didn't want any more accidents, so he'd made up the feeds himself.'

'You're brilliant, George.'

His ready laugh came back.

'Don't forget the water tank, eh? You can lift the lid . . . where the plank floats, remember? You could dope all those horses at once with one quick cupful of mischief, couldn't you?'

CHAPTER ELEVEN

Leslie Brown told us adamantly that no one could possibly have tampered with either the fodder or the water.

'When did the grooms last fill the buckets?' I asked.

During the morning, she said. Each groom filled the bucket for his own horse, when he wanted to. All of them had been in there, seeing to their charges.

The horses' drinking-water tank had been topped up, she said, by a hosepipe from the city's water supply during the first twenty minutes of our stop in Thunder Bay, in a procedure that she herself had supervised.

George nodded and said the whole train had been re-watered at that point.

'Before Thunder Bay,' I said, 'could anyone have put anything in the water?'

'Certainly not. I've told you over and over again, I am here all the time.'

'And how would you rate all the grooms for trust-worthiness?' I said.

She opened her mouth and closed it again and gave me a hard look.

'I am here to supervise them,' she said. 'I didn't know any of them before yesterday. I don't know if any of them could be bribed to poison the water. Is that what you want?'

'It's realistic,' I said with a smile.

She was unsoftened, unsoftenable.

'My chair, as you see,' she said carefully, 'is next to the water tank. I sit there and watch. I do not think . . . I repeat, I do not believe, that anyone has tampered with the water.'

'Mm,' I said calmingly. 'But you could ask the grooms, couldn't you, if they've seen anything wrong?'

She began to shake her head automatically, but then stopped and shrugged. 'I'll ask them, but they won't have.'

'And just in case,' I said, 'in case the worst happens and the horses prove to have been interfered with, I think I'll take a sample of what's in the tank and also what's in their buckets at this moment. You wouldn't object to that, Ms Brown, would you?'

She grudgingly said she wouldn't. George elected himself to go and see what could be done in the way of sample jars and presently returned with gifts from the Chinese cook in the dome car, in the shape of four rinsed-out plastic tomato-sauce bottles rescued from the rubbish bin.

George and Leslie Brown took a sample from the

tank, draining it, at the dragon's good suggestion, from the tap lower down, where the buckets were filled. I visited Voting Right, Laurentide Ice and Upper Gumtree, who all graciously allowed me to dip into their drink. With Leslie Brown's pen, we wrote the provenance of each sample on the sauce label and put all four containers into a plastic carrier bag which Leslie Brown happened to have handy.

Carrying the booty, I thanked her for her kindness in answering our questions, and helping, and George and I retreated.

'What do you think?' he said, as we started back through the train.

'I think she now isn't as sure as she says she is.'

He chuckled. 'She'll be doubly careful from now on.'

'As long as it's not already too late.'

He looked as if it were a huge joke. 'We could get the tank emptied, scrubbed and refilled at Winnipeg,' he said.

'Too late. If there's anything in it, it was there before Thunder Bay, and the horses will have drunk some of it. Some horses drink a lot of water . . . but they're a bit fussy. They won't touch it if they don't like the smell. If there're traces of soap in it, for instance, or oil. They'd only drink doped water if it smelled all right to them.'

'You know a lot about it,' George commented.

'I've spent most of my life near horses, one way and another.'

We reached his office where he said he had some paperwork to complete before we stopped fairly soon for ten minutes at Kenora. We would be there at five-twenty, he said. We were running thirty minutes behind the Canadian. There were places the race train didn't really need to stop, he said, except to keep pace with the Canadian. We needed always to stop where the trains were serviced for water, trash and fuel.

I had nowhere on our journey to and from the horse car seen the man with the gaunt face. George had pointed someone out to me in the dayniter, but he was not the right person: grey-haired, but too ill-looking, too old. The man I was looking for, I thought, was fifty-something, maybe less, still powerful; not in decline.

In a vague way, I thought, he had reminded me of Derry Welfram. Less bulky than the dead frightener, and not as smooth, but the same stamp of man. The sort Filmer seemed to seek out naturally.

I sat for an hour in my roomette looking out at the unvarying scenery and trying to imagine anything else that Filmer might have paid to have done. It was all the wrong way round, I thought: it was more usual to know the crime and seek the criminal, than to know the criminal and seek his crime.

The four sample bottles of water stood in their plastic carrier on my roomette floor. To have introduced something noxious into that tank, gaunt-face would certainly have to have bribed a groom. He wasn't one of the grooms himself, though perhaps he had been one, somewhere, sometime. The grooms on the train were all younger, thinner and from what I'd seen of them in their uniform T-shirts less positive. I couldn't imagine any of them having the nerve to stand up to Filmer and demand their money.

I spent the brief stop at the small town of Kenora hanging out of the open doorway past George's office, watching him, on the station side of the train, walk a good way up and down outside while he checked that all looked well. The Lorrimores' car, it appeared, was still firmly tacked on. Up behind the engine, two baggage handlers were loading a small pile of boxes. I hung out of the door on the other side of the train for a while, but no one was moving out there at all.

George climbed back on board and closed the doors, and presently we set off again to our last stop before Winnipeg.

I wished intensely that I had the power to see into Filmer's mind. I ached to foresee what he was planning. I felt blind, and longed for second sight. Failing such superhuman qualities, however, there was only as usual ordinary observation and patience, and they both seemed inadequate and tame.

I went along to the dining car where I found that Zak had already positioned some of the actors at the tables for the cocktail-hour double-length scene. He and Nell were agreeing that after the scene the actors would leave again (all except Giles-the-murderer), even though they didn't like being banished all the time and were complaining about it.

Emil, laying tablecloths, said that wine alone was included in the fare, all other cocktails having to be paid for, and perhaps I'd better just serve the wine; he and Oliver and Cathy would do the rest. Fine by me, I said, distributing ashtrays and bud vases. I could set the wine glasses also, Emil said. Glasses for red wine and for white at each place.

The passengers drifted in from their rooms and the dome car and fell into by now predictable patterns of seating. Even though to my mind Bambi Lorrimore and Daffodil Quentin were as compatible as salt and strawberries, the two women were again positioned opposite each other, bound there by the attraction between their men. When I put the wineglasses on their table, Mercer and Filmer were discussing world-wide breeding in terms of exchange rates.

Daffodil told Bambi there was a darling little jewellery store in Winnipeg.

Xanthe was still clinging to Mrs Young. Mr Young looked exceedingly bored.

Sheridan had struck up an acquaintanceship with the actor-murderer Giles, a slightly bizarre eventuality which might have odd consequences.

The Upper Gumtree Unwins and the Flokati couple seemed locked in common interest: whether the instant friendship would wither after their mutual race would be Wednesday evening's news.

Most of the other passengers I knew only vaguely, by face more than by name. I'd learned their names only to the extent that they owned horses in the horse car or had touched bases with Filmer, which came to only about half. They were all in general pleasant enough, although one of the men sent nearly everything back to the kitchen to be reheated, and one of the women pushed the exceptional food backwards and forwards across her plate with flicking movements of her fork, sternly remarking that plain fare was all anyone needed for godliness. What she was doing among the racing fraternity, I never found out.

Zak's long scene began with impressive fireworks as soon as everyone in the dining car had been served with a drink.

A tall man dressed in the full scarlet traditional uniform of the Royal Canadian Mounted Police strode into the dining car and in a conversation-stopping voice said he had some serious information for us. He had come aboard at Kenora, he said, because the body of a groom from this train called Ricky had been found lying beside the railway lines near Thunder Bay. He had been wearing his Race Train T-shirt, and he had identification in his pocket.

The passengers looked horrified. The Mountie's impressive presence dominated the whole place and he sounded undoubtedly authentic. He understood, he said, that the groom had been attacked earlier, in Toronto, when he foiled the kidnapping of a horse, but he had insisted on making the journey nevertheless, having been bandaged by a Miss Richmond. Was that correct?

Nell demurely said that it was.

Among the actual owners of the horses, disbelief had set in the quickest. Mercer Lorrimore enjoyed the joke. Mounties, when investigating, didn't nowadays go around dressed for parades.

'But we are in Manitoba,' Mercer could be heard saying in a lull, 'they've got that right. We passed the boundary with Ontario a moment ago. The Mounted Police's territory starts right there.'

'You seem to know all about it,' our Mountie said. 'What do you know about this dead groom?'

'Nothing,' Mercer said cheerfully.

I glanced briefly at Filmer. His face was hard, his neck rigid, his eyes narrow; and I thought in a flash of Paul Shacklebury, the lad dead in his ditch. Stable lads in England . . . grooms in Canada: same job. What had Paul Shacklebury known about Filmer . . . ? Same old unanswerable question.

'And why was he killed?' the Mountie asked. 'What did he know?'

I risked a glance, looked away, Filmer's mouth was a tight line. The answer to the question had to be in his tautly-held head at that moment and it was as inaccessible to me as Alpha Centauri.

Zak suggested that Ricky had identified one of the hijackers. Perhaps, he said, the hijackers had come on the train. Perhaps they were among the racegoers, waiting another chance to kidnap their quarry.

Filmer's neck muscles slowly relaxed, and I realized that for a moment he must have suspected that the scene had been specifically aimed at him. Perhaps he spent a lot of his time reacting in that way to the most innocent of remarks.

Mavis and Walter Bricknell demanded that the Mountie should keep their own precious horse safe.

The Mountie brushed them aside. He was taking over the enquiry into the death of Angelica Standish, he said. Two deaths connected to the same train could be no coincidence. What was the connection between Angelica and Ricky?

Zak said that *he* was in charge of the Angelica investigation.

No longer, said the Mountie. We were now in the province of Manitoba, not Ontario. His territory, exclusively.

Zak's intended scene of investigation into Angelica's murder had been upstaged by the reality of the Lorrimores' car and then aborted by the long stop at Thunder Bay. Passing the questioning to the Mountie bridged the void neatly, and the Mountie told us that the reason that Steve, Angelica's business manager, also her lover, had not turned up at Toronto station was because he too was dead, struck down in his apartment by blows to the head with a mallet.

The audience received the news of still more carnage

with round eyes. The said Steve, the Mountie went on, seemed to have been in bed asleep at the time of his murder, and the Ontario police were wanting to interview Angelica Standish as a suspect.

'But she's dead!' Mavis Bricknell said.

After a pause, Donna said she and Angelica had talked for maybe two hours between Toronto and Sudbury, and Donna was sure Angelica couldn't have murdered Steve, she was lost without him.

Maybe, the Mountie said, but if she was as upset as all that, why had she come on the train at all? Couldn't it have been to escape from having to realize that she'd killed her lover?

Giles-the-murderer calmly enquired whether any murder weapon had been found after Angelica had been killed.

Also, Pierre asked, wouldn't Angelica's murderer have been covered with blood? The whole toilet compartment had been splashed.

Zak and the Mountie exchanged glances. The Mountie said grudgingly that a blood-covered rolled-up sheet of plastic had been found on the track near the area where Angelica must have been battered, and it could have been used as a poncho, and it was being investigated for blood type and fingerprints.

Donna said couldn't Steve and Angelica both have been killed by a mallet? That would make her innocent, wouldn't it? She couldn't believe that anyone as nice as Angelica could have been mixed up in an insurance swindle.

What? What insurance swindle?

I glanced involuntarily at Daffodil, but if there had been a flicker of her eyelids, I had missed it.

Donna in confusion said she didn't know what insurance swindle. Angelica had just mentioned that Steve was mixed up in an insurance swindle, and she was afraid that was why he had missed the train. Donna hadn't liked to probe any further.

Sheridan Lorrimore, saying loudly that Angelica had been a bitch, made a lunging grab at the pistol sitting prominently in a holster on the Mountie's hip. The Mountie, feeling the tug, turned fast and put his hand down on Sheridan's wrist. It was a movement in a way as dextrous as John Millington on a good day, speaking of razor-sharp reactions, more like an athlete than an actor.

'That gun's mine, sir,' he said, lifting Sheridan's wrist six inches sideways and releasing it. 'And, everybody, it's not loaded.'

There was a general laugh. Sheridan, universally unpopular and having made a boorish fool of himself yet again, looked predictably furious. His mother, I noticed, had turned her head away. Mercer was shaking his.

The Mountie, unperturbed, said he would be proceeding vigorously with the enquiries into both Angelica's and Ricky's deaths and perhaps he would have news for everyone in Winnipeg. He and Zak went away together, and Donna drifted around from table to table for a while telling everyone that poor Angelica had really been very sweet, not a murderess, and she, Donna, was dreadfully upset at the suggestion. She wrung out a real tear or two. She was undoubtedly an effective actress.

'What do you care?' Sheridan asked her rudely. 'You only met her yesterday morning and she was dead before dinner.'

Donna looked at him uncertainly. He'd sounded as if he really believed in Angelica's death.

'Er . . .' she said, 'some people you know at once.' She moved on gently and presently disappeared with disconsolate-looking shoulders down the corridor beside the kitchen. Sheridan muttered under his breath several times, making the people he was sitting with uncomfortable.

Emil and his crew, including me, immediately began setting the tables round the passengers for dinner, and were soon serving warm goat's cheese and radicchio salads followed by circles of rare Chateaubriand with snow peas and matchstick carrots and finally rich orange sorbets smothered in fluffy whipped cream and nuts. Most of the passengers persevered to the end and looked as though it were no torture.

My suggestion to Angus, while we were dishwashing after the battle, that maybe his food could have been injected somehow with a substance that even now could be working away to the detriment of everyone's health was received by him with frosty amusement. Absolutely impossible, he assured me. I had surely noticed that nearly all the ingredients had come on to the train *fresh*? He was *cooking* this food, not bringing it in pre-frozen packs.

I assured him truthfully that I had been impressed by his skill and speed, and I thought his results marvellous.

'You actors,' he said more indulgently, 'will think of any impossible thing for a plot.'

Everyone got off the train at Winnipeg, one thousand, four hundred and thirteen miles along the rails from Toronto.

Two large motor horseboxes were waiting for the horses, which were unloaded down and loaded up ramps. The grooms and Leslie Brown led the horses across from train to van and saw them installed and then, carrying holdalls, themselves trooped on to a bus which followed the horseboxes away towards the racetrack.

A row of buses waited outside the station to take the racegoers away to a variety of outlying motels, and a long new coach with darkly tinted windows was set aside for the owners. A few of the owners, like the Lorrimores and Daffodil and Filmer, had arranged their own transport separately in the shape of chauffeur-driven limousines, their chauffeurs coming over to the train to carry their bags.

The crew, after everyone else had left, tidied away into secure lockers every movable piece of equipment and goods, and then joined the actors in the last waiting bus. The Mountie, I was interested to see, was among us, tall and imposing even with his scarlet and brass buttons tucked away in his bag.

George came last, carrying an attaché case of papers and looking over his shoulder at the train as if wondering if he'd forgotten anything. He sat in the seat across the aisle from me and said the cars would be backed into a siding for two days, the engine would be removed and used elsewhere, and there would be a security guard on duty. In the siding, the carriages would be unheated and unlit and would come to life again only about an hour before we left on the day after tomorrow. We'd been able to keep the same crew from coast to coast, he said, only because of the two rest breaks along the way.

The owners and some of the actors were staying in the Westin Hotel which had, Nell had told everyone during dinner, a ballroom and an indoor pool on the roof. There was a breakfast room set aside for the train party where a piece of the mystery would unravel each morning. Apart from that, everyone was on their own: there were good shops, good restaurants and good racing. Transport had been arranged to and from the racecourse. We would all come back to reboard the train after the Jockey Club Race Train Stakes on Wednesday, and cocktails and dinner would be served as soon as we'd rolled out of the station. The party, in good humour, applauded.

I had decided not to stay in the same hotel as any of the groups of owners, actors, racegoers or crew, and asked Nell if she knew of anywhere else. A tall order, it seemed.

'We've put people almost everywhere,' she said doubtfully, 'but only a few actors will be at the Holiday Inn . . . why don't you try there? Although actually . . . there *is* one place we haven't booked anyone into, and that's the Sheraton. But it's like the Westin – expensive.'

'Never mind, I'll find somewhere,' I said, and when the crew bus, after a short drive, stopped and disgorged its passengers, I took my grip and vanished on foot and, after asking directions, made a homing line to where no one else was staying.

In my buttoned-up grey VIA raincoat, I was unexceptional to the receptionists of the Sheraton: the only problem, they said, was that they were full. It was late in the evening. The whole city was full.

'An annexe?' I suggested.

Two of them shook their heads and consulted with each other in low voices. Although they had no single rooms left, they said finally, they had had a late cancellation of a suite. They looked doubtful. I wouldn't be interested in that, they supposed.

'Yes, I would,' I said and gave them my American

Express card with alacrity. So Tommy the waiter carefully hung up his yellow waistcoat with its white lining and ordered some wine from room service and in a while after a long easing shower slept for eight solid hours and didn't dream about Filmer.

In the morning, I telephoned Mrs Baudelaire and listened again to the almost girlish voice on the wire.

'Messages for the invisible man,' she said cheerfully. 'Er . . . are you still invisible?'

'Mostly, yes, I think.'

'Bill says Val Catto would like to know if you are still invisible to the quarry. Does that make sense to you?'

'It makes sense, and the answer is yes.'

'They're both anxious.'

'And not alone,' I said. 'Will you tell them the quarry has an ally on the train, travelling I think with the racegoers. I've seen him once and will try to photograph him.'

'Goodness!'

'Also will you ask them whether certain numbers, which I'll tell you, have any significance in the quarry's life.'

'Intriguing,' she said. 'Fire away.'

'Well . . . three numbers I don't know. Three question marks, say. Then one-five-one.'

'Three question marks, then one-five-one. Right?'

238

'Right. I know it's not his car's number plate, or not the car he usually travels in, but ask if it fits his birthday in any way, or his phone number, or anything at all they can think of. I want to know what the first three digits are.'

'I'll ask Bill right away, when I've finished talking to you. He gave me some answers to give you about your questions yesterday evening.'

'Great.'

'The answers are that Mr and Mrs Young who own Sparrowgrass are frequent and welcome visitors to England and are entertained by the Jockey Club at many race meetings. They were friends of Ezra Gideon. Val Catto doesn't know if they know that Ezra Gideon sold two horses to Mr J. A. Filmer. Does that make sense?'

'Yes,' I said.

'I'm glad you understand what I'm talking about. How about this one, then?' She paused for breath. 'Sheridan Lorrimore was sent down – expelled – from Cambridge University last May, amid some sort of hushed-up scandal. Mercer Lorrimore was over in England at that time, and stayed and went racing at Newmarket in July, but the Jockey Club found him grimmer than his usual self and understood it was something to do with his son, although he didn't say what. Val Catto is seeing what he can find out from Cambridge.'

'That's fine,' I said.

DICK FRANCIS

'Sheridan Lorrimore!' she said, sounding shocked. 'I hope it's not true.'

'Brace yourself,' I said drily.

'Oh dear.'

'How well do you know him?' I asked.

'Hardly at all. But it does no good, does it, for one of our golden families to hit the tabloids.'

I loved the expression, and remembered she'd owned a magazine.

'It demeans the whole country,' she went on. 'I just hope whatever it was will stay hushed up.'

'Whatever it was?'

'Yes,' she said firmly. 'For his family's sake. For his mother's sake. I know Bambi Lorrimore. She's a proud woman. She doesn't deserve to be disgraced by her son.'

I wasn't so sure about that: didn't know to what extent she was responsible for his behaviour. But perhaps not much. Perhaps no one deserved a son like Sheridan. Perhaps people like Sheridan were born that way, as if without arms.

'Are you still there?' Mrs Baudelaire asked.

'I sure am.'

'Bill says the Lorrimores' private car got detached from the train on Sunday evening. Is that really true? There's a great fuss going on, isn't there? It's been on the television news and it's all over the papers this morning. Bill says it was apparently done by some lunatic for reasons unknown, but he wants to know if you have any information about it that he doesn't have.'

I told her what had happened: how Xanthe had casually nearly walked off into space.

'Tell Bill the quarry sat relaxed and unconcerned throughout both the incident and the enquiry held at Thunder Bay yesterday morning, and I'm certain he didn't plan the uncoupling. I think he did plan *something* though, with his ally on the train, and I think Bill should see that they guard the train's horses very carefully out at the track.'

'I'll tell him.'

'Tell him there's a slight possibility that the horses' drinking water was tampered with on the train, before it got to Thunder Bay. But I think that if it had been, the horses should have been showing distress by last night, which they weren't. I can't check them this morning. I suppose if there's anything wrong with them, Bill will know pretty soon. Anyway, I took four samples of the drinking water which I will take to the races this evening.'

'Good heavens.'

'Tell Bill I'll get them to him somehow. They'll be in a package with his name on it.'

'Let me write some of this down. Don't go away.'

There was a quiet period while she put down the receiver and wrote her notes. Then she came back on the line and faithfully repeated everything I'd told her, and everything I'd asked.

'Is that right?' she demanded, at the end.

'Perfect,' I said fervently. 'When in general is it a good time for me to phone you? I don't like to disturb you at bad moments.'

'Phone any time. I'll be here. Have a good day. Stay invisible.'

I laughed, and she'd gone off the line before I could ask her about her health.

A complimentary copy of a Winnipeg newspaper had been slipped under my sitting-room door. I picked it up and checked on what news it gave of the train. The story wasn't exactly all over the front page, but it started there with photographs of Mercer and Bambi and continued inside, with a glamorous backlit formal shot of Xanthe, which made her look a lot older than her published age, fifteen.

I suspected ironically that the extra publicity given to the Great Transcontinental Mystery Race Train hadn't hurt the enterprise in the least. Blame hadn't been fastened on anyone except some unknown nutter back in the wilds of Ontario. Winnipeg was full of racegoing visitors who were contributing handsomely to the local economy. Winnipeg was pleased to welcome them. Don't forget, the paper prominently said, that the first of the two Celebration of Canadian Racing meetings would be held this evening with the regular post time of 7 p.m., while the second meeting, including the running of the Jockey Club Race Train Stakes would be tomorrow afternoon, post time 1.30. The afternoon had been declared a local holiday, as everyone knew, and it would be a fitting finale to the year's thoroughbred racing programme at Assiniboia Downs. (Harness racing, it said in brackets, would hold the first meeting of its winter season the following Sunday.)

I spent most of the day mooching around Winnipeg, seeing a couple of owners once in a shop selling Eskimo sculptures, but never coming face to face with anyone who might know me. I didn't waste much time trying to see what Filmer did or where he went, because I'd quickly discovered that the Westin Hotel was sitting over an entrance to a subterranean shopping mall that stretched like a rabbit warren in all directions. Shopping, in Canada, had largely gone underground to defeat the climate. Filmer could go in and out of the Westin without a sniff of fresh air, and probably had.

There were racetrack express buses, I found, going from the city to the Downs, so I went on one at about six o'clock and strolled around at ground level looking for some way of conveying to Bill Baudelaire the water samples which were now individually wrapped inside the nondescript plastic carrier.

It was made easy for me. A girl of about Xanthe's age bounced up to my side as I walked slowly along in front of the grandstand, and said, 'Hi! I'm Nancy. If that's for Clarrie Baudelaire, I'll take it up if you like.'

'Where is she?' I asked.

'Dining with her dad up there by a window in the

243

Clubhouse.' She pointed to a part of the grandstand. 'He said you were bringing her some thirst quenchers, and he asked me to run down and collect them. Is that right?'

'Spot on,' I said appreciatively.

She was pretty, with freckles, wearing a bright blue tracksuit with a white and gold studded belt. I gave her the carrier and watched her jaunty back view disappear with it into the crowds, and I was more and more sure that what she was carrying was harmless. Bill Baudelaire wouldn't be calmly eating dinner with his daughter if there were a multi-horse crisis going on over in the racecourse stables.

The Clubhouse, from where diners could watch the sport, took up one whole floor of the grandstand, glassed in along its whole length to preserve summer indoors. I decided not to go in there on the grounds that Tommy would not, and Tommy off duty in Tommy's off-duty clothes was what I most definitely wanted to be at that moment. I made some Tommy-sized bets and ate very well in the (literally) below-stairs bar, and in general walked around, racecard in hand, binoculars around neck, exactly as usual.

The daylight faded almost imperceptibly into night, electricity taking over the sun's job smoothly. By seven, when the first race was run, it was under floodlighting, the jockeys' colours brilliant against the backdrop of night.

There were a lot of half-familiar faces in the crowds;

the enthusiastic racegoers from the train. The only one of them that I was interested in, though, was either extremely elusive, or not there. All the techniques I knew of finding people were to no avail: the man with his gaunt face, grey hair and fur-collared parka was more invisible than myself.

I did see Nell.

In her plain blue suit she came down from the Clubhouse with two of the owners who seemed to want to be near the horses at ground level. I drifted after the three of them to watch the runners come out for the third race and wasn't far behind them when they walked right down to the rails to see the contest from the closest possible quarters. When it was over, the owners turned towards the stands, talking animatedly about the result, and I contrived to be where Nell would see me, with any luck, making a small waving motion with my racecard.

She noticed the card, noticed me with widening eyes, and in a short while detached herself from the owners and stood and waited. When without haste I reached her side, she gave me a sideways grin.

'Aren't you one of the waiters from the train?' she said.

'I sure am.'

'Did you find somewhere to sleep?'

'Yes, thank you. How's the Westin?'

She was staying with the owners; their shepherd, their smoother-of-the-way, their information booth.

'The hotel's all right – but someone should strangle that rich . . . that arrogant . . . that *insufferable* Sheridan.' Disgust vibrated in her voice as she suddenly let go of some clearly banked-up and held-back emotion. 'He's unbearable. He's spoiling it for others. They all paid a fortune to come on this trip and they're entitled not to be upset.'

'Did something happen?' I asked.

'Yes, at breakfast.' The memory displeased her. 'Zak put on the next scene of the mystery and Sheridan shouted him down *three* times. I went over to Sheridan to ask him to be quiet and he grabbed my wrist and tried to pull me on to his lap, and I overbalanced and fell and hit the table hard where he was sitting, and I caught the cloth somehow and pulled it with me and everything on it landed on the floor. So you can imagine the fuss. I was on my knees, there was orange juice and broken plates and food and coffee everywhere and Sheridan was saying loudly it was my fault for being clumsy.'

'And I can imagine,' I said, seeing resignation more than indignation now in her face, 'that Bambi Lorrimore took no notice, that Mercer hurried to help you up and apologize, and Mrs Young enquired if you were hurt.'

She looked at me in amazement. 'You were there!'

'No. It just figures.'

'Well . . . that's exactly what happened. A waiter came to deal with the mess, and while he was kneeling there Sheridan said loudly that the waiter was sneering at him and he would get him fired.' She paused. 'And I suppose you can tell me again what happened next?'

She was teasing, but I answered, 'I'd guess Mercer assured the waiter he wouldn't be fired and took him aside and gave him twenty dollars.'

Her mouth opened. 'You *were* there.'

I shook my head. 'He gave me twenty dollars when Sheridan shoved me the other evening.'

'But that's awful.'

'Mercer's a nice man caught in an endless dilemma. Bambi's closed her mind to it. Xanthe seeks comfort somewhere else.'

Nell thought it over and delivered her judgement, which was much like my own.

'One day, beastly Sheridan will do something his father can't pay for.'

'He's a very rich man,' I said.

CHAPTER TWELVE

'It's nothing to do with his birthday, nor with his telephone numbers, nor addresses, past or present, nor his bank accounts, nor his national insurance.'

Mrs Baudelaire's light voice in my ear, passing on the bad news on Wednesday morning.

'Val Catto is working on your quarry's credit card numbers now,' she said. 'And he wants to know why he's doing all this research. He says he's looked up your quarry's divorced wife's personal numbers also and he cannot see one-five-one anywhere, with or without three unknown digits in front.'

I sighed audibly, disappointed.

'How important is it?' she asked.

'It's impossible to tell. It could be pointless, it could solve all our problems. Empty box or jackpot, or anywhere in between. Please would you tell the Brigadier that one-five-one is the combination that unlocks the right-hand latch of a black crocodile briefcase. We have three unknowns on the left.'

'Good gracious,' she said.

'Could you say I would appreciate his instructions?'

'I could, young man. Why don't you just steal the briefcase and take your time?'

I laughed. 'I've thought of that, but I'd better not. Or not yet, anyway. If the numbers have any logic, this way is safest.'

'Val would presumably prefer you didn't get arrested.'

Or murdered, perhaps, I thought.

'I would say,' I agreed, 'that getting myself arrested would lose me my job.'

'You'd no longer be invisible?'

'Quite right.'

'And I'm afraid,' she said, 'that I have some more negative news for you.'

'What is it?' I asked.

'Bill says the samples of water you sent him were just that, water.'

'That's good news, actually.'

'Oh? Well, good, then.'

I reflected. 'I think I'll phone you again this evening before we leave Winnipeg.'

'Yes, do,' she agreed. 'The further west you go the bigger the time change and the longer it takes to get replies from Val Catto.'

'Mm.'

Mrs Baudelaire couldn't ring the Brigadier in the middle of his night, nor in the middle of hers. Toronto, where she lived, was five hours behind London,

Winnipeg six, Vancouver eight. At breakfast time in Vancouver, London's office workers began travelling home. Confusing for carrier pigeons.

'Good luck,' she said. 'I'll talk to you later.'

I was used by now to her abrupt disappearances. I put my receiver down, hearing only silence on the line, and wondered what she looked like, and how deeply she was ill. I would go back to Toronto, I thought, and see her.

I sped again on the bus to the races and found that overnight Assiniboia Downs had sprouted all the ballyhoo of Woodbine: T-shirt stalls, banners and be-sashed bosoms saying 'Support Canadian Racing' included.

I again spent most of the afternoon looking for gaunt-face, coming in the end to the conclusion that whatever he was doing on the train he wasn't travelling because of an overpowering interest in racing. The racegoers from the train were on the whole easily identifiable as they all seemed to have been issued with large red and white rosettes with 'Race Train Passenger' emblazoned on them in gold: and the rosettes proved not to be confined to those in the front half of the train because I came across Zak wearing one too, and he told me that everyone had been given one, the owners included, and where was mine?

I didn't know about them, I said. Too bad, he said, because they entitled everyone to free entry, free racecards and free food. They were gifts from the racecourse, he said. Nell should have one for me, he thought.

I asked him how the scene from the mystery had fared that morning, as Nell had described what had happened the day before.

'A lot better without that bastard Sheridan.'

'Wasn't he there?'

'I got Nell to tell his father that if Sheridan came to breakfast we wouldn't be putting on our scene, and it did the trick. No Sheridan.' He grinned. 'No Lorrimores at all, in fact.' He looked around. 'But they're all here, Sheridan included. They were getting out of a stretch limo when we rolled up in our private bus. That's where we were given these rosettes; on the bus. How did you get here, then?'

'On a public bus.'

'Too bad.'

His batteries were running at half-speed, neither highly charged up nor flat. Under the mop of curls his face, without the emphasizing make-up he wore perpetually on the train, looked younger and more ordinary: it was David Flynn who was at the races, not Zak.

'Are all the actors here?' I asked.

'Oh, sure. We have to know what happens here today. Have to be able to talk about it to the owners tonight. Don't forget, it's a racing mystery, after all.'

I thought that I had forgotten, in a way. The real

mystery that I was engaged in tended to crowd the fiction out.

'What are you betting on in our race?' he asked. 'I suppose Premiere will win. What do you think?'

'Upper Gumtree,' I said.

'It's supposed to be half asleep,' he objected.

'It's got a nice face,' I said.

He looked at me sideways. 'You're crazy, you know that?'

'I am but mad north-north-west.'

'When the wind is southerly,' he said promptly, 'I know a hawk from a handsaw.' He laughed. 'There isn't an actor born who doesn't hope to play Hamlet.'

'Have you ever?'

'Only in school. But once learned, never forgotten. Shall I give you my "To be or not to be"?'

'No.'

'You slay me. See you tonight.'

He went off with a medium spring to his step and I saw him later with his arms round Donna's shoulders, which wasn't (as far as I knew) in his script.

Most of the owners came down from the Clubhouse to watch the saddling of the runners in the Jockey Club Race Train Stakes, and all the sportier of them wore the rosettes.

Filmer didn't: there was no light-heartedness in him. Daffodil, however, had fastened hers to her cleavage, the red, white and gold popping out now and again past the long-haired chinchillas. Mrs Young wore hers boldly on her lapel. Mr Young's wasn't in sight.

The Unwins, rosetted, were showing uninhibited pleasure in Upper Gumtree, who did in fact have a nice face, and wasn't unacceptably sleepy. Upper Gumtree's trainer hadn't made the journey from Australia, and nor had his usual jockey: Canadian substitutes had been found. The Unwins beamed and patted everyone within reach including the horse, and Mr Unwin in his great antipodean accent could be heard calling his jockey 'son', even though the rider looked older by far than the owner.

In the next stall along things were a great deal quieter. Mercer Lorrimore, unattended by the rest of his family, talked pleasantly with his trainer, who had come from Toronto, and shook hands with his jockey, the same one who had ridden for him at Woodbine. Premiere, the favourite, behaved like a horse that had had a fuss made of him all his life; almost, I thought fancifully, as arrogantly as Sheridan.

The owners of Flokati were showing Mavis and Walter Bricknell-type behaviour, fluttering about in a nervous anxiety that would be bound to affect the horse if it went on too long. Their ineffective-looking trainer was trying to stop the owners from straightening the number cloth, tidying the forelock over the headband, tweaking at the saddle and shoving their big rosettes with every ill-judged movement near the horse's affronted nostrils. A riot, really. Poor Mr and Mrs Flokati; owning the horse looked an agony, not a joy.

Mr and Mrs Young, like Mercer Lorrimore, had shipped their Winnipeg runners, two of them, by road. They, old hands at the owning game, stood by with calm interest while their pair, Soluble and Slipperclub, were readied, Mrs Young speaking with her sweet expression to one of the jockeys, Mr Young more impassively to the other.

Daffodil Quentin's runner, Pampering, had been flown in with five others owned by people on the train, all of whom were strolling around with rosettes and almost permanently smiling faces. This was, after all, one of the highlights of their journey, the purpose behind the pizzazz. I learned that the Manitoba Racing Commission had moreover by mid-afternoon given each of them not only a champagne reception and a splendid lunch but also, as a memento, a framed group photograph of all the owners on the trip. They were living their memories, I thought, here and now.

Television cameras all over the place recorded everything both for news items that evening and for the two-hour Support Canadian Racing programme which posters everywhere announced was being made for a gala showing coast to coast after the triple had been completed in Vancouver.

The Winnipeg runners went out on to the track to bugle fanfares and cheers from the stands and were pony-escorted to the starting gate.

Mercer Lorrimore's colours, red and white like the rosette he had pinned on gamely 'For the Sake of Canadian Racing', could be seen entering the outermost stall. Daffodil's pale blue and dark green were innermost. Upper Gumtree, carrying orange and black, started dead centre of the eleven runners and came out of the stalls heading a formation like an arrow.

I was watching from high up, from the upper part of the grandstand, above the Clubhouse floor to which the owners had returned in a chattering flock to watch the race. Through my binoculars-camera the colours down on the track in the chilly sunshine looked sharp and bright, the race easy on that account to read.

The arrow formation soon broke up into a ragged line, with Premiere on the outside, Pampering on the inner and Upper Gumtree still just in front. The Youngs' pair, split by the draw, nevertheless came together and raced the whole way side by side like twins. Flokati, in pink, made for the rails as if needing them to steer by, and four of the other runners boxed him in.

Going past the stands for the first time, the Unwins' Upper Gumtree still showed in front but with Premiere almost alongside; Pampering was on the inside tugging his jockey's arms out. Doing their best for the glory of Canada, the whole field of eleven swept round the bend and went down the far side as if welded together, and it still seemed when they turned for home that that was how they might finish, in a knot.

They split apart in the straight, one group swinging wide, the red and white of Premiere spurting forward with the Youngs' pair at his quarters and Upper Gumtree swerving dramatically through a gap to take the rails well ahead of Pampering.

The crowd bounced up and down. The money was on Premiere. The yelling could have been heard in Montreal. The Canadian racing authorities were again getting a rip-roaring brilliant finish to a Race Train Stakes . . . and Mercer, putting his brave face on it, again came in second.

It was the Unwins, in the stratosphere of ecstasy, who led Upper Gumtree into the winners' circle. The Unwins from Australia who were hugging and kissing everyone near enough (including the horse). The Unwins who had their photographs taken each side of their panting winner, now covered across the shoulders by a long, triumphant blanket of flowers. The Unwins who received the trophy, the cheque and the speeches from the President of the racecourse and the top brass of the Jockey Club; whose memories of the day would be the sweetest.

Feeling pleased for them, I lowered the binoculars through which I'd been able to see even the tears on Mrs Unwin's cheeks, and there below me and in front of the grandstand was the man with the gaunt face looking up towards the Clubhouse windows.

Almost trembling with haste, I put the binoculars up again, found him, activated the automatic focus, pressed the button, heard the quiet click of the shutter: had him in the bag.

It had been my only chance. Even before the film had wound on, he'd looked down and away, so that I could see only his forehead and his grey hair; and within two seconds, he'd walked towards the grandstand and out of my line of vision.

I had no idea how long he'd been standing there. I'd been too diverted by the Unwins' rejoicings. I went down from the upper grandstand as fast as I could, which was far too slowly because everyone else was doing the same thing.

Down on ground level again, I couldn't see gauntface anywhere. The whole crowd was on the move: one could get no length of view. The Race Train event had been the climax of the programme and although there was one more race on the card, no one seemed to be much interested. A great many red and white rosettes, baseball caps, T-shirts and balloons were on their way out of the gates.

The Unwins' entourage was disappearing into the Clubhouse entrance, no doubt for more champagne and Press interviews, and probably all the other owners would be in there with them. If gaunt-face had been looking up at the Clubroom windows in the hope of seeing Filmer – or of Filmer seeing him – maybe Filmer would come down to talk to him and maybe I could photograph them both together, which might one day prove useful. If I simply waited, it might happen.

I simply waited.

Filmer did eventually come down, but with Daffodil. They weren't approached by gaunt-face. They climbed into their chauffeured car and were whisked away to heaven-knew-where, and I thought frustratedly about time and the little of it there was left in Winnipeg. It was already nearly six o'clock, and I wouldn't be able to find a one-hour photo lab open anywhere that evening; and I had to return to the Sheraton to collect my bag, and be back on the train by seven-thirty or soon after.

I retreated to the men's room and took the film out of the binoculars-camera, and wrote a short note to go with it. Then I twisted the film and note together into a paper towel and went out to try to find Bill Baudelaire, reckoning it might be all right to speak to him casually down on ground level since Filmer wasn't there to see. I'd caught sight of him in the distance from time to time all afternoon, but now when I wanted him his red hair wasn't anywhere around.

Zak came up to me with Donna and offered me a lift back to the city in their bus, and at that exact moment I saw not Bill Baudelaire himself but someone who might go among the owners, where Tommy couldn't.

'When does the bus go?' I asked Zak rapidly, preparing to leave him.

'Twenty minutes ... out front. It's got a banner on.

'I'll come ... thanks.'

I covered a good deal of ground rapidly but not running and caught up with the shapely back view of a dark-haired girl in a red coat with a wide gold and white studded belt.

'Nancy?' I said from behind her.

She turned, surprised, and looked at me enquiringly.

'Er ...' I said, 'yesterday you collected some thirst quenchers from me for Bill Baudelaire's daughter'

'Oh, yes.' She recognized me belatedly.

'Do you happen to know where I could find him now?'

'He's up in the Clubhouse, drinking with the winners.'

'Could you ... could you possibly deliver something else to him?'

She wrinkled her freckled teenage nose. 'I just came down, for some fresh air.' She sighed. 'Oh, all right. I guess he'd want me to, if you asked. You seem to be OK with him. What do you want me to give him this time?'

I passed over the paper-towel bundle.

'Instructions?' she asked.

'There's a note inside.'

'Real cloak and dagger goings-on.'

'Thanks, truly, and ... er ... give it to him quietly.'

'What's in it?' she asked.

'A film, with photos of today's events.'

She didn't know whether or not to be disappointed.

'Don't lose it,' I said.

259

She seemed to be more pleased with that, and flashing me a grin from over her shoulder went off towards the Clubhouse entrance. I hoped she wouldn't make a big production out of the delivery upstairs, but just in case she did I thought I wouldn't go anywhere where she could see me and point me out to any of the owners, so I left through the front exit gates and found the actors' bus with its 'Mystery Race Train' banner and faded inside into the reassembling troupe.

In general, the cast had backed Premiere (what else?) but were contented to have been interviewed on television at some length. A lot of Winnipeg's race crowd, Zak said, had asked how they could get on the train. 'I must say,' he said, yawning, 'with all the publicity it's had, it's really caught on.'

In the publicity and the success, I thought, lay the danger. The more the eyes of Canada and Australia and England were directed to the train, the more Filmer might want to discredit it. Might . . . might. I was guarding a moving shadow; trying to prevent something that might not happen, searching for the intention so as to stop it occurring.

The bus letting me off at a convenient corner in the city, I walked to the Sheraton and from a telephone there spoke to Mrs Baudelaire.

'Bill called me ten minutes ago from the track,' she said. 'He said you sent him a film and you didn't say where you wanted the pictures sent.'

'Is he calling you back?' I asked.

'Yes, I told him I'd be speaking to you soon.'

'Right, well, there's only one picture on the film. The rest is blank. Please tell Bill the man in the photo is the ally of our quarry. His ally on the train. Would you ask if Bill knows him? Ask if anyone knows him. And if there's something about him that would be useful if I knew, please will he tell you, to tell me.'

'Heavens,' she said. 'Let me get that straight.' She paused, writing. 'Basically, who is he, what does he do, and is what he does likely to be of help.'

'Yes,' I said.

'And do you want a copy of the photo?'

'Yes, please. Ask if there's any chance of his getting it to Nell Richmond at Chateau Lake Louise by tomorrow night or the next morning.'

'Difficult,' she commented. 'The mail is impossible.'

'Well, someone might be flying to Calgary tomorrow morning,' I suggested. 'They might even meet our train there. We get there at twelve-forty, leave at one-thirty. I suppose the time's too tight, but if it's possible, get Bill to address the envelope to the Conductor of the train, George Burley. I'll tell George it might come.'

'Dear young man,' she said, 'let me write it all down.'

I waited while she did it.

'Let me check,' she said. 'Either George Burley on the train or Nell Richmond at Chateau Lake Louise.'

'Right. I'll call you soon.'

'Don't go,' she said. 'I have a message for you from Val Catto.'

'Oh good.'

'He said ... now these are his exact words ... "Stolen evidence cannot be used in court but facts learned can be verified." ' The understanding amusement was light in her voice. 'What he means is, have a look-see but hands off.'

'Yes.'

'And he said to tell you to remember his motto.'

'OK,' I said.

'What is his motto?' she asked curiously, obviously longing to know.

'Thought before action, if you have time.'

'Nice,' she said, pleased. 'He said to tell you he was working hard on the unknown numbers, and you are not to put yourself in danger of arrest.'

'All right.'

'Phone me from Calgary tomorrow,' she said. 'By then it will be evening in England. Val will have had a whole day on the numbers.'

'You're marvellous.'

'And I'll be able to tell you when you'll get your photos.'

There was a click and she'd gone, and I could hardly believe that I'd ever doubted her as a relay post.

The train had come in from the sidings and stood in the station, warm and pulsing, its engines reattached, the horses and grooms on board and fresh foods and ice loaded.

It was like going back to an old friend, familiar and almost cosy. I changed into Tommy's uniform in my roomette and went along to the dining car where Emil, Oliver and Cathy welcomed me casually as if I were an accepted part of the crew. We began immediately laying the pink cloths and putting fresh flowers in the vases, and Angus in his tall white hat, whistling 'Speed Bonny Boat' amid clouds of steam, addressed his talents to wild rice and scallops in Parmesan sauce while Simone rather grimly chopped lettuce.

The passengers returned well before eight o'clock in very good spirits, Mercer bringing with him a porter wheeling a case of highly superior bubbles for toasting the Unwins' success. The Unwins themselves – and it was impossible for anyone to grudge them their moment – said over and over that it was great, just great that one of the horses actually on the train had won one of the races, it made the whole thing worthwhile, and the whole party, drifting into the dining car in true party mood, agreed and applauded.

Filmer, I was interested to see as I distributed glasses, was smiling pleasantly in all directions, when the last thing he probably wanted was the enormous smash-hit the train enterprise was proving.

Daffodil had changed into a sparkling crimson dress and showed no pique over Pampering finishing fifth.

She was being friendly as usual to Bambi, frostier in pale turquoise with pearls.

Mercer came to Emil and worried that the wine wasn't cold enough, but Emil assured him he had lodged all twelve bottles among the many plastic bags of ice cubes: by the time the train left the station, all would be well.

The Youngs, whose Slipperclub had finished third, were embraced by the hyperjoyous Unwins and were invited to their table, leaving the poor Flokatis to seek solace with others whose hopes had died on the last bend. Sheridan Lorrimore was telling a long-suffering good-natured couple all about his prowess at ice hockey and Xanthe, pouting and put out at having been temporarily deserted by Mrs Young, had ended up next to Giles-the-murderer whose real-life preference, I'd gathered, was for boys.

The train slid out of Winnipeg on time at eight-twenty and I put all my energies and attention into being an unexceptional and adequate waiter, even though always conscious of the ominous presence in the aisle seat, facing forward, three tables back from the kitchen end. I never met his eyes and I don't think he noticed me much, but we were all, Emil, Oliver, Cathy and I, becoming slowly and inevitably more recognizable to the passengers. Several of them enquired if we'd been to the races (we all had) and had backed the winner (no, we hadn't). Fortunately Mercer himself had had this conversation with Emil, which meant he felt no need to ask me also, so I escaped having to speak too much in my English accent at his table.

The party atmosphere went on all through dinner, prevailed through a short scene put on by Zak to explain that the Mountie had been left behind in Winnipeg for investigations on the ground and heated up thoroughly afterwards with more unsteady dancing and laughter in the dome car.

Nell wandered about looking slightly less starchy in a fuller-cut black skirt with her tailored white silk blouse, telling me in passing that Cumber and Rose wanted to give a similar party at Chateau Lake Louise.

'Who?' I said.

'Cumber and Rose. Mr and Mrs Young.'

'Oh.'

'I've spent most of the day with them.' She smiled briefly and went on her way. No clipboard, I noticed.

Cumber and Rose, I thought, collecting ashtrays. Well, well. Rose suited Mrs Young fine. Cumber was appropriate also, I supposed, though Mr Young wasn't cumbersome; perhaps a shade heavy in personality, but not big, not awkward.

Mercer and Bambi again invited Filmer and Daffodil into their private car, although it was Oliver, this time, who obliged them with a bowl of ice. Mercer came back after a while to collect the Unwins and the Youngs, and the general jollifications everywhere wore on without any alarms.

After midnight Nell said she was going to bed, and

265

I walked up the train with her to her roomette, almost opposite mine. She paused in the doorway.

'It's all going well, don't you think?' she said.

'Terrific.' I meant it. 'You've worked very hard.'

We looked at each other, she in executive black and white, I in my yellow waistcoat.

'What are you really?' she said.

'Twenty-nine.'

Her lips twitched. 'One day I'll crack your defences.'

'Yours are half down.'

'What do you mean?'

I made a hugging movement across my own chest. 'No clipboard,' I said.

'Oh . . . well . . . I didn't need it this evening.'

She wasn't exactly confused. Her eyes were laughing.

'You can't,' she said.

'Can't what?'

'Kiss me.'

I'd wanted to. She'd seen it unerringly.

'If you come into my parlour, I can,' I said.

She shook her head, smiling. 'I am not going to lose my credibility on this train by being caught coming out of the help's bedroom.'

'Talking in the corridor is almost as bad.'

'Yes, it is,' she said, nodding. 'So goodnight.'

I said with regret, 'Goodnight,' and she went abruptly into her own domain and closed the door.

With a sigh I went on a few steps further to George's office and found him as I'd expected, fully dressed, lightly napping, with worked-on forms pushed to one side beside an empty coffee cup.

'Come in,' he said, fully alert in an instant. 'Sit down. How's it going?'

'So far, so good.'

I sat on the facilities, and told him that the water samples from the horse car had been pure and simple H_2O.

'That'll please the dragon-lady, eh?' he said.

'Did you go to the races?' I asked.

'No, I've got family in Winnipeg, I went visiting. And I slept most of today, as I'll be up all night, with the stops.' He knew, however, that Upper Gumtree had won. 'You should see the party going on in the forward dome car. All the grooms are drunk. The dragon-lady's in a sober tizzy, eh?, because they tried to give a bucket of beer to the horse. They're singing gold rush songs at the tops of their voices in the dayniter and it's a wonder they haven't all rocked the train right off the rails, with the noise and the booze.'

'I guess it wouldn't be easy to rock the train off the rails,' I said thoughtfully.

'Easy?' George said. 'Of course it is. Go too fast round the curves.'

'Well ... suppose it was one of the passengers who wanted to stop the train getting happily to Vancouver, what could he do?'

He looked at me with bright eyes, unperplexed. 'Besides doping the horses' water? Do what they're doing in the mystery, I'd say. Throw a body off the train, eh? That would stop the parties pretty quick.' He chuckled. 'You could throw someone off the Stoney Creek bridge – that's a high curved bridge over Roger's Pass. It's a long way down into the gulch. Three hundred feet and a bit more. If the fall didn't kill them, the bears would.'

'Bears!' I exclaimed.

He beamed. 'Grizzly bears, eh? The Rocky Mountains aren't anyone's tame backyard. They're raw nature. So are the bears. They kill people, no trouble.' He put his head on one side. 'Or you could throw someone out into the Connaught Tunnel. That tunnel's five miles long with no lights. There's a species of blind mice that live in there, eating the grain that falls from the grain trains.'

'Jolly,' I said.

'There's a wine storage under the floor of your dining car,' he said with growing relish. 'They decided not to use it on this trip because opening it might disrupt the passengers. It's big enough to hide a body in.'

His imagination, I saw, was of a scarier dimension than my own.

'Hiding a body in the wine store,' I said politely, 'might indeed disrupt the passengers.'

He laughed. 'Or how about someone alive and tied up in there, writhing in agony?'

'Shouting his head off?'

'Gagged.'

'If we miss anyone,' I promised, 'that's where we'll look.' I stood up and prepared to go. 'Where exactly is the Stoney Creek bridge,' I asked, pausing in the doorway, 'over Roger's Pass?'

His eyes gleamed, the lower lids pouching with enjoyment. 'About a hundred miles further on from Lake Louise. High up in the mountains. But don't you worry, eh?, you'll be going across it in the dark.'

CHAPTER THIRTEEN

Everyone survived the night, although there were a few obvious hangovers at breakfast. Outside the windows, the seemingly endless rock, lake and conifer scenery had dramatically given way to the wide sweeping rolling prairies, not yellow with the grain that had already been harvested, but greenish grey, resting before winter.

There was a brief stop during breakfast at the town of Medicine Hat which lay in a valley and looked a great deal more ordinary than its name. The passengers dutifully put back their watches when Nell told them we were now in Mountain Time, but where, they asked, were the mountains?

'This afternoon,' she answered, and handed out the day's printed programme which promised 'Dreadful Developments in The Mystery' at eleven-thirty a.m., followed by an early lunch. We would reach Calgary at twelve-forty, where the horse car would be detached, and leave at one-thirty, heading up into the Rockies to Banff and Lake Louise. At Lake Louise, the owners would disembark and be ferried by bus to the Chateau, the huge hotel sitting on the lake's shore, amid 'Snowy Scenes of Breathtaking Beauty'. 'Cocktails and Startling Discoveries' would be offered at six-thirty in a private conference room in the hotel. Have a nice day.

Several people asked if we were now in front or behind the regular Canadian.

'We're in front,' I said.

'If we break down,' Mr Unwin said facetiously, 'it will be along to help us out.'

Xanthe, sitting next to him, didn't laugh. 'I wish we were behind it,' she said. 'I'd feel safer.'

'Behind the Canadian there are freight trains,' Mr Unwin said reasonably, 'and ahead of us there are freight trains. And coming the other way there are freight trains. We're not all alone on these rails.'

'No, I suppose not.' She seemed doubtful still and said she had slept much better again that past night in her upper bunk than she would have done in her family's own quarters.

I brought her the French toast and sausages she ordered from the menu and filled her coffee cup, and Mr Unwin, holding out his own cup for a refill, asked if I had backed his horse to win at Winnipeg.

'I'm afraid not, sir,' I said regretfully. I put his cup on the tray and poured with small movements. 'But congratulations, sir.'

'Did you go to the races?' Xanthe asked me without too much interest.

271

'Yes, miss,' I said.

I finished pouring Mr Unwin's coffee and put it by his place, then took my tray and coffee pot along to the next table where the conversation seemed to be about Zak's mystery rather than directly about horses.

'I think the trainer killed Angelica. And the groom too.'

'Why ever should he?'

'He wants to marry Donna for her money. Angelica knew something that would make the marriage impossible, so he killed her.'

'Knew what?'

'Maybe that he's already married.'

'To Angelica?'

'Well . . . why not?'

'But where does the dead groom come in?'

'He saw the murderer getting rid of the blood-spattered plastic.'

They laughed. I filled their cups and moved on and poured for Daffodil, who had an empty place on her far side. Daffodil, smoking with deep sucking lungfuls, sat with the Flokatis, and nobody else.

No Filmer.

I glanced back along the whole dining car, but couldn't see him anywhere. He hadn't come in while I was serving others, and he hadn't been at the kitchen and when I'd started.

Daffodil said to me, 'Can you bring me some vodka? Ice and lemon.'

'I'll ask, madam,' I said, and asked Emil, and it was he who civilly explained to her that the barman wouldn't be back on duty until eleven, and meanwhile everything was locked up.

Daffodil received the bad news without speaking but jabbed the fire out of her cigarette with some violent stabs and a long final grind. The Flokatis looked at her uncertainly and asked if they could help.

She shook her head. She seemed angry and near to tears, but determinedly in control.

'Give me some coffee,' she said to me, and to the Flokatis she said, 'I think I'll get off the train at Calgary. I think I'll go home.'

Small movements saved the day, as I would have spilled the brown liquid all over her hand.

'Oh no!' exclaimed the Flokatis, instantly distressed. 'Oh, don't do that. Your horse ran splendidly yesterday, even if it was only fifth. Ours was nearly last . . . and we are going on. You can't give up. And you have Laurentide Ice, besides, for Vancouver.'

Daffodil looked at them as if bemused. 'It's not because of yesterday,' she said.

'But why, then?'

Daffodil didn't tell them. Maybe wouldn't; maybe couldn't. She merely pursed her lips tight, shook her curly head, and dug out another cigarette.

The Flokatis having declined more coffee, I couldn't stay to listen any further. I moved across the aisle and stretched my ears, but the Flokatis seemed to get

273

nothing extra from Daffodil except a repeated and stronger decision to go home.

Nell in her straight grey skirt, clipboard in attendance, was still talking to passengers up by the kitchen end. I took my nearly empty coffee pot up there and made a small gesture onwards to the lobby, to where presently she came with enquiring eyebrows.

'Daffodil Quentin,' I said, peering into the coffee pot, 'is upset to the point of leaving the train. She told the Flokatis, not me . . . so you don't know, OK?'

'Upset about what?' Nell was alarmed.

'She wouldn't tell them.'

'Thanks,' she said. 'I'll see what I can do.'

Smoothing ruffled feelings, keeping smiles in place; all in her day's work. She started casually on her way through the dining car and I went into the kitchen to complete my mission. By the time I was out again with a full pot, Nell had reached Daffodil and was standing by her, listening. Nell appealed to the Youngs and the Unwins at adjacent tables for help, and presently Daffodil was out of sight in a bunch of people trying to persuade her to change her mind.

I had to wait quite a while to hear what was happening, but finally the whole little crowd, Daffodil among them, went out at the far end into the dome car and Nell returned to the lobby, relaying the news to me in snatches as I paused beside her on to-and-fro journeys to clear away the breakfast debris.

'Cumber and Rose . . .' The Youngs, I thought.

'Cumber and Rose and also the Unwins say there was nothing wrong last night, they all had a splendid time in the Lorrimores' car. Daffodil finally said she'd had a disagreement with Mr Filmer after the party had broken up. She said she had hardly slept and wasn't sure what to do, but there was no fun left in taking Laurentide Ice to Vancouver, and she couldn't face the rest of the journey. The Youngs have persuaded her to go up into the dome with them to think things over, but I honestly think she's serious. She's very upset.'

'Mm.' I put the last of the debris into the kitchen and excused myself apologetically from washing the dishes.

'How can Mr Filmer have upset Daffodil so much?' Nell exclaimed. 'She's obviously been enjoying herself, and he's such a nice man. They were getting on together so well, everyone thought.' She paused. 'Mr Unwin believes it's a lovers' quarrel.'

'Does he?' I pondered. 'I think I'll make a recce up the train. See if anything else is happening.'

Maybe Daffodil had made advances and been too roughly repulsed, I thought. And maybe not.

'Mr Filmer hasn't been in to breakfast,' Nell said. 'It's all very worrying. And last night everyone was so happy.'

If Daffodil's leaving the train was the worst thing that happened, I thought, we would have got off lightly. I left Nell and set off up the corridor, coming pretty soon to Filmer's bedroom door, which was uninformatively closed.

I checked with the sleeping-car attendant further along the car who was in the midst of folding up the bunks for the day and unfolding the armchairs.

'Mr Filmer? He's in his room still, as far as I know. He was a bit short with me, told me to hurry up. And he's not usually like that. He was eating something, and he had a thermos too. But then we do get passengers like that sometimes. Can't get through the night without raiding the icebox, that sort of thing.'

I nodded noncommittally and went onwards, but I thought that if Filmer had brought food and a thermos on board for breakfast, he must have known in Winnipeg that he would need them, which meant that last night's quarrel had been planned and hadn't been caused by Daffodil.

George Burley was in his office, writing his records.

'Morning,' he said, beaming.

'How's the train?'

'The forward sleeping-car attendants are threatening to resign, eh?, over the vomit in the bathrooms.'

'Ugh.'

He chuckled. 'I brought extra disinfectants aboard in Winnipeg,' he said. 'Train-sickness gets them, you know.'

I shook my head at his indulgence and pressed forward, looking as always for gaunt-face but chiefly aiming for the horses.

Leslie Brown, hollow-eyed from lack of sleep, regarded me with only half the usual belligerence.

'Come in,' she said, stepping back from her door. 'To be honest, I could do with some help.'

As I'd just passed several green-looking grooms being sorry for themselves in their section, I supposed at first she meant simply physical help in tending the horses, but it appeared that she didn't.

'Something's going on that I don't understand,' she said, locking the entrance door behind me and leading the way to the central space where her chair stood beside the innocent water tank.

'What sort of thing?' I asked, following her.

She mutely pointed further forward up the car, and I walked on until I came to the final space between the stalls, and there, in a sort of nest made of hay bales, one of the grooms half lay, half sat, curled like an embryo and making small moaning noises.

I went back to Leslie Brown. 'What's the matter with him?' I said.

'I don't know. He was drunk last night, they all were, but this doesn't look like an ordinary hangover.'

'Did you ask the others?'

She sighed. 'They don't remember much about last night. They don't care what's the matter with him.'

'Which horse is he with?'

'Laurentide Ice.'

I'd have been surprised, I supposed, if she'd said anything else.

'That's the horse, isn't it,' I asked, 'whose trainer sent separate numbered individual bags of food, because another of Mrs Quentin's horses had died because of eating the wrong things?'

She nodded. 'Yes.'

'And this boy was with the horse all the time in the barns at Winnipeg?'

'Yes, of course. They exercised the horses and looked after them, and they all came back to the train in horse vans yesterday after the races, while the train was still in the siding. I came with them. There's nothing wrong with any of the horses, I assure you.'

'That's good,' I said. 'Laurentide Ice as well?'

'See for yourself.'

I walked round looking at each horse but in truth they all appeared healthy and unaffected, even Upper Gumtree and Flokati who would have been excused seeming thin and fatigued after their exertions. Most of them had their heads out over the stall doors, a sure sign of interest: a few were a pace or two back, semi-dreaming. Laurentide Ice watched me with a bright glacial eye, in far better mental health than his attendant.

I returned to Leslie Brown and asked her the groom's name.

'Lenny,' she said. She consulted a list. 'Leonard Higgs.'

'How old is he?'

'About twenty, I should think.'

'What's he like, usually?'

'Like the others. Full of foul language and dirty jokes.' She looked disapproving. 'Every other word beginning with f.'

'When did all this moaning and retreating start?'

'He was lying there all night. The other boys said it was his turn to be in here, but it wasn't really, only he was paralytic, and they just dumped him in the hay and went back to the party. He started the moaning about an hour ago and he won't answer me at all.' She was disturbed by him, and worried, I thought, that his behaviour might be held to be her responsibility.

Rather to her surprise, I took off my yellow waistcoat and striped tie and gave them to her to hold. If she would sit down for a while, I suggested, I would try to sort Lenny out.

Meekly for her, she agreed. I left her perching with my badges of office across her trousered knees and returned to the total collapse in the hay.

'Lenny,' I said, 'give it a rest.'

He went on with the moaning, oblivious.

I sat down beside him on one of the hay bales and put my mouth near his one visible ear.

'Shut up,' I said, very loudly.

He jumped and he gasped and after a short pause he went back to moaning, though artificially now, it seemed to me.

'If you're sick from beer,' I said forcefully, 'it's your

own bloody fault, but I'll get you something to make you feel better.'

He curled into a still tighter ball, tucking his head down into his arms as if shielding it from a blow. It was a movement impossible to misconstrue: what he felt, besides alcohol sickness, was fear.

Fear followed Julius Apollo Filmer like a spoor; the residue of his passing. Lenny, frightened out of his wits, was a familiar sight indeed.

I undid the top buttons of my shirt, loosening the collar, and rolled up my cuffs, aiming for informality, and I slid down until I was sitting on the floor with my head on the same level as Lenny's.

'If you're shit-scared,' I said distinctly, 'I can do something about that, too.'

Nothing much happened. He moaned a couple of times and fell silent and after a long while, I said, 'Do you want help, or don't you? This is a good offer. If you don't take it, whatever you're afraid of will probably happen.'

After a lengthy pause he rolled his head round, still wrapped in his arms, until I could see his face. He was red-eyed, bony, unshaven and dribbling, and what came out of his slack mouth wasn't a groan but a croak.

'Who the bleeding hell are you?' He had an English accent and a habitual pugnacity of speech altogether at odds with his present state.

'Your bit of good luck,' I said calmly.

'Piss off,' he said.

280

'Right.' I got to my feet. 'Too bad,' I said. 'Go on feeling sorry for yourself, and see where it gets you.'

I walked away from him, out of his sight.

'Here,' he said, croaking, making it sound like an order.

I stayed where I was.

'Wait,' he said urgently.

I did wait, but I didn't go back to him. I heard the hay rustling and then a real groan as the hangover hit him, and finally he came staggering into view, keeping his balance with both hands on the green outside of Flokati's stall. He stopped when he saw me. Blinking, swaying, the Race Train T-shirt torn and filthy, he looked stupid, pathetic and spineless.

'Go back and sit down,' I said neutrally. 'I'll bring you something.'

He sagged against the green stall but finally turned round and shuffled back the way he'd come. I went down to Leslie Brown and asked if she had any aspirins.

'Not aspirins, but these,' she said, proffering a box from a canvas holdall. 'These might do.'

I thanked her, filled a polystyrene cup with water and went back to see how Lenny was faring: he was sitting on the hay with his head in his hands looking a picture of misery and a lot more normal.

'Drink,' I said, giving him the water. 'And swallow these.'

'You said you could help me.'

'Yes. Take the pills for a start.'

He was accustomed, on the whole, to doing what he was told, and he must have been reasonably good at his job, I supposed, to have been sent across Canada with Laurentide Ice. He swallowed the pills and drank the water and not surprisingly they made no immediate difference to his physical woes.

'I want to get out of here,' he said with a spurt of futile violence. 'Off this bleeding train. Off this whole effing trip. And I've got no money. I lost it. It's gone.'

'All right,' I said. 'I can get you off.'

'Straight up?' He was surprised.

'Straight up.'

'When?'

'At Calgary. In a couple of hours. You can leave then. Where do you want to go?'

He stared. 'You're having me on,' he said.

'No. I'll get you taken care of, and I'll see you get a ticket to wherever you want.'

The dawning hope in his face became clouded with confusion.

'What about old Icy?' he said. 'Who'll look after him?'

It was the first thought he'd had which hadn't been raw self-pity, and I felt the first flicker of compassion.

'We'll get another groom for old Icy,' I promised. 'Calgary's full of horse people.'

It wasn't exactly true. The Calgary I'd known had been one of the six biggest cities in Canada, half the size of Montreal and on a population par with central

Toronto. Time might have changed the statistics slightly, but probably not much. Calgary was no dusty old-west cattle town, but a skyscrapered modern city set like a glittering oasis in the skirts of the prairies: and the Stampede, in which one July I'd worked as a bronco rider, was a highly organized ten-day rodeo with a stadium, adjacent art and stage shows and all the paraphernalia and razzamatazz of big-time tourist entertainment. But Calgary, even in October, definitely had enough horse people around to provide a groom for Laurentide Ice.

I watched Lenny Higgs decide to jettison his horse, his job and his unbearable present. Fearful that I would bungle the whole business because I'd never before actually tried this sort of unscrambling myself, I strove to remember John Millington's stated methods with people like the chambermaid at Newmarket. Offer protection, make any promise that might get results, hold out carrots, be supportive, ask for help.

Ask for help.

'Could you tell me why you don't want to go on to Vancouver?' I said.

I made the question sound very casual, but it threw him back into overall panic, even if not into the foetal position.

'No.' He shivered with intense alarm. 'Piss off. It's none of your effing business.'

Without fuss I withdrew from him again, but this

283

time I went further away, beyond Leslie Brown, right down to the exit door.

'Stay there,' I said to her, passing. 'Don't say anything to him, will you?'

She shook her head, folding her thin arms over my waistcoat and across her chest. The dragon, I thought fleetingly, with the fire in abeyance.

'Here,' Lenny shouted behind me. 'Come back.'

I didn't turn round.

He wailed despairingly at the top of his voice, 'I want to get off this train.'

It was, I thought, a serious cry for help.

I went back slowly. He was standing between Flokati's stall and Sparrowgrass's, swaying unsteadily, watching me with haggard eyes.

When I was near him, I said simply, 'Why?'

'He'll kill me if I tell you.'

'That's rubbish,' I said.

'It isn't.' His voice was high. 'He said I'd effing die.'

'Who said?'

'Him.' He was trembling. The threat had been of sufficient power for him to believe it.

'Who is him?' I asked. 'One of the owners?'

He looked blank, as if I were talking gibberish.

'Who is him?' I asked again.

'Some bloke . . . I never saw him before.'

'Look,' I said calmingly, 'let's go back, sit on the hay, and you tell me why he said he'd kill you.' I pointed over his shoulders towards the bales and with a sort of exhausted compliance he stumbled that way and flopped into a huddled mess.

'How did he frighten you?' I asked.

'He . . . came to the barns . . . asked for me.'

'Asked for you by name?'

He nodded glumly.

'When was this?'

'Yesterday,' he said hoarsely. 'During the races.'

'Go on.'

'He said he knew all about old Icy's food being in numbered bags.' Lenny sounded aggrieved. 'Well, it wasn't a secret, was it?'

'No,' I said.

'He said he knew why . . . because Mrs Quentin's other horse died . . .' Lenny stopped and looked as if an abyss had opened before him. 'He started saying I done it . . .'

'Done what?'

Lenny was silent.

'Said you'd poisoned Mrs Quentin's other horse?' I suggested.

'I never did it. I didn't.' He was deeply agitated. 'I never.'

'But this man said you did?'

'He said I would go to jail for it, and "they do bad things to boys like you in jail", he said.' He shivered. 'I know they do. And he said . . . "Do you want AIDS, because you'll get it in jail, a pretty boy like you." '

Pretty, at that moment, he did not look.

'So what next?' I prompted.

'Well, I . . . Well, I . . .' he gulped. 'I said I never did it, it wasn't me . . . and he went on saying I'd go to jail and get AIDS and he went on and on . . . and I told him . . . I told him . . .'

'Told him what?'

'She's a nice lady,' he wailed. 'I didn't want to . . . he made me . . .'

'Was it Mrs Quentin,' I asked carefully, 'who poisoned her horse?'

He said miserably, 'Yes, No. See . . . she gave me this bag of treats . . . that's what she said they were, treats . . . and to give them to her horse when no one was looking . . . See, I didn't look after that horse of hers, it was another groom. So I gave her horse the bag of treats private, like . . . and it got colic and blew up and died . . . Well, I asked her, after. I was that scared . . . but she said it was all dreadful, she'd no idea her darling horse would get colic, and let's not say anything about it, she said, and she gave me a hundred dollars, and I didn't . . . I didn't want to be blamed, see?'

I did see.

I said, 'So when you told this man about the treats, what did he say?'

Lenny looked shattered. 'He grinned like a shark . . . all teeth . . . and he says . . . if I say anything about him to anybody . . . he'll see I get . . . I get . . .' He finished in a whisper, 'AIDS.'

I sighed. 'Is that how he threatened to kill you?'

He nodded weakly, as if spent.

'What did he look like?' I asked.

'Like my dad.' He paused. 'I hated my dad.'

'Did he sound like your dad?' I asked.

He shook his head. 'He wasn't a Brit.'

'Canadian?'

'Or American.'

'Well,' I said, running out of questions, 'I'll see you don't get AIDS.' I thought things over. 'Stay in the car until we get to Calgary. Ms Brown will get one of the other grooms to bring your bag here. The horse car is going to be unhitched from the train, and the horses are going by motor van to some stables for two days. All the grooms are going with them, as I expect you know. You go with the other grooms. And don't worry. Someone will come to find you and take you away, and bring another groom for Icy.' I paused to see if he understood, but it seemed he did. 'Where do you want to go from Calgary?'

'I don't know,' he said dully. 'Have to think.'

'All right. When the someone comes for you, tell him then what you want to do.'

He looked at me with a sort of wonderment. 'Why are you bothering?' he asked.

'I don't like frighteners.'

He shuddered. 'My dad frightened the living day-lights out of people... and me and Mum... and someone stabbed him, killed him... served him right.' He paused. 'No one ever helped the people he frightened.' He paused again, struggling for the unaccustomed word, and came up with it. 'Thanks.'

With tie and buttons all correctly fastened, Tommy went back to the dining car. Zak was just finishing a scene in which old Ben, the groom who had been importuning Raoul for money on Toronto station, had been brought in from the racegoers' part of the train to give damning (false) evidence against Raoul for having doped the Bricknells' horses, a charge flatly denied by Raoul who contrived to look virtuous and possibly guilty, both at the same time. Sympathy on the whole ended on Raoul's side because of Ben's whining nastiness, and Zak told everyone that a Most Important Witness would be coming to Chateau Lake Louise that evening to give Damaging Testimony. Against whom? some people asked. Ah, said Zak mysteriously, vanishing towards the corridor, only time would tell.

Emil, Oliver, Cathy and I set the tables for lunch and served its three courses. Filmer didn't materialize, but Daffodil did, still shaken and angry as at breakfast. Her suitcase was packed, it appeared, and she was adamant about leaving the party at Calgary. No one, it seemed, had been able to find out from her exactly what the matter was, and the lovers' tiff explanation had gained ground.

I served wine carefully and listened, but it was the

288

appealing prospect of two days in the mountains rather than Daffodil's troubles that filled most of the minds.

When Calgary appeared like sharp white needles on the prairie horizon and everyone began pointing excitedly, I told Emil I would do my best to return for the dishwashing and sloped off up the train to George's office.

Would the credit-card telephone work in Calgary? Yes, it would. He waved me towards it as the train slowed and told me I'd got fifty minutes. He himself, as usual, would be outside, supervising.

I got through to Mrs Baudelaire, who sounded carefree and sixteen.

'Your photograph is on its way,' she said without preamble. 'But it won't get to Calgary in time. Someone will be driving from Calgary to Chateau Lake Louise later this afternoon, and they are going to take it to your Miss Richmond.'

'That's great,' I said. 'Thank you.'

'But I'm afraid there's been no word from Val Catto about your numbers.'

'It can't be helped.'

'Anything else?' she asked.

'Yes,' I said. 'I need to talk to Bill direct.'

'What a shame. I've been enjoying this.'

'Oh,' I said. 'Please . . . so have I. It's only that it's more than a message and question and answer. It's long . . . and complicated.'

'My dear young man, don't apologize. Bill was still

in Winnipeg ten minutes ago. I'll call him straight away. Do you have a number?'

'Um, yes.' I read her the number on the train's handset. 'The sooner the better, would you tell him?'

'Talk to you later,' she said, and went away.

I waited restlessly through ten wasted minutes before the phone rang.

Bill's deep voice reverberated in my ear. 'Where are you?'

'On the train in Calgary station.'

'My mother says it's urgent.'

'Yes, but chiefly because this cellular telephone is in the Conductor's office and only works in cities.'

'Understood,' he said. 'Fire away.'

I told him about Daffodil's departure and Lenny Higgs's frightened collapse; about what she had not said, and he had.

Bill Baudelaire at length demanded, 'Have I got this straight? This Lenny Higgs said Daffodil Quentin got him to give her horse something to eat, from which the horse got colic and died?'

'Strong supposition of cause and effect, but unprovable, I should think.'

'Yes. They had an autopsy and couldn't find what caused the colic. It was the third of her dead horses. The insurers were very suspicious, but they had to pay.'

'Lenny says she told him she would never do any harm to her darling horses, but she gave him a hundred dollars to keep quiet.'

THE EDGE

Bill groaned.

'But,' I said, 'it might have been because she'd had two dead horses already and she was afraid everyone would think exactly what they did think anyway.'

'I suppose so,' he said. 'So where are we now?'

'Going on past experience,' I said, 'I would think – and this is just guessing – that after midnight last night, our quarry told Daffodil that her groom had spilled the beans, and would spill them again to order in public, and that he would see she was warned off at the very least if she didn't sell him ... or give him ... her remaining share in Laurentide Ice.'

He said gloomily, 'You all know him better than I do, but on form I'd think you may be right. We'll know for sure, won't we, if he applies to change the partnership registration before the Vancouver race.'

'Mm,' I agreed. 'Well, if you – the Ontario Racing Commission – feel like giving Daffodil the benefit of the doubt over her horses ... and of course you know her better than I do, but it seems to me she may not be intentionally wicked, but more silly ... I mean there's something immature about her, for all her fifty years or so ... and some people don't think it's all that wicked to defraud insurance companies, perfectly respectable people sometimes do it ... and I believe all three horses would have been put down sooner or later, wouldn't they? Anyway, I'm not excusing her if she's guilty, but explaining how she might feel about it ...'

291

'You've got to know her remarkably well.'

'Er . . . I've just . . . noticed . . .'

'Mm,' he said dryly. 'Val Catto said you notice things.'

'Well . . . I, er, don't know how you feel about this, but I thought that if we spirited Lenny Higgs away, sort of, he wouldn't be around to be threatened, or to be a threat to Daffodil, and if you could tell her somehow that Lenny Higgs had vanished and will not be spilling any beans whatsoever . . . if you could square it with your conscience to do that . . . then she doesn't need to part with her half-share and we will have foiled at least one of our quarry's rotten schemes. And that's my brief, isn't it?'

He breathed out lengthily, as a whistle.

I held the line and waited.

'Is Lenny Higgs still on the train?' he asked eventually.

'Unless he panics, he's going with the other grooms and horses to their stabling here. I told him someone would come to fetch him and look after him and give him a free ticket to wherever he wants to go.'

'Now, hold on . . .'

'It's the least we can do. But I think we should follow it up, and positively know his exact ultimate destination, even fix him up with a job, because we in our turn may want him to give evidence against the man who frightened him. If we do, we don't want to have to find him worldwide. And if you can send

292

someone to help him, get them to take along a copy of the photo you've had printed for me, because I'm pretty certain that's the man who frightened him. Lenny should turn to jelly, if it is.'

CHAPTER FOURTEEN

There was unfortunately a fair amount of dishwashing still to do when I returned to the kitchen so I lent a slightly guilty hand but kept walking out with glasses and cloths into the dining car so that I could see what was going on outside the windows.

Daffodil, attended by Nell and Rose and Cumber Young (he carrying her two suitcases), was helped down from the dome car by station staff and went off slowly into the main part of the station. Daffodil's curls were piled as perkily high as usual but her shoulders drooped inside the chinchillas, and the glimpse I had of her face showed a forlorn lost-child expression rather than a virago bent on revenge. Nell was being helpful. Rose Young exuded comfort: Cumber Young looked grim.

'Are you drying glasses or are you not?' Cathy demanded. She was pretty, bright-eyed and quick, and also, at that moment, tired.

'Intermittently,' I said.

Her momentary ill-temper dissolved. 'Then get an

intermittent move on or I won't be able to go over to the station before we leave.'

'Right,' I said, and dried and polished several glasses devotedly.

Cathy giggled. 'How long are you going to keep this up?'

'To the end, I guess.'

'But when is your scene?'

'Ah . . .' I said, 'that's the trouble. Right at the end. So I'll be drying dishes to Vancouver.'

'Are you the murderer?' she asked teasingly.

'Most definitely not.'

'The last time we had an actor pretending to be a waiter, he was the murderer.'

'The murderer,' I said, 'is that passenger you give the best portions to. That good-looking single man who's nice to everyone.'

Her eyes stretched wide. 'He's an owner,' she said.

'He's an actor. And don't give him away.'

'Of course I won't.' She looked slightly dreamy-eyed, though, as if I'd passed on good news. I didn't like to disillusion her about her or any girl's prospects with the gorgeous Giles; she would find out soon enough.

The chores finally done, Cathy skipped away to the delights of the station and in her place I helped Emil and Oliver stow and lock up all the equipment, as when everyone disembarked at Lake Louise the train was again going to be standing cold and silent in sidings for two days before the last stretch westwards to the Pacific.

Some but not all of the passengers had gone ashore, so to speak, at Calgary, and those who had been in the station came wandering back in good time, including the Youngs. Of Filmer there was no sign, nor of the gaunt-faced man. The dining car half filled again with people who simply preferred sitting there, and from those I heard that the horse car had been safely detached from the train and had been towed away by the engine, leaving the rest of us temporarily stranded.

The regular Canadian, they told each other, which had arrived on time thirty-five minutes after us, was the train standing three tracks away, its passengers stretching their legs like our own. The Canadian, it seemed, had changed from threat to friend in the general perception; our *doppelgänger* and companion on the journey. The passengers from both had mingled and compared notes. The Conductors had met for a talk.

There was a jerk and a shudder through the train as the engine returned and reattached, and soon afterwards we were on our way again, with passengers crowding now towards the dome car's observation deck to enjoy the ascent into the mountains.

Filmer, slightly to my surprise, was among those going through the dining car, and right behind him came Nell who looked over Filmer's shoulder at me and said, 'I've got a message for you from George Burley.'

'Excuse me, miss,' I said abruptly, standing well back between two tables to let Filmer go by, 'I'll be right with you.'

'What?' She was puzzled, but paused and stepped sideways also to let others behind her walk on through the car. Filmer himself had gone on without stopping, without paying Nell or me the least attention, and when his back was way down the car and well out of earshot of a quiet conversation, I turned back to Nell with enquiry.

'It's a bit of a mix-up,' she said. She was standing on the far side of the table from me, and speaking across it. 'Apparently the telephone in George Burley's office was ringing when he got back on board, and it was a woman wanting to speak to a Mr Kelsey. George Burley consulted his lists and said there was no Mr Kelsey on board. So whoever it was asked him to give a message to me, which he did.'

It must have been Mrs Baudelaire phoning, I thought: no one else knew the number. Bill himself could never be mistaken for a woman. Not his secretary . . .? Heaven forbid.

'What's the message?' I asked.

'I don't know if between us George Burley and I have got it right.' She was frowning. 'It's meaningless, but . . . zero forty-nine. That's the whole message, zero

forty-nine.' She looked at my face. 'You look happy
enough about it, anyway.'

I was also appalled, as a matter of fact, at how close
Filmer had come to hearing it.

I said, 'Yes, well . . . please don't tell anyone else
about the message, and please forget it if you can.'

'I can't.'

'I was afraid not.' I hunted around if not for explanations at least for a reasonable meaning. 'It's to do,' I
said, 'with the border between Canada and America,
with the Forty-Ninth Parallel.'

'Oh, sure.' She was unsure by the look of things, but
willing to let it go.

I said, 'Someone will bring a letter to the Chateau
sometime this evening addressed to you. It will have a
photo in it. It's for me, from Bill Baudelaire. Will you
see that I get it?'

'Yes, OK.' She briefly glanced at her clipboard. 'I
wanted to talk to you anyway about rooms.' A passenger or two walked past, and she waited until they
had gone. 'The train crew are staying in the staff annexe
at Chateau Lake Louise and the actors will be in the
hotel itself. Which do you want? I have to write the list.'

'Our passengers will be in the hotel?'

'Ours, yes, but not the racegoers. They're all getting
off in Banff. That's the town before Lake Louise. The
owners are all staying in the Chateau. So am I. Which
do you want?'

'To be with you,' I said.

'Seriously.'

I thought briefly. 'Is there anywhere else?'

'There's a sort of village near the station about a mile from the Chateau itself, but it's just a few shops, and they're closing now at this time of the year, ready for winter. A lot of places are closed by this time, in the mountains.' She paused. 'The Chateau stands by itself on the lake shore. It's beautiful there.'

'Is it big?' I asked.

'Huge.'

'OK. I'll stay there and risk it.'

'Risk what?'

'Being stripped of my waistcoat.'

'But you won't wear it there,' she assured me.

'No . . . metaphorically.'

She lowered the clipboard and clicked her pen for writing.

'Tommy Titmouse,' I said.

Her lips curved. 'T. Titmuss.' She spelled it out. 'That do?'

'Fine.'

'What are you really?'

'Wait and see,' I said.

She gave me a dry look but no answer because some passengers came by with questions, and I went forward into the dome car to see how firmly Julius Apollo would appear to be seated, wondering whether it would be safe to try to look inside his briefcase or whether I should most stringently obey the command not to risk being arrested. If he hadn't hoped I would look, the Brigadier wouldn't have relayed the number. But if I looked and got caught looking, it would blow the whole operation.

Filmer was nowhere to be seen.

From the top of the staircase, I searched again through the rows of backs of heads under the dome. No thick black well-brushed thatch with a scattering of grey hairs. Bald, blond, tangled and trimmed, but no Filmer.

He wasn't in the downstairs lounge, and he wasn't in the bar where the poker school was as usual in progress, oblivious to the scenery. That left only the Lorrimores' car. . . . He had to be with Mercer, Bambi and Sheridan. Xanthe was with Rose and Cumber Young, watching the approach of the distant white peaks under a cloudless sky.

I walked irresolutely back towards Filmer's bedroom, wondering whether the disinclination I felt to enter it was merely prudence or otherwise plain fear, and being afraid it was the latter.

I would have to do it, I thought, because if I didn't I'd spend too much of my life regretting it. A permanent D minus in the balance sheet. By the time I left the dining room and started along the corridor past the kitchen, I was already feeling breathless, already conscious of my heart, and it was not in any way good for self-confidence. With a dry mouth I crossed the chilly shifting join between cars, opening and closing the doors, every step bringing me nearer to the risky commitment.

Filmer's was the first room in the sleeping car beyond the kitchen. I rounded the corner into the corridor with the utmost reluctance and was just about to put my hand to the door handle when the sleeping-car attendant, dressed exactly as I was, came out of his roomette at the other end of the car, saw me, waved and started walking towards me. With craven relief I went slowly towards him, and he said, 'Hi,' and how was I doing.

He was the familiar one who'd told me about Filmer's private breakfast, who'd shown me how to fold and unfold the armchairs and bunks, the one who looked after both the car we were in and the three bedrooms, Daffodil's among them, in the dome car. He had all afternoon and nothing to do and was friendly and wanted to talk, and he made it impossible for me to shed him and get back to my nefarious business.

He talked about Daffodil and the mess she had made of her bedroom.

Mess?

'If you ask me,' he said, nodding, 'she'd had a bottle of vodka in her suitcase. . . . There was broken glass all over the place. Broken vodka bottle. And the mirror over the washbasin. In splinters. All over the place. I'd guess she threw the vodka bottle at the mirror and they both broke.'

'A bore for you to have to clear that up,' I said.

He seemed surprised. 'I didn't clear it. It's still like that. George can take a look at it.' He shrugged. 'I don't know if the company will charge her for it. Shouldn't be surprised.'

He looked over my shoulder at someone coming into the car from the dining car.

'Afternoon, sir,' he said.

There was no reply from behind me. I turned my head and saw Filmer's back view going into his bedroom.

Dear God, I thought in horror: I would have been in there with his briefcase open, reading his papers. I felt almost sick.

I sensed more than saw Filmer come out of his bedroom again and walk towards us.

'Can I help you, sir?' the sleeping-car attendant said, going past me, towards him.

'Yes. What do we do about our bags at Lake Louise?'

'Leave it to me, sir. We're collecting everyone's cases and transporting them to the Chateau. They'll be delivered to your room in the Chateau, sir.'

'Good,' Filmer said, and went back into his lair, closing the door. Beyond the merest flicker of a glance at about waist level, he hadn't looked at me at all.

'We did the same with the bags at Winnipeg,' the sleeping-car attendant said to me resignedly. 'You'd think they'd learn.'

'Perhaps they will by Vancouver.'

'Yeah.'

I left him after a while and went and sat in my own roomette and did some deep breathing and thanked every guardian angel in the firmament for my deliverance, and in particular the angel in the sleeping-car attendant's yellow waistcoat.

Outside the window, the promise of the mountains became an embrace, rocky hillsides covered with tall narrow pines crowding down to the railway line winding through the valley of the Bow River. There were thick untidy collections of twigs sitting like Ascot hats on the top of a good many telegraph poles, which looked quite extraordinary; one of the passengers had said the hats were osprey nests, and that the poles were made with platforms on especially to accommodate them. Brave birds, I thought, laying their eggs near to the roaring trains. Hair-raising entertainment for the hatchlings.

Our speed had slowed from the brisk prairie rattle to a grunting uphill slither, the train taking two hours to cover the seventy miles from Calgary to Banff. When it stopped there, in the broad part of the valley, the snow-topped peaks were suddenly revealed as standing around in a towering, glistening, uneven ring, the quintessential mountains rising in bare majestic rocky grandeur from the thronging forested courtier foothills. I felt then, as most people do, the strong lure of high mysterious frozen places and, Filmer or not, I found myself smiling with pleasure, light-hearted to the bone.

It had been noticeably warm in Calgary, owing, it

was said, to the föhn winds blowing down from the mountains, but in Banff it was suitably cold. The engine huffed and puffed about and split the train in two, taking the racegoers and all the front part off to a siding and coming back to pick up just the owners' quarters; the three sleeping cars, the dining car, the dome car and the Lorrimores'. Abbreviated and much lighter, these remains of the train climbed at good speed for another three-quarters of an hour and triumphantly drew up beside the log-cabin station of Lake Louise.

With great cheerfulness the passengers disembarked, shivering even in their coats after the warmth of the cars, but full of expectation, Daffodil forgotten. They filed on to a waiting bus, while their suitcases were loaded into a separate truck. I clung to a fraction of hope that Filmer would leave his briefcase to be ferried in that fashion, but when he emerged from the train the case went with him, clutched firmly in his fist.

I told Nell I would walk up the mile or so from the station so as not to arrive until everyone had booked in and cleared the lobby. She said I could travel up anyway with the crew in their own bus, but I entrusted my bag to her keeping and in my grey regulation raincoat, buttoned to the neck, I enjoyed the fresh cold air and the deepening harvest gold of the late afternoon sunlight. When I reached the lobby of the grand Chateau, it was awash with polite young Japanese couples on honeymoon, not the Unwins, the Youngs and the Flokatis.

Nell was sprawled in a lobby armchair as if she would never be able to summon the energy to rise again, and I went and sat beside her before she'd realized I was there.

'Is everyone settled?' I asked.

She sighed deeply and made no attempt at moving. 'The suite I had reserved for the Lorrimores had been given to someone else half an hour before we got here. The people are not budging, the management are not apologizing, and Bambi is not pleased.'

'I can imagine.'

'On the other hand, we are sitting with our backs to one of the greatest views on earth.'

I twisted round and looked over the back of the chair, and saw, between thronging Japanese, black and white mountains, a turquoise blue lake, green pines and an advancing glacier, all looking like painted stage scenery, awesomely close and framed by the windows.

'Wow,' I said, impressed.

'It won't go away,' Nell said, after a while. 'It'll all still be there tomorrow.'

I flopped back into the chair. 'It's amazing.'

'It's why people have been coming here to stare for generations.'

'I expected altogether more snow,' I said.

'It'll be knee-deep by Christmas.'

'Do you have any time off here?' I asked.

305

She looked at me sideways. 'Five seconds now and then, but almost no privacy.'

I sighed lightly, having expected nothing else. She was the focus, the centre round which the tour revolved: the most visible person, her behaviour vivisected.

'Your room is in one of the wings,' she said, handing me a card with a number on it. 'You just have to sign in at the desk and they'll give you the key. Your bag should be up there already. Most of the actors are in that wing. None of the owners.'

'Are you?'

'No.'

She didn't say where her room was, and I didn't ask. 'Where will you eat?' she said doubtfully. 'I mean . . . will you sit with the actors in the dining room?'

I shook my head.

'But not with the owners . . .'

'It's a lonely old life,' I said.

She looked at me with sudden sharp attention, and I thought ruefully that I'd told her a good deal too much.

'Do you mean,' she asked slowly, 'that you do this all the time? Play a part? Not just on the train?'

'No,' I smiled. 'I work alone. That's all I meant.'

She almost shivered. 'Are you ever yourself?'

'Sundays and Mondays.'

'Alone?'

'Well . . . yes.'

Her eyes, steady and grey, looked only moderately

troubled. 'You don't seem unhappy,' she observed, 'being lonely.'

'Of course not. I choose it, mostly. But not when there's an alluring alternative hiding behind a clipboard.'

The armour lay on her lap at that moment, off duty. She smoothed a hand over it, trying not to laugh.

'Tomorrow,' she said, retreating into common sense, 'I'm escorting a bus load of passengers to a glacier, then to lunch in Banff, then up a mountain in cable cars.'

'And may it keep fine for you.'

'The Lorrimores have a separate chauffeur-driven car.'

'Has anyone else?'

'Not since Mrs Quentin's left.'

'Poor old Daffodil,' I said.

'Poor?' Nell exclaimed. 'Did you know she smashed the mirror in her room?'

'Yes, I heard. Is Mr Filmer going on the bus trip?'

'I don't know yet. He wanted to know if there's an exercise gym because he likes lifting weights. The bus is simply available for anyone who wants to go. I won't know everyone who'll be on it until we set off.'

I would have to watch the departure, I thought, and that could be difficult as I would be half familiar to all of them by now and could hardly stand around invisibly for very long.

'The Unwins have come down into the hall and are heading towards me,' Nell said, looking away from me.

'Right.'

I stood up without haste, took the card she'd given me to the desk, and signed the register. Behind me, I could hear the Unwins' Australian voices telling her they were going for a stroll by the shore and it was the best trip they'd ever taken. When I turned round, holding my own key, they were letting themselves out through the glass doors to the garden.

I paused again beside Nell who was now standing up. 'Maybe I'll see you,' I said.

'Maybe.'

I smiled at her eyes. 'If anything odd happens . . .'

She nodded. 'You're in room six sixty-two.'

'After Vancouver,' I said, 'what then?'

'After the races I'm booked straight back to Toronto on the red-eye special.'

'What's the red-eye special?'

'The overnight flight.'

'So soon?'

'How was I to know I wouldn't want to?'

'That'll do fine,' I said, 'for now.'

'Don't get ideas,' Nell said sedately, 'above your lowly station.'

She moved away with a mischievous glint and I went contentedly up to the sixth floor in the wing where there were no owners, and found that the room allocated to me was near the end of the passage and next door to Zak's.

His door was wide open with Donna and Pierre standing half in, half out.

'Come on in,' Donna said, seeing me. 'We're just walking through tonight's scene.'

'And we've a hell of a crisis on our hands,' Pierre said. 'We need all the input we can get.'

'But Zak might not . . .' I began.

He came to the door himself. 'Zak is taking suggestions from chimpanzees,' he said.

'OK. I'll just take off my coat.' I pointed. 'I'm in the room next along.'

I went into my room which proved to have the same sweeping view of the mountains, the lake, the trees, and the glacier, and it was if anything more spectacular than in the lobby from being higher up. I took off the raincoat and the uniform it had hidden, put on a track-suit and trainers, and returned to Zak's fray.

The crisis was the absence of an actor who was supposed to have arrived but had sent apologies instead.

'Apologies!' Zak fumed. 'He broke his goddam arm this morning and he's not coming. I ask you! Is a broken arm any sort of excuse?'

The others, the whole troupe, were inclined to think not.

'He was supposed to be Angelica's husband,' Zak said.

'What about Steve?' I asked.

'He was her lover, and her business partner. They were both killed by Giles because they had just found out he had embezzled all the capital and the bloodstock business was bankrupt. Now Angelica's husband comes on the scene to ask where her money is, as she hasn't changed her will and he inherits. He decided to investigate her death himself because he doesn't think either the Mounties or I have done a good enough job. And now he isn't even *here*.'

'Well,' I said, 'why don't you discover that it is *Raoul* who is really Angelica's husband and who stands to inherit, which gives him a lot of motive as he doesn't know yet that Giles has embezzled the money, does he? No one does. And Raoul is only free to marry Donna because Angelica is dead, which can give the Bricknells hysterics. And how about if Raoul says the Bricknells themselves have been doping their horses, not Raoul, but they deny it and are very pleased that he should be judged guilty of everything now they know he can't marry their daughter because he is probably a murderer and will go to jail? And how about if it was the Bricknells' horse that was really supposed to be kidnapped, but by Giles, as you can later discover, so that he could sell it and gain enough to skip the country once he got safely to Vancouver?'

They opened their mouths.

'I don't know that it actually makes sense,' Zak said eventually.

'Never mind, I don't suppose they'll notice.'

'You cynical son-of-a . . .'

'I don't see why not,' Donna said. 'And I can have a nice weepy scene with Pierre.'

'Why?' Zak said.

'I like doing them.'

They all fell about, and in a while walked through dramatic revelations (received by Zak from Outside Sources) of Raoul's marriage to Angelica five years earlier, which neither had acknowledged at Toronto station because, Raoul said unconvincingly, they were both shocked to find the other there, as he wanted to meld with Donna as she with Steve.

They all went away presently to get into their character clothes, and from Zak, very much later, I heard that the whole thing, played at the tops of their voices, had been a galvanic riot. He came to my door with a bottle in each hand, Scotch for him, red wine for me, and sank exhaustedly into an armchair with an air of having nobly borne the weight of the world on his shoulders and bravely survived.

'Did you have any dinner?' he said, yawning. 'Didn't see you.'

'I had some sent up.'

He looked at the television programme with which I'd passed the time.

'Rotten reception in these mountains,' he said. 'Look at that idiot.' He stared at the screen. 'Couldn't act his way out of a paper bag.'

We drank companionably and I asked if the party were all generally happy without Daffodil Quentin.

'The dear in the Mont Blanc curls?' he said. 'Oh, sure. They were all in a great mood. That man who used to be with her all the time was dripping charm all over Bambi Lorrimore and that nutter of a son of hers didn't open his mouth once. Those Australians are still in the clouds . . .'

He described the reactions of some of the others to the evening's scene and then said he would rely on me for another scintillating bit of scrambled plot for the next night. Not to mention, he added, a denouement and finale for the night after, our last on the train. The mystery had to be solved then before a gala dinner of epic proportions comprising five courses produced by Angus by sleight of hand.

'But I only said it all off the top of my head,' I said.

'The top of your head will do us all fine.' He yawned. 'Tell you the truth, we need a fresh mind.'

'Well . . . all right.'

'So how much do I pay you?'

I was surprised. 'I don't want money.'

'Don't be silly.'

'Um,' I said. 'I do earn more than Tommy.'

He looked at me over his whisky glass. 'You don't really surprise me.'

'So thanks a lot,' I said, meaning it, 'but no thanks.'

He nodded and left it: the offer honourably made, realistically declined. Anything he would have paid me would have come directly out of his own pocket: impossible to accept.

'Oh!' he said, clearly hit by a shaft of memory, 'Nell asked me to give you this.' He dug into a pocket and produced a sealed envelope which he handed over. It said 'Nell Richmond' on the outside, and 'Photographs, do not bend.'

'Thanks,' I said, relieved. 'I was beginning to think it hadn't got here.'

I opened the envelope and found three identical prints inside, but no letter. The pictures were clear, sharp and in black and white owing to the fast high-definition film I habitually used in the binoculars-camera. The subject, taken from above, was looking upwards and to one side to a point somewhere below the lens, so that one couldn't see his eyes clearly; but the sharply jutting cheekbones, the narrow nose, the deep eye sockets, the angled jawbone and the hairline retreating from the temples, all were identifiable at a glance. I handed one of the prints to Zak, and he looked at it curiously.

'Who is it?' he said.

'That's the point. Who is he? Have you seen him on the train?'

He looked again at the picture which showed, below the head, the shoulders and neck, with the sheepskin collar of the padded jacket over a sweater of some sort and a checked shirt unbuttoned at the top.

'A tough-looking man,' Zak said. 'Is he a militant union agitator?'

I was startled. 'Why do you say that?'

'Don't know. He has the look. All intensity and aggression. That's what I'd cast him as.'

'And is that how you'd also act a union agitator?'

'Sure.' He grinned. 'If he was described in the script as a troublemaker.' He shook his head. 'I haven't seen him on the train or anywhere else that I know of. Is he one of the racegoers, then?'

'I don't know for sure, but he was at Thunder Bay station and also at Winnipeg races.'

'The sleeping-car attendants will know.'

I nodded. 'I'll ask them.'

'What do you want him for?'

'Making trouble.'

He handed back the photograph with a smile. 'Type-cast,' he said, nodding.

He ambled off to bed, and early the next morning I telephoned Mrs Baudelaire who sounded as if she rose with the lark.

I asked her to tell Bill the photos had arrived safely.

'Oh, good,' she said blithely. 'Did you get my message with the numbers?'

'Yes, I did, thank you very much.'

'Val called with them from London, sounding very pleased. He said he wasn't having so much success with whatever it was that Sheridan Lorrimore did at Cambridge. No one's talking. He thinks the gag is cash for the new library being built at Sheridan's old college. How immoral can academics get? And Bill said to tell you that they went round to the Winnipeg barns with that photo, but no one knew who the man was, except that he did go there asking for Lenny Higgs. Bill says they will ask all the Ontario racing people they can reach and maybe print it in the racing papers coast to coast.'

'Great.'

'Bill wants to know what name you're using on the train.'

I hesitated, which she picked up at once with audible hurt. 'Don't you trust us?'

'Of course I do. But I don't trust everyone on the train.'

'Oh, I see.'

'You were right to send the message to Nell.'

'Good, then.'

'Are you well?' I asked.

The line said, 'Have a nice day, young man,' and went dead.

I listened to her silence with regret. I should have known better. I did know better, but it seemed discourteous never to ask.

With her much in mind I dressed for outdoors, hopped down the fire stairs and found an inconspicuous way out so as not to come face to face with any passengers who were en route to breakfast. In my woolly hat, well pulled down, and my navy zipped jacket, I found a good vantage point for watching the front door, then wandered round a bit and returned to the watching point a little before bus-boarding time for the joy-trip to Banff. Under the jacket I had slung the binoculars, just in case I could get nowhere near, but in fact, from leaning against the boot of an empty, parked, locked car where I hoped I looked as if I was waiting for the driver to return, I had a close enough view not to need them.

A large ultra-modern bus with tinted windows rolled in and stationed itself obligingly so that I could see who walked from the hotel to board it, and very soon after, when the driver had been into the hotel to report his arrival, Nell appeared in a warm jacket, trousers and boots and shepherded her flock with smiles into its depths. Most of the passengers were going sightseeing, it seemed, but not all.

Filmer didn't come out. I willed him to: to appear without his briefcase and roll away for hours: to give me a chance of thinking of some way to get into his room in safety. Willing didn't work. Julius Apollo didn't seem to want to walk on a glacier or dangle in a cable car, and stayed resolutely indoors.

Mercer, Bambi and Sheridan came out of the hotel together, hardly looking a light-hearted little family, and inserted themselves into a large waiting chauffeur-driven car which carried them off immediately.

No Xanthe. No Xanthe on the bus either. Rose and

Cumber Young had boarded without her. Xanthe, I surmised, was back in the sulks.

Nell, making a note on her clipboard and looking at her watch, decided there were no more customers for the bus. She stepped inside it and closed the door and I watched it roll away.

CHAPTER FIFTEEN

I walked about on foot in the mountains thinking of the gifts that had been given me.

Lenny Higgs. The combinations of the locks of the briefcase. Nell's friendship. Mrs Baudelaire. The chance to invent Zak's scripts.

It was the last which chiefly filled my mind as I walked round the path which circled the little lake; and the plans I began forming for the script had a lot to do with the end of my conversation with Bill Baudelaire, which had been disturbing.

After he'd agreed to arrange a replacement groom for Laurentide Ice, he said he'd tried to talk to Mercer Lorrimore at Assiniboia Downs but hadn't had much success.

'Talk about what?' I asked.

'About our quarry. I was shocked to find how friendly he had become with the Lorrimores. I tried to draw Mercer Lorrimore aside and remind him about the trial, but he was quite short with me. If a man was found innocent, he said, that was an end of it. He thinks good of everyone, it seems – which is saintly but not sensible.' Bill's voice went even deeper with disillusion. 'Our quarry can be overpoweringly pleasant, you know, if he puts his mind to it, and he had certainly been doing that. He had poor Daffodil Quentin practically eating out of his hand, too, and I wonder what she thinks of him now.'

I could hear the echo of his voice in the mountains. 'More saintly than sensible.' Mercer was a man who saw good where no good existed. Who longed for goodness in his son, and would pay for ever because it couldn't be achieved.

The path round the lake wound up hill and down, sometimes through close-thronging pines, sometimes with sudden breath-stopping views of the silent giants towering above, sometimes with clear vistas of the deep turquoise water below in its perfect bowl. It had rained during the night so that the whole scene in the morning sunshine looked washed and glittering; and the rain had fallen as snow on the mountaintops and the glacier which now appeared whiter, cleaner and nearer than the day before.

The air was cold, descending perceptibly like a tide from the frozen peaks, but the sun, at its autumn highest in the sky, still kept enough warmth to make walking a pleasure, and when I came to a place where a bench had been placed before a stunning panorama of lake, the Chateau and the mountain behind it, it was warm enough also to pause and sit down. I brushed some raindrops off the seat and slouched on the bench, hands in pockets, gazed vaguely on the picture-postcard spectacle, mind in second gear on Filmer.

I could see figures walking about by the shore in the Chateau garden, and thought without hurry of perhaps bringing out the binoculars to see if any of them was Julius Apollo. Not that it would have been of much help, I supposed, if he'd been there. He wouldn't be doing anything usefully criminal under the gaze of the Chateau's serried ranks of windows.

Someone with quiet footsteps came along the path from the shelter of the trees and stopped, looking down at the lake. Someone female.

I glanced at her incuriously, seeing a backview of jeans, blue parka, white trainers and a white woollen hat with two scarlet pompoms: and then she turned round, and I saw that it was Xanthe Lorrimore.

She looked disappointed to find the bench already occupied.

'Do you mind if I sit here?' she said. 'It's a long walk. My legs are tired.'

'No, of course not.' I stood up and brushed the raindrops off the rest of the bench, making a drier space for her.

'Thanks.' She flopped down in adolescent gawkiness and I took my own place again, with a couple of feet between us.

She frowned. 'Haven't I seen you before?' she asked. 'Are you on the train?'

'Yes, miss,' I said, knowing that there was no point in denying it, as she would see me again and more clearly in the dining room. 'I'm one of the crew.'

'Oh.' She began as if automatically to get to her feet, and then, after a moment, decided against it out of tiredness, and relaxed. 'Are you,' she said slowly, keeping her distance, 'one of the waiters?'

'Yes, Miss Lorrimore.'

'The one who told me I had to pay for a Coke?'

'Yes, I'm sorry.'

She shrugged and looked down at the lake. 'I suppose,' she said in a disgruntled voice, 'all this is pretty special, but what I really feel is *bored*.'

She had thick almost straight chestnut hair which curved at the ends over her shoulders, and she had clear fine skin and marvellous eyebrows. She was going to be beautiful, I thought, with maturity, unless she let the sulky cast of her mouth spoil not just her face but her life.

'I sometimes wish I was poor like you,' she said. 'It would make everything simple.' She glanced at me. 'I suppose you think I'm crazy to say that.' She paused. 'My mother would say I shouldn't be talking to you anyway.'

I moved as if to stand up. 'I'll go away, if you like,' I said politely.

'No, don't.' She was unexpectedly vehement and surprised even herself. 'I mean ... there's no one else to talk to. I mean ... well.'

'I do understand,' I said.

'Do you?' She was embarrassed. 'I was going to go on the bus, really. My parents think I'm on the bus. I was going with Rose ... Mrs Young ... and Mr Young. But he ...' She almost stopped, but the childish urge in her to talk was again running strong, sweeping away discretion. 'He's never as nice to me as she is. I think he's tired of me. Cumber, isn't that a stupid name? It's Cumberland, really. That's somewhere in England where his parents went on their honeymoon, Rose says. Albert Cumberland Young, that's what his name is. Rose started calling him Cumber when they met because she thought it sounded cosier, but he isn't cosy at all, you know, he's stiff and stern.' She broke off and looked down towards the Chateau. 'Why do all those Japanese go on their honeymoons together?'

'I don't know,' I said.

'Perhaps they'll all call their children Lake Louise.'

'They could do worse.'

'What's your name?' she asked.

'Tommy, Miss Lorrimore.'

She made no comment. She was only half easy in my company, too conscious of my job. But above all, she wanted to talk.

'You know my brother, Sheridan?' she said.

I nodded.

'The trouble with Sheridan is that we're too rich. He thinks he's better than everyone else because he's richer.' She paused. 'What do you think of that?' It

322

was part a challenge, part a desperate question, and I answered her from my own heart.

'I think it's very difficult to be very rich very young.'

'Do you really?' She was surprised. 'It's what everyone wants to be.'

'If you can have everything, you forget what it's like to need. And if you're given everything, you never learn to save.'

She brushed that aside. 'There's no point in saving. My grandmother left me millions. And Sheridan too. I suppose you think that's awful. He thinks he deserves it. He thinks he can do anything he likes because he's rich.'

'You could give it away,' I said, 'if you think it's awful.'

'Would you?'

I said regretfully, 'No.'

'There you are, then.'

'I'd give some of it away.'

'I've got trustees and they won't let me.'

I smiled faintly. I'd had Clement Cornborough. Trustees, he'd told me once austerely, were there to preserve and increase fortunes, not to allow them to be squandered, and no, he wouldn't allow a fifteen-year-old boy to fund a farm for pensioned-off racehorses.

'Why do you think it's difficult to be rich?' she demanded. 'It's easy.'

I said neutrally, 'You said just now that if you were poor, life would be simple.'

'I suppose I did. I suppose I didn't mean it. Or not really. I don't know if I meant it. Why is it difficult to be rich?'

'Too much temptation. Too many available corruptions.'

'Do you mean drugs?'

'Anything. Too many pairs of shoes. Self-importance.'

She put her feet up on the bench and hugged her knees, looking at me over the top. 'No one will believe this conversation.' She paused. 'Do you wish you were rich?'

It was an unanswerable question. I said truthfully in evasion, 'I wouldn't like to be starving.'

'My father says,' she announced, 'that one's not better because one's richer, but richer because one's better.'

'Neat.'

'He always says things like that. I don't understand them sometimes.'

'Your brother Sheridan,' I said cautiously, 'doesn't seem to be happy.'

'Happy!' She was scornful. 'He's never happy. I've hardly seen him happy in his whole life. Except that he does laugh at people sometimes.' She was doubtful. 'I suppose if he laughs, he must be happy. Only he despises them, that's why he laughs. I wish I *liked* Sheridan. I wish I had a terrific brother who would look after me and take me places. That would be fun.

Only it wouldn't be with Sheridan, of course, because it would end in trouble. He's been terrible on this trip. Much worse than usual. I mean, he's embarrassing.' She frowned, disliking her thoughts.

'Someone said,' I said without any of my deep curiosity showing, 'that he had a bit of trouble in England.'

'Bit of trouble! I shouldn't tell you, but he ought to be in jail, only they didn't press charges. I think my father bought them off . . . and anyway, that's why Sheridan does what my parents say, right now, because they threatened to let him be prosecuted if he as much as squeaks.'

'Could he still be prosecuted?' I asked without emphasis.

'What's a statute of limitations?'

'A time limit,' I said, 'after which one cannot be had up for a particular bit of law-breaking.'

'In England?'

'Yes.'

'You're English, aren't you?' she asked.

'Yes.'

'He said, "Hold your breath, the statute of limitations is out of sight." '

'Who said?'

'An attorney, I think. What did he mean? Did he mean Sheridan is . . . is . . .'

'Vulnerable?'

She nodded. ' . . . for ever?'

'Maybe for a long time.'

325

'Twenty years?' An unimaginable time, her voice said.

'It would have to have been bad.'

'I don't know what he did,' she said despairingly. 'I only know it's ruined this summer. Absolutely ruined it. And I'm supposed to be in school right now, only they made me come on this train because they wouldn't leave me in the house alone. Well, not alone, but alone except for the servants. And that's because my cousin Susan Lorrimore, back in the summer, she's seventeen, she ran off with their chauffeur's son and they got married and there was an *earthquake* in the family. And I can see why she did, they kept leaving her alone in that huge house and going to Europe and she was bored out of her skull and, anyway, it seems their chauffeur's son is all brains and cute, too, and she sent me a card saying she didn't regret a thing. My mother is scared to death that I'll run off with some . . .'

She stopped abruptly, looked at me a little wildly and sprang to her feet.

'I forgot,' she said. 'I sort of forgot you are . . .'

'It's all right,' I said, standing also. 'Really all right.'

'I guess I talk too much.' She was worried and unsure. 'You won't . . .'

'No. Not a word.'

'Cumber told me I ought to mind my tongue,' she said resentfully. 'He doesn't know what it's like living in a mausoleum with everyone glowering at each other and Daddy trying to smile.' She swallowed. 'What would you do,' she demanded, 'if you were me?'

'Make your father laugh.'

She was puzzled. 'Do you mean ... make him happy?'

'He needs your love,' I said. I gestured to the path back to the Chateau. 'If you'd like to go on first, I'll follow after.'

'Come with me,' she said.

'No. Better not.'

In an emotional muddle that I hadn't much helped, she tentatively set off, looking back twice until a bend in the path took her out of sight, and I sat down again on the bench, although growing cold now, and thought about what she'd said, and felt grateful, as ever and always, for Aunt Viv.

There wasn't much wrong with Xanthe, I thought. Lonely, worried, only half understanding the adult world, needing reassurance, she longed primarily for exactly what Mercer himself wanted, a friendly united family. She hadn't thought of affronting her parents by cuddling up to a waiter; very much the reverse. She hadn't tried to put me into a difficult position: had been without guile or tricks. I wouldn't have minded having a younger sister like her that I could take places for her to have fun. I hoped she would learn to live in peace with her money, and thought that a month or so of serving other people in a good crew like Emil, Oliver and Cathy would be the best education she could get.

After a while I scanned the whole Chateau and its gardens with the binoculars but I couldn't see Filmer, which wasn't really surprising, and in the end I set off again to walk, and detoured up on to the foot of the glacier, trudging on the cracked, crunchy, grey-brown-green fringe of the frozen river.

Laurentide Ice, one of the passengers had knowledgeably said early on, was the name given to one of the last great polar ice sheets to cover most of Canada twenty thousand years before. Daffodil, nodding, had said her husband had named the horse because he was interested in prehistory, and she was going to call her next horse Cordilleran Ice, the sheet that had covered the Rockies. Her husband would have been pleased, she said. I could be standing at that moment on prehistoric Cordilleran ice perhaps, I thought, but if glaciers moved faster than history, perhaps not. Anyway, it gave a certain perspective to the concerns of Julius Apollo.

Back at the Chateau, I went upstairs and drafted a new scene for the script, and I'd barely finished when Zak came knocking to enquire for it. We went into his room where the cast had already gathered for the rehearsal, and I looked round at their seven faces and asked if we still had the services of begging Ben, who was missing from the room. No, we didn't, Zak said. He had gone back to Toronto. Did it matter?

'No, not really. He might have been useful as a messenger, but I expect you can pretend a messenger.'

They nodded.

'Right,' Zak said, looking at his watch. 'We're on stage in two and a half hours. What do we do?'

'First,' I said, 'Raoul starts a row with Pierre. Raoul is furious to have been discovered to be Angelica's husband, and he says he positively knows Pierre owes thousands in gambling debts which he can't pay, and he knows who he owes it to, and he says that that man is known to beat people up who don't pay.'

Raoul and Pierre nodded. 'I'll put in some detail,' Raoul said. 'I'll say the debts are from illegal racing bets, and I've been told because they were on the Bricknells' horses, OK?'

'OK?' Zak said to me.

'Yes, OK. Then Raoul taunts Pierre that his only chance of getting the money is to marry Donna, and Walter Bricknell says that if Donna's so stupid as to marry Pierre, he will not give her a penny. He will in no circumstances pay Pierre's debts.'

They all nodded.

'At that point, Mavis Bricknell comes screaming into the cocktail room saying that all her beautiful jewels have been stolen.'

They all literally sat up. Mavis laughed and clapped her hands. 'Who's stolen them?' she said.

'All in good time,' I smiled. 'Raoul accuses Pierre, Pierre accuses Raoul, and they begin to shove each other around, letting all their mutual hatred hang out. Finally Zak steps in, breaks it up, and says they will all go and search both Pierre's room and Raoul's room for the jewels. Zak, Raoul, Pierre and Mavis go off.'

They nodded.

'That leaves,' I said. 'Donna, Walter Bricknell and Giles in the cocktail room. Donna and Walter have another argument about Pierre, Donna stifles a few tears and then Giles comes out of the audience to support Donna and say she's been having a bad experience, and he thinks it's time for a little good feeling all round.'

Giles said, 'OK, good. Here we go.'

'Then,' I said, 'Zak and the others return. They haven't found the jewels. Giles begins to comfort Mavis as well. Mavis says she lived for her collection, she loved every piece. She's distraught. She goes on a bit.'

'Lovely,' Mavis said.

'Walter,' I went on, 'says he can't see any point in jewellery. His jewellery is his horses. He lives for his horses. He says extravagantly that if he couldn't go racing to watch his horses, he'd rather die. He'd kill himself if he couldn't have horses.'

Walter frowned but eagerly nodded. He hadn't had much of a part so far: it would give him a big scene of his own, even if one difficult to make convincing.

'Walter then says Raoul is ruining his pleasure in his horses, and ruining the journey for everyone, and he gives him the formal sack as his trainer. Raoul protests, and says he hasn't deserved to be fired. Walter says Raoul is probably a murderer and a jewel thief and has been cheating him with his horses. Raoul in a rage tries to attack Walter. Zak hauls him off. Zak tells everyone to cool down. He says he will organize a search of everyone's bedrooms to see if the jewels can be found, and he will consult with the hotel's detective and call in the police if necessary. Everyone looks as if they don't want the police. End of scene.'

I waited for their adverse comments and altering suggestions, but there were very few. I handed my outline to Zak who went over it again bit by bit with the actors concerned, and they all started murmuring, making up their own words.

'And what happens tomorrow?' Zak asked finally. 'How do we sort it all out?'

'I haven't written it down yet,' I said.

'But you do have it in mind? Could you write it this evening?'

I nodded twice.

'Right,' he said. 'We'd better all meet here tomorrow after breakfast. We'll have to do a thorough walk through, maybe two or even three, to make sure we get it all right. Tie up the loose ends, that sort of thing. And don't forget, everybody, tomorrow we'll be back in the dining car. Not so much room for fighting and so on, so make it full of action tonight.'

'Tomorrow Pierre gets shot,' I said.

'Oh boy, oh boy,' Pierre said.

'But not fatally. You can go on talking.'

'Better and better.'

'But you'll need some blood.'

'Great,' Pierre said. 'How much?'

'Well . . .' I laughed. 'I'll let you decide where the bullet goes, and how much gore you think the passengers can stand, but you'd better be going to live, at the end of it.'

They wanted to know what else I had in store, but I wouldn't tell them: I said they might give the future away by accident if they knew, and they protested they were too professional to do that. But I didn't altogether trust their improvising tongues, and they shrugged and gave way with fair grace.

I watched the walk through which seemed to go pretty well, but it was nothing, Zak assured me afterwards, to the actual live performance among the cocktails.

He came back to my room at eleven, as on the previous night, drinking well-earned whisky exhaustedly.

'Those two, Raoul and Pierre, they really gave it a go,' he said. 'They both learned stage fighting and stunts at drama school, you know. They'd worked out the fight beforehand, and it was a humdinger. All over the place. It was a shame to break it up. Half the passengers spilled their cocktails with Raoul and Pierre rolling and slogging on the floor near their feet and we had to give everyone free refills.' He laughed. 'Dear Mavis put on the grand tragedy for reporting the theft of the jewels and poured on some tremendous pathos later over losing all her happy memories of the gifts that were bound up in them. Had half the audience in tears. Marvellous. Then Walter did his thing quite well considering he complained to me that no one in their right mind would kill themselves because they couldn't go racing. And afterwards, would you believe it, one of the passengers asked me where we got the idea from, about someone killing themselves because they couldn't go racing.'

'What did you say?' I asked with a jerk of anxiety.

'I said I picked it out of the air.' He watched me relax a shade and asked, 'Where *did* you get it from?'

'I knew of someone not long ago who did just that.' Thirteen days ago . . . a lifetime.

'Crazy.'

'Mm.' I paused. 'Who asked you?'

'Can't remember.' He thought. 'It might have been Mr Young.'

Indeed it might, I thought. Ezra Gideon had been his friend.

It might have been Filmer. Ezra Gideon had been his victim.

'Are you sure?' I asked.

He thought some more. 'Yep, Mr Young. He was sitting with that sweet wife of his, and he got up and came across the room to ask.'

I drank some wine and said conversationally, 'Did anyone else react?'

Zak's attention, never far below the surface, came to an intuitive point.

'Do I detect,' he said, 'a hint of Hamlet?'

'How do you mean?' I asked, although I knew exactly what he meant.

'The play's the thing, wherein I'll catch the conscience of the King? Right? Is that what you were up to?'

'In a mild way.'

'And tomorrow?'

'Tomorrow too,' I agreed.

He said broodingly, 'You're not going to get any of us into trouble, are you? Not sued for slander, or anything?'

'I promise not.'

'Perhaps I shouldn't let you write tomorrow's script.'

'You must do what you think best.' I picked the finished script off the table beside me and stretched forward to hand it to him. 'Read it first, then decide.'

'OK.'

He put his glass down and began reading. He read to the end and finally raised a smiling face.

'It's great,' he said. 'All my original ideas with yours on top.'

'Good.' I was much relieved that he liked it, and thought him generous.

'Where's the Hamlet bit?' he asked.

'In loving not wisely but too well.'

'That's Othello.'

'Sorry.'

He thought it over. 'It seems harmless enough to me, but . . .'

'All I want to do,' I said, 'is open a few specific eyes. Warn a couple of people about the path they're treading. I can't, you see, just walk up to them and say it, can I? They wouldn't take it from Tommy. They probably wouldn't take it from anybody. But if they see something acted . . . they can learn from it.'

'Like Hamlet's mother.'

'Yes.'

He sipped his whisky. 'Who do you want to warn about what?' he said.

'Better I don't tell you, then nothing's your fault.'

'What are you really on the train for?' he asked, frowning.

'You know what. To keep everyone happy and foil the wicked.'

'And this scene will help?'

'I hope so.'

'All right.' He made up his mind. 'I don't object to foiling the wicked. We'll give it our best shot.' He grinned suddenly. 'The others will love the Hamlet angle.'

I was alarmed. 'No . . . please don't tell them.'

'Why ever not?'

'I want the passengers to think that any similarity of the plot to their own lives is purely coincidental. I don't want the actors telling them afterwards that it was all deliberate.'

He smiled twistedly. 'Are we back to slander?'

'No. There's no risk of that. It's just . . . I don't want them identifying me as the one who knows so much about them. If anyone asks the actors where the plot came from, I'd far rather they said it was you.'

'And dump me in the shit?' He was good-humoured, however.

'No one could have suspicions about you.' I smiled faintly. 'Apart from foiling villainy, success for me means hiding behind Tommy to the end and getting off the train unexposed.'

'Are you some sort of spy?'

'A security guard, that's all.'

'Can I put you in my next plot? In my next train mystery?'

'Be my guest.'

He laughed, yawned, put down his glass and stood up.

'Well, pal, whoever you are,' he said, 'it's been an education knowing you.'

Nell telephoned to my room at seven in the morning. 'Are you awake?' she said.

'Wide.'

'It snowed again in the night. The mountains are white.'

'I can see them,' I said, 'from my bed.'

'Do you sleep with your curtains open?'

'Always. Do you?'

'Yes.'

'Are you dressed?' I asked.

'Yes, I am. What's that to do with anything?'

'With defences, even over the telephone.'

'I hate you.'

'One can't have everything.'

'Listen,' she said severely, smothering a laugh. 'Be sensible. I phoned to ask if you wanted to walk down again to the station this afternoon when we board the train, or go down on the crew bus?'

I reflected. 'On the bus, I should think.'

'OK. That bus goes from outside the staff annexe at three-thirty-five. Take your bag with you.'

'All right. Thanks.'

'The whole train, with the horses and racegoers and everything, comes up from Banff to arrive at Lake Louise station at four-fifteen. That gives the passengers plenty of time to board and go to their bedrooms again and begin to unpack comfortably before we leave Lake Louise on the dot of four-thirty-five. The regular Canadian comes along behind us as before and leaves Lake Louise at ten past five, so we have to make sure everyone is boarded early so that our train can leave right on time.'

'Understood.'

'I'm going to tell all this to the passengers at breakfast, and also that at five-thirty we're serving champagne and canapés to everyone in the dining car, and at six we'll have the solution to the mystery, and after that cocktails for those who want them, and then the gala banquet. Then the actors return for photos and post-mortems over cognac. It all sounds like hell.'

I laughed. 'It will all work beautifully.'

'I'm going into a nunnery after this.'

'There are better places.'

'Where, for instance?'

'Hawaii?'

There was a sudden silence on the line. Then she said, 'I have to be back at my desk . . .'

'We could take the desk too.'

She giggled. 'I'll find out about shipment.'

'Done, then?'

'No . . . I don't know . . . I'll let you know in Vancouver.'

'Vancouver,' I said, 'is tomorrow morning.'

'After the race, then.'

'And before the red-eye special.'

'Do you ever give up?'

'It depends,' I said, 'on the signals.'

CHAPTER SIXTEEN

Filmer clung closely to his briefcase during the transit from Chateau to train at Lake Louise, although he had allowed his larger suitcase to be brought down with everyone else's to be arranged side by side in a long line at the station, waiting to be lifted aboard by porters.

From among the bunch of crew members, Emil, Oliver, Cathy, Angus, Simone, the barman and the sleeping-car attendants, I watched Filmer and most of the passengers disembark from the bus and check that their bags were in the line-up. The Lorrimores, arriving separately with their chauffeur, brought their cases with them, the chauffeur stacking them in an aloof little group.

A freight train clanked by, seemingly endless. A hundred and two grain cars, Cathy said, counting. A whole lot of bread.

I thought about Mrs Baudelaire to whom I'd been talking just before leaving the Chateau.

'Bill said to tell you,' she said, 'that Lenny Higgs did turn to jelly and is being safely taken care of, and a new groom has been engaged for Laurentide Ice with the approval, by telephone, of his trainer. They told the trainer that Lenny Higgs had done a bunk. Bill has left Winnipeg and has come back to Toronto. He says he has been consulting with the Colonel as a matter of urgency, and they agree that Bill will see Mrs Daffodil Quentin as soon as possible. Does that all make sense?'

'Indeed it does,' I said fervently.

'Good, then.'

'Is Bill still going to Vancouver?' I asked.

'Oh, yes, I think so. Monday evening, I believe, ready for the race on Tuesday. He said he would be back here again on Wednesday. All these time changes can't be good for anybody.'

'Canada is so huge.'

'Five thousand five hundred and fourteen kilometres from side to side,' she said primly.

I laughed. 'Try me in miles.'

'You'll have to do your own sums, young man.'

I did them later, out of curiosity: three thousand four hundred and twenty-six miles, and a quarter.

She asked if I had any more questions, but I couldn't think of any, and I said I would talk to her again from Vancouver in the morning.

'Sleep well,' she said cheerfully.

'You too.'

'Yes.' There was reservation in her voice, and I realized that she probably never slept well herself.

'Sweet dreams, then,' I said.

'Much easier. Goodnight.'

She gave me no time, as usual, to answer.

The train hooted in the distance: one of the most haunting of seductive sounds to a wanderer. That, and the hollow breathy boom of departing ships. If I had any addiction, it was to the setting off, not the arrival.

Headlights bright in the ripening afternoon sunlight, the huge yellow-fronted engine slowed into the station with muted thunder, one of the engineers, as he passed us, looking down from his open window. The engineers were the only crew that hadn't come the whole way from Toronto, each stretch of track having its own specialists.

There being no sidings at Lake Louise, the abbreviated train that had brought us there had been returned to Banff for the two mountain days, with George Burley going with it, in charge. He returned now with the whole train, his cheerful round figure climbing down in the station and greeting the passengers like long-lost friends.

With a visible lifting of spirits and freshening enjoyment, the whole party returned upwards to their familiar quarters; the Lorrimores, a glum quartet stepping on to their private railed platform entrance at the very rear of everything, being the only sad note. Nell went along to speak to them, to try to cheer them up. Mercer stopped, answered, smiled: the others simply went on inside. Why bother with them, I thought. One would get no thanks. Yet one would always bother, somehow, for Mercer, the blind saint.

Filmer boarded through the open door at the end of his sleeping car and through his window I saw him moving about in his room. Hanging up jackets. Washing his hands. Ordinary things. What made one man good, I wondered, and another man bad: one man to seek to build, the other to frighten and destroy? The acid irony was that the bad might feel more satisfied and fulfilled than the good.

I walked along to the car where my roomette was, dumped my bag there and took off my raincoat to reveal the familiar livery beneath. Only one more night of Tommy. One dinner, one breakfast. Pity, I thought; I'd been getting quite fond of him.

George came swinging aboard as the train moved off in its quiet way, and he greeted me with a pleased chuckle.

'We're lucky to have heat on this train, eh?' he said.

'Why?' I asked. 'It's very warm.'

'They couldn't start the boiler.' He seemed to think it a great joke. 'You know why?'

I shook my head.

'No fuel.'

I looked blank. 'Well . . . they could surely fill up?'

'You bet your life,' he said. 'Only the tank had been filled two days ago, eh?, when we went down to Banff. Or was supposed to have been. So we had a look, and there were a few drips trickling from the bottom drain which is only opened for sluicing through the tank, which isn't done often, eh?' He looked at me expectantly, his eyes bright.

'Someone stole the fuel?'

He chuckled. 'Either stole it from the tank, or never loaded it in the first place, and opened the drain to be misleading.'

'Was there a lot of oil on the ground?' I asked.

'Not a bad detective, are you? Yes, there was.'

'What do you think, then?'

'I think they never loaded the right amount, probably just enough to get us a fair way out of Lake Louise, then they opened the drain a bit to persuade us the fuel had run away by accident along the track, eh? Only they got it wrong. Opened the drain too much.' The laugh vibrated in his throat. 'What a fuss, eh?, if the train went cold in the mountains! The horses would freeze. What a panic!'

'You don't seem too worried.'

'It didn't happen, did it?'

'No, I guess it didn't.'

'We would have filled the tank again at Revelstoke, anyway,' he said. 'It would have ruined this gala banquet of yours, eh? But no one would have died. Doubt if they'd even have got frostbite, not like they might in January. The air temperature up here will fall below zero after sunset, soon, but the track goes through the valleys, not up the peaks, eh? And there'd be no wind chill factor, inside the cars.'

'Very uncomfortable, though.'

'Very.' His eyes gleamed. 'I left them all buzzing around like a wasp's nest in Banff, trying to find out who did it.'

I wasn't as insouciant as he was. I said, 'Is there anything else that can go wrong with this train? Is there for instance any *water* in the boiler?'

'Never you mind,' he said comfortingly. 'We checked the water. The top tap ran. That tank's full, just as it should be. The boiler won't blow up.'

'What about the engine?'

'We checked every inch of everything, eh? But it was just some greedy ordinary crook stealing that oil.'

'Like the ordinary crook who unhitched the Lorrimores' car?'

He thought it over sceptically. 'I'll grant you that this particular train might attract psychos, as the publicity would be that much greater, and more pleasing to them, but there is no visible connection between the two things.' He chuckled. 'People will steal anything, not just oil. Someone stole eight of those blue leather chairs in the dining car, once. Drove up to the dining car while it was standing unused in the sidings at Mimico in Toronto, drove up in a van saying "Furniture Repairs" on the side, and simply loaded up eight good chairs, eh? Last that was ever seen of them.'

He turned away towards the paperwork spread out on his table, and I left him to go along to the dining car, but I'd taken only two paces when I remembered gaunt-face, and I fetched his photograph and went back to George.

'Who is he?' he asked, frowning slightly. 'Yes, I'd say he might be on the train. He was down in Banff, in the sidings . . .' He thought, trying to remember. 'This afternoon, eh?' he exclaimed suddenly. 'That's it. While they were joining up the train. See, the horses had come up from Calgary this morning as the first car of a freight train. They dropped the horse car in the sidings. Then our engine picked up the horse car and then the racegoers' cars . . .' He concentrated. 'This man, he was down on the ground, rapping on the horse-car door with a stick, and when the dragon-lady came to the door and asked what he wanted, he said he had a message for the groom looking after the grey horse, so the dragon-lady told him to wait and she came back with a groom, only he said it wasn't the right groom, and he, the groom, eh?, said the other groom had left in Calgary and he had taken over, and then your man in the photo walked off. I didn't see where he went to. I mean, it wasn't important.'

I sighed. 'Did the man look angry, or anything?'

'I didn't notice. I was there to ask Ms Brown if everything was in order in the horse car before we set off, and she said it was. She said all the grooms were in the horse car with their horses, looking after them, as they had been all day, and they would stay there until after we left. She looks after the horses well, eh?, and the grooms, too. Can't fault her, eh?'

'No.'

He held out the photograph for me to take back, but I told him to keep it, and asked diffidently if he would check with the racegoers' sleeping-car attendants, if he had time, to find out for sure whether or not gaunt-face had come all the way from Toronto among the passengers.

'What's he done? Anything yet?'

'Frightened a groom into leaving.'

He stared. 'Not much of a crime, eh?' His eyes laughed. 'He won't do much jail time for that.'

I had to agree with him. I left him to his enjoyment of human failures and went towards the dining car, passing as I did so the friendly sleeping-car attendant who was again resting himself in the corridor, watching the changing perspectives of the snowy giants.

'I don't see this usually,' he said in greeting. 'I don't usually come further west than Winnipeg. Grand, isn't it?'

I agreed. Indeed it was.

'What time do you bring the beds down?' I asked.

'Any time after the passengers have all gone along to the dining car. Half of them are in their rooms here, now, changing. I've just taken extra towels to two of them.'

'I'll give you a hand with the beds later, if you like.'

'Really?' He was surprised and pleased. 'That would be great.'

'If you do your dome-car rooms first,' I said, 'then

when you come back through the dining car, I'll follow you and we can do these.'

'You don't have to, you know.'

'Makes a nice change from waiting at table.'

'And your scene,' he said, smiling in understanding, 'what about that?'

'That comes later,' I promised him.

'All right, then. Thanks very much.'

'Pleasure,' I said, and swung along past Filmer's closed door, through the heavy doors of the cold and draughty join, into the heat of the corridor beside the kitchen, and finally to the little lobby between kitchen door and tables where Emil, Oliver and Cathy were busy unboxing the champagne flutes.

I picked up a cloth and began polishing. The other three smiled.

In the hissing heat of the kitchen, Angus and Simone were arguing, Angus having asked Simone to shell a bowlful of hard-boiled eggs which she refused to do, saying he must do it himself.

Emil raised amused eyebrows. 'She is getting crosser as time goes by. Angus is a genius and she doesn't like it.'

Angus, as usual seeming to have six hands all busy at once, proved to be making dozens of fresh canapés on baking trays ready for ten minutes in a scorching oven. Crab and Brie together in thin layers of pastry, he said of one batch, and chicken and tarragon in another, cheese and bacon in a third. Simone stood with her hands on her hips, a hoity-toity tilt to her chin. Angus had begun ignoring her completely, which was making things worse.

The passengers as usual came to the dining car well before the appointed hour, but seemed perfectly happy just to sit and wait. The theatrical entertainment outside the windows anyway claimed all eyes and tongues until the shadows grew long in the valleys and only the peaks were lit with slowly fading intensity, until they too were extinguished into darkness. Evening came swift and early in the mountains, twilight being a matter of a lingering lightness in the sky, night growing upwards from the earth.

A real shame, most of the passengers complained to Nell, that the train went through the best scenery in Canada in the dark. Someone in a newspaper, they were saying as I distributed the champagne glasses, had said that it was as if the French kept the lights off in the Louvre, in Paris. Nell said she was really sorry, she didn't write the timetables, and she hoped everyone had been able to see a mountain or two at Lake Louise, which everyone had, of course. Most had gone up one, Sulphur Mountain, to the windy summit, in four-seater glass containers on wires. Others had said no way, and stayed at the bottom. Filmer, sitting this time with the ultra-rich owners of Redi-Hot, was saying pleasantly that no, he hadn't been on the bus tour, he'd been content to take his exercise in the gym at Lake Louise.

Filmer had come into the dining room from the

dome-car end, not from his bedroom, and he arrived wearing a private smirk which sent uncomfortable shivers along my nerves. Any time Julius Apollo looked as pleased with himself as that, it was sure to mean trouble.

The Lorrimores arrived in a group and sat together at one table, the offspring both looking mutinous and the parents glum. Xanthe, it was clear, hadn't yet made Mercer laugh. Rose and Cumber Young were with the Upper Gumtree Unwins and the Flokati people were with the owners of Wordmaster. It was interesting, I thought, that the owners of the horses tended to be attracted to each other, much as if they belonged to a brotherhood which clung naturally together.

Perhaps Filmer had understood that. Perhaps it was why he had made such efforts to go on the train as an owner: because being an owner of one of the horses gave him standing, gave him credibility, gave him a power base. If that was what he intended, he had achieved it. Everyone on the train knew Mr Julius Filmer.

Emil popped the champagne corks. Angus whizzed his succulent hot appetizers from oven to serving trays, seeming to summon from nowhere the now peeled and sliced eggs topped with caviare and lemonskin twists on Melba toast circles. We set off from the kitchen in a small procession, Emil and I pouring the bubbles, Oliver and Cathy doing the skilful stuff with silver serving tongs, giving everyone little platefuls of the hors-d'oeuvre they preferred.

Nell was laughing at me silently. Well, she would. I kept a totally straight face while filling her glass and also that of Giles who was sitting beside her in the aisle seat, ready for action.

'Thank you,' Giles said in a bored voice when his glass was full.

'My pleasure, sir,' I said.

He nodded. Nell smothered her laughing mouth against her glass and the people sitting opposite her noticed nothing at all.

When I reached the Lorrimores, Xanthe was perceptibly anxious. I poured into Bambi's glass and said to Xanthe, 'For you, miss?'

She gave me a flicker of a glance. 'Can I have Coke?'

'Certainly, miss.'

I poured champagne for Mercer and for Sheridan, and went back to the kitchen for the Coke.

'You have to pay for it,' Xanthe said jerkily to her father when I returned.

'How much?' Mercer asked. I told him, and he paid. 'Thank you,' he said.

'A pleasure, sir.'

He looked abstracted, not his usual placatory self. Xanthe risked another semi-frightened glance at me and seemed to be greatly reassured when I didn't refer in any way to our encounter above the lake. The most I gave her was the faintest of deferential smiles, which even her mother couldn't have disapproved of, if she had seen it: but she, like Mercer, seemed more than usually preoccupied.

I went on to the next table and hoped that Filmer's smirk and Mercer's gloom were not connected, although I was afraid that they might be. The smirk had been followed into the dining room by the gloom.

When Angus's canapés had been devoured to the last melting morsel and the champagne glasses refilled, Zak arrived with a flourish for the long wrap-up scene. First of all, he said, he had to announce that a thorough search of the rooms in the Chateau had produced no sign of Mavis Bricknell's jewels.

Commiserations were expressed for Mavis, the passengers entering into the fantasy with zest. Mavis accepted them gratefully.

Raoul came bursting into the dining car, furious with Walter Bricknell who was looking upset enough already.

It was too much, Raoul loudly said. It was bad enough Walter firing him as his trainer when he had done nothing to deserve it, but now he had found out that Walter had sent a letter from the Chateau to the racing authorities saying his horse, Calculator, wouldn't be running in his, Walter's, name at Vancouver, and that Raoul wouldn't be credited as trainer.

'It's unfair,' he shouted. 'I've trained the horse to the minute for that race. I've won five races with

351

him for you. You're cheating me. You're damned ungrateful. I'm going to complain to the Jockey Club.'

Walter looked stony. Raoul had another go. Walter said he would do what he liked, Calculator was his. If he wanted to sell it ... or give it away ... that was entirely his own business and nobody else's.

'You said yesterday,' Raoul yelled, 'that if you didn't have horses, if you couldn't go racing, you'd kill yourself. So kill yourself. Is that what you're going to do?'

Everyone looked at Walter in shocked disbelief.

Zak invited Walter to explain. Walter said it was none of Zak's business. Everything on the train was his business, Zak said. 'Could we all please know,' he asked Walter, 'who the new owner of Calculator is going to be?'

No, no one could ask. Mavis, bewildered, did ask. Walter was rude to her, which no one liked. Walter realized that no one liked it, but said he couldn't help it, he was getting rid of Calculator, and since the horse was in his name only, not Mavis's, she couldn't do anything about it. Mavis began to cry.

Donna went to her mother's defence and verbally attacked her father.

'You be quiet,' he said angrily. 'You've done enough harm.'

Pierre put his arm round Donna's shoulders and told Walter not to talk to his daughter that way. He, Pierre, would borrow some money to pay his gambling debts, he said, and really work this time and save until it was paid off, and he would never let Donna take a penny from her father, and when he was out of debt he and Donna would get married and there was nothing Walter could do to stop them.

'Oh, Pierre,' Donna wailed, and hid her face against his chest. Pierre, in snow-white shirtsleeves, put both arms round her, stroked her hair and looked very manly, handsome and protective. The audience approved of him with applause.

'Oh, goody,' Cathy said from beside me. 'Isn't he cute?'

'He sure is.'

We were standing in the little lobby, watching from the shadows and, by a malign quirk of fate, all the faces I was most interested in were sitting with their backs to me. Filmer's neck, not far off, was rigid with tension, and Cumber Young, one table further along, had got compulsively to his feet when Raoul had told Walter to kill himself, and only slowly subsided, with Rose talking to him urgently. Mercer, just over midway along, sitting against the far right-hand side wall, had his head bowed, not watching the action. He couldn't help but hear, however. The actors were all courting laryngitis, making sure that those in the furthest corners weren't left out.

Mavis had a go at Walter, first angry, then pleading, then saying she might as well leave him, she obviously didn't count with him any more. She prepared to go.

Walter, stung beyond bearing, muttered something to her that stopped her dead.

'*What?*' she said.

Walter muttered again.

'He says he's being *blackmailed*,' Mavis said in a high voice. 'How can anyone blackmail someone into getting rid of a horse?'

Filmer, pinned against the left-hand wall by the Unwins in the aisle seats, sat as if with a rod up his backbone. Mercer turned his head to stare at Walter. Mercer had his back towards Filmer, and I wondered whether he'd sat that way round on purpose so as not to see his recent friend. He was sitting beside Sheridan and opposite Bambi. Xanthe sat opposite her brother, both in aisle seats. I could see both of the female faces, where I wanted to see the male. I would have done better, I supposed, to have watched from the far end, but on the other hand they might have seen me watching: watching them instead of the action.

Walter, under pressure, said loudly that yes, he was being blackmailed, and by the very nature of blackmail he couldn't say what about . . . he categorically refused to discuss it further. He had good and sufficient reasons and he was angry and upset enough about losing his horse without everyone attacking him.

And who was he losing it to? Zak asked. Because whoever's name turned up on the race card at Vancouver as the owner, he or she would be the blackmailer.

Heads nodded. Walter said it wasn't so. The black-mailer had just said he must give the horse away.

'Who to?' Zak asked insistently. 'Tell us. We'll soon know. We'll know at the races on Tuesday.'

Walter, defeated, said, 'I'm giving the horse to Giles.'

General consternation followed. Mavis objected. Giles was a very nice, comforting fellow, but they hardly knew him, she said.

Raoul said bitterly that Walter should have given *him* the horse. He'd worked so hard . . .

Giles said that Walter had asked him, Giles, to have the horse, and of course he'd said yes. After the race on Tuesday, he would decide Calculator's future.

Walter looked stony. Giles was being frightfully nice.

Donna suddenly detached herself from Pierre and said rather wildly, 'No, Daddy, I won't let you do it. I understand what's happening . . . I won't let it happen.'

Walter told her thunderously to shut up. Donna wouldn't be stopped. It was her fault that her father was being blackmailed and she wouldn't let him give his horse away.

'Be quiet,' Walter ordered.

'I stole Mother's jewels,' she said miserably to everyone. 'I stole them to pay Pierre's debts. They said he would be beaten up if he didn't pay. Those jewels were going to be mine anyway, one day, they're in Mother's will . . . so I was only stealing from myself really . . . but then, he guessed . . .'

'Who guessed?' Zak demanded.

355

'Giles,' she said. 'He saw me coming out of Mother's room. I suppose I looked scared . . . maybe guilty. I had her jewels in a tote bag. I suppose it was afterwards, when Mother came to say someone had stolen them, that he guessed. . . . He made me give them to him . . . he said he'd have me arrested otherwise, and my parents wouldn't like that . . .'

'Stop him!' Zak yelled peremptorily as Giles made a dash for the lobby, and Raoul, a big fellow, intercepted him and twisted his arm up behind his back. Giles displayed pain.

Zak invited Walter to talk.

Walter, distressed, said that Giles had threatened to prove publicly that Donna had stolen the jewels if Walter wouldn't give him the horse. Even if Walter refused to press charges against his daughter, Giles had said, everyone would know she was a thief. Walter confessed that Giles had said, 'What is one horse against your daughter's reputation?' Walter thought he'd had no choice.

Donna wept. Mavis wept. Half the audience wept.

Filmer was rigid. Also Mercer, Bambi and Sheridan; all unmoving in their seats.

'It wasn't sensible to love your daughter so much,' Raoul said. 'She stole the jewels. You shouldn't cover up for her. Look where it got you. Into the hands of a blackmailer, and losing the horse you love. And did you think it would stop there, with just one horse? You've got two more in my care, don't forget.'

'Stop it,' Mavis said, defending Walter now. 'He's a wonderful man to give up his dearest possession to save his daughter.'

'He's a fool,' Raoul said.

During this bit, Zak came to the lobby as if to receive a message and went back into the centre of the dining car opening an envelope and reading the contents.

He said the letter was from Ben, who had begged for money, did they remember? They remembered.

Ben, Zak said, had run away off the train because he was frightened, but he had left this letter to be opened after he'd gone. Zak read the letter portentously aloud.

'I know who killed Ricky. I know who threw him off the train. Ricky told me he knew who killed that lady, Angelica someone. Ricky saw the murderer with a lot of plastic rolled into a ball. He didn't know he was a murderer then, like. This man came up the train into the part where the grooms are and he was in the join part between two sleeping cars and he pushed the plastic out through one of the gaps, until it fell from the train, and then he saw Ricky looking at him. Ricky didn't think much of it until we were told about Angelica someone, and the plastic with her blood on, and then he was afraid, and told me. And then he was thrown off the train. I know who it was, I knew who must have did it, but I wasn't saying. I didn't want to end up dead beside the railway tracks. But now I'm safe out of here I'll tell you, and it's that good-looking one they was calling Giles on Toronto station. I saw him there too, same as Ricky. It was him.'

Zak stopped reading and Giles, struggling in Raoul's grip, shouted that it was rubbish. Lies. All made up.

Raoul showed signs of breaking Giles's arm on account of him having killed Angelica, who was his wife, even if they had separated.

How could a groom like Ben make up anything like this? Zak said, waving the note. He said it was time someone searched Giles's room on the train for the jewels, and for anything else incriminating.

'You've no right. You've no search warrant. And this man is breaking my arm.'

'You murdered his wife, what do you expect?' Zak said, 'and I don't need a search warrant. I'm chief of the railway detectives, don't forget. On trains, I investigate and search where I like.' He marched off past me and went swaying down the corridor, pausing down at the end of the kitchen wall where he'd left a sports bag full of props, and soon came marching back. The other actors, meanwhile, had been emoting in character over the disclosure of Giles as murderer as well as blackmailer. Zak took the sports bag, it seemed to me by accident, to the table across from the Lorrimores. The people sitting at the table cleared the glasses and empty plates into a stack and Zak, dumping the bag on the pink cloth, unfastened a few zips.

To no one's surprise, he produced the jewels. Mavis was reunited with them, with joy slightly dampened by knowing who had stolen them. Reproachful looks, and so on.

Zak then discovered a folder of papers.

'*A-HAH!*' he said.

Giles struggled, to no avail.

Zak said, 'Here we have the motive for Angelica's murder. Here's a letter to Giles from Steve, Angelica's lover and business partner, complaining accusingly that he has been checking up, and Giles, in his capacity of bloodstock agent, has not bought the horses that he says he has, that Angelica and Steve have given him the money for. Steve is saying that unless Giles comes up with a very good explanation he is going to the police.'

'Lies,' Giles shouted.

'It's all here.' Zak waved the letter, which everyone later inspected, along with Ben's note. They were accurately written: Zak's props were thorough. 'Giles embezzled Angelica and Steve's money,' he said, 'and when they threatened him with disgrace, he killed them. Then he killed the groom, who knew too much. Then he blackmailed Walter Bricknell, who was too fond of his daughter. This man Giles is beneath contempt. I will get the conductor of the train to arrange for him to be arrested and taken away in Revelstoke, where we stop in two hours.'

He walked towards the lobby again.

Giles, finally breaking free of Raoul, snatched a gun

that Zak was wearing in a holster on his hip and waved it about. Zak warned, 'Put it down. This gun is loaded.'

Giles shouted at Donna, 'It's all your fault, you shouldn't have confessed. You spoiled it all. And I'll spoil you.'

He pointed the gun at Donna. Pierre leapt in front of her to save her. Giles shot Pierre, who had, it transpired, chosen a romantic shoulder for the affected part. He clapped a hand to his snow-white shirt which suddenly blossomed bright red. He fell artistically.

The audience truly gasped. Donna knelt frantically beside Pierre, having a grand dramatic time. Giles tried to escape and was subdued, none too gently, by Zak and Raoul. George Burley appeared on the scene, chuckling non-stop, waving a pair of stage handcuffs. As Zak later said, it was a riot.

CHAPTER SEVENTEEN

Emil said there was enough champagne for everyone to have half a glass more, so he and I went around pouring while Oliver and Cathy cleared the hors d'oeuvre plates, straightened the cloths and began setting the places for the banquet.

I glanced very briefly at Filmer. He looked exceedingly pale, with sweat on his forehead. One hand, lying on the tablecloth, was tightly clenched. Beside him, the Redi-Hots were enthusing over Zak who was standing beside their table agreeing that Pierre was a redeemable character who would make good. Zak gave me a smile and stepped to one side to let me fill the Redi-Hots' glasses.

Filmer said, in a harsh croaking voice, 'Where did you get that story?'

As if accepting a compliment, Zak answered, 'Made it up.'

'You must have got it from somewhere.' He was positive and angry. The Redi-Hots looked at him in surprise.

'I always make them up,' Zak said lightly. 'Why . . . didn't you enjoy it?'

'Champagne, sir?' I said to Filmer. I'd grown very bold, I thought.

Filmer didn't hear. Mrs Redi-Hot passed me his glass which I replenished. She passed it back. He didn't notice.

'I thought it a great story,' she said. 'What a wicked revolting murderer. And he was so nice all along . . .'

I stepped around Zak with a glimmer of eye contact in which I gave him my devout thanks for his discretion, and he accepted them with amusement.

At the next table Rose Young was protesting to Cumber that it had to have been a coincidence about committing suicide after getting rid of your best horse . . . and Ezra had sold his horse, she said, not given it away because he was being blackmailed.

'How do we know he wasn't?' Cumber demanded.

The Unwins were listening open-mouthed. I filled all their glasses quietly, unnoticed in their general pre-occupation.

'Who now has Ezra's horses, that's what I want to know,' Cumber said truculently. 'And it'll be easy enough to find out.' He spoke loudly: loudly enough, I thought, for Filmer to hear him, if he were listening.

Emil had beaten me to it with the Lorrimores, but they made a remarkable picture. Mercer's forearms rested on the table as he sat with his head bowed. Bambi, a glitter of tears in the frosty eyes, stretched out a hand, closed it over one of Mercer's fists, and stroked his knuckles with comforting affection. Xanthe was saying anxiously, 'What's the matter with everybody?' and Sheridan looked blank. Not supercilious, not arrogant, not even alarmed: a wiped blank slate.

There were a good many people in the aisle, not only the service crew but also the actors who, still in character, were finishing off the drama in the ways they felt happy with: Walter and Mavis, for instance, agreeing that Pierre had saved Donna's life and couldn't be all bad, and maybe he would marry Donna . . . if he stopped gambling.

Threading his way through all this came the sleeping-car attendant on his way to do the bunks in the dome car. He nodded to me with a smile as he passed, and I nodded back: and I thought that my main problem would probably be that the play had been all too successful, and that the people most upset by it wouldn't stay sitting down for dinner.

I wandered back to the kitchen where Angus's octopus act was reaching new heights and hoped especially that Filmer's physical reactions wouldn't get him restlessly to his feet and force him to leave.

He didn't move. The rigidity in his body very slowly relaxed. The impact of the play seemed to be lessening, and perhaps he really believed that Zak had made it all up.

I set the two tables nearest to the kitchen: automatically folded the napkins and arranged knives and forks.

The sleeping-car attendant came back eventually from the dome car, and I left my place settings unfinished and followed him.

'Are you sure?' he asked over his shoulder. 'They seem pretty busy in the dining car.'

'It's a good time,' I assured him. 'Fifteen minutes to dinner. How about if I start from this end, then I'll just stop and go back if I feel guilty.'

'Right,' he said. 'Do you remember how to fold the chairs?'

He knocked on Filmer's door.

'The people are all along in the dining car, but knock first just in case,' he said.

'OK.'

We went into Filmer's room.

'Fold the chair while I'm here, so I can help if you need it.'

'OK.'

I folded, a shade slowly, Julius Apollo's armchair. The sleeping-car attendant gave me a pat on the shoulder and left, saying he would start from the far end, as he usually did, and we might meet in the middle.

'And thanks a lot,' he said.

I waved a hand. The thanks, did he but know it, were all mine. I left the door open and pulled Filmer's bed down into the night position, smoothing the bottom sheet, folding down a corner of the top sheet, as I'd been shown.

I groped into Filmer's wardrobe space, gripped the black crocodile briefcase and rested it on the bed.

Zero-four-nine. One-five-one.

My fingers trembled with the compulsion for speed.

I aligned the little wheels, fumbling where I needed precision. Zero-four-nine . . . press the catch.

Click!

One-five-one. Press the catch. Click! The latches were open.

I laid the case flat on the bottom sheet, pushing the upper sheet back a little to accommodate it, and I lifted the lid. Heart thumping, breathing stopped.

The first thing inside was Filmer's passport. I looked at it briefly and then more closely, getting my suspended breath back in a jerky sort of silent laugh. The number of Filmer's passport was H049151. Hooray for the Brigadier.

I laid the passport on the bed, and looked through the other papers without removing them or changing their order. They were mainly a boring lot: all the bumf about the train trip, a few newspaper pages about the races, then a newspaper cutting from a Cambridge local paper about the building of a new library in one of the colleges, thanks to the generosity of Canadian philanthropist Mercer P. Lorrimore.

My God, I thought.

Beneath the clipping was a letter – a photocopy of a letter. I read it at breakneck speed, feeling danger creep up my spine, feeling my skin flood with heat.

365

It was short. Typewritten. There was no address at the top, no date, no salutation and no signature. It said:

As requested I examined the cadavers of the seven cats found pegged out, eviscerated and beheaded in the College gardens. I can find nothing except for wilful wickedness. These were not cult killings, in my opinion. The cats were killed over a period of perhaps three weeks, the last one yesterday. Each one, except the last, had been hidden under leaves, and had been attacked after death by insects and scavengers. They were all alive when they were pegged out, and during evisceration. Most, if not all, were alive at decapitation. I have disposed of the remains, as you asked.

I could see my hand trembling. I tipped up the next few sheets of paper which were reports from stock-brokers, and then, at the very bottom, I came across a small yellow memo sticking to a foolscap-size paper headed CONVEYANCE.

The memo said, 'You will have to sign this, not Ivor Horfitz, but I think we can keep it quiet.'

I looked a shade blankly at the legal words on the deed: ' . . . all that parcel of land known as SF 90155 on the west side of . . .' and heard the sleeping-car attendant's voice coming nearer along the corridor.

'Tommy . . . where are you?'

I flicked the case shut and pushed it under the bed's

top sheet. The passport was still in view. I shoved it under the pillow, walked out of the door hastily and closed it behind me.

'You've been ages in there,' he said, but tolerantly. 'Couldn't you undo the bed?'

'Managed it finally,' I said, dry-mouthed.

'Right. Well, I didn't give you any chocolates.' He handed me a box of big silver-wrapped bonbons. 'Put one on each pillow.'

'Yes,' I said.

'Are you all right?' he asked curiously.

'Oh, yes. It was hot in the dining car.'

'True.' He went back towards his end of the car, unsuspicious. Heart still thumping I returned to Filmer's room, retrieved his passport from under the pillow, replaced it in the briefcase, shut the locks, twirled the combination wheels, realized I hadn't noticed where they'd been set when I came in, hoped to hell that Filmer didn't set them deliberately, put the case back as I'd found it, straightened the bed and put the chocolate tidily where it belonged.

I went out of the room, closed the door and walked two paces towards the next door along.

'Hey, you,' Filmer's voice said angrily from close behind me. 'What were you doing in there?'

I turned. Looked innocent . . . felt stunned.

'Making your bed ready for the night, sir.'

'Oh.' He shrugged, accepting it.

I held the box of sweets towards him. 'Would you like an extra chocolate, sir?'

'No, I wouldn't,' he said, and went abruptly into his bedroom.

I felt weak. I waited for him to come out exploding that I'd meddled with his belongings.

Nothing . . . nothing . . . happened.

I went into the room next door, folded the armchairs, lowered both beds, turned back the sheets, delivered the sweets. All automatic, with a feeling of total unreality. I'd twice come too close to discovery. I had no great taste, I found, for the risks of a spy.

I was disturbed, in a way, by my pusillanimity. I supposed I'd never thought much about courage: had taken it for granted . . . physical courage, or physical endurance, anyway. I'd been in hard places in the past, but these risks were different and more difficult, at least for me.

I did the third bedroom, by which time the sleeping-car attendant, much faster, had almost finished the rest.

'Thanks a lot,' he said cheerfully. 'Appreciate it.'

'Any time.'

'Did you do your scene?' he asked.

I nodded. 'It went fine.'

Filmer came out of his room and called, 'Hey, you.'

The sleeping-car attendant went towards him. 'Yes, sir?'

Filmer spoke to him, his voice obliterated, as far as

I was concerned, by rail noise, and went back into his room.

'He's not feeling well,' the sleeping-car attendant reported, going back towards his own roomette. 'He asked for something to settle his stomach.'

'Do you have things like that?'

'Antacids, sure. A few simple things.'

I left him to his mission and went back to the dining car, where Emil greeted me with raised eyebrows and thrust into my hands a trayful of small plates, each bearing a square of pâté de foie gras with a thin slice of black truffle on top.

'We missed you. You're needed,' Emil said. 'The crackers for the pâté are on the tables.'

'Right.'

I went ahead with the delivery, going to the Redi-Hots' table first. I asked Mrs Redi-Hot if Mr Filmer would be coming back: should I put his pâté in his place?

She looked a little bewildered. 'He didn't say if he was coming back. He went out in a hurry... he trampled on my feet.'

'Leave the pâté,' Mr Redi-Hot said. 'If he doesn't come back, I'll eat it.'

With a smile I put some pâté in Filmer's place and went on to the Youngs' table, where Cumber had stopped talking about Ezra Gideon but looked dour and preoccupied. Rose received her pâté with a smile and made attempts not to let Cumber's moroseness spoil the occasion for the Unwins.

Cathy had taken pâté to the Lorrimores who sat in glum silence except for Xanthe who could be heard saying exasperatedly, 'This is supposed to be a *party*, for God's sakes.'

For the rest of the passengers, that was true. The faces were bright, the smiles came easily, the euphoria of the whole journey bonded them in pleasure. It was the last night on the train and they were determined to make it a good one.

Nell was moving down the aisle handing out mementos: silver bracelets made of tiny gleaming railway carriages for the women, onyx paperweights set with miniature engines for the men. Charming gifts, received with delight. Xanthe clipped on her bracelet immediately and forgot to look sullen.

Emil and I collected the wrapping-paper debris. 'Miss Richmond might have waited until after dinner,' Emil said.

We served and cleared the rest of the banquet: a salad of sliced yellow tomatoes and fresh basil, a scoop of champagne sorbet, rare roast rib of beef with julienned vegetables and finally apple snowballs appearing to float on raspberry purée. About six people, including Rose Young, asked how to make the apple snowballs, so I enquired of Angus.

He was looking languid and exhausted, but obliging. 'Tell them it's sieved apple purée, sugar, whipped cream, whipped white of egg. Combine at the last minute. Very simple.'

'Delicious,' Rose said, when I relayed the information. 'Do bring out the chef for us to congratulate him.'

Emil brought out and introduced Angus to prolonged applause. Simone sulked determinedly in the kitchen. Rose Young said they should all thank the rest of the dining-car crew who had worked so hard throughout. Everyone clapped: all most affecting.

Xanthe clapped, I noticed. I had great hopes for Xanthe.

I managed to stop beside Nell's ear.

'Xanthe's longing to have a good time,' I said. 'Couldn't you rescue her?'

'What's the matter with the others?' she asked, frowning.

'Xanthe might tell you, if she knows.'

Nell flashed me an acutely perceptive glance. 'And you want me to tell you?'

'Yes, please, since you ask.'

'One day you'll explain all this.'

'One day soon.'

I went back to the kitchen with the others to tackle the mountainous dishwashing and to eat anything left over, which wasn't much. Angus produced a bottle of Scotch from a cupboard and drank from it deeply without troubling a glass. Apart from Simone, who had disappeared altogether, there was very good feeling in the kitchen. I wouldn't have missed it, I thought, for a fieldful of mushrooms.

When everything was scoured, polished and put away, we left Angus unbelievably beginning to make breads for breakfast. I stood in the lobby for a while, watching the dining-car slowly clear as everyone drifted off to the dome-car lounge for laughter and music. The Lorrimores had all gone, and so had Nell and the Unwins and the Youngs. Out of habit I began to collect, with Oliver, the used napkins and tablecloths, ready to put out clean ones for breakfast, and presently Nell came back and sat down wearily where I was working.

'For what it's worth,' she said, 'Xanthe doesn't know what has thrown her parents into such a tizzy. She says it can't have been something Mr Filmer said in the lounge before cocktails because it sounded so silly.'

'Did she tell you what he said?'

Nell nodded. 'Xanthe said Mr Filmer asked her father if he would let him have Voting Right, and her father said he wouldn't part with the horse for anything, and they were both smiling, Xanthe said. Then Mr Filmer, still smiling, said, "We'll have to have a little talk about cats." And that was all. Mr Filmer went into the dining car. Xanthe said she asked her father what Mr Filmer meant, and he said, "Don't bother me, darling." ' Nell shook her head in puzzlement. 'So anyway, Xanthe is now having a good time in the dome-car lounge and the rest of the family have gone off into their own car, and I'm deadly tired, if you want to know.'

'Go to bed, then.'

'The actors are all along in the lounge having their photos taken,' she said, dismissing my suggestion as frivolous. 'They came up trumps tonight, didn't they?'

'Brilliant,' I said.

'Someone was asking Zak who had tried to kidnap which horse at Toronto station.'

'What did he say?' I asked, amused. It was the loosest of the loose ends.

'He said it had seemed a good idea at the time.' She laughed. 'He said they'd had to change the script because the actor who was supposed to play the part of the kidnapper had broken his arm and couldn't appear. Everyone seemed to be satisfied. They're all very happy with the way it ended. People are kissing Donna and Mavis. Mavis is wearing the jewels.' She yawned and reflected. 'Mr Filmer didn't have any dinner, did he? Perhaps I'd better go and see if he's all right.'

I dissuaded her. Antacids were taking care of it, I said. What one could give a man for a sick soul was another matter.

From his point of view, he had made his move a fraction too early, I thought. If he hadn't already made the threat, the play wouldn't have had such a cataclysmic effect either on him or on Mercer. Mercer might have been warned, as I'd intended, might have been made to think: but I couldn't have foreseen that it would happen the way it had, even though Filmer's smirk and Mercer's gloom had made me wonder. Just as well, perhaps, that I hadn't known about the cats when I invented the theft of the jewels. I might have been terribly tempted to hit even closer to home. Tortured horses, perhaps?

'What are you hatching now?' Nell demanded. 'You've got that distant look.'

'I haven't done a thing,' I said.

'I'm not so sure.' She stood up. She was wearing, in honour of the banquet, a boat-necked black blouse above the full black skirt, a pearl choker round her neck. Her fair hair was held back high in a comb, but not plaited, falling instead in informal curls. I thought with unnerving intensity that I didn't want to lose her, that for me it was no longer a game. I had known her for a week and a day. Reason said it wasn't long enough. Instinct said it was.

'Where are you staying in Vancouver?' I asked.

'At the Four Seasons Hotel, with all the passengers.'

She gave me a small smile and went off towards the action. Oliver had finished clearing the cloths and was laying clean ones, to leave the place looking tidy, he said. I left him to finish and made my way up the train to talk to George Burley, passing Filmer's closed door on the way.

The sleeping-car attendant was sitting in his roomette with the door open. I poked my head in and asked how the passenger was, who'd asked for the antacid.

'He went up the train a while ago, and came back. He didn't say anything, just walked past. He must be all right, I guess.'

I nodded and went on, and came to George sitting at his table with his endless forms.

'Come in,' he invited, and I took my accustomed seat. 'I showed that photo,' he said. 'Is that what you want to know about?'

'Yes.'

'He's definitely on the train. Name of Johnson, according to the passenger list. He has a roomette right forward, and he stays in it most of the time. He eats in the forward dome-car dining room, but only dinner, eh? He was in there just now when I went up to the engine, but he'd gone when I came back. A fast eater, they say. Never goes for breakfast or lunch. Never talks to anyone, eh?'

'I don't like it,' I said.

George chuckled. 'Wait till you hear the worst.'

'What's the worst?'

'My assistant conductor – he's one of the sleeping-car attendants up front – he says he's seen him before, eh?'

'Seen him where?'

George watched me for effect. 'On the railways.'

'On the – do you mean he's a *railwayman*?'

'He can't be sure. He says he looks like a baggage

handler he once worked with on the Toronto to Montreal sector, long time ago. Fifteen years ago. Twenty. Says if it's him, he had a chip on his shoulder all the time, no one liked him. He could be violent. You didn't cross him. Might not be him, though. He's older. And he doesn't remember the name Johnson, though I suppose it's forgettable, it's common enough.'

'Would a baggage handler,' I said slowly, 'know how to drain a fuel tank . . . and uncouple the Lorrimores' car?'

George's eyes gleamed with pleasure. 'The baggage handlers travel on the trains, eh? They're not fools. They take on small bits of freight at the stops and see the right stuff gets off. If you live around trains, you get to know how they work.'

'Is there a baggage handler on this train?'

'You bet your life. He's not always in the baggage car, not when we're going along. He eats, eh? He's always there in the stations, unlocking the doors. This one's not the best wc've got, mind. A bit old, a bit fat.' He chuckled. 'He said he'd never seen this man Johnson, but then he's always worked Vancouver to Banff, never Toronto to Montreal.'

'Has the baggage handler or your assistant talked to Johnson?'

'My assistant conductor says the only person Johnson talks to is one of the owners who raps on Johnson's door when he goes along to see his horse. He went up there this evening not long ago, and they

had some sort of row in the corridor outside my assistant's roomette.'

'George! Did your assistant hear what it was about?'

'Important, is it?' George said, beaming.

'Could be, very.'

'Well, he didn't.' He shook his head regretfully. 'He
said he thought the owner told Johnson not to do
something Johnson wanted to. They were shouting, he
said, but he didn't really listen, eh? He wasn't
interested. Anyway, the owner came back down here,
he said, and he heard Johnson say, "I'll do what I
frigging like," very loudly, but he doesn't think the
owner heard, as he'd gone by then.'

'That's not much help,' I said.

'It's easier to start a train going downhill than to
stop it, eh?'

'Mm.'

'It's the best I can do for you.'

'Well,' I said. 'We do know he's on the train, and we
know his name may or may not be Johnson, and
we know he may or may not be a railwayman, and I
know for certain he has a violent personality. It sounds
as if he's still planning something and we don't know
what. I suppose you are certain he can't get past the
dragon-lady?'

'Nothing is certain.'

'How about if you asked the baggage handler to sit
in with her, with the horses?'

He put his head on one side. 'If you think she'd stand for it?'

'Tell her it's to keep the horses safe, which it is.'

He chuckled. 'Don't see why not.' He looked at his watch. 'Sicamous is coming up. I'll go up there outside, when we stop. Three or five minutes there. Then it'll be time to put the clocks back an hour. Did your Miss Richmond remember to tell everyone?'

'Yes. They're all on Pacific time already, I think. Getting on for midnight.'

We had stopped towards the end of dinner in a small place called Revelstoke for half an hour for all the cars to be refilled with water. At Kamloops, a far larger town, we would stop at two in the morning very briefly. Then it was North Bend at five-forty, then the last stretch to Vancouver, arriving at five past ten on Sunday morning, a week from the day we set off.

We slowed towards Sicamous while I was still with George.

'After here, though you won't see it,' he said, 'we follow the shoreline of Shuswap Lake. The train goes slowly.'

'It hasn't exactly been whizzing along through the Rockies.'

He nodded benignly. 'We go at thirty, thirty-five miles an hour. Fast enough, eh? Uphill, downhill, round hairpin bends. There are more mountains ahead.'

He swung down on to the ground when the train

stopped and crunched off forward to arrange things with the baggage handler.

It was snowing outside: big dry flakes settling on others that had already fallen, harbingers of deep winter. The trains almost always went through, George had said.

I thought I might as well see how the revelries were going but it seemed that, unlike after the Winnipeg race, most people were feeling the long evening was dying. The lounge in the dome car was only half full. The observation deck was scarcely populated. The poker school, in shirtsleeves, were counting their money. The actors had vanished. Nell was walking towards me with Xanthe whom she was seeing safely to bed in the upper bunk behind the felt curtains.

'Goodnight,' Nell said softly.

'Sleep well,' I replied.

'Goodnight,' Xanthe said.

I smiled. 'Goodnight.'

I watched them go along the corridor beside the bar. Nell turned round, hesitated, and waved. Xanthe turned also, and waved. I waved back.

Gentle was the word, I thought. Go gentle into this good night . . . No, no! It should be, 'Do not go gentle into that good night.' Odd how poets' words stuck in one's head. Dylan Thomas, wasn't it? *Do not go gentle into that good night* . . . because that good night was death.

*

The train was slowly going to sleep.

There would be precious little peace, I thought, in the minds of the Lorrimores, father, mother and son. Little peace also in Filmer who would know now from Johnson that the departure of Lenny Higgs had robbed him of the lever to be used against Daffodil; who could have doubts at the very least about Mercer's future reactions; who would know that Cumber Young would find out soon who had taken Ezra Gideon's horses; who would realize he was riding a flood tide of contempt. I wished him more than an upset stomach. I wished him remorse, which was the last thing he would feel.

I wandered back through the train past George's office, which was empty, and stretched out in my own room on the bed, still dressed, with the door open and the light on, meaning just to rest but stay awake: and not surprisingly I went straight to sleep.

I awoke to the sound of someone calling 'George . . . George . . .' Woke with a start and looked at my watch. I hadn't slept long, not more than ten minutes, but in that time the train had stopped.

That message got me off the bed in a hurry. The train should have been moving; there was no stop scheduled for almost an hour. I went out into the passage and found an elderly man in a VIA grey suit like George's peering into the office. The elderly man looked at my uniform and said urgently, 'Where's George?'

'I don't know,' I said. 'What's the matter?'

'We've got a hot box.' He was deeply worried. 'George must radio to the despatcher to stop the Canadian.'

Not again, I thought wildly. I went into George's office, following the VIA Rail man who said he was the assistant conductor, George's deputy.

'Can't you use the radio?' I said.

'The Conductor does it.'

The assistant conductor was foremost a sleeping-car attendant, I supposed. I thought I might see if I could raise someone myself, as George would have already tuned in the frequency, but when I pressed the transmit switch, nothing happened at all, not even a click, and then I could see why it wouldn't work . . . the radio was soaking wet.

There was an empty coffee cup beside it.

With immense alarm, I said to George's assistant, 'What's a hot box?'

'A hot axle, of course,' he said. 'A journal-box that holds the axle. It's under the horse car, and it's glowing dark red. We can't go on until it cools down and we put more oil in.'

'How long does that take?'

'Too long. They're putting snow on it.' He began to understand about the radio. 'It's wet . . .'

'It won't work,' I said. Nor would the cellular telephone, not out in the mountains. 'How do we stop the Canadian? There must be ways, from before radio.'

'Yes, but . . .' He looked strained, the full enormity

381

of the situation sinking in. 'You'll have to go back along the track and plant fusees.'

'Fusees?'

'Flares, of course. You're younger than me . . . you'll have to go . . . you'll be faster.'

He opened a cupboard in George's office and pulled out three objects, each about a foot in length, with a sharp metal spike at one end, the rest being tubular with granulations on the tip. They looked like oversized matches, which was roughly what they were.

'You strike them on any rough or hard surface,' he said. 'Like a rock, or the rails. They burn bright red . . . they burn for twenty minutes. You stick the spike . . . throw it . . . into the wooden ties, in the middle of the track. The driver of the Canadian will stop at once when he sees it.' His mind was going faster almost than his tongue. 'You'll have to go half a mile, it'll take the Canadian that much time to stop . . . Hurry, now . . . half a mile at least. And if the engineers are not in the cab . . .'

'What do you mean,' I asked aghast, 'if they're not in the cab?'

'They aren't always there. One of them regularly flushes out the boiler . . . the other could be in the bathroom . . . If they aren't there, if they haven't seen the fusees and the train isn't stopping, you must light another flare and throw it through the window into the cab. Then when they come back, they'll stop.'

I stared at him. 'That's impossible.'

'They'll be there, they'll see the flares. Go now. Hurry. But that's what you do if you have to. Throw one through the window.' He suddenly grabbed a fourth flare from the cupboard. 'You'd better take another one, just in case.'

'In case of what?' What else could there be?

'In case of bears,' he said.

CHAPTER EIGHTEEN

With a feeling of complete unreality I set off past the end of the train and along the single railway track in the direction of Toronto.

With one arm I clasped the four flares to my chest, in the other hand I carried George's bright-beamed torch, to show me the way.

Half a mile. How long was half a mile?

Hurry, George's assistant had said. Of all unnecessary instructions . . .

I half walked, half ran along the centre of the track, trying to step on the flat wood of the ties, the sleepers, because the stones in between were rough and speed-inhibiting.

Bears . . . my God.

It was cold. It had stopped snowing, but some snow was lying . . . not enough to give me problems. I hadn't thought to put on a coat. It didn't matter, movement would keep me warm. Urgency and fierce anxiety would keep me warm.

I began to feel it wasn't totally impossible. After all,

it must have been done often in the old days. Standard procedure still, one might say. The flares had been there, ready. All the same, it was fairly eerie running through the night with snow-dusted rocky tree-dotted hillsides climbing away on each side and the two rails shining silver into the distance in front.

I didn't see the danger in time, and it didn't growl; it wasn't a bear, it had two legs and it was human. He must have been hiding behind rocks or trees in the shadow thrown by my torch. I saw his movement in the very edge of my peripheral vision after I'd passed him. I sensed an upswept arm, a weapon, a blow coming.

There was barely a hundredth of a second for instinctive evasion. All I did as I ran was to lean forward a fraction so that the smash came across my shoulders, not on my head.

It felt as if I had cracked apart, but I hadn't. Feet, hands, muscles were all working. I staggered forward, dropped the flares and the torch, went down on one knee, knew another bang was travelling. Thought before action . . . I didn't have time. I turned towards him, not away. Turned inside and under the swinging arm, rising, butting upwards with my head to find the aggressive chin, jerking my knee fiercely to contact between the braced legs, punching with clenched fist and the force of fury into the Adam's apple in his throat. One of the many useful things I'd learned on

385

my travels was how to fight dirty, and never had I needed the knowledge more.

He grunted and wheezed with triple unexpected pain and dropped to his knees on the ground, and I wrenched the long piece of wood from his slackening hand and hit his own head with it, hoping I was doing it hard enough to knock him out, not hard enough to kill him. He fell quietly face down in the snow between the rails, and I rolled him over with my foot, and in the deflected beam of the torch which lay unbroken a few paces away, saw the gaunt features of the man called Johnson.

He had got, I reckoned, a lot more than he was used to, and I felt intense satisfaction which was no doubt reprehensible but couldn't be helped.

I bent down, lifted one of his wrists and hauled him unceremoniously over the rail and into the shadows away from the track. He was heavy. Also the damage he'd done me, when it came to lugging unconscious persons about, was all too obvious. He might not have broken my back, which was what it had sounded like, but there were some badly squashed muscle fibres somewhere that weren't in first-class working order and were sending stabbing messages of protest besides.

I picked up the torch and looked for the flares, filled with an increased feeling of urgency, of time running out. I found three of the flares, couldn't see the fourth, decided not to waste time, thought the bears would have to lump it.

Must be light-headed, I thought. Got to get moving. I hadn't come anything like half a mile away from the train. I swung the beam back the way I'd come, but the train was out of sight round a corner that I hadn't noticed taking. For a desperate moment I couldn't remember which direction I'd come from: too utterly stupid if I ran the wrong way.

Think, for God's sake.

I swung the torch both ways along the track. Trees, rocks, silver parallel rails, all exactly similar.

Which way? *Think.*

I walked one way and it felt wrong. I turned and went back. That was right. It felt right. It was the wind on my face, I thought. I'd been running before into the wind.

The rails, the ties seemed to stretch to infinity. I was going uphill also, I thought. Another bend to the right lay ahead.

How long did half a mile take? I stole a glance at my watch, rolling my wrist round which hurt somewhere high up, but with remote pain, not daunting. Couldn't believe the figures. Ten minutes only . . . or twelve . . . since I'd set off.

A mile in ten minutes was ordinarily easy . . . but not a mile of sleepers and stones.

Johnson had been waiting for me, I thought. Not for me personally, but for whomever would come running from the train with the flares.

Which meant he knew the radio wouldn't work.

I began actively to worry about George being missing.

Perhaps Johnson had fixed the hot box, to begin with.

Johnson had meant the trains to crash with himself safely away to the rear. Johnson was darned well not going to succeed.

With renewed purpose, with perhaps at last a feeling that all this was really happening and that I could indeed stop the Canadian, I pressed on along the track.

George's voice floated into my head, telling me about the row between Johnson and Filmer. Filmer told Johnson not to do something; Johnson said, 'I'll do what I frigging like.' Filmer could have told him not to try any more sabotage tricks on the train, realizing that trouble was anyway mounting up for him, trouble from which he might not be able to extricate himself if anything disastrous happened.

Johnson, once started, couldn't be stopped. 'Easier to start a train running downhill than to stop it, eh?' Johnson with a chip on his shoulder from way back; the ex-railwayman, the violent frightener.

I had to have gone well over half a mile, I thought. Half a mile hadn't sounded far enough: the train itself was a quarter-mile long. I stopped and looked at my watch. The Canadian would come in a very few minutes. There was another curve just ahead. I mustn't leave it too late.

I ran faster, round the curve. There was another

curve in a further hundred yards, but it would have to do. I put the torch down beside the track, rubbed the end of one of the flares sharply against one of the rails, and begged it, implored it, to ignite.

It lit with a huge red rush for which I was not prepared. Nearly dropped it. Rammed the spike into the wood of one of the ties.

The flare burned in a brilliant fiery scarlet that would have been visible for a mile, if only the track had been straight.

I picked up the torch and ran on round the next bend, the red fire behind me washing all the snow with pink. Round that bend there was a much longer straight: I ran a good way, then stopped again and lit a second flare, jamming its point into the wood as before.

The Canadian had to be almost there. I'd lost count of the time. The Canadian would come with its bright headlights and see the flare and stop with plenty of margin in hand.

I saw pinpoint lights in the distance. I hadn't known we were anywhere near habitation. Then I realized the lights were moving, coming. The Canadian seemed to be advancing slowly at first ... and then faster ... and *it wasn't stopping.* ... There was no screech of brakes urgently applied.

With a feeling of dreadful foreboding, I struck the third flare forcefully against the rail, almost broke it, felt it whoosh, stood waving it beside the track, beside the other flare stuck in the wood.

The Canadian came straight on. I couldn't bear it, couldn't *believe* it. . . . It was almost impossible to throw the flare through the window . . . the window was too small, too high up, and moving at thirty-five miles an hour. I felt puny on the ground beside the huge roaring advance of the yellow bulk of the inexorable engine with its blinding lights and absence of brain.

It was there. Then or never. There were no faces looking out from the cab. I yelled in a frenzy, 'Stop', and the sound blew away futilely on the bow wave of parting air.

I threw the flare. Threw it high, threw it too soon, missed the empty black window.

The flare flew forward of it and hit the outside of the windscreen, and fell on to the part of the engine sticking out in front; and then all sight of it was gone, the whole long heavy silver train rolling past me at a constant speed, making the ground tremble, extinguishing beneath it the second flare I'd planted in its path. It went on its mindless way, swept round the curve, and was gone.

I felt disintegrated and sick, failure flooding back in the pain I'd disregarded. The trains would fold into each other, would concertina, would heap into killing chaos. . . . In despair, I picked up the torch and began to jog the way the Canadian had gone. I would have to face what I hadn't been able to prevent . . . have to help

390

even though I felt wretchedly guilty ... couldn't bear the thought of the Canadian ploughing into the Lorrimores' car ... someone would have warned the Lorrimores ... oh God, oh God ... someone *must* have warned the Lorrimores ... and everyone else. They would all be out of the train, away from the track ... Nell ... Zak ... everybody.

I ran round the curve. Ahead, lying beside the track, still burning, was the flare I'd thrown. Fallen off the engine. The first flare that I'd planted a hundred yards ahead before the next curve had vanished altogether, swept away by the Canadian.

There was nothing. No noise, except the sighing wind. I wondered helplessly when I would hear the crash. I had no idea how far away the race train was; how far I'd run.

Growing cold and with leaden feet, I plodded past the fallen flare and along and round the next bend, and round the long curve following. I hadn't heard the screech of a metal tearing into metal, though it reverberated in my head. They must have warned the Lorrimores, they must. ... I shivered among the freezing mountains from far more than frost.

There were two red lights on the rails far ahead. Not bright and burning like the flares, but small and insignificant, like reflectors. I wondered numbly what they were, and it wasn't until I'd gone about five more paces that I realized that they weren't reflectors, they were *lights* ... stationary lights ... and I began running faster again, hardly daring to hope, but then seeing that they were indeed the rear lights of a train . . . a train . . . it could be only one train . . . there had been no night-tearing crash. . . . The Canadian had stopped. I felt swamped with relief, near to tears, breathless. It had stopped . . . there was no collision . . . no tragedy . . . it had *stopped*.

I ran towards the lights, seeing the bulk of the train now in the torch's beam, unreasonably afraid that the engineers would set off again and accelerate away. I ran until I was panting, until I could touch the train. I ran alongside it, sprinting now, urgent to tell them not to go on.

There were several people on the ground up by the engine. They could see someone running towards them with a torch, and when I was fairly near to them, one of them shouted out authoritatively, 'Get back on the train, there's no need for people to be out there.'

I slowed to a walk, very out of breath. 'I . . . er . . .' I called, 'I came from the train in front.' I gestured along the rails ahead, which were vacant as far as one could see in the headlights of the Canadian.

'What train?' one of them said, as I finally reached them.

'The race train.' I tried to breathe. Air came in gasps. 'Transcontinental . . . mystery . . . race train.'

There was a silence. One of them said, 'It's supposed to be thirty-five minutes ahead of us.'

'It had . . .' I said, dragging in oxygen, 'a hot box.'

It meant a great deal to them. It explained everything.

'Oh.' They took note of my uniform. 'It was you who lit the fusees?'

'Yes.'

'How far ahead is the other train?'

'I don't know. . . . Can't remember . . . how far I ran.'

They consulted. One, from his uniform, was the Conductor. Two, from their lack of it, were the engineers. There was another man there; perhaps the Conductor's assistant. They decided – the Conductor and the train driver himself decided to go forward slowly. They said I'd better come with them in the cab.

Gratefully, lungs settling, I climbed up and stood watching as the engineer released the brakes, put on power and set the train going at no more than walking pace, headlights bright on the empty track ahead.

'Did you *throw* one of the fusees?' the engineer asked me.

'I didn't think you were going to stop.' It sounded prosaic, unemotional.

'We weren't in the cab,' he said. 'The one you threw hit the windscreen and I could see the glare all the way down inside the engine where I was checking a valve. Just as well you threw it . . . I came racing up here just in time to see the one on the track before we ran over it. Bit of luck, you know.'

'Yes.' Bit of luck . . . deliverance from a lifetime's regret.

'Why didn't the Conductor radio?' the Conductor said crossly.

'It's out of order.'

He tut-tutted a bit. We rolled forward slowly. There was a bend ahead to the right.

'I think we're near now,' I said. 'Not far.'

'Right.' The pace slowed further. The engineer inched carefully round the bend and it was as well he did, because when he braked at that point to a halt, we finished with twenty yards between the front of the Canadian's yellow engine and the shining brass railing along the back platform of the Lorrimores' car.

'Well,' the engineer said phlegmatically, 'I wouldn't have wanted to come round the corner unawares to see *that*.'

It wasn't until then that I remembered that Johnson was somewhere out on the track. I certainly hadn't spotted him lying unconscious or dead on the ground on the return journey, and nor obviously had the Canadian's crew. I wondered briefly where he'd got to, but at that moment I didn't care. Everyone climbed down from the Canadian's cab, and the crew walked forward to join their opposite numbers ahead.

I went with them. The two groups greeted each other without fuss. The race train lot seemed to take it for granted that the Canadian would stop in time. They didn't discuss flares, but hot boxes.

The journal-box which held the nearside end of the rear-most of the six axles of the horse car had overheated, and it had overheated because, they surmised, the oil inside had somehow leaked away. That's what was usually wrong, when this happened. They hadn't yet opened it. It no longer glowed red, but was too hot to touch. They were applying fresh snow all the time. Another ten minutes, perhaps.

'Where's George Burley?' I asked.

The race train baggage handler said no one could find him, but two sleeping-car attendants were still searching for him. He told the others that it was a good thing he'd happened to be travelling in the horse car. He had smelled the hot axle, he said. He'd smelled that smell once before. Terrible smell, he said. He'd gone straight forward to tell the engineer to stop at once. 'Otherwise the axle would have broken and we could have had a derailment.'

The others nodded. They all knew.

'Did you warn any of the passengers?' I asked.

'What? No, no, no need to wake them up.'

'But . . . the Canadian might not have stopped . . .'

'Of course it would, when it saw the fusees.'

Their faith amazed and frightened me. The Conductor of the Canadian said that he would radio ahead to Kamloops and both trains would stop there again, where there were multiple tracks, not just the one. Kamloops, he thought, would be getting worried soon that the race train hadn't arrived, and he went off to inform them.

I walked back behind the horse car and boarded

the race train, and almost immediately met George's assistant who was walking forward.

'Where's George?' I said urgently.

He was worried. 'I can't find him.'

'There's one place he might be.' And please let him be there, I thought. Please don't let him be lying miles back in some dreadful condition beside the track.

'Where?' he said.

'In one of the bedrooms. Look up the list. In Johnson's bedroom.'

'Who?'

'Johnson.'

Another sleeping-car attendant happened to arrive at that point.

'I still can't find him,' he said.

'Do you know where Johnson's room is?' I asked anxiously.

'Yes, nearly next to mine. Roomette, it is.'

'Then let's look there.'

'You can't go into a passenger's room in the middle of the night,' he protested.

'If Johnson's there, we'll apologize.'

'I can't think why you think George might be there,' he grumbled, but he led the way back and pointed to a door. 'That's his.'

I opened it. George was lying on the bed, squirming in ropes, fighting against a gag. Very much alive.

Relieved beyond measure, I pulled off the gag which was a wide band of adhesive plaster firmly stuck on.

'Dammit, that hurt, eh?' George said. 'What took you so long?'

George sat in his office, grimly drinking hot tea and refusing to lie down. He was concussed, one could see from his eyes, but he would not admit that the blow to his head that had knocked him out had had any effect. As soon as he was free of the ropes and had begun to understand about the hot box, he had insisted that he and the Conductor from the Canadian had a talk together in the forward dome car of the race train, a meeting attended by various other crew members and myself.

The despatcher in Kamloops, the Canadian's Conductor reported, had said that as soon as the race train could set off again, it would proceed to Kamloops. The Canadian would follow ten minutes later. They would also alert a following freight train. The race train would remain at Kamloops for an hour. The Canadian would leave Kamloops first so that it fell as little behind its timetable as possible. After all the journal-boxes of the race train had been checked for heat, it would go on its way to Vancouver. There wouldn't be any enquiry at Kamloops as it would be past three in the morning – Sunday morning – by then. The enquiry would take place at Vancouver.

Everyone nodded. George looked white, as if he wished he hadn't moved his head.

The race train's engineer came to say that the box had been finally opened, it had been dry and the oily waste had burned away, but all was now well, it was cool and filled again, it was not dripping out underneath, and the train could go on.

They wasted no time. The Canadian's crew left and the race train was soon on the move again as if nothing had happened. I went with George to his office and then fetched him the tea, and he groggily demanded I tell him from start to finish what was going on.

'You tell me first how you came to be knocked out,' I said.

'I can't remember. I was walking up to see the engineers.' He looked puzzled. 'First thing I knew, I was lying there trussed up. I was there for ages. Couldn't understand it.' He hadn't a chuckle left in him. 'I was in Johnson's roomette, they said. Johnson did it, I suppose. Jumped me.'

'Yes.'

'Where is he now?'

'Heaven knows.' I told George about Johnson's attacking me and how I'd left him, and how I hadn't seen him anywhere on the way back.

'Two possibilities,' George said. 'Three, I suppose. Either he buggered off somewhere or he's getting a ride on the Canadian right now.'

I stared. Hadn't thought of that. 'What's the third?' I asked.

A tired gleam crept into George's disorientated eyes.

'The mountain where we stopped,' he said. 'That was Squilax Mountain. Squilax is the Indian word for black bear.'

I swallowed. 'I didn't see any bears.'

'Just as well.'

I didn't somehow think Johnson had been eaten by a bear. I couldn't believe in it. I thought I must have been crazy, but I hadn't believed in bears all the time I'd been out there on Black Bear Mountain.

'Know something?' George said. 'The new rolling stock can't easily get hot boxes, the axles run on ball-bearings, eh?, not oily waste. Only old cars like the horse car will always be vulnerable. Know what? You bet your life Johnson took most of the waste out of that box when we stopped in Revelstoke.'

'Why do you say oily waste?' I asked.

'Rags. Rags in the oil. Makes a better cushion for the axle than plain oil. I've known one sabotaged before, mind. Only that time they didn't just take the rags out, they put iron filings in, eh? Derailed the train. Another railwayman with a grudge, that was. But hot boxes do happen by accident. They've got heat sensors with alarm systems beside the track in some places, because of that. How did that Johnson ever think he'd get away with it?'

'He doesn't know we have a photo of him.'

George began to laugh and thought better of it. 'You kill me, Tommy. But what was my assistant thinking of, sending you off with the fusees? It was his job, eh? He should have gone.'

'He said I'd go faster.'

'Well, yes, I suppose he was right. But you weren't really crew.'

'He'd forgotten,' I said. 'But I thought he might have warned the Lorrimores . . . and everyone else . . . to get them out of danger.'

George considered it. 'I'm not going to say he should. I'm not going to say he shouldn't.'

'Railwaymen stick together?'

'He's coming up to his pension. And no one was as much as jolted off their beds, eh?'

'Lucky.'

'Trains always stop for flares,' he said comfortably.

I left it. I supposed one couldn't lose a man his pension for not doing something that had proved unnecessary.

We ran presently into Kamloops where the axles were all checked, the radio was replaced, and everything else went according to plan. Once we were moving again, George finally agreed to lie down in his clothes and try to sleep; and two doors along from him I tried the same.

Things always start hurting when one has time to think about them. The dull ache where Johnson's piece of wood had landed on the back of my left shoulder was intermittently sharply sore: all right when I was standing up, not so good lying down. A bore. It would be stiffer still, I thought, in the morning. A pest for serving breakfast.

I smiled to myself finally. In spite of Johnson's and Filmer's best efforts, the great Transcontinental Mystery Race Train might yet limp without disaster to Vancouver.

Complacency, I should have remembered, was never a good idea.

CHAPTER NINETEEN

It was discomfort as much as anything which had me on my feet again soon after six. Emil wouldn't have minded if I'd been late, as few of the passengers were early breakfasters, but I thought I'd do better in the dining car. I stripped off the waistcoat and shirt for a wash and a shave, and inspected in the mirror as best I could the fairly horrifying bruise already colouring a fair-sized area across my back. Better than on my head, I thought resignedly. Look on the bright side.

I put on a clean shirt and the spare clean waistcoat and decided that this was one VIA Rail operative who was not going to polish his shoes that morning, despite the wear and tear on them from the night's excursions. I brushed my hair instead. Tommy looked tidy enough, I thought, for his last appearance.

It wasn't yet light. I went forward through the sleeping train to the kitchen where Angus was not only awake but singing Scottish ballads at the top of his voice while filling the air with the fragrant yeasty smell of his baking. The dough, it seemed, had risen satisfactorily during the night.

Emil, Oliver, Cathy and I laid the tables and set out fresh flowers in the bud vases, and in time, with blue skies appearing outside, poured coffee and ferried sausages and bacon. The train stopped for a quarter of an hour in a place called North Bend, our last stop before Vancouver, and ran on down what the passengers were knowledgeably calling Fraser Canyon. Hell's Gate, they said with relish, lay ahead.

The track seemed to me to be clinging to the side of a cliff. Looking out of the window by the kitchen door, one could see right down to a torrent rushing between rocky walls, brownish tumbling water with foam-edged waves. The train, I was pleased to note, was negotiating this extraordinary feat of engineering at a suitably circumspect crawl. If it went too fast round these bends, it would fly off into space.

I took a basket of bread down to the far end just as Mercer Lorrimore came through from the dome car. Although Cathy was down there also, he turned from her to me and asked if I could possibly bring hot tea through to his own car.

'Certainly, sir. Any breads?'

He looked vaguely at the basket. 'No. Just tea. For three of us.' He nodded, turned and went away. Cathy raised her eyebrows and said with tolerance, 'Chauvinist pig.'

Emil shook his head a bit over the private order but

made sure the tray I took looked right from his point of view, and I swayed through on the mission.

The lockable door in the Lorrimores' car was open. I knocked on it, however, and Mercer appeared in the far doorway to the saloon at the rear.

'Along here, please.'

I went along there. Mercer, dressed in a suit and tie, gestured to me to put the tray on the coffee table. Bambi wasn't there. Sheridan sprawled in an armchair in jeans, trainers and a big white sweatshirt with the words MAKE WAVES on the front.

I found it difficult to look at Sheridan pleasantly. I could think of nothing but cats. He himself still wore the blank look of the evening before, as if he had opted out of thinking.

'We'll pour,' Mercer said. 'Come back in half an hour for the tray.'

'Yes, sir.'

I left them and returned to the dining car. The chill within Bambi, I thought, was because of the cats.

Nell and Xanthe had arrived during my absence.

'My goodness, you look grim,' Nell exclaimed, then, remembering, said more formally, 'Er . . . what's for breakfast?'

I got rid of the grimness and handed her the printed menu. Xanthe said she would have everything that was going.

'Has George told you that we're running late?' I asked Nell.

404

'No. His door was shut. Are we? How much?'

'About an hour and a half.' I forestalled her question. 'We had to stop in the night at Kamloops to get George's radio fixed, and then we had to wait there for the Canadian to go ahead of us.'

'I'd better tell everyone, then. What time do we get to Vancouver?'

'About eleven-thirty, I think.'

'Right. Thanks.'

I almost said, 'Be my guest,' but not quite. Tommy wouldn't. Nell's eyes were smiling, all the same. Cathy chose that exact moment to go past me with a tray of breakfasts: or not exactly past, but rather against me where it seemed to hurt most.

'Sorry,' she said contritely, going on her way.

'It's OK.'

It was difficult always to pass in the swaying aisle without touching. Couldn't be helped.

Filmer came into the dining room and sat at the table nearest to the kitchen, normally the least favourite with the passengers. He looked as if he'd spent a bad night. 'Here, you,' he said abruptly at my approach, having apparently abandoned the Mister-Nice-Guy image.

'Yes, sir?' I said.

'Coffee,' he said.

'Yes, sir.'

'Now.'

'Yes, sir.'

I gave Xanthe's order to Simone who was stiffly

laying a baking sheet of sausages in the oven in silent protest at life in general, and I took the coffee pot, on a tray, to Filmer.

'Why did we stop in the night?' he demanded.

'I believe it was to fix the radio, sir.'

'We stopped twice,' he said accusingly. 'Why?'

'I don't know, sir. I expect the Conductor could tell you.'

I wondered what he'd do if I said, 'Your man Johnson nearly succeeded in wrecking the train with you in it.' It struck me then that perhaps his enquiry was actually anxiety: that he wanted to be told that nothing dangerous had happened. He did seem marginally relieved by my answer and I resisted the temptation of wiping out all that relief by telling him that the radio had been sabotaged, because the people at the next table were listening also. Spreading general gloom and fright was not in my brief. Selective gloom, selective fright . . . sure.

Others, it seemed, had noticed the long stops in the night, but no one seriously complained. No one minded letting the Canadian go on in front. The general good humour and the party atmosphere prevailed and excused everything. The train ride might be coming to an end, but meanwhile there was the spectacular gorge outside to be exclaimed over, the city of Vancouver to be looked forward to, the final race to promise a sunburst of a conclusion. The Great Transcontinental Race Train, they were saying, had been just that: great.

After half an hour or so, I went back to the Lorrimores' car to fetch the tray of teacups. I knocked on the door, but as there was no answer I went anyway along to the saloon.

Mercer was standing there looking bewildered.

Looking haggard. Stricken with shock.

'Sir?' I said.

His eyes focused on me vaguely.

'My son,' he said.

'Sir?'

Sheridan wasn't in the saloon. Mercer was alone.

'Stop the train,' he said. 'We must go back.'

Oh *God*, I thought.

'He went out . . . on to the platform . . . to look at the river . . .' Mercer could hardly speak. 'When I looked up . . . he wasn't there.'

The door to the platform was closed. I went past Mercer, opened the door and went out. There was no one on the platform, as he'd said.

There was wind in plenty. The polished brass top of the railings ran round at waist height, with both of the exit gates still firmly bolted.

Over the right-hand side, from time to time, there were places which offered a straight unimpeded hundred-foot drop to the fearsome frothing rocky river below. Death beckoned there. A quick death.

I went into the saloon and closed the door.

Mercer was swaying with more than the movement of the train.

'Sit down, sir,' I said, taking his arm. 'I'll tell the Conductor. He'll know what to do.'

'We must go back.' He sat down with buckling legs. 'He went out . . . and when I looked . . .'

'Will you be all right while I go to the Conductor?'

He nodded dully. 'Yes. Hurry.'

I hurried, myself feeling much of Mercer's bewildered shock, if not his complicated grief. Half an hour earlier, Sheridan hadn't looked like someone about to jump off a cliff; but then I supposed that I'd never seen anyone else at that point, so how would I know? Perhaps the blank look, I thought, had been a sign, if anyone could have read it.

I hurried everywhere except through the dining car, so as not to be alarming, and when I reached George's room I found the door still shut. I knocked. No reply. I knocked again harder and called his name with urgency. '*George!*'

There was a grunt from inside. I opened the door without more ado and found him still lying on the bed in his clothes, waking from a deep sleep.

I closed his door behind me and sat on the edge of his bed, and told him we'd lost a passenger.

'Into Fraser Canyon,' he repeated. He shunted himself up into a sitting position and put both hands to his head, wincing. 'When?'

'About ten minutes ago, I should think.'

He stretched out a hand to the radio, looking out of the window to get his bearings. 'It's no use going back, you know. Not if he went into the water from this height. And the river's bitter cold, and you can see how fast it is . . . and there's a whirlpool.'

'His father will go, though.'

'Of course.'

The despatcher he got through to this time was in Vancouver. He explained that Mercer Lorrimore's son – that was right, *the* Mercer Lorrimore – his twenty-year-old son had fallen from the rear of the race train into Fraser Canyon somewhere between Hell's Gate and a mile or two south of Yale. Mercer Lorrimore wanted the train stopped so that he could go back to find his son. He, George Burley, wanted instructions from Montreal. The despatcher, sounding glazed, told him to hang on.

There was no chance now, I thought, of reaching Vancouver without a disaster. Sheridan was a disaster of major proportions, and the Press would be at Vancouver station for all the wrong reasons.

'I think I'd better go back to Mercer,' I said.

George nodded gingerly. 'Tell him I'll come to talk to him when I get instructions from Montreal, eh?' He rubbed a hand over his chin. 'He'll have to put up with stubble.'

I returned to the dining car and found Nell still sitting beside Xanthe. I said into Nell's ear, 'Bring Xanthe into the private car.'

She looked enquiringly into my face and saw nothing comforting, but she got Xanthe to move without alarming her. I led the way through the dome car and through the join into the rear car, knocking again on the unlocked door.

Mercer came out of his and Bambi's bedroom further up the corridor looking grey and hollow-eyed, a face of unmistakable calamity.

'Daddy!' Xanthe said, pushing past me. 'What's the matter?'

He folded his arms round her and hugged her, and took her with him towards the saloon. Neither Nell nor I heard the words he murmured to her, but we both heard her say sharply, 'No! He couldn't!'

'Couldn't what?' Nell said to me quietly.

'Sheridan went off the back platform into the canyon.'

'Do you mean . . .' she was horrified ' . . . that he's *dead*?'

'I would think so.'

'Oh *shit*,' Nell said.

My feelings exactly, I thought.

We went on into the saloon. Mercer said almost mechanically, 'Why don't we stop? We have to go back.' He no longer sounded, I thought, as if he expected or even hoped to find Sheridan alive.

'Sir, the Conductor is radioing for instructions,' I said.

He nodded. He was a reasonable man in most circumstances. He had only to look out of the window to know that going back wouldn't help. He knew that it

410

was practically impossible for anyone to fall off the platform by accident. He certainly believed, from his demeanour, that Sheridan had jumped.

Mercer sat on the sofa, his arm around Xanthe beside him, her head on his shoulder. Xanthe wasn't crying. She looked serious, but calm. The tragedy for Xanthe hadn't happened within that half-hour, it had been happening all her life. Her brother had been lost to her even when alive.

Nell said, 'Shall we go, Mr Lorrimore?' meaning herself and me. 'Can I do anything for Mrs Lorrimore?'

'No, no,' he said. 'Stay.' He swallowed. 'You'll have to know what's decided . . . what to tell everyone . . .' He shook his head helplessly. 'We must make some decisions.'

George arrived at that point and sat down in an armchair near Mercer, leaning forward with his forearms on his knees and saying how sorry he was, how very sorry.

'We have to go back,' Mercer said.

'Yes, sir, but not the whole train, sir. Montreal says the train must go on to Vancouver as scheduled.'

Mercer began to protest. George interrupted him. 'Sir, Montreal say that they are already alerting all the authorities along the canyon to look out for your son. They say they will arrange transport for you to return, you and your family, as soon as we reach Vancouver. You can see . . .' he glanced out of the window ' . . . that the area is unpopulated, eh?, but there are often

411

people working by the river. There is a road running along quite near the canyon, as well as another railway line on the other side. There's a small town over there called . . . er . . .' he coughed ' . . . Hope. It's at the south end of the canyon, eh?, where the river broadens out and runs more slowly. We're almost at that point now, as you'll see. If you go to Hope, Montreal says, you will be in the area if there is any news.'

'How do I get there?' Mercer said. 'Is there a train back?'

George said, 'There is, yes, but only one a day. It's the Super-continental. It leaves Vancouver at four in the afternoon, passes through Hope at seven.'

'That's useless,' Mercer said. 'How far is it by road?'

'About a hundred and fifty kilometres.'

He reflected. 'I'll get a helicopter,' he said.

There was absolutely no point in being rich, I thought, if one didn't know how to use it.

The logistics of the return were making Mercer feel better, one could see. George told him that the train we were on would speed up considerably once we were clear of the canyon, and that we'd·be in Vancouver in two hours and a half. They discussed how to engage a helicopter; Mercer already had a car meeting him at the station. Nell said Merry & Co would arrange everything, as they had indeed already arranged the car. No problem, if she could reach her office by telephone. George shook his head. He would relay the message by radio through Montreal. He brought out a notepad to write down Merry & Co's number and the instruction 'Arrange helicopter, Nell will phone from Vancouver.'

'I'll phone from the train,' she said.

George stood up. 'I'll get moving then, Mr Lorrimore. We'll do everything possible.' He looked big, awkward and unshaven, but Mercer had taken strength from him and was grateful. 'My sympathy,' George said, 'to Mrs Lorrimore.'

The tray of empty teacups still lay where I'd left it on the coffee table. I picked it up and asked if there was anything I could bring them, but Mercer shook his head.

'I'll come and find you,' Xanthe said, 'if they need anything.' She sounded competent and grown up, years older than at breakfast. Nell gave her a swift, sweet glance of appreciation, and she, George and I made our way back into the dome car, George hurrying off to his radio and Nell sighing heavily over what to say to the other passengers.

'It'll spoil the end of their trip,' she said.

'Try them.'

'You're cynical.'

'Pretty often.'

She shook her head as if I were a lost cause and went into the dining room with the bad news, which was predictably greeted with shock but no grief.

'Poor Xanthe,' Rose Young exclaimed, and Mrs Unwin said, 'Poor Bambi.' The sympathy stage lasted ten seconds. The deliciously round-eyed 'Isn't it dreadful?' stage went on all morning.

Julius Apollo Filmer was no longer in the dining room and I wished he had been as I would like to have seen his reactions. Chance would seem to have robbed him of his lever against Mercer; or would he reckon that Mercer would still sacrifice one horse to preserve the reputation of the dead? Filmer could read it wrong, I thought.

There was a cocktail party scheduled for that evening in the Four Seasons Hotel for Vancouver's racing bigwigs to meet the owners: would it still be held, several anxiously asked.

'Certainly,' Nell answered robustly. 'The party and the race will go on.'

No one, not even I, was cynical enough to say, 'Sheridan would have wished it.'

I helped clear away the breakfast and wash the dishes and pack everything into boxes for sending back to the caterers in Toronto, and when we'd finished I found that Nell had collected gratuities from the passengers to give to the waiters, and Emil, Cathy and Oliver had split it four ways. Emil put a bundle of notes into my hand, and he and the others were smiling.

'I can't take it,' I said.

Emil said, 'We know you aren't a waiter, and we

know you aren't an actor, but you have worked for it. It's yours.'

'And we know you've worked all morning although it's obvious you've hurt your arm,' Cathy said. 'I made it worse . . . I'm real sorry.'

'And it would all have been very much harder work without you,' Oliver said. 'So we thought we'd like to give you a present.'

'And that's it,' Cathy added, pointing to the notes.

They waited expectantly, wanting my thanks.

'I . . . er, I don't know . . .' I kissed Cathy suddenly; hugged her. 'All right. I'll buy something to remember us by. To remember the journey. Thank you all very much.'

They laughed, pleased. 'It's been fun,' Cathy said, and Emil added ironically, 'But not every week.'

I shook Emil's hand, and Oliver's. Kissed Cathy again. Shook hands with Angus. Was offered Simone's cheek for a peck. I looked round at their faces, wanting to hold on to the memory.

'See you again,' I said, and they said, 'Yes,' and we all knew it was doubtful. I went away along the swaying corridor, taking Tommy to extinction and, as often in the past, not looking back. Too many regrets in looking back.

In the sleeping cars everyone was packing and holding impromptu parties in each other's rooms, walking in and out of the open doors. Filmer's door was shut.

Nell was in her roomette, with the door open, packing.

'What's wrong with your arm?' she said, folding one of the straight skirts.

'Is it so obvious?'

'Most obvious when Cathy bumped into you with her tray. The shock went right through you.'

'Yes, well, it's not serious.'

'I'll get you a doctor.'

'Don't be silly.'

'I suppose,' she said, 'Mercer won't run his horse now on Tuesday. Such a shame. That *damned* Sheridan.'

The biblical description, I thought, was accurate.

'Xanthe,' Nell said, putting the skirt in her suitcase, 'says you were kind to her at Lake Louise. Did you really say something about the corruption of self-importance? She said she learned a lot.'

'She grew up this morning,' I said.

'Yes, didn't she?'

'If we go to Hawaii,' I said, 'you can wear a sarong and a hibiscus behind your ear.'

She paused in the packing. 'They wouldn't really go,' she said judiciously, 'with a clipboard.'

George came out of his office and told her the cellular telephone was now working, if she wanted to make her calls, and I went into my roomette and changed out of uniform into Tommy's outdoor clothes, and packed everything away. The train journey might be finished, I was thinking, but my real job wasn't.

416

There was much to be done. Filmer might be sick, but it was sick sharks that attacked swimmers, and there could still be a dorsal fin unseen below the surface.

Nell came out of George's office and along to my door.

'No helicopter needed,' she said. 'They've found Sheridan already.'

'That was quick.'

'Apparently he fell on to a fish ladder.'

'You're kidding me.'

'No, actually.' She stifled a laugh, as improper to the occasion. 'George says the ladders are a sort of staircase hundreds of metres long that are built in the river because the salmon can't swim upstream to spawn against the strength of the water, because the water flows much faster than it used to because a huge rockfall constricted it.'

'I'll believe it,' I said.

'Some men were working on the lower ladder,' she said, 'and Sheridan was swept down in the water'

'Dead?' I asked.

'Very.'

'You'd better tell Mercer.'

She made a reluctant face. 'You do it.'

'I can't. George could.'

George agreed to go with the good bad news and hurried off so as to be back at his post when we reached the station.

'Did you know,' I said to Nell, 'that Emil, Cathy and Oliver wanted to share their tips with me?'

'Yes, they asked me if I thought it would be all right. I do hope,' she said with sudden anxiety, 'that you accepted? They said you'd been great. They wanted to thank you. They were so pleased with themselves.'

'Yes,' I said, relieved to be able to. 'I accepted. I told them I'd buy something to remind me of them and the trip. And I will.'

She relaxed. 'I should have warned you. But then, I guess . . . no need.' She smiled. 'What are you really?'

'Happy,' I said.

'Yuk.'

'I try hard, but it keeps breaking out. My boss threatens to fire me for it.'

'Who's your boss?'

'Brigadier Valentine Catto.'

She blinked. 'I never know when you're telling the truth.'

Catto, I thought. Cats. Sobering.

'I have just,' I said slowly, 'been struck by a blinding idea.'

'Yes, you rather look like it.'

Time, I thought. Not enough of it.

'Come back,' Nell said. 'I've lost you.'

'You don't happen to have a world air timetable with you, do you?'

'There are several in the office. What do you want?'

'A flight from London to Vancouver tomorrow.'

She raised her eyebrows, went into George's office, consulted on the telephone and came out again.

'Air Canada leaves Heathrow 3 p.m., arrives Vancouver 4.25.'

'Consider yourself kissed.'

'Are you still a waiter, then, in the eyes of the passengers?'

There were passengers all the time in the corridor.

'Mm,' I said thoughtfully, 'I think so. For another two days. To the end.'

'All right.'

George returned and reported that all three of the Lorrimores had received the news of Sheridan calmly and would go to the hotel as planned, and make arrangements from there.

'Poor people,' Nell said. 'What a mess.'

I asked George what he would be doing. Going back to Toronto, of course, possibly by train, as soon as the various VIA enquiries were completed, which would be tomorrow. Couldn't he stay for the race, I asked, and go back on the Tuesday evening? He wasn't sure. I took him into his office and convinced him, and he was chuckling again as the train slowed to a crawl and inched into the terminus at Vancouver.

The wheels stopped. Seven days almost to the hour since they'd set off, the passengers climbed down from the travelling hotel and stood in little groups outside, still smiling and still talking. Zak and the other actors moved among them, shaking farewell hands. The actors had commitments back in Toronto and weren't staying for the race.

Zak saw me through the window and bounced up again into the sleeping car to say goodbye.

'Don't lose touch, now,' he said. 'Any time you want a job writing mysteries, let me know.'

'OK.'

'Bye, guy,' he said.

'Bye.'

He jumped off the train again and trailed away beneath his mop of curls towards the station buildings, with Donna, Pierre, Raoul, Mavis, Walter and Giles following like meteorites after a comet.

I waited for Filmer to pass. He walked on his own, looking heavy and intent. He was wearing an overcoat and carrying the briefcase and not bothering to be charming. There was a firmness of purpose in his step that I didn't much like, and when Nell took a pace forward to ask him something he answered her with a brief turn of his head but no break in his stride.

When he'd gone, I jumped down beside Nell who was carefully checking other passengers off against a list on the clipboard as they passed. It was a list, I discovered by looking over her shoulder, of the people catching the special bus to check into the Four Seasons Hotel. Against Filmer's name, as against all the others, I was relieved to see a tick.

'That's everyone,' Nell said finally. She looked

towards the rear of the train. 'Except the Lorrimores, of course. I'd better go and help them.'

I stepped back on board to collect my gear and through the window watched the little solemn party pass by outside: Mercer, head up, looking sad, Bambi expressionless, Xanthe caring, Nell concerned.

Some way after them I walked forward through the train. It was quiet and empty, the racegoers having flooded away, the surly cook gone from the centre diner, the dayniter no longer alive with singing, the doors of the empty bedrooms standing open, the Chinese cook vanished with his grin. I climbed down again and went on forward, past the baggage car where I collected my suitcase from the handler, and past the horse car, where Leslie Brown was leaning out of the window, still a dragon.

'Bye,' I said.

She looked at me, as if puzzled for a second, and then recognized me: Calgary and Lenny Higgs were three days back.

'Oh, yes . . . goodbye.'

The train was due to shunt out backwards, to take the horses and the grooms to a siding, from where they would go by road to Exhibition Park. Ms Brown was going with them, it seemed.

'Good luck at the races,' I said.

'I never bet.'

'Well . . . have a good time.'

She looked as if that were an unthinkable suggestion.

I waved to her, the stalwart custodian, and went on past the engine where the engineer was a shadowy figure high up beyond his impossibly small window, went on into the station.

The Lorrimores had been interrupted by people with notebooks, cameras and deadlines. Mercer was being civil. Nell extricated the family and ushered them to their car, and herself climbed into the long bus with the owners. I hung back until they'd all gone, then travelled in a taxi, booked in at the Hyatt and telephoned England.

The Brigadier wasn't at home in Newmarket. I could try his club in London, a voice said, giving me the familiar number, and I got connected to the bar of the Hobbs Sandwich where the Brigadier, I was relieved to hear, was at that moment receiving his first-of-the-evening well-watered Scotch.

'Tor!' he said. 'Where are you?'

'Vancouver.' I could hear the clink of the glasses and the murmurings in the background. I pictured the dark oak walls with the gentlemen in the pictures with side-whiskers, big pads and little caps, and it all seemed far back in time, not just in distance.

'Um,' I said. 'Can I phone you again when you're alone? This is going to take some time. I mean, soon, really.'

'Urgent?'

'Fairly.'

422

'Hold on. I'll go upstairs to my bedroom and get them to transfer the call. Don't go away.'

I waited through a few clicks until his voice came quietly on the line again without sound effects.

'Right. What's happened?'

I talked for what seemed a very long time. He punctuated my pauses with grunts to let me know he was still listening, and at the end he said, 'You don't ask much, do you? Just for miracles.'

'There's an Air Canada flight from Heathrow at three tomorrow afternoon,' I said, 'and they'll have all day and all Tuesday to find the information, because when it's only eleven in the morning in Vancouver on Tuesday, it'll be seven in the evening in England. And they could send it by fax.'

'Always supposing,' he said drily, 'that there's a fax machine in the Jockey Club in Exhibition Park.'

'I'll check,' I said. 'If there isn't, I'll get one.'

'What does Bill Baudelaire think of all this?' he asked.

'I haven't talked to him yet. I had to get your reaction first.'

'What's your phone number?' he asked. 'I'll think it over and ring you back in ten minutes.'

'Thought before action?'

'You can't fault it, if there's time.'

He thought for twice ten minutes, until I was itchy. When the bell rang, I took a deep breath and answered.

'We'll attempt it,' he said, 'as long as Bill Baudelaire

agrees, of course. If we can't find the information in the time available, we may have to abort.'

'All right.'

'Apart from that,' he said, 'well done.'

'Good staff work,' I said.

He laughed. 'Flattery will get you no promotion.'

CHAPTER TWENTY

I was looking forward to talking to Mrs Baudelaire. I dialled her number and Bill himself answered.

'Hello,' I said, surprised. 'It's Tor Kelsey. How's your mother?'

There was a long, awful pause.

'She's ill,' I said with anxiety.

'She . . . er . . . she died . . . early this morning.'

'Oh . . . no.' She couldn't have, I thought. It couldn't be true. 'I talked to her yesterday,' I said.

'We knew . . . she knew . . . it would only be weeks. But yesterday evening there was a crisis.'

I was silent. I felt her loss as if she'd been Aunt Viv restored to me and snatched away. I'd wanted so very much to meet her.

'Tor?' Bill's voice said.

I swallowed. 'Your mother . . . was great.'

He would hear the smothered tears in my voice, I thought. He would think me crazy.

'If it's of any use to you,' he said, 'she felt like that about you, too. You made her last week a good one.

425

She wanted to live to find out what happened. One of the last things she said was . . . "I don't want to go before the end of the story. I want to see that invisible young man . . ." She was slipping away . . . all the time.'

> Do not go gentle into that good night,
> Old age should burn and rave at close of day:
> Rage, rage against the dying of the light . . .

'Tor?' Bill said.

'I'm so very sorry,' I said with more control. 'So sorry.'

'Thank you.'

'I don't suppose . . .' I said, and paused, feeling helpless.

'You suppose wrong,' he replied instantly. 'I've been waiting here for you to phone. We would both fail her if we didn't go straight on. I've had hours to think this out. The last thing she would want would be for us to give up. So I'll start things off by telling you we've had a telex from Filmer announcing that he is the sole owner of Laurentide Ice, but we are going to inform him that the Ontario Racing Commission are rescinding his licence to own horses. We're also telling him he won't be admitted to the President's lunch at Exhibition Park.'

'I'd . . . er . . . like to do it differently,' I said.

'How do you mean?'

I sighed deeply and talked to him also for a long

time. He listened as the Brigadier had, with intermittent throat noises, and at the end he said simply, 'I do wish she'd been alive to hear all this.'

'Yes, so do I.'

'Well,' he paused. 'I'll go along with it. The real problem is time.'

'Mm.'

'You'd better talk to Mercer Lorrimore yourself.'

'But . . .'

'No buts. You're there. I can't get there until tomorrow late afternoon, not with all you want me to do here. Talk to Mercer without delay, you don't want him coming back to Toronto.'

I said with reluctance, 'All right.' But I had known that I would have to.

'Good. Use all the authority you need. Val and I will back you.'

'Thank you . . . very much.'

'See you tomorrow,' he said.

I put the receiver down slowly. Death could be colossally unfair, one knew that, but rage, rage . . . I felt anger for her as much as grief. Do not go gentle into that good night . . . I thought it probable, if I remembered right, that the last word she'd said to me was 'Good night'. Good night dear, dear Mrs Baudelaire. Go gentle. Go sweetly into that good night.

I sat for a while without energy, feeling the lack of sleep, feeling the nagging pain, feeling the despondency

427

her death had opened the door to: feeling unequal to the next two days, even though I'd set them up myself.

With an effort, after an age I got through to the Four Seasons Hotel and asked for Mercer, but found myself talking to Nell.

'All the calls are being re-routed to me,' she said. 'Bambi is lying down. Mercer and Xanthe are on their way to Hope in the helicopter, which was reordered for him, so that he can identify Sheridan's body which is being taken there by road.'

'It all sounds so clinical.'

'The authorities want to make sure it's Sheridan before they make any arrangements.'

'When will Mercer and Xanthe be back, do you know?'

'About six, they expected.'

'Um . . . the Jockey Club asked me to fix up a brief meeting. Do you think Mercer would agree to that?'

'He's being terrifically helpful to everyone. Almost too calm.'

I thought things over. 'Can you get hold of him in Hope?'

She hesitated. 'Yes, I suppose so. I have the address and the phone number of where he was going, but I think it's a police station . . . or a mortuary.'

'Could you . . . could you tell him that on their return to the hotel, a car will be waiting to take him straight on to a brief meeting with the Jockey Club? Tell him the Jockey Club send their sincere condolences and ask for just a little of his time.'

'I guess I could,' she said doubtfully. 'What about Xanthe?'

'Mercer alone,' I said positively.

'Is it important?' she asked, and I could imagine her frowning.

'I think it's important for Mercer.'

'All right.' She made up her mind. 'Xanthe can take the phone calls for her mother, then, because I have to go to this cocktail party.' A thought struck her. 'Aren't some of the Jockey Club coming to the party?'

'Mercer won't want to go. They want a quiet talk with him alone.'

'OK then, I'll try to arrange it.'

'Very many thanks,' I said fervently. 'I'll call back to check.'

I called back at five o'clock. The helicopter was in the air on its way back, Nell said, and Mercer had agreed to being picked up at the hotel.

'You're brilliant.'

'Tell the Jockey Club not to keep him long. He'll be tired . . . and he's identified Sheridan.'

'I could kiss you,' I said. 'The way to a man's heart is through his travel agent.'

She laughed. 'Always supposing that's where one wants to go.'

She put her receiver down with a delicate click. I did not want to lose her, I thought.

The car I sent for Mercer picked him up successfully and brought him to the Hyatt, the chauffeur telling him, as requested, the room to go straight up to. He rang the doorbell of the suite I'd engaged more or less in his honour, and I opened the door to let him in.

He came in about two paces and then stopped and peered with displeasure at my face.

'What is this?' he demanded with growing anger, preparing to depart.

I closed the door behind him.

'I work for the Jockey Club,' I said. 'The British Jockey Club. I am seconded here with the Canadian Jockey Club for the duration of the race train Celebration of Canadian Racing.'

'But you're . . . you're . . .'

'My name is Tor Kelsey,' I said. 'It was judged better that I didn't go openly on the train as a sort of security agent for the Jockey Club, so I went as a waiter.'

He looked me over. Looked at the rich young owner's good suit that I'd put on for the occasion. Looked at the expensive room.

'My God,' he said weakly. He took a few paces forward. 'Why am I here?'

'I work for Brigadier Valentine Catto in England,' I said, 'and Bill Baudelaire over here. They are the heads of the Jockey Club Security Services.'

He nodded. He knew them.

'As they cannot be here, they have both given me their authority to speak to you on their behalf.'

'Yes, but . . . what about?'

'Would you sit down? Would you like . . . a drink?'

He looked at me with a certain dry humour. 'Do you have any identification?'

'Yes.' I fetched my passport. He opened it. Looked at my name, at my likeness, and at my occupation: investigator.

He handed it back. 'Yes, I'll have a drink,' he said, 'as you're so good at serving them. Cognac if possible.'

I opened the cupboard that the hotel had supplied at my request with wine, vodka, Scotch and brandy, and poured the amount I knew he'd like, even adding the heretical ice. He took the glass with a twist of a smile, and sat in one of the armchairs.

'No one guessed about you,' he said. 'No one came anywhere near it.' He took a sip reflectively. 'Why were you on the train?'

'I was sent because of one of the passengers. Because of Julius Filmer.'

The ease that had been growing in him fled abruptly. He put the glass down on the table beside him and stared at me.

'Mr Lorrimore,' I said, sitting down opposite him, 'I am sorry about your son. Truly sorry. All of the Jockey Club send their sympathy. I think though that I should tell you straight away that Brigadier Catto, Bill Baudelaire and myself all know about the . . . er . . . incident . . . of the cats.'

He looked deeply shocked. 'You can't know!'

'I imagine that Julius Filmer knows also.'

He made a hopeless gesture with one hand. 'However did he find out?'

'The Brigadier is working on that in England.'

'And how did *you* find out?'

'Not from anyone you swore to silence.'

'Not from the college?'

'No.'

He covered his face briefly with one hand.

'Julius Filmer may still suggest you give him Voting Right in exchange for his keeping quiet,' I said.

He lowered the hand to his throat and closed his eyes. 'I've thought of that,' he said. He opened his eyes again. 'Did you see the last scene of the mystery?'

'Yes,' I said.

'I haven't known what to do . . . since then.'

'It's you who has to decide,' I said. 'But . . . can I tell you a few things?'

He gave a vague gesture of assent, and I talked to him, also, for quite a long time. He listened with total concentration, mostly watching my face. People who were repudiating in their minds every word one said didn't look at one's face but at the floor, or at a table, at anything else. I knew, by the end, that he would do what I was asking, and I was grateful because it wouldn't be easy for him.

When I'd finished, he said thoughtfully, 'That mystery was no coincidence, was it? The father blackmailed because of his child's crime, the groom murdered because he knew too much, the man who would kill himself if he couldn't keep his racehorses ... Did you write it yourself?'

'All that part, yes. Not from the beginning.'

He smiled faintly. 'You showed me what I was doing ... was prepared to do. But beyond that ... you showed Sheridan.'

'I wondered,' I said.

'Did you? Why?'

'He looked different afterwards. He had changed.'

Mercer said, 'How could you see that?'

'It's my job.'

He looked startled. 'There isn't such a job.'

'Yes,' I said, 'there is.'

'Explain,' he said.

'I watch ... for things that aren't what they were, and try to understand, and find out why.'

'All the time?'

I nodded. 'Yes.'

He drank some brandy thoughtfully. 'What change did you see in Sheridan?'

I hesitated. 'I just thought that things had shifted in his mind. Like seeing something from a different perspective. A sort of revelation. I didn't know if it would last.'

'It might not have done.'

'No.'

'He said,' Mercer said, ' "Sorry, Dad." '

It was my turn to stare.

'He said it before he went out on to the platform.' Mercer swallowed with difficulty and eventually went on. 'He had been so quiet. I couldn't sleep. I went out to the saloon about dawn, and he was sitting there. I asked him what was the matter, and he said, "I fucked things up, didn't I?" We all knew he had. It wasn't anything new. But it was the first time he'd said so. I tried . . . I tried to comfort him, to say we would stand by him, no matter what. He knew about Filmer's threat, you know. Filmer said in front of all of us that he knew about the cats.' He looked unseeingly over his glass. 'It wasn't the only time it had happened. Sheridan killed two cats like that in our garden when he was fourteen. We got therapy for him. . . . They said it was the upheaval of adolescence.' He paused. 'One psychiatrist said Sheridan was psychopathic, he couldn't help what he did . . . but he could, really, most of the time. He could help being discourteous, but he thought being rich gave him the right . . . I told him it didn't.'

'Why did you send him to Cambridge?' I asked.

'My father was there, and established a scholarship. They gave it to Sheridan as thanks – as a gift. He couldn't concentrate long enough to get into college otherwise. But then . . . the Master of the college said they couldn't keep him, scholarship or not, and I understood . . . of course they couldn't. We thought he would be all right there . . . we so hoped he would.'

They'd spent a lot of hope on Sheridan, I thought.

'I don't know if he meant to jump this morning when

he went out on the platform,' Mercer said. 'I don't know if it was just an impulse. He gave way to impulses very easily. Unreasonable impulses . . . almost insane, sometimes.'

'It was seductive, out there,' I said. 'Easy to jump.'

Mercer looked at me gratefully. 'Did you feel it?'

'Sort of.'

'Sheridan's revelation lasted until this morning,' he said.

'Yes,' I said. 'I saw . . . when I brought your tea.'

'The waiter . . .' He shook his head, still surprised.

'I'd be grateful,' I said, 'if you don't tell anyone else about the waiter.'

'Why not?'

'Because most of my work depends on anonymity. My bosses don't want people like Filmer to know I exist.'

He nodded slowly, with comprehension. 'I won't tell.'

He stood up and shook my hand. 'What do they pay you?' he asked.

I smiled. 'Enough.'

'I wish Sheridan had been able to have a job. He couldn't stick at anything.' He sighed. 'I'll believe that what he did this morning was for us. "Sorry, Dad . . ." '

Mercer looked me in the eyes and made a simple statement, without defensiveness, without apology.

'I loved my son,' he said.

435

On Monday morning, I went to Vancouver station to back up George Burley in the rail company's dual enquiry into the hot box and the suicide.

I was written down as 'T. Titmuss, Acting Crew', which amused me and seemed to cover several interpretations. George was stalwart and forthright, with the ironic chuckles subdued to merely a gleam. He was a railwayman of some prestige, I was glad to see, who was treated with respect if not quite deference, and his were the views they listened to.

He gave the railway investigators a photograph of Johnson and said that while he hadn't actually seen him pour liquid into the radio, he could say that it was in this man's roomette that he had awakened bound and gagged, and he could say that it was this man who had attacked Titmuss, when he, Titmuss, went back to plant the flares.

'Was that so?' they asked me. Could I identify him positively?

'Positively,' I said.

They moved on to Sheridan's death. A sad business, they said. Apart from making a record of the time of the occurrence and the various radio messages, there was little to be done. The family had made no complaint to or about the railway company. Any other conclusions would have to be reached at the official inquest.

'That wasn't too bad, eh?' George said afterwards.

'Would you come in uniform to the races?' I asked.

'If that's what you want.'

'Yes, please.' I gave him a card with directions and instructions and a pass cajoled from Nell to get him in through the gates.

'See you tomorrow, eh?'

I nodded. 'At eleven o'clock.'

We went our different ways, and with some reluctance but definite purpose I sought out a doctor recommended by the hotel and presented myself for inspection.

The doctor was thin, growing old and inclined to make jokes over his half-moon glasses.

'Ah,' he said, when I'd removed my shirt. 'Does it hurt when you cough?'

'It hurts when I do practically anything, as a matter of fact.'

'We'd better have a wee X-ray then, don't you think?'

I agreed to the X-ray and waited around for ages until he reappeared with a large sheet of celluloid which he clipped in front of a light.

'Well, now,' he said, 'the good news is that we don't have any broken ribs or chipped vertebrae.'

'Fine.' I was relieved and perhaps a bit surprised.

'What we do have is a fractured shoulder blade.'

I stared at him. 'I didn't think that was possible.'

'Anything's possible,' he said. 'See that,' he pointed, 'that's a real granddaddy of a break. Goes right across, goes right through. The bottom part of your left

437

scapula,' he announced cheerfully, 'is to all intents and purposes detached from the top.'

'Um,' I said blankly. 'What do we do about it?'

He looked at me over the half-moons. 'Rivets,' he said, 'might be extreme, don't you think? Heavy strapping, immobility for two weeks, that'll do the trick.'

'What about,' I said, 'if we do nothing at all? Will it mend?'

'Probably. Bones are remarkable. Young bones especially. You could try a sling. You'd be more comfortable though, if you let me strap your arm firmly skin to skin to your side and chest, under your shirt.'

I shook my head and said I wanted to go on a sort of honeymoon to Hawaii.

'People who go on honeymoons with broken bones,' he said with a straight face, 'must be ready to giggle.'

I giggled there and then. I asked him for a written medical report and the X-ray, and paid him for them, and bore away my evidence.

Stopping at a pharmacy on my way back to the hotel, I bought an elbow-supporting sling made of wide black ribbon, which I tried on for effect in the shop, and which made things a good deal better. I was wearing it when I opened my door in the evening, first to the Brigadier on his arrival from Heathrow, and then to Bill Baudelaire, from Toronto.

Bill Baudelaire looked around the sitting room and commented to the Brigadier about the lavishness of my expense account.

'Expense account, my foot!' the Brigadier said, drinking my Scotch. 'He's paying for it himself.'

Bill Baudelaire looked shocked. 'You can't let him,' he said.

'Didn't he tell you?' the Brigadier laughed. 'He's as rich as Croesus.'

'No . . . he didn't tell me.'

'He never tells anybody. He's afraid of it.'

Bill Baudelaire, with his carroty hair and pitted skin, looked at me with acute curiosity.

'Why do you do this job?' he said.

The Brigadier gave me no time to answer. 'What else would he do to pass the time? Play backgammon? This game is better. Isn't that it, Tor?'

'This game is better,' I agreed.

The Brigadier smiled. Although shorter than Bill Baudelaire, and older and leaner, and with fairer, thinning hair, he seemed to fill more of the room. I might be three inches taller than he, but I had the impression always of looking up to him, not down.

'To work, then,' he suggested. 'Strategy, tactics, plan of attack.'

He had brought some papers from England, though some were still to come, and he spread them out on the coffee table so that all of us, leaning forward, could see them.

'It was a good guess of yours, Tor, that the report on the cats was a computer print-out, because of its lack of headings. The Master of the college had a call from Mercer Lorrimore at eight this morning . . . must have been midnight here . . . empowering him to tell us everything, as you'd asked. The Master gave us the name of the veterinary pathology lab he'd employed and sent us a fax of the letter he'd received from them. Is that the same as the one in Filmer's briefcase, Tor?'

He pushed a paper across and I glanced at it. 'Identical, except for the headings.'

'Good. The path lab confirmed they kept the letter stored in their computer but they don't know yet how anyone outside could get a printout. We're still trying. So are they. They don't like it happening.'

'How about a list of their employees,' I said, 'including temporary secretaries or wizard hacker office boys?'

'Where do you get such language?' the Brigadier protested. He produced a sheet of names. 'This was the best they could do.'

I read the list. None of the names was familiar.

'Do you really need to know the connection?' Bill Baudelaire asked.

'It would be neater,' I said.

The Brigadier nodded. 'John Millington is working on it. We're talking to him by telephone before tomorrow's meeting. Now, the next thing,' he turned to me. 'That conveyance you saw in the briefcase. As you suggested, we checked the number SF 90155 with the Land Registry.' He chuckled with all George Burley's enjoyment. 'That alone would have been worth your trip.'

He explained why. Bill Baudelaire said, 'We've got him, then,' with great satisfaction: and the joint Commanders-in-Chief began deciding in which order they would fire off their accumulated salvoes.

Julius Apollo walked into a high-up private room in Exhibition Park racecourse on Tuesday morning to sign and receive, as he thought, certification that he was the sole owner of Laurentide Ice, which would run in his name that afternoon.

The room was the President of the racecourse's conference room, having a desk attended by three comfortable armchairs at one end, with a table surrounded by eight similar chairs at the other. The doorway from the passage was at mid-point between the groupings, so that one turned right to the desk, left to the conference table. A fawn carpet covered the floor, horse pictures covered the walls, soft yellow leather covered the armchairs: a cross between comfort and practicality, without windows but with interesting spotlighting from recesses in the ceiling.

When Filmer entered, both of the Directors of Security were sitting behind the desk, with three senior members of the Vancouver Jockey Club and the British Columbia Racing Commission seated at the conference table. They were there to give weight to the proceedings and to bear witness afterwards, but they had chosen to be there simply as observers, and they had agreed not to interrupt with questions. They would take notes, they said, and ask questions afterwards, if necessary.

Three more people and I waited on the other side of a closed door which led from the conference table end of the room into a serving pantry, and from there out again into the passage.

When Filmer arrived I went along the passage and locked the door he had come in by, and put the key in the pocket of my grey raincoat, which I wore buttoned to the neck. Then I walked back along the passage and into the serving pantry where I stood quietly behind the others waiting there.

A microphone stood on the desk in front of the Directors, with another on the conference table, both of them leading to a tape recorder. Out in the serving pantry, an amplifier quietly relayed everything that was said inside.

Bill Baudelaire's deep voice greeted Filmer, invited him to sit in the chair in front of the desk, and said, 'You know Brigadier Catto, of course?'

As the two men had glared at each other times without number, yes, he knew him.

'And these other gentlemen are from the Jockey Club and Racing Commission here in Vancouver.'

'What *is* this?' Filmer asked truculently. 'All I want is some paperwork. A formality.'

The Brigadier said, 'We are taking this opportunity

to make some preliminary enquiries into some racing matters, and it seemed best to do it now, as so many of the people involved are in Vancouver at this time.'

'What are you talking about?' Filmer said.

'We should explain,' the Brigadier said smoothly, 'that we are recording what is said in this room this morning. This is not a formal trial or an official enquiry, but what is said here may be repeated at any trial or enquiry in the future. We would ask you to bear this in mind.'

Filmer said strongly, 'I object to this.'

'At any future trial or Jockey Club enquiry,' Bill Baudelaire said, 'you may of course be accompanied by a legal representative. We will furnish you with a copy of the tape of this morning's preliminary proceedings which you may care to give to your lawyer.'

'You can't do this,' Filmer said. 'I'm not staying.'

When he went to the door he had entered by, he found it locked.

'Let me out,' Filmer said furiously. 'You can't do this.'

In the serving pantry Mercer Lorrimore took a deep breath, opened the door to the conference room, went through and closed it behind him.

'Good morning, Julius,' he said.

'What are you doing here?' Filmer's voice was surprised but not overwhelmingly dismayed. 'Tell them to give me my paper and be done with it.'

'Sit down, Julius,' Mercer said. He was speaking into

the conference table microphone, his voice sounding much louder than Filmer's. 'Sit down by the desk.'

'The preliminary enquiry, Mr Filmer,' the Brigadier's voice said, 'is principally into your actions before and during, and in conjunction with, the journey of the race train.' There was a pause, presumably a wait for Filmer to settle. Then the Brigadier's voice again, 'Mr Lorrimore . . . may I ask you . . . ?'

Mercer cleared his throat. 'My son Sheridan,' he said evenly, 'who died two days ago, suffered intermittently from a mental instability which led him sometimes to do bizarre . . . and unpleasant . . . things.'

There was a pause. No words from Filmer.

Mercer said, 'To his great regret, there was an incident of that sort, back in May. Sheridan killed . . . some animals. The bodies were taken from where they were found by a veterinary pathologist who then performed private autopsies on them.' He paused again. The strain was clear in his voice, but he didn't falter. 'You, Julius, indicated to my family on the train that you knew about this incident, and three of us . . . my wife Bambi, my son Sheridan and myself . . . all understood during that evening that you would use Sheridan's regrettable act as leverage to get hold of my horse, Voting Right.'

Filmer said furiously, 'That damned play!'

'Yes,' Mercer said. 'It put things very clearly. After Sheridan died, I gave permission to the Master of my son's college, to the British Jockey Club Security Service, and to the veterinary pathologist himself, to find out how that piece of information came into your possession.'

'We did find out,' the Brigadier said, and repeated what a triumphant John Millington had relayed to us less than an hour ago. 'It happened by chance ... by accident. You, Mr Filmer, owned a horse, trained in England at Newmarket, which died. You suspected poison of some sort and insisted on a post-mortem, making your trainer arrange to have some organs sent to the path lab. The lab wrote a letter to your trainer saying there was no foreign substance in the organs, and at your request they later sent a copy of the letter to you. One of their less bright computer operators had meanwhile loaded your letter on to a very private disk which she shouldn't have used, and in some way chain-loaded it, so that you received not only a copy of your letter but copies of three other letters besides, letters which were private and confidential.' The Brigadier paused. 'We know this is so,' he said, 'because when one of our operators asked the lab to print out a copy for us, your own letter and the others came out attached to it, chain-loaded into the same secret document name.'

The pathologist, Millington had said, was in total disarray and thinking of scrapping the lab's computer for a new one. 'But it wasn't the computer,' he said. 'It was a nitwit girl, who apparently thought the poison enquiry on the horse was top secret also, and put it on the top-secret disk. They can't sack her, she left weeks ago.'

'Could the pathologist be prosecuted for the cover-up?' the Brigadier had asked.

'Doubtful,' Millington had said, 'now that Sheridan's dead.'

Filmer's voice, slightly hoarse, came out of the loud-speaker into the pantry. 'This is rubbish.'

'You kept the letter,' the Brigadier said. 'It was dynamite, if you could find who it referred to. No doubt you kept all three of the letters, though the other two didn't concern criminal acts. Then you saw one day in your local paper that Mercer Lorrimore was putting up money for a new college library. And you would have had to ask only one question to find out that Mercer Lorrimore's son had left that college in a hurry during May. After that, you would have found that no one would say why. You became sure that the letter referred to Sheridan Lorrimore. You did nothing with your information until you heard that Mercer Lorrimore would be on the Transcontinental Race Train, and then you saw an opportunity of exploring the possibility of blackmailing Mr Lorrimore into letting you have his horse, Voting Right.'

'You can't prove any of this,' Filmer said defiantly.

'We all believe,' said Bill Baudelaire's voice, 'that with you, Mr Filmer, it is the urge to crush people and make them suffer that sets you going. We know you could afford to buy good horses. We know that for you simply owning horses isn't enough.'

'Save me the sermon,' Filmer said. 'And if you can't put up, shut up.'

'Very well,' the Brigadier said. 'We'll ask our next visitor to come in, please.'

Daffodil Quentin, who was standing beside George in the pantry and had been listening with parted mouth and growing anger, opened the dividing door dramatically and slammed it shut behind her.

'You unspeakable toad,' her voice said vehemently over the loudspeaker.

Attagirl, I thought.

She was wearing a scarlet dress and a wide shiny black belt and carrying a large shiny black handbag. Under the high curls and in a flaming rage, she attacked as an avenging angel in full spate.

'I will never give you or sell you my half of Laurentide Ice,' she said forcefully, 'and you can threaten and blackmail until you're blue in the face. You can frighten my stable lad until you think you're God Almighty, but you can't from now on frighten *me* – and I think you're contemptible and should be put in a zoo.'

CHAPTER TWENTY-ONE

Bill Baudelaire, who had persuaded her to come with him to Vancouver, cleared his throat and sounded as if he were trying not to laugh.

'Mrs Quentin,' he said to the world at large, 'is prepared to testify . . .'

'You bet I am,' Daffodil interrupted.

' . . . that you threatened to have her prosecuted for killing one of her own horses if she didn't give . . . *give* . . . you her remaining share of Laurentide Ice.'

'You used me,' Daffodil said furiously. 'You bought your way on to the train and you were all charm and smarm and all you were aiming to do was ingratiate yourself with Mercer Lorrimore so you could sneer at him and cause him pain and take away his horse. You make me puke.'

'I don't have to listen to this,' Filmer said.

'Yes, you damned well do. It's time someone told you to your face what a slimy putrid blob of spit you are and gave you back some of the hatred you sow.'

'Er,' Bill Baudelaire said. 'We have here a letter from

Mrs Quentin's insurance company, written yesterday, saying that they made exhaustive tests on her horse that died of colic and they are satisfied that they paid her claim correctly. We also have here an affidavit from the stable lad, Lenny Higgs, to the effect that you learned about the colic and the specially numbered feeds for Laurentide Ice from him during one of your early visits to the horse car. He goes on to swear that he was later frightened into saying that Mrs Quentin gave him some food to give to her horse who died of colic.' He cleared his throat. 'As you have heard, the insurance company are satisfied that whatever she gave her horse didn't cause its death. Lenny Higgs further testifies that the man who frightened him, by telling him he would be sent to prison where he would catch AIDS and die, that man is an ex-baggage handler once employed by VIA Rail, name of Alex Mitchell McLachlan.'

'*What*!' For the first time there was fear in Filmer's voice, and I found it sweet.

'Lenny Higgs positively identifies him from this photograph.' There was a pause while Bill Baudelaire handed it over. 'This man travelled in the racegoers' part of the train under the name of Johnson. During yesterday, the photograph was shown widely to VIA employees in Toronto and Montreal, and he was several times identified as Alex McLachlan.'

There was silence where Filmer might have spoken.

'You were observed to be speaking to McLachlan . . .'

'You bet you were,' Daffodil interrupted. 'You were talking to him . . . arguing with him . . . at Thunder Bay, and I didn't like the look of him. This is his picture. I identify it too. You used him to frighten Lenny, and you told me Lenny would give evidence against me, and I didn't know you'd *frightened* the poor boy with such a terrible threat. You told me he hated me and would be glad to tell lies about me . . .' The enormity of it almost choked her. 'I don't know how you can live with yourself. I don't know how anyone can be so full of *sin*.'

Her voice resonated with the full old meaning of the word: an offence against God. It was powerful, I thought, and it had silenced Filmer completely.

'It may come as an anticlimax,' the Brigadier said after a pause, 'but we will now digress to another matter entirely. One that will be the subject of a full stewards' enquiry at the Jockey Club, Portland Square, in the near future. I refer to the ownership of a parcel of land referred to in the Land Registry as SF 90155.'

The Brigadier told me later that it was at that point that Filmer turned grey and began to sweat.

'This parcel of land,' his military voice went on, 'is known as West Hillside Stables, Newmarket. This was a stables owned by Ivor Horfitz and run by his paid private trainer in such a dishonest manner that Ivor Horfitz was barred from racing – and racing stables –

for life. He was instructed to sell West Hillside Stables, as he couldn't set foot there, and it was presumed that he had. However, the new owner in his turn wants to sell and has found a buyer, but the buyer's lawyers' searches have been very thorough, and they have discovered that the stables were never Horfitz's to sell. They belonged, and they still do legally belong, to you, Mr Filmer.'

There was a faint sort of groan which might have come from Filmer.

'That being so, we will have to look into your relationship with Ivor Horfitz and with the illegal matters that were carried on for years at West Hillside Stables. We also have good reason to believe that Ivor Horfitz's son, Jason, knows you owned the stables and were concerned in its operation, and that Jason let that fact out to his friend, the stable lad Paul Shacklebury who, as you will remember, was the subject of your trial for conspiracy to murder, which took place earlier this year.'

There was a long long silence.

Daffodil's voice said, murmuring, 'I don't understand any of this, do you?'

Mercer, as quietly, answered: 'They've found a way of warning him off for life.'

'Oh good, but it sounds so dull.'

'Not to him,' Mercer murmured.

'We'll now return,' Bill Baudelaire's voice said more loudly, 'to the matter of your attempt to wreck the train.' He coughed. 'Will you please come in, Mr Burley?'

I smiled at George who had been listening to the Horfitz part in non-comprehension and the rest in horrified amazement.

'We're on,' I said, removing my raincoat and laying it on a serving counter. 'After you.'

He and I, the last in the pantry, went through the door. He was wearing his grey uniform and carrying his conductor's cap. I was revealed in Tommy's grey trousers, grey and white shirt, deep-yellow waistcoat and tidy striped tie. Polished, pressed, laundered, brushed: a credit to VIA Rail.

Julius Filmer saw the Conductor and a waiter he'd hardly noticed in his preoccupation with his own affairs. The Brigadier and Bill Baudelaire saw the waiter for the first time, and there was an awakening and realization on each of their faces. Although I'd told them by now that I'd worked with the crew, they hadn't truly understood how perfect had been the bright camouflage.

'Oh, that's who you are!' exclaimed Daffodil who was sitting now in one of the chairs round the conference table. 'I couldn't place you, outside.'

Mercer patted her hand which lay on the table, and gave me the faintest of smiles over her head. The three Vancouver bigwigs took me at face value, knowing no different.

'Would you come forward, please?' Bill Baudelaire said.

George and I both advanced past the conference table until we were nearer the desk. The two Directors were seated behind the desk, Filmer in the chair in front of it. Filmer's neck was rigid, his eyes were dark, and the sweat ran down his temples.

'The Conductor, George Burley,' Bill Baudelaire said, 'yesterday gave VIA Rail an account of three acts of sabotage against the race train. Disaster was fortunately averted on all three occasions, but we believe that all these dangerous situations were the work of Alex McLachlan who was acting on your instructions and was paid by you.'

'No,' Filmer said dully.

'Our enquiries are not yet complete,' Bill Baudelaire said, 'but we know that the VIA Rail offices in Montreal were visited three or four weeks ago by a man answering in general to your description who said he was researching for a thesis on the motivations of industrial sabotage. He asked for the names of any railroad saboteurs so that he could interview them and see what made them tick. He was given a short list of people no longer to be employed on the railroads in any capacity.'

Heads would roll, the VIA Rail executive had said. That list, although to be found in every railway station office in the country, should *never* have been given to an outsider.

'McLachlan's name is on that list,' Bill Baudelaire observed.

Filmer said nothing. The realization of total disaster showed in every line of his body, in every twitch in his face.

'As we said,' Bill Baudelaire went on, 'McLachlan travelled on the train under the name of Johnson. During the first evening, at a place called Cartier, he uncoupled Mr Lorrimore's private car and left it dead and dark on the track. The railroad investigators believe he waited in the vicinity to see the next train along, the regular transcontinental Canadian, come and crash into the Lorrimores' car. He had always been around to watch the consequences of his sabotage in the past: acts he had been sent to prison for committing. When the race train returned to pick up the Lorrimores' car, he simply reboarded and continued on the journey.'

'He shouldn't have done it,' Filmer said.

'We know that. We also know that in speech you continually mixed up Winnipeg with Vancouver. You instructed McLachlan to wreck the train before Winnipeg, when you meant before Vancouver.'

Filmer looked dumbfounded.

'That's right,' Daffodil said, sitting up straight, 'Winnipeg and Vancouver. He got them mixed up all the time.'

'In Banff,' Bill Baudelaire said, 'someone loosened the drain plug on the fuel tank for the boiler that provides steam heat for the train. If it hadn't been discovered, the train would have had to go through a freezing evening in the Rockies without heat for horses or passengers. Mr Burley, would you tell us at first hand about both of these occurrences, please?'

George gave his accounts of the uncoupling and the missing fuel with a railwayman's outrage quivering in his voice.

Filmer looked shrunken and sullen.

'During that last evening,' Bill Baudelaire said, 'you decided to cancel your instructions to McLachlan and you went forward to speak to him. You had a disagreement with him. You told him to do no more, but you had reckoned without McLachlan. He really is a perpetual saboteur. You misunderstood his mentality. You could start him off, but you couldn't stop him. You were responsible for putting him on the train to wreck it, and we will make that responsibility stick.'

Filmer began weakly to protest, but Bill Baudelaire gave him no respite.

'Your man McLachlan,' he said, 'knocked out the Conductor and left him tied up and gagged in the roomette he had been given in the name of Johnson. McLachlan then put the radio out of order by pouring liquid into it. These acts were necessary, as he saw it, because he had already, at a place called Revelstoke, removed oily waste from the journal-box holding one of the axles under the horse car. One of two things could then happen: if the train crew failed to notice the axle getting red hot, the axle would break, cause damage, possibly derail the train. If it were discovered, the train would stop for the axle to be cooled. In either case, the Conductor would radio to the despatcher in Vancouver, who would radio to the Conductor of the regular train, the Canadian, coming along behind, to tell him to stop, so that there shouldn't be a collision. Is that clear?'

It was pellucid to everyone in the room.

'The train crew,' he went on, 'did discover the hot axle and the engineers stopped the train. No one could find the Conductor, who was tied up in Johnson's roomette. No one could radio to Vancouver as the radio wouldn't work. The only recourse left to the crew was to send a man back along the line to light flares, to stop the Canadian in the old historic way.' He paused briefly. 'McLachlan, a railwayman, knew this would happen, so when the train stopped he went himself along the track, armed himself with a piece of wood and lay in wait for whoever came with the flares.'

Filmer stared darkly, hearing it for the first time.

'McLachlan attacked the man with the flares, but by good fortune failed to knock him out. It was this man here who was sent with the flares.' He nodded in my direction. 'He succeeded in lighting the flares and stopping the Canadian.' He paused and said to me, 'Is that correct?'

'Yes, sir,' I said. Word-perfect, I thought.

He went on, 'The race-train engineers cooled the

journal-box with snow and refilled it with oil, and the train went on its way. The Conductor was discovered in McLachlan's roomette. McLachlan did not reboard the train that time, and there will presently be a warrant issued for his arrest. You, Mr Filmer, are answerable with McLachlan for what happened.'

'I told him not to.' Filmer's voice was a rising shout of protest. 'I didn't want him to.'

His lawyers would love that admission, I thought.

'McLachlan's assault was serious,' Bill Baudelaire said calmly. He picked up my X-ray and the doctor's report, and waved them in Filmer's direction. 'McLachlan broke this crewman's shoulder blade. The crewman has positively identified McLachlan as the man who attacked him. The Conductor has positively identified McLachlan as the passenger known to him as Johnson. The Conductor has suffered concussion, and we have here another doctor's report on that.'

No doubt a good defence lawyer might have seen gaps in the story, but at that moment Filmer was beleaguered and confounded and hampered by the awareness of guilt. He was past thinking analytically, past asking how the crewman had escaped from McLachlan and been able to complete his mission, past wondering what was conjecture with the sabotage and what was provable fact.

The sight of Filmer reduced to sweating rubble was the purest revenge that any of us – Mercer, Daffodil, Val Catto, Bill Baudelaire, George Burley or I – could

457

have envisaged, and we had it in full measure. Do unto others, I thought drily, what they have done to your friends.

'We will proceed against you on all counts,' the Brigadier said magisterially.

Control disintegrated in Filmer. He came up out of his chair fighting mad, driven to lashing out, to raging against his defeat, to pushing someone else for his troubles, even though it could achieve no purpose.

He made me his target. It couldn't have been a subconscious awareness that it was I who had been his real enemy all along: much the reverse, I supposed, in that he saw me as the least of the people there, the one he could best bash with most impunity.

I saw him coming a mile off. I also saw the alarm on the Brigadier's face and correctly interpreted it.

If I fought back as instinct dictated, if I did to Filmer the sort of damage I'd told the Brigadier I'd done to McLachlan, I would weaken our case.

Thought before action; if one had time.

Thought could be flash fast. I had time. *It would be an unexpected bonus for us if the damage were the other way round.*

He had iron-pumping muscle power. It would indeed be damage.

Oh well . . .

I rolled my head a shade sideways and he punched me twice, quite hard, on the cheek and the jaw. I went back with a crash against the nearby wall, which wasn't all that good for the shoulder blade, and I slid the bottom of my spine down the wall until I was sitting on the floor, knees bent up, my head back against the paintwork.

Filmer was above me, lunging about and delivering another couple of stingingly heavy cuffs, and I thought, come on, guys, it's high time for the arrival of the cavalry, and the cavalry – the Mounties – in the shape of George Burley and Bill Baudelaire obligingly grabbed Filmer's swinging arms and hauled him away.

I stayed where I was, feeling slightly pulped, watching the action.

The Brigadier pressed a button on the desk which soon resulted in the arrival of two large racecourse security guards, one of whom, to Filmer's furious astonishment, placed a manacle upon the Julius Apollo wrist.

'You can't do this,' he shouted.

The guard phlegmatically fastened the hanging half of the metal bracelet to his own thick wrist.

One of the Vancouver top brass spoke for the first time, in an authoritative voice. 'Take Mr Filmer to the security office and detain him until I come down.'

The guards said, 'Yes, sir.'

They moved like tanks. Filmer, humiliated to his socks, was tugged away between them as if of no account. One might almost have felt sorry for him . . . if one hadn't remembered Paul Shacklebury and Ezra Gideon for whom he had had no pity.

Daffodil Quentin's eyes were stretched wide open.

She came over and looked down at me with compassion.

'You poor boy,' she said, horrified. 'How perfectly *dreadful*.'

'Mr Burley,' Bill Baudelaire said smoothly, 'would you be so kind as to escort Mrs Quentin for us? If you turn right in the passage, you'll find some double doors ahead of you. Through there is the reception room where the passengers and the other owners from the train are gathering for cocktails and lunch. Would you take Mrs Quentin there? We'll look after this crewman . . . get him some help. . . . And we would be pleased if you could yourself stay for lunch.'

George said to me, 'Are you all right, Tommy?' and I said, 'Yes, George,' and he chuckled with kind relief and said it would be a pleasure, eh?, to stay for lunch.

He stood back to let Daffodil lead the way out of the far door, and when she reached there she paused and looked back.

'The poor boy,' she said again. 'Julius Filmer's a *beast*.'

The Vancouver Jockey Club men rose and made courteous noises of sympathy in my direction; said they would hand Filmer on to the police with a report of the assault; said we would no doubt be needed to make statements later. They then followed Daffodil, as they were the hosts of the party.

When they'd gone, the Brigadier switched off the machine that had recorded every word.

'Poor boy, my foot,' he said to me. 'You chose to let him hit you. I saw you.'

I smiled a little ruefully, acknowledging his perception.

'He couldn't!' Mercer protested, drawing nearer. 'No one could just let himself be . . .'

'He could and he did.' The Brigadier came round from behind the desk. 'Quick thinking, Brilliant.'

'But why?' Mercer said.

'To tie the slippery Mr Filmer in tighter knots.' The Brigadier stood in front of me, put a casual hand down to mine and pulled me to my feet.

'Did you truly?' Mercer said to me in disbelief.

'Mm.' I nodded and straightened a bit, trying not to wince.

'Don't worry about him,' the Brigadier said. 'He used to ride bucking broncos, and God knows what else.'

The three of them stood as in a triumvirate, looking at me in my uniform, as if I'd come from a different planet.

'I sent him on the train,' the Brigadier said, 'to stop Filmer doing whatever he was planning.' He smiled briefly. 'A sort of match . . . a two-horse race.'

'It seems to have been neck and neck now and then,' Mercer said.

The Brigadier considered it. 'Maybe. But our runner had the edge.'

*

461

Mercer Lorrimore and I watched the races from a smaller room next to the large one where the reception was taking place. We were in the racecourse President's private room, to which he could retire with friends if he wanted to, and it was furnished accordingly in extreme comfort and soft turquoise and gold.

The President had been disappointed but understanding that Mercer felt he couldn't attend the lunch party so soon after his son's death, and had offered this room instead. Mercer had asked if I might join him, so he and I drank the President's champagne and looked down from his high window to the track far below, and talked about Filmer, mostly.

'I liked him, you know,' Mercer said, wonderingly.

'He can be charming.'

'Bill Baudelaire tried to warn me at Winnipeg,' he said, 'but I wouldn't listen. I really thought that his trial had been a travesty, and that he was innocent. He told me about it himself . . . he said he didn't bear the Jockey Club any malice.'

I smiled. 'Extreme malice,' I said. 'He threatened them to their faces that he would throw any available spanner into their international works. McLachlan was some spanner.'

Mercer sat down in one of the huge armchairs. I stayed standing by the window.

'Why was Filmer prosecuted,' he asked, 'if there was such a poor case?'

'There was a cast-iron case,' I said. 'Filmer sent a

particularly vicious frightener to intimidate all four prosecution witnesses, and the cast iron became splinters. This time ... this morning ... we thought we'd stage a sort of preliminary trial, at which the witnesses couldn't have been reached, and have it all on record in case anyone retracted afterwards.'

He looked at me sceptically. 'Did you think I could be intimidated? I assure you I can't. Not any more.'

After a pause I said, 'You have Xanthe. Ezra Gideon had daughters and grandchildren. One of the witnesses in the Paul Shacklebury case backed away because of what she was told would happen to her sixteen-year-old daughter if she gave evidence.'

'Dear God,' he said, dismayed. 'Surely he'll be sent to prison?'

'He'll be warned off, anyhow, and that's what he wants least. He had Paul Shacklebury killed to prevent it. I think we will have got rid of him from racing. For the rest ... we'll have to see what the Canadian police and VIA Rail can do, and hope they'll find McLachlan.'

Let McLachlan not be eaten by a bear, I thought. (And he hadn't been: he was picked up for stealing tools from a railway yard in Edmonton a week later, and subsequently convicted with Filmer of the serious ancient offence of attempted train-wrecking, chiefly on the evidence of a temporary crew member in his VIA Rail clothes. VIA put me on their personnel list retroactively, and shook my hand. Filmer was imprisoned despite his defence that he had not given specific

instructions to McLachlan on any count and had tried
to stop him before the end. It was proved that he had
actively recruited a violent saboteur: any later possible
change of mind was held to be irrelevant. Filmer never
did find out that I wasn't a waiter, because it wasn't a
question his lawyers ever thought to ask, and it went
much against him with the jury that he'd violently
attacked a defenceless rail employee without provo-
cation in front of many witnesses even though he knew
of the broken scapula. The Brigadier kept a straight
face throughout. 'It worked a treat,' he said afterwards.
'Wasn't Daffodil Quentin a trouper, convincing them
the poor boy had been brutally beaten for no reason
except that he'd saved them all from being killed in
their beds? Lovely stuff. It made nonsense of the
change-of-heart defence. They couldn't wait to find
Filmer guilty after that.' McLachlan in his turn swore
that I'd nearly murdered him, out on the track. I said
he'd tripped and knocked himself out on the rails.
McLachlan could produce no X-rays and wasn't
believed, to his fury. 'Broken bone or not, that waiter
can fight like a goddam tiger,' he said. 'No way could
Filmer beat him up.' Filmer, however, had done so. It
had been seen, and was a fact.)

On the Tuesday of the Jockey Club Race Train
Stakes at Exhibition Park, with the trial still months
ahead, and the feel of Filmer's fists a reality not a
memory, the racecourse President came into his private
room to see Mercer and me and to show us that if

we drew the curtains along the right-hand side wall, we could see into the reception room.

'They can't see into here,' he said. 'It's one-way glass.' He pulled strings and revealed the party. 'I hear the meeting went well this morning except for the end.' He looked at me questioningly. 'Mr Lorrimore and Bill Baudelaire asked that you be treated as a most honoured guest . . . but shouldn't you be resting?'

'No point, sir,' I said, 'and I wouldn't miss the great race for anything.'

Through the window one could fascinatingly see all the faces grown so familiar during the past ten days. The Unwins, the Redi-Hots, the Youngs . . .

'If I might ask you – ?' I said.

'Ask the world, according to Bill Baudelaire and Brigadier Catto.'

I smiled. 'Not the world. That young woman over there in the grey suit, with the fair hair in a plait and a worried expression.'

'Nell Richmond,' Mercer said.

'Would you mind if she came in here for a while?'

'Not in the least,' the President said, and within minutes could be seen talking to her. He couldn't have told her who to expect in his room, though, because when she came in and saw me she was surprised and, I had to think, joyful.

'You're on your feet! Daffodil said the waiter was hurt badly.' Her voice died away and she swallowed. 'I was afraid . . .'

465

'That we wouldn't get to Hawaii?'

'Oh.' It was a sound somewhere between a laugh and a sob. 'I don't think I like you.'

'Try harder.'

'Well . . .' She opened her handbag and began to look inside it, and glanced up and saw all the people next door. 'How great,' she said to Mercer. 'You're both with us, even if you're not.' She produced a folded piece of paper and gave it to me. 'I have to go back to sort out the lunch places.'

I didn't want her to go. I said, 'Nell . . .' and heard it sound too full of anxiety, too full of plain physical battering, but it was past calling back.

Her face changed. The games died away.

'Read that when I've gone,' she said. 'And I'll be there . . . through the glass.'

She went out of the President's room without looking back and soon reappeared among the others. I unfolded the paper slowly, not wanting it to be bad news, and found it was a telex.

It said:

RICHMOND, FOUR SEASONS HOTEL, VAN-COUVER. CONFIRM YOUR TWO WEEKS VACATION STARTING IMMEDIATELY.
MERRY. HAVE A GOOD TIME.

I closed my eyes.

'Is that despair?' Mercer said.

I opened my eyes. The telex still read the same way. I handed it to him, and he read it also.

'I dare say,' he said ironically, 'that Val Catto will match this.'

'If he doesn't, I'll resign.'

We spent the afternoon companionably and watched the preliminary races with the interest of devotees. When it was time for the Jockey Club Race Train Stakes Mercer decided that, Sheridan or not, he would go down to see Voting Right saddled, as he could go and return by express elevator to our eyrie to watch the race.

When he'd gone and the room next door had mostly emptied, I looked down on the flags and the banners and the streamers and balloons and the razzamatazz with which Exhibition Park had met the challenge of Assiniboia Downs and Woodbine and thought of all that had happened on the journey across Canada, and I wondered whether I would find flat-footing round British racecourses in the rain a relaxation or a bore, wondered if I would go on doing it; thought that time would show me the way, as it always had.

I thought of Mrs Baudelaire, whom I would never meet, and wished she could have watched this next race; thought of Aunt Viv with gratitude.

Mercer came back looking happy: happier in a peaceful way, as if he had settled ghosts.

'Daffodil is amazing,' he said. 'She's down there

467

holding court, kissing Laurentide Ice, laughing, on top of the world. There seems to be no difficulty in the horse running, even though half still presumably belongs to Filmer.'

'It's in Daffodil's name on the racecard,' I said.

'So it is. And the Youngs . . . Rose and Cumber . . . with Sparrowgrass, and the people with Redi-Hot. It's like a club, down there. They were pleased, they said, that I had come.'

They genuinely would be, I thought. The party was incomplete without Mercer.

There was a large television set in the President's room, through which one could hear the bugles preceding the runners to the track and hear crowd noises and the commentary. Nothing like being down near the action, but better than silence. The race was being broadcast live throughout Canada and recorded for the rest of the world, and there was a long spiel going on about the Growing International Flavour of Canadian Racing, and how the Great Transcontinental Mystery Race Train had awakened enormous interest everywhere and was altogether A Good Thing For Canada.

Mercer, who had been prepared to do a lot for Canadian racing, watched Voting Right lead the pre-race parade, the horse on the screen appearing larger to us than the real one far down on the track.

'He's looking well,' he told me. 'I do hope . . .' He

stopped. 'I think he may be the best of all my horses. The best to come. But he may not be ready today. It's perhaps too soon. Sparrowgrass is favourite. It would be nice for the Youngs . . .'

We watched Sparrowgrass prance along in his turn.

'Cumber Young has found out it was Filmer who bought . . . or took . . . Ezra Gideon's horses. If Cumber had been up here this morning, he'd have torn Filmer limb from limb.'

'And been in trouble himself,' I said.

'As Filmer is now?'

'Yes, roughly speaking.'

'Rough is the word.' He looked at me sideways, but made no further comment.

'Watch the horses,' I said mildly. Not the lumps that were swelling.

With a wry twitch of the lips, he turned his attention back to Redi-Hot who looked fit to scorch the dirt, and to Laurentide Ice, the colour of his name.

Nine of the ten runners had travelled on the train. The tenth was a local Vancouver horse bought by the Unwins for the occasion. Not as good a prospect as Upper Gumtree, but the Unwins had wanted to take their part in the climax.

All of the owners and Nell, precious Nell, came to watch the race in the glassed-in part of the stands slanting down in front of the window of the President's room, so that it was over their excited heads that

Mercer and I saw the horses loaded into the stalls and watched the flashing colours sprint out.

'All the way across Canada,' Mercer said as if to himself, 'for the next two minutes.'

All the way across Canada, I thought, in worry and love and grief for his son.

Voting Right shot out of the gate and took a strong lead.

Mercer groaned quietly, 'He's running away.'

Laurentide Ice and Sparrowgrass, next, weren't in a hurry but kept a good pace going, their heads together, not an inch in it. Behind them came five or six in a bunch, with Redi-Hot last.

The sing-song commentary on the television read off the time of the first quarter-mile covered by Voting Right.

'Too fast,' Mercer groaned.

At the half-mile, Voting Right was still in front, still going at high speed, ahead by a full twenty lengths.

'It's hopeless,' Mercer said. 'He'll blow up in the home stretch. He's never been ridden this way before.'

'Didn't you discuss it with the jockey?'

'I just wished him luck. He knows the horse.'

'Maybe the horse has been inspired by the train travel,' I said flippantly.

'To come all this way . . .' Mercer said, taking no notice. 'Oh well, that's racing.'

'He hasn't exactly blown up yet,' I pointed out.

Voting Right was far in front, going down the back stretch a good deal faster than the race train had gone through the Rockies, and he didn't know he was going too fast, he simply kept on going.

The jockeys on Sparrowgrass, Laurentide Ice, Redi-Hot and the others left their move on the leader until they'd come round the last bend and spread out across the track to give themselves a clear run home.

Then Laurentide Ice melted away as Mrs Baudelaire had said he would, and Redi-Hot produced a spurt, and Sparrowgrass with determination began to close at last on Voting Right.

'He's going to lose,' Mercer said despairingly.

It looked like it. One couldn't say for certain, but his time was too fast.

Voting Right kept right on going. Sparrowgrass raced hard to the finish, but it was Voting Right, as Mrs Baudelaire had predicted, Voting Right who had the edge, who went floating past the post in a record time for the track; the best horse Mercer would ever own, the target kept safe from Filmer.

Sheridan lay in untroubled eternity, and who was to say that Mercer wasn't right, that in his impulsive way the son hadn't died to give his father this moment.

Mercer turned towards me, speechless, brimming to overflowing with inexpressible emotion, wanting to laugh, wanting to cry, like all owners at the fulfilment of a dreamed-of success. The sheen in his eyes was the

471

same the world over: the love of the flying thoroughbred, the perfection of winning a great race.

He found his voice. Looked at me with awakening
humour and a good deal of understanding.

'Thank you,' he said.

COMEBACK

With heartfelt thanks
to
JENNY HALL
Veterinary Surgeon
and to
PETER SPICELEY
and
PHILIP GRICE
British Consuls

CHAPTER ONE

I'm Peter Darwin.

Everyone asks, so I may as well say at once that no, I'm not related to Charles.

I was in fact born Peter Perry, but John Darwin, marrying my widowed mother when I was twelve, gave me, among many other things, a new life, a new name and a new identity.

Twenty years rolled like mist over the memories of my distant childhood in Gloucestershire, and now I, Peter Darwin, was thirty-two, adopted son of a diplomat, in the diplomatic service myself.

As my stepfather's postings and later my own were all at the whim of the Foreign Office, I'd mostly lived those twenty years abroad in scattered three- or four-year segments, some blazing, some boring, from Caracas to Lima, from Moscow to Cairo to Madrid, housed in Foreign Office lodgings from one-bedroom concrete to gilt-decked mansions, counting nowhere home.

Friendships were transitory. Locals, left behind.

Other diplomats and their children came and went. I was rootless and nomadic, well used to it and content.

'Look us up if you're ever in Florida,' Fred Hutchings said casually, leaving Tokyo to be consul in Miami. 'Stay for a day or so if you're passing through.'

That 'day or so', I thought wryly, was a pretty good indicator of the warmth of our feelings for each other: tepid to luke.

'Thanks,' I said.

He nodded. We'd worked together for months without friction. He half-meant the invitation. He was trained in politeness, as we all were.

My own posting, when it came through nearly a year later, was surprisingly to England, to the Foreign and Commonwealth Office in Whitehall.

'*What?*' My stepfather in Mexico City chuckled with pleasure on the phone when I told him. 'Private secretary! Well done! The pay's rotten. You'll have some leave first, though. Come and see us. Your mother misses you.'

So I spent nearly a month with them and then set off to England via Miami, which was why, after a delayed flight and a missed connection, I found myself with twenty-four hours to kill and the echo of Fred Hutchings' invitation in my head. Why not, I thought, and on an impulse found his number from Enquiries, and phoned him.

His answering voice sounded genuinely welcoming and I pictured him on the other end of the line; forty, plump, freckled, eager, with a forehead that perspired under the slightest nervous pressure. The mildness of my liking for him flooded belatedly back, but it was too late to retreat.

'Great, great,' he was saying heartily. 'I'd ask you here for the night but the children aren't well. How about dinner, though? Get a taxi to The Diving Pelican on 186th street, North Miami Beach. I'll meet you there about eight. How's that?'

'Splendid,' I said.

'Good. Good. Great to see old friends.' He told me the address of the restaurant again, carefully. 'We eat there all the time. Come to think of it . . .' his voice brightened enthusiastically '. . . two of our friends there are going to England tomorrow too. You'll like them. Maybe you'll all be on the same plane. I'll introduce you.'

'Thank you,' I said faintly.

'A pleasure.' I could feel him beaming with goodwill down the wire. 'See you, then.'

With a sigh I replaced the receiver, booked myself and my bags into the airport hotel for the night and in due course taxied as instructed to the rendezvous.

The Diving Pelican, less striking than its name, glowed dimly at one end of a dark row of shops. There seemed to be few other signs of neighbourhood life, but the twenty or so parking spaces in front were full. I pulled open the outwards-opening door, stepped into a small entrance hall and was greeted by a young woman with a bright smile who said 'And how are you today?' as if she'd known me for years.

'Fine,' I said, and mentioned Fred.

The smile grew wider. Fred had arrived. Fred, it seemed, was good news.

He was sitting alone at a round table spread with a cream lace cloth over a pink underlay. Stainless steel flatware, pink napkins, unfussy wine glasses, little oil lamps, carnation in a bud vase, the trappings of halfway up the scale. Not very large overall, the place was pleasantly packed. Not a pelican in sight, diving or otherwise.

Fred rose to his feet to pump my hand and the smiling lady pulled out a chair for me, producing a shiny menu and showing her molars.

'Great, great,' Fred was saying. 'Sorry I'm alone but Meg didn't want to leave the children. They've got chickenpox.'

I made sympathetic noises.

'Covered in spots, poor little buggers,' Fred said. 'Like some wine?'

We ate our salads first in the American way and drank some reasonable red. Fred, at my prompting, told me about life in his consulate, mostly a matter, he said, of British tourists complaining of lost documents, stolen money and decamping boyfriends.

'They'll con you rigid,' Fred said. 'Sob stories by the dozen.' With a sly gleam of amusement he looked at me sideways. 'People like you, smooth two-a-penny first secretaries used to embassy life, you'd fall for the wet-handkerchief routine like a knockover. All half of them want is a free ticket home.'

'You've grown cynical, Fred.'

'Experienced,' he said.

Always expect a lie, my stepfather had said right back at the beginning of my enlightenment into what his job entailed. Politicians and diplomats, he'd said, are liars until proved different. 'You too?' I asked, dismayed, and he'd smiled his civilized smile and educated me. 'I don't lie to you or your mother. You will not lie to us. If you hear me tell an untruth in public you will remain calm and keep your mouth shut and work out why I said it.'

We got on fine from the start. I couldn't remember my natural father, who had died when I was a baby, and I had no hang-ups about anyone taking his place. I'd longed to have a father like other boys, and then suddenly there was this big stranger, full of jokes, who'd swept like a gale into our single-parent only-child existence and carried us off to the equator before we could gasp. It was only gradually, afterwards, that I realized how irrevocably he'd changed me, and how fortunate I had been.

Fred said, 'Where have they posted you, after your leave?'

'Nowhere. I mean, England. Private secretary.'

'Lucky old you!' There was a jealous edge to his voice at my promotion, all of a piece, I thought, with his jibe about two-a-penny gullible young men in embassies: and he'd been one himself in the past.

'Perhaps I'll get Ulan Bator after that,' I said. Ulan Bator was the pits with everyone. It was heavily rumoured that instead of a car there the ambassador got issued an official yak. 'No one gets plums in a row.'

Fred flicked me a rueful smile, acknowledging that I'd seen his envy, and welcomed our seafood fettucini with yum-yum noises and a vigorous appetite. Fred had recommended the house speciality. I'd been persuaded, and in fact it was good.

Midway through, there was a small burst of clapping and Fred, pausing with fork in the air, exuded pleasure.

'Ah,' he said proprietorially. 'Vicky Larch and Greg Wayfield. They're the friends I told you about, who are going to the UK tomorrow. They live just round the corner.'

Vicky Larch and Greg Wayfield were more than friends; they were singers. They had come into the restaurant without fanfare through curtains at the far end, she dressed in a white sequinned tunic, he in a Madras-checked tailored jacket, both in light coloured trousers. The only thing really surprising about them was their age. They were mature, one might perhaps say, and no longer slim.

I thought reprehensibly that I could have done without the embarrassment of having to applaud earnest elderly amateurs all the way back to England. They fiddled around with amplifying equipment and tapped microphones to make sure they were working. Fred nodded encouragingly to them and to me and happily returned to his pasta.

They got the equipment going and ran a tape: soft sweet music from old stage shows, well known, undemanding, a background to food. Greg Wayfield hummed a few bars after a while and then began to sing the words, and I looked up from my fettucini in surprise because this was no geriatric disaster but a good true voice, gentle, virile and full of timbre.

Fred glanced at my expression and smiled with satisfaction. The song ended, the diners applauded, and there was more tape. Then, again without announcement or fuss, the woman smoothed into a love song, the words a touch sad, moody, expressed with the catchy syncopated timing of long experience. Dear heavens, I thought with relief, they're pros. Good old pros, having a ball.

They sang six songs alternately and finished with a duet, and then to enthusiastic clapping they threaded a way round the tables and sat down with Fred and me.

Fred made introductions. Half-standing, I shook the singers' hands across the lace cloth and said with perfect honesty how much I'd enjoyed their performance.

'They'll sing again,' Fred promised, pouring wine for them as if from long habit. 'This is just a break.'

At close quarters they looked as wholesome and

old-fashioned as their act, he still handsome, she with the air of a young chanteuse trapped in a grand-motherly body.

'Did you sing in night clubs?' I asked her, as she sat beside me.

Her blue eyes widened. 'How did you know?'

'Something about your phrasing. Intimate. Designed for shadowy late-night spaces. Something about the way you move your head.'

'Well, yes, I did clubs for years.' She was amused, aware of me physically despite her age. Once a woman, always a woman, I thought.

Her hair was white, a fluffy well-cut helmet. She had good skin lightly made up and her only real concession to theatricality lay in the silky dark up-curling false lashes, second nature to her eyes.

'But I retired ages ago,' she said, lowering the lids and raising them in harmless coquetry. 'Had a bunch of babies and got too fat. Too old. We sing here just for fun.'

Her speaking voice was English, without regional accent, her diction trained and precise. Under the mild banter she seemed serene, secure and sensible, and I revised my gloomiest views of the next night's journey. Flight attendants could be chatted up another time, I supposed.

Greg said, 'My wife would flirt with a chair leg,' and they both looked at me indulgently and laughed.

'Don't trust Peter,' Fred cautioned them ironically.

'He's the best liar I know, and I've met a few, believe me.'

'How unkind,' Vicky said disbelievingly. 'He's a lamb.'

Fred made a laughing cough and checked that we all were in fact booked on the same flight. No doubt about it. British Airways' jumbo to Heathrow. Club class, all of us.

'Great. Great,' Fred said.

Greg, I thought, was American, though it was hard to tell. A mid-Atlantic man: halfway accent, American clothes, English facial bones. Part of the local scenery in Miami, he had presence but not his wife's natural stage charisma. He hadn't been a soloist, I thought.

He said, 'Are you a consul too, Peter?'

'Not at the moment.'

He looked perplexed, so I explained. 'In the British foreign service you take the title of your present job. You don't take your rank with you. You can be a second or first secretary or a consul or counsellor or a consul-general or a minister or a high commissioner or an ambassador in one place, but you'll very likely be something different in the next. The rank stays with the job. You take the rank of whatever job you're sent to.'

Fred was nodding. 'In the States, once an ambassador always an ambassador. "Mr Ambassador" for ever. Even if you've only been an ambassador to some tiny country for a couple of years and are back to being a dogsbody, you keep the title. The British don't.'

'Too bad,' Greg said.

'No,' I disagreed, 'it's better. There's no absolutely clear-cut hierarchy, so there's less bitching and less despair.'

They looked at me in astonishment.

'Mind you,' Fred said to them with mock confidentiality, 'Peter's father's an ambassador at the moment. Between the two of them, they've held every rank in the book.'

'Mine are all lower,' I said smiling.

Vicky said comfortingly, 'I'm sure you'll do well in the end.'

Fred laughed.

Greg pushed away his half-drunk wine and said they'd better get back to work, a popular move with the clientele, always quick to applaud them. They sang another three songs each, Greg finishing quietly with a crooning version of 'The Last Farewell', the lament of a sailor leaving his South Seas love to go back to storms and war at sea round Britain. Shut your eyes, I thought, listening, and Greg could be the doomed young man. It was a masterly performance; extraordinary. A woman at the next table brought out a handkerchief and wiped away surreptitious tears.

The diners, sitting transfixed over long-cooled cups of coffee, gave Greg the accolade of a second's silence before showing their pleasure. Sentimental it might all be, I thought, but one could have too much of stark unsugared realism.

The singers returned to our table, accepting plaudits on the way, and this time drank their wine without restraint. They were pumped up with the post-performance high-level adrenalin surge of all successful appearances of any sort, and it would take them a while to come down. Meanwhile, they talked with animation, scattering information about themselves and further proving, if it were necessary, that they were solidly good, well-intentioned people.

I'd always found goodness more interesting than evil, though I was aware this wasn't the most general view. To my mind, it took more work and more courage to be good, an opinion continually reinforced by my own shortcomings.

He had trained originally for opera, Greg said, but there weren't enough roles for the available voices.

'It helps to be Italian,' he said ruefully. 'And so few of any generation really make it. I sang chorus. I would have starved then rather than sing "The Last Farewell". I was arrogant, musically, when I was young.' He smiled with forgiveness for his youth. 'So I went into a banking house as a junior junior in the trust department and eventually began to be able to afford opera tickets.'

'But you went on singing,' I protested. 'No one could sing as you do without constant practice.'

He nodded. 'In choirs. Sometimes in cathedrals and

so on. Anywhere I could. And in the bathroom, of course.'

Vicky raised the eyelashes to heaven.

'Now they both sing here two or three times a week,' Fred told me. 'This place would die without them.'

'Hush,' Vicky said, looking round for outraged proprietorial feelings but fortunately not seeing any. 'We enjoy it.'

Greg said they were going to England for a month. One of Vicky's daughters was getting married.

Vicky's daughter?

Yes, she said, the children were all hers. Two boys, two girls. She'd divorced their father long ago. She and Greg were new together: eighteen months married, still on honeymoon.

'Belinda – she's my youngest – she's marrying a veterinary surgeon,' Vicky said. 'She was always mad about animals.'

I laughed.

'Well, yes,' she said, 'I hope she's mad about him, too. She's worked for him for ages, but this came on suddenly a few weeks ago. So, anyway, we're off to horse country. He deals mostly with horses. He acts as a vet at Cheltenham races.'

I made a small explosive noise in my throat and they looked at me enquiringly.

I said, 'My father and mother met at Cheltenham races.'

They exclaimed over it, of course, and it seemed a

bit late to say that my mother and *stepfather* met at Cheltenham races, so I let it pass. My real father, I thought, was anyway John Darwin: the only father I could remember.

Fred, reflecting, said, 'Didn't your father spend his entire youth at the races? Didn't you say so in Tokyo, that time you went to the Japan Cup?'

'I expect I said it,' I agreed, 'though it was a bit of an exaggeration. But he still does go when he gets the chance.'

'Do ambassadors usually go to the races?' Vicky asked doubtfully.

'This particular ambassador sees racecourses as the perfect place for diplomacy,' I said with ironic affection. 'He invites the local Jockey Club bigwigs to an embassy party and they in turn invite him to the races. He says he learns more about a country faster at the races than in a month of diplomatic handshaking. He's right, too. Did you know they have bicycle parks at Tokyo racecourse?'

Greg said, 'Er . . . uh . . . I don't follow.'

'Not just car parks,' I said. 'Motorcycle parks and bicycle parks. Rows and rows of them. They tell you a lot about the Japanese.'

'What, for instance?' Vicky asked.

'That they'll get where they want to go one way or another.'

'Are you being serious?'

'Of course,' I said with mock gravity. 'And they have

a baby park at the races too. You leave your infant to play in a huge bouncing Donald Duck while you bet your money away in a carefree fashion.'

'And what does this tell you?' Vicky teased.

'That the baby park draws in more than enough revenue to fund it.'

'Don't worry about Peter,' Fred told them reassuringly. 'He's got this awful quirky mind, but you can rely on him in a crisis.'

'Thanks,' I said dryly.

Greg asked a few things about our time in Japan. Had we enjoyed it, for instance. Very much, we both said. And did we speak the language? Yes, we did. Fred had been a first secretary in the commercial department, spending his time oiling the wheels of trade. My own job had been to learn what was likely to happen on the political scene.

'Peter went to the lunches and cocktail parties,' Fred said, 'drinking saké out of little wooden boxes instead of glasses.'

The customs and cadences of Japan still flowed strongly in my head, barely overlaid by the month in Mexico City. It was always an odd feeling of deprivation, leaving behind a culture one had striven intensely to understand. Not exactly post-partum blues, but departing-from-post blues, definitely.

The diners in the restaurant had gradually drifted away, leaving the four of us as the last to leave. Vicky and Greg went off to pack up their equipment and, as

14

a matter of course, Fred and I divided the bill between us to the last cent.

'Do you want it in yen?' I asked.

'For God's sake,' Fred said. 'Didn't you change some at the airport?'

I had. A habit. Fred took the notes and handed me some coins in return, which I pocketed. The Foreign Office was permanently strapped for cash and our basic pay came nowhere near the level of status and responsibility given us. I wasn't complaining. No one ever entered the diplomatic service to get mega-rich. Fred said he would run me back to the airport to save me having to pay for another taxi, which was good of him.

Vicky and Greg returned, she carrying a large white handbag a-glitter with multicoloured stones outlined in thin white cord and he following with a large squashy hold-all slung boyishly from one shoulder. We all four left the restaurant and stood for a while outside the door saying goodnights, Vicky and Greg making plans to find me the following day.

On the wall beside the door, a glassed frame held a sample menu flanked by two eight-by-ten black-and-white photographs of the singers, both taken, it was clear, a long time previously.

Vicky saw the direction of my eyes and made a small sad moue, philosophical with an effort. Her likeness, a striking theatre-type glossy with her head and shoulders at a tilt, bright light shining on the forehead, stars in the eyes, tactful shadows over the beginnings of double chin, must have been from twenty years earlier at least. Greg's no nonsense straight-ahead smile had few photographic tricks and was very slightly out of focus as if enlarged from a none-too-clear print. It too was an earlier Greg, thinner, positively masculine, strongly handsome, with a dark, now-vanished moustache.

Impossible to guess at Vicky's character from that sort of picture, but one could make a stab at Greg's. Enough intelligence, the complacency of success, a desire to please, an optimistic nature. Not the sort to lie about people behind their backs.

Final goodnights. Vicky lifted her cheek to me for a kiss. Easy to deliver.

'Our car's down there,' she said, pointing to the distance.

'Mine's over there,' Fred said, pointing the other way.

We all nodded and moved apart, the evening over.

'They're nice people,' Fred said contentedly.

'Yes,' I agreed.

We climbed into his car and dutifully fastened the seat-belts. He started the engine, switched on the lights, backed out of the parking space and turned the car to the general direction of the airport.

'Stop!' I yelled abruptly, struggling to undo the hampering seat-belt buckle so easily done up.

'*What?*' Fred said, jamming foot on brake but not understanding. 'What the hell's wrong?'

I didn't answer him. I got the wretched belt undone

16

at last, swung open the car door and scrambled out, running almost before I had both feet on the ground.

In the passing beam of Fred's headlights as he'd turned the car, I'd seen the distant sparkle of Vicky's sequinned tunic and seen also that she was struggling, falling, with a dark figure crowding her, cutting half of her from my sight, a figure of unmistakable ill-will . . . attacking.

I sprinted, hearing her cry out shrilly.

I myself yelled 'Vicky, Vicky' in an attempt to frighten off the mugger but he seemed glued to her like a leech, she on the ground and kicking, he close on her, hunched and intent.

No sign of Greg.

I reached the man over Vicky, cannoning into him to knock him away. He was heavier than I'd thought and not easily deterred, and far from running from me, he seemed to view me as merely another mug to be robbed. He jabbed a strong fist at my face, a blow I ducked from nothing but instinct, and I tried catching him by the clothes and flinging him against a parked car.

No success. He connected with a fist to my chest that left me breathless and feeling as if he'd squashed my heart against my backbone. The face above the fists was a matter of darkness and narrow eyes: he was shorter than I and thicker.

I was losing the fight, which made me angry but not

much more effective. It was hostility I was up against, I thought, not just greed. Behind the robbery, hatred.

Vicky, who had crawled away moaning, suddenly rose to her feet as if galvanized and came up behind our assailant. I saw her eyes momentarily over his shoulder, stretched wide with fear and full of determination. She took aim and kicked at him hard. He hissed fiercely with pain and turned towards her and I in turn kicked him, targeting nowhere special but hitting the back of his knee.

Vicky had her long scarlet nails up, her fingers bent like a witch. There was bright red blood in splashes down her tunic. Her mouth was stretched open in what looked in that dim light like the snarl of a wolf, and out of it came a shriek that began in the low register and rose to a fortissimo scream somewhere above high G.

It raised the hairs on my own neck and it broke the nerve of the thief. He took a stumbling step to go round her and then another, and belatedly departed at a shambling run.

Vicky fell weakly into my arms, the fighting fury turning fast to shakes and tears, her triumphant voice roughened and near incoherence.

'God. Oh God ... There were two of them ... Greg ...'

Headlights blazed at us, fast advancing. Vicky and I clutched each other like dazzled rabbits and I was bunching muscles to hurl us both out of the way when tyres squealed to a stop and the black figure emerging like a silhouette through the bright beam resolved itself into the solid familiarity of Fred. The consul to the rescue. Good old Fred. I felt a bit lightheaded, and stupid because of it.

'Is she all right?' Fred was asking me anxiously. 'Where's Greg?'

Vicky and I declutched and the three of us in unison looked for Greg.

He wasn't hard to find. He was lying in a tumbled unconscious heap near the rear wheel on the far side of what turned out to be his and Vicky's dark blue BMW.

There was a stunned moment of disbelief and horror. Then, crying out, Vicky fell on her knees beside him and I squatted down and felt round his neck, searching for the pulse under his jaw.

'He's alive,' I said, relieved, straightening.

Vicky sniffed in her tears, still crying with distress. Fred, ever practical, said, 'We'd better get an ambulance.'

I agreed with him, but before we could do anything a police car wailed with its siren down the road and drew up beside us, red, white and blue lights flashing in a bar across the car's roof.

A big man in midnight-blue trousers and shirt with insignia stepped out, bringing his notebook to the ready and telling us someone had just reported a woman screaming and what was it all about. Fast, I thought.

Response time, spectacular. He had been cruising near by, he said.

Greg began moaning before anyone could answer and struggled to sit up, appearing dazed and disoriented and startlingly old.

Vicky supported him round the shoulders. Looking at her with pathos and pain and gratitude, he saw the blood on her tunic and said he was sorry.

'*Sorry!*' Vicky exclaimed blankly. 'What for?'

He didn't answer, but one could see what he meant: sorry that he hadn't been able to defend her. It was encouraging, I thought, that he seemed to know where he was and what had happened.

The policeman unclipped a hand-held radio from his belt and called for the ambulance and then, with notable kindness, asked Vicky just what had occurred. She looked up at him and tried to answer, but the phrases came out unconnectedly and on jagged half-hysterical breaths, as if from splintered thoughts.

'Greg's wallet . . . well, they banged his head on the car . . . shadows . . . didn't see them . . . he was trying . . . you know, he was trying to take my *rings* . . . the plane tickets . . . it's my daughter's wedding . . . I'd've killed him . . .' She stopped talking as if aware it was gibberish and looked lost.

'Take your time, ma'am,' the policeman said. 'When you're ready.'

She took a visibly deep breath and tried again. 'They were waiting . . . behind the car . . . I could kill them . . .

They jumped on Greg when he went round . . . I hate them . . . I hope they die . . .'

There were high-coloured patches of extreme stress over her cheekbones and more strong flush marks on her jaw and down her neck. Blood on her neck, also; quite a lot of it.

'You're doing good,' the policeman said.

He was about my age, I thought, with a natural kindness not yet knocked out of him by the system.

'My ear hurts,' Vicky said violently. 'I could kill him.'

I supposed we'd all noticed but not done much about the source of the blood on her tunic. One of her lobes was jaggedly cut and steadily oozing. She turned her head slightly, and the other ear shimmered suddenly in the car's lights, revealing a large aquamarine ringed by diamonds.

'Your earring,' Fred exclaimed, fishing his pockets for a handkerchief and not finding one. 'You need a bandage.'

Vicky put a finger tentatively to her torn ear and winced heavily.

'The *bastard*,' she said, her voice shaking. 'The bloody bastard. He tugged . . . he just *ripped* . . . he's torn right through my ear.'

'Shouldn't earrings come off more easily than that?' the policeman asked uncritically.

Vicky's voice, high with rage and shock, said, 'We bought them in Brazil.'

'Er . . .' the policeman said, lost.

21

'Vicky,' Fred said soothingly, 'what does it matter if they came from Brazil?'

She gave him a bewildered look as if she couldn't understand his not understanding.

'They don't have butterfly clips on the back,' she told him jerkily. 'They have butterfly *screws*. Like a nut and bolt. So they don't fall off and get lost. And so people can't steal them . . .' Her voice died away into a sob, a noise it seemed suddenly that she herself disapproved of, and she sniffed again determinedly and straightened her shoulders.

Hanging on to her courage, I thought. See-sawing towards disintegration, hauling herself back. Agitation almost beyond her control, but not quite.

'And another thing,' she wailed, misery and anger fighting again for supremacy. 'They stole my handbag. It's got my passport . . . and, oh *hell*, my green card . . . and our tickets . . .' A couple of tears squeezed past her best resolutions. 'What are we going to *do*?'

The distress-filled plea was answered pragmatically by Fred who said he wasn't consul for nothing and he'd get her to her daughter's wedding willy-nilly.

'Now, ma'am,' the policeman said, uninterested in travel arrangements, 'can you give a description of these two men?'

'It was dark.' She seemed angry with him suddenly. Angry with everything. She said furiously, 'They were dark.'

'Black?'

'No.' She was uncertain, besides angry.

'What then, ma'am?'

'Dark skinned. I can't think. My ear hurts.'

'Clothes, ma'am?'

'Black . . . What does it matter? I mean . . . they were so quick. He was trying to pull my rings off . . .'

She extended her fingers. If the stones were real they were worth stealing.

'My engagement ring,' she explained. 'Bastard didn't get it, thanks to Peter.'

The urgent whipping siren of a dazzlingly lit ambulance split the night and paramedics spilled out purposefully, taking charge with professional heartiness and treating Vicky and Greg like children. The policeman told Vicky he would be following them to the hospital and would take a proper statement once her ear and Greg's head were fixed, but she didn't seem to take it in.

Two more police cars arrived fast with flashing lights and wailing sirens, disgorging enough navy figures to arrest half the neighbourhood, and Fred and I found ourselves with our hands on the car roof being frisked while insisting that we were not in fact the muggers but instead the British consul, friends and witnesses.

The kindly original cop looked back fleetingly and said something I couldn't hear in the bustle, but at least it seemed to blunt the sharpest of suspicions. Fred loudly reiterated his identity as British consul, a statement he was this time asked in a bullish fashion to substantiate. He was allowed to fetch out an oversized credit card which announced – with photograph – his diplomatic status, thereby inducing a reluctant change of attitude.

Greg was on his feet. I took a step towards him and was stopped by a midnight-blue arm.

'Ask him for his car keys,' I said. 'If his car stays out here all night it will be stolen.'

Grudgingly the midnight-blue presence yelled over his shoulder, and presently the information percolated back that Greg had dropped the keys by the car when he was attacked. Midnight-blue went to look, found the keys and, after consultation, gave them to Fred.

The uniforms seemed to be doing things at great speed which no doubt came from much practice and was a regular pace for such an occasion. Vicky and Greg were helped into the ambulance which at once departed, followed immediately by the first policeman. Other policemen fanned out into the surrounding area to search for the muggers should they still be around and hiding. Fat chance, I thought.

One of the new bunch wrote down my name under Fred's and paused over the address I gave him: the Foreign and Commonwealth Office, Whitehall, London, England.

'Diplomatic immunity, like him?' He jerked his head in Fred's direction.

'I'll help if I can,' I said.

He sucked his teeth a bit and asked what I'd observed.

I told him, in fair detail.

Had I seen this mugger at close quarters?

Well yes, I said, since he'd hit me.

Description?

'Dark skinned.'

'Black?'

I found the same difficulty as Vicky over the skin colour.

'Not West Indian or African,' I said. 'Maybe Central American. Maybe Hispanic. He didn't speak. I can't tell you any better.'

'Clothes?'

'Black.' I thought back, remembering how I tried to throw him, re-feeling the cloth that I'd clutched. 'I'd say black jeans, black cotton sweatshirt, black sneakers. When he ran off he wasn't easy to see.'

I made my guesses at his age, height, weight and so on but I couldn't remember his face well enough to be sure I'd recognize him in other clothes, in daylight.

Midnight-blue shut his notebook and produced two cards with his name on, one for Fred, the other for me. He would be grateful, he indicated, if we would present ourselves at his police station the following morning at ten a.m., and he gave us the impression that had it not been for the sheltering umbrella of the Foreign Office, the request would have been an order.

The scattered searchers returned without a mugger

but with, surprisingly, Vicky's torn-out earring, which they'd found on the ground. Bagged and labelled, it was solemnly retained in police custody. There was no sign, it seemed, of a capacious white bejewelled handbag or Greg's wallet or his shoulder-slung hold-all.

As fast as they'd arrived, the midnight-blues departed, leaving a sudden deafening silence in which Fred and I stood and looked at each other a touch dazedly, deciding what to do next.

The few curious local inhabitants faded back through their doors, their interest-level in the noise and glittering red, white and blue illuminations having been remarkably low throughout, as though the circus were too familiar to bother with; though this, Fred commented ruefully, was supposed to be a quiet residential area.

'You'd better drive the BMW to the hospital,' Fred said, 'and collect them and take them home.'

'Um . . .'

'I can't do it,' he said reasonably. 'I promised Meg I wouldn't be late. She's got her hands full . . . the children were crying because their spots are itching.'

'Won't the hospital send them home in an ambulance?' I asked.

Fred looked at me pityingly. 'This is not the National Health Service. This is pay-through-the-nose country.'

'Oh, all right. Where's the hospital?'

He began to give me directions but shrugged finally

and said I'd better follow him, so he led me to the entrance, pointed to it emphatically through his open window and, without pausing for more speech, zoomed away towards the chickenpox.

I found Greg and the friendly policeman sitting glumly side by side in the waiting area, Greg looking drained and grey, the policeman glowing with health and watching the passing nurses in the same sort of way that I did, once I settled myself in the next seat.

'How are you feeling?' I asked Greg: an unnecessary question.

'Tired,' he said, 'but my head's all right. They say there's only a bruise. Got to rest a bit, that's all.'

I nodded. 'I brought your car,' I said. 'I'll drive you home.'

He said limply, 'Thanks.'

Conversation lapsed. The ratio of middle aged to nubile nurses proved to be ten to one. Disappointing.

After a long time Vicky reappeared, sitting in a wheelchair pushed by a (middle-aged) nurse and accompanied by a young doctor whose smudged white coat spoke of long hours on duty. Vicky, wearing a large white bandage like an ear-muff above the bloodstained sparkling tunic, held a tissue to her mouth and had her eyes shut. Her face, cleaned of make-up, appeared lined and pudgy. The false eyelashes had been removed. The trouper persona was in abeyance; the grandmother alone inhabited the body.

The young doctor told Greg that his wife was fine,

he'd stitched the ear under local anaesthetic, it should heal without trouble, he'd given her painkillers, sedatives and antibiotics and she should come back later that day to have the dressing changed. Vicky opened her eyes and looked no better.

I glanced at my watch and found it was very nearly two o'clock. Time flies, I thought wryly, when one's having a good time.

The doctor departed and the policeman gently asked Vicky questions which she answered in a low voice without emotion. After a while he produced a card with his name on it and asked her and Greg to go to the police station at ten in the morning to complete their statements.

'You too,' he said to me.

'Your pals have already given me a card.' I showed it to him. He peered at it and nodded. 'Same place, same time.'

He said goodnight to us and left, his kindness, I saw, a habitual way of getting things done, not a deep compassion for each individual. Much better, all the same, than a brusque automatic universal disregard of sensibilities.

A nurse reappeared to push Vicky to the doorstep, but no further. Hospital care and hospital insurance stopped right there, she firmly said. We persuaded her merely to let me fetch the car to the door, rather than have Vicky walk to the car, a concession she made with impatience. Both Greg and Vicky were beyond caring.

They chose to sit together in the back of the car, and I asked for the most elementary instructions on how to get to their home, like which way out of the gate. It was amazing we ever reached the house as Vicky closed her eyes again and kept them shut, and Greg kept drifting off to sleep, waking when I stopped and asking where we were. You tell me, I said.

I stifled the beginnings of irritation and drove with care and we did at last pull up in a semi-circular drive outside their front door. Greg fortunately still had the house keys in his pocket, and I didn't think it was exactly the moment to speculate aloud as to whether the thieves had acted on the knowledge they must have found in their possession and come to rob and destroy while their victims were in the hospital.

Telling the couple to stay where they were for a moment, I got Greg to give me the key, and fed it into the lock with some foreboding. All was dark and quiet inside, however, and when I felt around and found the light switch, all was also revealed as undisturbed.

Feeling exposed to predators and half-ready for another attacking rush from the many surrounding bushes, I tried to hurry Greg and Vicky into the house without actually scaring them into paralysis, but they were agonizingly slow. It wasn't until we were all safely inside with the door locked behind us that I began in any way to relax.

They lived in a one-storey house, most of the rooms flowing into each other without doors. No heating

29

problems, of course, in South Florida. I went round checking that all the curtains were drawn, finding that the Wayfield taste in interior decorating ran to bright floral prints and mahogany.

Returning to find them both sitting in the chairs nearest the front door, as if their legs could take them no further – the life force at its lowest ebb – I suggested they made themselves a hot sweet drink before they went to bed. I, I said, would phone for a taxi.

They looked at me in horror.

'Oh no,' Vicky said, near to tears. 'Stay here. Please do. I hate to say it, but I feel so shaky and shivery. And I'm scared. I can't help it. They might come here. I've realized they must know our address.'

Greg reached across for her hand and squeezed it. He didn't actually say he was scared but he too begged me to stay.

'You chased them off before,' Vicky said. 'They won't come if you're here.'

I thought with longing of a quiet bed in the airport hotel but saw I couldn't abandon them to a panic-filled night. I'd known them for less than six hours; felt I'd been with them for ever.

'I'll stay,' I said, 'but it wasn't I who chased them off. You,' I said to Vicky, 'you did it yourself with that brilliant scream.'

I remembered her as she looked then, a white-haired witch with scarlet raking nails and brilliant eyes, the personification of all the dark female powers that had petrified men from pre-history.

'You were magnificent,' I said: frightening, I might have added, if I'd wanted to admit it.

She brightened a little at the memory, a movement in the eyes. 'It wasn't just the scream,' she said. 'It was the kick.'

I asked in awakening understanding, 'Where?'

She looked down at her shoes, high-heeled with sharply pointed toes.

'Where do you think?' she said. 'I used to be a dancer too. High kicks. I was behind him. I aimed for just below the bottom of his spine. I was so angry I'd have killed him if I could.' She looked up, a smile somewhere near, full of revengeful satisfaction. 'I was right on target. It was a doozie, hard and straight. He had his legs apart, balancing himself to clobber you.' She paused, then finished it with a nod. 'I got him in the balls.'

CHAPTER TWO

Two nights later I flew to England. Across the aisle Vicky and Greg slumbered peacefully, blanketed to their chins, heads together, babes in the wood.

'Peter, it wouldn't hurt you to put your journey off for one more day,' Fred had said. 'It isn't as if you've got anything to go *to*, especially. And Greg and Vicky are badly shaken by all this, you know they are.'

Fred was at his most earnest, almost evangelical in his desire to do good. Rather, in his desire that *I* should do good. I thought of a T-shirt I'd once owned which read 'Stress is what happens when your gut says NO and your mouth says YES I'D BE GLAD TO', and Fred asked me what I was smiling at.

'Nothing, really.'

'Then you'll wait a day?'

'Yes, all right.'

'Great. Great. I was sure you would. I told them I was sure you would. They can't possibly go tonight, you can see that.'

We were in his office at the time, in the consulate in

Miami, on the day after the mugging. The night had passed undisturbed by marauders but it had been an exhausted pair that had pottered round the kitchen in dressing-gowns that morning to assemble much needed breakfasts. Vicky's car was throbbing, Greg's forehead was dark with bruises and both were suffering from depression.

'All my credit cards . . .' Greg said wearily. 'There's so much to *do*.' He picked up the telephone and passed on the bad news to the companies.

I thought of my bags sitting unattended in my unused room and phoned the hotel: no problem at all, I could pick up the luggage later but they would charge me for the past night regardless. Fair enough, I agreed.

Once they were dressed, I drove Vicky and Greg to meet Fred and keep the police appointment, a session that taxed the Wayfields' remaining stamina sorely. The only bright spot for Vicky was the return of her earring, though it would be a long time, she guessed, before she could wear it.

'I don't want to keep thinking of last night,' she said vehemently during the interview, but the friendly policeman carried on asking friendly persistent questions none the less. Finally they let all four of us go, and Fred in his car led the rest of us in the BMW across town to his official domain.

The consulate proved to be a modest suite of offices high in a glass-walled tower. British firms and holiday-makers had clamoured for it to be opened, but funding it, it was rumoured in the service, Fred said, had meant closing its equivalent in some other place from where the tourist tide had ebbed.

Arriving on the 21st floor we squeezed through tall doors into a small entrance and waiting area already filled by an indignant family who'd been robbed at Disneyworld and a man in a wheelchair who'd been brought in by the police as he couldn't remember where he was staying in Florida and had been found dazed and alone in the street repeating an English address.

Behind a glass partition, two good-looking young women, trying to sort everything out, welcomed the sight of Fred with relief.

'Bomb-proof glass, of course,' Fred said to me, and signalled the girls to let us in through the electronic glass door. 'Carry on,' he said to them, which they did most competently, it seemed to me.

Beyond the anti-terrorist door, the available space had been cleverly divided to allow for all the familiar sections of embassy life, but in miniature. Records room, cypher room, conference room, individual offices, large busy secretaries' room, kitchen, and a more spacious office with the best view for the man in charge.

This efficient layout was staffed by Fred himself, he said, along with the two super-secretaries and two vice-consuls, one of whom was involved in trade, the other, currently out on a job, in delicate areas like the unlawful movement of drugs.

Fred parked Greg and Vicky in a conference room just big enough for a round table surrounded by dining chairs and then, his forehead sweating, beckoned me into his private sanctum and shut the door.

'They won't be able to leave today,' he said. 'They' had become shorthand for Greg and Vicky. 'Tickets, easy. But there's her passport, and she has to go to the hospital and she's only half packed, she said.'

'And new locks for their house,' I agreed.

'So you could stop another day and help them, couldn't you?'

I opened my mouth and shut it again and it was then that Fred had warmed to his persuasion.

Fred and I were of equal rank in the service, consuls and first secretaries both being (if one equated things to the army) like colonels.

As in the army, the next step up was the big one. First secretaries and consuls abounded, but counsellors and consul-generals and ministers led towards the peak of the pyramid: there were at least six hundred consuls and probably more first secretaries around the world but only about a hundred and fifty ambassadors.

Fred looked out of his window at the wide spectacular view of palm trees, glittering blue sea and downtown sky-scraper Miami and told me he'd never been happier.

'I'm glad, Fred,' I said, meaning it.

He turned with a self-deprecating smile, his plumpish body soft but his mind as agile as an acrobat.

35

'We both know you'll go higher than me in the end,' he said.

I made disclaiming motions but he brushed them aside.

'But here,' he went on, 'for the first time ever, I'm in charge. It's a great feeling. Terrific. I just wanted to tell you. I can't tell many people. They wouldn't understand. But you do, don't you?'

I slowly nodded. 'I've never really been totally in charge myself except now and then for a day or so. There's always someone to report to.'

'This is much better.' He grinned, looking almost boyish. 'Think of me sometimes while you're scuttling round in Whitehall.'

I thought of him as I sat in the jumbo with Greg and Vicky asleep across the aisle. I'd probably learned more about him in the last few days than in all the time in Tokyo, and certainly I liked him better. Being his own chief seemed to have sharpened the outlines of his character and smoothed away a lot of nervous mannerisms and maybe one day even the sweating forehead would remain dry.

Somehow or other he had persuaded me not only to travel to England with his distressed friends but to deliver them safely to their daughter in Gloucestershire. I was aware that if they'd been going to somewhere like Northumberland my response might have been different, but there had been a tug of curiosity about returning to the county of my childhood.

Two weeks remained of my leave and I hadn't planned to do anything in them definitely except find myself somewhere in London to live. So to Gloucestershire – why not?

I rented a car at Heathrow when we arrived in the morning and drove the pathetically grateful Wayfields westward in the general direction of Cheltenham and the racecourse, Vicky having said that her daughter lived close to the track itself.

As Vicky hadn't been there before and my own memory was hazy, I stopped a couple of times to consult the map provided with the car, but we arrived in the general area at about noon without getting lost and drew up at a garage to ask for final directions.

'The vets' place? Turn right, go past the fire station . . .'

The road ran through an uneasy mix of centuries, the mellow and old elbowed into the shade by aggressive shopfronts and modernized pubs. Not a village, more a suburb: no cohesive character.

'The vets' place' was a substantial brick building set back from the road, allowing enough parking space in front for not only several cars but a horsebox. A large horsebox, in fact, was parked there. Did vets no longer make house calls?

I stopped the rented car on a spare piece of tarmac and helped Vicky unwind to her feet. She was suffering already from jet-lag, from a metabolism telling her she'd been awakened at two in the morning, never mind that it had said seven on the local clocks. There were dark smudges under her eyes and a sag in her facial muscles and an overall impression of exhaustion.

A white plastic shield on a headband neatly covered her repaired ear but a lot of fluffy bounce had gone out of the white hair around it. She looked a tired old woman, and even the attempt at lipstick in the car as we neared our destination in no way disguised the true state of affairs.

The weather hardly helped. Straight from the warmth of Florida to a grey cold windy late February day in England was a shiversome enough transition for anyone; on top of their injuries, it was debilitating.

Vicky wore a dark green trouser suit with a white blouse, inadequate for the English out-of-doors, and had had no energy for brightening things with jewellery or gold chains. Simply getting onto the aeroplane had been enough.

Greg did his best to be her mainstay but, despite his protestations, it was clear that being knocked unconscious and helpless had shaken him to the foundations. He had left the humping of all the suitcases entirely to me and apologized six times for feeling weak.

I didn't in any way think that either of them should have snapped back like elastic. The muggers had been strong, purposeful enemies, and the single punch I'd taken had been like a jab from a pole. Moreover, the police had depressed us all by their opinion that the muggers would not be discovered or caught: the savage hostility we'd felt from them wasn't unusual, it appeared. Vicky was more or less advised not to wear screwed-on earrings in future.

'To make it easier for them to rob me?' she asked with tired sarcasm.

'Better wear fakes, ma'am.'

She'd shaken her head. 'No fun, when you have the real thing.'

Outside the vets' place, Greg extricated himself from the car and all three of us went over to the brick building and in through a glassed entrance door to a lobby. This brown-carpeted space was furnished with two chairs and a counter for leaning on while one talked with the young woman in an office on the far side of it.

She was sitting at a desk and speaking on a telephone.

We waited.

Eventually she made some notes, disconnected, turned an enquiring face in our direction and said, 'Yes?'

'Belinda Larch . . .' Vicky said tentatively.

'Not in, I'm afraid.' The reply was crisp: not impolite exactly, but not helpful either. Vicky looked as if it wouldn't take much to bring her to tears.

I said to the young woman, 'Perhaps you could tell

us where we could find her. This is her mother, just arrived from America. Belinda is expecting her.'

'Oh yes.' She wasn't moved to any show of excessive welcome. 'Supposed to have arrived yesterday, I thought.'

'I telephoned,' Vicky said miserably.

'Sit down,' I said to her. 'You and Greg sit on these two chairs and wait, and I'll find Belinda.'

They sat. I'd been taking care of them for so long now that if I'd said 'lie down on the floor', they might have done it.

'Right,' I said to the girl. 'Where do I find her?'

She began to answer with the same sort of underlying obstructiveness and then saw something in my expression which changed her mind. Very prudent, I thought.

'Well, she's in the hospital section assisting the vets. You can't go in there. They're operating on a horse. I'm sorry, but you'll have to wait.'

'Can you phone her?'

She started to say no, looked at the Wayfields, looked at me, and with raised eyebrows picked up the receiver.

The conversation was short but produced results. The girl put down the phone and drew a labelled bunch of keys out of a drawer.

'Belinda says she can't get out for an hour at least but these are the keys of the cottage where her mother will be staying. She says to go there and she'll come as soon as she can.'

'And where's the cottage?'

'The address is on that label and on the key ring. I don't know where it is.'

Thanks for very little, I thought. I escorted Greg and Vicky back to the car and sought directions from passers-by. Most proved equally uninformed but I finally got a reliable pointer from a telephone repair man up a pole and drove away from the bustle, up a hill, round a bend and down the first turning on the left.

'It's the first house along there on the right,' I'd been told from aloft. 'You can't miss it.'

I did in fact nearly miss it because it wasn't my idea of a cottage. No thatched roof and roses round the door. No quaint little windows or bulging whitewashed walls. Thetford Cottage was a full-blown house no older than Vicky or Greg.

I braked the car doubtfully, but there was no mistake: the words 'Thetford Cottage' were cut into square stone pillars, one each side of imposing iron gates. I stopped, got out, opened the gates and drove through and stopped again on the gravelled expanse inside.

It was a weathered grey three-storey edifice built of stone from the local Cotswold hills, roofed in grey slate and painted brown round the windows. The one surprise in its otherwise austere façade was a roofed balcony over the front entrance, with a stone balustrade and a glimpse of long windows behind.

Vicky got out of the car uncertainly, holding on to my arm, blown by the wind.

'Is this the place?' she said doubtfully.

She looked around at the bare flower beds, the leafless trees and bedraggled grass, her shoulders sagging ever more forlornly.

'Surely this isn't the place . . .?'

'If the key fits, it is,' I said, trying to sound encouraging; and indeed the key did fit, and turned easily in the lock.

The house was cold inside with a deep chill speaking of no recent heating. We stood in a wood-floored hall looking around at a lot of closed doors and a polished wood staircase leading to undiscovered joys above.

'Well,' I said, shivering myself. 'Let's see what we've got.'

I opened one of the doors purposefully, expecting vistas at least, and found it was a cloakroom.

'Thank God for that,' Greg said with relief, eyeing the comforts within. 'Excuse me, Peter.' He brushed past me, went in and closed the door behind him.

'That's one of us satisfied,' I said, moved nearly to a giggle. 'Now let's find a fire.'

A pair of double doors led into a large drawing-room, another door into a dining-room, a third into a small sitting-room with armchairs, television and, the gods be thanked, a fire that lit with switches, not paper, wood and coal.

Turned on, it warned up nicely and put on a show of flickering flames. Vicky subsided speechlessly into an armchair near it and sat huddled and shaking, looking ill.

'Back in a moment,' I said, and made tracks up the staircase, looking for blankets or anything warm. All the doors upstairs were again closed. The first I opened revealed a bathroom. I must be a water diviner, I thought. The second held twin beds, unmade, the bed-clothes neatly stacked on each.

Better than blankets: duvets. Royal blue, scattered with white daisies. I gathered the pair of them into my arms and negotiated the bare polished wooden stairs downwards, thinking that they were a skating rink for the unwary.

Vicky hadn't moved. Greg stood over her, looking helpless.

'Right,' I said, handing them the duvets, 'You tuck these round you and I'll see what's in the kitchen in the way of hot drinks.'

'Johnnie Walker?' Greg suggested.

'I'll look.'

I'd left all the hall doors open, though two were as yet unexplored. One led to a capacious broom, garden-ware and flower vase store, the other to a cold antiseptic kitchen of white fitments round a black-and-white tiled floor. On a central table stood the first signs of recent human life: an unopened box of tea bags, some artificial sweeteners and a tartan-printed packet of shortbread.

The refrigerator was empty except for a carton of milk. The cupboards on inspection held, besides the normal clutter, a large quantity of home-made marmalade, serried ranks of condensed soups and several stacks of tinned fish, mostly tuna.

I went back to Vicky and Greg, who now sat dumbly in royal blue scattered with white daisies.

'Tea bags or instant coffee?' I asked.

'Tea,' Vicky said.

'Johnnie Walker?' Greg repeated hopefully.

I smiled at him, warming to him, and went on the quest. No alcohol, however, in the dining-room cupboards, none in the kitchen, none in the drawing-room. I made tea for both of them and carried it, along with the shortbread and the bad news, to the little sitting-room.

'You mean, no drink *anywhere*?' Greg exclaimed, dismayed. 'Not even beer?'

'I can't find any.'

'They've locked it up,' Vicky said unexpectedly. 'Bet they have.'

They, the owners, whoever they were, might have done so, I supposed, but they'd left their store cupboards stocked and unprotected, and I hadn't come across any unopenable spaces.

Vicky drank her tea holding the cup with both hands,

as if to warm them. The room itself by then was perceptibly warmer than the rest of the house and I began to think of roaming round switching on every heater I could find.

Action was frustrated by the arrival of a car outside, the slam of a door and the rapid entrance into the house of a young woman in a hurry. Belinda, one supposed.

We heard her voice calling 'Mother?' followed by her appearance in the doorway. She was slim in stone-washed jeans topped by a padded olive green jacket. Pretty in a fine-boned scrubbed sort of way. Maybe thirty, I thought. Her light brown hair was drawn up into a pony tail that seemed more utilitarian than decorative and she looked worried, but not, it soon appeared, on her mother's account.

'Mother? Oh good, you got here.'

'Yes, dear,' Vicky said wearily.

'Hello Greg,' Belinda said briefly, going over to him and giving him a dutiful peck. Her mother got the same treatment in turn: a kiss on the cheek but no deeply loving welcoming hug.

'Well, Mother, I'm sorry, but I can't stay,' she said. 'I'd arranged to have yesterday free, but you being a day late . . ' She shrugged. 'I have to go back. The horse died. They have to do a post-mortem.' She stared hard at her mother. 'What's the matter with your ear?'

'I told you on the phone . . .'

'Oh yes, so you did. I'm so worried about the horses . . . Is the ear all right now? By the way, we're

45

getting married in church instead of the registrar's office, and we're having the reception here in this house. I'll tell you about it later. I have to go back to the hospital now. Make yourselves comfortable, won't you? Get some food in, or something. I brought some milk etcetera yesterday.' Her gaze sharpened from vague to centre upon myself. 'Sorry, didn't catch your name?'

'Peter Darwin,' I obliged.

'Peter,' Vicky said forcefully, 'has been our lifeline.'

'Oh? Well, good. Nice of you to have helped them.' Her gaze slid away, encompassing the room in general. 'The Sandersons who own the house have gone to Australia for a couple of months. They're renting it to you quite cheaply, Mother, and I've engaged the caterers ... You always said you wanted me to have a proper wedding and I decided it would be a good idea after all.'

'Yes, dear,' Vicky said, accepting it meekly.

'Three weeks tomorrow,' Belinda told her. 'And now, Mother, I really have to run.'

I abruptly recalled a conversation I'd had long ago in Madrid, with my father.

'A child who calls its mother "Mother", wants to dominate her,' he said. 'You will never call your mother "Mother".'

'No, Dad.'

'You can call her Mum, Darling, Mater, Popsie or

46

even silly old cow, as I heard you saying under your breath last week, but *never* Mother. Understood?'

'Yes, Dad.'

'And why did you call her a silly old cow?'

Lying to him was fairly impossible: he always saw through it. Swallowing, I told him the truth. 'She wouldn't let me go to Pamplona to run with the bulls because I'm only fifteen.'

'Quite right. Your mother's always right. She's made a good job of you and one day you'll thank her. And never call her Mother.'

'No, Dad.'

'Mother,' Belinda said, 'Ken says we'll have dinner together soon. He meant it to be tonight, but with all this worry . . . I'll phone you later.'

She gave a brief wave, turned and departed as speedily as she'd come.

After a short silence Vicky said valiantly, 'She was a really sweet baby, very cuddly and loving. But girls grow up so independent . . .' She paused and sighed, 'We get on quite well really as long as we don't see each other too much.'

Greg gave me a sideways look and made no comment, though I saw that he felt much as I did about the off-hand welcome. Belinda, I thought, was as self-centred as they come.

'Right,' I said cheerfully, 'we may as well get your cases in, and if you like I'll go to the shops.'

A certain amount of bustle at least partially filled

the emotional vacuum, and after a while Vicky felt recovered just enough to investigate upstairs. The large bed in what was clearly the Sandersons' own domain at least looked ready for occupation, though their clothes still filled the cupboards. Vicky said apathetically that she would unpack later the cases I'd carried up for her but meanwhile she was going to sleep at once, in her clothes, on the bed.

I left Greg fussing over her and went downstairs, and presently he followed, agitated and displeased.

'Belinda's a pain in the ass,' he said. 'Vicky's crying. She doesn't like being in someone else's house. And I feel so helpless.'

'Sit down by the fire,' I said. 'I'll go foraging.'

When I came to think of it, I hadn't been shopping regularly for food in England since I'd been at Oxford, and not much then. I was more accustomed to eating what I was given: the sort of life I led was rarely domestic.

I drove back to the straggly suburb and bought all the essentials I could think of, and felt like a stranger in my own country. The inside layouts of shops were subtly different from my last brief visit four years earlier. The goods available were differently packaged. Colours were all brighter. Even the coins had changed shape.

I found I'd lost, if I'd ever really known, any clear idea of what things in England should cost. Everything seemed expensive, even by Tokyo standards. My ignorance puzzled the shop assistants as I was obviously English, and it was altogether an unexpectedly disorienting experience. What on earth would it be like, I wondered, for someone to return after half a century, return to the world of my parents' childhood, a time that millions still clearly remembered.

Every child had chilblains in the winter back then, my mother said; but I hadn't known what a chilblain was.

I collected some scotch for Greg and a newspaper and other comforts and headed back to Thetford Cottage, finding things there as I'd left them.

Greg, dozing, woke up when I went in and came shivering out into the hall. The whisky brightened his eye considerably and he followed me into the kitchen to watch me stow the provisions.

'You should be all right now,' I said, closing the fridge.

He was alarmed. 'But surely you're staying?'

'Well . . . no.'

'Oh, but . . .' His voice deepened with distress. 'I know you've done a lot for us, but please . . . just one more night?'

'Greg . . .'

'Please. For Vicky's sake. *Please*.'

For his sake too, I saw. I sighed internally. I liked them well enough and I supposed I could stay one night there and start my rediscovery of Gloucestershire in the morning, so again, against my gut reaction, I said yes.

Vicky woke at six thirty in the evening and came tottering down the stairs complaining of their slipperiness.

Greg and I had by that time lowered the scotch level, read the newspapers from cover to cover and found out how the television worked. We'd listened to the news, which was all of death, as usual. Amazing how many ways there were of dying.

Belinda had not telephoned.

At seven, however, a car arrived outside and the daughter herself came in as before, managerial rather than loving. This time, however, she had brought her affianced.

'Mother, you met Ken two or three years ago, you remember.'

'Yes dear,' Vicky said kindly, though she'd told me she couldn't bring him to mind. She offered him her cheek for a kiss, and after the fleetest of pauses received one.

'And this is Greg,' Belinda said. 'I suppose he's my stepfather.' She laughed briefly. 'Odd having a stepfather after all these years.'

'How do you do?' Ken said politely, shaking Greg's hand. 'Glad to meet you, sir.'

Greg gave him an American smile that was all front

with reservations hidden, and said he was sure pleased to be in England for the happy occasion.

Ken, at that moment, looked a long way from happy. Anxiety vibrated in his every gesture, not a simple nervousness at meeting his future in-laws but a much deeper, overriding bunch of worries, too intense to be covered.

He was tall, thin, sandy and wiry looking, like a long-distance runner. A touch of Norwegian, perhaps, about the shape of the head and the light blue of his eyes. Fair hair on the point of thinning. I guessed his age at nearing forty and his dedication to his job as absolute.

'Sorry,' Belinda said to me, not sounding contrite. 'Can't remember your name.'

'Peter Darwin.'

'Oh yes.' She glanced towards Ken. 'Mother's helper.'

'How do you do?' He shook my hand perfunctorily. 'Ken McClure,' he said.

It sounded very familiar. 'Kenny?' I said doubtfully.

'No. Ken. Kenny was my father.'

'Oh.'

None of them paid any attention but I felt as if I'd been kicked in the subconscious by sleeping memory. Kenny McClure. I knew about Kenny McClure – but what did I know? – from a long time ago.

He'd killed himself.

The knowledge came back abruptly, accompanied

51

by the curiosity I'd felt about it as a child, never having known before that people could kill themselves, and wondering how he had done it and what it felt like.

Kenny McClure had acted as veterinary surgeon at Cheltenham races. I knew I'd driven round the track with him in his Land-Rover a few times, but I couldn't now recall what he'd looked like.

Ken had made an attempt at dressing for the occasion in a suit, shirt and tie but with one black shoe and one brown. Belinda had come in a calf-length blue woollen dress under the padded olive jacket and, having made the effort herself, was critical of Vicky, who hadn't.

'Mother, honestly, you look as if you'd slept in those clothes.'

'Yes dear, I did.'

Belinda impatiently swept her upstairs to find something less crumpled and Greg offered Ken some scotch.

Ken eyed the bottle with regret. 'Better not,' he said. 'Driving, and all that.'

A short silence. Between the two of them there was no instant rapport. Eye contact, minimal.

'Belinda told us,' Greg said, finally, 'that you've had some trouble with a horse today.'

'It died.' Ken had clamped a lid tight over his seething troubles and the strain came out in staccato speech. 'Couldn't save it.'

'I'm real sorry.'

52

Ken nodded. His pale eyes turned my way. 'Not at my best this evening. Forgotten your name.'

'Peter Darwin.'

'Oh yes. Any relation to Charles?'

'No.'

He considered me. 'I suppose you've been asked before.'

'Once or twice.'

He lost interest, but I thought that in other circumstances he and I might have done better together than he with Greg.

Ken tried, all the same. 'Belinda says you were both mugged, sir, you and ... er ... Mother.'

Greg made a face at the memory and gave him a brief account. Ken raised a show of indignation. 'Rotten for you,' he said.

He spoke with a Gloucestershire accent, not strong, but recognizable. If I tried, I'd still be able to speak that way easily myself, though I'd lost it to my new father's Eton English soon after I had met him. He'd told me at once that I had a good ear for languages, and he'd made me learn French, Spanish and Russian intensively all through my teens. 'You'll never learn a language as naturally as now,' he said. 'I'll send you to school in England for two final years to do the university entrance, but to be truly multi-lingual you must learn languages where they're spoken.'

I'd consequently breathed French in Cairo, Russian in Moscow, Spanish in Madrid. He hadn't envisaged

Japanese. That had been a quirk of Foreign Office posting.

Vicky and Belinda having reappeared, Vicky in red this time, Ken led the way in his car to a small country inn with a restaurant attached. He took Belinda with him and I again drove the rental car with Vicky and Greg sitting together in the back, an arrangement that led Belinda to conclude that 'helper' meant chauffeur. She gave me sharply disapproving looks when I followed the group into the bar and accepted Ken's offer of a drink before dinner.

We sat round a small dark table in a corner of a room heavily raftered and furnished in oak. The level of light from the red-shaded wall lamps was scarcely bright enough for reading the menus and there was an overall warmth of atmosphere that one met nowhere else on earth but in a British pub.

Belinda stared at me from over her glass. 'Mother says you're a secretary. I can't understand why she needs one.'

'No, dear,' Vicky began, but Belinda made a shushing movement with her hand.

'Secretary, chauffeur, general helper, what does it matter?' she said. 'Now that you're here, Mother, I can look after you perfectly well myself. I'm sorry to be frank, but I don't see how you justify the expense of someone else.'

Greg and Vicky's mouths dropped open and both of them looked deeply embarrassed.

'Peter . . .' Vicky's words failed her.

'It's OK,' I reassured her, and to Belinda I said peacefully, 'I'm a civil servant. A private secretary in the Foreign Office. Your mother isn't paying me. I'm literally here just to help them over the few sticky days since they were attacked. I was coming to England in any case, so we travelled together. Perhaps I should have explained sooner. I'm so sorry.'

An apology where there was no fault usually defused things, I'd found. The Japanese did it all the time. Belinda gave a shrug and twisted her mouth. 'Sorry, then,' she said in my general direction but not actually looking at me. 'But how was I to know?'

'I did tell you . . .' Vicky began.

'Never mind,' I said. 'What's good on this menu?'

Belinda knew the answer to that and began to instruct her mother and Greg. Ken's thoughts had been on a distant travel throughout, but he made a visible effort then to retrieve the evening from gloom, and to some extent succeeded.

'What wine do you like with dinner . . . um . . . Mother?' he asked.

'Don't call me mother, call me Vicky.'

He called her Vicky easily, without the 'um'. She said she preferred red wine. Any. He could choose.

Vicky and Ken were going to be all right, I thought, and was glad for Vicky's sake. Belinda softened enough over dinner to put a glow on the thin beauty that had to be attracting Ken, and Greg offered a toast to their marriage.

'Are you married?' Ken asked me, clinking glasses with Vicky.

'Not yet.'

'Contemplating it?'

'In general.'

He nodded, and I thought of the young English-woman I'd left behind in Japan who had settled for a bigger fish in the diplomatic pond. The English girls on the staff of the embassies abroad were often the high-grade products of fashionable boarding schools, intelligent and good looking as a general rule. Liaisons between them and the unmarried diplomats made life interesting all round but often ended discreetly, without tears. I'd said fond farewells in three different countries, and not regretted it.

By the time coffee arrived, the relationships among Greg, Vicky, Belinda and Ken had taken the shape they were likely to retain. Vicky, like a rose given water, had revived to the point of flirting very mildly with Ken. Ken and Greg remained outwardly cordial but inwardly stiff. Belinda bossed her mother, was reserved with Greg and took Ken for granted. A pretty normal set up, all in all.

Ken still retreated every five minutes or so for brief seconds unto his consuming troubles but made no attempt to share them. He talked instead about a horse he'd bought two years earlier for peanuts to save it from being put down.

'Nice horse,' he said. 'It cracked a cannon bone. The owner wanted it put down. I told him I could save the horse if he'd pay for the operation but he didn't want the expense. Then, of course, the horse would have to rest a year before racing. All too much, the owner said. Put it down. So I offered him a bit more than he would have got from the dog-food people and he took it. I did the operation and rested the horse and put it in training and it won a nice race the other day, and now Ronnie Upjohn, that's the owner, won't speak to me except to say he'll sue me.'

'What a pig,' Vicky said indignantly.

Ken nodded. 'Luckily I got him to sign a paper at the time, saying he understood an operation might save the horse but that he preferred to have it put down, so he hasn't a chance of winning. He won't sue in the end. But I guess I've lost a client.'

Ronnie Upjohn, I thought.

I knew that name too. Couldn't attach any immediate information to it, except that it was linked in my vague memory with another name: Travers.

Upjohn and Travers.

Who or what was Upjohn and Travers?

'We're planning on running the horse here at Cheltenham in a couple of weeks,' Ken said. 'I'm giving it to Belinda and it'll run in her name, and if it wins it'll be a nice wedding present for both of us.'

'What sort of race?' I asked, making conversation.

'A two-mile hurdle. Are you a racing man?'

'I go sometimes,' I said. 'It's years since I went to Cheltenham.'

'Peter's parents met on Cheltenham racecourse,' Vicky said, and after Belinda and Ken's exclamations of interest I gave them all a version of the facts that was not the whole truth but enough for the casual chat of a dinner party among people one didn't expect to get close to.

'My mother was helping out with some secretarial work,' I said. 'My father blew into her office with a question, and bingo, love at first sight.'

'It wasn't at first sight with us,' Belinda said, briefly touching Ken's hand. 'Fiftieth or sixtieth sight, more like.'

Ken nodded. 'I had her under my feet for months and never really saw her.'

'You were getting over that frightful Eaglewood girl,' Belinda teased him.

'Izzy Eaglewood isn't frightful,' Ken protested.

'Oh, you know what I mean,' his fiancée said; and of course, we did.

Izzy Eaglewood, I thought. A familiar name, but out of sync. Something different. Eaglewood was right, but not Izzy. Why not Izzy? What else?

Russet!

I almost laughed aloud but, from long training, kept an unmoved face. *Russet* Eaglewood had been the

58

name to giggle over in extremely juvenile smutty jokes. What colour are Russet Eaglewood's knickers? No colour, she doesn't wear any. Russet Eaglewood doesn't need a mattress; she *is* one. What does Russet Eaglewood do on Sundays? Same thing, twice. We had been ignorant of course, about what she actually did. We called it 'IT', and IT in fact applied to anybody. Are they doing IT? Giggle, giggle. One day – one unimaginable day – we would find out about IT ourselves. Meanwhile IT went on apace throughout the racing world, and indeed everywhere else, we understood.

Russet Eaglewood's father had been one of the leading trainers of steeplechasers: it had been that fact, really, that had made the scurrilous stories funniest.

The knowledge came crowding back. The Eaglewoods had had their stables at the end of our village, half a mile from our little house. Their horses clattered through the village at dawn on their way up to the gallops, and I'd played in the stable yard often with Jimmy Eaglewood until he got hit by a lorry and died after three hushed weeks in a coma. I could remember the drama well, but not Jimmy's face. I couldn't clearly remember any of the faces; could dredge up only the sketchiest of impressions.

'Izzy Eaglewood ran off with a guitarist,' Belinda said disapprovingly.

'Nothing wrong with guitarists,' Vicky said. 'Your father was a musician.'

'Exactly. Everything wrong with guitarists.'

Vicky looked as if defending the long-divorced husband from Belinda's jokes was an unwelcome habit.

I said to Ken, 'Have you heard Vicky and Greg sing? They've lovely voices.'

He said no, he hadn't. He looked surprised at the thought.

'Mother,' Belinda said repressively, 'I do wish you wouldn't.'

'Wouldn't sing?' Vicky asked. 'But you know we enjoy it.'

'You're too old for it.' More than a jibe, it was a plea.

Vicky studied her daughter and said with sad enlightenment, 'You're embarrassed, is that it? You don't like it that your mother brought you up by singing in night clubs?'

'Mother!' Belinda cast a horrified glance at Ken, but Ken, far from being shocked, reacted with positive pleasure.

'Did you really?'

'Yes, until time put a stop to it.'

'I'd love to hear you,' Ken said.

Vicky beamed at him.

'Mother, please don't go around telling everyone,' Belinda said.

'Not if you don't like it, dear.'

Shout it from the rooftops, I wanted to say: Belinda should be proud of you. Stop indulging your daughter's every selfish snobbish whim. Vicky's sort of love, though, forgave all.

Ken called for the bill and settled it with a credit card but, before we could rise to go, a buzzer sounded insistently somewhere in his clothes.

'Damn,' he said, feeling under his jacket and unclipping a small portable telephone from his belt. 'I'm on call. Sorry about this.'

He flipped open the phone, said his name and listened, and it was obviously no routine summons to a sick animal because the blood left his face and he stood up clumsily and fast and literally swayed on his feet, tall and toppling.

He looked wildly, unseeingly, at all of us sitting round the table.

'The hospital's on fire,' he said.

CHAPTER THREE

The vets' place was on fire, but actually not, as it turned out, the new hospital itself which lay separately to the rear. All one could see from the road, though, was the entrance and office block totally in flames, scarlet tongues shooting far skywards from the roof with showers of golden sparks. It was a single-storey building, square, extensive, dying spectacularly, at once a disaster and majestic.

Ken had raced off frantically from the restaurant alone, driving like the furies, leaving the rest of us to follow and thrusting Belinda into suffering fiercely from feelings of rejection.

'He might have waited for me.'

She said it four times aggrievedly but no one commented. I broke the speed limit into the town.

We couldn't get the car anywhere near the vets' place. Fire appliances, police cars and sightseers crowded the edges of the parking area and wholly blocked the roadway. The noise was horrendous. Spotlights, streetlights, headlights threw deep black shadows behind the milling helpers, and the flames lent orange haloes to the firemen's helmets and shone on spreading sheets of water and on the transfixed faces outside the cordoned perimeter.

'Oh, God, the horses...' Belinda, leaving us at a run as soon as our car came willy-nilly to a halt, pushed and snaked a path through to the front, where I briefly spotted her arguing unsuccessfully with a way-barring uniform. Ken was out of sight.

Great spouts of water rose in plumes from hoses and fell in shining fountains onto the blazing roof, seeming to turn to steam on contact and blow away into the black sky. The heat, even from a distance, warmed the night.

'Poor things,' Vicky said, having to shout to be heard.

I nodded. Ken had enough worry beside this.

There were the thuds of two explosions somewhere inside the walls, each causing huge spurts of flame to fly outwards through the melted front windows. Acrid smoke swirled after them, stinging the eyes.

'Back, back,' voices yelled.

Two more thuds. Through the windows, with a searing roar like flame-throwers, sharp brilliant tongues licked across the parking space toward the spectators, sending them fleeing in panic.

Another thud. Another fierce jet-burst of flames. A regrouping among the firemen, heads together in discussion.

The whole roof fell in like a clap of thunder, seeming

to squeeze more flames like toothpaste from the windows, and then, dramatically, the roaring inferno turned to black gritty billowing smoke and the pyrotechnics petered out into a wet and dirty mess, smelling sour.

Ash drifted in the wind, settling in grey flakes on our hair. One could hear the hiss of water dousing hot embers. Lungs coughed from smoke. The crowd slowly began to leave, allowing the three of us to get closer to the ruined building to look for Belinda and Ken.

'Do you think it's safe?' Vicky asked doubtfully, stopping well short. 'Weren't those bombs going off?'

'More like tins of paint,' I said.

Greg looked surprised. 'Does paint explode?'

Where had he lived, I wondered, that he didn't know that, at his age.

'So does flour explode,' I said.

Vicky gave me a strange look in which I only just got the benefit of the doubt as to my sanity, but indeed air filled with flour would flash into explosion if ignited. Many substances diffused in a mist in air would combust. Old buddies, oxygen, fuel and fire.

'Why don't you go back to the car,' I suggested to Vicky and Greg. 'I'll find the other two. I'll tell them I'm driving you back to the house.'

They both looked relieved and went away slowly with the dispersing throng. I ducked a few officials, saw no immediate sign of Belinda and Ken but found on the right of the burnt building an extension of the parking area that led back into a widening space at the rear. Down there, movement, lights and more people.

Seeing Ken briefly and distantly as he hurried in and out of a patch of light, I set off to go down there despite warning shouts from behind. The heat radiating from the brick wall on my left proved to be of roasting capacity, which accounted for the shouts, and I did hope as I sped past that the whole edifice wouldn't collapse outwards and cook me where I fell.

Ken saw me as I hurried towards him and stood still briefly with his mouth open looking back where I'd come.

'Good God,' he said, 'did you come along there? It isn't safe. There's a back way in.' He gestured behind him and I saw that indeed there was access from another road, as evidenced by a fire engine standing there that had been dealing with the flames from the rear.

'Can I do anything?' I said.

'The horses are all right,' Ken said. 'But I need ... I need ...' He stopped suddenly and began shaking, as if the enormity of the disaster had abruptly overwhelmed him once the need for urgent action had diminished. His mouth twisted and his whole face quivered.

'God help me,' he said.

It sounded like a genuinely desperate prayer, applying to much more than the loss of a building. I was no great substitute for the deity, but one way or another I'd helped deal with a lot of calamities. Crashed bus-loads of British tourists for instance, ended up, figuratively speaking, on embassy doorsteps, and I'd mopped up a lot of personal tragedies.

'I'll take Vicky and Greg back to the house, and then come back,' I said.

'Will you?' He looked pathetically grateful even for the goodwill. He went on shaking, disintegration not far ahead.

'Just hold on,' I said, and without wasting time left by the rear gate, hurrying along the narrow road there and getting back to the main road via an alley, finding that by luck I'd come out only a few steps from the car. Vicky and Greg made no objections to being taken home and left. They hoped Belinda would forgive them, but they were going to bed to sleep for a week, and please would I ask her not to wake them.

I glanced at them affectionately as they stood drooping in the polished hall of Thetford Cottage. They'd had a rough time, and when I thought of it, looking back, they hadn't seriously complained once. I said I'd see them in the morning and took the front door key with me at their request, leaving them to shut the door behind me.

Finding a way round to the back road, I returned to the vets' place from the rear and smelled again the pervading ashy smoke that stung in the throat like tonsillitis. The rear fire engine had wound in its hoses and departed, leaving one man in yellow oilskins and helmet trudging around to guard against the ruins heating up to renewed spontaneous life.

I took brief stock of what lay in the unburnt area: a new-looking one-storey building with electric lights shining from every window, a row of stable boxes set back under an overhanging roof, all empty, with their doors open, and a glass-walled thirty-yard passage connecting the burnt and unburnt buildings. That last was extraordinarily mostly untouched, only the big panes nearest the heat having shattered.

A good many people were still hurrying about, as if walking slowly would have been inappropriate. The first urgency, however, was over; what was left was the usual travail of getting rid of the debris. No bodies to go into bags this time, though, it seemed. Look on the bloody bright side.

As Ken was nowhere to be seen and a door to the new building stood open, I went inside to look for him and found myself in an entrance hall furnished as a waiting-room with about six flip-up chairs and minimum creature comfort.

Everything, including the tiled floor and a coffee machine in a corner, was soaking wet. A man trying to get sustenance from that machine gave it a smart kick of frustration as if its demise after all else was insupportable.

'Where's Ken?' I asked him.

He pointed through an open door and attacked the machine again, and I went where directed, which proved to be into a wide passage with doors down each side, one of them open with light spilling out. I found Ken in a smallish office along there, a functional room already occupied by more people than the architect had intended.

Ken was standing by the uncurtained window, still trembling as if with cold. A grey-haired man sat gloomily behind a metal desk. A woman with a dirt-smudged face stood beside him, stroking his shoulder. Two more men and another woman perched on office furniture or leaned against walls. The room smelled of the smoke trapped in their clothes and it was chilly enough to make Ken's shivers reasonably physical in origin.

The heads all turned my way when I appeared in the doorway, all except Ken's own. I said his name, and he turned and saw me, taking a second or two to focus.

'Come in,' he said, and to the others added, 'he's a helper.'

They nodded, not querying it. They all looked exhausted and had been silent when I got there as if sandwiched in shock between hectic crisis activity and facing the resumption of life. I'd seen a lot of people in that suspended state, starting from when I was twenty-three, in my first posting, and in a far-flung consulate with the consul away I had had to deal alone with a British-chartered aeroplane that had clipped a woody hillside after dark and had scattered broken bodies among splintered trees. Among other things, I'd been out there at dawn trying to stop looters. Relatives then came to the city to identify what they could and to cling to me numbly for comfort. Talk about growing up fast. Nothing, since that, had been worse.

The man who had been kicking the coffee machine came into the office, passed me, and slid down to sit on the floor with his spine against the wall.

'Who are you?' he asked, looking up.

'Friend of Ken's.'

'Peter,' Ken said.

The man shrugged, not caring. 'Coffee machine's buggered,' he announced.

His eyes were red-rimmed, his hands and face dirty, his age anywhere from thirty to fifty. His news was received with apathy.

The grey-haired man behind the desk seemed to be the senior in rank as well as years. He looked round at the others and wearily said, 'Suggestions?'

'We go to bed,' the coffee-machine man said.

'Buy a better computer,' one of the other men offered. 'When the records are saved on back-up disks, in future store them in a vault.'

'A bit late for that,' said one of the women, 'since all the records are burnt.'

'The new records, then.'

'If we have a practice,' Ken said with violence.

That thought had occurred to the others who went on looking gloomy.

'How did the fire start?' I asked.

69

The grey-haired man answered with deep tiredness. 'We were having the place painted. We ourselves have a "no smoking" rule, but workmen with cigarettes . . .' He left the sentence unfinished, the scenario too common for comment.

'Not arson, then,' I said.

'Are you a journalist?' one of the women demanded.

'No, definitely not.'

Ken shook his head. 'He's a diplomat. He fixes things.'

None of them looked impressed. The women said that a diplomat was the last thing they needed but the grey-haired man said that if I had any practical suggestions, to give them.

I said with hesitation. 'I would leave someone here all night with all the lights on.'

'Well . . . why?'

'Just in case it was arson.'

'It couldn't have been arson,' the grey man said. 'Why would anyone want to burn our building?'

One of the other men said, 'They wouldn't get far trying to burn this hospital. We had it all built of flame-retardant materials. It's supposed to be fire-proof.'

'And it didn't burn,' the woman said. 'The fire doors held in the passage. The firemen poured tons of water on all that end . . .'

'And buggered the coffee machine,' the man on the floor said.

There were a few wan smiles.

'So we still have our hospital,' the grey-haired man told me, 'but we've lost the pharmacy, the lab, the small-animal surgeries and, as you heard, every record we possessed. The tax situation alone . . .' He stopped, shaking his head hopelessly. 'I think the going to bed suggestion was a good one, and I propose we adopt it. Also if anyone will stay here all night, please volunteer.'

They'd all had too much, and no one spoke.

After an appreciable pause, Ken said jerkily, 'I'll stay if Peter will.'

I'd let myself right in for it, I thought. Oh well. 'OK,' I said.

'Who's on call?' the grey-haired man asked.

'I am,' Ken said.

'And I am,' a dark-haired young woman added.

The grey hair nodded. 'Right. Ken stays. Everyone else, sleep.' He rose to his feet, pushing himself up tiredly with hands flat on the desk. 'Council of war here at nine in the morning.' He came round the desk and paused in front of me. 'Whoever you are, thanks.' He briefly shook my hand. 'Carey Hewett,' he said, introducing himself.

'Peter Darwin.'

'Oh. Any relation to . . .?'

I shook my head.

'No. Of course not. It's late. Home, everyone.' He led the way out of the office and the rest drifted after him, yawning and nodding to me briefly but not giving their names. None of them expressed any curiosity, let

71

alone reservations, about the stranger they were so easily leaving on their property. They trusted Ken, I supposed, and by extension, any friend of Ken's.

'Where's Belinda?' I asked, as the last of them disappeared.

'Belinda?' Ken looked temporarily lost. 'Belinda . . . went with the horses.' He paused, then explained. 'We had three horses out in the boxes. Patients. Needing nursing care. We've sent them to a trainer who had room in his yard. Belinda went to look after them.' Another pause. 'They were upset, you see. They could smell the smoke. And we didn't know . . . I mean, the hospital might have burnt too, and the boxes.'

'Yes.'

He was still faintly trembling.

I said, 'It's pretty cold in here.'

'What? I suppose it is. The firemen said not to turn the central heating on until we'd had it checked. It's gas-fired.'

'Gas-fired in the office building too?'

'Yes, but it was all switched off. It always is at night. The firemen asked.' He stared at me. 'They made a point of shutting off the mains.' The shakes came back strongly. 'It's all a nightmare. It's . . . it's . . .'

'Yes,' I said, 'sit down.' I pointed to the grey-haired man's padded chair behind the desk, the only remotely comfortable perch in sight.

Ken groped his way onto it and sat as if his legs had given way. He had the sort of long loose-jointed limbs that seem always on the point of disconnecting from the hip bone, the thigh bone, the ankle bone – the skeleton coming apart. The longish Norwegian head accentuated it, and the thin big-knuckled fingers were an anatomy lesson in themselves.

'Apart from the fire,' I said, 'what's the problem?'

He put his elbows on the desk and his head in his hands and didn't answer for at least a minute. When he finally spoke his voice was low and painfully controlled.

'I operate on horses about five times a week. Normally you'll lose less than one out of every two hundred on the table. For me, that means maybe one or at most two deaths a year. You can't help it, horses are difficult under anaesthetic. Anyway,' he swallowed, 'I've had four die that way in the last two months.'

It seemed more like bad luck to me than utter tragedy, but I said, 'Is that excessive?'

'You don't understand!' The pressure rose briefly in his voice and he stifled it with an effort. 'The word goes round like wildfire in the *profession*. People begin to snigger. Then any minute the public hears it and no one's sending horses to you any more. They ask for a different vet. It takes years to build a reputation. You can lose it like *that*.' He snapped the long fingers. 'I *know* I'm a good surgeon. Carey knows it, they all know it, or I'd be out already. But they've got themselves to consider. We're all in it together.'

I swept a hand round the empty office.

'The people who were here . . .?'

73

Ken nodded. 'Six vets in partnership, including me, and also Scott, the anaesthetist. And before you ask, no, I can't blame *him*. He's a good technician and a trained veterinary nurse, like Belinda.'

'What happened this morning?' I asked.

'Same thing,' Ken said miserably. 'I was putting some screws in a split cannon bone. Routine. But the horse's heart slowed and his blood pressure dropped like a stone and we couldn't get it back.'

'We?'

'Usually it would have been just Scott, Belinda and me, but today we had Oliver Quincy assisting as well. And that was because the owner insisted, because he'd heard the rumours. And still the horse died, and I can't . . . I don't . . . it's my whole *life*.'

After an interval I said, 'I suppose you've checked all the equipment and the drugs you use.'

'Of *course*, we have. Over and over. This morning we double-checked *everything* before we used it. Triple-checked. I checked, Scott checked, Oliver checked. We each did it separately.'

'Who checked last?'

'I did.' He said it automatically, then understood the significance of what I was asking. He said again, more slowly, 'I checked last. I see that maybe I shouldn't have. But I wanted to be sure.'

The remark and action, I thought, of an innocent man.

I said, 'Mightn't it have been more prudent, in the

circumstances, to let one of the other vets see to the cannon bone?'

'What?' He looked at me blankly, then understood my ignorance, and explained. 'We're partners in a big general practice but we all have our own specialities. Carey and the two women are small-animal vets, though Lucy Amhurst does sheep and ponies as well. Jay Jardine does cattle. I do horses. Oliver Quincy is a general large-animal man working with both Jay and me, though he does mostly medical work and only minor surgery, almost never here in the hospital. Castrations, things like that. They're done on site.'

He had almost stopped shaking, as if the unburdening and explanations themselves had released the worst of the pressure.

'We're all interchangeable to some extent,' he said. 'I mean, we can all stitch up a gash whether it is a ferret or a carthorse. We know all the usual animal diseases and remedies. But after all that, we specialize.' He paused. 'There aren't all that number of surgeons like me in the whole country, actually. I get sent cases from other vets. This hospital has earned a reputation we can't afford to lose.'

I reflected a bit and asked, 'Have there been any over-the-top calamities in the dog and cat departments?'

Ken shook his head in depression. 'Only horses.'

'Racehorses?'

'Mostly. But a couple of weeks ago there was an

Olympic-standard show-jumper – and that didn't die during an operation. I had to put it down.' He looked into tormented space. 'I'd done a big repair job on its near hind a week earlier where it had staked itself breaking a jump, and it was healing fine back at home, and then they asked me out to it as the whole leg had swelled like a balloon, and the tendon was shot to hell. The poor thing couldn't put its foot to the ground. I gave it painkillers and brought it here and opened the leg up, but it was hopeless . . . the tendon had disintegrated. There wasn't anything to repair.'

'Does that happen often?' I asked.

'No, it damn well doesn't. The owner was furious, his daughter was in tears, there was a hullabaloo all over the place. They'd insured the horse, thank God, otherwise we would have had another lawsuit on our hands. We've had to insure ourselves against malpractice suits just like American doctors. You get some very belligerent people these days in the horse world. They demand perfection a hundred per cent of the time, and it's impossible.'

I had a vague feeling that he'd glossed over some fact or other, but decided it was probably to do with a technicality he knew I wouldn't understand. I wasn't in a position, anyway, to demand that he tell me his every thought.

The night grew colder. Ken seemed to have retreated into introspection. I felt a great desire to make up for some of the sleep I'd missed. No one would come to set fire to the hospital. It had been a stupid idea of mine to suggest it.

I shook myself mentally awake and went out into the passage. All quiet, all brightly lit. I walked back to the entrance hall and checked that the departing vets had locked the front door when they left.

All secure.

Although wet, the entrance hall was distinctly warmer than the passage and the office. I put my hand on the wall nearest the burned building and felt the heat in it, which was of a comforting level rather than dangerous. The solid door to the glass-walled connecting passage was fastened with bolts and bore an engraved strip of plastic with the instruction 'Keep This Fire Door Shut'. The door's surface was warmer than the wall, but nowhere near to frying eggs.

A third door led from the entrance hall into a spartan roomy washroom and a fourth opened onto cleaning materials. No arsonists crouching anywhere.

Passing the defunct coffee machine, I went back to the office and asked Ken to show me round the rest of the hospital. Lethargically he rose and told me that the office we were in was used by whoever was operating in the theatre for writing notes of the procedures used, together with drugs prescribed. The notes, he added with a despairing shake of the head, were then taken to the secretarial section and stored in files.

'Not in the computer?' I asked, flicking a finger at a monitor which stood on a table near the desk.

'In the main computer in the office, yes, but our secretary enters only the date, the name of the animal, owner, type of surgery and a file number. It takes too long to type in all the notes and, besides, mistakes creep in. If anyone wants to refer back, they just call up the file number and go and find their actual notes.' He gestured helplessly. 'Now all the files are bound to have gone. So has the computer itself, I suppose. This terminal is dead, anyway. So there will be no records any more to prove that all the operations when the horses died were normal regular procedures.'

I reflected that on the other hand if in fact there had been any departure from regular procedures, all records of that too had conveniently vanished. Yet I did believe in Ken's distress, otherwise what was I doing wandering round an animal hospital in the middle of the night looking for people playing with matches.

'What's absolutely *irritating*,' Ken said, 'is that the architect we engaged for the hospital told us the office wasn't up to his standards of fire proofing. He said we should install heavy fire doors everywhere and frankly we didn't want to, they slow you up so much. We knew we'd simply prop them open. But there you are, he was right. He insisted on at least fire proof doors at each end of the connecting passage, and the firemen say those doors – and the length of the passage – saved the hospital.'

'Why is the passage so long?'

'Something to do with what's under the ground. It

wasn't suitable for foundations any nearer. So we had to have the passage, or else run from building to building in the rain.'

'Lucky.'

'So it turned out.'

'How old is the hospital?'

'Three or four years,' Ken said. 'Three and a half, about.'

'And you all use it?'

He nodded. 'Not for minor things, of course. Often it's because of some sort of emergency. Dog run over, that sort of thing. There's a small-animal wing. Otherwise there are – were – the two small-animal surgeries over in the main building for vaccinations and so on.' He paused. 'God, it's all so depressing.'

He led the way out of the office and into the central passage. The floors throughout were of black grey-streaked vinyl tiles, the walls an unrelenting white. The hospital hadn't been designed, of course, to soothe human patient anxieties: severe practicality reigned along with the fire-retardant ethos.

Nothing was made of wood. Doors were metal everywhere, set into metal frames, painted brown. A row of three on the left-hand side were store rooms, Ken said. All the doors were locked. Ken opened them and we checked inside: all quiet.

On the right, past the office, lay another much bigger double room, one half housing X-ray developing equipment and the other a movable X-ray machine on wheels. There was also a simple bed in there, with folded blankets, looking unused, and a closed door giving access from the car park for patients.

'We have to keep all these doors locked, including the office,' Ken said grimly. 'We've found things walking out of here when we're all busy in the theatre. You wouldn't believe what some people will steal.'

Looting was a built-in instinct, I thought.

Immediately beyond the X-ray room there was what should have been a heavy fire door blocking our way. It was present, but had been opened flat against the wall and held there by a substantial wedge. Ken saw me eyeing it and shrugged.

'That's the problem. We can't open these doors with our arms full of equipment. The firemen closed that door earlier, when they first came, but someone's opened it since. Force of habit.'

Past the habit, there was an extra-wide door straight ahead. The passage itself turned right.

'That door,' Ken said, pointing ahead, 'is the entry to the theatre area from this side. The passage goes round to an outside door.'

He unlocked the theatre door, pressed rows of switches to light our path, and led the way into a vestibule with doors on either side and another across the end.

'Changing rooms right and left,' Ken said, opening the doors and pointing. 'Then we go ahead into the central supply of gowns and gloves and so on. We'd better put gowns and shoecovers on, if you don't mind, in the interests of cleanliness in the operating room.'

He handed me a pair of plastic disposable shoecovers and a sort of cotton overall, dressing in similar himself, and then supplied us also with hats like shower caps and masks. I began to feel like a hospital movie, only the eyes emoting. 'Instruments and drugs are in here too,' he went on, showing me locked glass-fronted cupboards. 'This cupboard here opens both ways, from this side and from inside the operating room. The drug cupboard has two locks and unbreakable glass.'

'A fortress,' I commented.

'Carey took advice from our insurers as well as the police and the fire inspectors. They all had a go.'

Ken pointed to a door in the left-hand wall. 'That leads towards the small-animal operating room or theatre.' A door to the right, he showed me, opened to a scrub room. 'You can go through the scrub room into the operating room,' he said, 'but we'll go straight in from here.'

He pushed open double swing doors ahead – not locked, for once – and walked into the scene of his disasters.

It was unmistakably an operating theatre, though the wide central table must have been almost nine feet long with an upward pointing leg at each corner, like a four-poster bed. There were unidentifiable (to me) trolleys, carts and wheeled tables round the walls, all of metal. I had an impression of more space than I'd expected.

Without ado, Ken skirted the table and went to the far wall where, after another clinking of keys, a whole section slid away to reveal another room beyond. I followed Ken into this space and found that the floor was spongy underfoot. I remarked on it, surprised.

Ken, nodding, said, 'The walls are padded too,' and punched his fist against one of the grey plastic-coated panels which lined the whole room. 'This stuff is like the mats they put down for gymnasts,' he said. 'It absorbs shocks. We anaesthetize the horses in here, and the padding stops them hurting themselves when they go down.'

'Cosy,' I said dryly.

Ken nodded briefly and pointed upwards. 'See those rails in the ceiling, and those chains hanging down? We fasten the horse's legs into padded cuffs, attach the cuffs to the chains, winch up the horse and he travels along the rails into the theatre.' He pointed back through the sliding door. 'The rails guide the horse right over the table. Then we lower him into the position we want. The table is wheeled too, and can be moved.'

One lived and learned I thought. One learned the most extraordinary things.

'You have to support . . . er, to *carry* . . . the head, of course,' Ken said.

'Of course.'

He rolled the wall-door into place again and

relocked it, then went across the spongy floor to another door, again padded, but opening this time into a short corridor which we crossed to enter what Ken called the preparation room. There was a clutter of treatment carts round the walls there, and more cupboards.

'Emergency equipment,' he explained briefly. 'This is reception, where the horses arrive.' He stepped out of the shoecovers and gestured to me to do the same, throwing them casually into a discard bin. 'From here we go back into the corridor and down there into the outside world.'

A gust of wind blew specks of ash in through the widening opening of the outside door and Ken gestured me to hurry through after him, relocking as usual behind us.

Each of Ken's keys had a coloured tag with a stick-on label, identifying its purpose in the general scheme of things. Ken clanked like an old-time gaoler.

Outside, we were still under a wide roof which covered a good-sized area in front of a row of four new-looking boxes stretching away to the left. All the box doors stood open, as I'd seen before, the patients having left.

'That's about it,' Ken said, looking around. 'We unload the sick animals just here and usually take them straight into reception. There's often not much time to lose.'

'Nearly always horses?' I asked.

He nodded. 'Occasionally cattle. Depends on the value of the beast, whether the expense is justified. But yes, mostly horses. This is hunting country, so we get horses staked and also we get barbed wire injuries. If we can't sew them up satisfactorily in their home stable, we bring them here. Abdominal wounds, that sort of thing. Again, it depends on love, really.'

Reflecting, I asked, 'How many horses are there in your area?'

'Can't tell exactly. Between us we're the regular vets of, say, half a dozen or more racing stables, five riding schools, a bunch of pony clubs, countless hunting people, showing people, eventers, and people who just keep a couple of hacks about the place . . . oh, and a retirement home for old steeplechasers. There are a whole lot of horses in Gloucestershire.'

'A whole lot of love,' I commented.

Ken actually smiled. 'It keeps us going, no doubt of it.' The smile faded. 'Up to now.'

'Law of averages,' I said. 'You'll go months now without another death.'

'No.'

I listened to the hopelessness and also the fear, and wondered if either of those emotions sprang from facts he hadn't told me.

'There won't be anyone out here in the boxes,' he said.

'We may as well look.'

He shrugged and we walked along the row and

found it indeed deserted, including the small feed and tack rooms at the end. Everywhere was noticeably swept and clean, even allowing for the fire.

'That's it, then,' Ken said, turning back.

He closed and bolted the empty boxes as we passed them and, at the end, made not for the door into the treatment areas but to another set back to the left of it, which led, I discovered, into the off-shoot of the black-tiled passage. From there, through uncurtained windows, one could look out to where the fire engine had been. A long line of pegs on the wall opposite the windows held an anorak or two, a couple of cloth caps and a horse's head collar. Pairs of green wellies stood on the floor beneath, with a row of indoor shoes on a shelf above.

Ken wiped his own shoes carefully on a mat and waited while I did the same, then opened yet another door, at which point we were only a few steps and a couple of turns away from where we'd started. Ken took the gowns back to the changing room and returned to comment on the silence everywhere in a building usually full of bustle.

I agreed that we could relax on the score of ill-intentioned intruders for the moment and rather regretted having offered an all-night service. Cold was a problem I hadn't given much thought to, and although it was by then nearing three o'clock it would presumably get colder still before dawn.

'How about us borrowing those anoraks?' I suggested, 'and wrapping ourselves in blankets.'

'Yes, we could,' he began to say, but was forestalled by the same muffled noise as in the restaurant, the chirp of the telephone on his belt.

He looked at me blankly for a second, but pulled out the phone and flipped it open.

'Hewett and Partners,' he said. 'Yes... Ken speaking.'

I wouldn't have thought he could grow much paler, but he did. The shakes returned as badly as ever.

'Yes,' he said. 'Well... I'll come straight away.'

He clipped the phone back on to his belt with fumbling fingers and tried with three or four deep breaths to get himself back into control, but the pale blue eyes were halfway to panic.

'It's the Vernonside Stud,' he said. 'They've a broodmare with colic. The stud groom's been walking her round but she's getting worse. I'll have to go.'

'Send someone else,' I suggested.

'How can I? If I send someone else, I've as good as resigned.'

He gave me the wild unseeing stare of a courage-racking dilemma and, as if he indeed had no choice, unhesitatingly went down the passage and into the drugs room where he rapidly gathered an armful of bottles, syringes and other equipment to take out to his car. His fingers trembled. He dropped nothing.

'I'll be gone an hour at least,' he said, 'that's if I'm

lucky.' He gave me a brief glance. 'Do you mind staying here? It's a bit of an imposition . . . I hardly know you, really.'

'I'll stay,' I said.

'Phone the police if anything happens.'

He set off fast along the passage in the direction of the coats-on-pegs and over his shoulder told me that I'd get no incoming calls to worry about because they'd be re-routed in the exchange to his own portable phone – always their system for whoever was on duty at night.

'You can make calls out,' he said, taking down an anorak, shaking off his shoes and sliding into wellies. 'You'd better have my keys.' He threw me the heavy bunch. 'See you.'

He sped out of the far door letting its latch lock with a click behind him, and within seconds I heard his car start up and drive away.

When I couldn't hear him any longer, I tried on the remaining olive green anorak, but it would have fitted a small woman like Belinda and I couldn't get it on. I settled for a blanket from the X-ray room and, wrapped to the chin, sat on the padded chair in the office, put my feet up on the desk and read an article in a veterinary journal about oocyte transfers from infertile mares into other mares for gestation, and the possible repercussions in the thoroughbred stud book.

This was not, one might say, riveting entertainment.

A couple of times I made the rounds again, but I no longer expected or feared to find a new little bonfire.

I did go on wondering whether the office building had been torched or not, but realized that it was only because of Ken's general troubles that arson had seemed possible.

I read another article, this time about enzyme-linked immuno-sorbent assay, a fast antibody test for drugs in racehorses. It was the only reading matter of any sort in sight. I had a readaholic friend who would read bus timetables if all else failed. Hewett and Partners didn't use buses.

I eyed the telephone. Who could I call for a chat at three in the morning? It would be nine o'clock at night in Mexico City. A good time for the parents. Better not.

I dozed over an account of 3-D computer scanning of bone stress factors in hocks and awoke with a start to hear someone rapping on the window with something hard, like a coin.

A face accompanied the hand, coming close to the glass, and a voice shouted, 'Let me in.'

He pointed vigorously in the direction of the rear door and as I went along the passage I remembered that he was the one who'd been kicking the coffee machine and so could be presumed to be on the side of the angels.

He came in stamping his feet and complaining of the cold. He held two large thermos flasks and explained that in the rush he'd forgotten his keys.

'But not to worry, Ken said you were here.'

'Ken?' I asked.

He nodded. 'He's on his way back here with the mare.' He thrust the thermos flasks into my grasp and kicked off his boots, reaching up for a pair of indoor shoes on the shelf above the pegs. Slipping his feet into those he took off his padded jacket. Then he said, 'God, it's freezing in here,' and put it on again. 'Ken's phoning Belinda, and I'm to get the theatre ready.'

He was moving as he talked. 'I hate these middle-of-the-night emergencies.' He reached the central passage. 'I hate buggered coffee machines.' He marched into the office, took one of the thermoses back, unscrewed its inside top and used it as a cup. The coffee steamed out and smelled like comfort while he drank.

'Want some?' he asked, wiping his mouth on the back of his hand.

'Please.'

He filled the container again and handed it to me carefully. Hot sweet instant; strong and milky. Better than champagne at that moment.

'Great,' I said, screwing the emptied cap back on the thermos.

'Right. I take it you know nothing about anaesthetizing horses?'

'Nothing.'

'Can't be helped. Are these Ken's keys? Good.'

He picked up the bunch and exited rapidly. He was tall, wide shouldered, dark haired, roughly forty, and he moved jerkily as if there was far more explosive power available in his muscles than he needed.

I followed him into the passage and found him unlocking one of the store rooms.

'OK,' he said. 'Maintenance fluids.' He went in and reappeared with several large plastic bags full of clear liquid. 'Do you mind carrying these?' He didn't wait for an answer but pushed them into my care and dived back for more of the same, setting off down the passage at a great rate. Cursing under his breath, he unlocked the wide door leading to the vestibule and the theatre.

'I hate all these doors,' he said, stacking the bags of fluid inside the two-way cupboard that led into the operating room. He then hooked the door back against the wall. 'Do you mind putting on a gown and shoe-covers?'

We donned the whole paraphernalia, and when we were clad he went backwards through the double swing doors into the theatre itself and held one for me to follow.

'Good.' He bustled about. 'Ventilator.' He rolled one of the metal carts from against the wall to the head of the operating table. 'Horses can't breathe very well on their own when they're under anaesthetic,' he said. 'Most animals can't. Or birds, for that matter. You have to pump air into them. Do you want to know all this?'

'Carry on.'

He flicked me a brief glance and saw I was genuinely interested.

'We pump the anaesthetic in with oxygen,' he said. 'Halothane usually. We use the minimum we can, just a light anaesthesia because it's so difficult for them.'

He expertly linked together the tubes of the ventilator and plugged an electric lead into a socket in the floor.

'We went through all this ad infinitum yesterday morning,' he said. 'Checked every valve, checked the pump, checked the oxygen, which comes in from outside cylinders when we turn on this tap.' He showed me. 'Sometimes the heart starts failing and there's not a damn thing one can do about it. We've had our fair share of those recently.' He stopped his narrative abruptly, as if remembering I didn't wholly belong there. 'Anyway, I'm checking everything twice.'

He darted in and out readying other things that he didn't explain and I stood around feeling that I ought to be helping, but out of ignorance couldn't.

There was the sound of a car door slamming outside. Scott – it had to be Scott, the anaesthetist – lifted his head at the sound and rolled enough wall to one side to allow us access to the padded room. He crossed the spongy floor with his power-packed stride and unlocked the door to the corridor. With myself still at his heels (snapping off the shoecovers) we went down there and emerged into the brisk air and found Ken in anorak and wellies letting down the rear ramp of a small horsetrailer that had been towed there by a Land-Rover.

'Scott, good,' Ken said, letting the ramp fall with a

clang. 'I had to drive the damn thing myself. They've two mares foaling at this moment at Vernonside and no staff to spare. They're stressed beyond sense. This mare is dying on her feet and she's carrying a foal worth God knows what by Rainbow Quest.'

He sped into the trailer to fetch his patient, who came lumbering backwards down the ramp looking sicker than I'd known was possible with animals. Heavy with foal, she was bloatedly fat. Her head hung low, her brown skin glistened with sweat, her eyes were dull and she was making groaning noises.

'She's full of painkillers,' Ken said. He saw me standing there and in black distress said, 'Her heart's labouring. She's swollen with gas and there's feedback up from her stomach. That means her gut's obstructed. It means she'll die probably within an hour if I don't operate on her, and quite likely if I do.'

'You'd be safer with a second opinion,' I said.

'Yes. I phoned Carey on my way back here, asking him to get someone, or come himself. He said to trust my own ability. And he said I'm the best horse surgeon in this area. I do know it, even if I don't usually say it.'

'So you'll go ahead,' I said.

'Got no choice, have I? Just look at her.'

He handed the mare's leading rein to Scott, who said, 'Belinda's not here yet.'

'She's not coming,' Ken said. 'I couldn't find her. I phoned the trainer who's got our horses in his yard

92

and he said he didn't know where she was sleeping and he wasn't going around at this hour looking for her.'

'But . . .' Scott said, and fell silent.

'Yes. But.' Ken looked directly at me. 'What I want *you* to do is watch and make notes. A witness. Just write down what I tell you and what Scott tells you. Do you faint at the sight of blood?'

I thought of the broken bodies on the hillside.

'No,' I said.

CHAPTER FOUR

In the padded room, while Scott held her by the head collar, Ken with sensitive fingers found the mare's jugular vein and pushed into it what looked like a long hypodermic needle covered with plastic and an end connector that remained outside on the skin.

'Catheter,' he said, removing the needle and leaving the plastic sleeve in the vein.

I nodded.

'Intravenous drip,' he enlarged, fastening to the catheter a tube from one of the bags of fluid that Scott was busily suspending from the ceiling. 'You have to keep the body fluids up.'

He went briefly to the operating room, returning with a small syringeful of liquid which he injected into the mare's neck via the catheter.

'Half a cc of Domosedan,' he said, spelling it for me as I wrote on a pad on a clipboard. 'It's a sedative to make her manageably dozy. Mind you, don't get within reach of her feet. Horses kick like lightning, even in this state. Go behind that half-wall, out of reach.'

I stood obediently behind a free-standing section of padded wall that allowed one to see the action while being shielded from trouble: rather like the shelter provided in bullrings for humans to escape the horns.

'What do you do with the syringe now?' I asked.

'Throw it away. It's disposable.'

'Keep it,' I said.

Ken gave me a pale blue stare, considered things, and nodded.

'Right.'

He took the syringe into the operating room and put it in a dish on one of the tables round the walls. He wore what I did: his own shoes covered with disposable covers, green cotton trousers, short-sleeved green shirt, a lab coat over them, surgical mask dangling round his neck, a soft white cap like a shower cap over his hair.

Scott, in similar clothes, rubbed a hand down the mare's nose, fondling her ears and making soothing noises. Slowly some of the jangle loosened in her beleaguered brain, peace perceptibly creeping in until she was quiet and semi-conscious on her feet.

Ken, watching her closely, had come back carrying a larger syringe in another dish. 'Antibiotic,' he said, injecting. He went away to pick up a third.

'This is ketamine hydrochloride,' he said, returning and spelling it again for me. 'Sends her to sleep.'

I nodded. Scott shut the sliding door to the operating room, Ken temporarily disconnected the drip and with smooth skill injected the mare again through the catheter in her neck. Almost immediately the great body swung round in an uncoordinated arc, staggered, wavered and collapsed slowly sideways, one hind leg lashing out in a muscle spasm that spent itself harmlessly against the padding, the head flopping with a thump onto the spongy floor.

Dramatic, I thought; but routine, obviously, to Scott and Ken.

'Intubation,' Ken said to Scott.

Scott nodded and passed an impressively large tube into the mare's mouth and down her throat.

'For oxygen and halothane,' Ken told me briefly.

Scott opened the sliding door wide, went into the operating room with the syringe in the dish and returned with the padded cuffs for the mare's legs, and also bags to cover her feet.

Both men buckled these on, then pulled down the chains from the ceiling and linked them to the cuffs. Scott fetched a sort of canvas sling with handles for carrying the mare's head, and Ken without waste of time pressed buttons on a panel in the theatre wall to activate the winch.

The chains wound back and hoisted the half-ton horse effortlessly into the air. Scott supported her head in the sling while Ken reconnected the drip. Then Ken pressed another button and a high rolling trolley moved slowly along the ceiling rails, taking the dangling body, intravenous fluid and all, into the theatre.

The rails themselves positioned the patient directly

over the table. Ken pressed buttons. The chains length-
ened, letting down their burden inch by inch until the
mare was lying on her back with all four legs in the air,
her distended belly a brown rounded hump. Scott laid
her head down gently and then helped Ken hitch the
leg-cuffs to the four posts at the corners of the table
so that her legs were comfortably bent, not stiff and
straight. The two men worked without speaking,
moving smoothly through a manoeuvre often repeated.

'Ventilator on,' Ken said. 'Gas on.'

Scott fixed the tube in the horse's mouth to a tube
from the ventilator, then pressed a switch and turned a
tap, and the oxygen-halothane mixture began pumping
with slow insistent rhythm into the mare's lungs.

Ken asked me briefly, 'Do you understand all that?'

'Yes,' I said.

'Good. Now I'm going to slide another catheter into
her facial artery where it curves round the mandible.
It will directly monitor her blood pressure. Normally
Belinda would do this but today I'll do it myself.'

I nodded and watched his deft fingers push a small
tube into the mare's jaw and connect it to a metering
machine rolled into place by Scott. Both he and Scott
watched with clear anxiety the two lines which
appeared on a monitoring screen, but it seemed that
they were reassured, at least for the present.

'Final scrub,' Ken said at length. He looked at me,
'You'd better come and watch.'

I followed him into the scrub room where he

lengthily scrubbed his hands clean and dried them on a sterile towel. Then at his request I helped him put on a fresh sterile gown, tying the tapes for him. Finally he pushed his hands into sterile latex gloves. Everything came vacuum packed in separate envelopes, for one-use only.

'If this mare dies,' Ken said, 'I'm finished.'

'Stop thinking about it.'

He stood for a moment with all the strain showing in his eyes, then he blinked them a few times very positively and took a visibly deep breath.

'Come on, then.' He turned away and went towards the theatre, asking me to open the swing door for him so as not to contaminate himself.

He went first to where Scott stood, which was in front of the blood pressure screen, watching it.

'She's stabilized,' Scott said, his relief evident, 'and I've shaved her skin.' There was indeed now a shaved strip all along the mountainous belly.

Ken said to me, 'I need Scott to assist me. Will you stand by this screen? Watch it all the time. A horse's blood pressure is about the same as humans, ideally 120 over 80; but like humans, it drops under anaesthesia. If it drops below 70 millimetres of mercury, we're in trouble and an alarm will go off. We should be safe between 80 and 90, where we are now. Watch that line there. And that counter, that's the heart rate. If there's any change in either of them, tell me immediately.'

'Right.'

'Write down the time, the heart rate and the blood pressure.'

I nodded, and wrote.

He went round to the other side of the table where Scott brought forward instruments on rolling carts and created what Ken called a sterile area in the room. He and Scott between them took disposable green cloths out of sterile packaging and laid them all over the horse's abdomen, leaving visible only a narrow shaved section on top.

'All set?' Ken asked Scott, and Scott nodded.

It was the last moment that Ken could have drawn back, but the commitment in his mind had been made long before.

'Incision,' he said, dictating to me while he picked up a scalpel and with precision suited the deed to the word. 'Ten inches, beside the umbilicus.'

I wrote fast what he'd said and switched my gaze back to what he was doing. Scott, meanwhile, went off to scrub.

'Watch the blood pressure,' Ken said fiercely, not even raising his eyes. 'Don't watch me, watch the monitor between writing.'

I watched the monitor, which remained steady. I still couldn't help taking fascinated second-long glances at a process I'd expected to be horrifying, but wasn't in the least. For one thing, there was little smell, when I'd somehow been prepared for stench, nor, with retractors, clamps, forceps and swabs, even a great deal of bleeding.

'Cutting along the linea alba,' Ken said, continuing his running commentary. 'That's the central fibrous ridge between muscle groups. If you cut through there into the abdominal cavity, you get little bleeding.' He looked at Scott, who had returned, and without being asked Scott held out a long rubber sleeve-glove which he pulled on over Ken's right hand and arm up to the armpit. 'Watertight,' Ken explained to me briefly, 'and of course sterile, for going into the abdomen.'

What I hadn't begun to envisage were the extraordinary contents of an equine tum. From out of the quite small incision popped a large ridged bit of intestine and in its wake Ken slowly began to pull a loop of vast tube ten or more inches in diameter, seemingly endless, pink, bulbous and glistening. My eyes, I suppose, were equally huge with astonishment.

'Watch the screen,' Ken said. 'This is the colon, now distended by gas. The equine colon's not held in place by connecting tissue like in humans, it just zig-zags free. Half of all cases of twisted gut are colon trouble.' He pulled out at least another yard of the enormous tube and gave it to Scott to support in a green cloth while he felt around in the cavity it had come from.

'The mare's less than a month from foaling,' he said. 'It's a good sized foal.' He was silent for a moment or two, then said unemotionally, 'If she collapses and I can't save her, I'll deliver the foal here and now by caesarean section. It might have a chance. It's got a good strong heartbeat.'

Scott glanced at him quickly and away, knowing, I thought, a good deal more than I did about the risks of such a procedure.

From time to time, as the drip bag emptied, Scott replaced it with a full one from the two-way cupboard, asking me to fetch it for him and to throw the empty one away.

'Screen?' Ken asked after every change.

'Same,' I said.

He nodded, intent, slowly feeling his way round the internal organs, his eyes in his fingertips.

'Ah,' he said finally. 'Here we are. God, what a twist.' He brought some part I couldn't see up into his own vision but still just inside the mare and made an instantaneous decision to cut out the tangled obstruction altogether.

'Eyes on the screen *all the time*,' he instructed me sharply.

I obeyed him, seeing his actions only in peripheral vision.

Supplied with instruments by Scott, he worked steadily, attaching clamps, clipping, removing tissue, swabbing, stitching, making occasional noises in his throat but otherwise not talking. Time passed. Eventually he took two clamps off and watched the results unwaveringly.

'Monitor?'

'Steady.'

He murmured to himself and finally looked up. 'All right. The obstruction's excised and the gut repaired. No leaks.' He seemed to be fighting down hope he couldn't help. 'Ready to close up.'

I glanced at the great length of huge intestine looped over Scott's arm and couldn't see how on earth they were going to stuff it all back into the body cavity.

As if reading my mind Ken said, 'We'll empty the colon.' Scott nodded. Ken asked me to fetch an open dustbin which stood against one wall and to position it near him beside the table. Next he wanted me to slot a tray into the table, rather like tray-tables in aeroplanes. A colon tray, he said.

He nodded his thanks. 'You're a non-sterile area,' he said, almost cheerfully. 'Go back to the screen, will you?'

He straightened the colon until part of it was on the tray and over the bin, then swiftly made a slit, and he and Scott began systematically to squeeze out all of the contents.

This time it did smell, but only like a stable yard, quite fresh and normal. For some reason I found myself wanting to laugh: the process was so incredibly prosaic and the bin so incredibly full.

'Monitor,' Ken said severely.

'Steady.'

Scott washed the now empty, flabby and lighter tubing with fluid, and Ken, in a fresh gown and gloves, stitched up the slit he'd made in it; then, carefully folding it into zig-zags, he returned the large gut to its rightful position inside. He did a quick half-audible check list on the abdomen, almost like a pilot coming in to land and, still with deftness and care, fastened the incision together in three layers, first the linea alba with strong separately knotted stitches, then the subcutaneous tissue with a long single thread, finally closing the skin with a row of small steel staples, three to an inch. Even the stapler came separately packed, sterile and throwaway, made mostly of white plastic, handy and light.

After the briefest of pauses, when he'd finished, Ken pulled his mask down and gave me a look of shaky triumph.

'She's made it so far,' he said. 'Scott, gas off.'

Scott, who had put a lid on his odorous bin and rolled it away, had also been round to the ventilator to turn off the halothane.

'Blood pressure?' Ken asked.

'No change,' I said.

'Ventilator off,' Scott said. 'Disconnect the catheter?'

Ken nodded. 'She's got a strong heart. Write down the time,' he said to me, and I looked at my watch and added the time to my notes.

'Ninety-one minutes from incision to finish,' I said.

Ken smiled with the professional satisfaction of star work well done, the doubts and shakes in abeyance.

He lightheartedly peeled off the green sterile cloths from the mare's round body and threw them into a bin.

He and Scott unclipped the mare's legs from the bed posts. Then the hoist, with Scott supporting her head, lifted her up off the table. In reverse order she rolled along the rails and through the sliding door into the padded room, where Ken brought over an extra panel of padding and placed it on the floor. The hoist lowered the mare onto that until she lay on her side comfortably, her legs relaxing into their normal position.

Scott removed the padded cuffs from her legs and put a rope halter on her head, leading the rope through a ring on top of the half-wall so that someone standing behind the wall could partly control her movements and stop her staggering about too much.

'She'll take twenty minutes or so to wake up slowly,' Ken said. 'Maybe in half an hour she'll be on her feet, but she'll be woozy for a good while. We'll leave her here for an hour after she's standing, then put her in the stable.'

'And is that it?' I asked, vaguely surprised.

'Well, no. We'll leave in the stomach tube to make sure nothing's coming back up the wrong way, like it was before – reflux, it's called – and because we can't give her anything to eat or drink for at least twelve hours, we'll continue with the intravenous drip. Also we'll continue with antibiotics and a painkiller-sedative and we'll monitor her heart rate, and tonight if everything's OK we'll take out the stomach tube and try her with a handful of hay.'

Hay, after all that, seemed like bathos.

'How long will you keep her here?' I asked.

'Probably a week. It knocks them over a bit, you know, a major op like that.'

He spoke with earnest dedication, a doctor who cared. I followed him back into the operating room and through to the vestibule, where he stripped off all the disposable garments and threw them into yet another bin. Scott and I did the same, Ken walking back immediately to take a continuing look at his patient.

'He won't leave her,' Scott said. 'He always wants to see them wake up. How about that coffee?'

He strode off towards the office to return with the thermoses and all three of us drank the contents, watching the mare until movement began to come back, first into her head and neck, then into her forelegs, until with a sudden heave she was sitting sideways, her forelegs bearing the weight of her neck and head, the hindlegs still lying on the padding.

'Good,' Ken said. 'Great. Let's get behind the wall now.' He suited the action to the word and took hold of the steadying rope.

The mare rested in the same position for another ten minutes, and then, as if impelled by instinct, staggered onto all four feet and tottered a step or two, weaved a bit at the end of the rope and looked as if she might fall, but stayed upright. I supposed she might have been feeling sore, disoriented and in her own way puzzled, but she was clearly free of the terrible pain of the colic.

Ken said, 'Thanks,' to me, and rubbed his eyes. 'You gave me confidence, don't know why.'

He handed Scott the rope and left him watching the mare, jerking his head for me to follow him back into the operating room.

'I want to look at something,' he said. 'Do you mind if I show you?'

'Of course not.'

He went over to the table where the dishes still lay with the spent syringes in them: not three dishes now, but four. The fourth contained a large unidentifiable bit of convoluted bloody tissue with flapping ends of wide tube protruding, the whole thing pretty disgusting to my eyes.

'That's what I took out of the mare,' Ken said.

'*That?* It's huge.'

'Mm.'

I stared at it. 'What is it?'

'A twisted bit of intestine, but there's something odd about it. Wait while I get some gloves, and I'll find out.'

He went and returned with clean gloves, and then with strong movements of fingers and a spatula he slightly loosened the fearsome knot in which one loop of intestine had tightened round another like a noose, throttling the passage of food altogether. Incredibly,

106

there seemed to be a thread wound in among the tissue: pale strong thread like nylon.

Frowning, Ken spread some of the cut edges apart to look at the contents, astonishment stiffening in his face.

'Just look at this,' he said disbelievingly, and I peered through his hands into the gap he was holding open and saw, with an astonishment beyond his own, a three-inch diameter semi-circular needle, the strong sort used for stitching carpet.

He spread open another few inches and we could both see that the needle was threaded with the nylon. The needle, passing round and round in the intestine, had effectively stitched it into the knot.

'We have this happen from time to time with cats and dogs,' Ken said. 'They swallow sewing needles that have fallen to the floor and literally stitch themselves together. I've never known it in a horse. No needles carelessly dropped in their vicinity, I suppose.' He looked at it, fascinated. 'I don't think I'll take it out, it's more interesting in situ.' He paused, thinking deeply. 'It's a real curiosity and I'll organize photos of it for our records and maybe veterinary magazines, but to do that I need to keep this in good condition, and bugger it, the fridge was in the other building, in the path lab there. The lab was by the rear door. We didn't go to the expense of another lab in the hospital. I mean, there was no point.'

I nodded. I said, 'What if you take it home?'

'I'm not going home. After I've set up the mare's drip, I'll catch quick naps on the bed in the X-ray room. I do that, sometimes. And I'll watch the monitor until Belinda arrives.'

'What monitor?' I asked.

'I hope to God it still works,' he said. 'It's connected to a monitor in the main building as well.' He saw I was going to ask the question again, and answered it. 'There's a closed circuit television camera in the intensive care box, the nearest stall this end, with a monitor in the office here and another at the main reception desk. Well, there used to be. It's so we can check on the patient all the time without forever going out there.'

I looked at the cause of the mare's troubles.

'I could put that in the fridge at Thetford Cottage,' I said briefly, 'if we labelled it conspicuously not to be touched.'

'Christ.' His pale face crinkled with amusement. 'All right, why not.'

He carefully wrapped the piece of gut and in the office tied on a luggage label with a cogent message to deter curiosity in future parents-in-law.

The television circuit, when he pressed switches without much hope, proved in fact to be working, though there was nothing at present on the screen but night and a section of barred window in the empty stall.

'If only tomorrow was that simple,' he said.

*

I slept at Thetford Cottage for four hours as if drugged and was awakened by a gentle persistent tapping on the bedroom door. Rousing reluctantly, I squinted at my watch and managed a hoarse croak, 'Yes?'

Vicky opened the door with an apology and said Ken had phoned to ask if I would go down to the hospital.

'Not another emergency, for God's sake.' I sat up, pushed my fingers through my hair and looked back with awe at the night gone by.

'It's some sort of meeting,' she said. 'I didn't want to wake you but he said you wouldn't mind.'

She had taken off the ear-shield and had washed her hair, which was again white and fluffy, and she looked altogether more like Vicky Larch, singer.

'Are you feeling better?' I asked, though it was obvious.

'Much,' she said, 'though still not right, and Greg's the same. It's going to take us days. And I don't like this house, which is ungrateful of me.'

'It's unfriendly,' I agreed. 'A personality clash.'

'And boring. Did you put that "don't touch on any account" parcel in the fridge?'

'Yes,' I said, remembering. 'It's some horse innards.' I explained about the burnt lab and Ken's need for them to be stored.

'Ugh,' she said.

She went away and I tottered into some clothes, jet-lagged myself if the truth were told. The face in the bathroom mirror, even when newly shaven, had tired, brownish-green eyes below the usual dark hair and eyebrows. Teeth freshly brushed felt big behind stiff facial muscles. I pulled a face at my familiar real self and practised a diplomatic expression to take to the meeting.

Diplomatic expression? Air of benign interest with giveaway-nothing eyes. Habit-forming, after a while.

Vicky in the kitchen had made me coffee and hot toast. I drank the coffee, kissed her cheek, and took the toast with me for the drive to the hospital, crunching gratefully all the way.

Chaotic activity filled the rear car park. A towing truck was trying to manoeuvre a Portakabin into a space already occupied by cars whose drivers were reversing all over the place to get out of the way. There were animals weaving in and out, mostly on leads, and people with anxious expressions or open mouths, or both.

I backed out of the mêlée and left the rented car in the road outside, walking in and being accosted by an agitated lady carrying a large cloth-covered birdcage who told me her parrot was sick.

Fighting down a laugh I said I was sorry about that.

'Aren't you one of the vets?' she demanded.

''Fraid not.'

'Where am I supposed to take my parrot?'

I managed the diplomatic expression but it was a close-run thing.

'Let's try that door over there,' I suggested, pointing

to the visitor's entrance in the hospital. 'I expect you'll find an answer there.'

'This fire's very inconvenient,' she said severely, 'and I do think they might have phoned to save me the journey.'

'The appointment book was burned,' I said.

She looked startled. 'I didn't think of that.'

From the rear, the main visible legacy of the flames was great black licks of soot above the frames where the windows had been and daylight itself showing in the openings because the space inside was open to the sky. There was still a lingering smell of doused ash, sour and acrid, leaving a taste in the mouth.

I steered the sick-parrot lady into the entrance hall, which had a chaotic quality all of its own with cats and barking dogs sitting on people's laps all round the walls and the centre filled by Carey Hewett in a white medical coat arguing with a fire officer, one of the women vets trying to sort out patient priority, yesterday's receptionist stolidly taking names and addresses and a large man in a tweed suit demanding Carey Hewett's attention.

Abandoning the parrot and all else, I threaded a way along to the office which was almost as full, though not as noisy.

The television monitor, I noticed at once, showed the mare standing apathetically in the box, her head a mass of tubes and tapes and leather straps with buckles. Poor old thing, I thought, but at least she was alive.

The people in the office weren't those of the night before. A motherly lady sat behind the desk answering non-stop enquiries on the telephone. 'Hewett and Partners ... Yes, I'm afraid the news of the fire is correct ... if it's urgent, we'll send Lucy today, otherwise we'll have a clinic running again by Monday ... Not urgent ... would you care to make an appointment?'

She was calm and reassuring, holding the disorganized practice together. Around her appeared to be an assortment of administrators, one audibly making a list of the most urgently needed replacements, another, a plaintive-looking man, demanding impossible details for insurance purposes of what had been lost.

Belinda was there, but not Ken. She noticed my arrival after a while and a spasm of annoyance crossed her thinly pretty face. The hair was scraped back, as before. No lipstick.

'What are you doing here?' she wanted to know. 'Can't you see we're busy?'

'Where's Ken?' I asked.

'Asleep. Leave him alone.'

I wandered out of the office and down the passage towards the operating theatre. The door of the X-ray room stood ajar: I looked in there, and there was no Ken asleep on the bed.

The access door to the operating suite was locked. I made the turns instead towards the anorak-and-wellies rear entrance and let myself out into the stable area, and there I found Ken leaning on the half-door of the first of the boxes, looking in at his patient.

He was drooping with tiredness, the line of his shoulders and neck a commentary on the limits of muscle power: at what point, I wondered, did they literally stop working.

'How's she doing?' I asked, reaching him.

He knew my voice without turning his head.

'Oh, hello. Thanks for coming. She's doing fine, thank God.'

She looked, of course, anything but fine to me. The intravenous drip led from a bag at the ceiling into her neck, another tube led out of one nostril and there was a muzzle over her nose (to stop her dislodging everything else).

'Her owner's coming,' Ken said. 'Carey says he's upset.'

'Understandable.'

Ken shook his head wearily. 'Not about her colic. About me. He'd heard the rumours. Apparently he told Carey he should have got a different surgeon.'

'He'll have to change his mind.'

'He'll take a look at her and he'll see her like this. He demanded I be here to talk to him, so I wanted you along for back up. Hope you don't mind?'

'A witness you wanted and a witness you've got.'

He finally turned his head my way and openly studied my face

'You've no obligation,' he said.

'I'm interested,' I said truthfully. 'How old are you?'

'Thirty-four, just,' he answered, surprised. 'Why?'

I'd thought him a good deal older, but it seemed tactless to say so. It was the elongated bone structure and the intimations of thinning hair that added the years; the opposite, I knew, of my own case, where people doubted my professional seniority as a matter of course.

'I'm thirty-three, almost,' I said as a quid pro quo, and after a moment, acknowledging the implicit as well as the factual information, he suddenly held out his hand to be shaken. The bond of mutual age was an odd one, but definitely existed. From that moment Ken and I, though not yet close friends, all the same became a team.

A good deal of bustle appeared to be going on behind us across the car park. The Portakabin had finally been positioned to everyone's satisfaction and the tow-truck disconnected. People were carrying flipped-up flip-up chairs from a van to the cabin, followed by trestle tables and a portable gas heater.

'Instant office,' Ken said, but it was more like instant clinic, as it was the animals with their owners who presently straggled across from the hospital, not the secretaries and administrators.

'Oliver Quincy and Jay Jardine are both out on calls,' Ken said, watching them. 'Scott's gone home to rest. Lucy's out with some sheep. I'm dead on my feet. That leaves Carey himself and Yvonne Floyd to deal with that lot, and we ought to have a nurse helping them, but she left in a huff last week.' He sighed. 'I suppose I shouldn't complain, but we have too much work.'

'How about Belinda?' I asked. 'She's here, I saw her.'

He nodded. 'She brought the other three horses back this morning.' He gestured along the row. 'Two of them go home today anyway. Belinda's looking after this mare chiefly, though I expect Carey will want her over with him.'

Belinda appeared at that moment to check on her charge, giving me an irritated glance which made Ken frown.

'Peter doesn't belong here,' Belinda said, 'and we don't need him.'

'I'm not so sure. Anyway, I asked him to come.'

Belinda bit off whatever rose into her mind to say and with compressed lips she opened the mare's door and went in. Over her shoulder, as if only then remembering, she said, 'Carey wants you in the entrance hall more or less five minutes ago.'

Ken gave her a fonder smile than I could have managed and set off round the outside of the building, taking it for granted that I would go with him.

Emptied of the cats, dogs, parrot and assorted owners, the entrance hall now held only Carey Hewett himself, the argumentative fireman, the woman vet, the receptionist and the bulky man in the tweed suit. Carey Hewett in his white coat seemed to be carrying on a multi-directional conversation addressing a sentence to each in turn, a grey-haired pivot of calm within fringes of hysteria.

'Yvonne, do the best you can. Use the drugs from my car. Use anything from the hospital drugs cupboard. We've new supplies coming this afternoon. No, of course we don't know any reason for it to burn down. Your mare came through the operation very well. Yvonne, better get moving, or we'll be here until bedtime . . . Oh, Ken, there you are.'

His gaze moved past Ken to me and paused for a second or two while he remembered. Then he gave me a nod and made no comment about my presence, probably because of the other voices talking in his ears.

The fireman gave up and went away. The two women walked over towards the Portakabin with a bravely resigned air of being thrown to the lions and the large importunate man finally held the field alone, swinging round to stare hard at Ken.

'Are you Ken McClure?'

Ken said he was.

Carey Hewett forestalled the large man as he drew breath and said to Ken. 'This is the mare's owner, Wynn Lees.'

Wynn Lees.

Again the extraordinary fizz of memory. I knew a lot about Wynn Lees, if it was the same person. The Wynn Lees of twenty-five years ago had been a cautionary tale freely used by my mother to scare me into good behaviour. 'If you hang out with that Gribble gang, you'll grow up to be like Wynn Lees.' 'If you smoke at your age . . . if you're cruel to insects . . . if you steal . . . if you play truant . . . if you throw stones at trains (all of which things I'd done) . . . you'll grow up like Wynn Lees.'

The present-day Wynn Lees had a fleshy obstinate look on his heavy face, the cheeks broken-veined from wind and weather, the head thrust forward on a thick neck. A bull of a man with no razor brains, he was saying belligerently to Ken, 'You had no right to operate on my mare without my say-so, and I certainly didn't give it.'

Carey Hewett said patiently, 'She'd be dead now if it weren't for Ken.'

'He had no permission,' Lees insisted doggedly.

'Yes, I did.' Ken said.

'Whose?' Lees demanded.

'Your wife's.'

The Lees mouth dropped again. 'My wife wouldn't do that.'

Ken explained. 'The stud groom had your phone number. He stood beside me while I tried it. Your wife answered.'

'When was that?' Lees interrupted.

'About a quarter past three this morning.'

'She couldn't have answered. She takes sleeping pills.'

'Well, she did answer. The stud groom will tell you.

She said you weren't at home and she didn't know where you were. I explained the mare had colic and needed an emergency operation. She asked how much it would cost, and I told her, and the stud groom himself told her it was the only way to save the mare's life, and the life of the foal. She said to go ahead.'

Wynn Lees looked more shaken than seemed sensible by his wife's wakefulness, and belatedly came around to acknowledging his debt to Ken.

'Well, if my wife said . . . and the mare's apparently all right . . . well then, no hard feelings.'

I didn't think the half-apology anywhere near good enough and nor, I sensed, did Ken, though from professional circumspection he swallowed it. Carey Hewett definitely relaxed inwardly and said he understood the operation had gone exceptionally well.

'How do you know?' Lees demanded, his truculence resurfacing like a conditioned reflex as though even the simplest statement was for him a cause of suspicion and challenge.

'I've read the notes,' Carey said.

'What notes?'

'Ken prudently asked his friend here to attend and take detailed notes of the whole procedure. There's no room for doubt. From start to finish the operation was impeccable.'

'Oh.' Lees looked momentarily baulked. 'Well, I need to see my property.'

'Certainly,' Carey said pacifically. 'Come this way.'

He took the owner out of the front door into the car park and turned left towards the stable. Ken and I followed, but halfway there I put my hand briefly on his arm and slowed him down a pace or two, to leave a gap wide enough for privacy.

'What is it?' Ken asked.

'Don't trust Wynn Lees.'

'Why not? I mean, he's obnoxious, that's all.'

'No, not all. Don't trust him. And don't tell him what you found in the horse's gut.'

'Why ever not?'

'In case he already knows.'

Ken gave me a stare of total astonishment but by then we were approaching the mare's box and within earshot of Lees himself.

Lees was as shocked by the mare's appearance as Ken had predicted but Carey tried to reassure him, and Belinda, who was still there, slapped the mare's rump energetically and told him the old girl was doing fine. Lees shrugged a couple of times and displayed none of the joy he should have felt at the life preserved. Not a good dissimulator, I thought. No good for the Foreign Office.

'Will the foal be born normally?' he asked.

Carey said 'Ken?' and Ken gave it as his opinion that he couldn't see any reason why not.

'Only a very skilful surgeon,' Carey said, 'could have performed such an operation successfully so late in the gestation period.'

Ken showed no embarrassment at the accolade. He knew his worth. False modesty didn't occur to him. His great fear earlier had been that he had somehow taken leave of his ability, and I guessed he had satisfactorily demonstrated to himself, as well as to Carey, that he hadn't. To me, of course, his impressive performance had indicated something quite different, but then I had by training a nasty suspicious mind.

'I expect the mare's insured,' I said neutrally.

I got swift glances from all three men, but it was Lees' attention that sharpened on my presence.

'Who did you say you were?' he demanded. 'It's none of your business if she's insured.'

'No, of course not,' I agreed. 'Just a random thought.'

Carey said to me in mild rebuke, 'You can't put a price on a Rainbow Quest foal,' and Lees opened his mouth, thought better of it and closed it again.

Instead he said to Ken, 'Did you find any reason for the colic?'

I didn't look at Ken. After the briefest of pauses he said, 'Colic's usually caused by a kink in the gut. If it persists, as it did in this case, you have to operate to straighten it. Sometimes, like in your mare, the gut's so badly knotted that the twisted piece is literally dying, and you have to cut it out.'

'It says in the notes,' Carey nodded, ' "Twisted portion of gut removed." '

The notes had ended with the mare's re-awakening. I hadn't recorded the discovery of the needle and thread,

120

meaning to add it later and not by then believing anyway that the notes were of great importance, once the mare had lived.

'What did you do with the excised bit?' Carey asked.

'It's in refrigeration,' Ken said, 'in case anyone wanted to see it.'

'Revolting!' Lees exclaimed. 'Throw it away.'

Carey nodded his assent and Ken promised nothing one way or the other.

Wynn Lees turned away from the box and, in what I interpreted as acceptance of things as they were, asked Carey to supervise the mare's convalescence.

Ken said nothing. Carey gave him an apprehensive glance and appeared grateful for his restraint. He told Lees that Ken, of course, was in charge of the mare but that he, Carey, would be available for consultation at all times. Lees still gave Ken an intense darkling look, transferring the end of it to me. I gave him back a grade one benign blandness and with satisfaction watched him shrug and write me off as of no significance.

He took his leave of Carey with minimum effusiveness, ignored Ken altogether, acted as if he hadn't seen Belinda in the first place, and marched across to drive away in a polished Roller.

Carey watched the departure with an unreadable expression of his own and, thanking Ken for his forbearance, took Belinda off towards the Portakabin. She went, looking back a few times over her shoulder in disapproval, not liking Ken to form even a transient link with anyone but herself. She would spend a miserable life, I thought, if she tried to build too many stockades.

Ken, unaware, said, 'Why don't you trust Mr Lees?'

'He acts as if he wanted the mare dead.'

Ken said slowly, 'You could look at it that way, I suppose. Do you mean . . . for the insurance?'

'Can't tell. It sounded as if he *had* insured the mare, but it would be a matter of which did be need most, the insurance money or the livestock.'

'The mare and foal,' Ken said without hesitation, as they would have been his own absolute priority. 'And he doesn't need the money, he was driving a Rolls, don't forget. I can't believe anyone would deliberately scheme to kill a horse by feeding it something to block its gut, because that's what you're saying, isn't it?'

'You're not that naive,' I said.

'Then I don't want to believe it.'

'That's not the same thing.'

'It's true,' he said thoughtfully, 'that I've never known a horse swallow a needle before.'

'Could you get a horse to swallow anything if it didn't want to?'

'Oh yes. Pack it in something round and slippery that would dissolve in the stomach or beyond, and then practically throw it down the horse's gullet, feeding some nuts or something very desirable to the animal immediately after. They used to give medicines that way. Horses can't vomit. Once they've swallowed something, it's for keeps.'

'Our Mr Lees,' I said, 'never dreamt that his wife would wake up and OK the op.'

'No.' Ken smiled. 'That was a shock, wasn't it? She sounded far from having taken a sleeping pill. I'm pretty sure she had a man with her. I heard his voice.'

We enjoyed the thought of Lees the cuckold: serve him right.

Ken yawned and said that as he was technically off duty he would go home for food and sleep. 'On call tonight, free tomorrow afternoon. I've promised to take Belinda to the races tomorrow. Care to come?'

'Belinda wouldn't want me.'

'What? Rubbish. See if Vicky and Greg would come too. Stratford-upon-Avon. Shakespeare and all that, just up their street. We could all go in my car. Why not? It's settled.' He smiled and yawned again. 'I like Vicky. Great old girl. I've drawn a winner in the mother-in-law stakes, don't you think?'

'You have,' I agreed.

'Bloody lucky. Greg's unreal, though. Clothes, not much else.'

Rather a good summing up, I thought. 'He can sing,' I said.

'So can blackbirds.' Ken's eyes glimmered. 'We'll never come to blows, Greg and I, but I can't take him down the pub for a jar.'

'Talking of jars . . .'

123

Ken looked at his watch and yawned. 'They'll still be open. What about it? Pie and a pint?'

'You're on.'

This civilized plan however was delayed by a fireman in full fig who came ambling round the corner to ask if the boss was around as they wanted to show him something 'out front'.

Ken fetched Carey from the Portakabin and the three of us trudged after the fireman back up the driveway I'd run down the night before. I put my hand on the brick side wall in passing: it was still warm to hot but no longer barbecue.

The scene 'out front' was reasonably orderly, with most vehicles parked out on the road and the car parking space given only to one police car and one large glittering fire appliance. There were also six firemen in fire-proof suits and three or four policemen in navy blue with checked bands on their peaked hats.

Seeing Carey Hewett arrive, one of the firemen came to meet him, followed immediately by a policeman. A small amount of handshaking took place, followed by an equal amount of headshaking as a prelude to the news that in the firemen's professional opinion, the fire had been set.

Carey looked blank.

'Arson,' the fireman said bluntly.

'I understand,' Carey said, 'but I just can't believe it. What makes you think so?'

The fireman explained in a healthy Gloucestershire

voice that it was still too hot in there – he gestured to the gutted walls – to look at everything carefully, but they had found some big bottles of cleaning fluid. Spot remover, that sort of thing.

This time not only Carey looked blank.

'Highly inflammable,' the fireman explained. 'It always says so on the bottle.'

'I expect we'd have spot remover,' Carey said dazedly, 'but I've no idea what's in the cleaning cupboard.'

'Ah, but this was three bottles, all empty. And you know what? If our chum had simply smashed the bottles to get at the contents, we might not have noticed, but these bottles had no caps on. And they weren't in any cupboard, we found them because they were in the big front room which, according to one of your young ladies, was where the two secretaries worked, and what mostly burned in there was paper which doesn't hold the heat so much. A bit of the roof fell at an angle against the wall in there, which gave us access, luckily.'

'I don't follow you,' Carey said.

The fireman gave the knowing look of one often confronted by villainy.

'We're experts, see, sir, at fires. Our chum made a common mistake in not screwing the caps back on. You'd be surprised how many times we find petrol cans with no caps. Firebugs are always in such a hurry they forget the caps. Then there's the paint. You were having the place painted inside, right? And some of the wood-work was being varnished?'

Carey nodded.

'Well, sir, there's paint tins in there with the lids off, same with pots of varnish, and good workmen don't leave empties about and certainly they don't leave lids off pots that've got paint in still.'

Carey said bemusedly, 'Someone said tins of paint had exploded.'

'It looks like it,' the fireman nodded. 'But as far as we can tell just now, those tins were all together, like, where the painters stored them, not lying round in your office.'

'In my office?' Carey repeated. 'Do you mean in my own office? I don't understand.'

'Your young lady drew a plan for us.' The fireman put a hand inside his tunic and brought out a tattered paper, holding it open for Carey to peer at. 'Isn't that where your own office was? In the front left-hand corner?'

Carey studied it for a few seconds, through his glasses. 'Yes, that's about right. I suppose ... is there any chance of anything being left in there to salvage?'

The fireman shook his head. 'Not a lot.'

Carey said forlornly, 'I was making some notes for a book.'

The fireman observed a decent interval of silence in face of such a disaster and then said they would know more by the next day when they'd been able to sift the rubble, but meanwhile they'd have to inform Carey's insurers that arson was suspected.

'We're insured against arson,' Carey said dully. 'We can rebuild and restock, but no amount of insurance can bring back my records. All those years of work . . .'

He broke off, looking tired and depressed. It wasn't his life's work, exactly, that had gone up in smoke, but the evidence of it had. I tried to imagine what a void like that would be like, but no one could, really, who hadn't suffered it.

Carey, the elder statesman of the practice, looked grey, spent and sad, standing dispiritedly in the small chilly breeze that had sprung up to ruffle our hair and sting in our noses.

CHAPTER FIVE

The journey to Stratford-upon-Avon races was short enough for Belinda to remain civil even if not cordial in my direction. She made no more remarks about my presence being unnecessary and seemed temporarily to have accepted that I would be part of the scenery for as long as I stayed around; and I'd been at pains to mention that I'd have to be reporting for work in London pretty soon.

'When?' Ken asked bluntly.

'I'll have to phone on Monday. They'll give me a date then.'

'I was hoping . . .' He stopped for a moment, glanced at me over his shoulder, and went on, 'How about a spot of detective work?'

'What about?' Belinda asked.

'This and that.'

'Ken!' She was reasonably exasperated. 'If you mean the things that have been going wrong in the practice, well, Peter can't begin to understand them in veterinary terms, can he? Far less explain them.'

'There was the fire, dear,' Vicky murmured.

'Yes, Mother, but the police will see to that.'

Belinda, sitting in the front passenger seat next to Ken, had come dressed in a chestnut leather skirt, big white sweater, knee-high boots and leather overcoat. She looked slender and pretty, her hair falling free to her shoulders, her mouth softened with colour. Ken patted her knee from time to time in appreciation.

I sat between Vicky and Greg in a bit of a crush in the back, uneasily rubbing hams with Greg and receiving mildly coquettish knee contacts from Vicky. She herself wore intense red to dramatize her white hair and apart from a small plaster on her ear, seemed back to normal in vitality, though complaining she kept going to sleep when you wouldn't expect.

I checked on the mare's health; Belinda knowledge-ably answered my enquiry. 'No sign of reflux, so we removed the stomach tube last night. This morning she's eating hay and drinking normally. So far, perfect.' She gave Ken an admiring glance, confident in her love.

Ken himself looked slightly less haunted, as if he'd put the worst of the anxieties on hold, and appeared determined that his passengers should enjoy the day, to the extent of making a slow sight-seeing detour through Stratford with glimpses of the theatre and swans and a plethora of black-and-white Tudor tim-bering, some of it actually genuine.

Inside the racecourse, the five of us split naturally apart, Greg and Vicky going off in search of lunch, leaving me on my own to wander about and enjoy the first steeplechase meeting I'd been to in years.

Cheltenham racecourse had been my childhood playground, my familiar backyard. My mother's 'help with secretarial work' had been full-time employment in the racecourse manager's office: her pay our livelihood. In school holidays, while she laboured at her desk, I was allowed by the manager to go almost everywhere on the course and in the buildings, 'as long as he isn't a nuisance' being the only proviso. As being a nuisance meant instant banishment to my grandmother (a tyrant) to spend endless boring days under her beady eye in her musty little bungalow, I endeavoured to be the opposite of a nuisance with fervent diligence, and on the whole succeeded.

Race days had been magic (and the cause of my truancy) and until John Darwin came along I had taken it for granted that one day I would be one of the jockeys rocketing over the jumps. I stood beside the fences entranced while the great horses thundered through the birch; I listened to the jockeys cursing during races and practised the words myself under the bedclothes; I read sporting newspapers, watched meetings on the box, knew the names and fortunes of every steeplechase horse, trainer and jockey in the business; fantasized eternally about being top jockey and winning all the top races, particularly the big one at home, the Cheltenham Gold Cup.

Two minor impediments damped the realistic prospects, though not the dreams. First, I had no pony of my own and could only snatch infrequent opportunities to ride at all, still less put in the concentrated practice I needed and longed for. Second, I faced the implacable determination of my mother that I shouldn't achieve my aim.

'It's in my blood,' I protested at ten, having just come across that exciting-sounding phrase. 'You can't say it isn't.'

'It may be in your blood, but look where it got your father.'

It had got my father into his grave. The man who'd sired me, whom I knew only from photographs, had been a jockey over jumps for one short year. Four winners to the good, he had ridden out as usual one morning with the string of horses, trotting along the road to the exercise gallops. His mount, they said, had shied at a bird flying out of a hedge; he himself was flung out of the saddle and into the path of a passing car and was already dead when the other lads dismounted to help him.

There were no headlines, none of the fuss that would have happened had he been killed in a race. My mother still kept the small paragraph from the local paper, yellowed by age, which gave the briefest details. 'Paul Perry, 21, aspiring jump jockey, died last Tuesday morning in Baydon Road, Lambourn, as a result of an accident involving the racehorse he was riding and a

131

passing car. Neither the horse nor the driver was injured. Perry leaves a widow and an infant son.'

The widow, barely twenty herself, was sustained through months to come by the charitable Injured Jockeys' Fund, a marvellous organization which eventually found for her, a trained secretary, the job at Cheltenham racecourse. Very appropriate, everyone said: a neat and useful solution. The Perry kid – myself – could grow up in his father's footsteps, in his father's world.

The benign thinking behind all this washed over me at the time without my realizing how much I owed to it, but it wasn't until I returned to England as Peter Darwin to try for Oxford that I understood why my memories of early childhood were chiefly happy. Whenever I gave anything to charity from then on, it was to the Injured Jockeys' Fund.

At Stratford, coming back to my long-dead father's world after a gap of twenty years, it seemed in some ways as if time itself had stood still. Up on the number boards, many of the jockeys' names were as they'd always been, yet these had to be the sons and daughters of the pack I'd idolized. In the racecard, the same thing with trainers, though in this case, as I progressively discovered, many were indeed the same old brigade.

J. Rolls Eaglewood, for instance, identified as he stood with his runner in the parade ring before the first race, was an old man with a walking stick on which he leant heavily. J. Rolls Eaglewood, father of Russet-of-the-no-knickers, was undoubtedly the same man, and was also related no doubt to Izzy, Ken McClure's one-time love.

I wouldn't have recognized him: his name alone remained stuck in a remote neural pathway, lighting up when one pressed the right button, a name associated not with a face but with power and threat.

Only the horses themselves were wholly unfamiliar, including their breeding; too many horse generations had turned over like pages. Many owners, however, were recognizably the same, witnesses to enduring pleasure and faith.

I looked through the racecard for Ronnie Upjohn, the owner threatening to sue Ken for daring to win with an Upjohn cast-off, but he had no runner that day.

Upjohn . . . and Travers. Upjohn and Travers.

They ran together in my mind like Abbott and Costello, but definitely without the laughs.

I turned away from the parade ring and began to thread a way through the throng to a good watching place in the stands. The racegoing crowd had changed not at all: there were perhaps fewer hats and more open-necked shirts, but the same manufacturers of overcoats and padded jackets were clearly healthily in business. The faces scurrying to beat the odds bore the same calculating anxiety, the bookmakers shouted from under the same fictitious name-boards, the snatches of overheard conversation exactly echoed the voices of a quarter-century ago.

133

' . . . Blew up turning into the straight . . .'
' . . . Couldn't ride in a cart with a pig net over it . . .'
' . . . Honest as a corkscrew . . .'
' . . . It's a bloody disgrace . . .'
' . . . The handicapper murdered him . . .'

I smiled to myself and felt like an alien returned to a loved-and-lost planet, and through not looking where I was going almost cannoned into two short men in navy overcoats, who happened to be Japanese.

I apologized in English. They bowed to me, unspeaking. I went on up to the stands.

The two Japanese, standing below and to the left of me in the area outside the weighing room, looked bewildered and lost, and I had a feeling I'd met one of them before, though a quick run-through of the government officials I'd usually worked with brought no enlightenment. I shrugged, looked away, watched the runners canter down to the post.

The jockey riding for J. Rolls Eaglewood wore purple and white and remained unexcitingly in mid-field throughout, the uneventful contest being won by the hot favourite, pulling up.

The crowd, roaring approval, streamed down from the stands to collect their winnings and, once the dust had settled, I glanced to where the Japanese had been standing.

They were still there, still looking lost, though they had by now been joined by a young woman who was trying to talk to them by signs. Black round heads together, the two men consulted each other earnestly and bowed a few times to their companion, but it was obvious that no one was understanding anything much.

The impulse to help was ingrained, I supposed. I strolled down from the stands and stopped a pace or two from the young woman who, at close quarters, looked impatient as well as harassed.

I said, 'Can I perhaps be of service?' Good old Foreign Office lingo.

She flicked me the briefest of glances which would have stopped Casanova and said with crisp disapproval, 'Not unless you speak Japanese.'

'Well, yes, I do. That's why I asked.'

She turned her full attention my way and metaphorically clutched the offered lifebuoy as one seeing escape from drowning.

'Then please,' she said, 'ask them what they want. They want something and they can't seem to be able to tell me what.'

I bowed to the Japanese and asked them the question. The extent of their relief at hearing their own language was almost comical, and so was their answer. I bowed and pointed out to them what they wanted, and they hurried away, bowing sketchily as they went.

The young woman watched open mouthed, crossly.

'They wanted the loo,' I said. 'They were bursting.'

'Why, for God's sake, didn't they say so!'

'With sign language?' I asked.

She stared at me, then melted inside and began to laugh.

'Thanks, then,' she said. 'What are you doing for the rest of the afternoon?'

'I'll be around, watching the races.'

'Can I send up smoke signals?'

'I'll look out for them,' I promised.

'I was supposed to bring three of them,' she said, talking easily, promoting me to instant friend. 'The third one speaks English. I've been showing them round London for three days and this morning Mr Kamato, he's the English speaker, had the squits. The other two didn't want to miss seeing Stratford and if you've ever tried explaining Anne Hathaway's cottage with your hands you'll understand the morning I've had. They're perfectly charming and they think I'm retarded.'

'Are they businessmen?' I asked.

'No, they're part of the Japanese Jockey Club.'

'Ah,' I said.

'What do you mean, ah?'

'I think I've met one of them before.'

'Really. Where?'

'In Japan. I used to work there.'

She gave me a bright assessing look and I in turn noted the small mouth, the huge blue eyes and the thick frizzed blond-streaked brown hair chopped off straight all round at ear-lobe level, except for an eyebrow-length fringe. The overall effect was slightly zany-doll, but the Japanese were wrong, the mind inside was no toy.

'I work for the British Jockey Club,' she said. 'I arrange things for visiting bigwigs. Transport, hotels, tourist traps, all that sort of thing. A general nanny.'

I could think of worse things than having my path smoothed by her.

'I'm Peter,' I said.

'Annabel.'

First names only meant no commitment beyond that afternoon but made a temporary sharing of her workload possible. The unspoken signalling was like a formal dance, I thought, with advances, retreats and do-si-dos. No one at that stage was going to break step.

We waited for the return of her charges.

'They are supposed to be watching these races from the directors' room,' she said, 'but they wanted to mix with the crowds. We had drinks up there.'

'Japanese feel at home in crowds.'

She said casually, 'What did you do in Japan?'

'Worked for the Foreign Office.'

She wrinkled her nose. 'As a career?'

'Mm.'

'I suppose you know the famous definition of a diplomat?'

I knew. Everyone in the foreign service knew. I quoted, 'An honest man sent to lie abroad for his country.'

She smiled. 'And do you?'

'Sometimes.'

'The Foreign Office stirs up more trouble than it's worth.'

'Who's that a quote from?'

She looked startled, then a shade defensive. 'My father, as a matter of fact.'

I didn't comment or argue. Every dogmatic opinion had a basis somewhere in truth, and there had been times when British along with other ambassadors had given wrong signals to would-be aggressors, indicating that opposition to intended tyranny might be slight or even non-existent. Both the Kaiser and Hitler had reportedly felt aggrieved when the supposedly acquiescent British Lion had awoken and roared.

Ambassadors from every country could get things wrong and often did: it depended both on their orders from home and on the information they'd been locally fed. My exact job in every posting had been to try to find out what was really going on behind the scenes in our host country and to keep my superiors up to date. In consequence, I went to local parties and dinners, and gave them myself, with the sole object of gathering and checking rumours, of learning who had leverage, who had ideals, who was ill with what, who was sleeping with whom, who was on drugs, who drank, who beat their wives, who was up-and-coming, who was gullible, who was greedy, who could be bought or blackmailed, who would be likely to crack or resign, whose information could sometimes be trusted, whose never, whose professed friendship might be genuine, whose not.

At that game I'd become fairly adept but it was impossible to get it right every time. Then, too, even if an ambassador were primed with impeccable gen, there was no guarantee the government back home would believe it or act in accordance. Hair-tearing in ignored embassies could reach epic proportions. No country on earth was exempt.

The Japanese Jockey Club came back and bowed several times, expressing especial pleasure when I said I recognized one of them. He apologized for not having immediately recognized me in turn. We went through a lot of platitudes and bowing. Finally I asked them if there was anything else I could achieve for them, and they said with visible eagerness that they would like hot weak tea with no milk and no sugar and – in a decorous shaft of humour – a Japanese tea ceremony to go with it. I, who had watched countless tea cere-monies and enjoyed them, asked if Miss Annabel could stand in, even though without kimono and obi. Their oriental eyes smiled. They said gravely that they would be delighted. I asked if they would like to return to the directors' room for the purpose, but it seemed they would not.

I said to Annabel, 'They're thirsty. They would like weak tea, no milk, no sugar. They would very much like you to get it for them down here.'

'Is that all they said?'

'Not really. In Japan, there are traditional tea cere-
monies as part of the entertainment some days at race
meetings. I think they're homesick.'

'I suppose,' she said, 'you wouldn't come with me?'

'Might consider it. Where's the tea-room?'

We tracked down the required liquid and over the
cups held a three-way conversation slowly. After that,
as I took my temporary leave, Annabel said, 'Why do
you bow to them more than they do to you? It's un-
English.'

'They are older. They are Jockey Club and we are on
a racecourse. They feel reassured, I am not humbled.'

'You are one crazy diplomat and can come to my
rescue anytime.'

I smiled at her and got a vivid smile back. Promising, I thought. She read my expression accurately,
curled her little mouth and shook her head.

Still promising, nevertheless.

She took her charges at their gestured request into
the Tattersalls enclosure to see the bookmakers at close
quarters, and I watched them from the stands as the
runners cantered down for the next race. She was taller
than the two men, and the combination of two black
and one frizzy blond heads was very easy to follow.
They moved slowly from bookmaker to bookmaker
pointing at the odds chalked on the boards until in
the end one of the men produced some money which
Annabel offered to a bookie. The bet was struck, the
ticket given. The trio went up into the Tattersalls stands

bchind the ranks of bookmakers and watched the race from there.

Greg and Vicky appeared at my side and tiredly said it was all very interesting, wasn't it? I diagnosed a slight case of boredom but Vicky said it wasn't boredom but the dearth of places to sit down. They had betted and lost in the first race, but at least the third race brought them a win, which sent them off to collect in less depression.

I didn't see Ken and Belinda at all and found later they'd walked down the course to be nearer the jumps. Annabel brought the Japanese to stand by the parade ring rails to watch the next lot of runners walk round and, far more from enjoyment than obligation, I joined them.

They were all pleased, the men almost effusively so: I'd become their dearest buddy in the West. They hoped I could tell them which of the horses in front of us would win the next race as they'd had to tear up their tickets after the last.

Sort out the fittest looking had long been my policy, thanks to my adopted name, so I watched the parade and pointed to a load of lean glossy muscle striding round phlegmatically with its head down. The Japanese bowed their thanks and hurried back to the bookies, who were a novelty for them, they said, and Annabel asked why I had picked the horse I had.

'It looks well,' I said.

'So you know about horses?'

141

'I wanted to be a jockey, once.'

She looked up at my height. 'There have been six-foot jockeys, I suppose.'

I nodded. 'But you might say I grew out of it in other ways.'

'What ways?'

'Total lack of opportunity.'

'I was a pony freak,' she said, nodding, 'and one fine day there was more to life than riding.'

She wore black and white all over: black boots and thin legs, checked skirt, white turtleneck, black short coat and a huge fluffy white scarf with black pompom fringes. She looked at times sixteen and at times double that and had an overall air of competence, when not hurling herself against language barriers.

'Do you live in London?' I asked.

'Fulham Road, if you can call that London. And you?'

'Homeless.'

I got a disillusioned stare worthy of the remark. 'Does that mean a grating in Trafalgar Square?'

'Are there any good gratings down Fulham way?'

She answered with a look which said games had gone far enough, and I thought to myself that, if I didn't start searching soon for somewhere to lay my head, a nice warm grating where hot air vented up from subterranean tunnels would have its attractions. I'd slept rough in the capital several times in my student days; guessed I was too old for it now.

The Japanese came back happily waving tickets and we all went up on the stands to watch the fittest. He survived to the last hurdle and there turned end over end in a flurry of legs.

I apologized. They said it wasn't my fault. The horse got up and galloped riderless past the stands, looking ready to go round twice more without panting. The Japanese put their useless tickets in their pockets along with their dashed hopes and decided that for the next race they would like to walk down to the fences, as they had seen other people do. I was ready to say I'd go with them when I spotted Ken walking alone and slowly, looking at his racecard, stopping in indecision.

'I'll be here when you come back,' I said hastily in two languages, 'but I have to speak to someone. Please, please excuse me.'

I left them in mid-bow and reached Ken before he moved off, slowing to a stop at his elbow.

'I want to talk to you,' I said.

'Fire away.' He lifted his gaze briefly from the racecard.

'Alone and uninterrupted.'

'But Belinda – '

'If you want me to do anything useful, I need some of your time.'

'All right.' He made up his mind. 'How about the bar?'

The bar turned out to be worse than useless because as we reached the door we came face to face with

J. Rolls Eaglewood, who was on his way out, limping along with his walking stick.

'Afternoon, sir,' Ken said. I hoped his tremble was detectable by me alone: I felt his panic flow across like a breeze. His impulse to turn and run couldn't have been clearer.

J. Rolls stopped dead, fixing a dire glare on Ken's face.

'You killed my horse,' he said.

Ken shook his head weakly. 'He died. We couldn't save him.'

'Sheer bloody incompetence, and I won't put up with it any longer.'

Eaglewood at close quarters, though thin, grey-haired and with age-freckled skin, still generated the power and threat I associated with his name. His voice held the rasp of one long used to instant obedience and he could and did score several patriarchal points over a vet less than half his age.

'I've put up with you this long because of my grand-daughter's infatuation with you,' he said, 'and out of respect, too, for your father's memory, but I've had to tell Carey that you're never to attend my horses again or I'll be transferring my business to another firm of vets, and I'd be sorry to do that after all these years, as I told him, but this slaughter has got to stop.'

Ken miserably made no attempt at defence. Eagle-wood gave him a brief fierce nod, gestured to him with his stick to get out of the way, and stumped off out of earshot.

'You see?' Ken said, shaking and as pale as ever. 'I can't even blame him. The horse that died on Thursday morning – with the split cannon bone – came from his stable.'

'It sounded as if it might not have been the first disaster.'

'You're right, it wasn't. Another of his died on the table about a month ago while I was doing respiratory tract surgery. And one died in its own box . . .' His voice took the by now familiar note of desperation. 'I didn't do anything wrong, I'm always careful. They just *died*.'

'Mm. Well, why don't you give me a complete chronological list of all the things that have ended badly? Also the names of all the owners and trainers and anything special or particular about them? If you're sure what you did was OK, we have to find another explanation.'

'What explanation?'

'Villainy, wouldn't you think?'

'But it's impossible. That's the trouble. I've checked everything over and over again. Gone over everything in my mind. I can't sleep . . . And what's the *point* of killing them?'

I sighed. 'Let's start with the list.'

'I'd need my notes – ' He broke off, freshly appalled. 'All my notes are *burnt*.'

145

We'd moved away from the door to the bar and stood in the area outside the weighing room. Several people, I'd noticed, gave Ken sidelong glances, but I thought it might have been only because of his visible distress until I later heard Eaglewood spreading his opinions far and wide. ' ... ruining a good old firm ...' and ' ... three of mine dead ... can't go on.' At what point, I wondered, did opinion become slander.

'What you've got to do,' I told Ken, 'is stop worrying what you did wrong, and start wondering how you would have set about killing the horses that died. Think about a needle and thread in a broodmare's gut. Think, in fact, of all the ways you know to commit equine murder.'

'But I ...' His voice tailed off indecisively.

'Knowledge isn't guilt,' I said. 'Knowing where to shove a dagger between the ribs doesn't mean you've done it.'

'But if you know how, then it *might* have been you.'

'So you do know ways.'

'Well ... every vet does.'

I looked at his long unhappy face with its troubled light eyes and understood his unwillingness to part with information that might sound like confession. It was the same hesitation I'd noticed on the night of the fire. I would get him to tell me in the end, I thought, but the sooner the safer, on the whole.

Over his shoulder I saw Belinda making her way

purposefully towards us and regretted not being hidden away in the depths of the bar.

'Think out the list,' I urged Ken. 'Meet me early tomorrow at the hospital. Alone.'

'How early?'

'Eight?'

'Well . . .' He turned to see what I was looking at. Belinda had six paces to go. 'All right,' he said. 'Eight.'

'Eight what?' Belinda asked, overhearing.

'Number eight in the next race,' I explained.

Ken closed his eyes.

'What's the matter?' Belinda asked.

'Nothing.' He opened his eyes again, smiling at her and fishing around for his wallet. 'Go and put a fiver on number eight for me, there's a darling. You know I don't like people to see me bet.'

'Eight hasn't a hope,' she said.

'All the same . . .'

'All right, but you're mad.'

She walked off towards the Tote windows and Ken at once said, 'Why don't you want Belinda there too, in the morning?'

'You'll tell me more and clearer on your own. I can ask her later for her impressions.'

He thought it over. 'You're probably right. And you're a shocking liar.'

'I thought I was quite good.'

'I mean, you shocked me. So fast.'

'Years of practice.'

147

'That's pretty shocking too.'

When Belinda returned we climbed the stands to watch the race and to everyone's blank surprise number eight came in first. The stunned crowd received the no-hoper's victory in silence, and Belinda stopped Ken's wide grin in its tracks by announcing a shade defiantly that she hadn't put his fiver on eight but on the favourite instead.

'People have been divorced for less,' Ken said, just about managing civility.

'Number eight was useless,' Belinda insisted. 'I wanted you to win.'

Number eight paid a fortune on the Tote, which caused a further chill between the betrothed. I left them fuming over the problem and made tracks for Annabel as she brought her retinue back to the paddock.

After twenty minutes apart we greeted each other as old friends. The expedition to the closer action had raised heartbeats, it appeared, and also quite clearly the spirits. The two Japanese talked animatedly between themselves about what looked fittest for the next race and Annabel and I looked at each other with a lot of unspoken questions.

When she finally asked, it was solely a search for information.

'Who,' she said, 'were you talking to when we came back? A tall thin man with fair hair and a tetchity girl.'

'Tetchity?'

She shrugged. 'Whatever.'

'Ken McClure and Belinda Larch. The wedding is three weeks today.'

She frowned, but not at that news. 'Is he a vet?'

'Yes, he is.'

'Friend of yours?'

'I met him the day before yesterday, and yes, to that extent, he is.'

I waited a bit, and she said, 'I owe you for your help. I wouldn't want you to make a mistake of getting too friendly with that vet. They were talking about him upstairs.'

'Who upstairs?'

'The directors and stewards. One of them was, anyway. He pointed him out to the others as they stood by the window having a drink before lunch. He said your friend would soon be disbarred from practising, or some such phrase, as he was killing horses left right and centre and was dishonest, sneaky and a disgrace to his profession.'

'As strong as that?'

'Stronger, if anything. There was a lot of hate in it.'

'Really?' I was interested. 'Who was he?'

'I was introduced to about eight people very fast and I was trying to present our chums here' – she pointed to her charges – 'so I can't remember his name, but I think he might have been one of the stewards.'

'Let's see,' I said, and turned my racecard back to page one, and there to my confusion found in the list

149

of stewards the name I'd searched all the inner pages for in vain.

R. D. Upjohn, Esq.

'Ronnie!' Annabel exclaimed. 'I still can't remember his last name, but they called him Ronnie.' She studied my face. 'Mean something to you?'

I told her why Ronnie Upjohn hated Ken McClure. 'Ken made him look a fool. Some men can't bear it.'

She listened with pursed mouth to the saga of the preserved cast-off that went on to win and said, 'I understand the spite and envy over the one that was saved, but how about the ones that died? It wasn't only Ronnie who'd heard about them, some of the others were nodding.'

'What does this Ronnie look like?' I asked.

'You're changing the subject!'

'I don't know why the horses died, and nor does Ken. We're working on it. Could you point out Ronnie Upjohn, by any chance?'

She shook the mop of hair. 'Stewards at race meetings all look alike.'

'That's what people say about the Japanese.'

'Oh no,' she said instantly, 'I'd know my three anywhere.' She looked at her watch. 'I really ought to take these two back upstairs, where all good little VIPs belong. Would you mind suggesting it?'

They went, it seemed to me, with polite resignation: they were having more fun down in the crowds with the doll of a girl. For me too, unexpectedly, the fizz went out of the hour with their departure, and I said to myself, 'Well, well, well, Peter my boy, take it easy, she'll have half London in tow, and besides that, you know nothing about her except the way she looks and talks . . .' and who really needed more? Everything had to begin *somewhere*, after all.

I rejoined Greg and Vicky on the stands and learned they'd at length found two seats in the bar and had stayed there for an hour making one gin and tonic last for ever and watching the races on closed-circuit television. They had backed two winners on quick forays to the Tote and had won a lot on number eight. 'My birthday's the eighth of the eighth month,' Vicky said. 'Eight's always my lucky number.' They'd quite enjoyed themselves after all, they said.

Belinda, looking glum, came to ask them dutifully if they were managing all right and was infuriated to be told of their winnings on number eight.

'The wretched animal's useless,' she protested, 'and Ken's kicking up the most ridiculous fuss.'

'Why, dear?' Vicky asked, perplexed.

'He gave me money to back eight for him and I put him on the favourite instead, and you'd think I'd lost him the crock of gold the way he's going on.'

'He's under a lot of pressure,' Greg said gently. 'You can see he is.'

'He's proud and he's stubborn,' Belinda said, 'and he's not speaking to me.' There was a sudden thin glitter of tears along her lower eyelids. She tossed her head as if to disclaim them and blinked hard, sniffing.

Vicky, looking relieved at this sign of emotion in her bossy daughter, said prosaically, 'He'll get over it.'

Belinda said, 'I offered to give him the wretched money he would have won. He says that's not the point. Well, if it's not, what is?'

'The point is his ego, dear,' Vicky said. 'You questioned his decision. Worse still, you overrode it. That's what's the matter with him, not the loss of his money.'

Belinda looked at her mother in wide-eyed silent astonishment, and I thought that it might even have been the very first time in her adult life that she'd really listened to what her mother said. After a long pause, her gaze slid from Vicky to me, and a good deal of acerbity returned to her expression.

'And you,' she said, not liking me, 'what do you say about it?'

'I'd say,' I said without emphasis, 'that he's too used to you obeying him without question in the course of your work.'

She gave me much the same stare that she'd bestowed on her mother.

'I wanted what was best for him,' she said.

And to prove your judgment superior, I thought, but knew better than to say it.

She changed the subject as if to defend her self-esteem from more analysis, and said, 'We all want to know who that weird looking woman is you've been talking to all afternoon.'

'We all' being Belinda's euphemism for 'I am consumed by curiosity'. Greg and Vicky looked mystified. They hadn't noticed Annabel, obviously.

'What woman?' Vicky in fact asked artlessly.

'She works for the Jockey Club,' I said. 'She escorts foreign official visitors. Today the visitors are Japanese. I helped her with translation, that's all.'

'Oh.' Belinda shrugged. 'Extraordinary of the Jockey Club to employ someone who dresses like that at the races.'

'Do point her out to me,' Vicky said.

Annabel however stayed out of sight until after the last race, when she came down from above and shepherded her charges towards the exit. She saw me hovering there (I was already keeping Ken and the others waiting) and came to my side with a small-mouthed grin.

'Ronnie Upjohn is that man there ahead of us, the one with the woman in the orange coat.' We walked on together out into the car park, followed by the two Japanese. 'I couldn't talk to him much, he was in and out all the time, and I was stuck with our friends, but he seems fairly ordinary. Dogmatic, of course. He thinks jockeys get away with murder, but who doesn't?'

'Who doesn't get away with murder, or who doesn't think jockeys do?'

'Take your pick.'

We arrived at a big car with a chauffeur waiting to carry away the very important Japanese. I bowed in farewell to the two men, keeping an eye on the departing orange coat.

'Go chase him,' Annabel said, 'if you must.'

I smiled at her blue eyes. 'I'll phone you,' I said.

'Do that.'

She followed her charges into the car and closed the door, and without delay I hurried after the orange coat as fast as I could without drawing stares.

The coat stopped beside a large grey car and the man, Ronnie Upjohn, unlocked the car doors. He then opened the boot, took off his hat, binocular case and overcoat and laid them inside. The orange coat, removed, followed. I had time to arrive and see Upjohn clearly before he folded himself into the car, and when he did it was into the front passenger seat, not behind the wheel. The orange-coat lady, now in grey with pearls, was the driver.

Ronnie Upjohn was sixtyish and basically unremarkable. I had to tick off features mentally to have any chance of knowing him elsewhere. Hair, grey. Forehead, medium height, lined. Eyebrows, medium bushy. Eyes, slightly drooping at outside edges, lids folded from age. Nose, large, a bit bulbous. Moustache, medium size, brownish. Mouth, firm. Jaw . . . I gave up. There wasn't anything memorable about his jaw. Moreover, he was by then inside the car and could be seen only through glass.

I turned away and started walking towards Ken's car across the main car park and found him standing with his arms folded, leaning on the car's roof and watching my antics with astonishment.

'Did you know who you were following?' he asked incredulously. 'That was Ronnie Upjohn.'

'I certainly hope so,' I said.

'But why?'

'I wanted to put a face to the name.' I paused. 'Apart from acting as a steward, what does he do?'

'Owns a few horses.' Ken thought it over. 'He's something in finance. In an office. I don't exactly know. He's semi-retired, I think. No lack of money. Probably inherited money: he has that feel. He's not over shrewd, I wouldn't say.'

'He's doing you no good just now,' I said.

Ken sighed. 'No one is.' He stood upright and prepared to get into the car. 'And I gave Belinda a right bollocking, and it wasn't as if I even knew the name of number eight, let alone believed it would win, and I upset her something dreadful and now I'm in the shit.'

I shook my head. 'Not really. All you have to do is pat her knee.'

I'd grown accustomed to him looking at me as if I'd taken leave of my senses, but on the drive home he did in fact wordlessly pat Belinda's knee, and she burst into tears, which resolved the quarrel instantly.

*

That evening, when they'd all gone out, I ate cheese on toast and drank some wine and telephoned my mother.

My parents had long ago set up a system for my calls to them from round the world which was, basically, if I would call, they would pay. I had myself only to get through and give them the number I was speaking from, and they would then call back. That way, I had to pay only for a maximum of three minutes though we might talk for an hour. My father had dryly remarked that it was the only way for them to make sure I was alive.

I counted out the money for three minutes to Mexico City and left it in an envelope by the phone in Thetford Cottage, and in short order, striking lucky, was talking to my mum.

I pictured her on the other end of the line, as beautiful as ever. She'd always had what I had grown to recognize as style, an inborn quality that had made the transition from efficient secretary to ambassador's wife look simple, a deserved progression. I listened with a familiar sense of security to her light voice, elegant and very young, ageless.

'Wynn Lees?' she repeated in disbelief after she'd phoned back. 'Why on earth do you want to know about Wynn Lees?'

Explaining took a fair amount of her money and left her both amused and alarmed.

'It's fascinating you've got to know Ken McClure,

but you seriously don't want to get mixed up with Wynn Lees, darling. He won't have changed his spots.'

'Yes, but *why*?' I asked. 'What did he do that was so awful?'

'Heavens, it was all so long ago.'

'But you used to tell me that if I didn't mend my ways I'd grow up like Wynn Lees, as if it was the worst fate in the world, and all I can dredge up about him is a vague impression that he went to prison.'

'Yes, he certainly did.'

'Well, what for?'

'For cruelty to horses.'

'For *what*?' I was stunned.

'The first time, it was for cruelty to horses. It happened long before you were born, when Wynn Lees was about twenty, I suppose. He and another youth cut off a horse's tongue. I think they did it about six times before they were caught. I didn't know about it until we moved to Cheltenham, and by that time Wynn Lees was over thirty and had been to prison again, but the second time was for fighting. Good heavens, I haven't thought about this for years. He was a horrible man. He used to come to the office sometimes because at that time he lived on the far side of the racecourse, though he went off to somewhere like Australia afterwards. He used to complain about the boundary fencing and I couldn't stand him. He'd be talking about wire and all I could think about were those horses dying because they'd had their tongues cut out. People used to say he'd paid for it and it was wild oats and all in the past, but I think people's pasts are *them*, and if it was in him to do that at twenty it's still in him at fifty or sixty, even if he wouldn't actually *do* it now, if you see what I mean. So if he's back in England, don't cross him, darling, just don't.'

'I'll try not to,' I promised. 'Who did he fight?'

'What? Oh . . . gracious . . . I can't remember. He'd not long come out of prison when we arrived in Cheltenham. You couldn't work on the racecourse without hearing about him all the time. Let me think . . . Oh yes!' She chuckled suddenly. 'It wasn't just for fighting. He'd attacked some man with a rivet gun and shot staples into him through his jeans. Stapled the jeans to the man. It sounds funny now but I think he'd accused the man of laying his girlfriend behind his back and he was making sure he wouldn't be able to take his trousers down again.'

'For God's sake!'

'Mm. I do remember now. The man with the staples in him had to go to hospital to get them taken out and they were mostly in the most painful of places, it was said, and touch and go whether he'd ever lay anyone again, let alone Wynn Lees' girlfriend.'

'Why didn't I ever hear about this?'

'Well, darling, you may have done but not from me. I wouldn't have told you. You were a baby at the time of the stapling. I can tell you though that you didn't like Wynn Lees at all. You used to hide if he came into the office if you were there. It was absolutely instinctive. You couldn't bear him. So I used him as a bogey-man without frightening you with what he'd actually done. I thought that the cutting off of horses' tongues would give you nightmares. I certainly wouldn't tell any child something like that even now, though no child grows up these days without knowing the world is full of horrors.'

'Thank you for not telling me,' I said. 'I'd have hated it.'

'You're a fairly rewarding child, now and then.'

Pat pat on the back. And why not? We'd always been friends.

'OK,' I said, 'let me try you with some more names. How about Ronnie Upjohn?'

'Upjohn . . .' Her voice was negative, without recognition.

'Upjohn and Travers,' I said. 'Who were Upjohn and Travers?'

'My darling, I haven't a clue. You were at school with a boy called Travers. That's what you used to call him, Travers, which was his surname. He used to come and play with you sometimes. His mother bred Siamese cats.'

'I don't remember him.'

'It's a long time ago. A world away.'

'I'm here in it now, in that world.'

'So you are. Isn't it odd?'

'Yes,' I agreed slowly. 'It is.'

159

'Who else have you met? Anyone else?'

'J. Rolls Eaglewood. The same man, but old and with a walking stick.'

'J. Rolls!' She laughed. 'I don't suppose you remember Russet.'

'No knickers,' I said.

'That's just the sort of thing you *would* remember.'

'I remember Jimmy being killed.'

'Poor boy. A nice kid.'

'J. Rolls has a touch of the tyrants,' I said.

'Always had. Ruled his yard like iron, and our village too. So the old monster's still training ... He would never hear a word against Russet. He sacked his jockey just for laughing at a joke someone made about her. There was the heck of a fuss. What happened to Russet?'

'I don't know yet. There's a granddaughter now, called Izzy. She was Ken McClure's girlfriend for a while.' I paused. 'Mum, did you ever know why Kenny McClure killed himself?'

After a brief silence she said, 'Depression, I suppose. It was a dreadful shock at the time. He was always popular. He used to take you round the course in his jeep. I never believed the rumours.'

'What rumours?'

'Something to do with drugs. With ordering the wrong drugs. Some dreadful drug. That's all it was, a rumour. People trying to explain why he would kill

160

himself when he was so well liked, and a good vet. It was really upsetting.'

'How did he kill himself?'

'Shotgun. Blew his head to pieces. Darling, don't make me remember, it made me feel ill for days at the time. Just thinking about it now brings it all back.'

'Sorry.'

The strength of her reaction surprised me. I'd never speculated about her love-life because as far as I knew it was non-existent between husbands. But at twenty-something, a widow and as striking as her photos bore witness, she must, as I now saw, have been at least ready and available for love. She'd been actively waiting, I thought, for a John Darwin.

Always alarmingly able to interpret my silences, my perceptive mother said, 'Kenny was married. It wasn't right for him to leave his wife and children. We both agreed on that. So it didn't last very long. It was over years before he killed himself. I saw him often, but we were just friends. Is that what you wanted to know?'

'I think so, yes.'

'I'd prefer you didn't tell your friend Ken.'

I smiled down the wire. 'OK, I won't.'

'He was a nice man, darling.'

'I trust your judgment.'

'You know,' she said tentatively, 'if you can help Ken in his troubles, it would be sort of fitting. Don't let him do what his father did. I would have given anything to know what was troubling Kenny ... to have stopped him. But he never told me ... we were no longer so close ... so help his son for me and Kenny, will you?'

I was extraordinarily moved. Parents were full of the most amazing surprises.

'I will help him,' I promised, 'if I can.'

I went along to the hospital at eight the next day determined to dig everything I could out of Ken, but instead of a quiet private chat early on a Sunday morning I found the whole place seething with activity.

A police barrier denied entry to the rear car park, which was itself full of police cars, with and without flashing lights.

An arm of the law also prevented my entry on foot. Across the tarmac I could see Carey Hewett in his by now familiar state of distress. I'd never seen him otherwise. Ken, in the same group, showed strain in every muscle.

'You can't go in, sir,' the law said.

I shouted, 'Ken!' which he heard. He lifted his head, waved and walked over.

'God knows what's happening,' he said. 'The fire service were apparently here all day yesterday with the insurance people, sifting through the mess looking for absolute proof of arson.'

'And did they find it?'

'They didn't say. But what they did find was a *body*.'

162

CHAPTER SIX

'Whose body?' I asked automatically.

'No one knows,' Ken said. 'Carey's just got here, a minute after I did.'

We talked across the barrier, the policeman saying that I, as an unauthorized person, couldn't be let in.

'I authorize him,' Ken said persuasively. 'I work here and I need him.'

The policeman wavered, took a quick look around, saw no senior officers or disapproval, and let me pass as if not quite noticing I'd taken the crucial step. I went across with Ken to join the group round Carey Hewett, who looked at me unseeingly and didn't question my being there.

He wore Sunday-morning casual clothes of checked shirt and maroon sweater, not his usual neat collar and tie under a white lab coat. Some of his air of authority was lost in consequence, and on top of that he looked a bewildered and worried man. He hadn't had time to shave, I guessed, seeing the dusting of grey beard, nor probably to have had breakfast, as he looked peaked and hungry. This last shock on top of what he had lost had noticeably aged him.

'I don't understand how anyone could have been in the building so late on Thursday,' he was saying. 'Everything was locked as usual when we left. And everyone has been accounted for. If anyone was in the building it wasn't one of our people.'

'Could have been the arsonist,' one of the men in the group said. 'It's been known for people to be trapped in their own fires.'

He was a plain-clothes policeman, I gradually discovered, though no one made clear introductions after my arrival and I never heard his name. Carey's tolerance of my presence gave me credence and in fact he mentioned later that he was quite glad Ken had a friend to support him, wishing ruefully that he had someone to lean on himself.

It appeared that a police pathologist was at that moment inside the burnt-out shell, but extreme care was having to be taken with shoring up all outer and inner walls as parts of the structure could be pushed over by the palm of a hand. I gathered gradually that the body had been found in the general area of what had previously been the pharmacy and had been burned beyond any chance of easy recognition. Even its sex hadn't yet been determined.

'They apparently found the body last night,' Ken told me as an aside, 'but the light was fading and as the place is so unsafe they decided to leave things alone until they could see what they were doing by daylight. So they posted police guards and came back this morning not long before I got here. What a bloody *mess!*'

'It could be worse,' I said.

'How do you mean?'

'It might have been one of you in there. One of you might have disturbed the arsonist and been bumped off for your pains.'

'I suppose so.' The thought didn't especially alarm him. 'There's often one of us around here at night when we've got patients in the boxes. Scott was in and out all day yesterday looking after the mare, and I came three times to check on her. Belinda and I both came by when we got back from Stratford and again last thing before bedtime. We saw the police here both times but I thought it was just because the building is dangerous.' He paused briefly. 'Scott should be back here at any minute.'

'So the mare's doing all right?'

'Fingers crossed.'

We left the group and went over to look at the two patients. They both seemed half asleep, standing quietly, alive and recovering

'What's wrong with this one?' I asked of the one next door to the mare.

'He had wind troubles. Couldn't get air down to his lungs under pressure because one side of his larynx is paralysed. Quite common in big horses. I put in a suture to hold that side of his larynx permanently open so he can breathe better when he's blowing hard. He could have gone home yesterday but his trainer's short-handed and wanted him to stay in our care until tomorrow. He's been no problem, thank God.'

'You operated on him here in the hospital?'

'Sure.'

'Full anaesthetic?'

'Yes. It's a fairly long procedure, fifty minutes or so. I did him on Wednesday morning. He'd been scheduled for the op for a couple of weeks. It wasn't an emergency.'

'Have the horses that died all been emergencies?'

He thought briefly and shook his head. 'One died out here of heart failure after a successful operation to remove a knee chip. Simple routine thirty-minute arthroscopy. I took out a chipped-off piece of bone from his knee.'

'He died out here?'

Ken nodded. 'It was a valuable colt. We took extra-special care. Scott stayed here all night after the op checking him regularly and watching the monitor. One minute he was all right. Next minute, dead.'

'That couldn't have been your fault.'

'Tell that to the owner. The horse was *here*. That was the trouble.'

'Did Scott actually see him fall?'

'No, I don't think so. To be honest, I think Scott went to sleep, though he swore blind he didn't. But it's hard to stay awake here all night when there's nothing happening. And he'd been working all day, too. He was awake when I left him which was when I checked the horse at about eleven. Scott phoned me in a panic about five, but I reckon the colt had been dead an hour or so by then. We did an autopsy, but,' he shrugged, 'we found nothing amiss. His heart had just stopped.'

'Is that common?'

'Not really. More common after a hard race. They sometimes die in the racecourse stables afterwards.'

'Did you make out that list?'

'Haven't had a minute.' He withdrew his attention from the patient that hadn't died and seemed as ambivalent as ever about the ones that had.

'What did you do wrong?' I said.

He opened his mouth with shock and closed it again.

'Nothing,' he said unconvincingly.

'*Something* must have been wrong.'

He made a movement of his head like the beginning of a nod, and then thought better of it.

I said, 'Why don't you just tell me?'

He gave me a lengthy unhappy look and shrugged his shoulders.

'The first one,' he began tentatively, his long face miserable, his mind still not totally committed, 'I thought afterwards . . . maybe I'd missed . . . but it seemed so illogical . . . and anyway, it wouldn't have been that that killed him, it would have worn off anyway in the end . . .'

'What, Ken? What would have worn off?'

'Atropine,' he said.

I could see why Belinda was so sure I wouldn't be able to sort out the veterinary puzzle. Atropine, to me, was merely a word I'd heard before and never bothered to look up.

'Is that a poison?' I asked.

His own doubt of me echoed my own. He said patiently, 'It's poisonous. It's belladonna. But it has its uses. It relaxes things. Stops spasms.'

'Stops the heart?'

He shook his head. 'Enough of it in a horse could cause ileus.'

I looked at him.

'Sorry. It could stop movement in the gut. That's what ileus means. So with enough atropine, the gut would stop working and become distended with fluid and gas and cause unrelenting pain, and you'd have no option but to take the horse to surgery. But you wouldn't find any obstructions or kinks or twists. You could get rid of a lot of the gas ... empty the colon like I did with the mare, and so on ... and close up, and the gut would start working again normally when the atropine wore off. Only that's not what happened. They both died under anaesthesia.'

'*Both?*'

'I can't be sure ...'

Irritatingly at that point, Scott yelled across to Ken from the gateway to come and tell the policemen to let

168

him in past the barrier. Ken obligingly went over and returned not only with Scott but with two others of the vets, Oliver Quincy and Lucy Amhurst, living proof that bad news travelled like lightning even before breakfast on Sundays.

'You know Peter, don't you?' Ken asked his two colleagues, bringing them across to the boxes, and they nodded to me uninterestedly and focused only on who it was who had died in the fire.

Oliver Quincy had been tipped off to the body's existence by a friend of his in the police. He had immediately phoned everyone else in the practice and, sure enough, almost before he'd finished saying so, another two arrived, Jay Jardine and Yvonne Floyd; they were followed closely by Belinda, alerted by Yvonne, not Ken, to her annoyance.

Once I'd sorted out who was who, I had no difficulty: the vets were easily distinguishable from each other, in contrast to the anonymity of Ronnie Upjohn the day before.

They moved by consensus in through the main door, Scott, Belinda and I following, and came to form a conference in the office, fetching along the chairs from the entrance hall to accommodate the behinds. Carey Hewett alone remained outside with officialdom: his partners said it couldn't be helped and held their palaver without him.

Lucy Amhurst demanded to know what was going on, which no one, of course, could tell her. 'We've

DICK FRANCIS

enough dead horses for a glue factory, we've arson and we've a body. It's not bloody funny.'

She was a positive, middle-aged, no-nonsense person with strong clean nails, a stocky countrywoman's body and years of goodwill to pony clubs in her eyes.

She sat in the desk chair as if by right and seemed to be accepted by the others as having seniority of tenure if not of age. She fixed a rather headmistressy gaze on me and said, 'Excuse me, we know you're a friend of Ken's and have been helping him, and I know Carey accepts you, but I think you might explain a bit more who you are. We don't know you, do you see? We don't necessarily want strangers overhearing what we have to say among ourselves.'

'I absolutely understand,' I said neutrally. 'I'll certainly leave if you would prefer it. But, um, I could perhaps help you in some way to find some answers.'

'Are you a private detective?' She frowned, not liking the idea.

'No. But detective work is what I do, more or less, all the time. I'm employed to find things out.'

'He's a civil servant,' Belinda said flatly. 'Some sort of secretary.'

As usual, the British had no idea of civil service ranks. Someone had once asked the Commissioner, the austere top-of-the-heap mandarin who himself appointed other mandarins to top jobs, at what hotel he worked and how could he be sure of hailing a taxi.

170

The vets didn't exactly ask my speed in shorthand and typing but pigeonholed me in that capacity.

'A snoop,' Jay Jardine said disapprovingly.

Lucy Amhurst gave me a judicial inspection. 'We can't afford anything extra at this point.'

I said, 'This would be a freebie for Ken and Belinda.'

A twitch of a smile moved her mouth. She looked round at the others with authority. 'Well, if he's a good snoop, why don't we accept his offer? We do need some answers, God knows. If he doesn't come up with anything, we'll be no worse off.'

There were shrugs. No one had passionate views. I quietly stayed and no one raised the subject again.

Jay Jardine, the cattle man, was thin, short, self-assertive and a fairly recent graduate from veterinary college. His conversation bristled with futuristic technology to the point where some of his colleagues asked for enlightenment. He was the youngest of the group and, it seemed to me, the least liked.

'Carey's dragging his feet,' he complained. 'We have to have lab space. You know we do. I phoned him yesterday evening again but he's still done nothing. I said I would do it myself but he says to leave it to him.'

'He has a lot on his mind,' Lucy Amhurst said.

'There are three or four facilities I can think of that would be willing to rent us space. If I don't get lab space we'll lose clients, can't he see that? I've already got to repeat a lot of tests and no one's pleased at the delay. Carey's too old to cope with all this, that's obvious.'

The others protested up and down the scale from outrage (Lucy) to anxiety (Yvonne Floyd).

'He's sixty, isn't he?' Yvonne said worriedly.

She was young enough, as I was, to think sixty unimaginably ancient, but my father at fifty-six was only four years off the compulsory retiring age for the Foreign Office, and he, as I knew well, was still at the top of his exceptional mental powers. It wasn't so much simple age that was at the bottom of Carey's possible indecisiveness, I thought, but emotional fatigue at having lost so much. More people in my admittedly limited experience had become ill or rudderless under extreme loss-stress than had bounced all the way back with a curse at fate.

Yvonne Floyd, thirtyish, wore a wedding ring and emphasized her femininity with a luxuriant mass of almost black hair from which artful tendrils curved forward onto her cheeks and neck. Even so early, even in spite of the disturbing reason for the summons, she wore lipstick and eyeliner and a skirt with a black lace-edged underslip which showed when she crossed her legs.

Oliver Quincy hardly took his eyes off the legs, though whether from lust or absent-mindedness I wasn't quite sure. Of all in the room, his response to calamity was the most relaxed. Though he, as the other vet occupied with horses, might have been most expected to share Ken's intense worries, he was the only one to try a joke.

'What four animals do women like most?'

'Shut up, Oliver,' Lucy said. 'We're not in the mood.'

'It's funny,' he insisted. 'It will cheer us all up.'

He was a brown-haired roly-poly sort of man in early middle-age with a more comforting aura than the others: a better bedside manner, one might say, which must have encouraged the owners of his patients.

'A woman's favourite animals,' he said carefully, 'are a mink in the cupboard, a jaguar in the garage, a tiger in the bed – and a jackass to pay for it all.'

I thought it hilarious, but no one laughed.

'I heard it last week,' Lucy said.

Belinda said crossly, 'How can you joke with some poor person lying dead over there?'

'That poor person probably scored an own-goal.'

Belinda and Oliver didn't get on, I saw, and reckoned it was because of her habitual jealousy of anyone sharing Ken's time.

Yvonne said anxiously, 'What will happen if the whole partnership falls to pieces?'

Everyone glanced at her and away, as if they'd all had the thought and hadn't wanted to express it.

Lucy after a pause said sturdily, 'We've got the Por-takabin. We can buy new supplies. The building's insured. We're all still alive. We've still got the hospital. Carey said all that himself. Of course the partnership won't fall to pieces.'

'If it does,' Oliver said easily, 'I'm hiring.'

'What do you mean?' Lucy asked.

'I'm talking *Quincy* and Partners,' he said. 'I'm the oldest of us here. We all need our jobs. We know all our clients. If Carey bows out, we go on as before, but without him. With me, instead, as senior partner.'

'He won't bow out,' Lucy said, upset.

Smart Jay Jardine said, 'We can bow him out. Tell him he's too old, he's lost our confidence. It's a great idea.'

'It's a lousy idea,' Ken protested. 'Carey built up this practice. It's *his*.'

'It's normal,' Oliver said. 'The young herd always gets rid of the old bull.'

'The old man won't stand for it,' Scott said forcefully. 'You'll see.'

'You're a good nurse,' Oliver told him. 'You'll have to choose to stay, or go.'

'We're all staying with Carey,' Scott asserted.

Oliver's mild-seeming gaze moved from Scott's face to Ken's. 'Quincy and Partners,' he said, 'can't be doing with a discredited surgeon. Sorry, and all that.'

There was a blank silence, then Lucy said with nervousness, 'Is this another of your jokes?'

Oliver might have laughed uproariously and told them he'd had them all on the hop, but he didn't.

'Who owns the hospital?' I asked.

The heads all turned my way, surprised at my speaking as much as by my question.

'Who owns the burned building?' I added. 'Who gets the insurance money?'

'The bank,' Lucy said doubtfully. 'Mostly.'

'The bank,' agreed Ken. 'They advanced the money to build both blocks. They hold the mortgage. All of us vets pay towards it every month out of our salaries.'

'Carey organized it all years ago,' Lucy said. 'I was the only one of us with him then. When I first joined, he ran the practice out of his own house but then his wife died and he wanted to move . . . Why do you ask?'

'I just wondered if anyone benefited especially if the whole place burned down.'

They thought about it, but one could see that it was basically caring for sick animals they were interested in, not finance. Even Oliver Quincy had an air of not having planned his insurrection in terms of cash.

Lucy took heart from his silence. 'We'll have to ask Carey,' she said with satisfaction. 'He's still in charge.'

The seeds of doubt had been sown though: one could see the eventual end of Carey's road writ plain on Quincy and Jardine, writ tentatively on Yvonne Floyd, writ unbelievingly on Lucy Amhurst and wretchedly on Ken. The words had been spoken and couldn't be retracted, and might work on them like dry rot, disintegrating their partnership from within.

Ken's prospects looked appalling. I understood clearly what he had seen all along. Carey's loyalty to him couldn't last for ever, and the others of necessity would ditch him. With such an ignominious departure hanging over him, no one at all reputable would take him on.

I thought of the Foreign Office in-joke of defining total unacceptability as 'turned down by Lagos'. Every country had the right to turn down a diplomat's posting to it. Absolutely no one ever chose to go to Lagos as Lagos ran Ulan Bator close in career non-advancement. Lagos had to take what it could get. To be offered to Lagos and *turned down* meant the ultimate in rejection and loss of face. Job prospects thereafter, nil.

Into the silence in which his five partners variously reviewed their futures, Carey himself put his grey head.

'Oh, there you all are,' he said, unreceptive to the atmosphere. 'The police want to see you over in the Portakabin. They've set up some sort of incident room in it although I told them we'd need that space for clinics tomorrow morning.'

His voice sounded tired. His manner looked defeated. I wondered how he would have acted if he'd known of the disaffection among his ranks: wondered if it would have stiffened him or caused complete collapse. No sensible way of finding out.

He, his partners and his nurses traipsed across the tarmac, Ken last. I walked beside Ken, slowing him down.

'The police will probably chuck me out,' I said. 'I'll wait for you back in the office if they do. This is all getting serious. You must tell me things without reservation.'

'It was always serious,' he objected.

'Terminal then.'

He swallowed, his sharp adam's apple making an up and down journey in his long pale neck.

'All right,' he said.

Belinda looked back to us, waited and tucked her arm through Ken's. To do her justice, she was still unfalteringly linking her star to his, believing in him absolutely.

We went into the Portakabin where a constable was taking names and asking everyone to sit on the flip-up chairs lining the walls. I gave my name and sat down like everyone else and stayed quiet for as long as possible.

The senior policeman in charge, middle-aged, local accent, air of sober reliability, still without a name as far as I was concerned, said he was interested in knowing who had left the main veterinary building last on Thursday, before the fire.

Yvonne Floyd said that when she left at seven only Carey, working in his office, had remained.

'Seven?' asked the law. 'Was that your normal time?'

'We hold small-animal clinics on Mondays and Thursdays from five to seven. I do Thursdays.'

The policeman looked at the lace-edged slip and the long crossed legs and quite likely decided to buy a dog. He slid his eyes away reluctantly and sought confirmation from Carey.

Yes, Carey agreed wearily. Thursday had been a long

bothersome day. The painters had been underfoot. A horse had died during an operation. He'd helped Yvonne with the clinic because they were short of a nurse, and then he'd had a good deal of telephoning and paperwork to see to. He hadn't left until after eight. At that time he'd checked every room to make sure he was the last, then he'd let himself out and locked the front door from the outside. He'd then walked back to the hospital, which was locked but had a light on in the office, and had gone on along to the stable boxes where he'd found Scott checking on the three inmates there. He'd said goodnight to Scott and driven home.

'And after that, sir?'

Carey looked nonplussed. 'Do you mean, what did I have for dinner? Things like that?'

'No, sir, not exactly. I meant, when did you find out that your place was on fire?'

'Oh, I see. The people who live over the shoe shop across the road, they phoned me. They said they'd already called the fire brigade.'

The policeman nodded as if he'd heard that already and asked which of us was Scott.

Scott identified himself, broad shouldered, lean, the power machine.

'Scott Sylvester, qualified veterinary nurse.'

'Large animals,' Carey supplemented.

'Did you see anyone around the place, sir, after Mr Hewett left?'

Scott said it had all been quiet. He'd settled his charges for the night and gone to the Red Lion just along the road for a few beers. It had been a rotten day, with the horse dying. Around closing time, someone had come into the pub and said the vets' place was on fire, so he'd belted back to help and found the fire department had got there first.

The policeman asked how many people had keys to the burned building.

'We all do,' Carey said. 'Also the senior secretary has some, and so do the cleaners, of course.'

The policeman took a patient breath. 'When do the cleaners come in?'

'Eight o'clock every weekday.'

'And er ... had they arrived when you left?'

'What?' Carey said, briefly puzzled. 'Oh no. They come at eight in the morning, not at night.'

The policeman made a note, which I speculated might be a memo to ask the cleaners if any of their number was missing. Vets' pharmacies held saleable drugs: a thieving cleaner might even have been issued with a shopping list. But a thief after drugs didn't necessarily explain the fire.

Carey said, 'I suppose it's impossible to tell if someone broke in through a window?'

The policeman nodded. 'Can you tell me if the internal doors were locked, sir?'

'Just the pharmacy and the path lab,' Carey said, shaking his head. 'We might close the other internal

179

doors, but we very seldom lock them. When I left on Thursday, only the pharmacy and path lab doors were locked.'

'Would they be spring locks, sir, or mortise?'

Carey looked blank. 'Mortise, I think.'

'Would you have keys with you now, sir?'

Carey nodded and produced a bunch as substantial as Ken's, if not even larger. Carey's too were labelled, and on request he identified the right keys to the policeman.

'Mortise locks,' the policeman said, nodding.

'What difference does it make?' Carey asked.

'You see, sir,' came the patient explanation, 'when wooden doors and frames burn away, the lock itself often doesn't. It falls to the floor and the heat may not melt it, you understand?'

Everyone nodded.

'The investigators now in your building have found a lock they think is lying in the position of the pharmacy door. It's a mortise lock, and it is in the *open* position.'

The significance of this information landed like lead in the communal consciousness, though no one said anything.

'We'd like to borrow your keys, sir, to find out if they have the right lock.'

Carey silently handed over the keys. The senior policeman handed them to his constable, showing him the key in question and telling him to take it over to the investigators, to wait there, and finally bring the keys back. The constable took the bunch and went away and the senior policeman then asked how many people had a key to the pharmacy.

'We all do,' Carey said, sighing.

'Including the senior secretary, sir?'

Carey nodded.

'And the cleaners?'

Carey said defensively, 'We have to keep the place spotless. And each cabinet has its own lock, of course. The secretary and cleaners don't have keys to those.'

'Glass-fronted cabinets, sir?'

Carey nodded.

'The investigators say there was a great deal of melted glass in that area. The room was totally gutted. The roof obliterated anything remaining, when it fell. The firemen have been pumping tons of water out of the ruins. There seems to be no chance of identifying anything in the pharmacy, which means we can't identify what's missing, if anything is. We can just ask you, all of you, to make a list of what you know was in the pharmacy, so that if any of it turns up in other hands, we can proceed further with our enquiries.'

'It's hopeless,' Lucy protested.

'Please try.'

I thought of a quick way to get at least some of the answers, but decided I would tell Carey later. If I drew attention to myself at that point, I thought, I could be turned out pretty fast, and it was definitely more interesting to be present.

Lucy asked, 'Is it true this body was in the pharmacy?'

'In that area,' the policeman confirmed.

'What do you mean, area?'

The policeman seemed to add up the pros and cons of answering but finally said that some of the internal walls had crumbled under the weight of the roof. The pharmacy, as a four-sided room, no longer existed.

'Oh God,' Lucy said.

Jay Jardine asked, 'How badly was the body burned?'

'An examination is still proceeding, sir.'

'How long will it take you to find out who he is?' Jay Jardine again.

'We can't tell, sir.' A brief pause. 'Some bodies are never identified.'

'But what about missing people?' Lucy asked.

'Vagrants, the homeless, runaways, migrant workers, madam, people like that never turn up on lists of missing people.'

'Oh.'

'And I'd like to ask all of you,' the policeman said, 'whether you know of anyone who holds a grudge against any or all of you. Have you dismissed anyone recently? Have you received any hate mail? Has anyone threatened you? Have you been engaged in any litigation? Have you in the course of your work come across anyone who holds you responsible for a pet's death? Do you know anyone you might think of as unbalanced or obsessed?'

'Wow,' Yvonne said. 'That covers half the human race.'

Oliver Quincy looked at Ken and said to the policeman, 'We've had several horses die in the hospital recently and the owners are screaming.'

'Details, sir?'

Carey took over, explaining the difficulties of equine anaesthesia. The policeman wrote notes.

'Have any of those owners threatened you, sir?'

Carey shook his head.

Ken said forcefully, 'If it had been those owners, it would have been the hospital they would have burned, and the body in it would have been mine.'

No one laughed.

'Did they threaten you, sir?' The policeman consulted his list. 'Kenneth McClure, equine surgeon?'

'Right. And I've received no threats. Not that sort of threat, anyway.'

'What sort, sir?'

'Oh, just that they'll never send a horse into my care again, that sort of thing.'

The policeman seemed to think that sort of threat more violent than Ken did, but then Ken was no doubt right: if he had been the target, it would have been he and the hospital under the torch.

The policeman flicked through his notes and after a

183

pause asked Carey, 'When you left the premises, sir, and checked the pharmacy door, was it already locked?'

'Yes,' Carey said. 'I told you.'

'So you did, sir. But what I mean is, who actually locked it? Was it you yourself who locked it earlier?'

Carey shook his head.

'I locked it,' Yvonne said. 'I locked it as usual after the clinic.'

The policeman glanced at the legs and suffered a spasm of regret, then pulled himself together, sighed and rubbed his fingers down his nose.

'And who locked the laboratory?'

'Probably I did,' Jay Jardine said. 'I had some tests in there that I didn't want to be disturbed.' He laughed with mirth. 'I suppose there's nothing left of those, either?'

'Very unlikely, sir.' The policeman cleared his throat. 'At what time were you last on the premises?'

Jay Jardine stared and took offence. 'Are you suggesting that *I* set fire to the place?'

'I'm trying to establish a pattern, sir.'

'Oh.' Jardine still looked annoyed. 'I locked up when I left at about four. I was called out to a sick cow. Anything else?'

'I'd like to make a list of where you all were during the evening.' The policeman turned to a fresh page in his spiral-bound notebook. 'Starting with Mr Hewett, please, sir.'

'I told you, I left after eight and went home.'

'How far away is home, sir?'

'Are all these questions necessary?' Carey protested. 'You surely can't think one of *us* started the fire?'

'We can't tell who started it, sir, but we'd like to eliminate as many people as possible.'

'Oh, I see. Well, I live five minutes away.'

'By car?'

'Of course, by car.'

'And you spent the evening with your wife?'

The policeman, not insensitive, observed the mental wince of everyone there and was ready for Carey's reply.

'My wife's dead.'

'Very sorry, sir. You were alone, then, sir?'

'I suppose so. I got some supper, played some music, read the newspaper. I don't think of it as being alone, but if you mean was anyone else there, no, they weren't.'

The policeman nodded, made a note and continued to the next name on his list.

'Mrs Amhurst?'

'Miss,' Lucy said.

The policeman gave her a slow reconnoitring look as if establishing a base against which to test her answers. A good detective, I thought, and very experienced.

'Thursday evening, madam?' he asked economically.

She answered straightforwardly, without Jardine's umbrage. 'I left here soon after lunch as I had about

185

four calls to make in the afternoon. The last was to some sheep up on a hill above Birdlip. I suppose I left there at dusk, say before seven, and then called on a basset hound I'd had in surgery in the morning. He was all right. I had a drink with the owners and went home. Didn't look at the time.'

'Do you live alone, madam?'

'My sister lives with me, but she's away on a cruise.'

'So that evening . . .?'

'Same as Carey, I suppose, though, in my case instead of music I watched some television.' She forestalled his next question humorously. 'Don't ask me what programme I watched, I've no idea. I'm afraid I've a habit of falling asleep in my chair after a long day.'

'How far away from here do you live, madam?'

'A mile and a quarter. In Riddlescombe.'

I looked at her with interest. Riddlescombe was the village where I'd lived with my mother, where the Eaglewoods still held sway. I hadn't realized it was quite so near to the outskirts of Cheltenham. Distances seemed greater, I supposed, to children.

The policeman consulted his list.

'Mrs Floyd?'

'Yes,' Yvonne said, uncrossing the spectacular legs and crossing them the other way. 'Like I told you, I went home at seven.'

'And home is?'

'Painswick Road. About a couple of miles from here.

My husband was away on business but the kids were in.'

'Er . . . how old are your children?'

'They're not mine. They're my husband's. Fifteen and sixteen. Boys. They listen to pop music and chew gum, hey man.' Her impersonation in the last few words brought the first cracking smiles of the morning.

'And could they vouch for you, madam?'

'*Vouch* for me?' She gave him a comical grin. 'They were doing their homework. How anyone can do homework with a million decibels battering their eardrums beats me, but they get fidgety in silence. They have a room each. Just as well. I always go up and tell them when I get in. They give me a wave. We get on pretty well.'

'So you went downstairs, madam, I'm guessing, and cooked some food and spent the evening more or less alone?'

'I suppose so. Read the day's letters and a magazine. Watched the news. Then Oliver phoned and said this place was on fire, so I hopped upstairs and told the boys why I'd be going out. They'd got their videos going by then but of course they wanted to come too but I wouldn't let them, it was already late and they had tests the next day. I told them to go to sleep. My name was shit.'

The policeman didn't bother to smother his smile and made the briefest of notes.

'Oliver Quincy, large animals?' he asked next.

'That's me,' Oliver said.

Oliver got the same contemplative inspection as Lucy.

'Sir, your evening?'

'Oh, well, I was bloody tired. We'd had that damned horse die and we'd had all sorts of post mortems, the real thing and endless checks of the equipment and we couldn't come up with anything wrong. But I was knackered by the end, we all were. I was supposed to be going to the rugby club annual dinner but I couldn't face the monkey suit and the speeches and the din, so I drove out to a pub and had a couple of pints and some bar food.'

'Did you pay with a credit card, sir?'

'No. Cash.'

'Are you married, sir?'

'My wife goes where she likes and so do I.'

There was something in his voice that belied the comfort-giving exterior, that belonged more to the ruthlessness with which he angled to supplant Carey.

'How did you hear the building was on fire, sir?'

'I phoned him,' Carey said. 'He was a long time answering but he was the first I'd tried to reach. I think of Oliver as my second-in-command. It was natural to get to him first and ask him to phone everyone else.'

None of them met any eyes. A real case of *et tu Brute* in the making. Poor old Carey.

'The phone was ringing when I got home,' Oliver confirmed, still not looking at his Caesar. 'I phoned

Yvonne, Lucy and Jay and told them, but got no answer from the others.'

'I was in the pub,' Scott said.

The policeman nodded, looking at his list.

'Mr McClure?' he asked.

'I took my fiancée, Belinda here, and her parents, out to dinner. Peter was with us too.'

The policeman again reviewed his list.

'Belinda Larch, qualified veterinary nurse? Peter Darwin, general assistant?'

We both silently nodded.

'And you three were together all evening, with Miss Larch's parents? In a restaurant?'

'Right,' Ken said. 'We were just about to leave when Lucy phoned me there.'

Lucy nodded. 'When we all got here I realized Ken was missing. I remembered he was on call, so I phoned his portable phone from the hospital office. Does all this matter?'

'Some things matter, some don't,' said our philosopher policeman. 'We can't tell yet.' He consulted the list. 'Mr Jay Jardine?'

Jay alone resented the questions. 'I told you.'

'Yes, sir. Could you go on from after the sick cow?'

With unsuppressed irritation, in snapping tight-mouthed syllables, Jay said he'd gone home and had a row with his live-in girlfriend. She'd stormed out to cry on her best friend's shoulder. So what.

So nothing, it seemed. His answer got written down

without comment and it appeared the present session of questions had come to an end. The constable conveniently returned at that moment with Carey's keys, speaking quietly into his senior officer's ear so that probably only Carey himself, who was nearest, could overhear.

The senior policeman nodded, turned and handed the bunch to its owner. Then, glancing round our expectant faces, he said matter-of-factly that the pharmacy key did fit the lock in question. As no one had expected it wouldn't, the news fell short of uproar. Carey, looking worried, said he *thought* he'd checked the door was locked, but he'd had so much else on his mind that now he couldn't swear...

'But I *did* lock it,' Yvonne said. 'I'm sure I did. I always do.'

'Don't worry too much about it, madam. It's quite easy to get duplicate keys cut and, frankly, between you, you already have so many keys in use here that I doubt if any would-be intruder would have much difficulty in borrowing and reproducing the whole bunch.'

Into a moderately stunned silence he poured a little professional advice. 'If you're thinking of rebuilding, sir, I would definitely consider electronic locks. No one can pop into the nearest hardware shop to copy that sort of key.'

He had to leave with his constable and Carey stood and went with them, leaving a roomful of thoughtfulness behind.

'I did lock it,' Yvonne repeated doubtfully. 'I always do.'

'Of course you did,' Oliver said. 'It's typical of Carey not to know whether he checked it or not. That's just what I mean. He's past it. The sooner we tell him, the better.' He stood up, stretching. 'There's no point in waiting about here. I'm off to play golf. Who's on call?'

'Carey is,' Lucy told him, 'and Ken.'

Oliver said without humour, 'Then let's hope it is a quiet Sunday.'

He walked purposefully out of the Portakabin, followed immediately by his chief admirer, Jay. Everyone else stood and in varying degrees of unsettlement moved in their wake. Scott, his internal dynamos whizzing again after the short inactivity, announced he was spending the day by the lake stripping down the engines of his speed boat in preparation for the water-skiing season, and marched briskly out of the rear of the car park. We heard the roar of his engine starting, and presently saw his strong figure riding a motorbike past the entrance.

'Does he always ride a bike?' I asked.

'He hasn't a car,' Ken said.

Lucy said tolerantly, 'He pumps iron, he's got pectorals you'd hardly believe, he's as physical as they come.'

'He's a good nurse,' Ken said to me. 'You saw him.' I nodded.

'Loyal to Carey, too,' Lucy went on approvingly. 'I

couldn't live the way he does, but he seems happy enough.'

'How does he live?' I prompted.

Yvonne answered. 'In a caravan park. He says he hates permanence. He's kind though. We took our boys to his lake one day last summer and he spent hours teaching them to ski.'

Lucy nodded. 'Such a mixture.'

'Unmarried?' I asked.

'A chauvinist,' Belinda stated, and the other two women nodded.

'We may as well all go home,' Yvonne said. 'Oliver was right, we can't do any more here.'

'I suppose not,' Lucy agreed reluctantly. 'It's all dreadfully upsetting.'

The two women walked together to the gate. Belinda urged Ken to come with her to Thetford Cottage because her mother was a disastrous cook and she, Belinda, had said she would do the Sunday lunch for everyone.

'You go on, darling,' Ken said, 'I just want to go over a few things with Peter.'

She went with bad grace, disliking it, delivering a parting shot about us not being late. Ken waved to her lovingly and walked purposefully ahead of me into the office.

'Right,' he said, settling into the chair behind the desk and stretching for a notepad to write on. 'No secrets, no reservations, and don't use what I tell you against me.'

'Not a chance.'

He must have heard more commitment in my voice than he expected, because he looked briefly puzzled and said, 'You've known me less than three days.'

'Mm,' I agreed, and thought about his father and my mother, and the promises I'd made her.

CHAPTER SEVEN

'Chronologically,' Ken said, 'if we're counting horses that've died when I wouldn't expect them to, the first one was months ago, last year, September, maybe. Without my notes I can't be certain.'

'What happened?' I said.

'I got called out to Eaglewood's at six one morning. The head lad phoned me. Old man Eaglewood was away for the night and the head lad was in charge. Anyway, he said one of the horses was down and extremely ill, so I went over there and he was by no means exaggerating. It was a three-year-old colt that I'd been treating for a strained tendon, but otherwise he'd been perfectly healthy. But he was lying on his side in his box in a coma, with occasional tremors and twitches in his muscles, obviously dying. I asked the head lad how long he'd been like that but he didn't know. He'd come in early to feed as usual, and found him in that state but with stronger spasms in the muscles.'

'What did you do?' I asked.

'I didn't know what was wrong with him, but he was too far gone to be helped. I just took some blood samples for analysis, and put him out of his misery.'

'And what *was* wrong with him?'

Ken shook his head. 'Everything in his blood was just about within normal limits though the blood sugar was low, but . . .' he stopped.

'But what?'

'Well, there were other things. It had been a good colt before the tendon injury. A winner several times over. Even if the tendon had mended decently it would have been surprising if he'd been as good again. I asked the head lad if he'd been insured, because you can't help wondering, but he didn't know. I asked old man Eaglewood later, but he said it wasn't my business. Then, before he died, the colt's heart rate was very high and there was swelling round his eyes.'

He paused. I said he would have to explain.

'He looked as if he'd been suffering for quite a while before I got there. I began to think about poisons, about what would cause spasms, high heart rate and coma. I thought a specialist lab's blood analysis would tell us, but it cost a lot and showed nothing. But horses don't die like that, I mean, not in the normal course of events. I talked it over with Carey several times and in the end he asked Eaglewood himself about the insurance, but it seemed the owner actually hadn't insured the colt at all.'

'But you weren't really satisfied?'

'Well, I mean, it was a mystery. I began thinking how the colt had behaved before the head lad found him, I mean, maybe for several hours alone in his box during the night; what he'd been like before he got to that final state. I wondered if he'd had seizures, perhaps like epileptic fits. The tremors at the end might have been just the last twitches of something absolutely terrible. I hate horses to suffer... If that colt had suffered the way I was imagining, and if it was the result of poison, I thought I'd never stop before I got whoever had done it prosecuted.' He shrugged. 'I never did get anyone prosecuted because there was no way of knowing who'd done it, but I woke up one morning with the answer in my head, and I'm certain that that colt was deliberately killed even if there wasn't an obvious reason for it.'

'So what killed him?' I asked, fascinated.

'Insulin,' he said, 'though I can't prove it.'

'*Insulin?*'

'Yes. Well, horses don't get diabetes, except so rarely it's almost never. You wouldn't give horses insulin for anything. If you gave a horse a big overdose, his blood sugar would fall catastrophically and he would go into hypoglycemic shock, with convulsions and then coma, and death would be inevitable. It fitted the symptoms of the colt. I began looking for mentions of insulin in veterinary case reports, but there isn't much anywhere about normal insulin levels in horses. As they don't get diabetes, there isn't the need for research. But I found enough to know better what to look for next time in the blood chemistry – if there is a next time. And I found that in America three or four racehorses had almost certainly been killed that way for the insurance. I showed Carey the case reports and we both told Oliver what I thought so that he would be on the look out, but we haven't come across it again.'

'It *must* have been for the insurance,' I said, pondering.

'But Mr Eaglewood said it wasn't insured.'

'Did he own the colt himself?'

'No. As a matter of fact it belonged to the man who owns the mare. Wynn Lees.'

I drew in a breath sharply enough for him to wonder why, and he sought for and found an explanation.

'I suppose it *is* a coincidence,' he said. 'But the mare didn't die.'

'But for you, she would have.'

'Have you still got that bit of gut?' he asked.

'I transferred it into the freezer,' I said.

'Oh.' He nodded. 'Good.'

'How much do you know about Wynn Lees?' I asked.

'Nothing much. I'd never met him before Friday morning. Why did you tell me not to trust him?'

I thought briefly about letting him know, but decided not to. Not yet. I might find a more oblique path. There were more ways of revealing truths than marching straight up to them, and if one could get a truth revealed without disclosing one's own hand in it, it gave one an advantage next time around.

Ken waited for his answer.

'Instinct,' I said. 'Natural antipathy. Hostile vibes. Call it what you like. He gave me the shivers.'

There was enough truth in all that to be convincing. Ken nodded and said the man had had much the same effect on himself.

After a moment I said, 'Is your mother still alive?'

'Yes, she is. Why do you ask?'

'I don't know... I just wondered if she'd had a chance yet of enjoying Greg and Vicky being here. They'd have a lot to talk about, with the wedding just ahead. And I'd like to meet her, too.'

He looked at me in dawning dismay. 'Why in hell haven't I arranged it? I must be mad. But there's been so much on my mind. How about today, for lunch?' He stretched a hand out to the phone. 'I'll ask the old lady at once.'

'Check with Belinda first, I should. Er... to make sure there's enough food.'

He gave me a sideways glance but saw the wisdom of asking Belinda first. It was actually Vicky who answered and who received the suggestion with enthusiasm, who said it was a lovely idea and that she would tell Belinda it was fixed. Ken disconnected with a smile and redialled, reaching his own parent and evoking a more moderate response. Ken was persuasive, his mother slowly let herself be persuaded. He would pick her up, he promised, and take her home afterwards, and she would be quite safe.

'My mother's not like Vicky,' he said, putting down the receiver. 'She likes things planned well in advance. I mean, at least days in advance, if not weeks. She thinks we're hurrying the wedding, but the truth is she's been against me marrying *anyone*.' He sighed. 'She'll never make friends with Belinda. She calls her Miss Larch half the time. Parents!'

'Do you remember your father?'

'Only vaguely. I was ten when he died so I ought to remember him clearly, but I don't. I know him from his photographs. I know he played with me and was fun. I wish ...' he paused, ' ... but what's the point of wishing? I wish I knew why he died.'

I waited without movement, and he said, 'He killed himself.' It was clearly still a painful thought. 'The older I get, the more I want to know why. I wish I could talk to him. Silly, isn't it?'

'No.'

'Anyway, it explains a lot about my mother.'

'I'll remember,' I said. I looked down at his notepad on which he'd written the single word 'insulin'. 'How about if you let me write the notes while you talk?'

He pushed the pad and pen across gladly. I turned to a new page and after a bit of thought he began again on the saga.

'The next one I can't explain was soon after

Christmas. That was the one I thought had been given atropine.'

'What sort of horse?' I asked, writing.

'Racehorse. A hurdler. Trained by Zoë Mackintosh out past Riddlescombe.'

'*Zoë* Mackintosh?'

'Quite a lot of women train,' Ken said reasonably.

Sure, I thought, but Mackintosh in my shadowy memory was a man.

'Is she a trainer's daughter?' I asked.

Ken nodded. 'Her father, old Mac, he's still there, but his memory's going. Zoë holds the licence and does what she wants when he isn't looking. He's a cantankerous old man and he's always breathing over her shoulder. She still employs Hewett and Partners because she's known Carey all her life – he and Mac are great buddies – but she's been shirty to me about the dead horses, and I can't blame her.'

'More than one?'

'Two. And I'd swear they were both given atropine. After the second one, I tackled Zoë about it and she practically threw me over her left shoulder. Very muscular lady, our Zoë. But it does no good to have her going round implying I'm crazy as well as incompetent, which she does.'

I thought it over.

'Were both these horses owned by the same person?' I asked.

'No idea.'

'And were they insured?'

'I don't think so. You'd have to ask Zoë or the owners, and frankly, I'm not going to.'

'You're scared of her!'

'You haven't met her.'

'What were the horses' names?'

'What a question! I'm always told their names but I can't remember them after I've finished treating them. Well, seldom. Only if they're in the top rank. I attend hundreds of horses in a year. They're filed under their names in the computer – well, they were – but to jog my own memory I write them down as, say, "Three-year-old filly, white socks, herring-gutted", then I know at once which horse I'm referring to.'

'Describe the atropine horses.'

'The first one, a bay four-year-old gelding, large white blaze down its nose. The second one, a five-year-old gelding, chestnut, two white socks in front, white face.'

'OK.' I wrote down the descriptions. 'How did they die?'

'Colic cases, both times the same. We had the colon out on the table, like you saw, and I was palpating – that's feeling – the smaller intestines for obstructions, and not finding any, and without warning their heart started to fail and their blood pressure dropped disastrously. The alarm signal went off and we'd lost them. Hopeless. But, like I told you, it does sometimes happen, so I didn't think much about the first one.'

'How many have died like that now?'

'Four in eight weeks.' He swallowed. 'It should be impossible.'

'Exactly the same way?'

'Yes, more or less.'

'How do you mean, more or less?'

'They weren't all colic operations. Like I told you, the last one was putting screws in a split cannon bone, and before that there was the respiratory tract, a tie-back like the one here now. Those two were both Eaglewood's, as I told you at Stratford.'

'Um,' I said, looking at my increasingly chaotic notes, 'Do you remember in which order they happened?'

'Well . . .' He thought. 'Put the insulin colt first, even though he didn't die here in the hospital.'

'OK.'

'Then Zoë Mackintosh's four-year-old.'

'Right.'

'Then . . . Eaglewood's respiratory tie-back.'

'OK,' I said. 'Do you ever do tubing? I remember being fascinated as a child that you could put a tube through into a horse's trachea so that it could breathe better, with a plug like a bath plug that you can put in and out of its neck – in for rest, out for galloping.'

'Not often. It's still done here sometimes, but you can't run tubed horses in America and it will end here soon.'

'And here, once upon a time, a tubed horse with the plug out galloped into a canal and drowned?'

'Ages ago,' he nodded, smiling, 'In the Grand National. It forgot to turn at the Canal Turn and made a proper balls of it.'

'Derby Day II in 1930,' I said, from the depths.

He was startled. 'How the hell do you know that?'

'I've an endless memory for trivia.' I said it as a joke, but realized it was more or less true. 'And trivia,' I said apologetically, 'means "three roads" in Latin. Wherever three roads met, the Romans put up notice boards with the news on. Little bits of information.'

'Jeez,' Ken said.

I laughed. 'Well, after the respiratory tie-back, what next?'

He thought for a good while. 'I suppose the next one was Nagrebb's show-jumper. The horse that staked itself, that I told you about. It splintered one of the jumps while they were schooling it at home, and when I went there it was still in the field with a sharp piece of wood a foot long driven into its near hind above the hock. There was blood pouring down its leg, and it was fearfully agitated and trying to wrench itself away from the two people holding its head collar. One of them was a groom and the other was the girl who rode it and she was in tears the whole time which didn't help the horse. Horses react to fear with fear. I think they can smell it. They're very receptive. Anyway, she was afraid he would have to be put down, and her father was jumping around yelling at me to *do* something, which upset the horse too. Between them, they'd

203

wound it up into such a state that the first thing I had to do was tranquillize it and wait until it calmed down and that wasn't popular either. In the end, I got old man Nagrebb to take his daughter into the house as I could manage well with just the groom. So after that I pulled the stake out of the leg and inspected the damage which was considerable but mainly muscular, with a few severed blood vessels but not the main artery or vein. Well, I did a clean-and-repair job and closed the skin with strong sutures. Staples, like you saw me use on the mare, aren't adequate for that sort of wound. It looked neat enough. I told the Nagrebbs the leg would be swollen and hot for a bit but with antibiotics it should heal satisfactorily, and I would take the sutures out after a week. They wanted me to promise the leg would be as good as new but how could I? I didn't know. I rather doubted it myself but I didn't tell them that. I said to give it time.'

He paused, thinking back, 'Well, then, as I told you, the leg was healing OK. I went out there several times. I took out the sutures. End of case. Then a day or two later, I got a panic call and went and found its lower leg and fetlock up like a balloon and the horse unable to put his foot to the ground. So we brought him here and I opened the leg because I was worried that infection had got into the tendon sheath and, like I told you, the tendon had literally disintegrated. There was nothing to repair. I'd never seen anything so bad. I got Carey to come and look at it because I thought

Nagrebb would take his word for it better than mine, because of course we had to put the horse down and it was this famous show-jumper. Nagrebb had insured it, so we told the insurers the horse couldn't be saved. They agreed to the lethal injection, which I gave. Then shortly after that, old man Nagrebb started complaining that I must have somehow damaged the fetlock and tendon myself when I repaired the stake wound but I know for certain I hadn't.'

He stopped again and looked at me earnestly. 'I'm going to tell you something because I promised I'd tell you everything, but you're not to think me raving mad.'

'You're not raving mad,' I said.

'All right. Well, you might say I brooded about that horse, about why its tendon disintegrated and, well, there is something that would make that happen.'

'What?' I asked.

'Some stuff called collagenase.' He swallowed. 'If you injected, say, two ccs of collagenase into a tendon you would get that result.'

'How, exactly?'

'It's an enzyme that dissolves collagen, which is what tendons and ligaments are made of.'

I stared at him. He stared apprehensively back.

'You are not raving mad,' I repeated.

'But you can't just go out and *buy* collagenase,' he said. 'It's supplied by chemical companies but it's only used in research laboratories. It's pretty dicey stuff. I mean, it would dissolve human tendons too. You wouldn't want to ram a needleful into your wrist.'

I felt like saying Jeez myself.

'You can buy it freeze-dried, in small bottles,' Ken said. 'I looked it up. You reconstitute it with one cc of water. You'd only need a small needle.'

Jeez again, I thought.

'What do you think?' he asked.

I thought he might possibly be in great danger, but all I said was, 'Go on to the next one.'

'Don't forget,' he said, 'that in between all those I saw dozens of other horses, racehorses, hunters and so on, that were quite all right. For every horse that died here, I operated on many others without incident. We get quite a few referrals from other veterinary practices, and none of them died. Telling the dead ones all at once makes it sound as if they were one after the other without interval.'

'I'll remember.'

'OK. Then the next one that died was the one out in the intensive care box that I told you about this morning.'

I nodded. He seemed to have finished with that one, but I asked, 'Who owned it?'

'Chap called Fitzwalter. Decent sort of man. Took it philosophically and didn't blame me.'

'And do you have reservations, or do you think that that one did die of natural causes?'

He sighed heavily. 'I took some of the colt's blood

206

for testing, though he'd been dead too long really. The results came back negative for any unexplained substance.'

I studied his pale worried face.

'Even if the tests were negative, do you have even a faint suspicion?'

'I suspect it because it happened.'

That seemed reasonable enough for the circumstances.

'And straight after that, the second Mackintosh horse came in, and it died on the table exactly like the first one.' He shook his head. 'It wasn't until after that second one that I thought of atropine. Because the pupils were dilated, you see. I thought I might have missed that the first time, or not seen the significance, anyway, because at that point there wasn't any *reason* to be suspicious.'

'No.' I sighed.

'Then last Thursday, the day you came, we lost the Englewood horse with the cannon bone. Just the same. Failing heart and diving blood pressure. I took blood samples before we began that operation and Oliver took more when the horse was beyond saving, but we'll never know the results of those as they were in the fridge in the path lab. I was going to send them to a professional lab for analysis.'

'Was there anything – anything at all – different in the two Mackintosh operations from the one I saw you do on the mare? Apart from not finding any physical obstructions, I mean?'

'Nothing, except naturally that it was Scott and Belinda who were with me, not you. Belinda runs the room, Scott does the anaesthetic. We always work that way.'

'Just the three of you?'

'Not always. Any of the others might come in. Lucy assists with ponies, sometimes. Oliver's often helping. I've assisted Jay with cows and bulls. Carey keeps an eye on things generally. He can turn his hand to any-thing if he has to, though nowadays he does small animals only. Yvonne, for all her glamour, is a neat delicate surgeon, a pleasure to watch. I've seen her put car-struck dogs and cats back together like jigsaw puzzles. Even a pet rabbit, for one little boy. She micro-stitched its half-severed leg back on. It was hopping around later.' He paused. 'The hospital has been our pride and joy, you see. Not many vets' practices have such good facilities. It's brought us a lot of outside work.'

'Go back to last Thursday morning,' I said. 'By then all of you were apprehensive over almost every oper-ation, right?'

He nodded mutely.

'So you checked everything twice. You had Oliver there. You were operating on a leg, not an abdomen. Go through it all in your mind, right from when the horse arrived. Don't skip anything. Go slowly. I'll just wait. Take your time.'

He raised no objections. I watched him think, watched the small movements in his facial muscles as he passed from procedure to procedure. Watched him shake his head and frown and finally move his whole body in distress.

'Absolutely nothing,' he burst out. 'Nothing, except –' He stopped, indecisively as if unconvinced by what he was thinking.

'Except *what*?' I asked.

'Well, Oliver was watching the screen, like you were. I glanced over a couple of times. I can't swear to it but I think now that the trace on the electrocardiograph – the line that shows the heartbeat – had changed slightly. I didn't stand and watch it. Perhaps I should have done, considering. But then, of course, the trace did change anyway because the heart wasn't working properly.' He frowned heavily, thinking it over. 'I'll have to look a few things up.'

'Here?' I asked, looking round the bare office.

'No, at home. All my books are at home. And thank God they are. Carey kept all his in his office so that we could all use them for reference if something cropped up we weren't sure of. What the fire didn't ruin, the water will have done.' He shook his head. 'Some of those books are irreplaceable.'

'Very bad luck,' I said.

'There's no saying the troubles are over, either.'

'Particularly not with an unknown body lying around.'

He rubbed a hand tiredly over his face. 'Let's go along to Thetford Cottage.'

'OK. But Ken . . .'

'What?'

'Until they find out whose body it is, well, don't go down any dark alleys.'

He stared. He didn't seem to have worried in the least about the body or seen it as any warning to be careful.

'It was the arsonist,' he protested.

'Maybe. But why was he setting fire to the place?'

'I've no idea. No one has.'

'It sounds to me as if the arsonist himself didn't know he was going to start a fire until just before he did it.'

'Why do you think that?'

'Cleaning fluid. Paint. They happened to be there. If you intended to set fire to a building, would you rely on breaking into it and finding inflammable liquids just lying around?'

He said slowly, 'No, I wouldn't.'

'So just take care.'

'You scare me, you know.'

'Good.'

He studied my face. 'I didn't expect you to be like this.'

'Like what?'

'So . . . so *penetrating*.'

I smiled lopsidedly. 'Like a carpet needle! But no one remembers everything all the time. No one sees the significance of things all at once. Understanding what you've seen comes in fits and starts and sometimes when you don't expect it. So if you remember anything else that you haven't told me about the dead horses, well, tell me.'

'Yes,' he said soberly, 'I will.'

Vicky did her best to charm Ken's mother – Josephine – but in truth they were incompatible spirits. Vicky, spontaneous, rounded, generous, essentially young despite the white hair, was having to break through to a defensive, plainly dressed angular woman in whom disapproval was a habit.

Belinda, taking refuge in the kitchen, was knocking back a huge bloody mary (to settle her nerves and stop her screaming, Ken said, mixing it for her) and in consequence seemed more human.

Greg and I batted some conversation around without saying anything worth remembering and eventually we all sat down to roast lamb with potatoes, peas, carrots and gravy, the sort of meal I'd almost forgotten existed.

It wasn't very difficult, once everyone had passed, poured and helped the food and was safely munching, to introduce the subject of Ken's brilliant work on the colicky mare being met with suspicion and ingratitude from its owner.

'A most extraordinary man,' I said. 'Wynn Lees, his name is. I didn't like him at all.'

Josephine McClure, sitting next to me, raised her head from the forkful she'd been about to eat and paid attention.

I went on, 'He showed no fondness for his mare. He didn't seem to care about her. It almost seemed as if he wanted her dead.'

'No one could be so heartless,' Vicky exclaimed.

Josephine McClure ate her forkful.

'Some people are born heartless,' I said.

Ken recounted the story of his having got permission to operate from Wynn Lees' wife. He chuckled. 'He said she couldn't have spoken to me in the middle of the night because she always took sleeping pills.'

Josephine McClure said tartly, 'Anyone married to Wynn Lees would take sleeping pills as a matter of course.'

God bless you, dear lady, I thought, and in an amused chorus with the others, begged her to enlarge.

'Ken,' she said severely, 'you didn't tell me you'd done any work for Wynn Lees. That name! Unforgettable. I thought he'd gone to live abroad. Stay away from him.'

Ken said, bemused, 'I didn't know you knew him.'

'I don't know him. I know *of* him. That's not the same.'

'What do you know *of* him?' I asked in my most persuasive voice. 'Do tell us.'

She sniffed. 'He tortured some horses and went to jail.'

Vicky exclaimed in horror, and I asked 'When?'

'Years ago. Probably forty years ago. It was a frightful scandal because his father was a magistrate.'

Ken looked at her open-mouthed. 'You never told me any of that.'

'There's never been any reason to. I haven't heard his name for years. I've never given him a thought. He'd gone away. But if your man was heartless to his mare, it must be the same person come back again. There can't be hundreds of people called Wynn Lees.'

'You have a good memory,' I said.

'I pride myself on it.'

'Ken's also been having a spot of trouble with Ronnie Upjohn,' I said. 'Do you know any scandal about *him*?'

'Ronnie Upjohn?' She frowned slightly. 'He used to know my husband. It's very stupid of him to complain about Ken winning with that horse. Ken told me about it.'

I said tentatively, 'Is he in business? Does he have a partner?'

'Oh, you mean old Mr Travers? No, that was Ronnie's father's partner.'

I held my breath.

213

Josephine cut up some meat and fed herself a mouthful.

'I've lost you,' Ken said. 'What are you talking about?'

'Old Mr Travers,' his mother said acidly, 'was a frightful lecher.'

Vicky looked captivated by the contrast between Josephine's censorious manner and the pithiness of her words. Vicky would have given 'lecher' a laugh. Josephine was serious. Greg, smiling, was maybe thinking that dried-up old Josephine needn't fear the attentions of lechers; yet she had been a happy wife once and there were still vestiges of that young woman, though her mouth might be pursed now and bitter.

'Upjohn and Travers,' I said.

'That's right.' She went on eating unemotionally.

'What sort of business was it?' I asked.

'I don't know. Something to do with finance.' Her voice said that finance to her was a closed book. 'Ronnie Upjohn's never done a day's work in his life, as far as I know. His father and old Mr Travers were rolling.'

'You know so much about all these people,' I said admiringly. 'How about the Eaglewoods?'

'Oh no, not the Eaglewoods,' Belinda said.

Josephine gave her future daughter-in-law a sharp glance and made a breathtaking statement. 'I suppose you're an advance on that Izzy girl.'

Belinda, although agreeing, looked astonished.

Backhander though it might be, she had received a compliment.

'What was wrong with Izzy Eaglewood?' I asked Josephine.

'Her mother.'

Vicky choked on some peas and needed her back patted.

When order had been restored, I said, 'What was wrong with Izzy Eaglewood's mother?'

Josephine compressed her lips but couldn't resist imparting knowledge. Now wound up, she would run and run.

She said, 'Izzy's mother was and is a tart.'

Vicky was fortunately not eating peas. She laughed delightedly and told Josephine she hadn't enjoyed a meal so much for ages. Josephine's pale cheeks faintly flushed.

'Hold on a bit,' Ken protested. 'It's not Izzy's fault what her mother is.'

'Heredity,' Josephine said darkly.

'Who is Izzy's mother?' I asked neutrally.

'Russet Eaglewood,' Josephine said. 'Such a silly name. Izzy is illegitimate, of course.'

'Leave it,' Ken begged her. He looked at me rather wildly, 'Change the subject, can't you?'

I said to Josephine obligingly, 'How about Zoë Mackintosh?'

'Who? Oh yes. Should have been born male. She's never made sheep's eyes at Ken as far as I know.'

'I didn't mean . . .' I shook my head and left it. 'I meant, are there any nice scandals about her or her family?'

'Her old father's going ga-ga, if you call that a scandal. He always was a villain. They said he would take a commission from bookmakers for telling them when a hot favourite of his wouldn't win.'

'Do go on,' said Vicky fervently.

'The Jockey Club could never prove it. Mackintosh was too slippery. I heard he lost a lot of his money a few months back in a property crash. You wouldn't think people could lose money in property the way the cost of houses goes up, but a lot of people around here did. I don't feel sorry for them, they shouldn't have been so greedy.'

'What happened?' I asked.

'I don't know exactly. A neighbour of mine lost everything. He said never guarantee a loan. I remember him saying it and I remember what he said. He's had to sell his house.'

'Poor man,' Vicky said.

'He should have had more sense.'

'Even millionaires can make that mistake,' I said. Josephine sniffed.

'How about the Nagrebb family?' I asked her.

'She's the show-jumper, isn't she? I've seen her on television. Ken looks after their horses.'

'And, um, Fitzwalter?'

'Never heard of him.' She finished her plateful, put

her knife and fork tidily together and turned to Ken. 'Isn't that man Nagrebb,' she asked, 'the one who got into trouble for training show-jumpers cruelly?'

Ken nodded.

'What did he do?' I asked.

'Rapped their shins with a pole, while they were jumping, to teach them to lift their legs higher,' Ken said. 'Difficult to prove. Show-jumpers are always rapping their legs, like hurdlers. Nagrebb's horses always had lumps and contusions on their shins. They're better these days, since he got a stiff warning.'

Belinda said, 'Nagrebb's daughter swore he didn't do it.'

Ken smiled. 'She does everything he tells her. She rode the horses while he hit their legs. She wants to win, and Daddy provides the wherewithal, and there's no way she's going to blow the whistle on him.'

'A wicked world,' Vicky said sadly.

Some degree of evil is the norm, my father had told me. Wholly good people are the aberration. What's aberration, I'd said. Look it up in the dictionary, then you'll remember it. Aberration, a deviation from what is common and normal. See the world as it is, he'd said, then see what good you can do in it. Lie abroad for your country. These inconsequential thoughts ended on the reflection that I, like Nagrebb's daughter, had been moulded by a father's cast of mind.

*

217

When the lunch party broke up I left Thetford Cottage and drove to Riddlescombe village to see how much I remembered. I'd had only vague pictures in my mind but it was a revelation how much was vividly familiar as I drove down the long straggly main street.

The post office, the garage, the pubs; all were still there. Time hadn't swept away the cottages or changed the stone houses. The pond I'd thrown stones into had shrunk as I had grown, and a small tree in whose bark I'd carved P.P. now spread limbs that would be shady in summer. I parked the car and walked, and remembered who had lived where and who had died and who had run away.

It was like walking back into a lost land that had existed for twenty years in mothballs. Henley's, the all-purpose shop, still apparently sold violent-coloured sweets and plimsoles and horror comics. Graffiti still shocked the prim in the bus shelter. Notices threatened bigger fines for litter. Volunteers were needed for rebuilding the games pavilion. The village, unlike the supermarket, was territory still well known, though the red telephone box had vanished and there was a bright new medical centre where the old doctor's house had been.

Untouched by centuries, let alone twenty years, stood the tiny ancient church to which I'd gone on Christmas mornings and not much any other time. Surrounded still by a low stone wall, a patch of grass, haphazard yews and weathered grey anonymous gravestones, it remained as always an expression of hope against hope for the life everlasting.

I supposed that in these days of normal evil it would be locked between services and I walked up its crunchy gravel path without expectation, but in fact the old latch clicked up with a familiar hollow clunk under my thumb and I pushed open the heavy wooden door to smell the musty mixture of hymn books, hassocks and altar flowers that I'd thought was the presence of God when I was six.

An elderly woman, straightening the pile of hymn books, looked round as I entered and said, 'You're too early. Evensong's three hours yet.'

Perhaps I could just look round, I suggested, and she said she saw no objection, if I was quiet. I could have ten minutes. After that she was leaving and would be turning out the lights.

I sat in a pew and watched her busy about the little turreted pulpit, running a duster over the brass rails of what I used to think of as a punch-and-judy stage, where the vicar popped into view from the chest up and read sonorous incomprehensible poetry that echoed richly off the walls.

Prayer now, I supposed, was what was really called for, but I had lost the habit and seldom felt the need. If there were spiritual sustenance within those walls, for me it lay in timelessness and silence which couldn't be achieved in the ten minutes.

I wandered to the rear of the church and read again

the small brass plaque still fixed high up incon-
spicuously.

Paul Perry. Years of birth and death. Rest in Peace.

My mother had persuaded the vicar to let it be put
there, even though Paul Perry had lived in Lambourn.
My mother had blown a kiss every Christmas Day to
the plaque, and although on this return I didn't do that,
I did wish him well, that very young horseman who'd
given me life.

I thanked the old woman. There was an offertory
box by the door, she said. I thanked her again and paid
my dues to the past, and walked on down the road to
the bungalow where we had lived.

It looked small, of course, and in the prosperous
village still seemed a poor relation. The paint was old,
the garden bare but tidy, the front gate, that I'd swung
on, missing altogether. I paused outside and wondered
whether or not to try to go in, but it would all be
different inside and I would have to start explaining,
and in the end I turned back with the old memories
undisturbed and strolled again to the car.

I decided, before I left, that I'd go up to the end of
the village, to the Eaglewood stables, and although
Sunday afternoon was a taboo time for visiting racing
stables I left the car outside and wandered in, hoping,
if anyone should see me from the windows, to look like
a lost tourist, harmless. A brief nostalgic look round
was all I intended – to see if I could better remember
the long-dead Jimmy.

In fact I got no more than six paces into the yard before being challenged with an authoritative 'Yes? Can I help you?'

I swivelled. The voice came from a thin fortyish woman in jeans and sweater who was up a stepladder fixing onto a stable wall a painted sign, bright white letters on newly varnished wood, saying 'Don't Feed the Horses'.

'Er,' I said, improvising, 'I'd been hoping to talk to Mr Eaglewood.'

'What about?'

I cleared my throat. 'About insurance.' The first thing that came into my head.

'This is an absolutely ridiculous time to do any such thing. Also we have all the insurance we need.' She regarded the sign with her head on one side, nodded to herself and came down the ladder. Another two signs, identical, were propped against the wall at its foot.

'About insuring the horses,' I said, beginning to see a purpose.

'Go away, will you? You're wasting your time.'

A chilly little breeze cooled the thin February sunshine and swirled her thick tawny hair across her face. Pushing it away, she was self-assured in her good looks. Her vitality and natural magnetism generated a force-field all of their own. She was instantly, to me at least, attractive.

She tried to pick up the ladder with one hand and

221

both signs with the other, and I caught one of the signs as it was sliding out of her grasp.

'Thanks,' she said briefly. 'Perhaps you wouldn't mind carrying it for me, though it won't get you anywhere except over there to the opposite wall.'

With a smile I followed her across the yard to where two hooks were screwed into the old brick wall at just above head height. She planted the ladder, went up a few rungs and manoeuvred the sign she was carrying until two hoops on its back engaged onto the two hooks. Once the sign hung flat against the wall she gave it the formal nod of approval and descended to the concrete underfoot.

She held out her hand for the sign I was still holding. 'Thanks,' she said. 'I can manage now.'

'I'll take it to where you want to put it.'

She shrugged, turned, and went off through an arch into a further, smaller yard beyond, and immediately I went through there I knew where the hay was stored and how to get through a tiny trapdoor into a roof space, and how to look down on the lads without their knowing that Jimmy and I were up there, spying on them. They never did anything worse than pee in the boxes; it was simply the secret of our presence that had absorbed me and Jimmy.

The third 'Don't Feed the Horses', also, was hung on pre-positioned hooks in an easily seen place.

'School parties come here once a term on projects,' she explained. 'We try to stop the little buggers handing out sweets to the inmates. For one thing, they can get their fingers bitten off, as I always warn them. They think it's clever not to listen.' She gave me a head-to-toe glance which felt like a moving X-ray through flesh and spirit. 'What sort of insurance?'

'Insuring the horses against death.'

She shook her head. 'We don't do that. It's a matter for the owners.'

'Perhaps Mr Eaglewood . . .'

'He's asleep,' she interrupted. 'And I'm the business manager. I run the finances. When the owners want to insure their horses we put them in touch with an agent. It's no use you talking to Mr Eaglewood. He leaves all such things to me.'

'Then . . . you couldn't tell me if Mr Wynn Lees insured the colt that died here in a coma last September?'

'*What?*'

I didn't repeat the question but watched a hundred speculations zip through her mind.

'Or,' I said, 'did the owner of the horse that died during a respiratory operation insure him beforehand? And – er . . . how long before the operation in which he died last Thursday did that horse split its cannon bone?'

She stared at me speechlessly as if not believing what she was hearing.

'Ken McClure is in a lot of trouble,' I said, 'and I don't think it's of his own making.'

She found her voice, which came out more with plain curiosity than anger.

'Just who are you?' she said.

'A friend of Ken's.'

'A policeman?'

'No, just a friend. The police rarely investigate the apparently normal deaths of horses.'

'What's your name?'

'Peter Darwin.'

'Any relation to Charles?'

'No.'

'Do you know who I am?' she asked.

I suggested slowly, 'Mr Eaglewood's daughter?'

I kept every vestige of a smile out of my face but she must have known her reputation.

'Whatever you've heard of me,' she said severely, 'revise it.'

'I have.'

She seemed fairly satisfied, and in any case I'd spoken the truth. I hadn't expected the brains.

'If you know Ken, you know he had a fling with my daughter,' she said.

'He's fond of her,' I said.

She shrugged philosophically. 'Izzy threw herself at him, poor little bitch. She's only seventeen, half his age. He treated her decently enough. She just grew out of it.'

'He won't hear a word against her ... or you.'

She tested that for cynicism, but seemed pleased enough.

'It's windy out here,' she said, 'and the lads will be along any minute for evening stables, making a racket. My father will be walking round. Why don't you and I go inside where we can talk quietly?'

Without waiting for my assent, she set off with the ladder to return it to a shed, and then led the way not to the big looming main house but to a small separate two-storey wing where she lived alone, she said.

'Izzy's gone off on a music course. She's much too impressionable. I expect hourly to hear she's met the perfect man. There's no such thing as a perfect man.'

Her taste in interiors ran to antique woods and classic fabrics, ultra-conservative, cool colour temperature; warm central heating. On the walls, original oils, mostly of horses. Overall, a relaxed accustomed prosperity.

She offered me an armchair and sat in another on the opposite side of the fireplace, her blue-clad legs crossed, a telephone and an address book on a small table at her elbow.

'There's no way I'm going to talk to Wynn Lees if I don't have to,' she said. 'We don't train for him any more and I won't have him in the yard. I can't understand why my father agreed to train the colt for him in the first place, knowing his reputation. But the colt died of seizures, didn't it? Or at least, Ken had to put it down.'

'Ken said that colt wasn't insured. Do you know if the other two were?'

225

'I never heard so.' She lifted the telephone receiver, looked up a number, pressed a succession of buttons, and spoke to the owner of the respiratory-tract horse, asking about insurance. The conversation seemed warm and friendly, and apparently the horse was not insured.

She repeated the conversation with the cannon-bone owner, with the same results.

'There were three days between the horse splitting its cannon bone and the operation,' she said. 'It was a stress fracture in a race. He seemed all right afterwards but the following day he was hopping lame. Ken came out with a portable X-ray and told us the bad news. My father discussed it with Ken and Carey and they both thought the leg could be screwed and the horse saved. The owner agreed to go ahead with the expense because the horse was still an entire and could be sent to stud if he didn't get back his racing form. So those two horses just simply died in the hospital. They weren't insured. My father and everyone else believes Ken was careless, if not plain negligent.'

I shook my head. 'I've watched him do a difficult and critical operation on a broodmare, and I know he couldn't be careless or negligent. He's punctiliously careful every inch of the way.'

She sat for a while thinking it over.

'Are you *seriously* saying,' she asked, 'that someone somehow engineered these two deaths?'

'Trying to find out.'

'And Ken can't suggest how?'

'Not yet.'

'But if it wasn't for insurance, what was the purpose?'

I sighed. 'To discredit Ken, perhaps.'

'But *why*?'

'He doesn't know.'

She looked at me broodingly. I thought she'd known a lot of lucky men, if the tales were true.

'Of course,' she said finally, 'someone else besides the owner could have insured those horses.'

'How?' I asked.

'We had an owner once who wouldn't pay the bills. In the end, he owed us a worrying amount. He wasn't doing well in his business and couldn't find the money. His best asset was the horse we were training for him, and eventually we could have claimed the horse against the bills, but we would have had to have sold it to get the money and my father thought he might win the Grand National and didn't want to part with him. Do you follow?'

'Yes,' I said.

'Well, he was due to run in a preliminary race and you know what it's like, horses can have accidents, and I was uneasy, so the day before the race I insured him for more than enough to cover what the owner owed us – and this is the point, I didn't tell the owner I'd done it.'

'And did the horse die?'

227

'Not in the race. He won it. He was killed in a motorway crash coming home.'

I made a sound of sympathy.

She nodded. 'Nothing could give us the horse back. The owner was astounded when I told him I'd done the insurance. I did it in his name and I suppose he could legally have taken all the money and not paid us after all, but he was honourable, just broke, and he gave us what he owed. But I *could* have insured the horse and never told him and pocketed all the money myself.'

I took a slow deep breath. 'Thank you,' I said.

'The insurers,' she said, 'might just possibly check that the name on the policy was the name of the registered owner, but even that's not certain, but they would never phone every owner to make sure the owner knew about and intended the insurance.'

'Never, anyway,' I said, 'unless they'd grown suspicious.'

'We haven't had any enquiry from any insurance company ever about proof of ownership.'

'Well,' I said, stirring. 'I can't thank you enough.'

'Like a drink?'

I listened carefully for overtones, for undertones, but there weren't any.

'That would be great,' I said.

'Scotch or wine?'

'Either.'

She rose fluidly, went over to a tray of bottles on a

table and returned with two glasses full of deep tannin-rich Bordeaux. A wine to match the woman, I thought: good staying quality, earthy, mature, great body.

'How long have you known Ken?' she asked, sitting down again.

I thought 'four days' might be inappropriate so I said merely, 'I've known his fiancée's mother longer,' which was accurate though not honest.

'Belinda!' my hostess said in wonderment. 'That bossy nurse. She's the last one I'd have picked for him.'

'She's not too bad.'

She shrugged. 'As long as they're happy.'

I drank some wine. 'They mentioned something about a boy who lived here long ago. Jimmy, wasn't it?'

Her face softened and she spoke with regret. 'My little brother.' She nodded. 'A proper little tearaway, he was.'

I willed her in silence to go on and after a moment she did. 'Always larking around with a boy from the village. They got into trouble for throwing stones at trains and a policeman in uniform came to tick Jimmy off, and the next day he was hit by a lorry and died later without regaining consciousness.' She smiled affectionately. 'Funny how some things still seem like yesterday.'

'Mm.'

'I was ten years older than Jimmy. My father had always wanted a son and he's never got over it.' She shook herself suddenly. 'I don't know why I'm burdening you with this.'

'I asked.'

'So you did.'

I was tempted to tell her I was the boy from the village but I still thought the anonymity of Peter Darwin, diplomat, might give me more chance of unravelling Ken's troubles, so I let the moment go by. She asked me in time what I did for a living, and I told her, and she asked about Japan and its ways.

'Everything possible's made from wood and paper,' I said, 'because trees grow and regrow. They are a frugal, orderly nation who continuously repress emotion from lack of space to scream and shout. Their houses are tiny. They work unremittingly hard. It's a male-dominated society and golf runs Shinto close as the observed religion.'

'But you speak with respect.'

'Oh yes. And with liking. I've left many friends there.'

'Will you go back there to live?'

'If I'm sent.'

She said with adult amusement, 'Do you always meekly go where you're sent?'

'It's a condition of the service and to me it's normal, so yes, I go.'

'I'd hate it. I grow roots in hotel rooms after one night.'

She refilled our glasses and went on talking,

switching on table lamps and drawing curtains as the light faded. I thought I had better leave but didn't make any move to, nor did I detect any 'that's enough' manoeuvres in her manner.

It's a wise man, I thought, who knows when he's being seduced.

Towards the end of the bottle came decision time. She'd made no overt suggestion, though by then all sorts of possibilities hung almost visibly in the air. I mentally ran through various forms of verbal invitation and came up with the least maudlin, the least lustful, the most humorous, the easiest to refuse.

Into a long smiling silence, lolling back in the armchair, I said casually, 'How about a bonk, then?'

She laughed. 'Is that Foreign Office standard phraseology?'

'Heard all the time in embassies.'

She'd long had the intention and I hadn't misread her.

'No strings,' she said. 'Passing ships.'

I nodded.

'Upstairs,' she said economically, taking my glass

So Russet Eaglewood and I enjoyed a lengthy nostrings bonk, and it was all true, not a knicker in sight.

CHAPTER EIGHT

The next morning, Monday, I went down to the hospital to meet Ken in the office and found he'd been called out to deal with an acute laminitis.

This information came from Oliver Quincy who had taken up the position he most coveted, the padded chair behind the desk.

'After that,' Quincy said, 'there's a wind op on Ken's schedule and this afternoon a referral from another practice, as long as they don't back out, so whatever you want will have to wait until after the next disaster.'

He wasn't especially friendly: the comforting bedside manner wasn't to be switched on and wasted on the declared ally of the man he intended to oust.

'What's your gripe against Ken, actually?' I asked.

'You know perfectly well. He fucks it up.'

'He's a good surgeon.'

'Was.' He stared at me judiciously. 'You've seen him operate just once. You know nothing. You're no judge. He shouldn't have let the cannon bone die last Thursday.'

'You were there. Could you have prevented it?'

'Of course not. Not my case. I wouldn't interfere in anyone else's case.'

'Why do you think the horse died?'

He went on staring and didn't answer. If he knew, he wasn't telling. If he'd known how to stop it, he hadn't told Ken. I didn't much like his company so wandered back into the car park and stood for a while watching the comings and goings of a full-blown small animals' session in the Portakabin.

Belinda was working there: I caught sight of her in her white lab coat as she came occasionally to the doorway, helping people with armfuls of cat or dog to manoeuvre up and down the steps.

The police had put a barrier across the back of the burned building, warning off foolhardy sightseers. Far away down the side drive I could see the unceasing activity of serious officialdom, still pecking away in search of guilt.

Over by the stable boxes, Scott was seeing to the unloading from a horse trailer of a skittish horse with flaring nostrils and tossing head, a horse full of vim and vigour looking not in the least ill. A groom with him led him into one of the empty boxes, bolting him in but leaving the top half of the door open. The horse's head appeared there immediately to watch the activity outside.

I strolled over as the trailer plus groom drove out

of the car park and asked Scott if the broodmare was still progressing.

'Doing well,' he said. 'Her owner's with her at this moment.'

'He's not?' I said, alarmed.

Scott said, shrugging, seeing no danger, 'He has every right. She's his property.'

The top half of the mare's box was also bolted back, and I went to it without delay and looked in.

Wynn Lees was standing there looking critically at the mare's big belly, his own pelvis thrust forward in such a way as to give him a big belly of his own. He saw the light change with my arrival to the doorway and turned enquiringly my way, his fleshy face already set in a scowl.

He barely remembered me from Friday morning except as some sort of assistant. He raised in me the same hackles as always.

'Get Carey to come here,' he said truculently. 'I'm not satisfied with this.'

I turned away and asked Scott for Carey's whereabouts. Over in the Portakabin for the clinic, Scott said, so I went over there and delivered the message.

'What does he want?' Carey asked, walking back with me.

'He said he wasn't satisfied.'

'He's a confounded nuisance, coming here like this.'

He went into the mare's box but all I could hear of the conversation were remarks concerning the continuation of antibiotics, the removal of the staples and the approaching birth of the foal. After a short while, both men came out not looking overly fond of each other, the one to leave in his Rolls, the other to go back to his invalids.

Scott and I looked over the door at the mare, who seemed quiet and unconcerned, and Scott decided to move her along the row to the far end box, to leave the intensive care box free for the new patients. I walked along with him as he led the great pregnant creature and asked another question.

'Last Thursday,' I said, 'when the cannon-bone horse died, did you notice anything you wouldn't expect in the trace on the screen? The electrocardiograph trace, I mean.'

'Nothing I hadn't seen before. Nothing to worry about.'

'Um . . . would you have seen it often before?'

'Often enough. Look,' he sounded aggrieved, 'is Ken trying to say it was my fault the horse died? Because I'll tell you straight, it wasn't.'

I said soothingly, 'Ken says you're a very good anaesthetist.'

'And anyway, Oliver was watching the screen as well as me, you know.'

'Mm.'

I thought back to my own stint in front of the screen. I'd been concerned only about the regularity and power of the heartbeats, not about the exact shape of the trace. Unless it had changed to a row of Donald Ducks I wouldn't have noticed, and by the sound of things, if there had been any change at all, it had been subtle enough not to have registered even with Ken until I'd jogged his memory long afterwards.

Scott led the mare into the box and bolted the bottom half of her door and before I could think of anything else to ask him a small plain white van swirled into the car park and pulled up with a jerk. Scott gave it a disparaging look and strode muscularly over to greet the driver.

'Took your time, didn't you?' he said.

'Now you look, mate . . .' The driver hopped out belligerently. 'My life's one long emergency call and I like a bit of appreciation.'

Carey in his white lab coat hurried out of the Porta-kabin again as if he'd been waiting for this minute and gave the van driver all the appreciation he felt was his due.

'Good. Good. Well done,' Carey was saying, going round to the van's rear doors. 'Take it all into the office in the hospital. We'll unpack and distribute from there.'

The van, it appeared, contained replacements for essentials destroyed in the burned pharmacy. It reminded me of the previous morning in the Portakabin and I went a few paces and offered Carey my sugges-tion for making the 'lost' list that the policeman had wanted.

'I just thought,' I said diffidently, 'that if you asked

all your suppliers to send duplicate invoices going back over, say, six months or whatever time you thought sensible, you'd have a pretty accurate inventory, allowing for daily or weekly usage.'

He looked at me vaguely for long enough for me to begin to wonder if the marbles were indeed leaking away, but then his gaze sharpened and came alive with understanding.

'Good idea. Yes. A comprehensive list from the wholesalers and no need for us to rack our brains. I wasn't sure what you meant, at first. Well done. Get Ken to see to it, will you?'

He bustled off after the driver, who was carrying armfuls of boxes into the hospital, and I thought ruefully that Ken wouldn't thank me for the extra work. I followed him into the office and found Scott there, inspecting and carefully checking off each arriving box against a delivery note running to several pages.

Oliver Quincy's contribution to the activity was practically nil. He was waiting, he grumbled, for the appearance of worm powders as he couldn't go on his morning's first errand without them. Once they'd been identified and marked present, he took what he needed and departed, and Carey gave his back view a look of puzzled disappointment.

Ken himself returned at that point, blowing in with a gale of enthusiasm for the renewed supplies.

'Did the wind-op horse come?' he asked.

'Out in a box,' Scott nodded.

'I thought they might cry off.'

Carey cleared his throat. 'I'm afraid I told him . . . I mean, I had to promise the owner I would . . . er . . . attend the procedure.'

Ken demanded, 'Do you mean, do the op yourself?'

'No. No. Just assist.' From his voice, though, it had been a close run thing.

Ken swallowed the insult to his ability as just another bitter pill in his mounting troubles and asked me to be there as well to take notes.

Scott looked surprised, Carey said it wasn't necessary, Ken stuck his toes in. 'Will you?' he said to me, and I said, 'Yes,' and it was fixed.

Lucy Amhurst came in on a search for the new drugs and gave me a nod of friendly acceptance.

'How's the sleuthing?' she asked.

'Brick on brick,' I said. 'Slowly.'

'What sleuthing?' Carey asked.

'Surely you remember?' Lucy said. 'We gave him the go-ahead yesterday morning to see what he could do for Ken. Oh no,' she exclaimed, 'you weren't there, of course.' I guessed she was herself remembering the anti-Carey conversation, as her cheeks went slowly red. 'We didn't see any harm in letting Peter find out whatever he could if it would help Ken.'

'No, that's fine,' Carey nodded. 'I agree.' To me he said, 'Go ahead. Do what you can. An amateur detective!'

'He's a civil servant,' Lucy said.

'A snoop,' Scott added, using Jay Jardine's word.

Carey raised an eyebrow at me in amusement, said he hoped the drains were up to snuff and went back to his dogs and cats, telling Ken to let him know when he was ready to operate.

'Drains?' Scott asked, mystified, after he'd gone.

'Red tape,' I said.

'Oh.'

Lucy, the wise woman, suggested Ken and Scott store the drugs somewhere safe, then took what she herself needed and followed Carey.

'Do you keep a list of who takes what?' I asked.

'We do normally,' Ken said. 'We have a book. Had.' He sighed. 'We all keep a stack of things in our cars, as you know. I'd never be sure at any given moment what I had.'

He decided to put everything on the shelves in one of the store rooms as the drugs cupboard wouldn't hold everything, and I helped him and Scott carry the boxes across and arrange them in logical order.

I wanted Ken's undivided attention for an hour, but didn't get it. He sat in the padded chair and insisted on writing his notes on the steeplechaser with laminitis that he'd just visited.

'Funny thing,' he said, pausing and looking up at me, 'they say the horse was quite all right yesterday.'

'What about it?' I asked.

'It reminded me . . .' He stopped, frowning, and went on slowly. 'You're making me see things differently.'

239

Do get on with it, I thought, but prodded him more gently. 'What have you thought of?'

'Another of Nagrebb's show-jumpers.'

'Ken.' Some of my impatience must have shown because he gave his shoulders a shake and said what was in his mind.

'One of Nagrebb's show-jumpers had laminitis . . .'

'What exactly is laminitis?'

'It's an inflammation of the lamina, which is a layer of tissue between the hoof wall and the bone of the foot. Sometimes it flares up and the sufferers hobble around, other times they seem perfectly all right. The condition makes them stiff. If you get the animal moving, exercising, the stiffness wears off, but it always comes back. So, anyway, one of Nagrebb's horses developed it and Nagrebb was annoyed I couldn't cure it. Then one day last autumn he called me out, and there was this same jumper in the field literally unable to move. Nagrebb said he'd left the horse out all night as it was warm enough, and in the morning he'd found him in this extreme stage of laminitis. It wasn't just in his two forefeet, as it had been, but in all four. Like I said, the poor animal simply couldn't move. I'd told Nagrebb not to give him too much grass as that always makes it worse, but he'd put him in the field anyway. I said we could try to save the horse, though frankly his feet were literally falling apart and it was a very poor prognosis. Nagrebb decided to put him out of his misery and called the knackers at once. But now, thanks to you,

240

I wonder . . . but even Nagrebb wouldn't do that . . . but
then there's that tendon . . .'

'*Ken!*' I said.

'Oh, yes. Well, you see, you could *give* a horse laminitis pretty easily.'

'How?'

'All you'd need to do is put a tube down into its
oesophagus and pour a gallon or so of sugar solution
into its stomach.'

'What – '

He anticipated the question. 'Several pounds of
sugar dissolved in water to make a syrup. A huge
amount of sugar or any carbohydrate all at once would
result in very severe laminitis not many hours later.'

God, I thought. No end to the villainous possibilities.

'The opposite of insulin,' I said.

'What? Yes, I suppose so. But the insulin colt was
Wynn Lees' at Eaglewood's.'

'You said it would be pretty easy to put a tube down
into a horse's oesophagus,' I remarked. 'Not for me, it
wouldn't.'

'Child's play for Nagrebb. He could do it with a
twitch. A twitch is . . .'

Yes, I nodded, I knew. A twitch was a tight short
loop of rope attached to a short length of pole and
twisted round the soft end of horse's nose and upper
lip. Held by that, any horse would stand still because
it was painful to move.

'If he did it,' I said, 'there's no way of finding out.'

241

Ken nodded gloomily. 'And what would be the point?'

'Insurance,' I said.

'You keep on about insurance.'

I brought a couple of folded sheets of paper out of my pocket and said I wanted to show him some lists.

'No, not now. Later. I simply want to do these notes before the op. I shouldn't have wasted all this time. Show me the lists later, OK?'

'OK.' I watched him scribble for a bit and asked if I could use the telephone, if he didn't mind. He pointed to it for acquiescence and I got through to the Foreign Office, reversing the charges.

It took a while to reach the right desk. I was reporting my presence in England, I said. When did they want me to darken the Whitehall doorway?

'Ah.' Papers were audibly shuffled. 'Here we are. Darwin. Four years in Tokyo. Accrued and terminal leave, eight weeks.' A throat was cleared. 'Where does that put you?'

'Three weeks today.'

'Fine.' Relief at the precision. 'Let's say . . . er . . . three weeks today, then. Splendid. I'm making a note.'

'Thank you very much.'

'Not at all.'

Smiling, I put down the receiver. They'd given me a fortnight longer than I expected, which meant I could go to Cheltenham races, held during the last of those weeks, without dereliction of duty.

Ken had finished his notes.

'One more quick one?' I asked, lifting the phone.

'Sure. Then we'll get started.'

I asked Enquiries for the Jockey Club and I asked the Jockey Club for Annabel.

'Annabel?'

'In public relations.'

'Hold on.'

Remarkably, she was there.

'It's Peter,' I said. 'How are the Japanese?'

'They leave today.'

'How about dinner tomorrow in London?'

'Can't do tomorrow. How about tonight?'

'Where will I find you?'

She sounded amused. 'Daphne's restaurant, Draycott Avenue.'

'Eight o'clock?'

'See you,' she said. 'Got to rush.' The phone disconnected before I could even say goodbye.

Ken looked at my expression. 'Two bits of good news in one morning! Like a cat that's tipped over the goldfish.' With awakening alarm he went on, 'You're not leaving, though, are you?'

'Not yet.' His alarm remained, so I added, 'Not if there's anything I can do.'

'I rely on you,' he said.

I could have said that to me what I was doing was like walking through a fog of confetti looking for one scarlet dot, but it would have increased his worries. I thought he wouldn't have minded much if his patient hadn't turned up that morning because in spite of his success with the broodmare he was again looking pale and apprehensive.

The operation however went smoothly from start to finish. Carey watched intently. I watched and took notes. Scott and Belinda moved expertly as Ken's satellites and the prancing horse, fast asleep, got its larynx firmed and widened to improve its breathing.

From behind the safe section of wall, we watched him wake in the recovery room, Scott holding the rope-through-the-ring to steady him. He staggered to his feet looking miserable but most decisively alive.

'Good,' Carey said, going off to the office. 'I promised to phone the owner.'

Ken gave me a glance of rueful relief, and he and I stripped off our gowns and left Scott and Belinda to clear the theatre again ready for the afternoon stint, while also checking on the patient continually.

'You all work hard,' I commented.

'We're under-staffed. We need a couple of dogs-bodies. Would you like a permanent job?'

He didn't expect an answer. We went into the office where Carey was giving his thumbs-up report and after Carey had gone he finally said it was time for my list.

I brought it, much creased from folding, out of my trousers pocket, smoothed it down on the desk and added to it one more line. We sat in the chairs side by side and I explained what he was seeing.

'The list on the left of the page,' I said, 'is of the owners and trainers whose horses have died with question marks, to say the least. The middle column is the various ways they may or may not have died. The list on the right is . . . well . . .'

Ken looked at the list on the right and protested immediately, as it named all his partners plus Belinda and Scott.

'They're not involved,' he insisted.

'All right. Look at the first and second columns, then.'

'OK.'

I'd written in table form:

Wynn Lees/ Eaglewood	Colt with Insulin	Put down in stable
Wynn Lees/ Vernonside Stud	Broodmare/ needle	(Alive)
Mackintosh	Colic from atropine?	Died on table
Mackintosh	Colic from atropine?	Died on table
Eaglewood	Respiratory tract	Died on table
Eaglewood	Cannon bone	Died on table
Fitzwalter	Chipped knee	Died in intensive care
Nagrebb	Show-jumper/ dissolved tendon	Put down on table

| Nagrebb | Show-jumper/ laminitis | Put down in field |

'Whew,' Ken said thoughtfully, reading to the end.

'Are there any others?'

'Not that I can think of.' He paused. 'We had one that broke its leg thrashing around when it came out of the anaesthetic after a successful colic operation. You've seen two satisfactory awakenings. They're not always so peaceful. We had to put that horse down.'

'All the horses that died on the table,' I pointed out, 'could have been there by appointment.' I forestalled his objection. 'If two were given atropine, their time was chosen. They weren't random emergencies.'

'No, I suppose not.'

'The respiratory job had been booked in well in advance,' I said, 'and that cannon bone was fractured three days before you screwed it.'

'How do you know?' he asked surprised. 'I thought he'd done it the day before.'

'It was a stress fracture in a race last Monday.'

'How do you know?' he repeated, mystified.

'I ... er ... drifted up to Eaglewood's stable yesterday afternoon and asked.'

'You did *what*? Didn't old Eaglewood throw you out?'

'I didn't see him. Someone in the stable yard told me.'

'Great God.'

'So all the deaths on the table very likely had a common premeditated cause, and it's up to you to work out what.'

'But I don't know.' His despair surfaced again. 'If I knew I wouldn't be in this mess.'

'I think you probably do know in some dark recess or other. I've great faith that one of these days a blinding light will switch on in your brain and make sense of everything.'

'But I've thought and thought.'

'Mm. That's where the third list comes in.'

'No.'

'It has to,' I said reasonably. 'Do any of Lees, Eaglewood, Mackintosh, Fitzwalter or Nagrebb have the knowledge to accomplish all this? Has any of them had the opportunity?'

He silently shook his head.

'The knowledge,' I said, 'is veterinary.'

'Let's stop this right away.'

'It's for your own sake,' I said.

'But they're my friends. My partners.'

Partners weren't always friends, I thought. He was still raising barriers against belief: a common enough mechanism encountered perennially in embassies.

I didn't want to antagonize him or force him into destructive self analysis. He would come to things in time. Understanding, as I'd grown to see it, was often a matter of small steps, small realizations, small sudden visitations of 'Oh, yes'. As far as Ken's problems were concerned I was still a long way from the 'Oh, yes' stage. I hoped that perhaps we might reach it together.

'Incidentally,' I said, 'you know the pharmacy list the police want?'

He nodded.

'Carey agrees it would be a good idea to ask your suppliers for copies of their invoices for six months back or maybe more. He asked me to ask if you would do it.'

He predictably groaned. 'One of the secretaries can do it.'

'I just thought,' I said diffidently, 'that if you did it yourself, you could get the invoices sent back to you personally.'

'What for?'

'Um . . . just suppose, for instance . . .' I came to it slowly. 'Just suppose someone here had ordered something like . . . collagenase.'

The pale eyes stared as if they would never blink. After a long pause he said, 'That wouldn't come from our regular wholesale suppliers. It would have to come from a chemical company dealing with research reagents for laboratory use only.'

'Do you deal with any of those companies for the laboratory here?'

'Well, yes, we do.'

A silence settled.

He sighed heavily. 'All right,' he said at length. 'I'll

write to them. I'll write to all I can think of. I hope they all come back negative. I'm sure they will.'

'Quite likely,' I agreed, and hoped not.

The afternoon's operation, with Carey coming in tired but vigilant and myself taking notes, passed off without crisis. The more accustomed I became to the general theatre routine the more impressed I was by Ken in action: his long-fingered hands were steady and deft, his whole oddly articulated height taking on an economical grace where one might have expected gangling clumsiness. His self-doubts seemed to evaporate every time once he had a scalpel in his hand and I supposed that that really was to be expected, because the doubts were thrust upon him from outside, not generated within.

He closed the incision with a neat row of staples and the hoist once again lifted the big inert body by its feet to transport it to the padded recovery room. Everyone followed and waited in safety behind the breast-high partition while the patient staggered and lunged back to consciousness, to stand in dumb and no doubt sore bewilderment.

'Good. Good,' Carey said again, sighing nevertheless. 'Nothing wrong with that.'

He still looked over-tired, I thought, still grey. He seemed to be functioning in irregular spurts of energy, not, like Scott, with inexhaustible stamina.

As if to confirm my impression, he rubbed a hand

249

over his face and round his neck, easing out stiffness, and said, 'I've asked Lucy to be on call instead of me. That makes Lucy and Jay tonight. Let's hope it's a quiet one. I'm going home.'

Ken and I went with him along to the office where he phoned the referring vets to tell them their horse was recovering normally. In his voice there was only a taking-it-for-granted tone; no hint of excessive relief. Oliver Quincy, who'd been writing notes all afternoon while monitoring the closed circuit television to check continually on the well-being of the morning's patient, said grumpily it was about time he was relieved.

'Jay's been spelling me,' he protested, 'but this isn't my job. It's Scott's or Belinda's.'

'We must all muck in,' Carey said, seeing no difficulty. 'Where's Jay now?'

'Taking what he wants of the new drugs. Yvonne and Lucy have been in doing that as well. I got them to write down what they took.'

'Good. Good,' Carey said.

Oliver gave him an unfriendly glance which he didn't notice, and said that as he had two calls to make on his way home, he'd better be going. Jay put his head in briefly with much the same message, and they left together, thick as thieves.

Ken began writing his own professional notes to supplement those I'd taken and through the window I watched Carey go out to his car and drive away. I borrowed the phone again and got through to Vicky, telling her I was going to London and not to be scared if she heard me coming back in the early hours, or even later. 'Thank you, dear,' she said. She sounded bored, I thought.

Ken looked up from his task. 'All right for some,' he said.

'You've got yours on the doorstep.'

He grinned. 'Is Annabel the girl at Stratford?'

'She is.'

'You don't waste time.'

'This is just a reconnaissance.'

'You know,' he said unexpectedly, 'I can't imagine you getting drunk.'

'Try harder.'

He shook his head in friendly evaluation. 'You wouldn't want to lose that much control.'

He surprised me, and not just because he was right.

'You've only known me since Thursday,' I said, repeating his own reservations.

'I basically knew you in half an hour.' He hesitated. 'Funny, that, Vicky told me the same.'

'Yeah,' I said. 'An open book.' I smiled and prepared to go. 'See you tomorrow.'

'See you.'

I left the hospital and walked across the car park to the car. I would be early for the planned meeting: I'd have time for buying newspapers with accommodation ads. I'd get to know how difficult it would be to find somewhere to live, and how expensive.

Belinda came out of the hospital and went into the intensive care box briefly to get it ready for the new incumbent. Leaving the first door wide open, she then took a look in the next box, where the morning's patient stood, and after that went along for a routine peek at the mare. I watched her trim capable figure and wondered if time and motherhood would soften or harden her caring instincts. Some nurses grew gentle, some unsympathetic. A toss up, I thought.

She unbolted the mare's door and went in, and came tearing out at high speed yelling, 'Ken, Ken.' She ran into the hospital and I thought, 'Oh, God, no,' and went over to the end box to see.

The big mare lay on her side.

There were no heaving breaths, no agitation in the limbs. The head lay floppily. The liquid eye looked grey, opaque, unseeing.

The mare was dead.

Ken came at a run, stricken. He fell on his knees beside her and put his ear to her brown body behind the shoulder, but one could see from his face that there was nothing to hear.

He sat back on his heels as moved and devastated as if she'd been a child, and I saw and understood his dedicated love of horses and the solicitude he unstintingly lavished on them without any thought or possibility of thanks.

I thought of the courage he'd dredged up to operate on that mare. Thought of the extreme skill he'd summoned to save her life while believing he was risking his own future. Felt impotently angry that so much holy nerve, so much artistry had gone to waste. In a way missing before, when I'd only heard about murdered horses but hadn't seen one, I felt personally engaged in avenging them. It was no longer just for Ken and to please my mother that I'd do my utmost to pierce the fog, but now too for the horses themselves, the silent splendid victims with no defence against predatory man.

'She shouldn't have died,' Ken said numbly. 'She was out of danger.'

It was a fraction too soon, I judged, to say I disagreed. Danger, in that place, wore many faces.

He smoothed his hand over the brown flank, then rose and knelt again, this time by her head, lifting the drooping eyelid, opening the mouth, peering down her throat.

'She's been dead for some time,' he said. He stood up wearily and trembled as of old. 'We'll never survive this. It's the absolute end.'

'It's not your fault.'

'How do I know? How does anyone know?'

Belinda, in the doorway, said defensively, 'She was all right at lunch time. When we brought the wind-op gelding out here I came along and checked, and she was eating hay, quite all right.'

Ken was only half listening. 'We'll have to have a post mortem,' he said dully. 'I'll see if I can get any blood.' He walked away disjointedly towards his car

253

and after a while returned with a case containing syringes, bottles and a supply of rubber gloves from the well-stocked boot.

'I phoned the knackers on the car phone,' he said. 'They're coming to fetch her. I told them we'd need to do a post-mortem at their place, and I'll have to get Carey and any number of outside vets to be there, and I don't think I'm going to do the post-mortem myself. I mean ... I can't. And as for what Wynn Lees will say ...'

His voice stopped; the shakes didn't.

'He was here this morning,' I said.

'Dear God.'

I described what I'd seen of Wynn Lees' visit. 'The mare was all right when he left. Scott moved her along to the end box afterwards and she was fine. You ask Carey.'

Ken looked down at the corpse. 'God knows what Carey will say about this.'

'If he's got any sense he'll start thinking about poison.'

It was Belinda who protested that I was being melo-dramatic, not Ken.

'But last time,' he said, taking the idea in his stride, 'when the Fitzwalter horse dropped dead out here, all the tests we could think of were negative. No poison. It cost us a lot in specialist lab fees, and all for nothing.'

'Try again.'

Without answering, he pulled on a pair of gloves

and tried with several syringes to draw blood from various areas in the mare's anatomy.

'How did you say you would give a horse atropine?' I asked.

'Inject it or scatter it on its feed. But this isn't atropine.'

'No, but test its feed anyway.'

He nodded. 'Makes sense. Water, too. Belinda, see if you can find two glass jars with tight lids. There ought to be some specimen jars in the cupboard under the drugs cupboard.'

Belinda went off without question, accustomed to being given orders in the line of duty. Ken shook his head over his task and muttered about the speed with which blood started decomposing after death.

'And the foal,' he said with a deep sigh. 'Such a *waste.*'

I said, 'What are we going to do with that needle you cut out of her gut?'

'God knows. What do you think? Does it matter any more?'

'It does if Wynn Lees ever mentions it.'

'But he hasn't.'

'No,' I agreed, 'but if he shoved it down her throat he must be *wondering* . . . He might just ask, one day.'

'All it would prove would be that he did want the mare dead and did his best to kill her, and he might be prosecuted for cruelty, but I wouldn't put any bets on a conviction. Every vet in the kingdom would testify that cats and dogs swallow sewing needles and stitch their guts into knots.'

He began to label the phials containing the pathetic samples of blood.

'I'll divide each sample into two and send them to two different labs,' he said. 'Double check.'

I nodded.

'Also we'll take umpteen sections of tissue from her organs at the post-mortem, and I tell you, there will be no results, like before, because we don't know what to look for.'

'You're such a pessimist.'

'With reason.'

He produced from the bag a large rectal thermometer and took the internal temperature, explaining it helped to indicate the time of death. Horses, because of their body mass, retained heat for hours and the result could be approximate only.

Belinda returned with two suitable jars into which she put and labelled samples of water from the half empty bucket and hay from the half empty net. There was no doubt that the mare had drunk and eaten from those sources.

Scott came fast on Belinda's heels and couldn't contain his feelings, a mixture of disbelief, rage and fear of being held responsible, as far as I could see.

'I put her in the box. I even gave her new water and fresh hay and she was right as rain. Peter will tell you. There's just no way she could be dead.'

No one bothered to say that, one way or another, she was.

Ken stripped off his gloves, finished packing the samples, snapped the case shut and stood up to his six foot four.

'Who's looking after this afternoon's patient?' he said. 'Scott, go and check at once. Belinda, set up the drip in the intensive care box. We can move him out here soon, then Scott can oversee him all evening. He's not to be left alone, even if I have to sit on a chair all night outside his door.' He gave me a wild look, still shattered for all his surface decisiveness. 'I'll have to tell Carey.'

I went with him into the office and listened to the fateful phone call. Carey on the other end received the news not with screeching fury but with silence.

'Carey?' Ken said anxiously. 'Did you hear what I said?'

It appeared that he had heard and was speechless.

Ken told him he'd talked to the knackers; told him he wanted an outside vet to do the post-mortem; told him Peter suggested they look for poison.

That last sentence produced a sharp reaction which I couldn't quite hear but which surprised and embarrassed Ken. He skipped on hurriedly to his opinion that the mare had been dead at least two hours when Belinda found her. Two hours, he said, clearly having done some thinking, meant a possible or probable period when he (Ken) and Carey and Belinda and Scott and Peter had all been together in the theatre, engaged in a long operation. Who knew, he said, what had been going on outside?

There was a lengthy issue of scratchy noises of disapproval from the telephone until finally Ken said, 'Yes. Yes, OK,' and slowly put down the receiver.

'He won't believe anyone deliberately killed the mare. He says you're panicking.' Ken looked at me apologetically. 'I suppose I shouldn't have told him what you think.'

'It doesn't matter. Is he coming here?'

He shook his head. 'He's going to fix the post mortem for tomorrow morning and he's going to tell Wynn Lees, which is one chore I'm very relieved to get out of.'

'Wynn Lees might know already.'

'Jeez.' Ken said.

I scorched the tyres to London not even in time for my appointment and with no chance of newspapers. I solved the problem of my sketchy if not non-existent knowledge of most of London by stopping at a multistorey car park as soon as I was off the M40 and letting a taxi find Draycott Avenue and Daphne's restaurant, which it achieved irritatingly slowly.

Annabel, efficiently, had arrived on time. I was seventeen minutes late. She was sitting primly at a table for two, a single glass of wine before her.

'Sorry,' I said, taking the opposite chair.

'Excuses?'

'A dead horse. A hundred miles. Dearth of taxis. Traffic.'

'I suppose that will do.' The small mouth curved. 'What dead horse?'

I told her in some detail and no doubt with heat.

'You care,' she said when I'd finished.

'Yes, I do. Anyway . . .' I shook my head dismissing it, 'did the oriental chums get off all right?'

She said they had. We consulted menus and chose, and I took stock of the surroundings and of herself.

She'd come dressed again in black and white: black skirt, loose harlequin back-and-white top with big black pompoms for buttons down the front. The cropped frizzy hair looked fluffy from recent washing and she wore gentle eye make-up and pale pink lipstick. I didn't know how much was normal to her or how much she'd done for the evening's benefit, but I definitely liked the result.

As at Stratford she effortlessly established a neutral zone around herself, across which she would be friendly to a point. The amusement in her big eyes was like a moat, I thought, dug for the deterrence of over-the-top attentions.

The narrow restaurant was packed and noisy, the waiters hurrying precariously holding big trays head high.

'Lucky to get a table,' I commented, looking round.

'I booked.'

I smiled. Effective public relations. 'I've no idea where I am,' I said. 'In terms of London, I mean.'

'Just off the Fulham Road, less than a mile from Harrods.' She considered me, her head on one side. 'Are you really looking for somewhere to live?'

'Three weeks today,' I said, nodding, 'I start work in Whitehall. What should I do if it's not to be a grating?'

'Are you rolling?'

I laughed. 'I've got a huge promotion in career terms at half the income I had before.'

'Impossible.'

I shook my head. 'In Tokyo, I had more than my salary again in cost of living supplements, entertainment allowances, free food and the use of a car. Over here, zilch. Severe drop in living standards, one might say. Over there I had diplomatic immunity if I got a parking ticket. Here, too bad, no immunity from anything, pay the fine. Britain, incidentally, is the only country in the world that doesn't give its diplomats diplomatic passports. There's a whole lot of no feather-bedding.'

'Poor dears.'

'Mm. So I need somewhere to lay my head, but not too many frills.'

'Will you share?'

'Anything, for a start.'

'I could put out a few feelers.'

'I'd be grateful.'

She ate snails, adept with the tongs. I, still uncertain of my way in my own country, had settled for safe old pâté and toast.

'Do you have a last name?' I asked, eating.

'Nutbourne. Do you?'

'Darwin. As in, but not descended.'

'You must always be asked.'

'Pretty often.'

'And, um, is your father, say, a bus driver?'

'Does it matter?'

'It doesn't *matter*. It's just interesting.'

'He's another diplomat, then. And yours?'

She chewed the last snail and put the tongs and fork down neatly.

'A clergyman,' she said. She looked at me carefully, waiting for a response. I guessed that was why she'd brought up occupations in the first place, to tell me that fact, not to worry about my own background.

I said judicially, 'Some perfectly good people are clergymen's daughters.'

She smiled, the eyes crinkling, the pink mouth an upturning arc. 'He wears gaiters,' she said.

'Ah. That's more serious.' And so it was. One trod softly around a bishop if one were a sensible little private secretary with good prospects in the Foreign Office, and especially around one who thought the Foreign Office did more harm than good. One didn't take any bishop's daughter lightly. It explained everything, I thought, about the touch-me-not aura:

she was vulnerable to gossip and wouldn't incur it needlessly.

'My father's an ambassador,' I said, 'to be fair.'

'Thanks,' she said.

'It doesn't mean we can't turn cartwheels naked in Hyde Park.'

'It does,' she said. 'The virtues of the fathers are visited on the children, just like sins. Millstones aren't in it.'

'They don't always deter.'

'They deter me,' she said flatly, 'for my own sake, as well as Dad's.'

'Why did you choose the Jockey Club?' I asked.

She smiled vividly. 'The old boy network heard of my existence and proposed it. They blinked a bit when they saw my clothes and still gulp politely. Otherwise we get on OK because I know what I'm doing.'

We progressed to Dover soles and I asked her if there was anyone in the Jockey Club who was a specialist in fraudulent insurance claims on dead horses.

She looked at me soberly. 'You think that's what's been happening?'

'Almost certainly, unless we have a fixated psychopath on the loose.'

She thought it over. 'I'm pretty good friends with the deputy director of the security service,' she said. 'I could ask him to meet you.'

'Could you? When?'

'If you'll just wait until I've finished my dinner, I'll phone him.'

Sleuthing took a step back while Annabel Nutbourne carefully cleared every particle from the fish bones and left a skeleton as bare as an anatomy lesson.

'Do you have suitors in droves?' I asked.

She flicked me an amused glance. 'Only one at a time.'

'How about now?'

'Don't they teach you diplomacy in the Foreign Office?'

The gibe was earned, I supposed. Where was the oblique approach that I'd practised so often? A cool honey-pot could make an instant fool of a healthy drone.

'Heard any good sermons lately?' I asked.

'It's better to be a buffoon than a lout, I suppose.'

'Do I say thanks?'

'If you have any sense.' She laughed at me, malice absent. There were fewer insecurities, I thought, beneath that confident exterior, than one met normally. I was more accustomed to drying eyes than being teased by them.

I thought of Russet Eaglewood, whose insecurities couldn't be guessed at and whose reputation had passed into legend. A selfish, generous, passionate, passive, devouring, laughing lover she'd been by turns, and Annabel might be all of those things if the time were right, but I didn't think I would loll back in my chair that evening and say 'How about a bonk, then?' to Miss Nutbourne.

She chose cappuccino coffee with nutmeg on top for us both and after that, while I paid the bill, she made the phone call.

'He says,' she reported, 'no time like the present.'

'Really?' I was as surprised as pleased. 'How lucky he's in.'

'In?' She laughed. 'He's never in. He just has a telephone growing out of his ear. I've ordered a taxi.'

Efficient transport, she said, was part of her job.

The deputy director of the security service of the Jockey Club met us in the entrance hall of a gaming club, and signed us in as guests. He was big in a useful way, broad shouldered, heavy topped, flat bellied, with long legs. The watchful eyes of his trade made me speculate on a police past, upper ranks.

'Brose,' Annabel said, rubbing his arm in greeting, 'this is Peter Darwin. Don't ask him, he isn't.' To me she said in introduction, 'John Ambrose. Call him Brose.'

He shook my hand; nothing indecisive about that, either.

'Do you understand blackjack?' he asked me.

'Twenty-one? More or less.'

'Annabel?'

'The same.'

Brose nodded and led us through swing doors into a wide stretch of gaming room where life was lived on green baize under bright low-slung lights. Slightly to my surprise it was noisy, and the stakes, I was relieved to find, weren't immediately ruinous. Brose steered us to a deserted blackjack table without a croupier and told us everything comes to him who waits.

'Order lemonade,' he said. 'I'll be back.'

He set off into the busy throng of punters who were determinedly putting little pieces of plastic where they believed their luck was, and we could see him from time to time leaning over people's shoulders and speaking into their ears.

'You wouldn't believe it,' Annabel said, 'but what he's doing is putting the fear of God into a lot of seamy characters from the racecourses. He goes round the clubs keeping tabs on them and they hate it. He says anyone sweating over losing is ripe for trouble, and besides that he gets told things on the quiet that put crooks out of business and keep racing at least halfway honest.'

'Did he literally mean lemonade?'

'Oh, I expect so. He doesn't drink alcohol and he has to account for everything he spends here. We wouldn't rate champagne.'

We settled for fizzy water instead and in time a few more people came to sit at our table where eventually a croupier appeared, broke open new packs, shuffled for ever, pushed the cards to a wheezy fat man to cut and then fed them into a shoe.

Most of the newcomers had brought chips with them. Annabel and I each bought twenty and played conservatively and in short order she'd doubled hers and I was down to two.

'You'll never win taking a card on fifteen,' Brose said in my ear. 'The odds are against it. Unless the dealer turns up a ten or face card, stick on twelve and bet the house will go bust.'

'That's not exciting,' I said.

'Nor is losing.'

I took his advice and the house went bust three times in a row.

'I've time for a drink,' he said. 'Want to talk?'

He led us to a railed-off corner section where at small tables hollow-eyed unfortunates sat drowning their mortgage money. A waitress without being asked brought Brose a glass of citron pressé which he despatched in a long smooth swallow.

'The air's kept dry here,' he said. 'Have you noticed? It makes everyone thirsty. Very good for trade. What is it exactly you want to know?'

I explained about Hewett and Partners' troubles with horses, though not in great detail except for the mare.

'She was carrying a foal by Rainbow Quest,' I said. 'Her owner's a weird man . . .'

'Name?' Brose interrupted.

'The owner? Wynn Lees.'

Brose grunted and his attention sharpened. 'There can't be two of them.'

'It's the same man,' I assured him.

'What's weird about him?' Annabel asked.

Brose said, 'He's a pervert. Not sexual, I don't mean. Cruel. He should never be allowed near horses. He got chucked out of Australia, our bad luck.'

I explained about the colic operation and told him about the needle, and I described the circumstance of the mare's death that afternoon.

'And these vets don't know what she died of?'

'Not yet, no. But why kill her? The foal was valuable, so was she.'

He looked at me with disillusion. 'You think Wynn Lees did it?'

'He was there in the morning, but she was alive when he left.'

He summoned a refill lemon with a raised finger and an unexpectedly sweet smile. The waitress brought his drink, purring.

'I'll tell you,' he said at length. 'I'd lay you odds the foal was not by Rainbow Quest.'

'Vernonside Stud said it was.'

'Vernonside Stud would believe what they were told. They're sent a broodmare with her name on her head-collar, right? So that's what they call her. She doubtless has papers with her, all in order. In foal to Rainbow Quest. Why doubt it?'

'OK then,' Annabel repeated. 'Why doubt it?'

'Because she's died the way she has.' He paused. 'Look, you own a decent broodmare, you send her to Rainbow Quest. She seems to be in foal and you take her home and put her in a field, very pleased, but somewhere along the line she slips it. It's often difficult to detect when that happens, but at some point you realize that all you have now is a barren year. But suppose an idea pops in your brain and you go out and buy some other unknown mare in foal to some obscure stallion. Well, now you have a mare in foal at about the right stage of gestation and you insure it as if it's your mare in foal to Rainbow Quest. If anyone checks, then yes, the visit to Rainbow Quest is fully documented. She goes to Vernonside Stud to have the foal because she's down for one of their stallions next. You have to act as a normal owner would. At that point, she's ready for the chop, poor beast, which is what she's got.' He paused to drink. 'These days paternity can be proved without doubt. If I were the insurance company, I'd make sure. Pity your vets didn't take tissue from the foal. Even though it's dead, they might still have got results.'

'They still could,' I said. 'The post mortem's tomorrow morning. I'll tell them.'

'What do you do with the real decent mare?' Annabel asked, fascinated.

'Ship it to some of your shady mates down under.'

I said, 'How do we find out which company carried the insurance? If, of course, you're right.'

Brose wasn't hopeful. 'You've got a problem there. There aren't exactly thousands of underwriters who'll take on horses, but any of them could. The non-marine syndicates at Lloyd's will insure anything from a kidnap ransom to a wet church fête. You ask them, they'll name you a price.'

'Perhaps one could send them all a cautionary letter.'

'You'll get yourself in trouble doing that.' Brose shook his head. 'What's your priority in all of this?'

'Um . . . to stitch Ken McClure's reputation together again and prove the horses' deaths weren't his doing.'

'Difficult,' he said.

'Is it impossible?' Annabel asked.

'Never say anything's impossible. Unlikely's better.'

'We also,' I said, 'have the vets' main building destroyed by arson with an unknown body in it.'

Brose listened impassively, Annabel open mouthed, to the extent of Hewett and Partners' problems.

'Carey Hewett, the senior partner, looks older by the hour. All the partners are tied together in a common mortgage on the burned building, but falling apart in loyalties. All their records were burned, including the back-up disks for the computer. Their chief remaining asset, the hospital, is gradually being boycotted by clients frightened by Ken operating on their horses. After today's disaster, that will accelerate. There isn't much time left for putting things right.'

Brose pursed his lips. 'I take it back. Impossible is the right word.'

'It would be really helpful,' I said, 'if you could give me a list of unidentifiable poisons.'

269

'If you can't identify them,' Brose said, 'you can't prove they were administered.'

Annabel raised her eyebrows. 'So they do exist?'

'I didn't say that,' Brose said.

'As good as.'

'Do they exist?' I asked.

'If they did,' Brose answered, 'and Annabel, I'm not saying that they do, then that's the sort of thing I'd not let out into common knowledge. What I will tell you is that all poisons are hard to find and identify if you have no general idea of what to look for.'

'Ken said that too,' I agreed.

'He's right.' Brose stood up. 'I'll just wish you luck. Keep me posted on Wynn Lees.' He thought briefly and changed his mind. 'Suppose I come to Cheltenham one day? It's not strictly a racing matter as such, but I might be able to suggest a few things.'

'Terrific,' I said, very pleased.

'Check with Annabel,' he said, 'and tomorrow I'll look at my diary.'

He patted Annabel on her rag-doll hair, nodded to me amiably and ambled off to instil fear into a few more unsuspecting wrong-doers.

Annabel held up her fistful of chips and said she felt like multiplying them, so we found a table with spaces and spent a fast hour in which she doubled her stake again and I lost my lot.

'You gamble too much at the wrong time,' she said, taking her half ton of plastic to the cashier to be changed back to spendable currency. 'You should have listened to Brose.'

'I had fun for my money.'

She put her head on one side. 'That sounds like an epitaph.'

'I'll settle for it,' I said, smiling.

We went back to the outer world where gambling was real and went in a taxi (Annabel phoned for it) to the house she shared in Fulham. The cab stopped outside and the driver waited resignedly to take me towards the M40.

She thanked me for the dinner. I thanked her for Brose.

'I'll phone you,' I said.

'Yes, do that.'

We stood on the pavement for a few moments. I kissed her cheek. I'd got that right, it seemed, from her little nod.

'Good luck with everything,' she said. 'It sounds as if you and the vets need a miracle.'

'A miracle would be fine.'

Instead, we got a nightmare.

CHAPTER NINE

Vicky had left a note on my pillow.

'Ken asks you to go to the hospital at nine a.m.'

With a groan, as the night had already half gone. I set my alarm, crawled under the daisy duvet and fell over black cliffs into sleep.

I dreamed of horses dying, their deaths somehow my fault. Awakening, I was relieved to shed the guilt, but a sense of unease remained and it was with a feeling of oppression I returned to the hospital.

At first sight, everything seemed relatively normal, even if gloomy under a scurrying cloudy sky. Cats and dogs went on arriving at the Portakabin. Lucy in a white coat gave me a wave as she crossed from the hospital. I went in through the rear door and found Ken in the office, pale and seething.

'What's the matter?' I said.

'Three referrals have cancelled for later this week. All breathing improvements. We need outside fees to keep the hospital going. They've all heard about the mare and they're now in a full-scale panic. On top of that I sat here until three this morning checking on yesterday's patients, then Scott took over. He promised blind he wouldn't go to sleep. So I came back ten minutes ago, and guess what? No Scott. He's sloped off somewhere for breakfast. It isn't my fault we haven't had the coffee machine mended.'

'How are the patients?'

'All right,' he said grudgingly, 'but that's not the point.'

'No,' I agreed. 'When's the post mortem on the mare?'

He looked at his watch. 'Carey said at ten. I suppose I'd better be there. Carey's called in a fellow from Gloucester to do it and he's more a butcher than a surgeon. The last person I'd have chosen. So I'll have to be there in case he does something diabolical.' Irritation and stress were plain in his voice. 'I wondered if you would mind finishing these letters to the pharmaceutical companies so that they can go out today. I was doing them last night.' He picked up a folder and slid out a bunch of papers. 'With the computer down I've had to get the names and addresses of some of the firms off the bottles and packets, if they're not supplied by the wholesalers who came yesterday. I've sent their letter already. Well, anyway, I wrote a general letter and at least our copier here is working, so I've made enough copies for every firm I could think of.'

He pushed them across the desk towards me, along

with another sheet of paper with the names and addresses.

'While I'm out, could you type in a company name at the top of each letter, and also do the envelopes. I know it's a ghastly chore but it was you who suggested it.'

'Mm,' I agreed. 'All right.'

'Thanks a lot.'

'I've got another suggestion,' I said.

He groaned.

'Take a tissue sample from the dead foal to do a test for paternity.'

He stared. I told him Brose's theory.

'To activate the insurance,' I said, 'the mare had to die. You inconveniently saved her life the first time, so someone had another go. If Brose is right, he, she, or they couldn't afford to have the foal born. Death had to occur before that, and as they probably didn't know exactly when the foal was due, they had to hurry.'

'It gets worse,' Ken said.

'You'd have to get a tissue sample from Rainbow Quest as well,' I said.

'Not difficult. Tissue matching is expensive, though. So is searching for poison, incidentally. Specialist labs cost the earth.'

'So you do think it was poison?'

'Well, it wasn't electrocution. She wasn't suffocated by a plastic bag. She didn't choke. I couldn't see any stab wounds. She shouldn't have died . . . something stopped her heart.'

Yvonne Floyd, coming into the office, overheard Ken's last words.

'Nerve gas?' she suggested ironically.

'So easy to get hold of,' Ken said.

'Smoke inhalation from a smouldering sofa?'

'I bet it wasn't,' Ken said, actually smiling.

'Only trying to help.'

Her presence lightened things always. She said she had an emergency dog case on its way in and had come over to ready things for the small-animal theatre.

'It'll need both Scott and Belinda, ideally.'

'Yes,' Ken said. 'They're around.'

'Great.'

She looked great herself in her white lab coat: white gleaming teeth, bright eyes, cloud of black hair.

She said, 'Belinda's asked me to be her matron of honour.'

'What?' Ken said, puzzled.

'At your wedding, nitwit. Sort of married brides-maid.'

'Oh.' He looked as if he'd forgotten the wedding altogether.

'I suppose you've got a best man?' she teased.

'Er . . .' Ken said. 'I've left everything to Belinda. It's her day.'

'Really, Ken,' she was mildly exasperated, 'you have to find your own best man.'

His gaze fell on me. 'How about it?'

'You must have other friends,' I said. 'Long-time friends.'

'You'll do fine,' he insisted, 'if you will.'

'But Belinda . . .'

'She's coming round, changing her mind about you,' Ken said. 'She'll be all right. Say you will.'

'OK.'

Yvonne was pleased. 'That's better. Don't forget your clothes, Ken. Or buttonholes.'

'Oh God,' he said. 'At a time like this, who can think of *buttonholes*?'

Yvonne smiled affectionately. 'Life goes on,' she said. 'We'll all come out of this all right, you'll see.'

She went out of the office and turned in the direction of the theatre.

'Terrific surgeon,' Ken said.

'Terrific legs.'

'Yes, I suppose so.' He was unmoved. After a pause he began to say, 'What are we going to do – ?'

There was a crash of a door slamming back against a wall and a clatter in the corridor and a groan.

'What's that?' Ken said alarmed, rising to his feet.

I being nearest to the door was first through it, Ken on my heels. Yvonne was coming towards us, weaving and stumbling, her eyes stretched wide, one hand clamped over her mouth. We went towards her to help her and she shook her head violently, tears coming into her eyes and her knees buckling.

'Yvonne,' Ken exclaimed, 'for God's sake, what's the matter?'

She took her hand away as if going to tell us and instead vomited violently onto the passage floor.

She leaned weakly against the wall, crying, her stomach heaving, looking as if she would pass out at any second. Ken and I moved instantly, one to each side of her, stepping round the vomit, to give her support.

She shook us off and, unable to speak, pointed with a wild sweep of an arm towards the theatre. Ken gave me a wide-eyed frightened glance and we went fearfully along there to see what had caused such an extreme reaction. It was the door to the vestibule that had crashed against the wall: it was still open. We went through and into the supply room and tried the door to the small-animal section, but it was locked. We pushed on through the swing doors leading to the big main operating room.

What we saw there brought me perilously near fainting myself.

Scott lay on the long equine operating table, on his back, his arms and legs in the air. Round each ankle and each wrist was buckled a padded cuff. Each cuff was attached to a chain, each chain came down from the hoist. He had been lifted onto the table like a horse.

He was dressed as always in blue jeans and sweater, and he still had shoes and socks on, and his wristwatch.

One might have thought it a joke, but there was about that energetic hard-muscled body an unaccustomed absolute stillness, a silence as lonely as the cosmos.

Ken and I stood one on each side of him, looking down on his face. His head was tipped back, his jaw jutting up. His eyes were unnervingly half-open, as if he were watching and waiting for our help. His mouth was closed. He was white.

'Christ,' Ken said under his breath, very pale.

I swayed. Told myself fainting was out of the question.

Scott's mouth had been securely fastened shut by a neat row of staples. Small silvery tacks. Nine of them.

The faintness ebbed. I'd seen a great many dead bodies before: it wasn't the fact of death but the barbarity that disturbed so radically. I swallowed and closed my teeth and breathed shallowly through my nose.

Ken said 'Christ' again and turned towards the controls of the hoist.

'Don't touch it,' I said.

He stopped and turned back. 'You're right, of course. But it's wrong to leave him like that.'

I shook my head. We had to leave him like that, and the one person who wouldn't care was Scott himself.

'We must get the police,' Ken said dully.

'Yes. And help Yvonne, and make sure no one else comes in here.'

'God.'

A stapler was lying on the floor near my feet. I left

it alone. There were no lights on; only daylight through frosted glass skylights. Everything looked clean and tidy, ready for work. It didn't matter any more, I thought, that we had gone without shoecovers into that sterile environment.

We went back into the corridor and along to Yvonne who was kneeling on the floor, her head against the wall. Ken squatted down beside her. She turned to him and clung, sobbing.

'He was . . . so good . . . to my boys.'

There were worse epitaphs. I went on past them into the office and picked up Ken's bunch of keys which were lying on the desk. The labels were all smudged from much use, but I found 'Theatre vestibule' and took it along the passage to see what it fitted.

Yvonne and Ken were standing. He was giving her his handkerchief, not especially clean, to wipe her ravaged face. He watched me go by with unseeing eyes, his mind, I guessed, like my own, unable to cast out the sight in the theatre.

The vestibule door, I supposed, was covered with everyone's fingerprints, but all the same I slotted the key into the lock without adding any more and found that the tongue turned easily. Using the key alone I closed and locked the door and then went round the corners, along the passage and out into the welcome fresh air.

The outside door leading to the large-animal reception room was closed. I sorted through the bunch for the key and fed it into the hole. I turned it to unlock the door, but nothing happened. Tried the other way: the bolt clicked audibly across. That made the whole theatre area safe from casual eyes, but everyone had keys ... it was all a disaster.

I turned back to the office, skirting the thin splashy patch of vomit. Ken, his arm round Yvonne, was helping her to the washroom off the entrance hall. I found a large piece of paper, wrote DO NOT ENTER on it, grabbed a roll of sticky tape and returned to the outside door. Even Oliver, I thought, sticking it on firmly, might obey that notice, or obey it at least long enough to come into the office to discover why it was there.

Returning to the office, I wrote a second notice and stuck it to the vestibule door, again without leaving finger marks. Then Ken came back from the entrance hall and together in the office we stood for a silent second simply looking at the telephone.

'It's going to be terrible,' he said.

'Mm.'

He sat in the chair behind the desk and picked up the receiver. 'Yvonne says Carey isn't here yet. He was calling in before the post mortem. Don't you think we should wait for him?'

'No, I don't think so.'

'What do I say, then?' he asked numbly. 'How can I say it?'

'Just say who you are, where you are, and that there's a man dead here. Speak slowly, it saves time.'

'You do it.' He gave me the receiver. 'I feel sick.'

I did it at dictation speed. Someone would come, they said.

In the pause before the police arrived, Carey himself turned up wanting to know why the don't enter notice was on the outside door.

'I didn't know there was one,' Ken said wearily.

'I put it there,' I said.

He nodded, understanding.

'Why?' Carey asked.

I found it difficult to tell him. While I did, he went even greyer. Ken gave him the desk chair and asked if he would like some water. Carey put his elbows on the desk and his head in his hands and didn't reply.

The telephone rang and because it was next to my hand I answered it.

'This is Lucy. Who's that?' a voice said.

'Peter.'

'Oh. Is Yvonne there?'

'Er . . . where are you?'

'In the Portakabin, of course.'

I remembered that the old building's number had been rerouted to a swaying wire connected to the temporary accommodation. The partnership's slender attachment to the well-organized past was about to be stretched to the limit.

'Yvonne's here,' I said, 'but not feeling well.'

'She was perfectly all right fifteen minutes ago.'

'Lucy, when you can, come over here.'

'I can't possibly. Belinda and I are knee deep in distemper jabs. Anyway, will you tell Yvonne her run-over dog has arrived outside our door here, but the poor thing's already dead. Ask her to come and talk to the owners, they're very upset.'

'She can't come,' I said.

She finally heard the calamity note in my voice. 'What's the matter?' she asked, her own alarm awakening.

'Get rid of the dogs. I'm not telling you on the phone, but it's catastrophic.'

After a brief silence, she simply replaced her receiver and a moment later I saw her through the window coming down the Portakabin steps and hurrying across to the entrance hall. She appeared in the office doorway prepared to be annoyed with me for frightening her.

One look at Carey's bent head, at Ken's extra pallor, at my own signs of strain, convinced her that fear was reasonable.

'What is it?' she asked.

I said, as the other two were mute, 'Scott's dead.'

'Oh no!' She was horrified. 'On his motorbike? I always told him he'd do himself in one day on that machine. Oh, poor man.'

'It wasn't on his bike,' I said. 'He's here, in the

theatre, and it looks ... well, it looks as if someone's killed him.'

She sat down abruptly on one of the chairs, her mouth open in protesting shock.

'Yvonne found him,' I said. 'She's in the washroom. She could do with your help.'

Strong sensible Lucy rose to her feet again and went on the errand.

Through the window, I saw Oliver Quincy arrive in his mud-spattered white car which he parked next to mine.

'Why don't the police come?' Ken asked fretfully.

The police, I thought, would take everything over. My glance fell on the folder of letters Ken had pushed my way in a long-ago different time-zone, and on impulse I picked it up and took it out to my car, meeting Oliver as he locked his own.

'I'd better warn you ...' I said slowly.

He interrupted brusquely, 'Warn me about what?'

'Ken and Carey can tell you,' I said. 'They're in the office.'

'Not *another* dead horse?'

I shook my head. He shrugged, turned away, and went into the office through the rear door, throwing an enquiring look at the don't enter notice as he passed it. I stowed the folder of letters in the boot and locked it, and turned to follow Oliver just as a police car drove into the car park.

It stopped outside the entrance hall and the same

plain-clothes policeman as before emerged from it, followed by the same constable. They looked around briefly and went in through the hospital's front door, and I decided to go back that way myself.

Lucy and Yvonne were coming out of the washroom together, both looking sick and shaky, as if Lucy's imagination had been as strong an emetic as Yvonne's actual experience. They sat unhappily on two of the chairs, each with a tissue to wipe her face, each sighing, both staring into space.

'The police have come,' I said.

'I left Belinda coping with the whole Portakabin,' Lucy said, sniffing and swallowing. 'I'll have to go back.' She stood up slowly as if suddenly older. 'We'll finish there as fast as we can.' She went out to the car park with little of the brave determination of four days ago.

'I ought to help her,' Yvonne said with difficulty, 'but I can't.'

'Much better to sit here for a bit.'

'You saw him, didn't you?'

I nodded.

'How could anyone do that?'

A question without answer.

'However will I sleep?' she said. 'I can't get him out of my mind. I think of him water-skiing, so expert and strong, so *alive*. And now like this . . .'

Jay Jardine in his self-assertive way strode positively into the entrance hall from up the central corridor and came to a halt at the sight of us.

'What the heck's going on?' he demanded. 'There's dog sick all over the passage and that bloody rude policeman in the office told me to come along here and wait. Why is he here again? Have they finally pinned a name on our corpse in the ashes?'

Yvonne groaned quietly and closed her eyes.

'For Christ's sake,' he was irritated, 'what's the matter?'

I told him.

He stared. Then he sat down, leaving a chair between himself and Yvonne. He said only, 'Too bad.'

The understatement of the day, I thought.

Jay said, 'The coffee machine's still buggered, I suppose.'

We all looked at it across the hall. The first words I'd heard Scott say, I remembered; were 'the coffee machine's buggered'. Poor Scott. There was still no coffee, nor likely to be any.

For a while, as we sat in limbo, there was little commotion, as if the stillness in the theatre had spread through the whole hospital. We could hear no voices from the office. We couldn't ourselves find much to say. Time passed.

Eventually two more plain-clothes police cars came to a halt outside the entrance door, the first spilling out its human contents, the second remaining closed. A thick-set man with the broken-veined complexion of a farmer ambled without great speed into the entrance hall, followed by an elderly man with a too-big suit, heavy black-rimmed glasses sliding down his nose, and the black top-opening bag of old-fashioned doctors.

The farmer-type asked briefly, 'The office?'

'Down the passage, first on the right,' Jay told him.

He nodded and went down there, and things began to happen, though none of them joyful. The second police car contained a photographer and other specialists who after a while followed their master under Jay's direction.

Ken came the other way, jerky, disjointed. 'They've gone into the operating room,' he said. 'Come outside, Peter. I need air.'

I went with him, looking at my watch. Nine-fifty. The morning had seemed a week long already. The air was brisk and cold.

'Did you remember the post mortem?' I asked.

'Carey did. He phoned them to go ahead without us.' He took a deep breath as if sucking life from the air, as if empty.

I said, 'Did you, um, ask him to get some foal tissue?'

He raised his eyebrows. 'I forgot it. Does it matter now?'

'Maybe more than before. You never know.'

'Oh, God.' He pulled his radio phone off his belt, looked up the number in a small pocket address book, and got through to the knackers. He told someone who seemed to have no problem understanding that he wanted properly labelled tissue samples and, as if struck by a thought, he added that he also wanted one of the foal's ears and the tail and some of the mare's mane.

'Why on earth the ear and tail?' I asked, as he put the phone away.

'Hair,' he said succinctly. 'You can get perfect DNA identification from hair, and of course hair doesn't decompose. To prove the foal's paternity you'd need its own hair, its dam's hair and its sire's hair. Or any tissue, really. You get the mare's DNA pattern, then you subtract that from the foal's pattern. What's left in the foal's DNA will be a match with the sire. It's a long expensive process but a genetic match is absolute proof.'

I looked up at the grey sky. 'Suppose whoever killed Scott left a hair on him?'

'Better if Scott fought and scratched. Murderers and rapists can be convicted by their scratched-off skin under their victim's fingernails. It's an exact science now.'

'Mm.' I half smiled. 'That works if you have a suspect.'

We watched the cat-and-dog brigade come and go.

'Will the police close us down?' Ken asked.

'God knows.'

'The second-wave policeman who came,' Ken said, 'he's a detective superintendent. The first lot wouldn't do anything until he'd got here, not when I described the state Scott was in. A blatant piece of buck-passing, it looked to me.'

'Prudent and proper, more like.'

'You're used to a hierarchy,' he said. 'I'm not.'

The Hewett and Partners set-up was a sort of mini-hierarchy in itself, I thought, but didn't press it. Instead I asked Ken if he owned a typewriter of any sort.

'Whatever for?'

'The letters. The envelopes. I can't use the office, it's full of police.'

'Oh, yes. Are we still going on with the letters?'

'We are indeed.'

He thought briefly. 'I've an old battered portable at home. Would that do?'

'Sooner the better,' I said, nodding. 'Where do you live?'

'We can't go now, though,' he protested. 'The police told me to wait.'

'They haven't told *me* to wait,' I said. 'Give me directions and keys and I'll pick up the typewriter and come back. Then I can get on with the letters as soon as possible.'

'But what will I say . . .?'

'If anyone complains, say I was hungry. I'll bring back some croissants or something.'

'There's actually a decent bakery two doors from where I live.'

'Fine.'

He gave me his house keys and told me where to find the typewriter, and as the dog and cat cars were still on the move I had no problem driving with them out of the car park. I'd have had more difficulty in getting in again without a sick animal as passenger if Ken, looking out for me, hadn't hurried across and told the policeman on gate duty that I belonged.

Ken's typewriter was by then locked in the boot, along with a packet of large envelopes and a sheet of stamps. I carried several big pâtisserie bags into the hospital and scattered sustenance all round, which everyone ate hungrily while protesting they had no appetite. Carbohydrates, as ever, were the easiest of sedatives. I ate two Danish pastries myself and even Yvonne gratefully chewed and said she felt better. Ken sat beside her and fell on my offerings ravenously.

'You weren't supposed to leave the premises, sir,' the familiar constable said reprovingly as I went along to the office.

'Sorry. Have a doughnut?'

He eyed the sugar-coated temptation with obvious longing but said he was on duty. No one else made any comment on my excursion. All the same, if I'd been disposing of vital evidence, I thought.

Carey ate a piece of sticky almond ring distractedly as if his brain wasn't quite aware of what his mouth was doing. He was still sitting in the same chair, still looking near collapse. Oliver eyed him like a predatory lion but meanwhile made do with double the cake. Jay Jardine, now in the office, stuffed down two doughnuts in quick succession and sucked the sugar off his fingers.

The door to the theatre vestibule, I'd noticed, was

shut and still bore my don't enter sign. I didn't want to think about what was going on behind it. I was just glad that I didn't have to deal with it.

Carey, Oliver and Jay were taciturn, each busy with his own thoughts. I returned to the more congenial company of Yvonne and Ken and time inched by as through the glass entrance doors we watched the flow of dogs diminish and finally dry. Lucy and Belinda, locking the door behind them, came down from the Portakabin and walked towards us across the tarmac.

Halfway, they stopped, their heads turning towards the gate. They stood unmoving, watching, then finally completed the traverse.

Lucy had tears in her eyes, coming into the entrance hall.

'They've taken him away,' she said. 'They backed an ambulance right up to the large-animal reception door. We couldn't see anything, thank God.'

Oliver and Jay came along the passage with messages. Carey had gone into the operating room at the police's request to tell them if anything struck him as being out of its ordinary place. Yvonne would please wait in the office for the police to ask her questions. They, Oliver and Jay, and also Lucy, could go out on their scheduled calls. Belinda, Oliver shrugged, could presumably do what she liked, they'd had no instructions about her one way or the other. Ken and Ken's friend should stay in the entrance hall. No one could enter or use the theatre until future notice. Someone,

Oliver said finally, should take a mop to the muck on the floor.

It was Lucy, predictably, who cleaned the passage, sweeping aside Yvonne's objections and Ken's and my half-hearted offers.

The crowd in the entrance hall broke up and scattered about its business until only I remained. Ken and Belinda were along at the stables checking on their horse patients. Yvonne was in the office with the door closed, reliving what she longed to forget. She came out crying, awkwardly accompanied by the constable.

'They want to see you next,' she said, gulping and wiping her eyes. 'They say I can go home but I'm due to attend some damned dog-lovers' lunch and lecture on the care of puppies. How can I?'

'Best if you do, perhaps. Make this morning seem unreal.'

'Sir . . .' the constable said, gesturing towards the office.

'Yes.' I gave Yvonne a hug. 'Go to the lunch.'

I left her trying to achieve a wan rain-washed smile and went where required, faithfully followed by the no-doughnut policeman.

The farmer-lookalike was standing by the window, head back, inspecting the cloud cover. He turned at my arrival and announced himself as Detective Superintendent Ramsey of the Gloucestershire police. His voice matched his appearance; an outdoor country

291

intonation, a canny poacher on the side of the game-keepers.

He checked a list. 'You are Peter Darwin, employed here as a general assistant?'

'Not employed,' I said. 'Unpaid helper.'

He raised his eyebrows, clicked open a pen and made a note.

'Are you employed elsewhere, sir?' The pen was poised.

'I'm on leave from the Foreign Office.'

He gave me a brief reassessing glance without pleasure, then wrote down the information and asked me what sort of unpaid help I'd been giving.

I told him that several horses had died in the hospital, that Ken McClure, my friend, was worried about it and that I was trying to help him find out why they'd died.

'And sir, have you succeeded?'

I said regretfully, 'No.'

'How long have you been trying?'

'Since last Thursday.'

He pursed his lips and shook his head slightly, forgiving me, it seemed, for not having achieved results in five days. He made another note, then looked up and began again.

'Do you think the deaths of the horses and the death of the anaesthetist are connected?'

I frowned. 'I don't know.'

'Do you think the deaths of the horses and the burning of the main building are connected?'

'I don't know.'

'Have you discussed any theories with anyone, sir?'

'I think it may not be safe to discuss theories round here.'

His eyes narrowed sharply. 'You saw Sylvester's body, I understand.'

'Yes.' I swallowed. 'How did he die?'

'All in good time,' he said blandly. 'When you were in the theatre, did you touch anything?'

'No.'

'Are you positive, sir?'

'Absolutely positive.'

'Did you see anything of note? Except Sylvester, of course.'

'There was a surgical stapler on the floor near the operating table.'

'Ah ... you know surgical staplers by sight?'

'I've seen Ken use one.'

He made another note.

'Also,' I said, 'I think all the doors were unlocked, which isn't usual. I went round outside to check the outer reception door, which is where the sick animals enter, and it was unlocked. I put the key in the hole and locked it to prevent anyone just walking in there and seeing Scott ...' I paused. 'And when Ken and I went into the theatre, the door to the padded room was open, and so was the one from there to the corridor and the reception room.'

He made a note. 'And was it you who put up the notices and locked the door between the passage here and the theatre?'

I nodded.

'So after you locked the doors, no one went in there?'

'I don't know for sure,' I said slowly. 'Everyone has keys.'

'Do you have keys?'

'No. I used Ken McClure's.'

'Where were you, sir, between nine last night and nine this morning?'

I almost smiled, the enquiry being classic. I said calmly, 'I went to London, to a private dinner. I was in the company of the Jockey Club's deputy director of security from eleven until two, then I drove back here to Cheltenham and went to bed. I'm staying with Ken McClure's fiancée's parents about a mile from here.'

He made short notes. 'Thank you, sir.'

'When did he die?' I asked.

'You don't expect me to answer that.'

I sighed. It had to have been after three, when Ken had left Scott in charge. Everyone's alibi would be the same and as hazy as mine: home in bed.

Superintendent Ramsey asked how long I would be staying with Ken McClure's fiancée's parents.

'It's in the air,' I said. 'Several more days, I should think.'

'We may need to speak to you again, sir.'

'Ken will know where I am, if I leave.'

He nodded, made one more note, thanked me in general and asked the constable to invite Ken to the office. As I went out into the passage, Carey and the policeman from Sunday, whose name I still didn't know, were coming out of the theatre vestibule. Carey walked heavily, grey head bowed, deep in distress.

He walked towards me unseeingly and turned into the office.

'There's nothing out of place,' he said leadenly to Ramsey.

The Sunday policeman followed Carey into the office and closed the door, and I and the constable left the hospital by the rear and found Ken and Belinda doing nothing much but leaning on the closed lower halves of the stable doors, aimlessly watching their patients recover.

'Your turn with the top brass,' I said to Ken.

He looked depressed.

'I'm going back to Thetford Cottage,' I said. 'I'll be there if you want me.'

Belinda said, 'I'm staying here with Ken.'

I smiled at her and after a second she smiled back, the wattage not blinding but an advance nevertheless.

*

Vicky and Greg were out when I reached the house. They had solved the boredom factor to some extent by making an arrangement to be driven on demand by a taxi firm, neither of them feeling confident enough to rent and drive a car themselves. 'The taxi drivers know where to go,' Vicky had said. 'They tell us what to do and see.'

I let myself in, took Ken's typewriter and the folder of letters up to my bedroom, and set to work.

Ken's letters, each made on the partnership writing paper and personally signed with his own sprawling signature, explained the police's need-to-know request for the pharmacy's burned contents and asked for the firm's cooperation. The letter was all right as far as it went, I thought, but as a candidate for the 'sometime or other' tray it got full marks. I slotted the first copy into the machine, typed in the first name on the address list at the top and rolled down to the bottom, below Ken's signature, to add an extra paragraph.

'This matter is of extreme urgency,' I wrote, 'as the police are concerned that certain dangerous, unusual and/or illegal substances may have been stolen prior to the arson, and may have passed into the general community. Please would you treat this request *with the utmost urgency* and send copies of all relevant invoices back by return of post in the stamped addressed envelope provided. Hewett and Partners expresses its profound appreciation of your kind and rapid participation.'

In Japan I'd have scattered a few 'respectfuls' around, but respect didn't seem to go down well with British commerce, as various mystified Japanese businessmen had told me. Bowing, too, for instance, produced not a contract but a squirm. In Japan it was the host who gave a gift to his guest, not the other way round. The opportunities for mutual embarrassment were endless.

I lavishly stamped a page-size envelope for the return information, addressing it to Hewett and Partners at Thetford Cottage (temporary office). The resulting missive looked official and commanding enough, I hoped, to get results.

Then I folded the letter and return envelope together, enclosing them in a business envelope addressed to the pharmaceutical firms. Without a copier or even carbons (which I hadn't thought of) it took me a fair while to type the extra paragraph on every letter and complete the task, but when they were all done I drove to the post office in the long shopping street and sent the whole enquiring bunch on its way.

Back in Thetford Cottage I made up on an hour's sleep and then on the off-chance phoned Ken's portable number.

He answered at once, 'Ken McClure.'

'Where are you?' I asked. 'It's Peter.'

'On my way to a dicky tendon. What do you need?'

'I thought we might go and see the Mackintoshes . . . or the Nagrebbs.'

He drew in an audible breath. 'You do think of vicious ways of passing the afternoon. No thanks.'

'Where do I find them?' I asked.

'You don't mean it?'

'Do you or don't you want your reputation back?'

After a silence he gave me directions. 'Zoë Mackintosh is a tigress and her old man's in dreamland. I'll meet you outside there in, say, fifteen minutes.'

'Fine.'

I drove through Riddlescombe and stopped on a hillside looking down on the Mackintoshes' village. Slate roofs, yellow-grey Cotswold stone walls, winter trees not yet swollen in bud. Charcoal and cream sky, heaped and hurrying. Sleeping fields waiting for spring.

The sense of actual déjà vu was immensely strong. I'd come over these hills before and seen these roofs. I'd run down the road where I now sat in the car. Jimmy and I, laughing ourselves sick over an infantile joke, had chucked off our clothes and splashed naked in the stream going down to the valley. I couldn't see the stream from where I sat but I knew it was there.

Near the appointed time for meeting Ken, I started the engine, released the brake and rolled down the hill. I still couldn't see the stream. Must have muddled the places, I thought, but I'd been so certain. I shrugged it away. Memory was unreliable enough after a week; hopeless after twenty years.

Ken met me at the entrance to the drive to a long grey house with gables and ivy. I'd been there before.

I knew the patterns on the folded-back wrought-iron entrance gates.

'Hi,' I said prosaically, getting out of my car.

'I hope you know what you're doing,' he said with resignation, looking out of the driver's window of his own car.

'Often,' I said.

'Oh God.' He paused. 'Zoë knows my car. She'll attack me.'

'Get in mine, then, coward.'

He climbed out of his car and folded his length in with me and put an arresting hand on mine when I moved to put the car in gear.

'Carey says he's resigning,' he said. 'I thought I'd better tell you.'

'That's unthinkable.'

'I know. I believe he does mean it, though. And he's all that holds us together.'

'When did he say he was resigning?'

'In the office. You know, after you left, when I went along there? Carey was there with that superintendent.'

I nodded.

'Carey had more or less collapsed. When I went in, the policeman was giving him a glass of water. Water! He should have had brandy. The moment he saw me he said he couldn't go on, it was all too much. I told him we needed him, but he didn't answer properly. All he said was that Scott had worked for the practice for ten or more years and we'd never find an anaesthetist like him.'

'And will you?'

He made a shrugging gesture that involved not just his shoulders but his neck and head.

'If Carey disbands the partnership,' he said, 'because that's what will happen if he resigns, we'll have to start again.'

'And to start again,' I pointed out, 'you need a clean slate. So we walk up the drive here and jerk the bell-pull.'

His long head turned slowly towards me.

'How do you know about jerking the bell-pull?'

I couldn't answer. I hadn't realized when I was speaking that I was drawing on memory.

'Figure of speech,' I said lamely.

He shook his head. 'You know things you couldn't know. I've noticed before. You knew my father's name was Kenny, that very first evening. How did you know?'

After a while I said, 'If I do any good for you, I'll tell you.'

'That's all?'

'That's all.'

I started the car, drove in through the gates and stopped in a circular gravelled area short of the house. Then, alone, I got out of the car and walked along the last piece of driveway. I jerked the bell-pull, which was a wrought iron rod with a gilded knob on the end. I knew, before I heard them, what the distant chimes would sound like inside the house.

I couldn't remember who should be opening the door, but it certainly wasn't the woman who did. Of indeterminate age she was sandy-coloured with dry curly hair, fair eyelashes, and noticeable down on her upper lip and lower jaw. Thin and strong, dressed in jeans, checked shirt and faded sweater, she made no attempt at personal show but was not unattractive, in an unconventional sort of way. She looked me up and down, and waited.

'Miss Zoë Mackintosh?' I asked.

'I'm not buying anything. Good afternoon.'

The door began closing.

'I'm not a salesman,' I said hastily.

'What then?' The door paused.

'I'm from Hewett and Partners.'

'Then why didn't you say so?' She opened the door wider. 'But I didn't send for anyone.'

'We're . . . er . . . working on the question of why two of your horses died in our hospital.'

'Bit late for that,' she said crisply.

'Could we possibly ask you a few questions?'

She put her head on one side. 'I suppose so. Who's we?'

I looked back to the car. 'Ken McClure's with me.'

'Oh, no. He killed them.'

'I don't think so,' I said. 'Couldn't you please listen?'

She hesitated. 'He told me some rubbish about atropine.'

'What if it wasn't rubbish?'

She gave me a straight uncompromising inspection, then made up her mind at least to hear the case for the defence.

'Come in, then,' she said, stepping back. She looked across to the car and said grudgingly, 'I told Ken he'd never set foot in here again, but he can come too.'

'Thank you.'

I made a beckoning arm movement to Ken but he approached warily and stopped a full pace behind me.

'Zoë . . .' he said tentatively.

'Yes, well, you've brought a devil's advocate, I see. So come in and get on with it.'

We stepped into a black-and-white tiled hallway and she closed the door behind us. Then she led the way across the hall, down a short passage and into a square room crowded with office paraphernalia, racing colours, photographs, sagging armchairs and six assorted dogs. Zoë scooped several dogs off the chairs and invited us to sit.

In an obscure way I thought the interior of the house was somehow wrong: it didn't smell the way it should, and there was an absence of sound. Zoë's room smelled of dogs. I couldn't get back past that, the way one can't remember a particular tune with a different one bombarding one's eardrums.

'Have you lived here long?' I asked.

She raised her eyebrows humorously, glancing round at the clutter.

'Doesn't it look like it?' she said.

'Well, yes.'

'Twenty-something years,' she said. 'Twenty-three, twenty-four.'

'A long time,' I agreed.

'Yes. So what about these horses?'

'I think they and several others died as a result of insurance swindles.'

She shook her head decisively. 'Our two weren't insured. Their owners don't let us forget it.'

I said, 'Horses can be insured without the owner or the trainer knowing.'

Her eyes slowly widened in memory. 'Russet Eaglewood did that once. Good job she did.'

'Yes, she told me.'

Ken gave me a hard stare.

Zoë reflected. 'So you went to see her about the Eaglewoods' dead horses?'

'Yours and theirs died in the same way.'

Zoë looked at Ken. I shook my head. 'Not his fault.'

'Whose then?'

'We're trying to find out.' I paused. 'The horses all died in the hospital, except perhaps one . . .'

'How many died?' she interrupted.

'Eight or nine,' I said.

'You're kidding!'

Ken protested, 'You shouldn't have told her.'

'One death could be put down to your carelessness,' I said. 'Perhaps even two. But *eight* unexplained deaths? Eight, when you are an expert surgeon? You've been carrying the can for someone else, Ken, and sensible people like Miss Mackintosh will realize it.'

The sensible Miss Mackintosh gave me an ironic glance but all the same looked on Ken as victim not villain from then on.

'To get the horses to the hospital, after they'd been insured, of course,' I said, 'they had to be made ill. Which is why we'd like you to concentrate hard on who had any opportunity to give your horses emergency-sized colic by feeding them atropine.'

Instead of answering directly she said, 'Did the Eaglewood horses have atropine?'

'No,' I said. 'They had appointments.'

She turned a gasp into a laugh. 'Who *are* you?' she asked.

'Peter. Friend of Ken's.'

'I'd say he's lucky.'

I gave her the ironic look back.

'All right,' she said. 'After Ken said that, even though I was furious, I did think about it. To be frank, any one of our lads would have fed their mothers to the horses for a tenner. A doctored apple? A quick agreement in the pub? Too easy. Sorry.'

'Worth a try,' Ken said.

A buzzer rasped loudly into the pause. 'My father,' Zoë said briefly, rising. 'I'll have to go.'

'I'd very much like to meet your father,' I said.

She raised fair bushy eyebrows. 'You're five years too late. But come if you like.'

She went out into the passage and we followed her back into the hall and in through double doors to a large splendid drawing-room whose far wall was glass from floor to ceiling. Just outside the glass was a mill wheel, a huge wooden paddle wheel, more than half of it visible, the lower part below floor level. It was decoration only; there was no movement.

'Where's the stream?' I said, and remembered what was wrong about the house. No musty smell of everlasting water. No sound of the mill wheel turning.

'There isn't one. It dried up years ago,' Zoë said, crossing the floor. 'They mucked around with the water table, taking too much for a bloody power station. Dad,' she finished, coming to a halt by a high-backed chair, 'you've got some visitors.'

The chair made no reply. Ken and I walked round to the front of it and met the man who had been Mac Mackintosh.

CHAPTER TEN

Mackintosh was small and wrinkled, an old dried apple of a horseman. Set in the weather-beaten face his startlingly deep blue eyes looked alert and intelligent enough, and it was only gradually one realized that the thoughts behind them were out of sequence, like a jumbled alphabet.

He was sitting facing the immobile wheel, looking through it, I supposed, to the field and hedge beyond. There was an impression that he'd sat there for a long time; that he sat there habitually. The arms of the chair, where his thin hands rested, had been patched and repatched from wear.

He said in a high scratchy voice, 'Have you forgotten evening stables?'

'Of course not, Dad,' Zoë said patiently. 'They're not for another half hour.'

'Who's that with you? I can't see faces against the light.'

'Good afternoon, Mr Mackintosh,' Ken said.

'It's Ken McClure,' Zoë informed him, 'and a friend of his.'

'Peter,' Ken said.

'I thought you said Ken,' Mackintosh complained testily.

'I'm Peter,' I said.

Zoë reintroduced everyone with clarity but it was doubtful if the old man grasped it, as he kept looking at me with bewilderment every few seconds.

'You said,' he told Zoë, 'that only Carey would come.'

'Yes, I know I did, but I've changed my mind. Carey will still come to play cards with you but Ken is back looking after the horses.' To us she quietly added, 'They've played cards together for years but it's a farce these days. Carey just pretends now, which is good of him.'

'What did you say?' Mackintosh asked crossly. 'Do speak up.'

'Where's your hearing aid, Dad?' Zoë asked.

'I don't like it. It whistles.'

Ken and I were both standing in front of him, between him and the window, and it seemed to displease him that he couldn't see the whole wheel as he kept moving his head to look round and beyond us. Ken must have sensed the same thing, because he turned sideways as if to minimize the obstruction.

The backlight from the window fell on half of Ken's bony face, the rest being still in shadow, and

Mackintosh sat up sharply in his chair and stared at him joyfully.

'Kenny!' he said, 'did you bring the stuff? I thought you were . . .' He broke off, fearfully confused. 'Dead,' he said faintly.

'I'm not Kenny,' Ken said, moved.

Mackintosh flopped back in the chair. 'We lost the money,' he said.

'What money?' I asked.

Zoë said, 'Don't bother him. You won't get a sensible answer. He's talking about the money he lost in a bad property investment. It preys on his mind. Every time anything worries him or he doesn't understand something, he goes back to it.'

I asked Ken, 'Is that what your mother was talking about?'

'Josephine?' Zoë involuntarily made a face. 'She always enjoys a good disaster. Sorry Ken, but it's true.' To me she added, 'Dad lost a small fortune, but he wasn't alone. The scheme looked all right on paper because you didn't have to invest any actual cash and it should have been a good return. Dozens of people guaranteed slices of a huge loan to build an entertainment and leisure centre between Cheltenham and Tewkesbury, and it did get built, but the location and the design of it were all wrong and so no one would use it or buy it and the bank called in all the loans. I can't bear to look at the damn thing. It's still unfinished and just rotting away, and half my inheritance is in it.' She stopped ruefully. 'I'm as bad as Dad, rabbiting on.'

'What was it called?' I asked.

'All our money,' Mackintosh said in his high voice.

'Porphyry Place,' Zoë said, smiling.

Ken nodded. 'A great white elephant, except a lot of it's dark red. I pass it sometimes. Rotten luck.'

'Ronnie Upjohn,' Mackintosh said gleefully, 'got his come-uppance.'

Zoë looked resigned.

'What does he mean?' I asked.

'Ronnie Upjohn is a steward,' she explained. 'For years he kept reporting Dad to the Jockey Club and accusing him of taking bribes from the bookies, which of course Dad never did.'

Mackintosh shrieked with laughter, his guilt plainly a satisfaction.

'Dad!' Zoë protested, knowing, I saw, that the charges were true.

'Ronnie Upjohn lost a packet.' Mackintosh shook with delight and then, under our gaze, seemed to lose the thread of thought and relapse into puzzlement. 'Steinback laid it off at a hundred to six.'

'What does he mean?' I asked Zoë again.

She shrugged. 'Old bets. Steinback was a bookie, died years ago. Dad remembers things but muddles them up.' She gave her father a look compounded of affection, exasperation and fear, the last, I guessed, the result of worry over the not-too-distant future. She and Russet Eaglewood had that in common: daughters holding together the crumbling lives of their fathers.

'As you're here,' Zoë said to Ken, 'would you like to look round at evening stables?'

Ken's pleased acceptance pleased Zoë equally. My mission of reinstatement seemed to have succeeded with her as with Russet. The world, however, remained to be conquered.

'Come on, Dad,' Zoë said, helping her father to his feet. 'Time for stables.'

The old man was physically much stronger than I'd somehow expected. Short, and with slightly bowed legs, he moved without hesitation and without stooping, heading straight down the big room in evident eagerness. The three of us followed him out into the tiled hall and passage, and down past the open door of Zoë's room. She put her head in there and whistled, and the six dogs came bounding out, falling over their own feet with excitement.

This enlarged party crammed into a dusty Land-Rover outside the back door and set off down a rear roadway which led to a brick-built white-painted stable yard a quarter mile distant. From a single-storey white house at one side, the head lad had emerged to join us, and I attended the ritual of British evening stables in an invited capacity for the first time ever.

It seemed familiar enough. The slow progress from box to box, the brief discussion between trainer, lad and head lad as to each horse's well-being, the pat and the carrot from the trainer, the occasional running of the trainer's hand down a suspect equine leg. Ken discussed the inmates' old injuries with Zoë and old man Mackintosh gave the head lad an unending stream of instructions which were gravely acknowledged but which sounded to me contradictory.

At one point I asked Zoë which boxes had been occupied by the two atropine colics.

'Reg,' she said to the head lad, 'talk to my friend here, will you? Answer any question.'

'*Any?*' he queried.

She nodded. 'He's on the side of the angels.'

Reg, small and whippy like Mackintosh himself, gave me a suspicious inspection and no benefit of any doubt. Reg, I thought, might be on the side of the devil.

I asked him anyway about the boxes. Reluctantly he pointed and identified them: numbers six and sixteen. The numbers were painted in black on the white wall above the door of each box. Nothing else to distinguish them from all the others.

Reg, carrying the bag of carrots, was handing them to Zoë and her father at each box and didn't want me getting in the way.

'Do you know anyone called Wynn Lees?' I asked him.

'No, I don't.' The answer was immediate, without pause for thought.

Old Mackintosh, taking a carrot, had also heard the question, and gave a different answer.

311

'Wynn Lees?' he said cheerfully in his high loud voice. 'He tacked a man's trousers to his bollocks.' He laughed long and hard, wheezing slightly. 'With a rivet gun,' he added.

I glanced at Ken. He was going rigid with shock, his mouth open.

'Dad!' Zoë protested automatically.

'True,' her father said. 'I think it was true, you know.' He frowned, troubled, as the memory slid away. 'I dream a bit, now and then.'

'Do you know him, sir?' I asked.

'Who?'

'Wynn Lees.'

The blue eyes sparkled at me. 'He went away . . . I expect he's dead. Six is Vinderman.'

'Come on, Dad,' Zoë said, moving along the row of boxes.

He said mischievously, as if reciting a nursery rhyme, 'Revised Edition, Wishywashy, Pennycracker, Glue.'

Zoë said, 'They don't want to be bothered with all that, Dad.'

I asked him lazily, 'What comes after Glue?'

'Faldy, Vinderman, Kodak, Boy Blue.'

I smiled broadly. He laughed happily, pleased.

'They're the names of horses he used to train long ago,' Zoë said. 'He forgets the names of today's.' She took his arm. 'Let's get on, the lads are all waiting.'

He went amenably, and we came to a horse that Zoë said had been much stronger and tougher since he'd been cut. For cut, read castrated, I thought. Most male steeplechasers were geldings.

'Oliver Quincy did it,' Zoë said.

Ken nodded. 'He's good at it.'

'He came out several times, did three or four of them. Dad likes him.'

Ken said neutrally, 'Oliver can be good company when he chooses.'

'Oliver?' Mackintosh asked. 'Did you say Oliver?'

'Yes, sir. Oliver Quincy.'

'He told me a joke. Made me laugh. I can't remember it.'

'He does tell jokes,' Ken agreed.

Oliver's joke had fallen flat on Sunday morning: 'what four animals did a woman like most?' My mother would love it, I thought.

We came to the last box. 'Poverty,' Mackintosh said, feeding a carrot to a chestnut with a white star. 'How's he doing, Reg?'

'Coming along fine, sir.'

'Is she still in season?' Zoë asked him.

Reg shook his head. 'She'll be fine for Saturday.'

'What's her name?' I asked. 'Shall I bet?'

'Metrella,' Zoë said, 'and don't. Well, thanks, Reg. That's all. I'll be down later.'

Reg nodded and Zoë swept everyone back into the Land-Rover except for the dogs, who bounded home at varying speeds in the wake.

313

Zoë invited us half-heartedly to go in for a drink and didn't mind when we declined.

'Come again,' Mackintosh said warmly.

'Thank you, sir,' Ken said.

I looked along the sweep of the fine mellow frontage, the mill wheel out of sight round the far end, the old stream gone for ever.

'Splendid house,' I said. 'A piece of history. I wonder who lived here before.'

'As it's been here two centuries, I can't tell you everyone,' Zoë said, 'but the people Dad bought it from were a family called Travers.'

Ken wanted to talk not about the Mackintoshes but about his session with the Superintendent, which had pressing priority in his mind. When we reached his car we sat on for a while in mine and he told me what had gone on in the office after I'd left.

'Superintendent Ramsey wanted to know if there were any surgical gloves missing. I ask you, how could we know? We buy them by the hundred pairs. We order more when we get low. Carey told him to stop asking, no one knew.'

'You and Carey were both there?'

'Yes, for a while. I told Ramsey we had several sizes of gloves. Yvonne uses size six and a half. Mine are much bigger. He asked dozens of questions. What are the gloves made of? Where do we buy them? How often do we count them? Where do we dispose of them? I asked him if he'd found any used gloves lying about, but he wouldn't say.'

While he drew breath, I said, 'What *are* they made of, then?'

'Latex. You've seen them often enough. Each pair is packed in its own sterile packet. You've seen me throw them in the bin. I mean, sometimes I might use three pairs during one operation. It always depends. So then he started on gowns, caps and masks. Same thing, except not so many sizes. We throw them away. We throw the packets away. All we could pretty well swear to was that there were no lab coats missing, because those aren't disposable, they go to the laundry. Ramsey said wasn't it extravagant to throw so much away. He has no understanding of sterile procedure. He'd never heard of shoecovers. After that army of doctors, police and photographers had marched through the operating room, any hope of deducing who'd been in there would have vanished, I would have thought.'

'Mm.'

'And why should he think anyone would need to be sterile to commit murder?'

'You told me yourself.'

'What do you mean?'

'So as not to leave any personal tell-tale litter on Scott. No hair, no skin, no fluff, no nothing.'

He blinked. 'Do you really believe that?'

315

'I don't know, but I'd guess they didn't find any fingerprints on the stapler, and took it from there.'

'It's all ghastly,' he said.

'What else did they ask?'

'They asked if I thought Scott had killed the horses.'

'Mm.'

'What do you mean, mm? He couldn't have done.' He was indignant at my response. 'He was a *nurse*.'

'And an anaesthetist.'

'You're as bad as the police.'

'It's always been a possibility,' I said reasonably. 'I'm not saying he killed them, I'm saying he had the ability and the opportunity. Just like you.'

He thought it over. 'Oh.'

'Maybe he found out who killed them,' I said.

Ken swallowed. 'I didn't believe you when you said things were dangerous. I mean killing horses is one thing but killing a man is different.'

'If you have the means to kill without trace, that's dangerous.'

'Yes, I see.'

'And Scott is the second person dead here.'

'The second? Oh, you mean the arsonist?'

'Everyone forgets him,' I said. 'Or her, of course.'

'Her?'

'How about the nurse who left in a huff?'

'Surely the police checked on her!'

'Yes, I expect so,' I reflected. 'How about us going to see Nagrebb?'

He hated the idea. 'Nagrebb's bad enough but his son's worse.'

'I thought you said he had a daughter.'

'He has. Two sons and a daughter. One of the sons is also a show-jumper and he's the meanest bastard that ever sat in a saddle.'

'That's saying something, with Wynn Lees about.'

'You'll be wanting to see *him* next!'

'Actually, no, I don't think so.'

'You've a vestige of sense left, then.'

'Well,' I said, 'who trained the Fitzwalter horse?'

'He trained it himself. He holds a permit.'

'Does he?' I didn't know why I should be surprised. Many owners of steeplechasers trained their own horses. 'I thought you said it was a colt.'

'Yes, it was. A three-year-old colt. It had run and won on the Flat as a two-year-old, and Fitzwalter bought it because he likes to get them going and run them as three- and four-year-old hurdlers and then put them over fences a bit later on.'

'What's he like?'

'Fitzwalter? Opinionated, but not too bad as a trainer. If you're thinking of going to see *him*, I don't mind coming with you. He took it quite well when his horse died.'

'Where does he live?'

'Five miles or so. Do you want me to phone, to see if he's home?'

'We might as well.'

'He hasn't stopped employing me, though. I mean, you don't have to persuade him, like the others. And how did you tame Zoë so quickly? She was positively putty. Not a claw in sight.'

'I don't know. I thought her attractive. She probably saw that.'

'*Attractive!*'

'In a way.'

'Astounding. Anyway, Fitzwalter engages us on a sort of contract basis, and it's still in operation.'

'Good, then can you drop in without his calling you out specifically?'

He nodded. 'I often pop in if I'm passing.'

'Let's pop, then.'

He consulted the small address book, phoned, got an affirmative answer, removed himself from my car to his own and led the way through country lanes and up a winding hill to a bare upland and a grey stone house. The house, unremarkable, stood next to about three acres of smashed and rotting cars, a jumbled rusting dump of old dreams.

We turned off the road into a straight drive which led past the house and ended by a small open-ended stable yard that looked as if it had been constructed from old sheds, a barn, a garage or two, and a henhouse.

'Fitzwalter's a scrap metal merchant,' Ken said unnecessarily as we got out of the cars. 'At weekends, that pile of junk is buzzing with crowds looking for parts, wheels, valves, seats, pistons, he sells anything.

Then he compresses the picked carcasses and ships them to be melted down. Makes a fortune.'

'An odd mixture, scrap metal and horses,' I said.

Ken was amused. 'You'd be surprised. Half the kids you see pot-hunting at horse shows and gymkhanas are funded this way. Well, OK, not half, but definitely some.'

In the yard, doors were open, lads carried buckets: evening stables were in full swing. Fitzwalter, whom Ken called and introduced simply as Fitz, came out of a garage-like stall and greeted us with a wave. He wore patched corduroys streaked blackly with oil and a big checked rough wool shirt. No jacket, despite the chill in the air. He had straight black hair, dark eyes and tanned skin, and was thin, energetic and perhaps sixty.

'You should see him at the races,' Ken said under his breath as we walked into the yard to join him. 'He has his suits made. Looks like a city gent.'

He looked more like a gipsy at that moment but his voice was standard English and his manner business-like. He excused himself from shaking hands as they were covered with sulphanilamide powder, instead wiping them casually on his trousers. He seemed pleased enough to see Ken and, nodding to include me, asked him to just take a quick look at the rash inside his mare's stifle.

We walked to the box he'd come out of, which proved to contain a pair of enormous chestnut hind-quarters and a flicking tail. Presumably she also had a head and the usual front half, but they were out of sight beyond. Ken and Fitz sidled unconcernedly past the kicking area, but I stayed back, out of reach.

Unable to hear the professional consultation within, I watched instead the activity out in the yard and listened to the clink and clank of the buckets.

I had no feeling here of familiarity. Memory held a blank.

'Try Vaseline instead,' Ken was saying, coming out. 'Keep the rash moist for a while, instead of trying to dry it up too soon. She's looking well otherwise.'

He and Fitzwalter moved across the expanse of packed earth and dead brown weeds and headed for the barn. In there, I discovered, following, were two roomy stalls strong enough for carthorses but each containing a good-looking narrow bay horse tied to the wall by its headcollar.

Ken and Fitzwalter looked at each in turn. Ken ran his hand down the legs. A good deal of nodding went on.

'How many horses do you train?' I asked Fitzwalter interestedly.

'Six at present,' he said. 'It's the busiest time of year, you see. I've room for seven, but we lost one a while back.'

'Yes, Ken told me. Bad luck.'

He nodded and asked Ken, 'Did you ever find out what hit him?'

'No, 'fraid not.'

Fitzwalter scratched his neck. 'Good little colt,' he said. 'Pity he had a chipped bone.'

'Did you have him insured?' I asked sympathetically.

'Yes, but not for enough.' He shrugged easily. 'Some I insure, some I don't. Most times the premium's too high so I don't insure. I risk it. With him, well, he was expensive when I bought him so I took some cover. Not enough, though. Win some, lose some.'

I smiled non-committally. He was perhaps lying, I thought.

'Decent insurance company, was it?' I asked.

'They paid up, that's the main thing.' He laughed briefly, showing his teeth, and led the way out of the barn. 'I'm running the five-year-old tomorrow at Worcester,' he said to Ken. 'What about a blood count to see if she's in good shape?'

'Sure,' Ken said, and returned forthwith to his car for the necessaries of collecting a blood sample, telling Fitzwalter he would borrow a neighbouring vet's lab for the count. 'Ours went up in smoke,' he said, 'if you remember.'

Fitzwalter nodded and thanked him and offered drinks, but we again declined. He looked at Ken speculatively, as he had been doing on and off all along, and came to a decision.

'One of my lads,' he said, 'told me a rumour that I really can't believe.'

Ken said, 'What rumour?'

'That you had one of your people murdered this

morning.' He inspected Ken's face and got his answer. 'Who was it? Not Carey!'

'Scott Sylvester, our anaesthetist,' Ken said, reluctantly.

'What happened?'

'We don't know,' Ken said, shying away from describing Scott's state. 'It'll be on the news . . . and in the papers.'

'You don't seem much worried,' Fitzwalter said critically. 'I was expecting you to tell me. When you didn't, I thought it couldn't be true. How was he killed?'

'We don't know,' Ken said uncomfortably. 'The police are trying to find out.'

'I don't like the sound of it.'

'It's devastating,' Ken agreed. 'We're trying to go on as normal but frankly I don't know how long we'll be able to.'

Fitzwalter's dark eyes looked into the distance, considering. 'I'll have to talk to Carey,' he said.

'Carey's very upset. Scott had been with us a long time,' Ken said.

'Yes, but *why* was he killed? You must know more than you're saying.'

'He was dead in the hospital when we arrived this morning,' Ken told him. 'In the operating theatre. The police came and took him away and asked us questions, but so far we don't have any answers and the police haven't told us what they think. It's all too soon. We'll know more tomorrow.'

'But,' Fitzwalter insisted, 'was he shot? Was there blood?'

'I don't think so,' Ken said.

'Not a shotgun?'

Ken shook his head.

'Suicide?'

Ken was silent. I said for him, 'It wasn't suicide.'

Fitzwalter's attention sharpened on me for the first time. 'How do you know?'

'I saw him. His wrists and ankles were tied. He couldn't have killed himself.'

He accepted my positive tone. 'Who are you, exactly?' he asked.

'Just a friend of Ken's.'

'Not involved in the practice?'

'Only visiting.'

'A vet?'

'Oh, no,' I said, 'far from it.'

He lost interest and turned back to Ken. 'I think it's extraordinary you didn't tell me first thing.'

'I try to forget it,' Ken said.

He could try, but it was impossible. I would never forget Scott's head. The memory had been coming back in flashes of nausea all day. It must have been the same for Ken.

Fitzwalter shrugged. 'I think I only met the man that time when the colt died. I reckoned he'd dropped off to sleep and not been watching properly, but it's unlikely he could have saved him anyway. That's the man, isn't it?'

Ken nodded.

'Well, I'm sorry.'

'Thanks,' Ken said. He sighed deeply. 'When it was just dead horses, life was simpler.'

'Yes, I heard you had an epidemic.'

'Everyone's heard,' Ken said despondently.

'And a fire and another body. I don't see how Hewett and Partners can survive.'

Ken didn't answer. The more anyone strung the disasters together the more impossible became the prospects. Even a quick solution to everything might not avoid the wreckage, and a quick solution lived in cloud-cuckooland.

'Time to go,' I said, and Ken nodded.

'How do we stand?' he asked Fitzwalter. 'You and I.'

Fitzwalter shrugged. 'I need a vet. You know the horses. I'll phone Carey. I'll see what can be worked out.'

'Thanks very much.'

Fitzwalter came halfway with us to the cars.

'Any time you want to scrap that old Ford,' he told Ken, 'I'll give you a price.'

Ken's car rattled with age and use but he looked indignant.

'There's miles in the old bus yet.'

Fitzwalter gave him a pitying shake of the head and turned away. Ken patted his old bus affectionately and folded his gangly height into it behind the wheel. We were both supposed to be returning to Thetford Cottage but it seemed he had as little eagerness as I.

'How about a pint?' he said. 'I haven't eaten all day and I feel queasy and I frankly can't talk to Greg for more than five minutes without rigor mortis.'

His last words disturbed him after he'd said them. Scott was everywhere in our minds.

'I'll follow you,' I said, and he nodded.

With the day darkening, we passed by the tangled metal dump, went down the winding hill and through the country lanes and ended in a quiet old pub where only the chronically thirsty were yet propping up the bar.

I couldn't face beer and settled for brandy in a lot of water, realizing I also hadn't eaten and was feeling more not less unsettled.

'It's hopeless, isn't it?' Ken said, staring into his glass. 'Talking to Fitz, I could see it. You give me hope sometimes, but it's an illusion.'

'How old is Nagrebb?' I asked.

'Not Nagrebb. I'm not going there.'

'Is he sixty or more?'

'He doesn't look it, but his son's over thirty. What does it matter?'

'All the owners or trainers of the dead horses have been men of sixty or more.'

He stared. 'So what?'

'So I don't really know. I'm just looking for similarities.'

'They all know me,' Ken said. 'They've got that in common.'

'Do they all know Oliver?'

Ken thought it over. 'I don't suppose he's met Wynn Lees. He probably knows the others. They all know Carey, of course.'

'Well, they would. But other things . . . is there anything else that links them?'

'I can't see the point really,' he said, 'but I suppose anything's worth a try.'

I said, 'We have a cruel-to-horses pervert, a ga-ga old man, a scrap metal dealer, an unscrupulous show-jumping trainer, the old tyrant father of Russet Eaglewood and a steward.'

'What steward?'

'Ronnie Upjohn.'

'But his horse *lived*.'

'He's the right age.'

'It's nonsense,' Ken said. 'You'll never get anywhere that way. A quarter of the population's over sixty.'

'I expect you're right.' I paused, then said, 'Did they all know your father?'

He gave me a slightly wild look but didn't shirk the question.

'Old Mackintosh obviously did,' he said. 'Wasn't that odd? I didn't know I looked so like him as all that.'

'Who else?'

326

'I don't know. He was a vet in this area, so I expect he knew most of them.'

'And of course he knew of Wynn Lees.'

'But it couldn't matter now, after all this time.'

'Just fishing around,' I said. 'Do they all know each other?'

He frowned. 'Eaglewood knows Lees and Mackintosh and Fitzwalter and Upjohn. Don't know about Nagrebb. The three trainers all know each other well, of course. They meet all the time at the races. Nagrebb's in a different world. So is Wynn Lees.'

'And all this started since Wynn Lees came back from Australia.'

'I suppose it did.'

Wholly depressed, we finished our drinks and drove to Thetford Cottage. Belinda, looking tired, had already told Vicky and Greg about Scott, so we passed a long subdued evening without cheer. Vicky offered to sing to raise our spirits but Belinda wouldn't let her. She and Ken left at ten and the rest of us went to bed in relief.

In the morning I went back to the hospital, drawn as if by a magnet, but there was nothing happening. The Portakabin doors were shut. The car park, usually overfilled, was half empty. There were two police cars by the hospital but no barrier to keep other cars out.

I parked near the front entrance and went in and

found Ken, Oliver, Jay and Lucy all sitting glumly silent in the office.

'Morning,' I said.

They couldn't raise a greeting between them.

'Carey's closed the practice,' Ken said, explaining the general atmosphere. 'He got the secretary to phone all the people with small-animal appointments to cancel them. She was doing it in the Portakabin when we arrived. Now she's in there answering the phone and telling people to find other vets.'

'I didn't think he would do this to us,' Lucy exclaimed. 'He didn't even ask us.'

'He hasn't the right,' Oliver said. 'It's a partnership. He can resign from it if he likes – and the sooner the better – but he can't just put us all out of work like this.'

Jay said, 'It isn't as if any of these disasters touched my cattle. I'm going to phone all my clients and tell them I've set up on my own.'

'Sometimes you need the hospital,' Ken said.

'I'll rent the theatre when I need it.'

'Good idea,' Oliver said.

I didn't bother to point out that as they jointly owned the hospital and each paid a share of the mortgage, it might not be as simple as they thought to disengage from it. Not my business, though.

'Is Carey here?' I asked.

They shook their heads. 'He came. He told us. We were speechless with shock. He left.'

'And the police? Their cars are here.'

'In the theatre,' Lucy said. 'Don't know what they're doing.'

As if on cue, the police constable appeared in the doorway and asked the vets to go with him to join the Superintendent. They trooped out and followed him up the passage and I might have tried to tack on unobtrusively, but the telephone on the desk gave me a better idea and I phoned Annabel at the Jockey Club instead.

'Oh, good,' she said when I announced myself, 'I didn't know how to reach you. Some people I know need a new tenant for their flat. Are you interested?'

'Fervently,' I said.

'When can you come?'

'This evening,' I said.

'Can you pick me up at my house at six?'

'I'll be there and I'm highly grateful.'

'Have to go now. Bye.'

'Bye,' I said, but she'd already gone. I put down the receiver thinking that life wasn't all doom and gloom after all.

Almost immediately the phone rang again and after a moment or two, as no one ran back from the theatre, I picked it up and said 'Hewett and Partners, can I help you?' just like Ken.

A voice on the other end said, 'This is the Parkway Chemical Company. We need to speak to Kenneth

McClure about a letter we received from him this morning.'

I said, 'I'm Kenneth McClure.' Lie abroad for your country . . . !

'Fine. Then I'm answering your query. I'm the sales manager, by the way. Condolences on your fire.'

'Thanks. It's a mess.'

'Will you be needing replacements for what you've lost?'

'Yes, we will,' I said. 'If you can send us the past invoices, we can make up a new shopping list.'

'Splendid,' he said. 'You will remember, though, won't you, that there are some substances we can't put in the post? Like last time, you'll have to send someone to collect it.'

'OK,' I said.

'Last time, according to our records, your messenger was a Mr Scott Sylvester. He's been vouched for, but if you send anyone else he'll need full identification and a covering letter from your partnership laboratory. Even Mr Sylvester will need identification. Sorry and all that, but we have to be careful, as you know.'

'Yes,' I said. 'Could you give us the copies of the invoices as soon as possible?'

'Certainly. We're getting them together at this moment. They'll go off today.'

'Could you also send us a copy of the delivery note that I'm sure you gave Scott Sylvester when he collected from you?'

'Certainly, if you like.'

'It would help us restore our records.'

'Of course. I'll assemble it straight away.'

'Thank you very much indeed.'

'No trouble. Glad to help.' He put the phone down gently and I stood thinking of the possible significance of what he'd told me.

Scott had personally collected at least one substance that couldn't be sent through the mail. It might be harmless. It might be anything. I'd wanted to ask the sales manager exactly what Scott had carried, but he'd talked as if I knew, and I hadn't wanted to make him suspicious. In the morning, or whenever the reply fell through the letterbox at Thetford Cottage, we would find out. Patience, I sometimes thought, was the hardest of virtues.

I reached Annabel's house on time at six and she opened the door to my ring.

The clothes this time were baggy black silk trousers and a big top that looked as if it were made of soft white feathers. She'd added silver boots, wide silver belt and silver earrings and carried a black swinging cape to put on to keep warm. Her mouth was pink and her eyes were smiling. I kissed her cheek.

'We may as well go straight on in your car,' she said. 'The people are expecting us.'

'Fine.'

She told me on the way that they were offering the self-contained flat at the top of their house.

'Because they live below, they want to make sure that their tenant is civilized and doesn't make a lot of noise. Although, of course, they can give you notice at any time.'

'You've lost me.'

'The rent acts, of course.'

I was unclear about the rent acts and got a brief lecture on how it was possible for the resident owner of a house to evict undesirable tenants just by claiming, in court if necessary, that the flat was required back for the owner's own use.

'I think I am what you call house-trained,' I said.

The flat itself was in an ancient mansion block, on the fourth of six floors and approached by a creaky old lift. The inhabitants were a bearded professor and his intimidated wife. The room they offered was large and old fashioned with a view of nearby roofs and fire escapes. I didn't like it much, but it was at least a foothold. We agreed on terms and I gave them a cheque for a deposit, and Annabel and I descended to the car.

'It's not awfully good,' she said doubtfully. 'I hadn't seen it before.'

'It's a start. I'll look around later for something else.'

It had the virtue at least of being within two miles of Annabel's house, and I hoped I might be crossing those two miles frequently. The bishop's daughter already had me thinking in such heavy unaccustomed words as permanent, for ever and commitment, and common sense told me it was far too soon for that. It had always been too soon; common sense had ever prevailed. Common sense had never come to grips with an Annabel.

'Six-forty,' she said, looking at her outsize black watch. 'Brose has fixed up someone for you to meet if you want to. It's about insuring horses.'

'Yes, please,' I said with interest.

'Brose says this man always drinks in a hotel bar near the Jockey Club's London quarters and he should be there about now. You could catch him before he leaves.'

'You're coming, I hope,' I said.

She smiled for answer and I drove while she gave directions to the rendezvous. It wasn't hard to find but achieving a parking space took up as much time as the journey and I was afraid we'd be too late.

Brose himself was in the bar, talking to a short bald man with a paunch and gold-rimmed glasses. Brose saw us come in, as it was hard to miss Annabel's arrival anywhere, and waved to us to join him.

'Thought you weren't coming,' the big man said.

'Parking,' Annabel told him succinctly.

'Meet Mr Higgins,' he said, indicating the paunch. 'His company insures horses.'

We shook hands, completing the introductions. Higgin's attention fastened on Annabel as if mesmerized while she twirled off the cape and rubbed a ruffling hand over her feathers.

'Er,' he said. 'Oh yes, horses.'

I bought drinks for everyone, a bearable pain in the cash flow since Brose, Annabel and I all chose citron pressé, much to the horror of Higgins with his double vodka and tonic. The bar was one of the dark sort, all dim lights and old wood, everything rich-looking and polished and pretending that the Edwardian age still existed, that horses pulled carriages outside in smoke-laden London fog.

Brose said, 'Your spot of bother's in the news. I was just telling Higgs about it. Out of hand, isn't it?'

'Pretty far,' I agreed.

'What's happened?' Annabel asked. 'What spot of bother?'

Brose looked at her kindly. 'Don't you watch the box? Don't you read the papers?'

'Sometimes.'

He said, 'The Hewett and Partners' anaesthetist was murdered sometime on Monday night. Didn't the pride of the Foreign Office tell you?'

'I'd have told her this evening,' I said.

Annabel listened in dismay to the short account Brose and I gave her. Brose had actually spoken to Superintendent Ramsey who'd informed him that enquiries were proceeding.

'That means they haven't a clue,' Brose said. 'I offered any service they needed, and that's where we stand.' He looked at me shrewdly. 'What do you know about it that I don't?'

The newspapers that I'd seen had printed nothing about hoists or staples and I'd supposed the police had their reasons for keeping quiet. I'd have told Brose then but Higgins was looking at his watch, drinking his vodka and showing signs of leaving, so I said to Brose, 'Tell you later,' and to Higgins, 'I really do want to know about insuring horses.'

The paunch resettled itself. I bought him a refill, which anchored him nicely.

'Brose suggested,' Higgins said in a fruity bass voice, 'that I just talk and if you want to ask anything, fire away.'

'Great,' I said.

'Insuring horses,' he began, 'is risk business. We don't do it except as a sideline, understand. Agents phone us and we make a deal. Premiums are high because the risks are high, understand?'

I nodded. 'Give us an example,' I said.

He thought briefly. 'Suppose you have a good Derby prospect, it's worth your while insuring it because of the possible future stud value. So we make a deal on how long the policy is to run for and exactly what it covers. That's accidental death usually, but it could include malicious damage, negligence and death from illness. Most horses don't die young from natural causes so that's not as risky as racing. We'd agree to a policy that included death from natural causes but we'd review

335

it every year and increase the premium. After ten years, except for stallions at stud, we might decline at any price, but generally racehorses live on well into their late teens, or middle twenties. That is, if nature takes its whole course. Many people put down their old horses earlier, if it's more humane.'

'Or cheaper,' Brose said dryly.

Higgins dispatched half his second drink with a nod of sad agreement.

'What about a broodmare?' I asked.

'In foal?'

'In foal to a top stallion.'

'Mm. We'd write a policy as long as the pregnancy was definitely established and proceeding normally. It isn't usual, but it could be done, especially if the stallion fee has to be paid whether there's a live foal or not. No foal, no fee is customary. How old a mare?'

'I don't know.'

'It would depend on her age and her breeding record.'

'I can tell you,' Brose said. 'She was nine and had been barren one year but had borne two healthy foals, one colt, one filly.'

Higgins raised his eyebrows until they rose above the gold rims of his glasses. I could feel my own eyebrows going up in unison.

'How do you know?' I asked.

'Peter, really. I'm a detective by trade.'

'Sorry.'

'I obtained the list of mares covered by Rainbow Quest last season and checked them. People with sires like Rainbow Quest are choosy about what mares they'll accept because they need foals of good quality to maintain the stallion's worth, so that the stud fees stay high.'

'It makes sense,' I agreed.

'So,' Brose said, 'I phoned the former owner of that mare you were supposed to have in the hospital and asked him how come he had sold her to Wynn Lees. He said his business was going bad and he needed to sell things. He'd sold his mare at the first decent offer. He'd never heard of Wynn Lees before that, he said, and he couldn't remember his name without being prompted. Utterly unbusinesslike, no wonder he was in trouble.'

'Was the mare in foal when he sold her?' I asked.

'He says so. Maybe she was, maybe she wasn't. Maybe he believed she was or maybe he was selling an asset he knew had vanished. Either way, he sold her to Wynn Lees.' He paused. 'Did you get tissue samples from the foal?'

I nodded. 'Hair. Also the mare's hair. They've been sent off to be matched. They need some of Rainbow Quest's too.'

'I'll get that for you,' Brose said. 'Which lab's doing the matching?'

'I'll have to ask Ken McClure.'

'Ask, and let me know.'

337

I thanked him profoundly. He didn't like fraud, he said.

Higgins nodded, saying, 'The temptation to kill an insured horse is one reason for the high premiums. Fraud is a major problem. Some of it is absolutely blatant but if we insure a horse and he breaks a leg, we have to pay, even if we think someone's come along with an iron bar and taken a swipe.'

'Did your company,' I asked, 'insure any horses that died during or after surgical operations?'

'Not recently,' he said. 'They don't often die during operations. I can't swear we haven't insured one in the past, but I can't recall that we've ever had to pay out for that. Mind you, I'm not saying other companies haven't. Do you want me to ask around?'

'Would you?'

'For Brose, sure.'

Brose said, 'Thanks, Higgs.'

I asked, 'Would you ever insure a horse specifically against dying during an operation?'

Higgins pursed his lips. 'I would, if it was already insured. I would charge an extra one per cent premium and pay up if the horse died.'

'It's all wicked,' Annabel said.

Brose and Higgins, tall and short, lean and fat, easy together like double-act comics, smilingly agreed with her. Higgins after a while said his goodbyes and left, but Brose stayed, saying at once, 'Go on about the murder.'

I glanced at Annabel.

'Tell the girl,' Brose said robustly, correctly reading my hesitation. 'She's not a drooping lily.'

'It's fairly horrific,' I said.

'If it's too gory, I'll stop you,' she said.

'There wasn't any blood.'

I explained about the hoist for lifting unconscious horses. Brose nodded. Annabel listened. I told them Scott had been lifted onto the operating table and left with his arms and legs in the air.

Brose narrowed his eyes. Annabel blinked several times.

'There's more,' Brose asserted, watching me.

I explained about vets stapling skin together after cuts and operations. I described the little staples. 'Not like staples for paper, exactly, though the same idea. Surgical staples are about an eighth of an inch wide, not narrow like ordinary staples. When you put the stapler against skin and squeeze, the staples go fairly deep before they fold round. It's hard to explain.' I paused. 'The staple ends up like a small squared ring. Only the top surface is visible. The rest is under the skin, drawing the two cut sides together.'

'Clear,' Brose said, though Annabel wasn't so sure.

'The staples are like unpolished silver in colour,' I said.

'Why all this about staples?' Annabel wanted to know.

I sighed. 'Scott's mouth was fastened shut by a row of staples.'

Her eyes went dark. Brose said, 'Now there's a thing,' and looked thoughtful.

'Before or after death?' he asked.

'After. No blood.'

He nodded. 'How was he killed?'

'Don't know. Nothing to be seen.'

'Like the horses?'

'Like the mare, perhaps.'

'You be careful,' Brose said.

'Mm.'

'He couldn't be in danger,' Annabel protested, looking alarmed.

'Couldn't he? What about all this fact-finding he's been doing?'

'Then stop it,' she told me adamantly.

Brose regarded her with quizzical eyes and she very faintly blushed. All the difficult words popped back into my mind unbidden. It's too quick, too soon, insisted common sense.

Brose stood up to his full height, patted Annabel's hair and told me he'd keep in touch. When he'd gone Annabel and I sat on, constantly talking though with many things unspoken.

She asked about my future in the service and I thought I heard a distant echo of an inquisition designed and desired by her father.

'Did you tell your parents about me?' I asked curiously.

'Well, yes. Just in passing. I was telling them about the Japanese.' She paused. 'So where will you go from this job in England?'

'Anywhere I'm sent.'

'And end up an ambassador?'

'Can't tell yet.'

'Isn't promotion to ambassador just a matter of Buggin's turn?' She didn't sound antagonistic but I reckoned that that question came straight from the bishop.

'Buggins,' I said, 'are very competent people.'

Her eyes laughed. 'Not a bad answer.'

'In Japan,' I said, 'all the men carry things around in bright carrier bags rather than in pockets or brief cases.'

'What on earth has that got to do with anything?'

'Nothing,' I said. 'I thought you might like to know.'

'Yes, my life is illuminated. It's overpowering.'

'In Japan,' I said, 'wherever Westerners don't go, the loos are often holes in the floor.'

'Riveting. Continue.'

'In Japan, every native person has straight black hair. All the women's names end in ko. Yuriko, Mitsuko, Yoko.'

'And did you sleep on the floor and eat raw fish?'

'Routine,' I agreed. 'But I never ate fugu.'

'What on earth is fugu?'

341

'It's the fish that's the chief cause of death from food poisoning in Japan. Fugu restaurants prepare it with enormous precautions but people still die . . .' My voice stopped as if of its own accord. I sat like stone.

'What is it?' Annabel asked. 'What have you thought of?'

'Fugu,' I said, unclamping my throat, 'is one of the deadliest of poisonous fish. It kills fast because it paralyses the neuromuscular system and stops a person breathing. Its more common name is the puffer fish. I think someone told me it takes so little to be lethal that it's virtually undetectable in a post mortem.'

She sat with the pink mouth open.

'The problem is,' I said, 'you can't exactly go out and buy a puffer fish in Cheltenham.'

CHAPTER ELEVEN

The evening with Annabel, full of laughter despite the grisly scene I'd transferred to her mind, ended like the earlier one, not with a bang but a kiss.

A brief kiss, but on the lips. She stood a pace away after it and looked at me doubtfully. I could still feel the soft touch of her mouth: a closed pink mouth, self-controlled.

'How about Friday?' I said.

'You must be tired of driving.'

'Soon it'll be two miles, not a hundred.'

If she hadn't wanted me two miles away she wouldn't have arranged it. I wondered if she felt as I did, a shade lightheaded but half afraid of a bush fire.

'Friday,' she agreed, nodding. 'Same time, same place.'

Wishing I didn't have to go, I drove back to Thetford Cottage, and there slept fitfully with unhappy, disconcerting dreams. I awoke thinking there was something in the dreams that I should remember, but the phantom movies slid quickly away. I'd never been good at remembering dreams. Couldn't imagine how anyone woke with total recall of them. I bathed and dressed and breakfasted with Vicky and Greg.

'You look tired,' Vicky said apologetically. 'If we hadn't been mugged in Miami, you wouldn't have got into this.'

And I wouldn't have gone to Stratford races, I thought, and I would never have met Annabel.

'I've no regrets,' I said. 'Are you happier now in this house?'

'Bored to death,' she said cheerfully. 'That wedding seems a long way off. I can't wait to go home.'

I hung around impatiently for the postman but he brought only one of the reply envelopes and that not the one from Parkway Chemicals. The only envelope to travel out and back in two days contained a whole bunch of invoices for things I'd never heard of. I put them back in the envelope and tried Ken's portable phone number.

He took his time answering. He yawned. 'I'm knackered,' he said. 'I was out at a racing stable half the night with a colic.'

'I thought the partnership was defunct.'

'So it might be,' he said, 'but I'm still a vet and horses still get sick and if I'm the only one available at three in the morning, well, I go.'

'You didn't have to operate, did you?'

'No, no. Managed to unknot him with painkillers and walking. He didn't leave home.'

344

'What trainer?'

'Not one you know. I promise you, this was a regular bona fide uncomplicated colic.'

'Great.' I told him one reply had come from a pharmaceutical company and, as far as I was concerned, it needed an interpreter. He said to give him half an hour and he would come to Thetford Cottage. Ask Vicky to feed him, he said.

When he arrived I ate a second breakfast with him in the uncosy kitchen, sitting on hard chairs round a white Formica-topped table. Vicky made toast as if on a production line.

'You two have the appetite of goats,' she said. 'It's not fair that you don't get fat.'

'You're an angel,' Ken said. Vicky sniffed, but she liked it.

Replete, Ken took the invoices out of the envelope and looked through them.

'They've sent a whole year's,' he observed. 'Let's see ... sodium, potassium, calcium, chlorine ... mm, these are the ingredients of Ringer's solution.'

'What's Ringer's solution?'

'An all-purpose maintenance fluid. The stuff in the drips.'

'Oh.'

'I use commercially prepared, ready-made sterile bags of fluid for operations,' he said, 'but we make our own in-house fluid for the drips out in the stable as it's much cheaper. In the pharmacy, Scott weighs out ...' He sighed.

'Scott weighed out these ingredients, which are white crystalline powders, and stored them ready in plastic bags. When we need some fluid, we add distilled water.'

He went on looking through the invoices and slowly began frowning.

'We've certainly used a lot of potassium,' he said.

'In the fluids?'

He nodded. 'It's customary to add extra potassium for diarrhoea cases because they get dehydrated and low in potassium. You can also inject it into ready-made drip bags.'

He sat staring into space, hit much as I had been by fugu.

I waited. He swallowed and slowly flushed, the exact opposite of his habit of going pale.

'I should have seen it,' he said.

'Seen what?'

'Potassium chloride. Oh God.' He transferred his unfocused gaze from the direction of the cooker and looked at me with horror. 'I should have seen it. Four times! I'm a disgrace.'

I couldn't tell whether his sense of shame was justified or not because I hadn't the knowledge. Knowing Ken, he'd be blaming himself excessively for any error and would take a long time to get over it.

I said, 'I always told you that you'd come face to face with realization. I told you that somewhere or other, you knew.'

'Yes, you did. Well, I think now that I do. I think

the four that died on the table died of excess potassium, which is called hyperkalemia, and I should have seen it at the time.'

'You weren't expecting the fluids to be wrong.'

'Even so . . .' He frowned. 'The serum samples from the last one that died were in the laboratory when it burned down. There's no way now of proving it, but the more I see . . .'

'Go on,' I said, as he stopped.

'The waves on the ECG, that I told you about, that looked different? There are P waves from the atria of the heart, and they had decreased in amplitude. The heart was slowing down.'

'Wasn't it Scott's job to tell you?'

'The captain's responsible for the ship. I always glance at the ECG, even when he's monitoring it. I simply never gave a thought that the slowing was due to excess potassium. I hadn't given them extra potassium.'

'Exactly,' I said. 'Who fetched the bags of drip, and who changed them when they were empty in all those four operations?' He knew I knew the probable answer, but I asked anyway.

After a moment he said, 'Scott.'

'Always Scott?'

He searched his memory. 'Oliver assisted once. He wanted to be there for the tie-back operation. He took Scott's place. It *can't* have been Scott that killed them.'

'Mm . . .' I pondered. 'How much potassium would you need?'

'It's a bit complicated. You'd have to bring the serum concentration to about eight to ten milliequivalents per litre . . .'

'Ken!'

'Um . . . well, the serum potassium would normally be four milliequivalents per litre or thereabouts, so you'd have to more than double it. To raise the four to six in a horse weighing one thousand pounds you'd need . . . er . . . Let's see . . .' He brought out a pocket calculator and did sums. 'Twenty-three point six eight grams of potassium in powder form. Dissolve that in water and add it to the fluid. When that bag's empty, repeat the process as the serum concentration is now up to eight. A third similar bag would do the trick. The operation would be well advanced by now so it would seem as if it was prolonged anaesthesia that had contributed to the collapse.'

He stood up compulsively and walked round and round the table.

'I should have realized,' he repeated. 'If we'd been using our in-house mixture I'd have tested it for errors, but what I used had come straight from the suppliers and they would never make such a gross mistake.'

I thought of all the bags of commercially prepared drips stacked in boxes in the hospital store room, one-litre and five-litre bags. For the operation on the mare, Ken had used four at least of the five-litre bags: horses in shock and pain, horses with complicated colic, all had to be given extra quantities of fluid, he'd told me,

348

to combat dehydration and maintain the volume of blood. I'd watched Scott methodically change the empty bags for full ones.

'You gave the mare a lot of extra fluids which were obviously the right stuff as she survived the operation,' I said. 'How many bags do you usually use?'

He pursed his lips, still walking, and gave me another not-so-simple answer. Perhaps there weren't any simple answers in veterinary medicine.

'In a routine operation on a healthy racehorse – like the screwed cannon bone – the rate of fluid administration would be three to five millilitres per pound of horse per hour, say about four litres an hour. The mare got fifteen an hour.'

'So you would use the five-litre bags for emergency colic operations and the single-litre bags for cannon bones?'

'More or less.' He thought. 'Mind you,' he said, 'you could probably also kill a horse by giving it too little fluid, or too much. Forty litres an hour of the normal commercial fluid would probably be lethal.'

The deadly opportunities were endless, it seemed.

'Well, all right,' I said. 'You think there was too much potassium in the bags of fluid. How did it get there? How did it get there for those four specific horses and for no others?'

He looked blank. 'It can't have been Scott. I won't believe it.'

'On the night of the mare's operation,' I said, 'Scott

came to the hospital while you were still on the way and I saw him collect the bags of fluid from the store and I helped him carry them along into the pharmacy room. He stacked them on the shelf there that can be reached from inside the theatre by opening the glass door.'

'Yes.'

'Did he have any routine for which bags he took?'

'Yes. Always in the order in which they arrived. Always the nearest or uppermost.'

'So if you wanted to add potassium you could do it in the store room, knowing which bags would be used next.'

Ken said with relief, 'Then it could have been anybody. It didn't have to be Scott.'

It could have been anyone, I reflected, who could go in and out of the store room without anyone thinking it inappropriate. That included all the partners, Scott, Belinda, the nurse who'd left in a huff and quite likely the secretaries and the cleaners. In the store room, there would have been no need to trouble with gowns and shoecovers and sterile procedures. The clear fluid inside the stiff plastic bags was itself sterile, and that was enough.

'I think we ought to talk to Superintendent Ramsey,' I said.

Ken made a face but no demur while I got busy on the phone and ended with an invitation to meet the policeman in the hospital office later that morning.

Ramsey, the farmer-type, listened patiently to the horse-death theory and how it affected Scott. He came with us into the store room to see how the bags of fluid were kept, the nearest to hand being always the next one used. He read the information printed on the plastic; contents and manufacturer.

He followed us along to the small pharmacy section where the bags were stacked on the shelf and he came into the operating room and saw how they could be reached when needed by opening the glass door.

No one actually mentioned the possibility that Scott had discovered who had doctored the bags; it hardly needed to be said.

'The horses are long gone,' Ramsey said ruminatively, back in the office. 'The last batch of tests was burned before investigation. The empty fluid bags were disposed of. There's no way of proving your theory.' He looked thoughtfully at each of us in turn. 'What else do you know that you don't know you know?'

'The riddle of the sphinx,' I said.

'I beg your pardon?'

'Sorry. It sounded like a riddle.'

'A riddle in a conundrum in a maze,' he said unexpectedly. 'A good deal of police work is like that.' He picked up the envelope containing the invoices. 'This wasn't a bad idea. Let me have the other answers when they come.'

We said we would, and I asked him if he knew yet

what had killed Scott. And if he yet knew who had been burned in the fire.

'We're proceeding,' he said, 'with our enquiries.'

I went to see Nagrebb.

Ken wouldn't come with me, but I wanted, out of curiosity if nothing else, to see the man who'd almost certainly cruelly killed two horses, one with laminitis, the other with a dissolved tendon. He and Wynn Lees hadn't cared if their horses died in agony. I'd seen Wynn Lees' mare suffering as I hadn't known horses could, and I'd felt bitterness and grief when she died. I couldn't prove her owner had fed her a carpet needle. I couldn't prove he'd injected his Eaglewood horse with insulin. I *believed* he had, with a revulsion so strong that I wanted never to be near him again.

Nagrebb instantly gave me the same feeling.

I'd imagined him large, bullish and unintelligent like Wynn Lees, so his physical appearance was a surprise. He was out in a paddock behind his house when, following Ken's reluctant instructions. I located his woodsy half-hidden gateposts and turned between them up a stretch of drive that curled round the house until it was out of sight of the road.

The paddock then revealed was fenced with once-white horizontal railings, a tempting path of escape, I would have thought, for any ill-used self-respecting show-jumper. Inside the paddock on well-worn grass a man and an auburn-haired woman stood beside a bright red-and-white show jump like a length of imitation brick wall exhorting another man on a dark muscly horse to launch himself over it. The horse ran out sideways to avoid jumping and received a couple of vicious slashes of a whip to remind him not to do it again.

At that point, all three noticed my arrival and offered only scowls as greeting, an arrangement of features which seemed as normal to them as walking about.

The man on the horse and the woman were young, I saw. The older man, noticeably top-heavy with legs too short for the depth of torso, strode grimly towards the paddock railings. Bald, sharp eyed, pugnacious; a Rottweiler of a man. I got out of the car and went close to the fence to meet him.

'Mr Nagrebb?' I asked.

'What do you want?' He stopped a few feet short of the fence, raising his voice.

'Just a few words.'

'Who are you? I'm busy.'

'I'm writing an article on causes of equine deaths. I thought you might help me.'

'You thought wrong.'

'You're so knowledgeable,' I said.

'What I know I keep to myself. Clear off.'

'I heard you might tell me about acute overnight laminitis,' I said.

His reaction in its way was proof enough. The sudden stillness, the involuntary contraction of muscles round the eyes, I'd watched them often when I'd asked seemingly innocuous questions in diplomatic circles about illicit, hidden sex lives. I knew alarm bells when I saw them.

'What are you talking about?' he demanded.

'Excessive carbohydrates.'

He didn't answer.

There must have been something about him that transmitted anxiety to the other two, as the young woman came running over and the man trotted across on the horse. She was fierce-eyed, a harpy; he as dark and well-muscled as his horse.

'What is it, Dad?' he asked.

'Man wants to know about sudden acute laminitis.'

'Does he, indeed.' His voice was like his father's; local Gloucestershire accent and aggressive. He knew, too, what I was talking about. I wasn't sure about the girl.

'I need first-hand accounts,' I said. 'It's for general public readership, not for veterinary specialists. Just your own words describing how you felt when you found your horse fatally crippled.'

'Tripe,' the son said.

'Last September, wasn't it?' I asked. 'Was he insured?'

'Fuck off,' the son said, bringing the horse right up to the fence and warningly raising his effective whip.

I thought it might be time to take this advice. I'd evaluated Nagrebb, which had been the point of the excursion, making my picture gallery of the old men complete. Ken's opinion of the son I would endorse any day. If the young woman were the daughter, she was the product of the family ethos but not, I thought, its powerhouse.

'Who sent you to us?' Nagrebb demanded.

'Hearsay,' I said. 'Fascinating stuff.'

'What's your name?'

'Blake Pasteur.' I said the first name that came into my head; the name of a colleague first secretary back in Tokyo. I didn't think Nagrebb would be checking the Foreign Office lists. 'Freelance journalist,' I said. 'Sorry you can't help me.'

'Piss off,' Nagrebb said.

I began to make a placatory retreat and that would have been the end of it except that at that moment another car swept round the house and came to a halt beside mine.

The driver climbed out. Oliver Quincy, to my dismay.

'Hello,' he said to me in surprise. 'What the hell are you doing here?' His displeasure was evident.

'Hoping for information for an article on equine deaths.'

'Do you know him?' Nagrebb demanded.

'Of course. Friend of Ken McClure's. Has his nose into everything in the hospital.'

The atmosphere took a chilly turn for the worse.

'I'm writing an article about the hospital,' I said.

'Who for?' Oliver said suspiciously.

'Anyone who'll buy it. And they will.'

'Does Ken know this?' Oliver exclaimed.

'It'll be a nice surprise for him. What are you doing here yourself?'

'None of your bloody business,' Nagrebb said, and Oliver answered simultaneously, 'Usual thing. Strained tendon.'

I tried to see into Oliver's mind, but failed. I guessed I was allied in his thoughts with Ken and Lucy Amhurst, the faithful upholders of Carey Hewett and Partners, the opponents of change. He was eyeing me with antagonism.

'Are you still in the partnership?' I asked.

'The partnership may dissolve,' Oliver replied, 'but horses still need attention.'

'That's what Ken says.'

Nagrebb's son, who'd been watching me more than listening, suddenly slid from his horse, handed the reins to his father, then bent down and ducked under the paddock railings to join Oliver and myself outside. At close quarters, the aggression poured out of him, almost tangible. His father twice over, I thought.

'You're trouble,' he said to me.

He held his whip in his left hand. I wondered fleetingly if he were left-handed. He more or less proved that he wasn't by hitting me very fast and hard with his fist, right-handedly, in the stomach.

356

I might as well have been kicked by a horse. I lost, it seemed to me, the power to breathe. I went down on one knee, doubled over, in virtual paralysis. It didn't much improve things when Nagrebb's son put his booted foot on my bent shoulder and toppled me over.

No one protested. I looked some dusty old grass in the eye. No succour there either.

Breath slowly returned to ease the suffocation and with it came impotent rage, some of it directed at myself for having precipitated the fracas. There was no point in trying to attack Nagrebb junior in my turn; I would be simply knocked down again. Words were my weapons, not arms. I'd never punched anyone in anger.

I got to my knees and to my feet. Nagrebb looked watchful and his son insufferably superior. Oliver was impassive. The girl was smiling.

I found enough breath to speak. Fought to keep my temper.

'Illuminating,' I said.

Not the wisest of remarks, on reflection, but the only sword I had. The son made another stab at me but I was ready for that one and parried his punch on my wrist. Even that was hard enough to numb my fingers. The only thing on the plus side, I thought, was that I hadn't disclosed any knowledge of collagen-dissolving enzymes and wasn't faced with collagenase-loaded syringes.

'Look,' I said, 'I'm a writer. If you don't want to be written about, well, I've got the message.'

I turned my back on them and walked the few steps to my car, trying not to totter.

'Don't come back,' Nagrebb said.

Not on your life, I thought. Not for my own life, either.

I opened the car door and eased painfully into the driver's seat. At the moment of impact, I'd felt as if my lungs had collapsed but with passing time the problem was soreness. Somewhere at the lower end of my sternum was an area of maximum wince.

They didn't try to stop me leaving. I started the car, reversed round Oliver's, and aimed for a straight line down the drive in ignominious defeat. Never engage an enemy, I thought, without buckler and shield.

When I got back to Thetford Cottage I sat for a while in the car, and Ken came out to see why.

He folded his height down to look in through the window which I opened for him.

'What's the matter?' he asked.

'Nothing much.'

'Something obviously is.'

I sighed. Winced. Smiled lop-sidedly. Pointed to my midriff.

'Nagrebb's son upset my solar plexus,' I said.

He was exasperated. 'I told you not to go there.'

'So you did. All my fault.'

'But why? Why did he hit you?'

'I asked about acute overnight laminitis.'

He looked shocked. 'That was a damn silly thing to do.'

'Mm. But the reaction was informative, don't you think? And by the way, Oliver was there, looking at strained tendons. Nagrebb had called him in.'

'Was Nagrebb himself there?'

'He was. Also a fierce red-haired girl who found it amusing that Nagrebb's son had knocked me down. They were all out in the paddock when I arrived.'

Ken nodded. 'That was Nagrebb's daughter. I warned you the son was poison.'

'You were right.'

Poison, I thought. I was on the point of telling Ken about fugu but the more I thought about it, the more it seemed far-fetched. Not fugu, then. But if one non-traceable poison existed, then so might others. Wait, I thought, for the delivery note from Parkway Chemicals.

I inched out of the car and stood gingerly upright. In every film I'd seen where people got punched six times in the stomach, they'd shaken it off like a tap from a feather. As I wasn't accustomed to the treatment, one punch felt like six attentions from a piledriver.

'He really hurt you,' Ken said, concerned.

'Oh well, as you say, I asked for it.'

We went into the house with my asking him not to embarrass me with Greg, Vicky or Belinda and he, now amused, promising not to.

*

On Friday morning, two more reply envelopes arrived but still not the one from Parkway Chemicals. I phoned Parkway, reached the sales manager and asked if all our copies had been sent.

'Why yes,' he confirmed, 'they went off to you yesterday.'

'Thanks very much.'

He didn't understand my urgency and I couldn't explain. Sending the copies after one extra day must have seemed immaterial to him. More patience required. Terrible.

I reached Ken on his phone and told him that two more pharmaceutical replies had arrived. Be right with you, he said.

When he came, he asked about the punch site.

'Recovering,' I said. 'What do we have today?'

He read the bunches of invoices, six months' worth from each place. He nodded, raised his eyebrows, nodded and lowered them.

'Nothing out of the ordinary,' was his comment on the first lot.

The second stack excited him.

'Jeez,' he said. 'Just look at this.'

He pushed the papers across the kitchen table, pointing to one line with a jabbing finger.

'Insulin! We ordered insulin! I can't believe it.'

'*Who* exactly ordered it?'

'Heaven knows.' He frowned. 'We don't have a separate pharmacist, the practice isn't – wasn't – big enough.

360

We make up various things ourselves in the pharmacy. Scott often did. Any of us did. When we use or take something, we write down what it is. There's a column for identifying the manufacturer if it's not something like maintenance fluids, painkillers and everyday needs that we get from wholesale suppliers. The secretary records the whole list in the computer and automatically reorders everything again in due time when stocks are low, unless we add a note not to.'

'So anyone,' I said, 'could write down insulin as having been used, and the secretary would automatically order it?'

'Christ,' he said, awed.

'When the orders arrive, who handles them?'

'One of the secretaries puts the parcels in the pharmacy. Any one of us opens them and puts the contents on the shelves. Most things have their regular space on the shelves and are often used. That's things like vaccines and ointments. Anything unusual or risky is in a special section. Was, of course. I keep seeing the pharmacy as it was and forgetting it's gone.'

'So if anyone unpacked a parcel containing insulin, that's where it would be put, the special section, available for the person who ordered it to pick up?'

'Dead easy,' he said.

He went on reading the invoices and reached something that stopped his breathing almost as effectively as Nagrebb's son had stopped mine.

'It's frightening,' he said hollowly. 'We ordered collagenase.'

'Who ordered it?'

'There's no way of telling.' He shook his head. 'After the secretary's entered the list in the computer, she shreds the paper as a precaution against anyone removing it from our rubbish bins and using the information to order drugs for themselves. We have to be careful about narcotics and amphetamines and the ingredients, for instance, of LSD.'

'Does the secretary know which of you ordered what?'

He nodded. 'She knows our signatures. We always initial for what we've used. She queries if we don't.'

'I suppose she wouldn't remember who initialled insulin and collagenase?'

'We could ask her, but she'd have no reason to remember.' He looked at the lists. 'Insulin was ordered six months ago. That figures. Wynn Lees' horse died last September, just after the order for insulin would have reached here. There was no hanging about.'

'And the collagenase?'

He looked up the date. 'Same thing. It was delivered here a few days after Nagrebb's horse staked itself.' He raised his eyes in puzzlement. 'No one could have staked a horse in that way on purpose.'

'How long do orders usually take to arrive?'

'Not long. A couple of days, especially if we send a special separate order marked "expedite".'

'I would think,' I said, 'that in the week between the staking repair and the disintegration of the tendon, the show-jumper was insured as sound and the collagenase ordered separately at speed.'

Ken rubbed his face.

I said, 'What's to stop anyone getting hold of a sheet of partnership writing paper, ordering insulin and collagenase, and getting the stuff sent to their own private address? Like I got all those envelopes sent here.'

'None of these companies would send any substance anywhere except to the partnership headquarters,' he said, thinking. 'They would never do it. There are strict rules.'

I sighed. We weren't much further forward, except that with every slow step it became more and more certain that someone had been using the partnership's own methods as a pathway to fraud.

'Do all veterinary partnerships follow your ordering procedure?' I asked.

'Shouldn't think so. Ours is pretty unusual, probably. But up to now it's been convenient and no trouble.'

'What about atropine?' I asked.

'We use that all the time after eye surgery to dilate the pupil. It would naturally appear now and then in small quantities on the invoices.'

In a repeat of the day before, I chased around by telephone until I reached Superintendent Ramsey.

'What is it?' he said, a touch impatiently.

363

'Answers from pharmaceutical companies.'

A short pause, then, 'Hospital office, three o'clock this afternoon.'

'Right,' I said.

In the event I met him alone, as Ken, notwithstanding the rumpus of rumours zig-zagging the neighbourhood like wasps, had been called out by a regular racehorse trainer client who wanted to check the blood count of several prospective runners. He and Oliver, Ken said, were continually busy with this procedure.

The superintendent too seemed to be alone, his car in the car park the only one present. I parked beside his and walked across the lonely tarmac and into the deserted building: no dogs, no cats, no partners. Ramsey was waiting for me in the office, having apparently unlocked the doors with a bunch of keys as big as Ken's. His thinning hair was windblown: he looked more than ever an out of doors man.

We sat by the desk and I gave him the invoices and explained the significance of insulin and collagenase, and the way they could be ordered.

He blinked. 'Repeat it, please.'

After I had, he looked pensive. For good measure I told him about the carpet needle and mentioned Brose's theory about the paternity of the dead foal.

He blinked again. 'You've been busy,' he said.

'I set out to clear Ken's reputation.'

'Hm. And you're telling me all this now,' he said in

his blunt way, 'because if I discover who killed the horses, I'll know who killed Scott Sylvester?'

'Yes.'

'You said you still have the carpet needle embedded in the piece of gut, and you've sent samples of the mare's and the foal's and the stallion's hair to a specialist lab for DNA matching. Is that right? And that mare was owned by Wynn Lees?'

I nodded.

'What else?' he asked.

'Atropine,' I said, and repeated Ken's convictions.

'Anything else?'

I hesitated. He bade me continue. I said, 'I've seen or been to visit the owners or trainers of all the suspiciously dead horses. I wanted to get the feel of them, to try to know if they are villains or not. To find out if they themselves were involved with their horses' deaths.'

'And?'

'Two are villains, one definitely isn't, one probably is, one may be but doesn't know it.'

He asked me about the last one, and I told him about old Mackintosh and his fade-in fade-out memory.

'He remembers,' I said, 'the order in which racehorses in a far-back time stood in the loose boxes in his stable yard. He recited them for me like an incantation. Six, he said, was Vinderman. Well, one of the horses which was probably given colic through atropine was stabled in box number six. I thought perhaps that if Mackintosh were provided with an apple, say, or a carrot – he gives his horses carrots every day – to feed especially to Vinderman, he would trot down to his stable and give it to the horse in box number six.'

He said doubtfully, 'Are you sure he would?'

'Of course I'm not sure, but I think it's possible. It's also possible that the head lad knows who visited box six – and box sixteen – bearing gifts. The head lad knows more than he's saying.' I then added, for no reason except that I had it on my mind, 'Mackintosh lives in an old mill house that used to belong to some people called Travers.'

Even experienced policemen don't have total control of their muscles. The subtle shift, the involuntary immobility, he could disguise them as little as Nagrebb. I had really surprised him.

'Travers,' I repeated. 'What does it mean to you?'

He didn't answer directly. 'Do *you* know anyone called Travers?' he asked.

I shook my head. The Travers I'd played with as a child was only a name my mother remembered, not anyone I knew.

He thought for a good time but told me nothing. The interview, he indicated by standing up, was over, the one-way flow of information at a temporary end. If any further drug lore should come my way, he said, he would like to have it.

'Where can I reach you tomorrow?' I asked. 'As it happens we found out that Scott went to a chemical company personally to collect something not allowed to be sent through the post. Tomorrow we should know what it was. The company sent the information off yesterday.'

Without waste of time he sat down again, wrote a number on a piece of memo paper and handed it to me, saying it would get him at any time.

'The postman comes at about ten,' I said. 'I'll have to get Ken there to interpret the chemical names into words I understand. After that I could call you.'

'Do it,' he nodded.

'Tell me about Travers,' I said persuasively. 'There was a financial firm of some sort long ago called Upjohn and Travers. The present Upjohn, Ronnie, he's about sixty. He acts as a steward at Stratford-upon-Avon races. He had an injured horse that he wanted Ken to put down a year or so ago. Ken said he could save the horse, and personally bought it from Upjohn, at not much more than a dead-meat price. The horse, since Ken's expert surgery, has won a race, and Upjohn is far from pleased. Illogical, but people are like that. Anyway, Ronnie Upjohn's father had a partner called Travers. All I know about him is hearsay from Ken's mother, Josephine, who described old man Travers as "rolling" and "a frightful lecher". He would be at least ninety now, I should think, if he's still alive.'

Ramsey closed his eyes as if to prevent my inspecting his thoughts. 'Anything else?' he said.

'Um . . . Porphyry Place.'

'That awful red monstrosity on the way to Tewkesbury? What about it?'

'Old Mackintosh lost money in it. So did Ronnie Upjohn and a lot of other people round here.'

He nodded a shade grimly, his eyes still shut, and I wondered fleetingly if he'd been among the unfortunates.

I went on conversationally, 'You don't have to be the owner of a horse to insure it. It can be insured without the owner knowing. The pay-out, sent in good faith by the company, never reaches the owner, who remains in ignorance from start to finish.'

His eyes opened. I saw that he well understood the implication.

'It's a big maybe,' I said, 'but maybe someone came up with a way of recovering their losses in Porphyry Place.'

He put a cupped hand over his mouth.

'Could you,' I asked, 'get from anywhere a list of the people who lost money guaranteeing those loans?'

'Don't tell me,' he said, ironic despite his training, 'that you haven't managed that yourself?'

'I don't know who to ask and I wouldn't have much chance of being told.'

'True.' A smile glimmered briefly. He didn't say whether or not he would obtain a list, nor whether he would show it to me if he did. Police the world over weren't renowned for sharing their information.

He rose to his feet again and came with me out to

the car park, carefully locking doors behind him. He seemed avuncular more than forbidding, but then bears could look cuddly. He might listen to me and reckon that Ken had killed the horses himself. Ken had at first been reluctant, if not afraid, to tell me how horses could be killed on the grounds that knowledge could be twisted into a presumption of guilt.

'I'll hear from you tomorrow,' Ramsey said, nodding and getting into his car.

'Right.'

He waited until I had started my own car and driven to the exit, almost as if shepherding me out. He needn't have worried that I'd go back: there was barely time to scorch the miles to the Fulham Road by six o'clock.

Annabel, relatively conservative in the silver cowboy boots below a straight black dress, opened her door and looked at her watch, laughing.

'Ten seconds late.'

'Abject apologies,' I said.

'Accepted. Where are we going?'

'You're the Londoner. You choose.'

She chose an adventure film and dinner in a bistro. The hero in the film got punched six times in the solar plexus and came up smiling.

The bistro had candles in Chianti bottles, red-checked tablecloths and a male gipsy singer with a flower behind his ear. I told Annabel about Vicky and

Greg's singing. Old fashioned but great voices. She would like to hear them, she said.

'Come down on Sunday,' I said on impulse.

'Sunday I see the bishop and his wife.'

'Oh.'

She looked down at her pasta, candlelight on her bouncy chopped-off hair, her eyes in shadow, considering.

'I only miss Sundays with them if it's important,' she said.

'This is important.'

She raised her eyes. I could see candle flames in them.

'Don't say it lightly,' she said.

'It's important,' I repeated.

She smiled briefly. 'I'll come on the train.'

'For country pub lunch?'

She nodded.

'And stay for the evening and I'll drive you home.'

'I can go back on the train.'

'No. Not alone.'

'You're as bad as my father. I can look after myself, you know.'

'All the same, I'll drive you.'

She smiled at her pasta. 'The bishop will have to approve of you in spite of your job.'

'I tremble to meet him.'

She nodded as if trembling were expected and asked how things were going in the practice. 'I can't get that poor man Scott out of my mind.'

I told her about the results from the pharmaceutical companies, which fascinated and alarmed her by turns. I told her that since Carey had dissolved the partnership, all the vets were rushing around like chickens without heads, looking after sick animals but with no central organization.

'But *can* anyone dissolve a partnership like that?'

'Heaven knows. The legal problems look knotty. Carey's exhausted and wants out. Half the others want him out. They jointly pay the mortgage on the hospital, which is currently shut. God help Ken if there's a middle of the night emergency.'

'What a mess.'

'Yup. It's a long way from here or now, though.'

'Mm.'

'So . . . er . . . does the bishop have any other daughters or sons?'

'Two of each.'

'Wow.'

'I'd guess,' she said, 'that you're an only child.'

'How do you know?'

'You don't need roots.'

I'd never thought of my nomadic life in that way, but perhaps it was solitariness that made the go-where-you're-sent discipline easy.

'How strong are yours?' I asked.

'I've never tried to pull them up.'

We looked at each other.

'I'll be in England for four years,' I said. 'After that,

371

a month or so every two years. If I reach sixty, I can
stay here always. Most diplomats buy a house here
somewhere along the line. My parents have one but I
can't live there now because it's leased to a company.
When my father retires in four years' time and the
lease runs out, they'll come back here to stay.'

She listened carefully.

'The Foreign Office pays for children to come home
from foreign postings and go to boarding schools,' I
said.

'Did you do that?'

'Only for my last two years.' I explained about
learning the languages in one's teens. 'Also I wanted
to stay with my parents. I like them and it's a multi-
everything life.'

A job description, I thought, was an odd sort of way
to tell her I was more than ordinarily interested in her
future. She seemed to have no trouble understanding.
It was also plain that this was to be no lusty rush into
uncontrollable sexual attraction and damn the consequences. Annabel wanted to be sure of her footing.

I drove her home and kissed her goodbye as before.
This time the kiss lasted longer and was a tingling
matter that made uncontrollable sex look totally desirable. I smiled at myself and at her, and she said she
would take whichever train on Sunday reached Cheltenham nearest to noon.

*

On Saturday morning the letter from Parkway Chemicals finally arrived, and to me looked like gobbledegook. While I waited for Ken, I read the few intelligible pieces of information supplied with the invoices.

The Parkway Chemical Company was in the business of selling biochemical organic compounds for research, and also diagnostic reagents. The company that had sent insulin and collagenase had had similar headings. Parkway Chemicals could be ordered by fax and by Freefone.

I read the few ordinary invoices but the only substance ordered that I recognized was fibrinogen, used to help blood clot.

The delivery note given to Scott had warnings stamped all over it.

'Extremly hazardous material.' 'For the use of qualified personnel.' 'Laboratory only.' 'Hand delivered.'

Scott had signed his name in acceptance.

The fuss, it seemed, was over three small ampoules of something called tetrodotoxin.

When Ken saw it he said immediately, 'Anything with the suffix "toxin" is poisonous.' He frowned over the details and read them aloud. 'Three ampoules one mg tetrodotoxin with sodium citrate buffer. Soluble in water. Read safety sheet.'

'What is it?' I asked.

'I'll have to look it up.'

Although the owners of Thetford Cottage weren't

book people, they did have a row of reference books and a small encyclopedia. Ken and I searched in vain for tetrodotoxin. The nearest the dictionary came to it was 'tetrode', a vacuum tube containing four electrodes, which hardly seemed to fit the case.

'I'd better go home for my books on poisons,' Ken said.

'OK.'

As I had the dictionary in my hands, and on the off chance, I looked up puffer fish. The entry read:

'**Puffer**, also called blowfish or globefish, capable of inflating the body with water or air until it resembles a globe, the spines in the skin becoming erected . . .'

So far, so good. It was the sting in the tail that had me gasping.

'. . . of the fish family *Tetraodontidae*.'

Puffer fish.

It was my old friend fugu after all.

CHAPTER TWELVE

'*Puffer fish?*' Ramsey said.

The superintendent had met us alone again in the empty hospital. It was rather as if he wanted to keep his sessions with Ken and me separate from whatever other enquiries he was making.

Ken had been home for his book on poisons.

'Tetrodotoxin,' he read aloud, 'is one of the most potent poisons known. It comes from the puffer fish and causes respiratory and cardiovascular failure through paralysis of the neuro-muscular system. A fatal dose is extremely small; only micrograms per kilogram of body weight. It is very unlikely to be detected by forensic examination.'

'Let me read that,' Ramsey said.

Ken gave him the book and we waited while he digested the bad news. Then he picked up the delivery note and read through it for the second or third time.

'You're telling me,' he said, 'that one milligram of this powder will kill a horse? One thousandth of a gram?'

'Yes, easily,' Ken said. 'A racehorse weighs approximately 450 kilograms. A microgram is *one millionth* of a gram. One of the ampoules would be enough to kill four horses, at a rough guess. So far, we've two dead, Fitzwalter's chipped knee and the broodmare.'

There was a dismayed pause while we each worked out that there might still be a good deal of the stuff lying around.

'Would you sprinkle the powder on the horse's food?' Ramsey asked.

'I suppose you could,' Ken said doubtfully, 'but it would be more usual to reconstitute it in water and inject it, preferably into a vein.'

'And wear surgical gloves while you do it,' I suggested.

'My God, yes.'

'Scott,' I said, 'must have known who had asked him to travel that distance to fetch the package. Must have known who he gave it to. He didn't necessarily know what was in it.' I paused and added, 'I guess he found out the hard way.'

'Jeez,' Ken said under his breath.

'Tell us,' I begged Ramsey. 'Just say yes or no. Did you find any needle puncture mark on Scott?'

He pursed his mouth. Looked at the question from north round to south. Consulted a mental rule book.

'You've been of considerable assistance,' he said finally. 'The answer is yes.' He checked some more with his inner self and squeezed out a few more sentences.

'Four days of tests have revealed the presence of treble a normal dose of soporific, taken in coffee. No other toxic material of any sort has so far been found. The needle puncture was into a vein on the back of the hand.'

At least, I thought, Scott had been asleep when he died. I reckoned he would have had to have been. All that explosive muscle power would have presented a daunting prospect to anyone wishing to creep up on him holding a death-laden syringe. Too much possibility of the tables being turned.

The symbolic closing of Scott's mouth, I thought, had been itself an unconscious declaration of motive. I'd never been involved with a murder before and understood little of the overpowering impulse to kill, but in the macabre state of Scott's body a compulsion of extreme magnitude was unmistakably visible. It hadn't been enough just to stop him talking: the raw statement must have sprung from subterranean urges too powerful to combat. In the depths of the psyche, logic foundered, caution dissolved, obsession swept all decency away.

Scott might have been an accomplice who finally objected. He might have discovered irregularities and threatened to reveal them. He might have tried a little dangerous blackmail. The brutality of the staples had been the violent response.

Ramsey, having once begun to divulge, continued, 'I see no harm in telling you what will be released to the press later today. We've identified the person burned in your fire.'

'You have?' Ken exclaimed. 'Who was it?'

Maddeningly, Ramsey answered the question crabwise. 'Usually if someone goes missing, it's reported. In this case, the person was not reported missing as his family believed he was away for a few days' fishing and at a trade conference. When he didn't return this Thursday evening at the expected time, the family discovered he hadn't been to the conference at all. They were alarmed and informed us at once. Owing partly to your information and your innuendos, sir,' he said to me, 'we speculated that the missing man and the unidentified body were one and the same. Dental records have now proved this to be the case.'

He stopped. Ken, disgusted, said, 'Come on man, who was it?'

Ramsey savoured his disclosures. 'A man, thirty-two years old, not on very good terms with his wife, who hadn't expected him to phone her from the conference. He was an insurance agent.' He paused. 'His name,' he said finally, 'was Travers. Theodore Travers.'

I knew my mouth fell open.

Theo, I thought. The Travers I'd played with, the Travers of the mill house, his name was Theo.

Dear God, I thought. Perhaps one should never go back to the scenery of one's childhood, perhaps never learn the fates of one's friends. To come back as a stranger into the future of one's past life, an adventure

378

that had at first pleased and captivated me, now seemed like a danger best left alone.

It was too late to wish I'd never returned. Since I had, in the most fortuitous unrolling of events, all I could do was try to leave the present state of Kenny's son in better shape than if I'd stayed away.

'Upjohn and Travers,' I said.

Ramsey nodded. 'We looked them up after you spoke of them yesterday. The firm no longer exists, and hasn't for many years, but in the days of old lecherous Travers, it was an insurance agency. It broke up when both Travers and Upjohn died.' He looked at me straightly. 'How did you hear, sir, of Upjohn and Travers?'

I said weakly, 'I don't know.'

Ken gave me a sharp-eyed look, trusting still, but ever more puzzled.

I must have heard the old firm's name at Theo's house, I supposed. I simply didn't know why it had stuck in my mind.

'Why,' I said, 'should an insurance agent be present in the veterinary building late in the evening?'

'Well, why?' Ramsey asked, as if knowing the answer.

'Someone let him in to discuss insurance schemes,' I said. 'Maybe illicit insurance of horses. Maybe they had an argument which ended either in the accidental or intentional death of Travers. Maybe the place was set on fire to cover it up.'

'That's a lot of maybes,' Ramsey observed, 'though I'm not saying you're wrong.'

Toss up the pieces, I thought, and they all came down in a jumble.

Ramsey ushered us out again and locked the doors, although presumably Ken had his own bunch in his pocket and could let us straight in again if he wanted. Ken seemed, however, to find the hospital oppressive and was happy to leave. We stood together by our cars in the car park and Ken said, 'What next?'

What happened next was one of those extraordinary flashes of ancient memory, tantalizingly incomplete most of the time but sometimes blindingly clear. Perhaps many different threads had to converge before the right synapse detonated. I remembered my threatening dream and knew I'd once heard my mother say more than she'd told me on the phone.

'Um,' I said breathlessly, 'how about if we go to see Josephine?'

'Whatever for?'

'To talk about your father.'

'No,' he protested, 'you can't.'

'I think we must,' I said, and told him in part what I wanted.

He looked upset, but drove to Josephine's home while I followed.

She lived on the top two floors of a fine big Edwardian house situated in a graceful semi-circular terrace in Cheltenham. Her drawing-room windows opened on to an ironwork balcony overlooking the wintry public garden in front. It could have been a delight, but Josephine's furnishings were stilted and unimaginative, as if not changed for decades.

Ken having forewarned her by telephone, she was pleased enough to see us. We had bought a bottle of sweet sherry on the way, Ken saying his mother liked it very much but wouldn't buy it for herself, repressed woman that she was. The gift, grudgingly accepted, was nevertheless immediately opened. Ken poured his mother a large glassful and two less exuberant slugs for himself and me. He made a face over his, but I could drink or eat anything by that time without showing dislike.

Disregard what you're actually putting into your mouth, my father had usefully instructed. If you know it's a sheep's eye, you'll be sick. Think of it as a grape. Concentrate on the flavour, not the origin. Yes, Dad, I'd said.

Josephine wore a grey skirt, prim cream shirt and a sludge green cardigan. There was a photograph in a silver frame on a side table showing her young, smiling, pretty. Beside her in the picture stood a recognizable version of the Ken I knew: same long head, long body, fair hair. Kenny in the picture smiled happily: the Ken I knew smiled seldom.

We sat down. Josephine pressed her knees together: to repulse lechers, I supposed.

381

Beginning was difficult. 'Was Ken's father a good sportsman?' I asked.

'How do you mean?'

'Er ... did he like fishing? My father fishes all the time.' My father would be amazed to hear it, I thought.

'No, he didn't like fishing,' Josephine said, raising eyebrows. 'Why do you ask?'

'Shooting?' I said.

She spluttered over the sherry, half choking.

'Do listen, Mother,' Ken said persuasively. 'We've never really known why Dad killed himself. Peter has a theory.'

'I don't want to hear it.'

'I think you do.'

I said, 'Did he shoot?'

Josephine looked at Ken. He nodded to her. 'Tell him,' he said.

She drank sherry. She would be all right once she'd started, I thought, remembering the unlocking of the gossip floodgates at lunch in Thetford Cottage; and so, hesitantly, it proved.

'Kenny,' she said, 'used to go shooting pheasants with the crowd.'

'Which crowd?'

'Oh, you know. Farmers and so on. Mac Mackintosh. Rolls Eaglewood. Ronnie Upjohn. Those people.'

'How many guns did Kenny have?'

'Only the one.' She shuddered. 'I don't like thinking about it.'

'I know,' I said placatingly. 'Where was he when he shot himself?'

'Oh dear. Oh dear.'

'Do tell him,' Ken said.

She gulped the sherry as a lifeline. Ken poured her more.

If the flash in my memory was right, I knew the answer, but for Ken's sake, it had to come from his mother.

'You've never told me where he died,' Ken said. 'No one would talk to me about him. I was too young, everyone said. Recently, now that I'm the age he was when he died, I want to know more and more. It's taken me a long time to face his killing himself, but now that I have, I have to know where and why.'

'I'm not sure about why,' she said unhappily.

'Where, then.'

She gulped.

'Go on, darling mother.'

The affection in his tone overthrew her. Tears streamed from her eyes. For a while she was completely unable to speak but eventually, bit by bit, she told him.

'He died ... he shot himself ... standing in the stream ... where it was shallow ... some way below the mill wheel ... on the Mackintosh place.'

The revelation rocked Ken and confirmed my vision. In memory, I heard clearly my weeping mother's voice, sometime soon after she'd heard the news, talking to a visitor while I hid out of sight. She'd said, 'He fell into the millstream and his brains washed away.'

'His brains washed away.' I'd stored that frightful phrase in deep freeze as a picture too awful to summon into consciousness. Now that I'd remembered it, the suppression surprised me. I'd have thought it was just the ghoulish sort of thing small boys would gloat over. Perhaps it was because it had made my mother cry.

'Do you know,' I asked gently, 'if his gun was in the stream with him?'

'Does it matter? Yes, it was. Of course, it was. Otherwise he couldn't have shot himself.'

She put down her glass, stood up abruptly, and went over to a mahogany bureau. From the top portion she retrieved a key with which she opened the lowest drawer, and from the lowest drawer produced a large polished wooden box. Another key was necessary to open that, but finally she brought it over and put it on the table beside her chair.

'I haven't looked at these things since just after Kenny died,' she said, 'but perhaps, for your sake, Ken, it's time.'

The box contained newspapers, typewritten sheets and letters.

The letters, on top, were expressions of sympathy. The crowd, as Josephine called them, had done their duty with warmth: they'd clearly liked Kenny. Mackintosh, Eaglewood, Upjohn, Fitzwalter – a surprise, that – and many from clients, friends and fellow vets. I

384

flipped through them. No letter from Wynn Lees, that I could see.

Towards the bottom, my heart skipped a bump. There, in her regular handwriting, was a short note from my mother.

My dear Josephine,

I'm so terribly sorry. Kenny was always a good friend and we shall miss him very much on the racecourse. If there's anything I can do, please let me know. In deepest sympathy,

Margaret Perry.

My poor young mother, weeping with grief, had had impeccable manners. I put her long-ago letter back with the others and tried to show no emotion.

Turning to the newspapers I found they varied from factual to garish and bore many identical pictures of the dead man. 'Well liked', 'respected', 'a great loss to the community'. Verdict at the inquest: 'not enough evidence to prove that he intended to take his own life'. No suicide notes. Doubts and questions. 'If he hadn't meant to kill himself, what was he doing standing in a stream in January with his shoes and socks on?' 'Typical of Kenny, always thoughtful, not to leave a mess for others to clean up.'

'I can't bear to read them,' Josephine said wretchedly. 'I thought I'd forgiven him, but I haven't. The disgrace! You can't imagine. It was hard enough being a widow, but when your husband kills himself it's the ultimate rejection, and everyone thinks it's your fault.'

'But it was an open verdict,' I said. 'It says so in the papers.'

'That makes no difference.'

'I thought there was a fuss about a drug he shouldn't have ordered,' I said. 'There's nothing about it here.'

'Yes, there is,' Ken said faintly. He'd been reading one of the typewritten sheets with his mouth open. 'You'll *never* believe this. And who on earth told you?'

'Can't remember,' I said erroneously.

He handed me the papers, looking pale and shattered. 'I don't understand it.'

I read in his footsteps. It seemed to be a letter of opinion, but had no heading and no signature. It was shocking and revelatory, and in a way inevitable.

It said baldly:

Kenneth McClure, shortly before his death, had ordered and obtained a small supply, ostensibly for research purposes, of the organic compound tetrodotoxin. A horse in his care subsequently died suddenly without apparent cause, consistent with tetrodotoxin poisoning. While not accusing him of having himself administered this extremely dangerous material, one had to consider whether the acquisition or dispensing of this substance could have engendered a remorse strong enough to lead to suicide. As it is impossible to know, I suggest we

do not put forward the possible explanation on the
grounds that it is alarmist.

In a shaking voice Ken asked his mother, 'Do you
know about this tetrodotoxin?'

'Is that what it was?' she asked vaguely. 'There was
an awful commotion but I didn't want to hear it. I didn't
want people knowing that Kenny had done wrong. It
was all too awful already, don't you see?'

What I saw quite clearly was that somewhere among
the old crowd the knowledge of the existence and dead-
liness of tetrodotoxin had been slumbering in abeyance
all these years, and something – perhaps the Porphyry
fiasco – had awakened it to virulence.

'Kenny!' old Mackintosh had said joyfully, when
we'd visited him. 'Did you bring the stuff?'

Kenny had, I judged. And then presumably had
repented and shot himself – or had decided to blow
the whistle, and had been silenced.

Scott, the messenger with his mouth shut. Travers,
the insurance agent burned to the teeth. Kenny, the vet
with his brains in the water and his gun with him,
washed clean of prints. Tetrodotoxin, arguably, had
been too much for any of them to stomach.

'Oh, God,' Ken said miserably, 'so that was why. I
wish now that I didn't know.'

'You know where,' I said, 'but not whether.'

'What do you mean?'

'I mean, he left no note. So the question is, did he

kill himself in the stream, or did someone shoot him on the bank so that he fell backwards into the water?' Mother and son were aghast. I went on regretfully, 'For one thing, how do you aim a shotgun at your head if you're knee deep? You can't reach the trigger, unless you use a stick. On the other hand, a shotgun let off at close quarters packs a terrific punch, easily enough to lift a man off his feet.'

Ken protested. 'That can't be right. Why should anyone kill him?'

'Why was Scott killed?' I asked.

He was silent.

'I think . . .' Josephine's voice quavered, 'awful that it is, I'd feel he hadn't betrayed me so terribly if he couldn't help it. If someone killed him. It's so long ago . . . but if he was killed . . . I'll feel better.'

Ken looked as if he couldn't understand her logic, but I knew my own mother, too, would be comforted.

Ken stayed with Josephine and I spent the afternoon aimlessly driving round the countryside, thinking. I stopped for a while on Cleeve Hill, overlooking Cheltenham racecourse, seeing below me the white rails, the green grass, the up-and-downhill supreme test for steeplechasers. The Grand National was a great exciting lottery, but the Cheltenham Gold Cup sorted out the true enduring stars.

The course, once familiar to me to the last blade of

grass, had metamorphosed into an alien creature. There were huge new stands and realigned smoothed-out tracks, and the parade ring had turned itself round and changed entirely. To one side a whole village of striped medieval-looking tents was being erected, no doubt for sponsors and private parties at the big meeting due to be held in less than two weeks. It would be odd, I thought, to walk again through those gates. The long-ago course and the long-ago child were echoes in the wind. The here and now, the new world, would be yesterday's ghost in its time.

I drove on. I drove past the ugly red lump of conspicuously sign-posted Porphyry Place and on into nice old Tewkesbury. I stopped by the River Severn and thought of Kenny's washed-away brains, and I tried to sort out everything I'd seen, everything I'd heard and everything I'd remembered since I'd come back.

The conviction that gradually emerged seemed to have been staring me in the face all along, saying, 'Here I am. Look at me.' It was theory, though, more than substance, so I could certainly *believe* but certainly not yet *prove*. Matching the foal's DNA might be helpful. Porphyry Place might cough up a name. Villainous old Mackintosh essentially knew, as I did, things he couldn't always call to mind.

Devising a revealing trap seemed the only solution, but I couldn't so far think of one that would work.

I drove back to Thetford Cottage in the dark and swept Greg and Vicky out to drinks and dinner in the giddy heights of Cheltenham. Vicky, coquettish, said Belinda would be middle-aged before herself. Greg smiled amiably. We talked about the wedding plans, which Ken had left to Belinda, and Belinda largely to her mother. There seemed an amazing amount to arrange. When I married Annabel, I thought, we would surely not need so much.

Dear heavens! I'd let that intention slip in unawares. When I married Annabel indeed! Much too soon, too soon for that.

A short while after we'd returned to the cottage, Ken telephoned.

'Where have you been?' he asked.

'Rioting in the town with Greg and Vicky.'

'That'll be the day. Look,' he sounded awkward, 'my mother's been crying buckets. You let loose a log-jam of grief. But, by God, I thank you. I don't know how you know the things you know, but as far as I'm concerned, my father can rest in peace.'

'I'm glad.'

'Since I got home,' he said, 'Carey phoned. He sounded pretty depressed. He wanted to know how things were going in the practice. I told him we needed him, but I honestly think he's stopped caring. Anyway, I told him about the invoices and what we'd been doing.'

'What did he say?'

'Nothing much. Just that we'd done well. I couldn't seem to get him interested. I think Oliver's right after

390

all. We'll have to regroup and work something out for ourselves.'

'Probably best.'

His voice sounded purposeful. 'I'm going to get all the others together to discuss it.'

'Good idea.'

'Anyway, thanks again,' he said. 'See you tomorrow, no doubt.'

Maybe, I thought, as he disconnected, but tomorrow Annabel would be coming and I wanted a private, not a family, lunch.

She came on the train nearest noon and we kissed a greeting as familiarly as if the eight days we'd known each other were eighty on a desert island. She wore a vast sweater of white stars on black over tight black stretchy trousers. Pink lipstick. Huge eyes.

'I've found a super pub for lunch,' I said, 'but we've got to make a short stop on the way. A tiny bit of sleuthing. Won't be long.'

'Never mind,' she said smiling. 'And I've brought you a present from Brose's friend Higgins to help you along.'

She took an envelope from a shiny black handbag and gave it to me. It contained, I found, a list of three insurance companies that had paid out on horses that had died off the racecourse during the past year. Alongside each company was a name and number for me to get in touch with, and at the bottom Higgins had written, 'Mention my name and you'll get the pukka gen. More to come next week.'

'Wonderful,' I said, very pleased. 'With these, we must be nearly home. I'll start phoning in the morning. It was boring old paperwork that put Al Capone in jail, don't forget. Paperwork's damning, as everyone knows only too well in the service, when we get things wrong.'

'Never sign anything,' she said ironically, 'and you'll stay out of trouble.'

We climbed into my car and set off to the horse hospital.

I said, 'Vicky took a message from the superintendent who's in charge of Scott's death saying he wants to see me briefly late this morning. Ken and I have talked to him at the hospital every day lately. It's getting to be a habit.'

'How are things going in general?'

'I'll tell you over lunch if you like, though there are better things to talk about. How's the bishop?'

'Cautious.'

I smiled. I was growing less cautious every time I saw her. The prospect of the spring and summer ahead, the feeling of life beginning, the shivering excitement deep down, all came together in a fizzing euphoria. Let it not be a mistake, I thought. In a few months we would know whether it would last for ever, if the attraction had glue. I'd never come near to thinking in such terms before. Perhaps it was true that one could know at once, when one met the right partner.

Perhaps she knew too. I saw in her the same glimmering acknowledgement, but also the certainty of her withdrawal if she should judge it a mistake. A mixture of fun, competence and reserve, that was Annabel. I began worrying that when I asked her, she wouldn't have me.

There was only one parked car by the front entrance of the hospital when we got there. Not Ramsey's usual car, not a car I knew.

'I don't think the superintendent's here yet, but someone is,' I said. 'Care to come in and look round?'

'Yes, I would. I've only ever seen the arrangements at Newmarket, before this.'

We went into the entrance hall and down the passage to the office, which was empty of everyone, not just policemen.

'Let's see how much is unlocked,' I suggested, and we continued on down the passage to the door of the theatre vestibule. It opened to the touch and we went through, with me pointing out the changing rooms and pharmacy cupboard to Annabel and saying at least we didn't need to bother with shoecovers and sterility or any of that jazz.

We went into the theatre and looked around. Annabel was enthusiastic about the hoist.

'In the place I saw in Newmarket, they stand the horse beside a table thing and strap him to it while he is still standing upright, conscious though sedated. Then when they've given the anaesthetic, they flip the table over to the horizontal position and hey presto, start cutting.'

The sliding door to the padded anaesthesia/recovery room was wide open to every passing germ. We went through there, Annabel exclaiming over the resilient floor and bouncing up and down a couple of times.

'What's that wall for?' she asked, pointing.

'The vets stand behind that when the horse comes round,' I explained. 'Apparently the patient thrashes around sometimes and the vets like to be out of kicking range.'

'Like bullrings,' she said.

'Exactly.'

There seemed to be no one about. We went on across the corridor and into the reception room with its array of equipment round the walls, all quiet and ready for use.

'Usually they're so careful about locking everything,' I said. 'The whole system's coming to bits.'

'Poor people.'

I tried the door leading to the outside world. That at least was secure.

I began to feel vaguely uneasy. The entire theatre area felt wrong, though I couldn't analyse why. I'd grown familiar with the place and it all looked the same. The difference was that I was now pretty sure who had murdered Scott, and felt anxious to tell

Ramsey immediately. It was unlike him not to be there already, though the 'late morning' of his message hadn't been pin-pointedly precise.

Perhaps I should have told Ken, I thought, but the damage had been done. Perhaps it wasn't such a good idea to be here on a Sunday morning.

'Let's go back to the office,' I said abruptly. 'I'll phone Ramsey's number and see how long before he gets here.'

'OK.'

I turned and led the way back through the padded room, heading for the passage. I went through into the theatre with all its life-saving and businesslike equipment and spoke over my shoulder.

'Have you ever been really ill in hospital?'

Annabel didn't answer.

I looked back and was flooded with horror, feeling adrenalin pour hot through my blood like a drench. She was down on her knees, her arms making uncoordinated movements, her head hanging low. Even as I sprinted back to her, she fell forward unconscious onto the spongy floor.

'Annabel!' I was agonized, bending over her, kneeling beside her, turning her, not knowing what was wrong with her, not knowing what help to get her, frenzied with worry.

I heard only at the last minute the rustle of clothes behind me and turned my head too late, too late.

A figure advanced from a bare yard away, a figure

in surgical gown, surgical gloves, surgical cap and mask. He carried a syringe which he jabbed like a dagger at my neck.

I felt the deep sting of the needle. I grabbed towards his clothes and he skipped back a pace, the eyes like grey pebbles over the mask.

I knew too late that he'd been hiding behind the bullring wall, that he'd darted out to inject Annabel, that he'd hidden again and come out of the other end to creep up behind me as I bent over her.

I knew, while clouds swiftly gathered in my brain, I knew as I went to inexorable sleep, that I'd been right. Small comfort. I'd been foolish as well.

The man in surgeon's clothes had murdered Scott.

An old grey man with all the veterinary knowledge in the world.

Carey Hewett.

I was lying on the floor, my nose pressed to the padding, smelling a mixture of antiseptic and horse. Awareness was partial. My eyelids weighed tons. My limbs wouldn't work, nor my voice.

The fact of being alive was in itself amazing. I felt as if awakening from ether, not death. I wanted to sink back into sleep.

Annabel!

The thought of her stormed through my half con-sciousness and quickened my sluggish wits towards order. With an enormous effort I tried to move, seeming to myself to fail.

I must have stirred. There was a fast exclamation above me, more breath than words. I realized that someone was touching me, moving my hands, hastening roughly.

Instinctive fear swamped me. Logical fear immediately followed. There was a clank of chains, and I knew that sound. The chains of the hoist.

No, I protested numbly. Not that. Not like Scott.

The physical effects of terror were at first an increase of the paralysis already plaguing me, but after that came a rush of useful bloody-mindedness that raced along like fire and set me fighting.

Flight was impossible. My limbs still had no strength. Equine padded cuffs had been strapped round my wrists. He clipped the chains onto the cuffs.

No, I thought.

My brain was one huge silent scream.

My eyes came open.

Annabel lay on the floor a few feet away, fast asleep. At least she looked asleep. Peaceful. I couldn't bear it. I'd brought her into appalling danger. I'd taken the message to meet Ramsey to be genuine. I should have been more careful, knowing that Ken had told Carey how much we'd discovered. Regrets and remorse thudded like piledrivers, relentlessly punishing.

Muscles recovered faster. I stretched the fingers of

one hand towards the buckles on the other wrist. The chains clinked from the movement.

Another exclamation from across the room and an impression of haste.

The hoist whined, reeling in the chains.

I couldn't get the buckles undone. Undid one, but there were two on each cuff.

The shortening chains tugged my wrists upwards, lifted my arms, pulled up my body, pulled me to my feet, pulled me higher until I dangled in the air. I shook my head desperately as if that itself would undo the frightful leadenness in my mind and clear away the remaining mists.

Carey stood inside the theatre and pressed the hoist's buttons. Raging and helpless I began to travel along the rails towards the sliding door, through that towards the huge operating table. I lunged towards Carey with my feet, but he was out of range of my futile swings and greyly intent on what he was doing.

His mercilessness and lack of emotion were unnerving. He wasn't gloating or cursing or telling me I shouldn't have meddled. He seemed to be approaching just another job.

'Carey,' I said, pleading, 'for God's sake.'

He might as well not have heard.

'I've told Ramsey it was you who murdered Scott.' I yelled it, all at once without control, petrified, pathetic, in shattering fear, believing I was lost.

He paid no attention. He was concentrating on the matter in hand.

He stopped the hoist when I was still short of the table and put his head on one side, considering. It was almost, I thought, as if he wasn't sure what to do next.

I understood as if in a revelation that he hadn't intended or expected me to be awake at that point, that Scott hadn't been watching him and shouting at him, that things weren't going entirely to plan.

The syringeful of what I hoped against hope had been simple anaesthetic had been at least half used on Annabel and he hadn't been able to put me out for as long as he'd meant.

He must have been disturbed to find me not alone. I guessed that perhaps he'd intended to lure me into the theatre by some noise or other and plump his needle in by surprise. Perhaps he'd thought I wouldn't be alarmed by a surgeon, if I'd seen him. Perhaps anything.

He made a decision and crossed to one of the wall tables upon which lay a kidney dish. He picked up a syringe that had been lying there, held it up to the light and squirted it gently until drops oozed out of the needle.

I didn't need telling that I was meeting the puffer fish.

Time really had come to an end if I just went on hanging there helplessly. He had to reach me with that needle to do any harm. All I had to do was stop him.

Imminent extinction gave me powers I would have said were impossible. As he started towards me, I bent my arms to raise myself and jackknife my body, bringing my knees to my chin, trying by straightening fiercely to get my feet onto the operating table to my left and behind me. The manoeuvre didn't really succeed but I did get my feet as far as the edge of the table, which gave me purchase to swing out towards Carey and try to knock away the syringe with my shoes.

He skipped backwards, carefully holding the syringe high. I swung futilely in the air, feeling wrenched and furious.

After a moment's thought, he pressed a hoist button and moved me a yard further from the table, towards him, towards the sliding door. Instantly, I repeated the jackknife, aiming this time straight at him. He retreated rapidly. My feet hit the wall where he had been and I pushed off from it violently, turning in the air, scything with my legs at the syringe.

I missed the high-held death but connected with Carey's head, by some chance with one foot each side of it. I tried to grip his head tight but the pendulum effect swung me away again. All that happened was that his surgical cap and mask were pulled off. The mask hung round his neck but the soft cap fell to the ground.

In an extraordinary way it seemed to fluster him. He put the hand holding the syringe to his head and drew it hastily away again. He was confused, his expression not venomous or evil, but showing double the exhaustion of recent days. Not plain tiredness, but psychic disintegration from too much stress.

Still as if nonplussed at things not going to plan, he bent down with his back to me to retrieve the fallen cap, and I, still futilely swinging, drew up my arms and knees and launched my feet with total desperation at Carey's backside.

The force of the connection was only slightly dissipated in the cloth of the surgical gown – no gloriously accurate success like Vicky's kick at the mugger – but it was hard enough to overbalance him, hard enough to send him staggering forward, and hard enough for him to crash his forehead against the sharp metal corner of one of the cabinets before he could straighten up.

He collapsed in a heap, stunned.

Feverishly I fought to undo the buckles of the constricting cuffs. I undid the left cuff first without thinking it out, as it was the one I'd tried to undo earlier. That wasn't too difficult, but it left me swinging from my right wrist alone, and undoing those buckles left-handed and up high cost enormous muscular effort. Sheer extreme panic gave me a strength beyond knowledge, a brute force like madness.

I sweated. Groaned. Struggled. Made my fingers overcome the opposing force of my weight.

My hands slid free at last and I fell, landing awkwardly, off balance, staggering, thinking immediately of a weapon, looking around for something to hit Carey's head with if he should stir, something to tie him with if he didn't.

Hurry. *Hurry*.

The solution was fitting and blindingly simple. I pushed the hoist buttons in my turn, lengthening the chains, still clipped to the cuffs, to their full extent. Then, very carefully, because of tetrodotoxin still a pinprick away, I pulled Carey's arms out from beneath him and bent them behind his back and fastened the cuffs to his wrists, but cross-buckled them so that they were held together, harder than ever to undo. He had a pulse. It throbbed in his wrists. Better, I thought, if he'd died.

I went to the controls and by degrees shortened the chains until they were just tight enough to lift Carey's latex glove-covered hands two or three inches clear of his back. When he woke in that position, he'd scarcely be able to pick his head off the floor.

Satisfied for the moment, but suffocating with anxiety, I ran into the padded room and over to Annabel.

She slept. I felt her pulse too. Strong enough. Alive.

'Oh Annabel.' I smoothed her hair, overwhelmed with feeling.

I felt like crying. Heroes who took six punches in the solar plexus and came up smiling never felt like crying.

I stumbled unsteadily back to the office and sent a

telephoned SOS to Ramsey to arrive with reinforcements. Went back to Annabel, sitting down beside her weakly with my back against the bullring wall, watching Carey through the sliding door for signs of murderous consciousness.

I held Annabel's hand, seeking comfort for myself as much as to give it.

She was alive. She would awake, as I had. She had to.

I loved her intensely.

No trap I could have devised would have revealed Carey as conclusively as the one he'd set for me.

Between intuition and probability I'd come to see that it had had to be Carey I was looking for, but until he'd attacked me I'd had no way of persuading anyone else to believe me. Carey was the grand old man, the father of the practice, the authority figure, the one respected and trusted above all others by the clients.

All those old men. His generation. All knowing each other for half a lifetime. All knowing the secrets.

Long ago, Ronnie Upjohn's father and Theo Travers's grandfather had been insurance agents who'd made a fortune, not the average state of affairs.

Long ago, Kenny McClure had ordered tetrodotoxin in order to pass it to the iniquitous Mackintosh, who everlastingly played cards with Carey. It was Carey, I judged, who'd persuaded Kenny, a vet but not his partner, to acquire the poison, and Kenny, baulking at what he'd done, had got shot for his pains.

Long ago, Wynn Lees had stapled an enemy's pants to his privates; had done his time and had gone to Australia.

The present troubles had begun after Wynn Lees' return, and perhaps he'd been the trigger that restarted the engine.

Carey had to have needed money. Not impossible that in the Porphyry crash he'd lost the savings that were to see him through old age. Not impossible to suppose he'd tried to get them back by using his professional knowledge.

Not impossible to guess that he'd somehow persuaded the third generation insurance man Travers to join him in growing rich, nor that Travers had wanted out like Kenny, and found that out meant dead.

Carey, I thought, had burned the building not just to postpone or avoid the identification of Travers, but also to cover all his own tracks. Orders, invoices, all the tell-tale paperwork had conveniently gone up in smoke, and particularly – I saw with awe – the blood samples taken that day when the cannon-bone horse was dying on the table. Those samples would have shown excessive potassium. The unexplained deaths in the operating room would suddenly have been explained. The hunt for the culprit would be on.

No one would ever have questioned Carey's going in and out of the store room where the intravenous drip fluids were kept. No one would ever question what chemicals Carey ordered. No one would think it odd if he went to see old friends and their horses, no one would worry if he were seen at Eaglewood's one night, checking on his patients while surreptitiously taking insulin with him.

Carey could go where he liked, do what he liked, unquestioned and unchallenged, unsuspected. After all, no senior veterinarian in his right mind would set out to destroy his chief surgeon's reputation, nor kill off a practice he'd spent a lifetime building. But Carey, I thought, had meant to make his money and go. Events had hurried him: Travers had precipitated the fire. Ken had saved the colicky mare from what should have been curtains. It had been necessary, from Carey's point of view, only to finish off the mare and close the mouth of the man who'd carried the poison. After that there was nothing to keep him and he'd smartly announced the end of the partnership. If Ken hadn't told him how much we'd found out, he would quite likely have been peacefully packing at that moment, rich again and ready to emigrate, not lying flat, face down in ultimate disaster.

Annabel stirred.

I felt enormous, heart-swelling thankful relief. I squeezed her hand and though she didn't squeeze back I thought that by then she could probably hear.

'Don't worry,' I said, 'I'm right here beside you. You're going to be all right very soon. Some bloody madman popped a bit of anaesthetic into you but you're coming out of it and everything's fine. Don't hurry. Things will improve very soon, I promise you.'

I went on trying to reassure her and in the end she opened her eyes and used them for smiling.

By the time Ramsey arrived, she was sitting snuggled in my arms but shivering with apprehension that the still prostrate figure in the surgical gown would come to life, jump up and still do us harm. He had jumped out at her from behind the wall, she said. She'd caught a horrified glimpse of him before he'd jabbed the needle into her neck.

'If he comes to life,' I said, 'I'll shorten the chains to pull his arms higher behind his back. I'll bend him double.'

'I don't like it.'

Nor did I. It seemed an age before the burly Superintendent appeared enquiringly through the door from the passage and stared in astonishment at the man on the floor.

I stood and went to meet him.

'What exactly gives?' he asked.

'I think,' I said, 'that that's your murderer. And be careful, because under him or near by there's a hypodermic syringe oozing something that may be very detrimental to your health.'

*

A week later, I phoned my mother and told her most of what had happened. Not Russet Eaglewood, not too much about Scott, not my frantic fight for life.

At the end she exclaimed, 'I can't believe a vet would kill horses!'

'Vets put down horses all the time.'

'That's different.'

'Not so very.'

'He must have been warped!'

'Oh, yes,' I said.

I thought of Carey as I'd briefly seen him last, lying securely strapped to a stretcher with a big swelling on his forehead. Eyes closed. Harmless looking. I heard later that he'd woken up concussed and been bewilderingly calm ever since. 'He's relieved, I reckon,' Ramsey said in a burst of unusual chattiness. 'They're often relieved when it's all over. Funny that.'

A syringe bearing traces of anaesthetic had been found on the floor behind the half-wall in the padded room.

The second syringe, whose needle Carey had tried to stick into me in the theatre, had rolled under a nearby table. Wary analysis proved the contents of that one to be indubitably tetrodotoxin. The empty ampoule, bearing the Parkway company's name and batch number in black letters and 'Extremely Hazardous' in red, lay in the kidney dish which had held the syringe.

'Smoking gun,' Ramsey said with satisfaction.

His search of Carey's house revealed a book on dangerous marine animals, among which puffer fish took a medal.

'Circumstantial,' Ramsey said.

Ramsey's list obtained from Porphyry Place showed Carey to have lost a sum that made me wince.

Higgins's insurance friends came up with every dead horse on our list: agent each time, Theodore Travers; recipients mostly fictitious, but also Wynn Lees, Fitzwalter and Nagrebb.

The expedited report on the DNA matching of the mare and foal with Rainbow Quest came back negative: nowhere near a match, he wasn't the sire, positively not. Wynn Lees, certain to be charged with fraud, had cannily skipped the country.

My mother said, 'What about Ken?'

'I had to tell him I'd lived here as a boy. He's wondered all the time how I knew so much.'

'You didn't tell him about me and his father?' she asked anxiously.

'No, not a word. It's better not known.'

'Ever the diplomat,' she said, teasing but relieved.

Ken and Belinda's wedding, I told her, was going ahead as planned. 'And that's just the word for it – planned. They're both so *practical* about it. No spark. But no doubts either, it seems.'

'Don't you give it much chance then?' she asked, sounding disappointed.

'Fifty fifty, I'd say. But Belinda's started calling her mother Vicky, not Mother. That might make all the difference.'

My own mother chuckled. 'You said I would like Vicky.'

'You'll love her.'

'We'll never meet.'

'I'll see you do.'

Ken himself, I told her, would emerge with his reputation in most part restored.

'There will be people,' I said, 'who might say he should have realized sooner why the horses were dying during operations. I can't judge that, not being a vet. But it looks like being all right in general. The partners all met and decided to carry on at once and sort out the legal details later, and the practice is renamed McClure Quincy Amhurst, which should steady the critics.'

'Wonderful!'

'And Mum,' I said, 'your Kenny . . .'

'Yes?'

'I found out why he died.'

There was a silence on the line, then she said, 'Tell me,' and I told her the theories, and that Josephine believed them and was comforted.

'Are your theories right?'

'Yes, I think so.'

A little pause. A voice gentle on a breath, 'Thanks, darling.'

I smiled. 'Do you want a daughter-in-law?' I asked.

'Yes! You know I do.'

'Her name is Annabel,' I said.